V. S. NAIPAUL

The Nightwatchman's Occurrence Book

V. S. Naipaul was born in Trinidad in 1932. He went to England on a scholarship in 1950. After four years at Oxford he began to write, and since then he has followed no other profession. He is the author of more than twenty books of fiction and nonfiction and the recipient of numerous honors, including the Nobel Prize in 2001, the Booker Prize in 1971, and a knighthood for services to literature in 1990. He lives in Wiltshire, England.

VINTAGE

INTERNATIONAL

ALSO BY V. S. NAIPAUL

The Nightwatchman's Occurrence Book

V. S. NAIPAUL

The Nightwatchman's Occurrence Book

And Other Comic Inventions

*

The Suffrage of Elvira

Mr Stone and the Knights Companion

A Flag on the Island

*

VINTAGE INTERNATIONAL

Vintage Books

A Division of Random House, Inc.

New York

FIRST VINTAGE INTERNATIONAL EDITION,
JUNE 2002

All but two of the shorter pieces in this collection have appeared in peri-
odicals in England or the United States. "The Enemy" was written in
part of my book *Miguel Street*. It was not used there, and some of the
episodes were developed in later books; the present story was published
in American *Vogue*. "The Raffle" was written for the London *Evening
Standard* series "Did it Happen?" The answer was no; the autobiographical detail is deliberately misleading. "A Flag on the Island" was specially
written for a film company. The story they required was to be "musical"
and comic and set in the Caribbean; it was to have a leading American
character and many subsidiary characters; it was to have much sex and
much dialogue; it was to be explicit.

In *The Suffrage of Elvira*, the song "My Heart and I" is quoted by per-
mission of Lawrence Wright Music Co. Ltd. The song "Swinging on a
Star" is quoted by permission of Edwin H. Morris & Co. Ltd and
Messrs Burke & Van Heusen Inc.

Author photograph © Jerry Bauer
Book design by Rebecca Aidlin

www.vintagebooks.com

Printed in the United States of America
10 9 8 7 6 5 4 3

CONTENTS

The Suffrage of Elvira

For Pat

Contents

Prologue: A Bad Sign

THAT AFTERNOON Mr Surujpat Harbans nearly killed the two white women and the black bitch.

When he saw the women he thought of them only as objects he must try not to hit, and he didn't stop to think how strange it was to see two blonde women forcing red American cycles up Elvira Hill, the highest point in County Naparoni, the smallest, most isolated and most neglected of the nine counties of Trinidad.

The heavy American bicycles with their pudgy tyres didn't make cycling up the hill easier for the women. They rose from their low saddles and pressed down hard on the pedals and the cycles twisted all over the narrow road.

Harbans followed in a nervous low gear. He didn't like driving and didn't feel he was ever in control of the old Dodge lorry banging and rattling on the loose dirt road. Something else about the lorry worried him. It was bright with red posters: *Vote Harbans for Elvira*. There were two on the front bumper; two on the bonnet; one on each wing; the cab-doors were covered except for an oblong patch which was painted HARBANS TRANSPORT SERVICE. The posters, the first of his campaign so far, had arrived only that morning. They made him shy, and a little nervous about the reception he was going to get in Elvira.

Just before the brow of the hill he decided he needed more power and stepped a little harder on the accelerator. At the same time the women wobbled into the middle of the road, decided they couldn't cycle up any further, and dismounted. Harbans stamped on his brakes, his left foot missed the clutch, and the engine stalled.

The bumper covered with two *Vote Harbans for Elvira* posters hit the back mudguard of one cycle and sent the cyclist stumbling forward, her hands still on the handlebars. But she didn't fall.

The women turned to the lorry. They were both young and quite remarkably good-looking. Harbans had seen nothing like it outside the cinema. Perhaps it was the effect of the sun-glasses they both wore. The trays of both cycles were packed with books and magazines, and from the top of each tray a stiff pennant said: AWAKE!

The taller woman, who had been knocked forward, composed herself quickly and smiled. 'Good brakes, mister.' She spoke with an American accent—or it might have been Canadian: Harbans couldn't tell. She sounded unreasonably cheerful.

'Fust time it happen,' Harbans said, almost in a whisper. 'Fust time in more than twenty years.' That wasn't hard to believe. He had the face of the extra-careful driver, thin, timid, dyspeptic. His hair was thin and grey, his nose thin and long.

The shorter woman smiled too. 'Don't look so worried, mister. *We*'re all right.'

In a difficult position Harbans had the knack of suddenly going absent-minded. He would look down at the grey hairs on the back of his hands and get lost studying them.

'Eh?' he said to his hands, and paused. 'Eh? All right?' He paused again. 'You sure?'

'We're *always* all right,' the taller woman said.

'We're Witnesses,' said the other.

'Eh?' But the legal sound of the word made him look up. 'You is. . . .' He waved a wrinkled hand. 'Election nonsense.' He was coy and apologetic; his thin voice became a coo. 'My head a little hot with worries. Election worries.'

The taller woman smiled back. 'We *know* you're worried.'

'We're Witnesses,' said the other.

Harbans saw the AWAKE! pennants for the first time and understood. The women dragged their red bicycles to the verge and waved him on. He managed somehow to move the Dodge off and got it to the top of Elvira Hill, where the black and yellow board of the Trinidad Automobile Association announces the district as 'The Elvira.' This is short for The Elvira Estate, named after the wife of one of the early owners, but everyone who knows the district well says Elvira.

From the top of Elvira Hill you get one of the finest views in Trinidad, better even than the view from Tortuga in South Caroni. Below, the jungly hills and valleys of the Central Range. Beyond, to the south, the sugar-cane fields, the silver tanks of the oil refinery at Pointe-à-Pierre, and the pink and white houses of San Fernando; to the west, the shining rice-fields and swamps of Caroni, and the Gulf of Paria; the Caroni Savannah to the north, and the settlements at the foot of the Northern Range.

Harbans didn't care for the view. All he saw about him was a lot of bush. Indeed, the Elvira Estate had long been broken up and only the tall immortelle trees with their scarlet and orange bird-shaped flowers reminded you that there was once a great cocoa estate here.

It was the roads of Elvira that interested Harbans. Even the election didn't make him forget to count the ruts and trenches and miniature ravines that made it hell to drive to Elvira. So far he had counted seven, and noted the beginnings of what promised to be a good landslide.

This consoled him. For years he had been able to persuade the chief engineer of County Naparoni to keep his hands off the Elvira roads. Big repairs were never attempted; even asphalt was not laid down, although the Pitch Lake, which supplies the world, is only thirty miles away. Harbans could depend on the hilly dirt roads of Elvira to keep the Harbans Transport Service busy carrying sand and gravel and blue-metal stone. Harbans owned a quarry too. Road works were always in progress in Elvira. That afternoon Harbans had counted three road-gangs—four men to a gang, two filling in the gaps in the road with a hammer and a light pestle, two operating the traffic signals. Respectful boys. When Harbans had passed they had stopped working, taken off their hats and said, 'Good luck, boss.'

At the small Spanish settlement of Cordoba he saw some labourers coming back from the day's work with muddy hoes and forks over their shoulders. They didn't wave or shout. The Spaniards in Cordoba are a reserved lot, more Negro than Spanish now, but they keep themselves to themselves.

Even so Harbans expected some small demonstration. But the labourers just stopped and stood at the side of the road and silently considered the decorated lorry. Harbans felt shyer than before, and a little wretched.

From Cordoba the road sloped down sharply to the old cocoa-house, abandoned now and almost buried in tall bush. The cocoa-house stood at the blind corner and it was only as he turned it that Harbans saw the black bitch, limping about idly in the middle of the road. She was a starved mongrel, her ribs stuck out, and not even the clangour of the Dodge quickened her. He was almost on top of her before he stamped on his brakes, stalling the engine once more.

'Haul your arse!'

Only his edginess made Harbans use language like that. Also, he believed he had hit her.

If he had, the dog made no sign. She didn't groan or whine; she didn't collapse, though she looked near it. Then Harbans saw that she had littered not long before. Her udders, raw and deflated, hung in a scalloped pink fringe from her shrunken belly.

Harbans sounded his horn impatiently.

This the dog understood. She looked up, but without great animation, limped to the side of the road with one foot off the ground and disappeared into the bushes in front of the cocoa-house.

It was only when he had driven away that Harbans thought. His first accidents in twenty years. The strange white women. The black bitch. The stalling of the engine on both occasions.

It was clearly a sign.

And not a good sign either. He had done all his bargaining for the election; the political correspondents said he had as good as won already. This afternoon he was going to offer himself formally to Baksh and Chittaranjan, the powers of Elvira. The bargains had only to be formally sealed.

But what did this sign mean?

Agitated, he drove into Elvira proper, where he was to find out. The first person he was going to call on was Baksh.

1. The Bakshes

DEMOCRACY HAD COME to Elvira four years before, in 1946; but it had taken nearly everybody by surprise and it wasn't until 1950, a few months before the second general election under universal adult franchise, that people began to see the possibilities.

Until that time Baksh had only been a tailor and a man of reputed wealth. Now he found himself the leader of the Muslims in Elvira. He said he controlled more than a thousand Muslim votes. There were eight thousand voters in County Naparoni, that is, in Elvira and Cordoba. Baksh was a man of power.

It was a puzzle: how Baksh came to be the Muslim leader. He wasn't a good Muslim. He didn't know all the injunctions of the Prophet and those he did know he broke. For instance, he was a great drinker; when he went to Ramlogan's rumshop he made a point of ordering white puncheon rum, the sort you have to swallow quickly before it turns to vapour in your mouth. He had none of the dignity of the leader. He was a big talker: in Elvira they called him 'the mouther'.

Chittaranjan, now, the other power in Elvira, was aloof and stiff, and whenever he talked to you, you felt he was putting you in your place. Baksh mixed with everybody, drank and quarrelled with everybody. Perhaps it was this that helped to make Baksh the Muslim leader, though the position should have gone in all fairness to Haq, a fierce black little man who wore a bristle of white beard and whiskers, and whose eyes flashed behind steel-rimmed spectacles when he spoke of infidels. Haq was orthodox, or so he led people to believe, but Haq was poor. He ran a grubby little stall, just twice the size of a sentry-box, stocked only with cheap sweets and soft drinks.

Baksh made money. It was hard not to feel that for all his conviviality Baksh was a deep man. He was a talker, but he did things. Like that shirt-making business. For months Baksh talked. 'Make two three dozen cheap khaki shirts,' he told them in Ramlogan's rumshop. 'Take them to Princes Town and Rio Claro on market day. A cool seventy dollars. Some damn fool or the other come up to you. You tell him that the shirts not really good enough for him. You say you going to make something especially to fit him pussonal. You pretend you taking his measure, and when you go back the next week you give the damn fool the same shirt. Only, you charge him a little extra.' He talked like that for months. And then one day he actually did it all as he had said. And made money.

He lived in a tumbledown wooden house of two storeys, an elaborate thing with jalousies and fretwork everywhere, built for an overseer in the days of the Elvira Estate; but he used to say that he could put up something bigger than Chittaranjan's any day he chose. 'Only,' he used to say, 'they just ain't have the sort of materials *I* want for my house. This Trinidad backward to hell, you hear.' He kept the designs of Californian-style houses from American magazines to show the sort of house he wanted. 'Think they could build like that in Trinidad?' he would ask, and he would answer himself: 'Naah!' And if he were at the door of his tailoring establishment he would spit straight across the ragged little patch of grass into the deep gutter at the roadside.

For a tailor he dressed badly and he said this was so because he was a tailor; anyway, 'only poorer people does like dressing up, to try and pretend that they ain't so poor.' He dressed his children badly because he didn't want them 'running about thinking they is superior to poorer people children'.

In June 1950, when Harbans drove into Elvira to see Baksh, there were seven young Bakshes. The eldest was seventeen; he would be eighteen in August. The boy's name was not generally known but everyone called him Foam, which was short for Foreman.

*

The decorated Dodge lorry came to a stop in a narrow trace opposite Baksh's shop. Harbans saw the sign:

M. BAKSH
London Tailoring Est.
Tailoring and Cutting
Suits Made and Repair at City Prices

A flock of poorer people's children, freed from school that Friday afternoon, had been running after the lorry ever since it entered the Elvira main road. Many of them were half-dressed according to the curious rural prudery which dictated that the top should be covered, not the bottom. They shouted, 'Vote Harbans for Elvira, man!' and made a chant of it. Harbans resented the whole thing as an indignity and was tempted to shoo the children away when he got out of the lorry, but he remembered the election and pretended not to hear.

He wasn't a tall man but looked taller than he was because he was so thin. He walked with a clockwork jerkiness, seeming to move only from the knees down. His white shirt, buttoned at the wrist, was newly ironed, like his trousers. The only rakish touch in his dress was the tie he used as a trousers-belt. Altogether, there was about him much of the ascetic dignity of the man who has made money.

Foam, Baksh's eldest son, sat at the Singer sewing-machine near the door, tacking a coat; an overgrown bony boy with a slab-like face: you felt that the moment he was born someone had clapped his face together.

Foam said, 'Candidate coming, Pa.'

'Let him come,' Baksh said. If Harbans had heard he would have recognized the casual aggressiveness he had been fearing all afternoon. Baksh stood at a counter with a tape-measure round his neck, consulting a bloated copy-book and making marks with a triangular piece of yellow chalk on some dark blue material. At one end of the counter there was a pile of new material, already cut. A yardstick, its brass tips worn smooth, was screwed down at the other end.

Light came into the shop only through the front door and didn't reach everywhere. Age had given the unpainted wallboards the barest curve; darkness had made them a dingy russet colour; both had given the shop a moist musty smell. It was this smell, warm and sharp in the late afternoon, not the smell of new cloth, that greeted Harbans when he walked over the shaky plank spanning the gutter and came into the yard.

Foam kept on tacking. Baksh made more marks on his cloth.

Two months, one month ago, they would have jumped up as soon as they saw him coming.

Harbans suffered.

'Aah, Baksh.' He used his lightest coo. '*How* you is?' He flashed his false teeth at Foam and added all at once, 'And how the boy is? He doing well? Ooh, but he looking too well and too nice.'

Foam scowled while Harbans ruffled his hair.

'Foam,' Baksh said, very gently, 'get up like a good boy and give Mr Harbans your bench.'

Baksh left his chalk and cloth and came to the doorway. He had the squat build of the labourer and didn't look like a leader or even like the father of seven children. He seemed no more than thirty. He seated Harbans and spat through the door into the gutter. 'Ain't got much in the way of furnishings, you see,' he said, waving his hands about the dark windowless room with its gloomy walls and high sooty ceiling.

'It matters?' Harbans said.

'It matter when you ain't have.'

Harbans said, 'Aah.' Baksh frightened him a little. He didn't like the solid square face, the thick eyebrows almost meeting at the

[15]

bridge of a thick nose, the thick black moustache over thick lips. Especially he didn't like Baksh's bloodshot eyes. They made him look too reckless.

Harbans put his hands on his thin knees and looked at them. 'I take my life in my hands today, Baksh, to come to see you. If I tell you how I hate driving!'

'You want some suit and things?'

'Is talk I want to talk with you, Baksh.'

Baksh tried to look surprised.

'Foam,' Harbans said, 'go away a lil bit. It have a few things, pussonal, I want to say to your father.'

Foam didn't move.

Baksh laughed. 'No, man. Foam is a big man now. Eh, in two three years we have to start thinking about marrying him off.'

Foam, leaning against the wall under a large Coca-Cola calendar, said, 'Not me, brother. I ain't in that bacchanal at all. I ain't want to get married.'

Harbans couldn't protest. He said, 'Ooh,' and gave a little chuckle. The room was too dark for him to see Foam's expression. But he saw how tall and wiry the boy was, and he thought his posture a little arrogant. That, and his booming voice, made him almost as frightening as his father. Harbans's hands began to tap on his knees. 'Ooh, ooh. Children, eh, Baksh?' He chuckled again. 'Children. What you going to do?'

Baksh sucked his teeth and went back to his counter. 'Is the modern generation.'

Harbans steadied his hands. 'Is that self I come to talk to you about. The modern world, Baksh. In this modern world everybody is one. Don't make no difference who you is or what you is. You is a Muslim, I is a Hindu. Tell me, that matter?' He had begun to coo again.

'Depending.'

'Yes, as you say, depending. Who you for, Baksh?'

'In the election, you mean?'

Harbans looked ashamed.

Baksh lay down on a low couch in the darkest corner of the dark room and looked up at the ceiling. 'Ain't really think about it yet, you know.'

'Oh. Ooh, who *you* for, Foam?'

'Why for you bothering the boy head with that sort of talk, man?'

Foam said, 'I for you, Mr Harbans.'

'Ooh, ooh. Ain't he a nice boy, Baksh?'

Baksh said, 'The boy answer for me.'

Harbans looked more ashamed.

Baksh sat up. 'You go want a lot of help. Microphone. Loud-speaking van. Fact, you go want a whole campaign manager.'

'Campaign what? Ooh. Nothing so fancy for me, man. You and I, Baksh, we is very simple people. Is the community we have to think about.'

'Thinking about them all the time,' Baksh said.

'Time go come, you know, Baksh, and you too, Foam, time go come when you realize that money ain't everything.'

'But is a damn lot,' Foam boomed, and took up his tacking again.

'True,' Harbans fluted.

'Must have a loudspeaking van,' Baksh said. 'The other man have a loudspeaking van. Come to think of it, you could use *my* loud-speaker.' He looked hard at Harbans. 'And you could use *my* van.'

Harbans looked back hard into the darkness. 'What you saying, Baksh? You ain't got no loudspeaker.'

Baksh stood up. Foam stopped tacking.

'You ain't got no loudspeaker,' Harbans repeated. 'And you ain't got no van.'

Baksh said, 'And you ain't got no Muslim vote.' He went back to his counter and took up the yellow chalk in a businesslike way.

'Haa!' Harbans chuckled. 'I was only fooling you. Haa! I was only making joke, Baksh.'

'Damn funny sorta joke,' Foam said.

'You going to get your van,' Harbans said. 'And you going to get your loudspeaker. You sure we *want* loudspeaker?'

'Bound to have one, man. For the boy.'

'Boy?'

'Who else?' Foam asked. 'I did always want to take up loud-speaking. A lot of people tell me I have the voice for it.'

'Hundred per cent better than that Lorkhoor,' Baksh said.

Lorkhoor was the brightest young man in Elvira and Foam's natural rival. He was only two-and-a-half years older than Foam but he was already making his mark on the world. He ran about the remoter districts of Central Trinidad with a loudspeaker van, advertising for the cinemas in Caroni.

'Lorkhoor is only a big show-offer,' Foam said. 'Ever hear him, Mr Harbans? "This is the voice of the ever popular Lorkhoor," he does say, "begging you and imploring you and entreating you and beseeching you to go to the New Theatre." Is just those three big words he knew, you know. Talk about a show-offer!'

'The family is like that,' Baksh said.

'We want another stand-pipe in Elvira,' Harbans said. 'Elvira is a big place and it only have one school. And the roads!'

Foam said, 'Mr Harbans, Lorkhoor start loudspeaking against you, you know.'

'What! But I ain't do the boy or the boy family nothing at all. Why he turning against a old man like me?'

Neither Baksh nor Foam could help him there. Lorkhoor had said so often he didn't care for politics that it had come as a surprise to all Elvira when he suddenly declared for the other candidate, the man they called Preacher. Even Preacher's supporters were surprised.

'But I is a Hindu,' Harbans cried. 'Lorkhoor is a Hindu. Preacher is Negro.'

Baksh saw an opening. 'Preacher giving out money hands down. Lorkhoor managing Preacher campaign. Hundred dollars a month.'

'Where Preacher getting that sort of money?'

Baksh began to invent. 'Preacher tell me pussonal'—the word had enormous vogue in Elvira in 1950—'that ever since he was a boy, even before this democracy and universal suffrage business, he had a ambition to go up to the Legislative Council. He say God send him this chance.' Baksh paused for inspiration. It didn't come. 'He been saving up,' Baksh went on lamely. 'Saving up for a long long time.' He shifted the subject. 'To be frank with you, Mr Harbans, Preacher have me a little worried. He acting too funny. He ain't making no big noise or nothing. He just walking about quiet quiet and brisk brisk from house to house. He ain't stick up no posters or nothing.'

'House-to-house campaign,' Harbans said gloomily.

'And Lorkhoor,' Foam said. 'He winning over a lot of stupid people with his big talk.'

Harbans remembered the sign he had had that afternoon: the women, the dog, the engine stalling twice. And he hadn't been half an hour in Elvira before so many unexpected things had happened. Baksh wasn't sticking to the original bargain. He was demanding a loudspeaker van; he had brought Foam in and Harbans felt that Foam was almost certain to make trouble. And there was this news about Lorkhoor.

'Traitor!' Harbans exclaimed. 'This Lorkhoor is a damn traitor!'

'The family is like that,' Baksh said, as though it were a consolation.

'I ain't even start my campaign proper yet and already I spend more than two thousand dollars. Don't ask me what on, because I ain't know.'

Baksh laughed. 'You talking like Foam mother.'

'Don't worry, Mr Harbans,' Foam said. 'When we put you in the Leg. Co. you going to make it back. Don't worry too much with Lorkhoor. He ain't even got a vote. He too young.'

'But he making a hundred dollars a month,' Baksh said.

'Baksh, we really *want* a loudspeaker van?'

'To be frank, boss, I ain't want it so much for the elections as for afterwards. Announcing at all sort of things. Sports. Weddings. Funerals. It have a lot of money in that nowadays, boss, especially for a poor man'—Baksh waved his hands about the room again—'who ain't got much in the way of furnishings, as you see. And Foam here could manage your whole campaign for eighty dollars a month. No hardship.'

Harbans accepted the loudspeaker van sorrowfully. He tried again. 'But, Baksh, I ain't want no campaign manager.'

Foam said, 'You ain't want no Muslim vote.'

Harbans looked at Foam in surprise. Foam was tacking slowly, steadily, drawing out his needle high.

Baksh said, 'I promise you the boy going to work night and day for you.' And the Muslim leader kissed his crossed index fingers.

'Seventy dollars a month.'

'All right, boss.'

Foam said, 'Eh, I could talk for myself, you hear. Seventy-five.'

'Ooh. Children, Baksh.'

'They is like that, boss. But the boy have a point. Make it seventy-five.'

Harbans hung his head.

The formal negotiations were over.

Baksh said, 'Foam, cut across to Haq and bring some sweet drink and cake for the boss.'

Baksh led Harbans through the dark shop, up the dark stairs, through a cluttered bedroom into the veranda where Mrs Baksh and six little Bakshes—dressed for the occasion in their school clothes—were introduced to him.

Mrs Baksh was combing out her thick black hair that went down to her hips. She nodded to Harbans, cleared her comb of loose hair, rolled the hair into a ball, spat on it and threw it into a corner. Then she began to comb again. She was fresh, young, as well-built as her husband, and Harbans thought there was a little of her husband's recklessness about her as well. Perhaps this was because of her modern skirt, the hem of which fell only just below the knee.

Harbans was at once intimidated by Mrs Baksh. He didn't like the little Bakshes either. The family insolence seemed to run through them all.

If it puzzled Harbans how a burly couple like Mr and Mrs Baksh could have a son like Foam, elongated and angular, he could see the stages Foam must have gone through when he looked at the other Baksh boys; Iqbal, Herbert, Rafiq and Charles. (It was a concession the Bakshes made to their environment: they chose alternate Christian and Muslim names for their children.) The boys were small-boned and slight and looked as though they had been stretched on the rack. Their bellies were barely swollen. This physique better became the girls, Carol and Zilla; they looked slim and delicate.

Baksh cleared a cane-bottomed chair of a pile of clothes and invited Harbans to sit down.

Before Harbans could do so, Mrs Baksh said, 'But what happen to the man at all? That is my ironing.'

Baksh said, 'Carol, take your mother ironing inside.'

Carol took the clothes away.

Harbans sat down and studied the back of his hands.

Mrs Baksh valued the status of her family and felt it deserved watching. She saw threats everywhere; this election was the greatest. She couldn't afford new enemies; too many people were already jealous of her and she suspected nearly everybody of looking at her with the evil eye, the *mal yeux* of the local patois. Harbans, with his thin face and thin nose, she suspected in particular.

Harbans, looking down at the grey hairs and ridge-like veins of his hands and worrying about the loudspeaker van and the seventy-five dollars a month, didn't know how suspect he was.

Foam came back with two bottles of coloured aerated water and a paper bag with two rock cakes.

'Zilla, go and get a glass,' Baksh ordered.

'Don't worry with glass and thing,' Harbans said appeasingly. 'I ain't all that fussy.' He was troubled. The aerated water and the rock cakes were sure not to agree with him.

The little Bakshes, bored up till then, began to look at Harbans with interest now that he was going to eat.

Zilla brought a glass. Foam opened a bottle and poured the bright red stuff. Zilla held the paper bag with the rock cakes towards Harbans. Foam and Zilla, the eldest Baksh children, behaved as though they had got to the stage where food was something to be handled, not eaten.

The little Bakshes hadn't reached that stage.

Baksh left the veranda and came back with a cellophane-wrapped tin of Huntley and Palmer's biscuits. He felt Mrs Baksh's disapproval and avoided her eye.

'Biscuit, Mr Harbans?'

The little Bakshes concentrated.

'Nice biscuits,' Baksh tempted, stubbornly. 'Have them here since Christmas.'

Harbans said, 'Give it to the children, eh?' He broke off a large piece of the rock cake and handed it to Herbert who had edged closest to him.

'Herbert!' Mrs Baksh exclaimed. 'Your eyes longer than your mouth, eh!'

'Let the poor boy have it,' Harbans cooed, and showed his false teeth.

She ignored Harbans's plea and faced Herbert. 'You don't care how much you shame me in front of strangers. You making him believe I does starve you.'

Herbert had already put the cake in his mouth. He chewed slowly, to show that he knew he had done wrong.

'You ain't shame?' Mrs Baksh pointed. 'Look how your belly puff out.'

Herbert stopped chewing and mumbled, 'Is only the gas, Ma.'

The other little Bakshes had their interest divided between their mother's anger and Harbans's food.

Harbans said, 'Ooh, ooh,' and smiled nervously at everybody.

Mrs Baksh turned to him. 'You eat those cakes up and drink the sweet drink and don't give a thing to any of these shameless children of mine.'

She used a tone of inflexible authority which was really meant for the little Bakshes. Harbans didn't know this. He ate and drank. The warm liquid stabbed down to his stomach; once there it tore around in circles. Still, from time to time he looked up from the aerated water and rock cake and smiled at Mrs Baksh and Baksh and Foam and the other little Bakshes.

The biscuits were saved.

At last Harbans was finished and he could leave. He was glad. The whole Baksh family frightened him.

Foam walked down the steps with Harbans. They had hardly got outside when they heard someone screaming upstairs.

'Herbert,' Foam said. 'He does always make that particular set of noise when *they* beat him.'

When Foam said *they* Harbans knew he meant Mrs Baksh.

Candidate and campaign manger got into the Dodge and drove on to see Chittaranjan.

2. The Bargain with Chittaranjan

EASILY THE MOST IMPORTANT person in Elvira was Chittaranjan, the goldsmith. And there was no mystery why. He looked rich and was rich. He was an expensive goldsmith with a reputation that had spread beyond Elvira. People came to him from as far as Chaguanas and Couva and even San Fernando. Everyone knew his house as the biggest in Elvira. It was solid, two-storeyed, concrete, bright with paint and always well looked after.

Nobody ever saw Chittaranjan working. For as long as Foam could remember Chittaranjan had always employed two men in the shop downstairs. They worked in the open, sitting flat on the concrete terrace under a canvas awning, surrounded by all the gear of their trade: toy pincers, hammers and chisels, a glowing heap of charcoal on a sheet of galvanized iron, pots and basins discoloured with various liquids, some of which smelled, some of which hissed when certain metals were dipped in them. Every afternoon, after the workmen had cleared up and gone home, children combed the terrace for silver shavings and gold dust. Even Foam had done so when he was younger. He hadn't got much; but some children managed, after years of collecting, to get enough to make a ring. Chittaranjan never objected.

No wonder Foam, like nearly everyone else, Hindu, Muslim, Negro, thought and spoke of his house as the Big House. As a Hindu Chittaranjan naturally had much influence among the Hindus of Elvira; but he was more than the Hindu leader. He was the only man who carried weight with the Spaniards of Cordoba (it was said he lent them money); many Negroes liked him; Muslims didn't trust him, but even they held him in respect.

'You ain't have nothing to worry about, Mr Harbans,' Foam said, speaking as campaign manager, as he and Harbans drove through Elvira. 'Chittaranjan control at least five thousand votes. Add that to the thousand Muslim votes and you win, Mr Harbans. It only have eight thousand voters in all.'

Harbans had been brooding all the way. 'What about that traitor Lorkhoor?'

'Tcha! You worrying with Lorkhoor? Look how the *people* welcoming you, man.'

And really, from the reception the lorry had been getting since it left Baksh's, it didn't look as though Harbans had anything to worry about. The news had gone around that he was in Elvira, campaigning at last. It was just after five o'clock, getting cool, and most people were at home. Children rushed to the roadside and shouted, 'Vote Harbans, man!' Women left their cooking and waved coyly from their front yards, and made the babies at their hips wave too.

Harbans was so morose he left it to Foam to wave and shout back, 'That's right, man! Keep it up!'

Foam's ebullience depressed Harbans more. The bargaining with Baksh had shaken him and he feared that Chittaranjan too might demand stiffer terms. Moreover, he was nervous about the Dodge; and the sweet drink and rock cakes he had had were playing hell with his inside.

'You shy, Mr Harbans,' Foam said. 'I know how it is. But you going to get use to this waving. Ten to one, before this election over, we going to see you waving and shouting to everybody, even to people who ain't going to vote for you.'

Harbans shook his head sadly.

Foam settled into the angle of the seat and the door. 'Way I see it is this. In Trinidad this democracy is a brand-new thing. We is still creeping. We is a creeping nation.' He dropped his voice solemnly: 'I respect people like you, you know, Mr Harbans, doing this thing for the first time.'

Harbans began to dislike Foam less. 'I think you go make a fust-class loudspeaking man, Foam. Where you learn all that?'

'Social and Debating Club. Something Teacher Francis did start up. It mash up now.' He stuck his long head out of the window and shouted encouragement to a group of children at the roadside. 'Soon as I get old enough, going up for County Council myself, you know, Mr Harbans. Sort of campaigning in advance. You want to know how I does do it? Look, I go in a café and I see some poorer people child. Buy the child a sweet drink, man.'

'Sweet drink, eh?'

'Yes, man. Buy him a sweet drink. Cost me six cents. But in five years' time it getting me one vote. Buy one sweet drink for a different child every day for five years. At the end of five years, what you have? Everybody, but everybody, man, saying, "We going to vote for Foam." Is the only way, Mr Harbans.'

'Is a lil too late for me to start buying sweet drink for poorer people children now.'

They were near Chittaranjan's now, and the Dodge slowed down not far from Ramlogan's rumshop.

Ramlogan, a big greasy man in greasy trousers and a greasy vest, was leaning against his shop door, his fat arms crossed, scowling at the world.

'Wave to him,' Foam ordered.

Harbans, his thin hands gripped nervously to the steering wheel, only nodded at Ramlogan.

'You have to do better than that. Particularly that Ramlogan and Chittaranjan don't get on too good.'

'Aah. But why this disunity in our people, Foam? People should be uniting these days, man.'

The Dodge came to a halt. Harbans struggled to put it in neutral.

Foam pointed. 'See that Queen of Flowers tree in Chittaranjan yard, just next door to Ramlogan?'

'Ooh, ooh, is a nice one.' It made him feel Chittaranjan must be a nice man. 'I didn't know that Chittaranjan did like flowers.'

'Chittaranjan *ain't* like flowers.'

Harbans frowned at the Queen of Flowers.

'Chittaranjan say flowers does give cough.'

'Is true.'

'Huh! Don't start talking to Chittaranjan about flowers, eh. Look at the Queen of Flowers again. Flowers in Chittaranjan yard. But look where the root is.'

The root was in Ramlogan's yard. But about eight inches from the ground the Queen of Flowers—just out of perversity, it seemed— had decided to change course. It made almost a right angle, went through the wide-meshed wire fence and then shot up and blossomed in Chittaranjan's yard.

'And look at that Bleeding Heart,' Foam went on. 'Root in Ramlogan yard, but the flowers crawling all up by Chittaranjan bedroom window. And look at the breadfruit tree. Whole thing in Ramlogan yard, but all the breadfruit only falling in Chittaranjan yard. And look at the zaboca tree. Same thing. It look like *obeah* and magic, eh?'

'Ooh, ooh.'

'Now, whenever Ramlogan plant a tree, he planting it right in the middle middle of his yard. But what does happen then? Look at that soursop tree in the middle of Ramlogan yard.'

It was stunted, wilting.

'Ramlogan blight. If you know, Mr Harbans, the amount of row it does have here on account of those trees. One day Chittaranjan say he want to cut the trees down. Ramlogan chase him with a cutlass, man. Another day Ramlogan say *he* want to go in Chittaranjan yard to collect the breadfruit and the zaboca and flowers from *his* trees. Chittaranjan take up a stick and chase Ramlogan all down Elvira main road.'

Harbans began to get worried about Chittaranjan.

All this while Ramlogan had been eyeing the lorry, heavy brows puckered over deep-set disapproving eyes, fat cheeks sagging sourly, massive arms still crossed. From time to time he hawked leisurely, and hissed out the spittle between the gap in his top teeth.

'Foam,' Harbans said, 'is a good thing I have a campaign manager like you. I only know about Elvira roads. I ain't know about the people.'

'It have nothing like the local expert,' Foam agreed. 'Look out, Mr Harbans, the lorry rolling in the drain!'

The lorry was moving forward, locked towards the gutter at the right. Harbans dived for the hand-brake and pulled it back with a loud ripping sound. 'Oh God, I did *know* I was taking my life in my hands today.' His alarm was double; he knew then that the sign he had had was being confirmed.

Ramlogan gave a short laugh, so sharp and dry it was almost like a word: 'Ha.'

The commotion brought Chittaranjan to his veranda upstairs. The half-wall hid most of his body, but what Foam and Harbans could see looked absurdly small and shrivelled. Spectacles with thin silver rims and thin silver arms emphasized Chittaranjan's diminutiveness.

Foam and Harbans got out of the lorry.

The awning of Chittaranjan's shop had been pulled back; the ground had already been combed that afternoon by children; and only two toy anvils set in the concrete terrace remained of the day's workshop.

'Is you, Mr Harbans?'

'Is me, Goldsmith.'

'Who is the little boy you have with you?'

'Campaign . . .' But Harbans was ashamed to go on. 'Baksh son.'

'And not so little either,' Foam muttered to himself. But he was anxious. He had been talking freely about Chittaranjan in the lorry, dropping the 'Mr,' but like nearly everyone else in Elvira he was awed by Chittaranjan, had been ever since he was a boy. He had never set foot in the Big House.

'What Baksh son want with me? He want to see me in any pussonal?'

'Not in any pussonal, Goldsmith. He just come with me.'

'Why he come with you?'

Harbans was beside himself with shyness.

'About the elections,' Foam boomed up.

'Ha,' Ramlogan said from his shop door. 'Ha.'

Chittaranjan turned to talk to someone in his veranda; then he shouted down, 'All right, come up the both of all-you,' and disappeared immediately.

Foam nudged Harbans and pointed to one side of Chitaranjan's yard. The ground under the breadfruit tree and the zaboca tree was mushy with rotting fruit. 'See what I did tell you,' Foam whispered. 'One frighten to eat it, the other 'fraid to come and get it.'

They went up the polished red steps at the side of the house and came into the large veranda. Chittaranjan was rocking in a morris rocking-chair. He looked even tinier sitting down than he did hunched over the ledge of the veranda wall. He didn't get up, didn't look at them, didn't greet them. He rocked measuredly, serenely, as though rocking gave him an exclusive joy. Every time he rocked, the heels of his sabots clacked on the tiled floor.

'Is a big big house you have here, Goldsmith,' Harbans cooed.

'Tcha!' Chittaranjan sucked his teeth. He had three gold teeth and many gold fillings. 'Biggest house in Elvira, that's all.' His voice was as thin as Harbans's, but there was an edge to it.

Harbans sought another opening. 'I see you is in your home clothes, Goldsmith. Like you ain't going out this evening at all.'

Like Foam, Harbans was struck by the difference between the appearance of the house and the appearance of the owner. Chittaranjan's white shirt was mended and remended; the sleeves had been severely abridged and showed nearly all of Chittaranjan's stringy arms. The washed-out khaki trousers were not patched, but there was a tear down one leg from knee to ankle that looked as though it had been there a long time. This shabbiness was almost grand. It awed at once.

Chittaranjan, rocking, smiling, didn't look at his visitors. 'What it have to go out for?' he asked at last.

Harbans didn't know what to say.

Chittaranjan continued to smile. But he wasn't really smiling; his face was fixed that way, the lips always parted, the gold teeth always flashing.

'If you ask me,' Chittaranjan said, having baffled them both into silence, 'I go tell you it have nothing to go out for.'

'Depending,' Foam said.

'Yes,' Harbans agreed quickly. 'Depending, Goldsmith.'

'Depending on what?' Chittaranjan's tone seemed to take its calmness from the evening settling on Elvira.

Harbans was stumped again.

Foam came to the rescue. 'Depending on who you have to meet and what you going to give and what you going to get.'

Chittaranjan relented. 'Sit down. The both of all-you. You want some sweet drink?'

Harbans shook his head vigorously.

Chittaranjan ignored this. 'Let me call the girl.' For the first time he looked at Harbans. 'Nelly! Nalini! Bring some sweet drink.'

'Daughter?' Harbans asked. As though he didn't know about Nalini, little Nelly; as though all Elvira didn't know that Chittaranjan wanted Nelly married to Harbans's son, that this was the bargain to be settled that afternoon.

'Yes,' Chittaranjan said deprecatingly. 'Daughter. One and only.'

'Have a son myself,' Harbans said.

'Look at that, eh.'

'Ambitious boy. Going to take up doctoring. Just going on eighteen.'

Foam sat silent, appreciating the finer points of the bargaining. He knew that in normal circumstances Chittaranjan, as the girl's father, would have pleaded and put himself out to please. But the elections were not normal circumstances and now it was Harbans who had to be careful not to offend.

Nelly Chittaranjan came and placed two wooden Negro waiters next to Harbans and Foam. She was small, like her father; and her long-waisted pink frock brought out every pleasing aspect of her slimness. She placed bottles of coloured liquid on the waiters; then went and got some tumblers.

Chittaranjan became a little more animated. He pointed to the bottles. 'Choose. The red one or the orange one?'

'Red for me,' Foam said briskly.

Harbans couldn't refuse. 'Orange,' he said, but with so much gloom, Chittaranjan said, 'You could have the red if you want, you know.'

'Is all right, Goldsmith. Orange go do me.'

Nelly Chittaranjan made a quick face at Foam. She knew him by sight and had had to put up with his daring remarks when she passed him on the road. Foam had often 'troubled' her, that is, whistled at her; he had never 'rushed' her, made a serious pass at her. She looked a little surprised to see him in her father's house. Foam, exaggeratedly relaxed, tried to make out he didn't value the honour at all.

She poured the sweet drinks into the tumblers.

Harbans looked carefully at the wooden waiter next to his chair. But in fact he was looking at Nelly Chittaranjan; doing so discreetly, yet in a way to let Chittaranjan know he was looking at her.

Chittaranjan rocked and clacked his sabots on the floor.

'Anything else, Pa?'

Chittaranjan looked at Harbans. Harbans shook his head.

'Nothing else, Nelly.'

She went inside, past the curtains into the big blue drawing-room where on one wall Harbans saw a large framed picture of the Round Table Conference with King George V and Mahatma Gandhi sitting together, the King formally dressed and smiling, the Mahatma in a loincloth, also smiling. The picture made Harbans easier. He himself had a picture like that in his drawing-room in Port of Spain.

Then Foam had an accident. He knocked the Negro waiter down and spilled his red sweet drink on the floor.

Chittaranjan didn't look. 'It could wipe up easy. Tiles, you know.'

Nelly came out, smiled maliciously at Foam and cleaned up the mess.

Chittaranjan stood up. Even in his sabots he looked no more than five feet tall. He went to a corner of the veranda, his sabots clicking and clacking, took up a tall chromium-plated column and set it next to Foam's chair.

'Kick it down,' he said. He looked flushed, as though he was going to break out in sweat.

Harbans said, 'Ooh.'

'Come on, Baksh son, kick this down.'

'Goldsmith!' Harbans cried.

Foam got up.

'Foam! What you doing?'

'No, Mr Harbans. Let him kick it down.'

The column was kicked.

It swayed, then sprang back into an upright position.

'You can't kick this down.' Chittaranjan took the ashtray with the weighted bottom back to its corner, and returned to his rocking-chair. 'Funny the modern things they making these days, eh? Something my brother in Port of Spain give me.' Chittaranjan looked at Harbans. 'Barrister, you know.'

Foam sat down in some confusion.

Harbans said, 'Your daughter look bright like anything, Goldsmith.'

'Tcha!' Chittaranjan didn't stop rocking. 'When people hear she talk, they don't want to believe that she only have sixteen years. Taking typing-lesson *and* shorthand from Teacher Francis, you know. She could take down prescription *and* type them out. This doctor son you have . . .'

'Oh, he ain't a doctor *yet*.'

'You shoulda bring him with you, you know. I like children with ambition.'

'He was learning today. Scholar and student, you see. But you must come and see him. He *want* to see you.'

'I want to see him too.'

So it was settled.

Harbans was so relieved that Chittaranjan had made no fresh demands, he took a sip of his orange liquid.

Chittaranjan rocked. 'You ain't have to worry about the election. Once I for you'—he made a small dismissing gesture with his right hand—'you win.'

'The boy father say he for me too.'

Chittaranjan dismissed Baksh with a suck of gold teeth. 'Tcha! What *he* could do?'

Foam's loyalty was quick. 'He control a thousand votes.'

Harbans made peace. 'In these modern days, everybody have to unite. I is a Hindu. You, Goldsmith, is a Hindu. Baksh is Muslim. It matter?'

Chittaranjan only rocked.

Foam said, 'We got to form a committee.'

Chittaranjan widened his smile.

'Committee to organize. Meetings, canvassers, posters.'

Harbans tried to laugh away Foam's speech. 'Things getting modern these days, Goldsmith.'

Chittaranjan said, 'I don't see how committee could bring in more votes than me. If I go to a man in Elvira and I tell him to vote for so-and-so, I want to see him tell me no.'

The cool threatening tone of Chittaranjan's last sentence took Harbans aback. He didn't expect it from such a small man.

'What about that traitor Lorkhoor?' he asked.

But he got no reply because at that moment a loud crash on the galvanized-iron roof startled them all. The Negro waiters shuddered. There was a sound of breaking glass.

From inside a woman's voice, weary, placid—Mrs. Chittaranjan's—said, 'Breadfruit again. Break a glass pane this time.'

Chittaranjan jumped up, his sabots giving the loudest clack. 'Is that son-of-a-bitch Ramlogan!' He ran to the veranda wall, stood on tiptoe and hunched himself over the ledge. Harbans and Foam looked out with him.

Ramlogan was picking his teeth with unconcern. 'Ha. Ha.'

'Ramlogan!' Chittaranjan shouted, his thin voice edged and carrying far. 'One of these days I going to mash up your arse.'

'Ha. You go mash up my arse? You ain't even got nothing to sit down on, and *you* go mash up *my* arse?'

'Yes, I go do it. I, Chittaranjan, go do it, so help me God!' He suddenly turned to Foam and Harbans, the fixed smile on his face, and screamed at them: 'Oh, God! Don't let that man provoke me, you hear! Don't let him provoke me!'

Ramlogan left his shop door and walked to the edge of his yard. 'Come down,' he invited, with savage amiability. 'Come down and mash up my arse. Come down and fight. Come down and cut down the breadfruit tree *or* the zaboca tree. Then we go see who is man.'

'Don't worry with the man, Pa,' Nelly Chittaranjan, inside. 'You don't see that the man just want you to low-rate yourself?'

Chittaranjan paid no attention. '*You* is a fighter?' he challenged. '*You?* You ever been to Port of Spain? Go to Port of Spain, ask somebody to show you where St Vincent Street is, walk down St Vincent Street, stop at the Supreme Court and ask them about Chittaranjan. *They* go tell you who is the fighter. Supreme Court know *you* as a fighter?'

Ramlogan hesitated. Chittaranjan had been an expert stick-fighter. He hadn't much of a reach but he made up for that by his nimbleness. And his stick-fighting had often got him into trouble with the police.

Ramlogan couldn't reply. He put his hands on the wire fence.

'Take your fat dirty hand offa my fence,' Chittaranjan snapped. 'A nasty blow-up shopkeeper like you want to put your hand on my fence?'

'All right, all right. One day I going to build my own fence, and then *you* don't touch it, I warning you.'

'But till then, take your fat dirty hand offa my fence.'

Then, unexpectedly, Ramlogan began to cry. He cried in a painful, belly-shaking way, pumping the tears out. 'You don't even want me to touch your fence now.' He wiped his eyes with the back of his big hairy hand. 'But you don't have to be so insultive with it. All right, you ain't want me. Nobody ain't want me. The candidate ain't want me. The three of all-you remain up there complotting against me, and you ain't want me to put my hand on your fence now. *I* don't control no votes, so nobody ain't want me. Just because I don't control no votes.' He stopped for breath, and added with spirit: 'Chittaranjan, the next time one of your wife chickens come in my yard, don't bother to look for it. Because that night I eating good.' He became maudlin again: 'I don't control no votes. Nobody don't want me. But everybody chicken think they could just walk in my yard, as if my yard is a republic.'

Sobbing, he retreated to his shop.

Chittaranjan went back to his rocking-chair. 'Mother arse,' he said, giving a bite to every consonant. 'For three years now, since the man come to live in Elvira, he only giving me provocation.' But Chittaranjan was as poised as before. His face was flushed; but the flush on Chittaranjan's face was, it seemed, as fixed as the smile.

Night fell.

Chittaranjan said, 'You go have to start a rum-account with Ramlogan.' The quarrel might not have been, to judge from Chittaranjan's calm.

Foam nodded. 'Only rumshop in Elvira, Mr Harbans.'

Harbans looked down at his hands. 'I have to buy rum for everybody?'

'Not *every*body,' Chittaranjan said.

Harbans changed the subject. 'What about that traitor Lorkhoor?'

'Lorkhoor ain't got no mind,' Chittaranjan said. 'But he can't worry me. Even supposing Lorkhoor win one thousand Hindu votes for Preacher, that still leave you three thousand Hindu votes. Now, three thousand Hindu votes and one thousand votes—you could depend on *me* for the Spanish votes—that give you four thousand votes.'

'Don't forget the thousand Muslim votes,' Foam boomed.

Chittaranjan acknowledged them distastefully. 'Make five thousand votes. You can't lose.'

'So is only five thousand now, eh?' Harbans said to Foam. 'In the lorry you tell me six thousand. I imagine tomorrow you go tell me four thousand and the day after you go tell me three thousand.'

'Mr Harbans!' Chittaranjan called. 'Mr Harbans, you mustn't talk like that!'

'Nobody can't fool me. I *know* this was going to happen. I had a sign.'

'Five thousand out of eight thousand,' Chittaranjan said. 'You can't lose. Majority of two thousand. Remember, I, Chittaranjan, is for you.'

'This Lorkhoor is a damn traitor!' Harbans exclaimed finally. He became calmer. He looked at Foam and Chittaranjan, smiled and began to coo: 'I sorry, Goldsmith. I sorry, Foam. I was just getting a little down-couraged, that is all.'

'Election fever,' Foam said. 'I know how it is.'

They settled other matters. Chittaranjan accepted the need for a committee, and they decided who were to be members of it. It pleased Harbans to see Chittaranjan growing less frigid towards Foam. At length he broke the news that Foam was the campaign manager. Chittaranjan took it well. It was not a post he coveted, because it was a paid post; everything he did for Harbans, he did only out of the goodness of his heart.

Before they left, Chittaranjan said, 'I coming up to Port of Spain to see that doctor son you have. I *like* ambitious children.'

'He *want* to see you too, Goldsmith.'

Foam and Harbans got into the Dodge.

A small oil lamp burned in Ramlogan's gloomy shop and the man himself was eating his dinner from an enamel plate on the counter.

'Wave to him,' Foam said.

Ramlogan waved back. 'Right, boss!' He was surprisingly cheerful.

'Funny man,' Harbans said, driving off.

'He always ready to play brave brave, but you never know when he going to start crying,' Foam said. 'He lonely really. Wife dead long time. Daughters don't come to see him.'

*

This time there was no waving and shouting. The youths sitting on the culverts and the half-naked children still straying about were dazzled by the headlights of the Dodge and recognized Harbans only when he had passed. Harbans drove warily. It was Friday evening and the main road was busy. The drinking was to begin soon at Ramlogan's rumshop; the other Friday evening excitement, Mr Cuffy's sermon, had already begun.

Foam pointed out Mr Cuffy's house. A gas lamp in the small rickety veranda lit up Mr Cuffy, an old Negro in a tight blue suit, thumping a Bible; and lit up Mr Cuffy's congregation in the yard below, a reverent Negro group with many women. The rumble of the Dodge obliterated Mr Cuffy's words, but his gestures were impassioned.

'Mr Cawfee is Preacher right hand man,' Foam said. 'Not one of those Negro people there going to vote for you, Mr Harbans.'

'Traitors! Elvira just full of traitors.'

Mr Cuffy and his congregation passed out of sight.

Harbans, thinking of the white women, the black bitch, the loud-speaker van, the seventy-five dollars a month, the rum-account with Ramlogan, the treachery of Lorkhoor, saw defeat and humiliation everywhere.

And then Foam shouted, 'Look, Mr Harbans! Preacher.'

Harbans saw. A tall Negro with high frizzy hair, long frizzy beard, long white robe; haloed in the light of the headlamps; walking briskly at the edge of the road, stamping his staff, the hem of his robe dancing above sandalled feet. They saw him leave the road, go across a yard, saw him knock; and as they drove past, saw the door opened for him.

'That is *all* he doing,' Foam said. 'Walking brisk brisk from door to door and knocking and going in and coming out and walking brisk brisk again.'

'What he does talk about when he go in?'

'Nobody ain't know, Mr Harbans. Nobody does tell.'

They stopped at Baksh's house and Foam got off.

'We go have the first committee meeting some time next week, Mr Harbans. It going to give you a encouragement.'

But Foam's hand was still on the door.

'Ooh, I was forgetting.' Harbans dipped into his hip pocket. 'Something. Nothing much, but is a beginning.'

'Is a encouragement,' Foam said, taking the note.

Harbans drove out of Elvira, past the abandoned cocoa-house, past Cordoba, up Elvira Hill, down Elvira Hill. At the bottom of the hill his headlights picked out the two white women on their bicycles.

'It don't mean nothing,' Harbans said to himself. 'I mustn't get down-couraged. It don't mean nothing at all.'

If he only knew, his troubles hadn't started.

3. The Writing on the Wall

IN SPITE OF WHAT HE HAD SAID to Harbans in the lorry about going up for the County Council, Foam hadn't been thinking of going into politics at all. But when Lorkhoor had suddenly begun to campaign for Preacher, Foam announced that he was going to campaign for Harbans. Mrs Baksh objected. But Baksh said, 'It going to be a good experience for the boy.' Baksh had already agreed to support Harbans for two thousand dollars. Foam, however, wanted to do some loudspeaking, like Lorkhoor; and Baksh himself had been talking for some time in Ramlogan's rumshop about the money to be made out of a loudspeaker. So when Harbans came that afternoon, Baksh hadn't said a word about the two thousand dollars but had asked instead for a loudspeaker van and for Foam to be campaign manager.

The rivalry between Foam and Lorkhoor began when Teacher Francis, the new headmaster of the Elvira Government School, formed the Elvira Social and Debating Club. Teacher Francis was a young red-skinned Negro who dazzled Elvira with his sharp city dress: sharkskin zoot suit, hot tie knotted below an open collar, two-toned shoes. He was young for a headmaster, but to be a headmaster in Elvira was to be damned by the Trinidad Education Department. (Teacher Francis had been so damned for parading his agnosticism in a Port of Spain school. He had drawn a shapeless outline on the blackboard and asked his class, 'Tell me, eh. That soul you does hear so much about, it look like that, or what?' One boy had been outraged. The boy's father complained to the Director of Education and Teacher Francis was damned to Elvira.) He formed the Elvira Social and Debating Club to encourage things of the mind. The idea was new and the response was big. Lorkhoor quickly became the star of the club. It was Lorkhoor who wrote most of the poems and stories which were read to the club, and one of Lorkhoor's poems had even been printed on the leader page of the *Trinidad Sentinel*, in the special type the *Sentinel* reserves for poetry and the Biblical quotation at the bottom of the leader:

Elvira, awake! Behold the dawn!
It shines for you, it shines for me . . .

In all the discussions, political and religious—Teacher Francis was still hot on religion—Lorkhoor shone and didn't allow Foam or anyone else to shine. Teacher Francis always backed up Lorkhoor; between them they turned the club into a place where they could show off before an audience. They made jokes and puns that went over the heads of nearly everyone else. One day Teacher Francis said, 'People like you and me, Lorkhoor, are two and far between.' Lorkhoor alone roared. At the next meeting Lorkhoor began a review of a film: 'The points in this film are two and far between—the beginning and the end.' People stopped coming to the club; those who came, came to drink—there were always two or three people in Elvira who were having a row with Ramlogan the rumshop owner—and the club broke up.

Teacher Francis and Lorkhoor remained thick. Teacher Francis felt Lorkhoor understood him. He said Lorkhoor was a born writer and he was always sending off letters on Lorkhoor's behalf to the *Sentinel* and the *Guardian* and the *Gazette*. So far nothing had come of that.

And then Foam was really cut up when Lorkhoor got that job advertising for the cinemas from a loudspeaker van. It was Foam who had heard of the job first, from Harichand the printer, a man of many contacts. Foam applied and had practically got the job when Lorkhoor, supported by Teacher Francis, stepped in. Lorkhoor pointed out that Foam was too young for a driving permit (which was true); that Foam's English wasn't very good (which was true). Lorkhoor pointed out that he, Lorkhoor, had a driving permit (which was true); and his English was faultless (which was an understatement). Lorkhoor got the job and said it was a degradation. But while he drove about Central Trinidad in his loudspeaker van, speaking faultless English to his heart's content, Foam had to remain in Elvira, an apprentice in his father's shop. Foam hated the stuffy dark shop, hated the eternal tacking, which was all he was allowed to do, hated Elvira, at moments almost hated his family.

He never forgave Lorkhoor. The job, which Lorkhoor called a degradation, was his by rights; he would have given anything to get it. And now the election gave him the next best thing. It gave him a loudspeaker of his own and took him out of the shop. He worked not so much for the victory of Harbans and the defeat of Preacher, as for the humiliation of Lorkhoor and Teacher Francis.

*

Even before the committee met, Foam set to work. He got a pot of red paint from Chittaranjan and went around Elvira painting culverts, telegraph poles and tree-trunks with the enthusiastic slogan, VOTE HARBANS OR DIE!

Mrs Baksh didn't like it at all. 'Nobody ain't listening to me,' she said. 'Everybody just washing their foot and jumping in this democracy business. But I promising you, for all the sweet it begin sweet, it going to end damn sour.'

She softened a little when the loudspeaker and the van came, but she still made it clear that she didn't approve. All Elvira knew about the van—it was another example of Baksh's depth—and Mrs Baksh was frightened by the very size of her fortune. She was tempting fate, inviting the evil eye.

Nobody else saw it that way. The little Bakshes clustered around the van while Foam and Baksh made arrangements for lodging it. To get the van into the yard they had to pull down part of the rotting wooden fence and build a bridge over the gutter. Some poorer people and their children came to watch. Baksh and Foam stopped talking; frowned and concentrated and spat, as though the van was just a big bother. And though it wasn't strictly necessary then, they put up the loudspeaker on the van. They spread a gunny sack on the hood, placed the loudspeaker on it and tied it down to the bumper with four lengths of rope.

Baksh spoke only one sentence during the whole of this operation. 'Have to get a proper stand for this damn loudspeaker thing,' he said, resentfully.

After dinner that evening, Foam, with his twelve-year-old brother Rafiq, went in the van to Cordoba, a good three miles away, to do some more slogans. The Spaniards watched without interest while he daubed VOTE HARBANS OR DIE!

The next evening he went to complete the job.

The first three words of his slogans had been covered over with whitewash and Cordoba was marked everywhere, in dripping red letters, DIE! DIE! DIE!

'That is Lorkhoor work,' Foam said.

Then Rafiq pointed to a wall. The first three words of the slogan were only partially covered over. Three strokes with a dry brush had been used, and between each stroke there was a gap, and the sign read: ──TE───N──DIE!

'Ten die,' Rafiq said.

'Come on, man,' Foam said. 'You letting a thing like that frighten you? You is a man now, Rafiq. And whatever you do,' Foam added, 'don't tell Ma, you hear.'

But that was the first thing Rafiq did.

'*Ten* die!' Mrs Baksh clapped her hand to her big bosom and sat on a bench, still holding the ash-rag with which she had been washing up.

Baksh swilled down some tea from a large enamel cup. 'It don't mean nothing, man. Somebody just trying to be funny, that's all.'

'Oh, God, Baksh, this election sweetness!'

The little Bakshes came into the kitchen.

'Don't mean nothing,' Baksh said. 'It say ten die. It only have nine of we in this house. The seven children and you and me. Was just a accident, man.'

'Was *no* accident,' Rafiq said.

'Oh, God, Baksh, see how the sweetness turning sour!'

'Is only that traitor Lorkhoor playing the fool,' Foam said. 'Let him wait. When *he* start putting up signs for Preacher . . .'

'How it could mean anything?' Baksh laughed. 'It say ten die and it only have nine of we here.'

Mrs Baksh became cooler. A thought seemed to strike her and she looked down at herself and cried, 'Oh, God, Baksh, how we know is only nine?'

*

Though he didn't care for the 'Ten die!' sign and for Mrs Baksh's fears, Foam didn't go out painting any more slogans. Instead he concentrated on the first meeting of the campaign committee.

He decided not to hold the meeting at Chittaranjan's house. The place made him too uncomfortable and he still remembered the malicious smile Nelly Chittaranjan had given him when he knocked his sweet drink over. His own house, the London Tailoring Establishment, was out of the question: Mrs Baksh didn't even want to hear about the election. He decided then to have the meeting in the old wooden bungalow of Dhaniram, the Hindu pundit, who had also been made a member of the committee. At least there would be no complications with Dhaniram's family. Dhaniram's wife had been paralysed for more than twenty years. The only other person in the house was a meek young daughter-in-law who had been deserted by Dhaniram's son only two months after marriage. That was some time ago. Nobody knew where the boy had got to; but Dhaniram always gave out that the boy was in England, studying something.

On the evening of the meeting Foam and Baksh, despite protests from Mrs Baksh, drove over in the loudspeaker van.

From the road Foam could see two men in the veranda. One was

Dhaniram, a large man in Hindu priestly dress lying flat on his belly reading a newspaper by an oil lamp. The other man drooped on a bench. This was Mahadeo.

Neither Dhaniram nor Mahadeo was really important. They had been drafted into the committee only to keep them from making mischief. Dhaniram was the best known pundit in Elvira, but he was too fond of gossip and religious disputation, and was looked upon as something of a buffoon. Mahadeo was an out and out fool; everybody in Elvira knew that. But Mahadeo could be useful; he worked on what remained of the Elvira Estate as a sub-overseer, a 'driver' (not of vehicles or slaves, but of free labourers), and as a driver he could always put pressure on his labourers.

When Foam and Baksh came into the veranda Dhaniram jumped up and the whole house shook. It was a shaky house and the veranda was particularly shaky. Dhaniram had kept on extending it at one end, so that the veranda opened out into something like a plain; there were gaps in the floor where the uncured, unplaned cedar planks had shrunk.

'Ah,' Dhaniram said, rubbing his hands. 'Campaign manager. Come to discuss the campaign, eh?'

Everything about the election thrilled Dhaniram. Words like campaign, candidate, committee, constituency, legislative council, thrilled him especially. He was a big exuberant man with a big belly that looked unnecessary and almost detachable.

Mahadeo didn't get up or say anything. He drooped on his bench, a plump little man in tight clothes, his large empty eyes staring at the floor.

There was an explosion of coughing inside the house and a woman's voice, strained and querulous, asked in Hindi, 'Who's there?'

Dhaniram led Foam and Baksh to the small drawing-room and made them look through an open door into a dark bedroom. They saw a woman stretched out on a four-poster. It was Dhaniram's wife. She was lying on her left side and they couldn't see her face.

'Election committee,' Dhaniram said to the room.

'Oh.' She didn't turn.

Dhaniram led Foam and Baksh back to the veranda and seated them on a bench opposite Mahadeo.

Dhaniram sat down beside Mahadeo and began to shake his legs until the veranda shook. 'So the goldsmith fix up, eh? Everything?'

Foam didn't understand.

'I mean, Chittaranjan see the boy? You know, Harbans son.'

'Oh, yes, that fix up,' Baksh said. 'Chittaranjan went to Port of Spain day before yesterday.'

Dhaniram lit a cigarette and pulled at it in the Brahmin way, drawing the smoke through his closed hand. 'Chittaranjan really believe Harbans going to let his son marry Nelly?'

Baksh seized this. 'You hear anything?'

Dhaniram shrugged his shoulders. 'We want some light. *Doolahin*, bring the Petromax,' Dhaniram called.

Baksh noted that though she had been deserted for so long, Dhaniram still called his daughter-in-law *doolahin*, bride.

'How Hari?' Baksh asked. 'He write yet?'

Hari was Dhaniram's son.

'Boy in England, man,' Dhaniram said. 'Studying. Can't study and write letters.'

The *doolahin* brought the Petromax. She looked a good Hindu girl. She had a small soft face with a wide mouth. About eighteen perhaps; barefooted, as was proper; a veil over her forehead, as was also proper. She hung the Petromax on the hook from the ceiling and went back to the kitchen, a smoky room boarded off at one corner of the vast veranda.

Baksh asked, 'How she taking it these days? Still crying?'

Dhaniram wasn't interested. 'She getting over it now. So Chittaranjan really believe that Nelly going to marry Harbans son?'

Mahadeo sat silent, his head bent, his full eyes staring at his unlaced black boots. Foam wasn't interested in the conversation. In the light of the Petromax he studied Dhaniram's veranda walls. There were many Hindu coloured prints; but by far the biggest thing was a large Esso calendar, with Pundit Dhaniram's religious commitments written in pencil above the dates. It looked as though Dhaniram's practice was falling off. It didn't matter; Foam knew that Dhaniram also owned the fifth part of a tractor and Baksh said that was worth at least two hundred dollars a month.

Harbans came, agitated, looking down at the ground, and Foam saw at once that something was wrong.

Dhaniram rose. Mahadeo rose and spoke for the first time: 'Good night, Mr Harbans.'

Dhaniram took Harbans into the drawing-room and Foam heard Harbans saying, 'Ooh, ooh, *how* you is, *maharajin?* We just come to talk over this election nonsense.'

But he looked dejected like anything when he came out and sat on a blanket on the floor.

Dhaniram shouted, '*Doolahin,* candidate here. We want some tea. What sort of tea you want, eh, Mr Harbans? Chocolate, coffee or green tea?'

'Green tea,' Harbans said distractedly.

'What happen, Mr Harbans?' Foam asked.

Harbans locked his fingers. 'Can't understand it, Foam. Can't understand it. I is a old old man. Why everybody down against me?'

Dhaniram was thrilled. He gave a little laugh, realized it was wrong, and tried to look serious. But his eyes still twinkled.

'I drive through Cordoba,' Harbans said, talking down to his hands, his voice thin and almost breaking. 'As soon as the Spanish people see the lorry, they turn their back. They shut their window. And I did think they was going to vote for me. Can't understand it, Foam. I ain't do the Spanish people nothing.'

'Is that traitor Lorkhoor,' Baksh said.

*

Then Chittaranjan came. He wore his visiting outfit and carried a green book in his hand. He seemed to know the house well because he didn't wait for Dhaniram to introduce him to the invalid inside.

[46]

As he came up the steps he shouted, 'How you feeling these days, *maharajin?* Is me, Chittaranjan, the goldsmith.'

When he came back out to the veranda, it seemed that Chittaranjan too had bad news. His smile was there, as fixed as his flush; but there was anger and shame in his narrow eyes.

'Dhaniram,' Chittaranjan said, as soon as he sat down and took off his vast grey felt hat, 'we got to make new calculations.'

Dhaniram took Chittaranjan at his word. *'Doolahin!'* he shouted. 'Pencil and paper. New calculations. Committee waiting. Candidate and committee waiting.'

Harbans looked at Chittaranjan. 'What I do the Spanish people for them to turn their back on me?'

Chittaranjan forced the words out: 'Something happen, Mr Harbans. This thing not going to be so easy . . .'

'It don't surprise me, Goldsmith,' Harbans interrupted. 'Loudspeaker van. Campaign manager. Rum-account. Lorkhoor. People turning their back on me. Nothing don't surprise me at all.'

The *doolahin* brought some brown shop-paper. 'I ain't have no pencil. I look everywhere.'

Dhaniram forgot about the election. 'But this is craziness, *doolahin*. I have that pencil six months now.'

'Is only a pencil,' the *doolahin* said.

'Is what *you* think,' Dhaniram said, the smile going out of his eye. 'Is more than just a pencil. Is the principle. Is only since you come here that we start losing things.'

'Your son, fust of all,' Baksh said.

Dhaniram looked at Baksh and the smile came into his eyes again. He spat, aiming successfully at a gap in the floor.

Foam said, 'This is the pencil you was looking for?' From the floor he picked up an indelible pencil of the sort used in government offices. A length of string was attached to a groove at the top.

Dhaniram began to rub himself. 'Ah, yes. Was doing the crossword just before you come in.'

The *doolahin* tossed her head and went back to her kitchen.

Harbans brooded.

All of a sudden he said, 'Chittaranjan, I thought *you* was the big controller of the Spanish vote?'

Everyone noticed that Harbans had called Chittaranjan by his name, and not 'goldsmith.' It was almost an insult.

Yet Chittaranjan didn't seem to feel it. He fidgeted with the book he had brought and said not a word.

Harbans, not getting an answer, addressed his hands. 'In the 1946 elections none of the candidates I know did spend all this money. I have to have loudspeaker van and rum-account with Ramlogan?'

Baksh looked offended. 'I know you mean me, boss. The moment you start talking about loudspeaker van. What you say about 1946 is true. Nobody did spend much money. But that was only the fust election. People did just go and vote for the man they like. Now is different. People learning. You have to spend on them.'

'Yes, you have to spend on them,' Dhaniram said, his legs shaking, his eyes dancing. He relished all the grand vocabulary of the election. 'Otherwise somebody else going to spend on them.'

Mahadeo, the estate driver, raised his right hand, turned his large eyes on Harbans and twitched his thick little moustache and plump little mouth. 'You spending your money in vain, Mr Harbans,' he said gently. 'We win already.'

Harbans snapped, 'Is arse-talk like that does lose election. (Oh God, you see how this election making me dirty up my mouth.) But you, Mahadeo, you go around opening your big mouth and saying Harbans done win already. You think that is the way to get people vote?'

'Exactly,' said Dhaniram. 'People go say, "If he done win, he ain't want my vote."'

'Foam,' Harbans said. 'How much vote you giving me today? Was six thousand when I first see you. Then was five thousand. Is *four* thousand today?'

Foam didn't have a chance to reply because Chittaranjan spoke up at last: 'Yes, Mr Harbans, is four thousand.'

Harbans didn't take it well. 'Look at the mess I getting myself in, in my old old age. Why I couldn't go away and sit down quiet and dead somewhere else, outside Elvira? Foam, take the pencil and paper and write this down. It have eight thousand votes in Naparoni. Four thousand Hindu, two thousand Negro, one thousand Spanish, and a thousand Muslim. I ain't getting the Negro vote and I ain't getting a thousand Hindu vote. That should leave me with five thousand. But now, Goldsmith, you say is only four thousand. Tell me, I beg you, where we drop this thousand vote between last week Friday and today?'

'In Cordoba,' Chittaranjan said penitently. 'You see for youself how the Spanish people playing the fool. Just look at this book.'

He showed the green book he had been turning over.

Mahadeo wrinkled his brow and read out the title slowly: '*Let—God—Be—True.*'

As a pundit Dhaniram regarded himself as an expert on God. He looked at the book quizzically and said, 'Hmh.'

'That is all that the Spanish talking about now,' Chittaranjan said, pointing to the book. 'I did know something was wrong the moment I land in Cordoba. Everywhere I look I only seeing red signs saying, "Die! Die!"'

'That is Lorkhoor work,' Foam said.

Chittaranjan shook his head. 'I don't know if any of all-you see two white women riding about on big red bicycles. If I tell you the havoc they causing!'

'Witnesses!' Harbans exclaimed. 'I know. I had a sign. I shoulda run them over that day.'

No one knew what he was talking about.

'Who they campaigning for?' Baksh asked. 'For Preacher?'

'For Jehovah,' Chittaranjan said. 'They can't touch the Hindus or the Muslims or the Negroes, but they wreaking havoc with the Spanish. Everywhere I go in Cordoba, the Spanish people telling me that the world going to end in 1976. I ask them how they know the date so exact and they tell me the Bible say so.'

[49]

Dhaniram slapped his thigh. 'Armageddon!' Pundit Dhaniram had been educated at one of the Presbyterian schools of the Canadian Mission where he had been taught hymns and other Christian things. He cherished the training. 'It make me see both sides,' he used to say; and even now, although he was a Hindu priest, he often found himself humming hymns like 'Jesus loves me, yes I know.' He slapped his thigh and exclaimed, 'Armageddon!'

'Something like that,' Chittaranjan said. 'And these white woman telling the Spanish that they mustn't take no part in politics and the Spanish taking all what these woman say as a gospel.' Chittaranjan sounded hurt. 'I telling you, it come as a big big pussonal blow, especially as I know the Spanish people so long. Look, I go to see old Edaglo, you know, Teresa father. The man is my good good friend. For years he eating my food, drinking my whisky, and borrowing my money. And now he tell me he ain't voting. So I ask him, "Why you ain't voting, Edaglo?" And he answer me back, man. He say, "Politics ain't a divine thing." Then he ask me, "You know who start politics?" You could imagine how that take me back. "Somebody start politics?" I say. He laugh in a mocking sorta way as though he know more than everybody else and say, "You see how you ain't know these little things. Is because you ain't study enough." He, Edaglo, talking like that to me, Chittaranjan! "Go home," he say, "and study the Bible and you go read and see that the man who start politics was Nimrod."'

'Who is Nimrod?' Baksh asked.

Pundit Dhaniram slapped his thigh again. 'Nimrod was a mighty hunter.'

They pondered this.

Harbans was abstracted, disconsolate.

Baksh said, 'What those woman want is just man, you hear. The minute they get one good man, all this talk about mighty hunting gone with the wind.'

Dhaniram was pressing Chittaranjan: 'You didn't tell them about Caesar? The things that are Caesar's. Render unto Caesar. That sort of thing.'

Chittaranjan lifted his thin hands. 'I don't meddle too much in all that Christian bacchanal, you hear. And as I was leaving, he, Edaglo, call me back. Me, Chittaranjan. And he give me this green book. Let God be true. Tcha!'

Mahadeo shook his head and clucked sympathetically. 'Old Edaglo really pee on you, Goldsmith.'

'Not only pee,' Chittaranjan said. 'He shake it.'

And having made his confession, Chittaranjan gathered about him much of his old dignity again.

*

'Even if the Spanish ain't voting,' Foam said, 'we have four thousand votes. Three thousand Hindu and one thousand Muslim. Preacher only getting three thousand. Two thousand Negro and a thousand Hindu. I don't see how we could lose.'

Dhaniram said, 'I don't see how a whole thousand Hindus going to vote for Preacher. Lorkhoor don't control so much votes.'

'Don't fool your head,' Foam said quickly. 'Preacher help out a lot of Hindu people in this place. And if the Hindus see a Hindu like Lorkhoor supporting Preacher, well, a lot of them go want to vote for Preacher. Lorkhoor going about telling people that they mustn't think about race and religion now. He say it ain't have nothing wrong if Hindu people vote for a Negro like Preacher.'

'This Lorkhoor want a good cut-arse,' Baksh said.

Chittaranjan agreed. 'That sort of talk dangerous at election time. Lorkhoor ain't know what he saying.'

Harbans locked and unlocked his fingers. 'Nothing I does touch does turn out nice and easy. Everybody else have life easy. I don't know what sin I commit to have life so hard.'

Everyone fell silent in the veranda, looking at Harbans, waiting for him to cry. Only the Petromax hissed and hummed and the moths dashed against it.

Then the *doolahin* thumped out bringing tea in delightfully ornamented cups so wide at the mouth that the tea slopped over continually.

Dhaniram said, 'Tea, Mr Harbans. Drink it. You go feel better.'
'Don't want *no* tea.'

Dhaniram gave his little laugh.

Two or three tears trickled down Harbans's thin old face. He took the cup, blew on it, and put it to his lips; but before he drank he broke down and sobbed. 'I ain't got no friends or helpers or nothing. Everybody only want money money.'

Mahadeo was wounded. 'You ain't giving *me* nothing, Mr Harbans.' He hadn't thought of asking.

Dhaniram, who had been promised something—contracts for his tractor—pulled at his cigarette. 'Is not as though you giving things to we pussonal, Mr Harbans. You must try and feel that you giving to the people. After all, is the meaning of this democracy.'

'Exactly,' said Baksh. 'Is for the sake of the community we want you to get in the Legislative Council. You got to think about the community, boss. As you yourself tell me the other day, money ain't everything.'

'Is true,' Harbans fluted. 'Is true.' He smiled and dried his eyes. 'You is all faithful. I did just forget myself, that is all.'

They sipped their tea.

To break the mood Dhaniram scolded his daughter-in-law. 'You was a long time making the tea, *doolahin*.'

She said, 'I had to light the fire and then I had to boil the water and then I had to draw the tea and then I had to cool the tea.'

She had cooled the tea so well it was almost cold. It was the way Dhaniram liked it; but the rest of the committee didn't care for cool tea. Only Harbans, taking small, noisy sips, seemed indifferent.

Dhaniram's wife called querulously from her room. The *doolahin* sucked her teeth and went.

Foam said, 'If Lorkhoor getting Hindus to vote for Preacher, I don't see why we can't get Negroes to vote for we.'

They sipped their tea and thought.

*

Dhaniram pulled hard at his cigarette and slapped his dhoti-clad thigh. 'Aha! Idea!'

They looked at him in surprise.

'It go take some money . . .' Dhaniram said apologetically.

Harbans took a long sip of cool tea.

'It go take some money. But not much. Here in Elvira the campaign committee must be a sort of social welfare committee. Supposing one of those Negroes fall sick. *We* go go to them. *We* go take them to doctor in *we* taxi. *We* go pay for their medicine.'

Chittaranjan sucked his teeth and became like the formidable Chittaranjan Foam had seen rocking and smiling in his tiled veranda. 'Dhaniram, you talking like if you ain't know how hard these Negroes is in Elvira. You ever see any Negro fall sick? They just does drop down and dead. And that does only happen when they about eighty or ninety.'

'All right. They don't get sick. But even you say they does dead sometimes. Well, two three bound to dead before elections.'

'You going to kill some of them?' Baksh asked.

'Well, if even *one* dead, *we* go bury him. *We* go hold the wake. *We* go take *we* coffee and *we* biscuits.'

Baksh said, 'And you think that go make the Negroes vote for you?'

'It go make them feel shame if they ain't vote for we,' Dhaniram said. 'And if they ain't vote, well, the next time they start bawling for help, they better not come round here.'

Mahadeo lifted his right hand as a warning that he was about to speak again. 'Old Sebastian is one Negro who look as though he might dead before elections.'

'Is a good idea,' Foam said. 'And every one of we could buy just one sweet drink for some Negro child every day until elections. Different child every day. And the parents. We mustn't only help them if they fall sick or if they dead. If they can't get a work or something. If they going to have a wedding or something. Take the goldsmith here. He could make a little present for Negroes getting married.'

Chittaranjan said animatedly, 'Foam, you talking as if I does make jewellery with my own gold. I ain't have no gold of my own. When people want things make, they does bring their own gold.'

And Chittaranjan destroyed an illusion which Foam had had since he was a boy; he had always believed that the gold dust and silver shavings the children collected from Chittaranjan's workshop belonged to Chittaranjan.

Harbans said, 'Foam, take the pencil and paper and write down all those who sick in Elvira.'

Dhaniram said, 'Mungal sick like anything.'

Mahadeo lifted his hand. 'It have a whole week now that Basdai and Rampiari ain't come out to work. They must be sick too.'

Harbans said, 'Mahadeo, you know you is a damn fool. You think is *Hindu* sick I want Foam to write down?'

Chittaranjan said, 'Like I say, it ain't have no Negro sick in Elvira.'

'All right.' Harbans was getting annoyed again. 'Who getting married?'

Chittaranjan said, 'Only Hindu and Muslim getting married. Is the wedding season now. The Negro people don't get married so often. Most of them just living with woman. Just like that, you know.'

Harbans said, 'And you can't damn well start taking round wedding-ring to those people as wedding present. So, all we could do is to keep a sharp look-out for any Negro who fall sick or who fall dead. That may you talk about, Mahadeo.'

'Sebastian?'

'Keep a eye on him.'

Foam said, 'I believe Mahadeo should handle the whole of that job. He could make a list of all Negro who sick or going to dead.'

'Yes.' And Harbans added sarcastically, 'You sure that job ain't too big for you, Mahadeo?'

Mahadeo stared at the floor, his big eyes filling with determination. 'I could manage, Mr Harbans. Old Sebastian is one Negro who bound to dead.'

They finished their tea and had some more. Then Harbans sent Foam to get the new posters he had brought in the lorry.

The posters said: HITCH YOUR WAGON TO THE STAR VOTE SURUJPAT ('PAT') HARBANS CHOOSE THE BEST AND LEAVE THE REST. And there was a photograph of Harbans; below that, his name and the star, his symbol.

Mahadeo said, 'It must make a man feel really big sticking his photo all over the place.'

Harbans, unwillingly, smiled.

Chittaranjan asked, 'Where you get those posters print?'

'Port of Spain.'

'Wrong move, Mr Harbans. You shoulda get that boy Harichand to print them.'

'But Harichand ain't got no sorta printery at all,' Harbans said.

'Never mind,' said Chittaranjan. 'People in Elvira wouldn't like that you get your posters print in Port of Spain when it have a Elvira boy who could do them.'

And then Harbans knew. No one in Elvira was fighting *for* him. All Elvira—Preacher, Lorkhoor, Baksh, Chittaranjan, Dhaniram and everybody else—all of them were fighting *him*.

He was nearly seized with another fit of pessimism.

But deep down, despite everything, he knew he was going to win. He cried and raged; but he wanted to fool, not tempt, fate. Then he thought of the sign he had had: the white women and the stalled engine, the black bitch and the stalled engine. He had seen what the first meant. The women had stalled him in Cordoba.

But the dog. What about the dog? Where was that going to stall him?

4. Tiger

SOME DAYS PASSED. The new posters went up. The campaign proceeded. Nothing terrible happened to Mrs Baksh. She became calmer
and Foam thought he could start painting slogans again. But now he
didn't paint VOTE HARBANS OR DIE! He had had his lesson; it was too
easy for the enthusiasm of the slogan to be mistaken for a threat. He
painted straight things like WIN WITH HARBANS and WE WANT HAR-
BANS.

One night when Baksh had taken out the loudspeaker van—he
said it was to do some campaigning but Mrs Baksh said it was to do
some drinking—one night Foam took up his pot of paint and a large
brush and went about Elvira, painting new slogans and refurbishing
old ones. He didn't take the excitable and untrustworthy Rafiq with
him. He took Herbert instead. Herbert was ten and politically and
psychically undeveloped. He didn't care for signs or election slogans; and while Foam painted Herbert whistled and wandered about.

Foam did his job with love. He painted even on houses whose
owners had gone to bed; and only when he had got as far as the old
cocoa-house did he decide it was time to go home.

Herbert hung back a little and Foam noticed that he was walking
in a peculiar way, arching his back and keeping his hands on his belly.
His belly looked more swollen than usual.

'Your belly hurting, Herbert?'

'Yes, man, Foam. Is this gas breaking me up.'

'Don't worry about it too much. All of we did get gas in we belly
when we was small. It does pass.'

'Hope so for truth, man.'

Lights were still on when they got home. They went around to the back of the house. The door was locked from the inside but it wasn't barred; and if you pressed on the middle and pulled and shook at the same time, it fell open. Foam put down the paint-pot and the brush.

'Herbert, when I press down, you pull hard and shake.'

Foam pressed down. Herbert, clutching his belly with one hand, pulled and shook with the other. The door unlocked, and as it did, something fell from Herbert's shirt. In the darkness Foam couldn't see what it was. When he pulled the door open and let out the thin light of the oil lamp inside, he saw.

It was a puppy.

A tiny rickety puppy, mangy, starved; a loose, ribby bundle on the ground. It made no noise. It tried to lift itself up. It only collapsed again, without complaint, without shame.

'Where you pick him up, Herbert?'

'Somewhere.'

'But you can't bring him home. You know how *they* don't like dogs.' *They* was Mrs Baksh.

'Is *my* dog,' Herbert said irrelevantly.

Foam squatted beside the puppy. None of the evening's adventures had disturbed the flies that had settled down for the night around the puppy's eyes. The eyes were rheumy, dead. The puppy itself looked half-dead. When Foam stroked the little muzzle he saw fleas jumping about. He pulled away his finger quickly.

'Take care, Foam. Is them quiet quiet dog does bite, you know.'

Foam stood up. 'You got to feed him good. But how you going to hide him from Ma?'

'*I* go hide him. Got a name for him too. Going to call him Tiger.'

Tiger tried to get up on his haunches. It was as if every tiny rib and every bone were made of lead. But he made it this time, and held the shaky pose.

'See! He recognize the name already,' Herbert said.

Tiger crumpled down again.

'Come on, Tiger,' Herbert said.

Tiger didn't respond.

'What you going to do with him?'

'Take him upstairs. Put him in the bed.'

'And what about Rafiq and Charles and Iqbal?' Foam asked, naming the other Baksh boys. 'Think they go want Tiger to sleep in the same bed with them?'

'We go see.'

The room in which they were was the room behind the tailor shop. It was the only part of the house Baksh had attempted to renovate and it smelled of new concrete and new cyp wood. There was a new concrete floor and a new staircase of rough unpainted planks that led to the upper floor. The whole thing was so makeshift because Baksh said he was thinking of pulling down the whole house one day and putting up something better and bigger. The room was called the store-room; but it was used as a dumping-ground for things the Bakshes didn't want but couldn't bring themselves to throw away.

Foam said, 'You can't take up the dog tonight. *They* still waking. What about hiding him under the steps until morning?'

He rummaged among the pile of rubbish under the staircase and brought out a condensed milk case stencilled STOW AWAY FROM BOIL-ERS, two smelly gunny-sacks and many old issues of the *Trinidad Sentinel*. He put the sacks in the case, the newspapers on the sack, and Tiger on the newspapers.

'Under the steps now.'

The door at the top of the stairs opened and some more light flowed down into the store-room.

Mrs Baksh said, 'What the two of all-you complotting and conspiring down there?'

'Nothing,' Foam said. 'We just putting away the paint and thing.'

'And we cleaning up the place,' Herbert added.

Mrs Baksh didn't take them up on that. 'You see your father?'

'Ain't he out with the loudspeaker?' Foam said.

'I know where he is. He just using this election as a big excuse to lift his tail and run about the place. And is what you doing too. Ha! This election starting sweet sweet for some people, but I promising you it going to turn sour before it end.'

She stood at the top of the stairs, broad and dominant.

Herbert, noisily storing away the paint-pot, pushed Tiger's box under the steps as well.

But Tiger had also to be fed.

Foam knew this. He walked up the steps. 'Herbert take in with one belly pain, Ma. All the way home he holding his belly and bawling. I think he hungry.'

'He ain't hungry one little bit. I don't know who ask him to walk about Elvira with all this dew falling.'

Herbert took his cue from Foam. He came out from under the steps, arched his back, and pressed his hands on his belly. 'God, man, how this gas breaking me up!'

Mrs Baksh said, 'But if a stranger hear this little boy talk they go believe I starving him. You ain't eat this evening, Herbert?'

'Yes, Ma.'

'You ain't eat one whole *roti?*'

'Yes, Ma.'

'You ain't eat *bhaji?*'

'Yes, Ma.'

'You ain't drink half a big pot of tea?'

'Yes, Ma.' Herbert drank enormous quantities of tea. He could drink two or three large enamel cups, and when visitors were present, four or five. Mrs Baksh used to boast to her sisters, 'I ain't see nobody to touch Herbert when it come to drinking tea.'

'You eat all that and you drink all that, and you still asking me to believe that you hungry?'

'Yes, Ma.'

'Look, boy! Don't answer me back like that, you hear. You standing up there with your little belly puff out and you looking at me in my face and you still bold and brave enough to challenge me? Don't think I forgetting how you shame me in front of that Harbans man, you know.'

Foam said, 'Is not his fault, Ma. Is the gas.'

'Gas! And the other modern thing is appendicitis. Nobody did have gas and appendicitis when I was small. It ain't gas. Is just the sort of gratitude I getting from my own children, after all the pinching and scraping and saving I does do. And tell me, for *who* I pinching and scraping and saving?'

She got no reply.

Her annoyance subsided. 'All right, come up and take out something. If you ain't careful you go get fat and blow-up like me. But I done see that is what you want. Dog eat your shame. Go ahead.'

She stood aside to let them pass and followed them to the grimy little kitchen. From a large blue enamel pot Herbert poured tea, stewed in condensed milk and brown sugar, into an enamel plate. He took half a *roti*, a dry unimaginative sort of pancake, broke it up and dropped the pieces into the tea.

Mrs Baksh stood over him. 'Go ahead. I want to see you eat up all of that.'

Herbert listlessly stirred the tea and *roti*.

'Is so hungry you was? Nobody ain't have to tell me about you, Herbert. Of all the seven children God give me, you have the longest tongue, and your eyes always longer than your tongue.'

Foam couldn't think of anything to get Mrs Baksh out of the kitchen. But distraction came. From one of the inner rooms came a shriek, and a girl's voice shouting, 'I going to tell Ma. Ma, come and see how Zilla pounding me up. She know I can't take blows and still she pounding me up.'

Mrs Baksh moved to the kitchen door. She lowered her voice with sardonic concern: 'Zilla, this evening you was telling me that you had a pain in your foot.' She left the kitchen and went inside. 'I go take away this pain from your foot. I go move it somewhere else.'

Herbert ran down the steps with the tea and *roti*. Upstairs Zilla was being punished. Tiger was unmoved by the screams and slaps and bumping about. When Herbert put the plate of tea and *roti* before him, he didn't know what to make of it. Slowly, instinct overcame inexperience. He sensed it was food. He sought to rise and approach it with dignity, on all four legs; but his legs trembled and folded under him. He let his muzzle lie on the chipped rim of the plate, edged out a tiny languid tongue and dipped it in the tea. Then he dragged the tongue back. He did this a few times; at last, with a show of strength that quite astonished Herbert, he got up on all four legs, trembly and shaky, remained upright, drank and ate.

'Go at it, Tiger boy,' Herbert whispered.

But Tiger ate in his own unemphatic way. Herbert expected him to wag his tail and growl at being handled while he ate; but Tiger ate without overt excitement or relish, philosophically, as though at any moment he expected to see the plate withdrawn as capriciously as it had come.

'Where that boy Herbert gone now?'

Herbert heard Mrs Baksh, and he heard Foam say, 'Went downstairs to bolt and bar the door. I tell him to go down.'

Tiger ate sloppily, squelchily.

Herbert waited, expecting Mrs Baksh to ask for the plate.

'But you and all, Foam, what happening to you? You want to bar the door and your father ain't come home yet?'

'I go call him up.'

The door at the top of the stairs opened, new light ran down the steps and striped Tiger's box, and Herbert heard Foam saying, 'Is all right, Herbert. Don't worry with the door. Come up.'

*

The room in which the five Baksh boys slept was called the brass-bed room because its only notable feature was a jangly old brass fourposter with a mildewed canopy that sagged dangerously under a mounting load of discarded boxes, clothes and toys. The four younger Baksh boys slept on the brass bed. Foam, as the eldest, slept by himself on an American Army canvas cot.

Herbert squeezed between Rafiq and Charles under the single floursack coverlet. He didn't like sleeping at the edge of the bed because he always rolled off. Iqbal, the youngest, held that position; he never rolled off.

Rafiq was still waking.

Herbert whispered, 'Tell you a secret if you promise not to tell.'

Foam, from the cot, said, 'Herbert, why you don't keep your mouth shut and go to sleep?'

Herbert waited.

He saw Rafiq kiss his crossed index fingers and put them to his eyes, to mean that his eyes would drop out if he told.

'Got a dog,' Herbert whispered. 'Not big, but *bad*.'

'*They* know?'

Herbert shook his head.

'How big?'

'Oh, he have to *grow* a little bit.'

'Call him Rex.'

'Nah. Calling him Tiger. Bad dog. Quiet too. Sort of thing, if *they* allow you, you could write up a signboard and hang it outside: Beware of Bad Dog.'

At that moment they heard the van drive into the yard and after a while they heard Baksh fumbling with the back door. Then there was a rattling and a stumbling, and Baksh began to curse.

Rafiq said, 'The old man drunk again.'

They heard him clattering hastily up the stairs, his curses becoming more distinct.

Then: 'Man!' Baksh cried. 'See a dog. Big dog. Downstairs.'

Herbert nudged Rafiq.

'Is all this campaigning and loudspeaking you doing,' Mrs Baksh said.

'Telling you, man. Big big dog. Downstairs. Walking about. Quiet quiet. Sort of guarding the steps.'

'You go start seeing hell soon, if you ain't careful,' Mrs Baksh said.

Herbert giggled.

'Who bite who?' Mrs Baksh asked. 'You bite the dog, or the dog bite you?'

Rafiq dug Herbert in the ribs.

They listened hopefully; but there was no further excitement. Mumblings from Baksh about the big dog; quiet sarcastic remarks from Mrs Baksh. But no blows; nothing being smashed or thrown through the window.

*

When Herbert got up the next morning, the brass bed was empty. Foam's cot was empty. He jumped out of bed—he slept in his ordinary clothes—and rushed to see what had happened to Tiger.

He had hardly set foot on the steps when Baksh said, 'You sleep well and sound? Come down, mister man. We waiting for you.'

Herbert knew it was all over.

Baksh was saying, 'But I tell you, man, I did see a big big dog here last night. And look how small it come this morning. Is only one thing. Magic. *Obeah.* But who want to put anything on me?'

Mrs Baksh was seated heavily on the cane-bottomed chair from the upstairs veranda. Baksh was standing next to her. In front of them the Baksh children were lined up, including Foam. Tiger's box had been dragged out from under the steps, and Tiger dozed fitfully, curled up on damp *Trinidad Sentinels.*

Mrs Baksh mocked, '"Who want to put anything on me?" Well, ten die. And with the dog it have ten of we in this house now.' Mrs Baksh was calm, ponderously calm. 'Baksh, you going to stand me witness that I tell you that this election beginning sweet sweet, but it going to end sour. You think Preacher is a fool? You think Preacher ain't know that you campaigning against him? You expect him to take that grinning and lying down?'

Baksh said, 'As usual, you didn't listen to *me*. You did think I was drunk. If you did come down last night you woulda see what I was telling you. Telling you, man, was a big big dog last night. Big big dog.'

Tiger half-opened one eye.

'See!' Baksh said. '*He* know. See how sly he looking at me.'

Herbert joined the line, standing beside Rafiq.

Mrs Baksh leaned back in her chair and looked broader than ever. Her bodice tightened and creased right across her bosom; her skirt tightened and creased across her belly. She folded her arms and then put one hand against her jaw. 'Foam, you bring the dog?'

'No, Ma.'

'Zilla, you bring the dog?'

Zilla began to cry.

'But why for you crying? If you ain't bring the dog, you ain't bring the dog, and that is that. You bring the dog?'

Zilla shook her head and sobbed loudly.

Tiger twitched an ear.

'Carol, you bring the dog?'

'Ma, you know I is not that sorta girl.'

And so the questioning went on.

'Herbert, you bring in any dog last night? Herbert, I asking you, you feed any dog outa one of my good good enamel plates that I does only feed humans on?'

'No, Ma.'

'Make sure, you know.'

'I ain't bring no dog, Ma.'

'All right. Foam, go and get the Bible. It in my bureau. Under the parcel with all the photos and the birth certificates.'

Foam went upstairs.

'Baksh, go and bring the shop key.'

Baksh went off with a lot of zest. 'Telling you, man. If only you did listen to me last night!'

'So!' Mrs Baksh sighed. 'So! *No*body ain't bring the dog. It just walk in through a lock door and jump in a condensed milk box.'

Foam and Baksh returned with Bible and key.

Mrs Baksh closed her eyes and opened the Bible at random. 'Ten die,' she sighed. 'Ten die.' She put the key on the open Bible. 'Foam, take one end of the key.'

Foam held one end of the key on the tip of his middle finger and Mrs Baksh held the other end. The Bible hung over the key.

'If nobody ain't going to take back what they say,' Mrs Baksh said, 'this is the only way to find out who bring the dog. All-you know what going to happen. If the Bible turn when I mention anybody name, we go know who bring the dog. Don't say I didn't warn you. Ready, Foam?'

Foam nodded.

Mrs Baksh said, 'By Saint Peter, by Saint Paul, Foam bring the dog.'

Foam replied, 'By Saint Peter, by Saint Paul, Foam *ain't* bring *no* dog.'

The Bible remained steady.

Mrs Baksh began again. 'By Saint Peter, by Saint Paul, Zilla bring the dog.'

Foam replied, 'By Saint Peter, by Saint Paul, Zilla *ain't* bring *no* dog.'

Mrs Baksh, leaning back in her chair, looked solemnly at the Bible, not at the little Bakshes. She fetched a deep sigh and began again, this time on Carol.

Foam's finger started to tremble.

Baksh looked on, pleased. The Biblical trial always appealed to him. Rafiq was excited. Herbert knew he was lost, but he was going to stick it out to the end. Tiger was dozing again, his thin muzzle between his thin front legs; the flies, energetic in the early morning, swarmed about him.

'By Saint Peter, by Saint Paul, Rafiq bring the dog.'

It was going to be Herbert's turn next. He had been through this sort of trial before. He knew he couldn't fool the Bible.

Foam's whole right hand was trembling now, from the strain of having a weight at his finger-tip.

'By Saint Peter, by Saint Paul, Rafiq *ain't* bring *no* dog.'

Another sigh from Mrs Baksh.

Baksh passed a hand over his moustache.

'By Saint Peter, by Saint Paul, Herbert bring the dog.'

'By Saint Peter, by Saint Paul, Herbert *ain't* bring no *dog*.'

The key turned. The Bible turned and fell. The key lay naked, its ends resting on the fingers of Foam and Mrs Baksh.

Rafiq said excitedly, 'I did know it! I did know it!'

Foam said, 'You did know too much.'

'Herbert,' Mrs Baksh said, 'you going to lie against the Bible, boy?'

Rafiq said, 'It must be *obeah* and magic. Last night he tell me it was a big big dog. And he say it was a *bad* dog.' The emphasis sounded sinister.

'Well,' Mrs Baksh said calmly, getting up and smoothing out the creases across her wide belly, 'before I do anything, I have to cut his little lying tail.' She spoke to Baksh, kindly: 'Man, let me see your belt a little bit, please.'

Baksh replied with equal civility: 'Yes, man.'

He undid his leather belt, pulling it carefully through the loops of his khaki trousers as though he wanted to damage neither trousers nor belt. Mrs Baksh took the belt. Herbert began to cry in advance. Mrs Baksh didn't look at him. She held the belt idle for some moments, looking down at it almost reflectively. On a sudden she turned; and lunged at Herbert, striking out with the belt, hitting him everywhere. Herbert ran about the small room, but he couldn't get out. The back door was still barred; the door that led to the tailor shop was still padlocked. Unhurried, Mrs Baksh stalked him. The belt gave her ample reach. Once she struck Baksh. She stopped and said, 'Och. Sorry, man.'

'Is all right, man. Mistake.'

Herbert bawled and screeched, making the siren-like noise that had so disturbed Harbans that Friday afternoon some weeks before. The other little Bakshes looked on with fascination. Even Foam was affected. Rafiq's excitement turned to horror. Zilla wept.

Then Foam called in his stern booming voice, 'All *right*, Ma.'

Mrs Baksh stopped and looked at him.

Baksh looked at him.

Mechanically Mrs Baksh passed the belt back to Baksh.

Herbert sat on the steps, his eyes and nose streaming. His sobs, half snuffle and half snort, came at regular intervals.

Tiger dozed on, his ears twitching.

Mrs Baksh sat down on the chair, exhausted, and began to cry. 'My own son, my biggest son, talking to me so!'

Baksh tried to soothe her.

'Go away. Is your fault, Baksh. Is this election sweetness that sweeten you up so. And now you seeing how sour it turning. You having people throwing all sorta magic and *obeah* in my house, you having all my sons lying to my face, and you having my biggest son talk to me like if I is his daughter. Is your fault, Baksh. This election sweetness done turning sour, I tell you.'

'You see, Foam?' Baksh said. 'It make you happy? Seeing your mother cry?'

'I ain't tell she nothing. She was going to bless the boy, that is all.'

'Take that dog outa my house!' Mrs Baksh screamed, her face twisted and inflamed. 'If that dog don't go, I go go.' She cried a lot more. 'Oh God, Baksh! Now I have to waste a whole day. Now I have to go and take Herbert and get the spirit off him.'

From the steps Herbert said, 'I ain't got *no* spirit on me.'

Baksh said, 'You keep your little tail quiet, mister man. Like you ain't had enough.' He said to Mrs Baksh, 'I can't think of nobody who could drive away a spirit as good as Ganesh Pundit. He was the man for that sort of thing. But he take up politics now.'

That reminded Mrs Baksh. 'This election sweetness! Man, I telling you, it turning sour.'

'Where you want me take the dog?' Foam asked.

'Just take him outa the house,' Mrs Baksh said, wiping her eyes. 'That is all I want. But don't take him away, in broad daylight. Is bad enough already having *obeah* coming inside here. Don't take it out for everybody to see. Ten die. What more Preacher have in mind than to make all of we come thin thin like that dog? And then for all ten of we to dead. What more?'

Baksh was struck by his wife's interpretation. 'Take that dog outa my house!' he ordered. 'And don't give that dog any of my food, you hear. That dog going to suck the blood outa all of we if you don't get him outa here quick sharp.'

Tiger woke up and looked dreamily at the scene.

*

Mrs Baksh took Herbert for a spiritual fumigation to a gentleman in Tamana who, following the celebrated mystic masseur Ganesh at a distance, dabbled in the mystic.

And when Baksh saw Preacher on the road that morning, walking as briskly as ever, he crossed himself.

5. Encounters

THINGS WERE CRAZILY MIXED up in Elvira. Everybody, Hindus, Muslims and Christians, owned a Bible; the Hindus and Muslims looking on it, if anything, with greater awe. Hindus and Muslims celebrated Christmas and Easter. The Spaniards and some of the Negroes celebrated the Hindu festival of lights. Someone had told them that Lakshmi, the goddess of prosperity, was being honoured; they placed small earthern lamps on their money-boxes and waited, as they said, for the money to breed. Everybody celebrated the Muslim festival of Hosein. In fact, when Elvira was done with religious festivals, there were few straight days left.

That was what Lorkhoor, Foam's rival, went around preaching from his loudspeaker van that morning; the unity of races and religions. Between speeches he played records of Hindi songs and American songs.

'People of Elvira, the fair constituency of Elvira,' Lorkhoor said. 'Unite! You have nothing to lose but you chains. Unite and cohere. Vote for the man who has lived among you, toiled among you, prayed among you, worked among you. This is the voice of the renowned and ever popular Lorkhoor begging you and urging you and imploring you and entreating you and beseeching you to vote for Preacher, the renowned and ever popular Preacher. Use your democratic rights on election day and vote one, vote all. This, good people of Elvira, is the voice of Lorkhoor.'

Lorkhoor took a good deal of pleasure in his unpopularity. He offended most Indians, Hindus and Muslims; and Preacher's Negro supporters looked on him with suspicion. Mr Cuffy didn't like Lorkhoor. Mr Cuffy was Preacher's most faithful supporter. Preacher was the visionary, Mr Cuffy the practical disciple. He was a grey-headed Negro who ran a shoe-repair shop which he called The United African Pioneer Self-Help Society. Every Friday evening Mr Cuffy held a prayer-meeting from his veranda. He wore his tight blue serge suit and preached with the Bible in one hand. On a small centre table he had a gas lamp and a framed picture of a stabbed and bleeding heart. On the last few Fridays, to ward off the evil he feared from Lorkhoor, Mr Cuffy had been giving resounding sermons on treachery.

So, when Lorkhoor's van came near, Mr Cuffy, some tacks between his purple lips, looked up briefly and muttered a prayer.

Lorkhoor stopped the van outside Mr Cuffy's shop and, to Mr Cuffy's disgust, made a long speech over the loudspeaker before jumping out. He was slim and tall, though not so tall or slim as Foam. He had a broad bony face with a thriving moustache that followed the cynical curve of his top lip and drooped down a bit further. He had grown the moustache after seeing a film with the Mexican actor, Pedro Armendariz. In the film Armendariz spoke American with an occasional savage outburst in Spanish; it was the Spanish outbursts that thrilled Lorkhoor. Teacher Francis loyally if sorrowfully agreed that the moustache made Lorkhoor look like the Mexican; but Lorkhoor's enemies thought otherwise. Foam called Lorkhoor Fu-Manchu; that was how Mr Cuffy thought of him too.

'Heard the latest, Mr Coffee?'

Here was another reason for Lorkhoor's unpopularity: his stringent determination to speak correct English at all times. He spoke it in a deliberate way, as though he had to weigh and check the grammar beforehand. When Lorkhoor spoke like that outside Elvira, people tried to overcharge him. They thought him a tourist; because he spoke correct English they thought he came from Bombay.

'Good *morning*,' Mr Cuffy said.

Lorkhoor recognized his social blunder. 'Morning, Mr Coffee.'

Mr Cuffy frowned, the wrinkles on his black face growing blacker. 'I is not something you does drink, sir.'

The people of Elvira called Mr Cuffy 'Cawfee'. Lorkhoor, a stickler for correctness, called him 'Coffee'. Mr Cuffy preferred 'Cawfee'.

'Heard the latest?'

'Ain't hear nothing,' Mr Cuffy said, looking down at the ruined black boot in his hand.

'Propaganda, Mr Cawfee. Blackmail and blackball.'

Mr Cuffy regarded Lorkhoor suspiciously; he thought his colour was being mocked.

'*Obeah*, Mr Cawfee.'

Mr Cuffy tacked a nail. 'God hath made man upright.'

'Yes, Mr Cawfee. However, this propaganda is pernicious.'

Mr Cuffy tacked another nail. 'But they had found out many inventions.'

'Something about a dog.'

'Ain't know nothing about no dog.'

'Could destroy the whole campaign, you know.'

'That go satisfy you, eh, Mr Lorkhoor? That go satisfy your heart?'

'Mr Cawfee, I'm only informing you that the opposition are spreading the pernicious propaganda that Preacher is working *obeah*.'

'Who give you the right to call the gentleman Preacher?'

'Mr Preacher, then.'

'Mr Preacher go look after everything. Don't worry your head too much, you.'

'Still, Mr Cawfee, keep your eyes open. Nip the rumour in the bud. And see if they try to work any *obeah* against us. Could frighten off many votes, you know, if they try to work any *obeah* and magic against Mr Preacher.'

Bicycle bells trilled from the road and Lorkhoor and Mr Cuffy saw two white women with sunglasses standing beside red pudgy-tyred American bicycles. Pennants from both cycles said AWAKE!

Mr Cuffy grumbled a greeting.

The shorter woman took a magazine from her tray and held it before her like a shield.

The taller woman said, 'Can we interest you in some good books?'

'I've read too many lately,' Lorkhoor said.

He was ignored.

Mr Cuffy looked down. 'Ain't want no magazine.' But his manner was respectful.

Miss Short said happily, 'Oh, we know you don't *like* us.'

Mr Cuffy looked up. 'You know?'

'Course we do. We're Witnesses.'

'This election business,' Mr Cuffy said. 'You in this election business, like everybody else?'

Miss Short curled her thin lips. 'We have nothing to do with politics.'

'It's not a divine institution,' said Miss Tall, 'but a man-made evil. After all, who started the politics you have in Elvira today?'

'British Government,' Mr Cuffy said. He looked puzzled.

The Witnesses rested their case.

'We had to fight for it,' Lorkhoor said.

Miss Short looked at him sympathetically. 'Why, I don't believe you're even a Christian.'

'Of course not,' Lorkhoor snapped. 'Look at Jacob. Defend Jacob. Defend Abraham.' It was something he had got from Teacher Francis.

'We *must* study the Bible together,' Miss Short said. 'What do you do Sunday afternoons?'

Mr Cuffy's puzzlement was turning to exasperation. 'Look, who you come to see? Me? Or he?'

Miss Tall said, 'The magazine my friend is holding shows how the prophecies in the Bible are coming true. Even the troubles of Elvira are in the Bible. Elections and all.'

'Who won?' Lorkhoor asked.

'Who *are* you?' Miss Short asked.

'I'm the village intellectual.' It was a tried sentence; it had the approval of Teacher Francis.

'We must study the Bible together.'

'Leave my election campaign alone first.'

Mr Cuffy's disapproval of Lorkhoor was melting into admiration.

'About this magazine,' Miss Tall persisted. 'You have no interest at all in seeing how the Bible's prophecies are coming true?'

'I'm not ambitious,' Lorkhoor said.

The women left.

'The devil ain't no fool,' Mr Cuffy said. 'He does send pretty woman to tempt us. But were I tempted?' He used the tone and grammar of his Friday evening sermons. 'No, sir, I were not.'

'You were not,' Lorkhoor said. 'But about this *obeah* affair, Mr Cawfee. If they try any fast ones, let me know. We have to plan move for move. And now we have those Witnesses encouraging people not to vote. We have to think of something to counter that as well.'

'You is really a atheist?'

'Freethinker really. Agnostic.'

'Oh.' Mr Cuffy looked reassured.

*

This Mahadeo, the estate-driver, was a real fool. He just had to make a list of sick and dying Negroes in Elvira—it was the only thing he could be trusted with—and he had to make a lot of noise about it.

That midday, shortly after Lorkhoor had left Mr Cuffy, Mahadeo, plump and sweating in his tight khaki driver's uniform, came up to Mr Cuffy's shop and tried to open a conversation with him. Mr Cuffy had relapsed into a mood of gloomy suspicion; opening a conversation with him was like opening a bottle of beer with your teeth. Mr Cuffy wasn't liking anything at all at that moment; he wasn't liking the Witnesses, wasn't liking this talk of *obeah*, wasn't liking Lorkhoor.

Mahadeo took off his topee. 'Working hard, Mr Cawfee?'

Silence. Mr Cuffy wasn't liking Mahadeo either.

Mahadeo scratched the mauve sweat-stains under his arms. 'Elections, Mr Cawfee.'

No reply.

'Progress, Mr Cawfee. Democracy. Elvira going ahead.'

'Why you don't go ahead yourself and haul your arse outa my yard?'

Mahadeo's eyes began to bulge, hurt but determined. 'One of the candidates want my help in the election, Mr Cawfee.'

Mr Cuffy grunted.

Mahadeo brought out his red pocket-notebook and a small pencil. 'I have to ask you a few questions, Mr Cawfee.' He tried some elementary flattery: 'After all, you is a very important man in Elvira.'

Mr Cuffy liked elementary flattery. 'True,' he admitted. 'It's God's will.'

'Is what I think too. Mr Cawfee, how your Negro people getting on in Elvira?'

'All right, I believe, praise be to God.'

'You sure, Mr Cawfee?'

Mr Cuffy squinted. 'How you mean?'

'*Every*body all right? Nobody sick or anything like that?'

'What the hell you up to, Mahadeo?'

Mahadeo laughed like a clerk in a government office. 'Just doing a job, Mr Cawfee. Just a job. If any Negro fall sick in Elvira, you is the fust man they come to, not true?'

Mr Cuffy softened. 'True.'

'And *no*body sick?'

'*No*body.' Mr Cuffy didn't care for the hopeful note in Mahadeo's voice.

Mahadeo's pencil hesitated, disappointed. 'Nobody deading or dead?'

Mr Cuffy jumped up and dropped the black boot. '*Obeah!*' he cried, and took up an awl. '*Obeah!* Lorkhoor was right. You people trying to work some *obeah*. Haul you tail outa my yard! Go on, quick sharp.'

'How you mean, *obeah?*'

Mr Cuffy advanced with the awl.

'Mr Cawfee!'

Mahadeo retreated, notebook open, pencil pointing forward, as protection. 'Just wanted to help, that is all. And this is the thanks I getting. Just wanted to help, doing a job, that is all.'

'Nobody ask for your help,' Mr Cuffy shouted, for Mahadeo was now well away. 'And listen, Mahadeo, one thing I promising you. If anybody dead, anybody at all, you going to be in trouble. So watch out. Don't try no magic. If anybody dead, anybody. *Obeah!*' Mr Cuffy bawled. '*Obeah!*'

Mr Cuffy sounded serious.

And now Mahadeo was really worried.

*

Mahadeo wouldn't have got into that mess if Baksh had kept his mouth shut. Mrs Baksh had warned him not to say anything about Tiger. But nothing like it had ever happened to him and he wanted people to know. Nearly everybody else in Elvira had some experience of the supernatural; when the conversation turned to such matters in Ramlogan's rumshop, Baksh had had to improvise.

As soon as Mrs Baksh and Herbert left for Tamana, Baksh went to see Harichand the printer and caught him before he started for his printery in Couva.

Harichand, the best-dressed man in Elvira, was knotting his tie in the Windsor style before a small looking-glass nailed to one of the posts in his back veranda. He listened carefully, but without excitement.

'Nothing surprising in what you say,' he said at the end.

'How you mean, man, Harichand? Was a big big dog . . .'

'If you think *that* surprising, what you going to think about the sign I had just before my father dead?'

'Sign, eh?' It was a concession, because Baksh had heard Hari-chand's story many times before.

'Two weeks before my father dead,' Harichand began, blocking his moustache with a naked razor-blade. 'Was a night-time. Did sleeping sound. Sound sound. Like a top. Eh, I hear this squeaky noise. Squeaky squeaky. Like little mices. Get up. Still hearing this squeaky noise. Was a moonlight night. Three o'clock in the morn-ing. Moonlight making everything look like a belling-ground. Dead and funny. Squeak. Squeak. Open the window. No wind at all. All the trees black and quiet. Squeak. Squeak. Road looking white in the moonlight. White and long. Squeak. Squeak. Lean out. No wind. Nothing. Only squeak, squeak. Look down. Something in the road. Black, crawling. Look down again. Four tiny tiny horses har-ness together. Big as little puppies. Black little horses. And they was pulling a funeral huss. Squeak. Squeak. Huss big as a shoebox.'

Harichand put away the razor-blade.

'Two weeks later, my father dead. Three o'clock in the morning.'

'But talking about puppies,' Baksh said. 'This thing was a big big dog last night. I just open the back door and I see it. Walking about in a funny limping way. You know how Haq does walk? Limping, as though he walking on glass? This dog was walking about like Haq. It ain't say nothing. It just look at me. *Sly.* I get one frighten and I run upstairs. In the morning is a tiny tiny puppy, thin, all the ribs show-ing. But the same coloration.'

Harichand bent down to shine his shoe. 'Somebody trying to put something on you.' His tone was matter-of-fact.

'Was a big dog, man.'

'Just don't feed it,' Harichand said.

'Feed it! Preacher ain't catching me so easy.'

'Ah, is Preacher, eh?' Harichand gave a knowing chuckle. 'Elec-tion thing starting already?'

'We helping out Harbans.'

'Harbans ain't getting *my* vote. Eh, the man ain't bring nothing yet for me to print.'

'How you could say that, man? We fixing up something for you.'

'Mark you, I ain't begging nobody. But if you want my vote, you want my printery. It have a lot of people who wouldn't like it if they know you wasn't treating me nice.'

'We fixing you up, man. So just don't feed it, eh?'

'Well, I waiting to see what all-you bringing. Just don't feed it. And try to get it outa the house.'

And then Baksh ran around telling his story to nearly everyone who wasn't too busy to listen. He had to listen to many stories in return. Etwariah, Rampiari's mother, told (in Hindi) how two days after her husband died she saw him standing at the foot of her bed. He looked at her and then at the baby—he had died the day Rampiari was born—and he cried a little before disappearing. Etwariah cried a lot when she told the story and Baksh had to cry too; but he couldn't keep on crying with Etwariah and in the end he had to leave, very rudely.

So it went on all morning. The story of Tiger got round nearly everywhere. Lorkhoor heard and told Mr Cuffy.

*

Before Rafiq went to school Foam called him to the little ajoupa at the back of the house and said, 'Rafiq, you is a nasty little good-for-nothing bitch.'

Rafiq began to sniffle.

'You pretending you ain't know why I calling you a bitch?'

'I ain't tell no lie.'

Foam slapped him. 'No, you ain't tell no lie,' he mimicked. 'But you tell.'

'The Bible turn for itself. I didn't have nothing to do with it.'

Foam slapped him again. 'How else Ma know, unless you did tell she about the dog?'

Rafiq began to cry. 'I didn't know she was going to bless Herbert.'

'When Herbert come back this evening from Tamana, I want

you to beg his pardon. And I want you to give him that red-and-blue top you hiding on top of the brass bed.'

'Is my top. I thief it from a boy at school. Big Lambie.'

'I want you to give Herbert the top.'

'Not going to give it. You could do what you like. Touch me again and I going to tell Ma.'

'Rafiq! What sorta obscene language you using? Where you pick up those words? Ma ever hear you using those sorta words?'

'What sorta words?'

'Again, Rafiq? I just have to tell Ma now.'

Rafiq understood blackmail. 'All right, I going to give the top to Herbert.'

*

One of the first things Foam bought with his campaign manager's salary was an expensive pair of dark glasses. He wore them whenever he took out the loudspeaker van.

He was cruising down Ravine Road—if you could cruise down any road in Elvira—when he saw Nelly Chittaranjan coming back from school. She was walking briskly, head a little high.

Foam slowed up and gave a little election speech. Nelly Chittaranjan turned and saw and turned away again, head a little higher.

Foam followed her with the van.

'Want a lift home, girl?'

She didn't reply. He followed.

'Foreman, I will kindly ask you to stop following me about.'

'Why you so formal? Is because you getting married to Harbans son? Call me Foam, man, like everybody else.'

'Some people in Elvira don't know their elders and betters.'

He gave a dry laugh. 'Ah, is because of the dark glasses that you can't recognize me!'

'Foreman, please drive off. Otherwise I will just have to tell my father.'

Foam sang:

[78]

'Tell, tell,
Till you belly full of rotten egg.'

'Simple things amuse small minds, I see.'

'Look, girl, you want this lift or you ain't want it? Don't waste my time. Is work I have to work these days.'

'Huh! I don't see what sort of work you could ever do.'

'I is your father boss in this election, you know.'

'Huh!' But she stopped.

The van stopped too. Foam rested an elbow on the door. 'Just managing Harbans campaign for him. That is all. Seventy-five dollars a month. See these glasses? Guess how much.'

'Sixty cents.'

'Garn. Twelve dollars, if you please.'

'Huh!'

'You like the old loudspeaking voice?' He gave a loud and vigorous demonstration.

'You mean to say you learn off all that by heart?'

'Nah! Just make it up as I go along. Want to hear some more?'

She shook her head. 'It *is* hot. You can give me a lift to the end of Ravine Road.'

'Only up to there, eh? Ah, you shame to let the old man see you with me.' He opened the door for her. 'Now that you is practically a married woman.'

He drove off with much noise, and settled down with one hand on the steering wheel, his back in the angle of the seat and door. He looked reposed and casual.

'So little Nelly getting married off, eh?'

He was embarrassing her.

'I don't see why you shame about it. You marrying a doctor, man. You could take down prescriptions *and* type them out. Especially with doctors' handwriting so hard to read.'

He had gone too far. It looked as though she might cry. 'I don't want to get married, Foreman.'

He hadn't thought of that. 'What you want to do then?'

'I want to go to the Poly.'

He couldn't make anything of that. 'Well, things could always mash up. From what I hear, Harbans ain't too anxious to see you as a daughter-in-law either.'

She wept. 'I want to go to the Poly.'

'Poly, eh?'

'In London. Regent Street.'

'Oh.' He spoke as though he knew it well. 'Teacher Francis been putting ideas in your head. Well, you never know what could happen between now and election day.' He paused. 'Look, you like dogs?'

Weeping, Nelly Chittaranjan remembered refinement. 'I adore dogs.'

Foam stamped on the brakes and brought the van to a noisy halt. 'Look, I ain't want that sort of talk. I ask you if you like dogs. You answer me yes or you answer me no. None of this educative nonsense, you hear. You ain't gone to the Poly yet.'

She stopped crying.

She said, 'I like dogs.'

'You is a nice girl. I have a dog—well, small dog, puppy really. Can't keep it home. You want to look after it?'

She nodded.

He was surprised. 'Giving it to you. Wedding present from Foam. What time you does stop taking lessons from Teacher Francis in the evening?'

'Half past eight.'

'See you at quarter to nine. Where we meet today.'

She got off at the end of the Ravine Road.

*

In the afternoon Chittaranjan put on his visiting outfit, left Mrs Chittaranjan to look after the two workmen downstairs, and went out to campaign for Harbans. Chittaranjan's visiting outfit was as special as his home clothes. Item number one was an untorn white shirt, size thirteen, with the sleeves carefully rolled up—not rolled, folded rather—and when it wasn't in use it hung on its own hanger in Chittaranjan's expensive, spacious and practically empty wardrobe. Chittaranjan was extra careful with his shirt. He didn't like to have it washed too often because that weakened the material; but he never liked keeping a shirt in use for more than two months at a time. He wore it as little as possible, and only on special occasions; Chittaranjan liked a shirt to grow dirty gradually and gracefully. Item number two was a pair of brown gaberdine trousers which he kept flat between *Trinidad Sentinels* under his mattress. Item number three was a pair of brown shoes, old, cracked, but glittering; this replaced the sabots he wore at home. The fourth and last item of Chittaranjan's visiting outfit was a vast grey felt hat, smooth, ribbonless, with only one stain, large, ancient and of oil, on the wide brim.

When Elvira saw Chittaranjan in this outfit, it knew he meant business.

Chittaranjan campaigned.

At first things went well. But then Chittaranjan found people a little less ready to commit themselves. They talked about *obeah* and magic and dogs. But they always yielded in the end. Only Rampiari's husband, who had cut his foot with a hoe, played the fool. At the best of times Rampiari's husband was a truculent lout; now he was in pain and ten times worse. He had been there in the morning when Baksh had come to Etwariah with the story of Tiger; and he made a big thing of it. He said he wasn't going to vote for anybody because he didn't want anybody to put any *obeah* on him, he didn't believe in this new politics business, politicians were all crooks, and nobody was going to do anything for him anyway.

Chittaranjan listened patiently, his hat on his knees.

When Rampiari's husband was finished, Chittaranjan asked: 'When you does want money borrow, Rampiari husband, who you does come to?'

'I does come to you, Goldsmith.'

'When you does want somebody to help you get a work, who you does come to?'

'I does come to you, Goldsmith.'

'When you want letter write to the Government, who you does come to?'

'I does come to you, Goldsmith.'

'When you want cup borrow, plate borrow, chair borrow, who you does come to?'

'I does come to you, Goldsmith.'

'When you want *any* sort of help, Rampiari husband, who you does come to?'

'I does come to you, Goldsmith.'

'So when *I* want help, who I must come to?'

'You must come to me, Goldsmith.'

'And when I want this help to put a man in the Legislative Council, who I must come to?'

'You must come to me, Goldsmith.'

'You see, Rampiari husband, the more bigger people *I* know, the more I could help *you* out. Now tell me, is beg I have to beg you for *your* sake?'

'You ain't have to beg, Goldsmith.'

Chittaranjan stood up and put his hat on. 'I hope your foot get better quick.'

'When you see Mr Harbans, Goldsmith, you go tell him, eh, how bad my foot sick.'

Chittaranjan hesitated, remembering Harbans's refusal to have anything to do with the Hindu sick or the Hindu dead.

Rampiari's husband said, 'Preacher coming to see me tomorrow.'

'What *Preacher* could do for you? A man like you ain't want only sympathy. You want a lot more.'

The sick man's eyes brightened. 'You never say a truer word, Goldsmith. *Whenever* I want help, I does come to you.'

Chittaranjan smiled; the sick man smiled back; but when he was outside Chittaranjan muttered, 'Blasted son of a bitch.'

Still, it was a successful afternoon, despite Rampiari's husband and all that talk about *obeah*.

But the *obeah* talk worried him. It could lose votes.

6. Encounters by Night

MRS BAKSH CAME BACK to Elvira, her mission accomplished. Herbert had received his spiritual fumigation; and she brought back mysterious things—in a small brown parcel—which would purify the house as well.

'Ganesh Pundit was really the man for this sort of mystic thing,' Baksh said. 'Pity he had to take up politics. Still, that show how good he was. The moment he feel he was losing his hand for that sort of thing, he give up the business.'

'The fellow we went to was all right,' Mrs Baksh said. 'He *jharay* the boy well enough.'

Herbert looked chastened indeed. His thin face was stained with tears, his eyes were still red, the edges of his nostrils still quivering and wet. He kept his mouth twisted, to indicate his continuing disgust with the world in general.

Mrs Baksh had been feeling guilty about Herbert. She said to Baksh, for Herbert to hear, 'Herbert didn't give the fellow much trouble you know. He behave like a nice nice boy. The fellow say that the fust thing to do when a spirit come on anybody is to beat it out. It ain't the person you beating pussonal, but the spirit.'

Herbert sniffed.

Baksh said, 'People ain't want to believe, you know, man, that the big big dog I see last night turn so small this morning. Nobody ain't want to believe at all at all. Everybody was surprise like anything.'

Mrs Baksh sank aghast into her cane-bottomed chair. 'But you know you is a damn fool, Baksh. You mean you went around *telling* people?'

'Didn't tell them *every*thing. Didn't mention nothing about Preacher or about *obeah*. Just say something about the dog. It ain't have nothing wrong if I tell about the dog. Look, Harichand tell me about the time he did see some tiny tiny horses dragging a tiny tiny funeral huss. Was a moonlight night. Three o'clock . . .'

'Everybody know about Harichand huss. But that was only a *sign*.'

'Sign, eh? And this thing—this dog business—that—that is *obeah* and magic, eh? Something bigger?'

'Yes, you damn fool, yes.'

'Nobody did believe anyway. Everybody thought I was lying.'

'You *was* lying, Pa,' Herbert said. 'Was a puppy last night and is a puppy today.'

Baksh was grateful for the diversion. 'Oh God! Oh God! I go show that boy!'

He tried to grab Herbert; but Herbert ducked behind Mrs Baksh's chair. He knew that his mother was in a sympathetic mood. And Baksh knew that in the circumstances Herbert was inviolate. Still, he made a show. He danced around the chair. Mrs Baksh put out a large arm as a barrier. Baksh respected it.

'Oh God!' he cried. 'To hear a little piss-in-tail boy talking to me like that! When I was a boy, if I did talk to my father like that, I woulda get my whole backside peel with blows.'

'Herbert,' Mrs Baksh said. 'You mustn't tell your father he lie. What you must say?'

'I must say he tell stories,' Herbert said submissively. But he perked up, and a faint mocking smile—which made him look a bit like Foam—came to his lips.

'No, Herbert, you mustn't even say that your father does tell stories.'

'You mean I mustn't say *any*thing, Ma?'

'No, son, you mustn't say anything.'

Baksh stuck his hands into his tight pockets. 'Next time you say anything, see what happen to you, mister man. I beat you till you pee, you hear.'

Herbert had a horror of threats of that sort; they seemed much worse than any flogging.

'I talking to you, mister man,' Baksh insisted. 'Answer me.'

Herbert looked at his mother.

She said, 'Answer him.'

He said, 'Yes, Pa.'

Baksh took his hands out of his pockets. He was mollified but continued to look offended. He couldn't fool Herbert though. Herbert knew that Baksh was only trying to prevent Mrs Baksh attacking *him*.

Baksh got in his blows first. 'You call yourself a mother, and this is the way you bringing up your children. To insult their father and call him liar to his face. This is what you *encouraging* the children to do, after they eating my food since they born.'

Mrs Baksh, tired and very placid now, said, '*You* carry them nine months in your belly? You nurse them? You clean them?'

Baksh's moustache twitched as he looked for an answer.

Before he found one Mrs Baksh returned to the counterattack. 'Who fault it is that this whole thing happen?' Her brow darkened and her manner changed. 'Is this election sweetness that sweeten you up, Baksh. But see how this sweetness going to turn sour sour. See.'

She was righter than she knew.

*

All that day Tiger remained in his box under the steps, dozing or lying awake and futile. Foam fed him surreptitiously; but Tiger was unused to food and in the afternoon he had an attack of hiccoughs. He lay flat on his side, his tiny ribs unable to contain the convulsions of his tiny belly. The hiccoughs shook him with more energy than he had ever shown; they lifted him up and dropped him down again on the sodden newspapers; they caused curious swallowing noises in his throat. His box became wetter and filthier. Foam, for all his toughness, was squeamish about certain things, and Tiger's box was never cleaned. But Foam fed Tiger, often and unwisely; and it gave him much pleasure when once, stretching out his hand and passing a finger down Tiger's muzzle, he saw Tiger raise his eyes and raise his tail.

And now he had to get rid of Tiger.

'Put him in a bag and take him away in the van,' Mrs Baksh said after dinner.

'Take him far,' Baksh added. 'Far far.'

'All *right*,' Foam said, with sudden irritation. 'All right, don't rush me. I going to take him so far, he not going to offend your sight *or* your heart.'

Mrs Baksh almost cried. 'Is only since the elections that this boy talking to me like that, you know.'

Baksh saw a chance to redeem himself. 'Boy, you know you talking to your mother? Who carry you for nine months in their belly? Who nurse you?'

Mrs Baksh said, 'Why you don't shut your tail, Baksh?'

'The two of all-you quarrel,' Foam said, and went downstairs.

He took a clean gunny sack, held it open and rolled it down to make a nest of sorts; lifted Tiger from his box, using newspaper to keep his hands clean, and put him in the nest.

Herbert tiptoed down the steps.

'Ey, Herbert. Come down and throw away this dirty box somewhere in the backyard. It making the whole house stink.'

'Foam, what you going to do with him?'

Foam didn't reply. His irritation lingered.

Tiger sprawled in the nest of sacking, heaving with hiccoughs.

'Foam, Tiger going to dead?'

Foam looked at Herbert. 'No. He not going to dead.'

'Foam! You not going to kill him?'

He didn't know what he was going to do. When he had spoken to Nelly Chittaranjan about Tiger, it was only to make conversation, to stop her from crying.

Tiger made choking noises.

Foam stood up.

'Foam! You not going to *kill* Tiger?'

Foam shook his head.

'Promise, Foam. Kiss your finger and promise.'

'You know I don't believe in that sort of thing.'

'Don't kill him, Foam. *You* don't believe in this *obeah* business, eh, Foam?'

Foam sucked his teeth. 'That boy give you the top?'

'Rafiq?' Herbert brightened. 'Yes, he give me the top.'

'Good, throw away that old box. It stinking.'

Herbert touched Tiger's nose with the tip of his index finger. Tiger's eyes didn't change; but his tail lifted and dropped.

*

Nelly Chittaranjan hadn't been thinking when she agreed to meet Foam that evening and take the dog. Now, sitting in Teacher Francis's drab drawing-room and only half listening while he talked, she wasn't so sure about the dog or about Foam. She didn't believe the dog existed at all. But the thought of meeting a boy at night in a lonely lane had kept her excited all afternoon. She had never walked out with any boy: it was wrong; now that she was practically engaged, it was more than wrong. Mr Chittaranjan was modern enough in many ways—the way he had given her education and the way he furnished his house and kept it shining with new paint—but he wasn't advanced enough to allow his only daughter to walk out with a boy before she was married. Nelly didn't blame him. She knew she was being married off so quickly only because she hadn't been bright enough to get into one of the girls' high schools like La Pique. Thinking of La Pique, she thought of the Poly, and then she thought of Harbans's son, the boy she was going to marry. She had seen him once or twice in Port of Spain when she had gone to stay with her aunt (the wife of the barrister, the donor of the chromium-plated ashtray in Chittaranjan's veranda). He was a fat yellow boy with big yellow teeth, a giggling gum-chewer, always taking out his wallet to show you his latest autographed picture of some American actress, and you were also meant to see the crisp quarter-inch wad of new dollar notes. Still, if she had to marry him, she had to; it was her own fault. She would have preferred the Poly though. Teacher Francis had met someone who had actually been. There were *dances* at the Poly! Foam didn't even know what the Poly was. But he was no fool. He couldn't talk as well as that Lorkhoor; but Lorkhoor was a big show-off; she preferred Foam. Foam was crazy. Those sunglasses. And those long speeches he shot right off the reel, just like that. She had wanted to laugh all the time. Not that the speeches were funny; it was the over-serious way Foam spoke them. And yet he could never make her feel that the whole thing was more than a piece of skylarking. A boy trying to be mannish! And making up that story about a dog, just to meet her!

Teacher Francis had to pull her up. 'But what making you laugh all the time so for, Miss Chittaranjan?' Teacher Francis reserved standard English only for prepared statements. 'I was saying, the thing about shorthand is practice. When *I* was studying it, I use to even find myself writing shorthand on my pillow.' That was how he always rounded off the lesson.

Nelly looked at the dusty clock on the ochre and chocolate wall. It was twenty past eight; she was meeting Foam at a quarter to nine.

But this was the time when Teacher Francis, the lesson over, his coat off, his tie slackened a little lower than usual, liked to talk about life. He was talking about the election. A bitter subject for him ever since Lorkhoor had, without warning or explanation, deserted him to campaign for Preacher.

'This new constitution is a trick, Miss Chittaranjan. Just another British trick to demoralize the people.'

Nelly, her pen playing on her pad, asked absently, 'Who you voting for, Teach?'

'Not voting for nobody at all.'

'You talking like the Witnesses now, man, Teach.'

He gave a sour laugh. 'No point in voting. People in Elvira don't know the *value* of their vote.'

Nelly looked up from her pad. 'It look to me that a lot of them know it very well, Teach.'

'Miss Chittaranjan, I don't mean nothing against your father, Miss Chittaranjan. But look at Lorkhoor. Before this election, I did always think he was going to go far. But now . . .' Teacher Francis waved a hand and didn't finish the sentence. 'Elvira was a good friendly place before this universal suffrage nonsense.'

'Teach! You mean to say you against democracy?'

He saw he had shocked her. He smiled. 'Is a thing I frown on, Miss Chittaranjan.'

'Teach!'

'I am a man of radical views, Miss Chittaranjan.'

Nelly put down her pen on her notebook. 'My father would be *very* interested, Teacher Francis.'

He saw the notebook. 'Miss Chittaranjan! You been taking down what I was saying, Miss Chittaranjan!'

She hadn't. But she snapped the book shut and rose.

'I was just throwing off ideas, Miss Chittaranjan. You mustn't think I is a fascist.'

She prepared to leave. '*I* don't think anything, Teacher Francis. But if my father hear that you don't approve of democracy or the elections, he wouldn't approve of me coming to you for lessons, I could tell you.'

It was what Teach feared.

'I was just talking, Miss Chittaranjan. Idea-mongering. Fact is, as a teacher, I have to be impartial.'

'I know what you mean. You want to play both sides.'

'No, Miss Chittaranjan, no.'

She didn't wait to hear any more.

He wandered about his bare, cheerless government house, feeling once again that, since the defection of Lorkhoor, Elvira had become a wilderness.

*

Ravine Road was pitch dark. There was no moon, no wind. The tall featureless bush hunched over the road on one side; on the other side the dry ravine was black, blank. When Foam turned off the head-lamps, all the night noises seemed to leap out at the van from the bush, all the croakings and stridulations of creatures he couldn't see, drowning the heaving of Tiger on the seat next to him.

Then the noises receded. Foam heard the beat of a motor engine not far away. Soon he saw headlights about two hundred yards down the slope where the road turned. The vehicle had taken the corner too quickly: the headlights made a Z. Then Foam was dazzled.

The driver shouted, 'Yaah!'

It was Lorkhoor.

'Yaah! We will bury Harbans! Yaah!'

Quick as anything, Foam put his head out of the window and shouted back, 'Put money where your mouth is! You traitor!'

'Yaah!'

And Lorkhoor was gone.

But Lorkhoor wasn't alone in his van. Foam was sure he had seen a woman with him; she had ducked when the van passed. He was really a shameless liar, that boy. He said it was a degradation to get mixed up with Elvira politics, yet he was campaigning for Preacher. He said he didn't care for women, that marriage was unnatural, and here he was driving out of Elvira at night with a woman who wasn't anxious to be seen.

'I too glad we not fighting on the same side this election,' Foam said aloud.

*

Nelly Chittaranjan came, coy but uneasy. 'Well, Foreman,' she said ironically. 'You bring this famous dog?'

He switched on the top light of the van.

'Oh God, Foreman! A dog!'

He didn't understand why she was annoyed.

'Is a mangy little mongrel puppy dog, Foreman. It sick and it stink.'

'For a little dog you calling him a lot of big names, you know.'

She was in a temper. 'Look at the belly, Foreman. Colic.'

'Is why I ask *you*. It ain't have nobody else in Elvira who would look after a sick dog.'

She couldn't go back on her word. But she was angry with Foam; she felt he had made a fool of her. What was she going to do with the dog anyway?

Foam said, 'Your father send a message. Committee meeting at your house. I could give you and your dog a lift.'

She got in without a word.

'For a educated girl, Miss Chittaranjan, you know you ain't got no manners? They not going to like that at the Poly. Nobody ever teach you to say thanks?'

She tossed her head, smoothed out her frock, edged away from Tiger, and sniffed loudly.

Foam said, 'You go get used to it.'

Then the trouble started.

They heard a curious noise at the side of the road. It was part gurgle, part splutter, part like a thirsty dog lapping up water.

Then a squeaky breathless voice exclaimed, 'This is the thing that does start the thing!'

Foam had some trouble in making out Haq, the Muslim fanatic. He got out of the van.

'Haq, you is a old *maquereau*. God give you the proper *maquereau* colour. Black. You so damn black nobody could see you in the night-time.'

Haq was trembling with excitement. His stick rapped the ground, he looked more bent than usual. 'You, Foreman Baksh, call me what you like. But I going to tell your father. For a Muslim you ain't got no shame. Going out with a kaffir woman.'

Nelly looked down at Tiger beside her; she was too stupefied to say or do anything.

Foam defended her. '*You* calling she kaffir? You make yourself out to be all this religious and all this Muslim and all this godly, and still you ain't got no shame. Dog eat your shame. You is a dirty old *maquereau*, old man.'

'This is the thing that does start the thing,' Haq repeated, his squeaky voice twittering out of control. For a precarious moment he lifted his weight off his stick and used the stick to point at Nelly. 'This is the thing.' He made a noise that could have been a titter or a sob, and leaned on his stick again. In the darkness all that Foam could see clearly of Haq were the whites of his eyes behind his glasses and his white prickly beard.

'What *thing* you see, *maquereau?*'

'I see everything.' Haq tittered, sobbed again. 'This is the thing that does start the thing.'

'Tell me what thing you see, *maquereau*.'

'All right, all right, you calling me rude words.' He whined one word and spat out another. 'You don't understand the hardship I does have to put up with.'

'You not getting one black cent from me, you nasty old *maquereau*.'

'I not young and strong like you. I is a old man. You calling me rude words and you want to see me cry. Well, all right. I go cry for you.'

And Haq began to cry. It sounded like chuckling.

'Cry, *maquereau*.'

Nelly spoke at last: 'Leave him, Foreman.'

'No, I want to see the old *maquereau* cry.'

Haq sobbed, 'I is a old man. All you people making Ravine Road a Lovers' Lane. First Lorkhoor and now you. All-you don't understand the hardship a old man does have.' He wiped his cheeks on his sleeve. Then he cried again. 'I is a widow.'

Foam got into the van.

'You tell anybody about this *thing* you see, Haq, and I promising you that you going to spend the rest of your days in a nice hospital. You go start using rubber for bones.'

Haq sobbed and gurgled. 'Kill me now self. You is young and

strong. Come on and kill me one time, and bury me right here in Ravine Road, all your Lovers' Lane.'

To start the engine Foam turned off the headlights. Again the noises sprang out from the bush and Haq cried out in the dark, 'Kill me, Foreman. Kill me.'

'*Maquereau*,' Foam shouted, and drove off.

He had enjoyed the encounter with Haq, a man he had never liked; because of Haq's tales he had often been flogged when he was younger.

But Nelly was feeling flat and frightened.

'Don't worry,' Foam said. 'He wouldn't say anything. Not after that tongue-lashing I give him.'

She was silent.

Between them Tiger heaved and croaked.

He dropped them both off at a trace not far from Chittaranjan's.

*

He found Mahadeo and Chittaranjan waiting for him. Chittaranjan had changed into his home clothes and, rocking in his own tiled veranda, was as dry and formidable as ever. Mahadeo was still in his khaki uniform.

There was no light in the veranda. Chittaranjan said they didn't need one, they didn't want to write anything, they only wanted to talk.

Presently Foam heard Nelly arrive. He heard her open the gate at the side of the shop downstairs and heard her come up the wooden steps at the back.

Chittaranjan called out, 'Is you, daughter?'

'Yes, Pa, is me.'

'Go and put on your home clothes,' Chittaranjan ordered. 'And do whatever homework Teacher Francis give you. No more running about for you tonight.'

Foam looked at Chittaranjan. He was smiling his fixed smile.

For some moments no one in the veranda said anything. Foam

was thinking about Tiger; Mahadeo was thinking about Mr Cuffy; Chittaranjan rocked and clacked his sabots on the floor.

At last Chittaranjan said to Foam, "This Mahadeo is a real real jackass.'

Mahadeo remained unmoved, his large eyes unblinking. He had just told Chittaranjan of his unhappy interview with Mr Cuffy that morning.

'I is a frank man,' Chittaranjan said, spreading out his palms on the arms of his rocking-chair. 'I does say my mind, and who want to vex, let them vex.'

Mahadeo wasn't going to be annoyed. He continued to look down at his unlaced boots, stroked his nose, cracked his fingers, passed his thick little hands through his thick oily hair and mumbled, 'I was a fool, I was a fool.'

Chittaranjan wasn't going to let him off so easily.

'Course you was a fool. And you was a double fool. And this boy father was a triple fool.'

'How you mean?' Foam asked.

Chittaranjan smiled more broadly. 'So your father was having trouble with a dog, eh?'

Foam looked down.

'And so your father think that the best way to get people votes is to run about saying that Preacher putting *obeah* and magic on him?' Chittaranjan was caustic, but bland. 'Tell me, that go make a *lot* of people want to vote against Preacher, eh?'

Mahadeo was still preoccupied with his morning adventure. 'It look, Goldsmith, like we have to give up that plan now for burying dead Negroes and looking after sick ones.'

For the first time in his life Foam heard Chittaranjan laugh, a short, corrosive titter. 'Eh, but Mahadeo, you smart, man. You work out that one all by yourself?'

Mahadeo smiled. 'Yes, Goldsmith.'

Foam was attending with only half a mind. He was straining to catch all the noises inside the house. The coolness he had shown in

Ravine Road was beginning to leave him in Chittaranjan's veranda; the thought of Haq unsettled him now. He heard sounds of washing-up; he heard Mrs Chittaranjan singing the theme song from the Indian film *Jhoola*.

Mahadeo was saying, 'Was a good plan though, Goldsmith. Goldsmith, ain't it did look to you that Sebastian was one Negro who was bound to dead before elections?'

Chittaranjan smiled and rocked and didn't reply.

Mahadeo suffered. He passed his hands through his hair and said, 'I sorry, Goldsmith. I was a fool, I was a fool.'

Inside Nelly was moving about. Foam heard the thump and slap of her slippers. Everything seemed all right so far.

Mahadeo scratched the back of his neck to indicate perplexity and contrition. Chittaranjan remained impassive. Mahadeo tried to crack his fingers again; but nothing came: they had been cracked too recently. 'Goldsmith, this new talk about *obeah* could frighten off a lot of votes.'

Chittaranjan spoke up. 'On one side we have the Witnesses telling people not to vote. And now this boy father decide to tell people that if they vote for Harbans, Preacher going to work magic and *obeah* on them. All-you go ahead. See if that is the way to win election.'

Mahadeo forgot his own error. 'In truth, Goldsmith, this boy father does talk too much.'

Foam was about to retort, but Chittaranjan challenged him: 'You got any sorta plan, Foam? To make the Spanish people vote, and to get other people to vote without getting frighten of Preacher *obeah*?'

Foam shook his head.

Chittaranjan rocked. 'I have a plan.'

They attended.

'It ain't Preacher who working *obeah*,' Chittaranjan said. 'Is the Witnesses. That is the propaganda we have to spread.'

'Is a master-idea,' Mahadeo said.

Foam was cautious. 'Just a minute, Goldsmith. All right, we go about saying that the Witnesses working *obeah*. But what Preacher going to say?'

Chittaranjan's gold teeth flashed in the pale light that came through the thickly curtained drawing-room doorway. 'You is a smart boy, Foam. You does ask the correct question. He'—Chittaranjan jerked his chin towards Mahadeo who stared stolidly at his boots—'he ain't have the brains to think of things like that.'

Mahadeo looked up and asked, 'What Preacher going to say, Goldsmith?'

Chittaranjan stopped rocking. 'Is like this. Preacher hoping to get some Spanish votes too. He wrong, but it good to let people hope sometimes. If the Spanish ain't voting, Preacher suffering. So, already Preacher hisself start saying that the Witnesses working *obeah*. If we say the same thing, the Witnesses ain't got a chance. People go start getting frighten of the Witnesses and we go get back all the votes of the Spanish people in Cordoba who saying they ain't voting because politics ain't a divine thing. Tcha!' Chittaranjan sucked his teeth; the ingratitude and stupidity of the Spaniards still rankled.

Mahadeo scratched the back of his head and passed a finger down his nose. 'You know what you have that we ain't have, Goldsmith? Is brains you have, Goldsmith.'

Chittaranjan snubbed Mahadeo. 'Wasn't my idea. Today I hear people talking about *obeah* and today I hear Lorkhoor going around saying that it wasn't Preacher working *obeah*, but the Witnesses. And I sit down and I hold my head in my two hands and I puzzle it out and I see that even out of this boy father stupidness, starting all this talk about dog and *obeah*, we could make some profit.'

Foam gave his approval. But he was a little bitter that it was Lorkhoor who had thought of a way to counter the Witnesses. After all, the Witnesses were to be defeated by talk of *obeah* and magic; and this *obeah* and magic was nothing other than Tiger, Herbert's Tiger.

Inside, footsteps were measured, ordinary. Mrs Chittaranjan was singing.

Tiger was going to be all right. At least for the night.

7. Dead Chicken

AND THE NEXT DAY, in spite of Chittaranjan's plan, Harbans was in trouble, big trouble.

The day began badly, you might almost say with an omen. Foam had an accident outside Chittaranjan's shop. Only a chicken was involved, but the repercussions of the accident were to shake Elvira before dusk.

It was just about midday when the accident happened. Ramlogan had closed his rumshop for the regulation hours from twelve to four. Chittaranjan's two workmen had disappeared somewhere into the back of the shop to eat—Mrs Chittaranjan gave them food and they ate squatting on the floor downstairs. Just then the two rival loud-speaker vans approached one another.

Foam gave his speech everything. 'People of Elvira, vote for the only honourable man fit to become an Honourable Member of the Legislative Council of Trinidad and Tobago. Vote for Mr Surujpat Harbans, popularly known to all and sundry as Pat Harbans. Mr Harbans is your popular candidate. Mr Harbans will leave no stones unturned to work on your behalf. People of Elvira, this is the voice of Foreman Baksh, popularly known to all and sundry as Foam, this is the voice of Foam Baksh asking you—not begging you or imploring you or beseeching you or entreating you—but asking you and telling you to vote for the honourable and popular candidate, Mr Pat Harbans. Mr Harbans will leave no stones unturned to help you.' There was a pause. 'But you must put him in fust.'

Then Lorkhoor spoke and Foam, honourably, remained silent. Lorkhoor said, in his irritating educated voice, 'Ladies and gentlemen of the fair constituency of Elvira, renowned in song and story, this is the voice of the renowned and ever popular Lorkhoor. Lorkhoor humbly urges every man, woman and child to vote for Mr Thomas, well known to you all as Preacher. Preacher will leave no stone unturned to help you. I repeat, ladies and gentlemen, no *stone* unturned.'

The vans were about to cross. Foam, remembering Lorkhoor's taunt the evening before, leaned out and shouted, 'Yaah! We going to bury Preacher! And he won't have nobody to preach at his funeral.'

Lorkhoor shouted back, 'When you bury him, make sure to leave no stone unturned.'

The vans crossed. Lorkhoor shouted, 'Foreman Baksh, why not speak English for a change?'

'Put money where your mouth is,' Foam retorted, although he knew that the words had no relevance to their present exchange. And as he spoke those words he pulled a little to the right to avoid Lorkhoor's van, felt a bump on his radiator, heard a short, fading cackle, and knew that he had damaged some lesser creature. He waited for the shouts and abuse from the owner. But there was nothing. He looked back quickly. It was a chicken, one of Chittaranjan's, or rather, Mrs Chittiranjan's. He drove on.

*

That happened just after noon. Less than three hours later a bread-fruit from Ramlogan's tree dropped so hard on Chittaranjan's roof that the framed picture of King George V and Mahatma Gandhi in the drawing-room fell.

Chittaranjan rushed to the kitchen window, pushed aside his wife from the enamel sink where she was scouring pots and pans with blue soap and ashes, and shot some elaborate Hindi curses at Ramlogan's backyard.

Ramlogan didn't retaliate, didn't even put his head out of his window.

Mrs Chittaranjan sighed.

Chittaranjan turned to her. 'You see how that man Ramlogan provoking me? You see?'

Mrs Chittaranjan, ash-smeared pot and ashy rag in hand, sighed again.

'You see or you ain't see?'

'I see.'

Chittaranjan was moved to further anger by his wife's calm. He put his head out of the Demerara window and cursed long and loud, still in Hindi.

Ramlogan didn't reply.

Chittaranjan was at a loss. He spoke to Mrs Chittaranjan. 'A good good picture. You can't just walk in a shop and get a picture like that every day, you know. Remember how much time I spend passe-partouting it?'

'Well, man, it have one consolation. The picture ain't break.'

'How you mean? It *coulda* break. Nothing in this house ain't safe with that man breadfruit dropping all over the place.'

'No, man. Why you don't go and hang back the picture up?'

'Hang it back up? Me, hang it back up? Look, *you* don't start provoking me now, you hear. I ain't know what I do so, for everybody to give me all this provocation all the time.'

'But, man, Ramlogan *ain't* provoking you today. The breadfruit fall, is true. But breadfruit ain't have a mind. Breadfruit don't stop and study and say, "I think I go fall today and knock down the picture of Mahatma Gandhi."'

'Stop giving me provocation!'

'And Ramlogan, for all the bad cuss you cuss him, he ain't even come out to answer you back.'

'Ain't come out! You know why he ain't come out? You know?' And running to the window, he shouted his own answer: 'Is because he ain't no fighter. You know who is the fighter? I, Chittaranjan, is the fighter.' He shook his short scrawny arms and beat on the enamel sink. Then he pulled in his head and faced Mrs Chittaranjan. 'My name in the Supreme Court for fighting. Not any stupid old Naparoni Petty Civil—ha!—but *Supreme* Court.' He sat on the paint-spotted kitchen stool and said ruminatively, 'I is like that. Supreme Court or nothing.' He chuckled. 'Well, if Ramlogan go on like this, Supreme Court going to hear from me again, that is all.' He spoke with rueful pride.

'Man, you know you only talking.' Mrs Chittaranjan was being provocative again.

Chittaranjan pursed and unpursed his lips. 'Only talking, eh?'

But he was quite subdued. Ramlogan's perverse silence had put him out. He sat smiling, frowning, his sabots on the cross-bar of the stool, his small sharp shoulders hunched up, the palms of his small bony hands pressing hard on the edges of the seat.

Mrs Chittaranjan returned to her pans. She scoured; the ash grated; she sang the song from *Jhoola*.

Chittaranjan said, slowly, 'Going to fix him up. Fix him good and proper. Going to put something on him. Something good.'

The singing stopped. 'No, man. You mustn't talk so. *Obeah* and magic is not a nice thing to put on anybody.'

'Nah, don't stop me, I begging you. Don't stop me. I can't bear *any* more provocation again.'

'Man, why you don't go and hang back the picture up?'

'Put something on him before *he* put something on we.'

Mrs Chittaranjan looked perturbed.

Chittaranjan saw. He drove home his point. 'Somebody try to put something on Baksh day before yesterday. Dog. Was big big in the night and next morning was tiny tiny. So high.'

'*You* see the dog?'

'You laughing. But I telling you, man, we got to put something on him before he put something on we. And it ain't we alone we got to think about. What about little Nalini?'

'Nelly, man? Little Nelly?'

His wife's anxiety calmed Chittaranjan. He got up from the stool. 'Going to hang back the picture up,' he announced.

He clattered down the wooden back steps in his sabots and went to the little dark cupboard behind the shop. In this cupboard he kept all sorts of things: pails and basins for his jewellery work, ladders and shears and carpenter's tools, paint-tins and brushes, tins full of bent nails he had collected from the concrete casings when his house was being built. There was no light in the cupboard—that was part of his economy. But he knew where everything was. He knew where the hammer was and where the nail-tin was.

When he opened the door a strong smell met his nostrils. 'That white lime growing rotten like hell,' he said. He felt for the hammer, found it. He felt for the nail-tin. His fingers touched something hard and fur-lined. Then something slimy passed over his hand. Then something took up the loose flesh at the bottom of his little finger and gave it a sharp little nip.

Chittaranjan bolted.

One sabot was missing when he stood breathless against the kitchen door.

'Man,' he said at last. 'Man, dog.'

'Dog?'

'Yes, man.'

'Downstairs?'

'Yes, man. Store-room. Lock up in the store-room.'

Mrs Chittaranjan nearly screamed.

'Just like the one Baksh say he see, man. They send it away but it come back. To we, man, to we.'

*

Ramlogan had heard the breadfruit fall and heard all the subsequent curses from Chittaranjan. But he didn't reply because a visitor had just brought him important news.

The visitor was Haq.

Haq had come at about half past two, gone around to that side of Ramlogan's yard which was hidden from Chittaranjan's, and beaten on the gate. The gate answered well: it was entirely made up of tin advertisements for Dr Kellogg's Asthma Remedy, enamelled in yellow and black.

Ramlogan shouted: 'Go away. I know who you is. And I know who send you. You is a police and your wife sick and you want some brandy really bad for she sake, and you go beg and I go sell and you go lock me up. And I know is Chittaranjan who send you. Go away.'

Chittaranjan had indeed caught Ramlogan like that once.

Haq drummed again. 'I is not a police. I is Haq. Haq.'

'Haq,' came the reply, 'haul your black arse away from my shop. You not getting nothing on trust. And too besides, is closing time.'

Haq didn't go away.

At length Ramlogan came out, smelling of Canadian Healing Oil, and unchained the gate. He had been having his siesta. He was wearing a pair of dirty white pants that showed how his fat legs shook when he walked, and a dirty white vest with many holes. And he was in his slippers: dirty canvas shoes open at the little toes, with the heels crushed flat.

'What the hell you want, black Haq?'

Haq put his face close up to Ramlogan's unshaved chin. 'When you hear me! When you hear me!'

Ramlogan pushed him away. 'You ain't bound and 'bliged to spit on me when you talk.'

Haq didn't seem to mind. 'When you hear,' he twittered, his lower lip wet and shining. 'Just wait until you hear. It not going to be black Haq then.'

Ramlogan was striding ahead, flinging out his legs, shaking and jellying from his shoulders to his knees.

They went to the room behind the shop. Here Ramlogan cooked, ate and slept. It was a long narrow room, just the size of the rumshop. *Trinidad Sentinels* covered the walls and sheltered many cockroaches. The one window was closed; the air was hot, and heavy with the sweet smell of Canadian Healing Oil.

Ramlogan said grumpily, 'You wake up a man when a man was

catching a little sleep, man,' and he lay down on his rumpled bed—a mattress thrown over some new planks—scratching easily and indiscriminately. He yawned.

Haq leaned his stick against the rum crates in a corner and eased himself into the sugar-sack hammock hanging diagonally across the room.

Ramlogan yawned and scratched. 'Before you start, Haq, remember one thing. No trust. Remember, no trust.'

He pointed to the only picture on his walls, a coloured diptych. In one panel Haq saw the wise man who had never given credit, plump—though not so plump as Ramlogan—and laughing and counting what looked like a fortune. In the other panel the incorrigible creditor, wizened, haggard, was biting his nails in front of an empty money chest. Ramlogan had a copy of this picture in his shop as well.

'In God we trust, as the saying goes,' Ramlogan glozed. 'In man we bust. *As* the saying goes.'

'I ain't come to beg,' Haq said. 'If you ain't want to hear what I have to say, I could just get up and walk out, you know.'

But he made no move to go.

He talked.

Ramlogan listened. And as he listened, his peevishness turned into delight. He rolled on his dirty bed and kicked up his fat legs. 'Oh, God, You is good. You is really good. Was this self I been waiting and praying for, for a long long time. Ha! So Chittaranjan is the fighter, eh? He in the Supreme Court for fighting, eh? Now we go show this Supreme Court fighter!'

Then the breadfruit fell. Then Chittaranjan cursed.

Haq waited. Ramlogan did nothing.

'Go on and tell him now,' Haq urged. 'Answer him back.'

'It could wait.' And Ramlogan began to sing: 'It could wait-ait, it could-ould wait-ait.'

He stopped singing and they both listened to Chittaranjan cursing. Ramlogan slapped his belly. Haq giggled.

'Let we just remain quiet like a chu'ch and listen to *all* that he have to say,' Ramlogan said. He clasped his hands over his belly, looked up at the sooty corrugated-iron ceiling, smiled and shut his eyes.

Chittaranjan paused. All that could be heard in Ramlogan's room was the whisking of cockroaches behind the *Trinidad Sentinels* on the wall.

Chittaranjan began again.

'He talking brave, eh, Haq? Let him wait. Haq, you black, but you is a good good friend.'

Haq was about to speak, but Ramlogan stopped him: 'Let we *well* listen.'

They listened until there was nothing more to listen to.

Haq said, 'Ramlogan, you is my good good friend too. You is the only Hindu I could call that.'

Ramlogan sat up and his feet fumbled for the degraded canvas shoes.

'I is a old man, Ramlogan. My shop don't pay, like yours. People ain't buying sweet drink as how they use to. I is a widow too. Just like you. But I ain't have your strength.'

'All of we have to get old, Haq.'

'That boy Foam say he going to send me to hospital.'

'Foam only full of mouth, like his father.'

'He did beg and beg me not to tell nobody. Wasn't for *my* sake I break my word.'

Ramlogan stood up, stretched, and passed his big hairy hands over his big hairy belly. He walked over to the rum crates and took out a quarter bottle.

'A good Muslim like you shouldn't drink, you know, Haq.'

Haq looked angrily from the quarter bottle to Ramlogan. 'I is a *very* old man.'

'And because you is very old, you want to take over my shop?' Ramlogan put back the bottle of rum. 'You done owing me more than thirty dollars which I know these eyes of mine never even going to smell again.'

It was true. Haq had caught Ramlogan when Ramlogan was new in Elvira.

Haq said, 'Is so it does happen when you get old. Give me.'

He took the rum, dolefully, and hid it in an inside pocket of his loose serge jacket. 'Sometimes, eh, Ramlogan, I could drop in by you for a little chat, like in the days when you did fust come to Elvira?'

Ramlogan nodded. 'You is a bad Muslim, Haq, and you is a bad drinker.'

Haq struggled to rise from his hammock. 'I is a old man.'

Ramlogan hurried him outside and chained the gate after him.

Haq came out well pleased, but trying hard to look dejected, to fool the two workmen in Chittaranjan's yard. They weren't looking at him; they were staring in astonishment at something he hadn't seen. He kept his eyes on the ground and fumbled with his jacket to make sure that his rum was safe. He limped a few paces; then, knowing that people would suspect equally if he appeared too dejected, he looked up.

And halted.

There, limping out of Chittaranjan's yard into the hot afternoon sun, was the animal all Elvira had heard about. Tiny, rickety. Dangerous. Tiger.

'Where that dog going?' Haq cried. And he hoped it wasn't to his place.

*

Tiger came out into the road and turned left.

It was nearly half past three. Children were coming back from school, labourers from the estate. Only people in government service were still at work; they would knock off at four.

The news ran through Elvira. Baksh's puppy, the *obeah*-dog, the one that had been sent away, was back.

Tiger limped on. Schoolchildren and labourers stood silently at the verge to let him pass. Faces appeared behind raised curtains. People ran up from the traces to watch. No one interfered with Tiger and he looked at no one. His hiccoughs had gone. He tottered, wobbled, and went on, as though some force outside him were pushing him on to a specific destination.

Mr Cuffy saw and was afraid.

Rampiari's husband was afraid. 'You is my witness, Ma,' he said to his mother-in-law, 'that when the goldsmith come yesterday to ask for my vote, I tell him I didn't want to meddle in this politics business. You is my witness that he beg and beg me to vote.'

Mahadeo, his thoughts on the sick and dying Negroes of Elvira, saw. When he passed Mr Cuffy he didn't look up.

Mr Cuffy shouted, 'Remember, Mahadeo, if anybody dead before this elections . . .'

Mahadeo walked on.

Tiger walked on.

Baksh, Mrs Baksh, Foam and all the six young Bakshes knew.

'Shut up the shop!' Baksh ordered. 'And shut up the gate. Nobody dog ain't walking in my yard as they well please.'

Mrs Baksh was pale. 'This sweetness, man, this election sweetness.'

Baksh said, 'Foam, I ain't want to get Bible and key again. You did or you didn't take away that dog last night?'

'I tell you, man.'

'Oh God, Foam! Things serious. Don't lie to me at this hour, you know.'

Foam sucked his teeth.

Herbert said, 'But we ain't even know is the same dog.'

'Yes,' Baksh said eagerly. 'Exactly. How we know is the same dog?'

Mrs Baksh beat her bosom. 'I *know*, Baksh.'

Tiger came on, indifferent as sea or sky. He didn't walk in the centre of the road, as people wished he would; he walked at the edge, as if he wished to hide in the grass.

Christians, Hindus and Muslims crossed themselves. To make sure, some Hindus muttered *Rama, Rama* as well.

Tiger came around the bend of the road.

'Is Tiger!' Herbert said.

'Sweetness! Sourness!'

Rafiq said, 'Ten die.'

'But look how small the mister man dog is, eh?' Baksh said. 'You know, he get even smaller now. Small as a rabbit and thin as a matchstick.'

Herbert said, 'Still, small as he is, he coming.'

'Herbert,' Mrs Baksh pleaded, 'you ain't cause enough trouble and misery?'

Baksh said, 'Not to worry, man. For all we know, the dog just going to walk straight past the house. After all, that fellow in Tamana did well *jharay* Herbert.'

'I *know*, Baksh. And everybody in Elvira know too. Look how they looking. They looking at the dog and then they looking at we. And they laughing in their belly, for all the serious face they putting on. Oh God, Baksh, this sweetness!'

Foam said, 'I don't see why all-you making this big set of fuss for. All I could see is a thin thin dog, break-up like hell, that look as though he ain't eat nothing since he born.'

Tiger staggered on.

Baksh said, 'Look, man. What you worried for? He ain't even trying to cross the road yet.'

'Baksh, I know. He go cross when he want to cross. That dog know his business, I telling you. Oh, Baksh, the mess you get me in!'

Herbert said, 'Oh. He ain't even stopping.'

Mrs Baksh, crying, asked, 'You want it to stop, Herbert? Just answer me that. My own child want the dog to stop?'

Herbert said, 'Well, it ain't stopping.'

'What I did tell you?' Baksh said. He laughed. 'Wonder *who* house little mister man dog going to. Come to think of it, you know, man, it ain't even the same dog. The one we did have had a white spot on the right foot in front. This one ain't have no white spot. Not the same dog really.' He turned his back to the veranda wall and faced his family. 'Don't know why everybody was getting so excited. All right, all right, the show over.' He clapped his hands and snapped his fingers at the young Bakshes. 'Show over. Back to your reading and your studies. Homework. Educate youself. Jawgraphy and jawme-try. Nobody did give *me* a opportunity to educate myself . . .'

'Dog coming back,' Foam said. 'He stop and turning.'

They all scrambled to look.

Tiger was limping brokenly across the road.

'Somebody feed that dog here!' Baksh shouted. 'Nobody not going to tell me that somebody ain't feed that dog here.'

Tiger dragged himself across the plank over the gutter. Then the strength that had driven him so far was extinguished; he collapsed on his side, his eyes vacant, his chest and belly heaving.

'He behaving as if he come home,' Herbert said.

'Herbert, my son, my own son,' Mrs Baksh said. 'What come over you, son? Tell me what they do to you, to make you *want* that dirty dog. Tell me, my son.'

Herbert didn't reply.

Mrs Baksh broke down completely. She cried and her breasts and belly shook. 'Something going to happen, Baksh. In this house.'

'Ten die,' Rafiq said.

Baksh slapped him.

'Suppose that dog just lay down there and dead,' Baksh said. 'Oh God, Foam, you want me to believe that you ain't feed that dog here? That dog behave too much as if he know where his bread butter, you hear.'

Foam shrugged his shoulders.

Baksh said, 'Man, what going to be the best thing? For the dog to live or dead?'

Mrs Baksh pressed her hands against her eyes and shook her head. 'I don't know, Baksh. I just don't know what is the best thing.'

But Herbert knew what he wanted. 'Oh, God,' he prayed, 'don't let Tiger dead.'

*

Ramlogan didn't know about Tiger's passage through Elvira. After Haq left he remained in his narrow dark room, savouring the news

Haq had brought. He couldn't go back to sleep. He remained on his bed, completely happy, looking up at the corrugated-iron roof until the alarm clock went off on the empty rum crate at his bedside. It was an alarm clock he had got many years before for collecting empty Anchor Cigarette packets; the dial had letters in the place of eleven numerals and read SMOKE ANCHOR 6. The dial was yellow and the glass, surprisingly uncracked, was scratched and blurred. Every midday when he shut his shop Ramlogan set the alarm for a quarter to four. That gave him time to anoint himself with Canadian Healing Oil, dress and make some tea before he opened the shop again at four.

That afternoon, routine became delicious ritual. He was lavish with the Canadian Healing Oil. He rubbed it over his face and worked it into his scalp; he poured some into his palm and held it to his nostrils to inhale the therapeutic vapours; the only thing Ramlogan didn't do with Canadian Healing Oil was drink it. He dressed leisurely, humming the song from *Jhoola*. He made his tea, drank it; and having some moments to spare, went out into his yard. The stunted and dead plants in the centre didn't offend him that afternoon, and he looked almost with love on the breadfruit tree and the zaboca tree at the edge of the yard. He was particularly fond of the zaboca tree. He had stolen it not long after he had come to Elvira, from a lorry that was carrying a whole load of small zaboca trees in bamboo pods. The lorry had had a puncture just outside his shop; he had gone out to look; and when the driver went off to look for a pump, Ramlogan had taken a bamboo pod and walked off with it into his own yard. The tree had grown well. Its fruit was high-grade. You could tell that by just looking at it. It was none of your common zaboca, all stringy and waterlogged. That afternoon it didn't grieve Ramlogan at all that he hadn't tasted one of the fruit.

It was time to open the shop. He climbed over the greasy counter, thinking, as he did so, that after the election, when Harbans had settled his account, he would get a nice zinc counter. And perhaps even a refrigerator. For lager. People were drinking more lager and it didn't do for him to keep ice wrapped up in the dirty sugar-sack. And sometimes the ice-lorry didn't even come.

He lifted the solid bar that kept the shaky front doors secure, humming the song from *Jhoola*. He remembered he had picked up the song from Mrs Chittaranjan next door, and stopped humming. He opened the doors, squinting against the sudden dazzle of the afternoon sun. He looked down.

Before him, laid squarely in the middle of his doorway, was a dead chicken.

8. Dead Dog

HE RECOGNIZED THE CHICKEN at once.

It was one of Mrs Chittaranjan's clean-necked chickens, white and grey, an insistent, impertinent thing that, despite repeated shooings and occasional lucky hits with stones and bits of wood and empty Canadian Healing Oil bottles, continued to come into his yard, eat his grass, dig up his languishing plants and leave its droppings everywhere, sometimes even in the back room and in the shop.

It was the chicken Foam had hit earlier that day.

Ramlogan had known the chicken since it was hatched. He had known its mother and managed to maim her in the leg when she came into his yard one day with all her brood. The rest of that particular brood had disappeared. They had been stolen, they had grown up and been eaten or they had just died. Only the hardy clean-necked chicken had survived.

For a moment Ramlogan was sad to see it lying dead at his feet. He looked up at Chittaranjan's veranda.

Chittaranjan was waiting for him. 'Look at it good, Ramlogan. It not going to worry you again. That fowl on *your* nasty conscience.'

Ramlogan was taken by surprise.

'You is a fat blow-up beast. You can't touch no human, so you take it outa a poor chicken. You is a bad wicked beast. Look at it good. Take it up. Cook it. Eat it. Eat it and get more fat. Ain't is that you say you want to do for a long long time? Now is your chance. Cook it and eat it and I hope it poison you. You kill it, you wicked beast, you Nazi spy.'

Ramlogan hadn't recovered. 'Who you calling a Nazi spy?'

'You. You is a Nazi spy. You is wuss than Hitler.'

'And because I is wuss than Hitler, you come and put this dead fowl on my doorstep?'

'But ain't it make your heart satisfy, you wuthless beast? Ain't it bring peace and satisfaction inside your fat dirty heart to see the poor little chicken dead?'

'Eh! But who tell you I kill your fowl? I ain't kill nobody fowl, you hearing me?'

'You is a wuthless liar.'

Ramlogan lifted his leg to kick the chicken from his doorstep. But something Chittaranjan said arrested him.

'Kick it,' Chittaranjan said. 'And I bet your whole fat foot drop off and rotten. Go ahead and kick it.'

Ramlogan was getting angry. 'You just want to put something on me, eh? You is a big big fighter, and all you could do is put magic and *obeah* on me, eh? You is a Supreme Court fighter?'

'What you asking me for? *You* ever see the inside of any court?'

Ramlogan strode over the dead chicken and walked slowly to the edge of his yard. He said, genially, 'Chittaranjan, come down a little bit. Come down and tell me I is a Nazi spy.'

And Ramlogan put his hand on the wire fence.

'Take your fat dirty hand offa my fence!'

Ramlogan smiled. 'Come down and take my hand off. Come down, take my hand offa your fence and tell me I is a Nazi spy.'

Chittaranjan was puzzled. Ramlogan had never before refused to take his hands off the fence. He had contented himself either with crying and promising to build his own fence, or with saying, 'All right, I taking my hand offa your fence, and I going inside to wash it with carbolic soap.'

'Come down,' Ramlogan invited.

'I not going to dirty my hands on you.' Chittaranjan paused. 'But is my fence still.'

Inspiration came to Ramlogan. 'Why you don't put a fence around your daughter too?'

He scored.

'Nalini?' Chittaranjan asked, and his tone was almost conversational.

'Yes, Nalini self. Little Nelly. Ha.' Ramlogan gave his dryest laugh.

'Ramlogan! What you want with my daughter?'

Ramlogan shook the wire fence. 'Ha. *I* don't want nothing with your daughter. But I know who want though.'

'Ramlogan! Who you is to take my daughter name in your mouth in vain? You, a man like you, who should be running about kissing the ground in case she walk on it.'

'*Walk?* Ha. Little Nelly tired with walking man. She lying down now.'

'Ramlogan! You mean you sell everything from that rumshop of yours? You ain't even keep back a penny shame? Is the sort of language to hear from a old, hardback, resign man like you?'

Ramlogan addressed Chittaranjan's workmen under the awning. They had been studiously inattentive throughout. 'Tell me, is something *I* make up?'

The workmen didn't look at him.

Ramlogan said, 'When girl children small, they does crawl, as the saying goes. Then they does start walking. Then they does lie down. *As* the saying goes. Ain't something I sit down and invent.'

'Who invent it?' Chittaranjan screamed. 'Your mother?'

Ramlogan said solemnly, 'Chittaranjan, I beg you, don't cuss my mother. Cuss me upside down as much as you want, but leave my mother alone.' He paused, and laughed. 'But if you want to learn more about Nelly, why you don't ask Foam?'

'Foam? Foreman? Baksh son?'

'Campaign manager. Ha. *Nice* boy. Nice *Muslim* boy.'

Chittaranjan lost his taste for battle. 'Is true? Is true, Ramlogan? You ain't making this up?'

'Why you asking me for? Ha. Ask little Nelly. Look, little Nelly coming back from school. Ask she.' Ramlogan pointed.

From his veranda Chittaranjan saw Nelly coming up the road.

'Proper student and scholar, man,' Ramlogan said. 'The girl going to school in the day-time and taking private lessons in the night-time. I know I is a Nazi spy, and I know I is a shameless hard-back resign man, but I is not the man to stand up between father and daughter.'

He gave the fence a final shake, went and picked up the chicken and flung it into Chittaranjan's yard. 'It get fat enough eating my food,' he said. 'Cook it and eat it yourself. Supreme Court fighter like you have to eat good.'

He went back to his counter.

Nelly had stayed behind at school, as she always did, to help correct the exercises of the lower classes and rearrange the desks after the day's upheaval. She was head pupil; a position more like that of unpaid monitor. On the way home she had heard about Tiger and seen him lying in the Bakshes' yard. She knew then that her parents must have found him and turned him out.

She overdid the cheerfulness when she saw Chittaranjan. 'Hi, Pops!'

Chittaranjan didn't like the greeting. 'Nalini,' he said sadly, 'don't bother to go round by the back. Come up here. I have something to ask you.'

She didn't like his tone.

'Oh dog, dog,' she muttered, going up the red steps to the veranda, 'how much more trouble you going to cause?'

*

The Bakshes in their dilemma—whether they wanted Tiger dead or alive—were fortunate to get the advice of Harichand the printer.

Harichand was coming home after his work in Couva. No taxi-driver cared to come right up to Elvira, and Harichand was dropped outside Cordoba. He had to walk the three miles to Elvira. He enjoyed it. It kept his figure trim; and when it rained he liked sport-ing the American raincoat he had acquired—at enormous cost, he said—on one of his trips to Port of Spain. He was the only man in Elvira who possessed a raincoat; everybody else just waited until the rain stopped.

Baksh was sitting in his veranda, looking out as if to find a solution, when he saw Harichand and pointed to Tiger prostrate in the yard.

'Ah, little puppy dog,' Harichand said cheerfully. 'Thought you did get rid of him.'

'It come back, Harichand.'

'Come back, eh?' Harichand stopped and looked at Tiger critically. 'Thin thing.' He stood up and gently lifted Tiger's belly with the tip of a shining shoe. 'Ah. Preacher put something strong on you if dog come back.'

'Come up, Harichand,' Baksh said. 'It have something we want to ask you.'

Harichand had an entirely spurious reputation as an amateur of the mystic and the psychic; but the thing that encouraged Baksh to call him up was the limitless confidence he always gave off. Nothing surprised or upset Harichand, and he was always ready with a remedy.

'I have a pussonal feeling,' Baksh began, seating Harichand on a bench in the veranda, 'I have a pussonal feeling that somebody feed that dog here.'

'Feed, eh?' Harichand got up again and took off his coat. His white shirt was spotless. One of Harichand's idiosyncrasies was to wear a clean shirt every day. He folded his coat carefully and rested it on the ledge of the veranda wall. Then he sat down and hitched up his sharply creased blue serge trousers above his knees. 'Somebody feed it, eh? But did tell you not to feed it. Wust thing in the world, feeding dog like that.'

Mrs Baksh came up. 'What go happen if the dog dead, Harichand?'

Harichand hadn't thought of that. 'What go happen, eh?' He

passed the edge of his thumb-nail along his sharp little moustache. 'If it dead.' He paused. 'Could be dangerous. You never know. You went to see somebody about it?'

She mentioned the name of the mystic in Tamana.

Harichand made a face. 'He all right. But he don't really *know*. Not like Ganesh Pundit. Ganesh was the man.'

'Is that I does always say,' Baksh said. He turned to Mrs Baksh. 'Ain't I did tell you, man, that Ganesh Pundit was the man?'

'Still,' Harichand said consolingly, 'you went to see somebody. He give you something for the house and he *jharay* the boy?'

'He well *jharay* him,' Mrs Baksh said. 'Baksh tell you about the sign, Harichand?'

'Sign? Funeral huss?'

'Not *that*,' Baksh said quickly. '*We* had a sign. Tell him, man.'

Mrs Baksh told about the 'Ten Die!' sign.

'Did see it,' said Harichand. 'Didn't know was *your* sign.'

Baksh smiled. 'Well, was *we* sign.'

Harichand said firmly, 'Mustn't let the dog dead.'

'But you did tell me not to feed him,' Baksh said.

'Didn't tell me about your sign,' said Harichand. 'And too besides, didn't exactly say that. Did just say not to feed it *inside* the house. Wust thing in the world, feeding dog like that inside.'

'Feed him outside?' Baksh asked.

'That's right. Outside. Feed him outside.'

Harichand stood up and looked down at Tiger.

'Think he go dead, Harichand?' Mrs Baksh asked.

'Hm.' Harichand frowned and bit his thin lower lip with sharp white teeth. 'Mustn't *let* him dead.'

Baksh said, 'He look strong to you, Harichand?'

'Wouldn't exactly *call* him a strong dog,' Harichand said.

Baksh coaxed: 'But is thin thin dogs like that does live and live and make a lot a lot of mischief, eh, Harichand?'

Harichand said, 'Trinidad full of thin dogs.'

'Still,' Baksh said, 'they *living*.'

Harichand whispered to Baksh, 'Is thin dogs like that does breed a lot, you know. And breed fast to boot.'

Baksh made a big show of astonishment, to please Harichand.

'Yes, man. Dogs like that. Telling you, man. See it with my own eyes.' Harichand caught Mrs Baksh's eye. He said, loudly, 'Just feed it outside. Outside all the time. Everything going to be all right. If anything happen, just let me know.'

He hung his coat lovingly over his left arm and straightened his tie. As he was leaving he said, 'Still waiting for those election printing jobs, Baksh. If Harbans want my vote, he want my printery. Otherwise . . .' And Harichand shook his head and laughed.

*

Soon Tiger was passing through Elvira again, this time in the loudspeaker van. Foam and Herbert were taking him, on instructions, to the old cocoa-house.

*

Chittaranjan called.

Baksh said, 'Going out campaigning, Goldsmith?'

For Chittaranjan was in his visiting outfit.

Chittaranjan didn't reply.

'Something private, eh, Goldsmith?'

And Baksh led Chittaranjan upstairs. But Chittaranjan didn't take off his hat and didn't sit down in the cane-bottomed chair.

'Something serious, Goldsmith?'

'Baksh, I want you to stop interfering with my daughter.'

Baksh knit his brows.

Chittaranjan's flush became deeper. His smile widened. His calm voice iced over: 'It have some people who can't bear to see other people prosper. I don't want nobody to pass over their *obeah* to me and I ain't give my daughter all that education for she to run about with boys in the night-time.'

'You talking about Foam, eh?'

'I ain't talking about Foam. I talking about the man who instigating Foam. And that man is you, Baksh. I is like that, as you know. I does say my mind, and who want to vex, let them vex.'

'Look out, you know, Goldsmith! You calling me a instigator.'

'I ain't want your *obeah* in my house. We is Hindus. You is Muslim. And too besides, my daughter practically engage already.'

'Engage!' Baksh laughed. 'Engage to Harbans son? You have all Elvira laughing at you. You believe Harbans going to let his son marry your daughter? Harbans foolish, but he ain't that foolish, you hear.'

For a moment Chittaranjan was at a loss.

'And look, eh, Goldsmith, Foam better than ten of Harbans sons, you hear. And too besides, you think *I* go instigate Foam to go around with *your* daughter? Don't make me laugh, man. Your daughter? When it have five thousand Muslim girl prettier than she.'

'I glad it have five thousand Muslim girl prettier than she. But that ain't the point.'

'How it ain't the point? Everybody know that Muslim girl prettier than Hindu girl. And Foam chasing *your* daughter? Ten to one, your daughter ain't giving the poor boy a chance. Let me tell you, eh, every Hindu girl think they in paradise if they get a Muslim boy.'

'What is Muslim?' Chittaranjan asked, his smile frozen, his eyes unshining, his voice low and cutting. 'Muslim is everything and Muslim is nothing.' He paused. 'Even Negro is Muslim.'

That hurt Baksh. He stopped pacing about and looked at Chittaranjan. He looked at him hard and long. Then he shouted, 'Good! Good! I glad! I glad Harbans ain't want no Muslim vote. Harbans ain't going to *get* no Muslim vote. You say it yourself. Negro and Muslim is one. All right. Preacher getting every Muslim vote in Elvira.'

Baksh's rage relaxed Chittaranjan. He took off his hat and flicked a finger over the wide brim. 'We could do without the Muslim vote.' He put on his hat again, lifted his left arm and pinched the loose skin just below the wrist. 'This is pure blood. Every Hindu blood is pure blood. Nothing mix up with it. Is pure Aryan blood.'

Baksh snorted. 'All-you is just a pack of kaffir, if you ask me.'

'*Madinga!*' Chittaranjan snapped back.

They traded racial insults in rising voices.

Mrs Baksh came out and said, 'Goldsmith, I is not going to have you come to my house and talk like that.'

Chittaranjan pressed his hat more firmly on his head. 'I is not *staying* in your house.' He went through the brass-bed room to the stairs, saying, 'Smell. Smell the beef and all the other nastiness they does cook in this house.' He matched the rhythm of his speech to his progress down the steps: 'A animal spend nine months in his mother belly. It born. The mother feed it. People feed it. It feed itself. It grow up. It come big. It come strong. Then they kill it. Why?' He was on the last step. 'To feed Baksh.'

Baksh shouted after him, 'And tell Harbans he have to win this election without the Muslim vote.'

'We go still win.'

And Chittaranjan was in the road.

'What I tell you, Baksh?' Mrs Baksh exclaimed. 'See how sour the sweetness turning?'

'Look, you and all,' Baksh said, 'don't start digging in my tail, you hear.'

Mrs Baksh smoothed her dress over her belly. 'Why you didn't talk to the goldsmith like that? No, you is man only in front of woman. But Baksh, you just put one finger on me, and Elvira going to see the biggest bacchanal it ever see.'

Baksh sucked his teeth. 'You talking like your mother. Both of all-you just have a lot of mouth.'

'Go ahead, Baksh. You finish already? Go ahead and insult the dead. This election make you so shameless. If it was to me that the goldsmith was talking, I woulda turn my hand and give him a good clout behind his head. *I* know that. But you, you make me shame that you is the father of my seven children.'

Bakish said irritably, trying to turn the conversation, 'You go ahead and talk. And let the goldsmith talk and let Harbans talk. But no Muslim ain't going to vote for Harbans. Just watch and see.'

*

It was growing dark when Foam and Herbert brought Tiger to the cocoa-house. Years before, labourers were paid to keep the very floor of the cocoa-woods clean; now the woods were strangled in bush that had spread out to choke the cocoa-house itself. When Foam was a child he had played in the cocoa-house, but it was too dangerous now and no one went near it.

Foam and Herbert broke a path through from the road to the house. They had brought a box, gunny sacks and food for Tiger. While Foam hunted about for a place safe enough to put Tiger, Herbert explored.

Herbert knew all about the ghost of the cocoa-house, but ghosts, like the dark, didn't frighten him. The ghost of the cocoa-house was a baby, a baby Miss Elvira herself had had by a negro servant at the time the cocoa-house was being built. The story was that she had buried it in the foundations, under the concrete steps at the back. Many people, many Spaniards in particular, had often heard the baby crying; some had even seen it crawling about in the road near the cocoa-house.

Herbert climbed to the ceiling and tried to push back the sliding roof: the roof was sliding so that the beans could dry in the sun and be covered up as soon as it began to rain. He pushed hard, but the wheels of the roof had rusted and stuck to the rails. He pushed again and again. The wheels grated on the rails, the whole house shook with a jangle of corrugated-iron sheets and a flapping of loose boards, and wood-lice and wood-dust fell down.

Herbert called out, 'Foam, the roof still working.'

'Herbert, why you so bent on playing the ass? Look how you make Tiger frighten.'

Tiger was indeed behaving oddly. He had staggered to his feet, for the first time since his marathon afternoon walk; and for the first time since he had been discovered, was making some sound. A ghost of a whine, a faint mew.

Herbert came down to see.

Tiger mewed and tottered around in his box, as though he were trying to catch his tail.

Herbert was thrilled. 'You see? He getting better.' He remembered Miss Elvira's baby. 'Dog could smell spirits, you know, Foam.'

The tropical twilight came and went. Night fell. Tiger's mews became more distinct. Whenever Foam stepped on the rotting floor the cocoa-house creaked. Outside in the bush croak was answering screech: the night noises were beginning. Tiger mewed, whined, and swung shakily about in his box.

Foam tried to force Tiger to lie down; the position seemed normal for Tiger; but Tiger wasn't going to sit down or lie down and he wasn't going to try to get out of his box either. The darkness thickened. The bush outside began to sing. Foam could just see the white spots on Tiger's muzzle. A bat swooped low through the room, open at both ends.

'Can't leave him here,' Foam said aloud. 'Herbert!'

But Herbert wasn't there.

'Herbert!'

He lit a match. For a moment the spurt of flame blinded him. Then the rotting damp walls, stained with the ancient stain of millions of cocoa-beans, defined themselves around him. He looked up at the roof.

'Herbert!'

He walked back to the box. Shadows flurried on the walls.

'Take it easy, Tiger.'

The match went out. He dropped it but didn't hear it fall. It must have gone through one of the holes in the floor.

'Herbert! You up on the roof? Boy, take care you don't fall and break your tail, you hear.'

He felt his way to the broken entrance. The house creaked, the galvanized-iron roof shivered.

'Herbert!'

In the night his voice sounded thinner. He couldn't see anything, only the blackness of bush all around. The road and the van were a hundred yards away.

Then: 'Foam! Foam!' he heard Herbert screaming, and ran back inside. The sudden rumbling of the house made him stop and walk. Tiger he couldn't see at all now, only heard him whining and striking against the sides of his box.

'Foam! Foam!'

He walked to the other end of the room, lighting matches to see his way across the holes in the floor.

'Look, Foam!'

He went down the solid concrete steps at the back. They were the only solid thing left in the cocoa-house. The ground sloped down from the road and the steps at the back were about eight feet high, nearly twice as high as those in front. A solid concrete wall supported the solid concrete steps. Foam lit a match. The surface of the steps was still smooth and new, as though it had been finished only the week before. Tall weeds switched against Foam's legs. The weeds were already damp with dew. The match flickered in his cupped hands.

'Look, Foam, under the steps here.'

Herbert was almost hysterical. Foam did what he had been told to do in such circumstances. He slapped Herbert, with great dexterity, back-hand and forward-hand. Herbert pulled in his breath hard and kept back his sobs.

Foam lit another match.

Under the steps he saw a dead dog and five dead puppies. The mother had its mouth open, its teeth bared. She was the dog Harbans had hit that afternoon weeks before.

Her eyes were horribly inanimate. Her chest and belly were

shrunken. Her ribs stood out, hard. Damp black earth stuck to her pink blotched dugs, thin and slack like a punctured balloon. The puppies were all like Tiger. They had died all over their mother, anyhow.

The match went out.

'She didn't have no milk or nothing to feed them,' Herbert said.

Foam squatted in the darkness beside the dead dog. 'You talking like a woman, Herbert. You never seen nothing dead before?'

'Everybody only know how to say, "Mash, dog!"' The words came between sobs. 'Nobody know how to feed it.'

'That is all you could think about, Herbert? Food? It look as if *they* right, you know.'

'What we going to do with them, Foam?'

Foam laughed. 'I got a master-idea, Herbert.' He got up and lit a match, away from the dead puppies. 'I going to get the cutlass.'

'What for, Foam?'

'Dig a hole and bury the mother. You coming with me or you staying here to cry over the dogs?'

'I coming with you, Foam. Don't go.'

They dug a shallow hole and buried the mother. Herbert trimmed a switch, broke it in two, peeled off the bark and tied the pieces into a cross. He stuck it on the grave.

Foam pulled it out. 'Where you learn that from?'

'Is how they does do it in the belling-ground, Foam.'

'Eh, but you turning Christian or something?'

Herbert saw his error.

'Come on now,' Foam said cheerfully. 'Help me take these dead puppies in the van.'

Foam's business-like attitude calmed Herbert. 'What we going to do with *five* dead puppies, Foam?'

Foam laughed. 'Ah, boy, you go see.'

Herbert trusted Foam. He knew that whatever it was, it was going to be fun.

'But what about Tiger, Foam? We could leave him here? He wouldn't grieve too much?'

Foam said confidently, 'Only place for Tiger now is right here. Don't worry about Tiger. He going to be all right.'

*

They got home late and found Baksh, Mrs Baksh and Zilla in the store-room. Teacher Francis was there too. Foam was surprised. Teacher Francis had come to the Baksh house only once before, to say that if Rafiq didn't buck up at school he was going to turn out just like Foam.

'Ah,' Baksh said heavily to Foam and Herbert. 'Campaign manager and little mister man. Where you was out so late? I did tell you to put away the dog or I did tell you to build a mansion for it?'

Herbert smiled. 'We was out campaigning.' He winked at Foam.

'That prove what I was saying about the elections, ma'am,' Teacher Francis said to Mrs Baksh. 'A little boy like Herbert ain't have no right to go out campaigning.'

Mrs Baksh was on her best behaviour for the teacher. 'Is what I does forever always keep on telling the father, Teach. Beg pardon, Teach.' She turned to the boys. 'All your food take out and waiting for all-you in the kitchen. It must be cold as dog nose now.'

Herbert went noisily up the stairs. Foam sucked his teeth and followed.

'I don't mean anything against you, Mr Baksh,' Teacher Francis went on, 'but the fact is, the *ordinary* people of Elvira don't really appreciate that voting is a duty and privilege.' That was part of the speech he had prepared for the Bakshes. 'Duty and privilege, ma'am.'

'Is what I does forever always keep on telling the father, Teach. Hear what the teacher say, Baksh? I been telling him, Teach, a hundred times if I tell him one time, that this election begin sweet sweet for everybody, but the same sweetness going to turn sour sour in the end. Zilla, you ain't hear me use those self-same words to your father?'

'Yes, Ma.'

'Yes, ma'am. Election bringing out all sort of prejudice to the surface. To the surface, ma'am.'

Mrs Baksh crossed her powerful arms and nodded solemnly. 'You never say a truer word, Teach. In all my born days nobody ever come to my own house—my own house, mark you—and talk to me like how the goldsmith come and talk to me this afternoon.'

Teacher Francis delivered the rest of his statement: 'I have been turning over this and similar ideas in my mind from time to time. From time to time. Yesterday evening I stated them in general terms—in general terms—to Miss Chittaranjan. Mrs Baksh, Miss Chittaranjan took down every word I said. *In shorthand.*'

Mrs Baksh opened her eyes wide, swung her head slowly, very slowly, from side to side and gave a cluck of horror. 'Look at that, eh, Teach. In shorthand.'

'You could trust somebody as stuck-up as Nelly Chittaranjan to do a low thing like that,' Zilla said.

'And Mrs Baksh, Miss Chittaranjan thinks I am a fascist.' He paused; he had come to the end of his statement. 'Mrs Baksh, I look like a fascist to you?'

'No, Teach. You ain't look like a fascist. Not to me anyway.'

Zilla said, 'Don't worry your head with Nelly Chittaranjan, Teach. She just a little too hot for man sheself. These small thin girls like Nelly Chittaranjan like man.'

'Beg pardon, Teach,' Mrs Baksh said. 'I have to talk to my sister here.' She turned to Zilla. 'Yes, *ma commère*? Small thin girls like man? How you know? You does like man yourself?' She turned to Teacher Francis again. 'Beg pardon, Teach. But these children these days is like if dog eat their mind and their shame.'

Zilla hung her head.

Teacher Francis came to the point. 'And then this evening, Mrs Baksh, Mr Chittaranjan come to see me. He come in cool cool and he tell me dry dry that Nelly not coming for no more lessons from me. It ain't the money I worried about, Mrs Baksh. Is the fact that I don't like people misunderstanding my views. I have to think of my job.'

It certainly wasn't the ten dollars a month alone that worried Teacher Francis. He knew that what Chittaranjan did today the rest of Elvira did tomorrow. If all the parents stopped sending their children to him for private lessons, he would be in a spot.

Foam, an enamel cup in his hands, came down the steps.

Teacher Francis was saying, 'That is why I come to see you, Mrs Baksh. I know how your husband and Mr Chittaranjan working on the same side in the elections, and I would be glad like anything if you could tell Mr Chittaranjan that I is not really a fascist. Fact is, I ain't taking no sides in this election at all.'

'Is the best best thing, God knows, Teach,' Mrs Baksh said.

Foam gave a loud dry laugh. 'Eh, Teacher Francis, why you want *we* to tell the goldsmith for? Why you don't ask Lorkhoor? He could run about telling it with his loud-speaking van.'

And Foam had his first triumph.

He had been waiting a long time to spurn a suppliant Teacher Francis. He had had extravagant visions of the moment. The reality seemed made to order, and was sweet.

Teacher Francis accepted the rebuke sadly. 'Lorkhoor let me down, man. Prove my point again, ma'am. Is the election that spoil Lorkhoor.'

But it had given Foam his first triumph.

'Lorkhoor is a damn traitor if you ask me,' Foam said.

'*Nobody* ain't ask you,' Baksh said. 'And look, eh, I ain't want to hear nobody bad-talking Lorkhoor in this house.'

Foam was baffled.

Baksh said, '*You*, you was out campaigning, eh? Campaigning for that dirty Hindu Harbans. Dog eat your shame? It look like dog eat *all* my children shame.'

Foam said, 'But look, look. What happening? Ain't you done take Harbans money and everything?'

If Teacher Francis hadn't been there Baksh would have spat. 'Money, eh? The money doing me a lot of good? A lot of good! Ten die. Big dog in the night turning tiny tiny in the morning. Send him away and he come back. A lot of good!'

Teacher Francis realized he had been talking in vain. Baksh was no good to him as an intermediary with Chittaranjan.

Foam said, 'Well, I take Harbans money and I give him my word. I going to still help Harbans.'

'I *want* you to help Harbans,' Baksh said. 'I going to help Preacher. I ain't stopping you doing nothing. You is a big man. Your pee making froth. How *much* votes you control, Foam?'

Teacher Francis, unhappy, bemused, got up and left.

Then Baksh told about Chittaranjan's visit.

'All right, you supporting Preacher,' Foam said, and Mrs Baksh noted that for the first time Foam was talking to his father man-to-man. 'Preacher could give you anything?'

Baksh smiled. 'It ain't *Preacher* who going to give me anything. Don't worry, you. I calculate everything already. Everything.'

9. The Retreat of the Witnesses

MAHADEO WAS A WORRIED MAN. He haunted Elvira, checking up on Negroes, anxious lest any of them fell ill or, worse, died.

Hindus misunderstood his purpose and resented his partiality. Rampiari's husband said, 'What the hell? Hindus does fall sick too.' And so, despite his strict instructions not to meddle with them, Mahadeo found himself making out a long list of sick Hindus to present to Harbans. That was one worry.

His big worry was Old Sebastian.

That evening in Dhaniram's veranda he had been pretty confident that Sebastian would die before polling day; and in the happy days before his interview with Mr Cuffy he had kept a hopeful eye on him. Every morning he passed Sebastian's hut and saw him sitting on a backless kitchen chair before his front door, a stunted unlit pipe in his mouth, making fish-pots from strips of bamboo, an inexplicable and futile occupation because Sebastian had no connexion whatever with the sea and the fish-pots only remained and rotted in his yard. Mahadeo would ask, 'How you feeling this morning, Sebastian?' And Sebastian would smile—he hardly spoke—showing his remaining teeth, isolated and askew as if some oral explosion had destroyed the others. In the afternoon Mahadeo would pass again, after the day's work on the estate, and repeat his question; and Sebastian would smile again.

Some days Mahadeo felt Sebastian wasn't going to die at all.

That was before Mr Cuffy.

Mahadeo distrusted and feared Mr Cuffy. He was old, he was black, he lived alone, he preached, and he read the Bible. And

Mahadeo could never forget a disquieting encounter he had had with him as a boy. One Saturday morning he had gone into Mr Cuffy's yard to watch Mr Cuffy whitewashing the walls of his house. Mr Cuffy frowned and muttered, but Mahadeo paid no attention. On a sudden Mr Cuffy had turned and vigorously worked the whitewash brush over Mahadeo's face.

And now Mr Cuffy was Sebastian's guardian.

Sebastian began to look very old and fragile. Mahadeo asked after his health with genuine concern and Sebastian suddenly revealed himself as a very sick man. He had aches and pains all over; stiff joints; and a dangerous stiffness in the neck. Everything that surrounded Sebastian seemed dangerous—the chair he sat on, the old thatched roof over his head. Mahadeo begged him to be careful with the penknife he used on his fish-pots, begged him not to lift heavy weights, begged him not to go for walks in the night dew, and not to get wet. Mahadeo backed up his advice with a shilling or so which Sebastian took easily, without acknowledgement, as though it was money from the government.

On the morning after Foam knocked down Mrs Chittaranjan's clean-necked chicken, Mahadeo, sweating in his tight khaki uniform, walked past Sebastian's hut.

And there was no Sebastian.

*

He forgot about the labourers on the estate waiting for him to measure out their tasks for the day. He hurried across the shaky bridge into Sebastian's yard. He had to warn Sebastian about that bridge: it was dangerous, made only of lengths of bamboo piled up with dirt. He knocked on Sebastian's door and there was no reply. He tried the door. It was locked. He walked around the hut, but every cranny in the walls was blocked up. That was what he himself had advised, to protect Sebastian from draughts.

'Sebastian!' Mahadeo called. 'You all right?'

There was a gap about three inches high running all around the hut between the walls and the eaves of the thatched roof. Mahadeo decided to climb. He would get up on the narrow window-ledge and hope it didn't come down with him. He tried to climb in full uniform. The dirt wall was too smooth to give him a grip and the tight khaki jacket hindered his arms. He took off the jacket, then took off his boots. Still, the wall was too smooth and the window-ledge too high to help him. He pressed the big toe of his right foot against the wall and tried again. He felt the wall give under his toe. He looked down. He had made a hole in Sebastian's wall, about eight inches from the ground. He went down on all fours and lowered his head. Some strands of tapia grass in the wall barred his view. He poked a finger in. Before he could pull away the grass he heard a shout from the road.

'Mahadeo! What the hell you think you doing?'

Still on all fours, he looked up. It was Mr Cuffy.

'Not doing nothing,' he said.

'Mahadeo, what get into you to make you play the ass so?'

Mahadeo rose and put his bare feet into his laceless boots.

'You see Old Sebastian this morning, Mr Cawfee?'

'Ain't see nobody,' Mr Cuffy said sullenly. '*What* you was look-ing for so?'

'Was Old Sebastian I was looking for, Mr Cawfee.'

'And is so you does always look for Sebastian? Look, Mahadeo, if anything happen to Sebastian, you go be surprise . . .'

At this moment Baksh shouted from a little way down the road, 'Hear about this thing at Cordoba, Mr Cawfee?'

'Going up there right now,' Mr Cuffy said.

'When I did tell people,' Baksh said, 'nobody did want to believe. Everybody did just run about saying Baksh is a big mouther, eh?'

'What happen at Cordoba?' Mahadeo asked.

Mr Cuffy looked at Mahadeo. It was the look he had given him when he pasted his face with the whitewash brush. 'Something *funny* happen up there last night, Mahadeo. I hear something about a dead.'

Mahadeo stared.

'Let him go and see for hisself,' Baksh said.

Mahadeo didn't wait. He ran as much as he could of the way to Cordoba. Even before he got there he saw the crowd blocking up the road. It was mostly a Spanish crowd—he could tell that by the dress—but there were people from Elvira as well.

The crowd made a wide circle around something in the road. The Spaniards were silent but uneasy; they actually seemed happy to have the outsiders from Elvira among them.

Mahadeo was stared at. A path was opened for him.

'Look,' he heard someone say in the acrid Spanish accent. 'Let him look good.'

*

Five dead puppies were symmetrically laid out on a large cross scratched right across the dirt road. One dead puppy was at the centre of the cross and there was a dead puppy at each of the four ends. Below was written, in huge letters:

AWAKE

And all around, on palings and culverts, Cordoba was still red with Foam's old, partly obliterated slogans: DIE! DIE!

Mahadeo, sweating, panting, gave a chuckle of relief.

The Spaniards looked at him suspiciously.

'I did think it was Sebastian,' Mahadeo said.

There were murmurs.

Mahadeo felt someone pull the sleeve of his uniform. He turned to see Sebastian, smiling, the empty pipe in his mouth. He almost embraced him. 'Sebastian! You here! You ain't there!'

The murmurs swelled.

Fortunately for Mahadeo, Baksh and Mr Cuffy came up just then, and almost immediately Foam arrived in the van and began to campaign.

Foam said, 'Is those Witnesses. They can't touch nobody else, so they come to meddle with the poor Spanish people in Cordoba. Telling them not to vote, to go against the government. Who ever see white woman riding around on red red bicycle before, giving out green books?'

Baksh wasn't thinking about politics. 'Aha!' he cried. 'Aha! Just look at those dogs. Said same coloration, said same shape, said same everything, as in *my* dog. But nobody did want to believe. Well, look now.'

Mr Cuffy crossed himself. 'Mahadeo, this is your work?'

'Ain't my work, Mr Cawfee. I just come and see it.'

'Want to know something?' Baksh said. 'For all the tiny those dogs look tiny this morning, they was big big dogs last night. I telling all-you, man. Come in that night. Eleven o'clock. Open the door. See this mister man dog, big big, walking about quiet quiet and *sly* . . .'

'Is those damn Witnesses,' Foam said.

'. . . next morning, is a tiny tiny puppy.'

'Jesus say,' Foam said, 'we have to give Caesar's things back to Caesar. Witnesses tell you different.'

'I always say this,' Mr Cuffy said. 'God hath made man upright, but they have found out many inventions.'

A Spaniard asked, 'But *what* they trying to do to we?'

'Do to you!' Foam said. 'Do to you! They ain't begin yet. Ain't they was talking about the world blowing up in 1976? And ain't you was listening? They was talking and you was listening. Well, look.' And he pointed to the puppies.

Baksh said, 'Nobody can't try nothing on me. I know how to handle them. *My* dog *didn't* dead.'

Harichand the printer came up, dressed for work.

'Ah,' he said. 'More puppy dogs.' He squatted and examined the ground like a detective. 'Dead, eh? Awake, eh?' He stood up. 'Witnesses. Serious. Very serious. Ganesh was the man to handle a thing like this.'

'But what we going to do, Mr Harichand?'

'Do, eh? What you going to do.' Harichand thought. 'Just don't feed no Witnesses,' he said decisively. 'Don't feed no Witnesses. Funny, five little puppy dogs like that. Like your dog, eh, Baksh?'

Baksh smiled. 'Tell them about it, Harichand. And tell them about the sign too.'

Harichand said, 'Yes, things really waking up in Elvira. But don't feed no Witnesses.'

Baksh said, 'But you did tell me it was Preacher who set the fust dog on me, Harichand.'

Harichand said quickly, 'Didn't exactly say it *that* way. Said *a* preacher was putting something on you. Didn't say what *sort* of preacher. What about those printing jobs, Baksh? If Harbans want my vote, he want my printery, I telling you.'

Baksh said, 'Harbans could haul his arse.'

Harichand laughed. 'Election thing, eh? You changing sides? Who you for now?'

Baksh said, 'Preacher. Eh, you ain't hear the bacchanal?'

Mr Cuffy spat loudly. *'Obeah! Obeah!'*

The Spaniards looked on in dismay.

'Obeah!' Mr Cuffy cried. 'That is what all-you trying to work. Lorkhoor, and now you, Baksh. Tomorrow I go hear that Harbans come over to Mr Preacher side too. All-you only making a puppet-show of Mr Preacher. Mahadeo!' Mr Cuffy called. 'You trying something, eh?'

'I ain't trying nothing, Mr Cawfee.' Mahadeo turned to Sebastian. 'Come on, Sebastian, let we go home.'

Sebastian, smiling, stepped away from Mahadeo's hand.

Mahadeo followed. 'Come, Sebastian, you only tireding out yourself. You should go home and rest, man.' He pressed a shilling into Sebastian's palm. Sebastian smiled and allowed himself to be led away.

Mr Cuffy shouted, 'Look after him good, you hear, Mahadeo.'

And then Chittaranjan was seen coming up to Cordoba.

He was in his visiting outfit.

*

Harbans—the candidate—heard about the row between Baksh and Chittaranjan and hurried down that noon to Elvira. He didn't want to inflame either of the disputants, so he went straight to Pundit Dhaniram to find out what was what.

That day Dhaniram was not being a pundit. He was in his other, more substantial role as the owner of one-fifth of a tractor. No dhoti and sacred thread; but khaki trousers, yellow sports shirt, brown felt hat and brown patent leather shoes. When Harbans drove up, Dhaniram was standing on his sunny front steps, humming one of his favourite hymns:

> What though the spicy breezes
> Blow soft o'er Ceylon's isle;
> Though every prospect pleases,
> And only man is vile;
> In vain with lavish kindness
> The gifts of God are strown;
> The heathen, in his blindness,
> Bows down to wood and stone.

He was about to leave, but he stayed to tell Harbans all about Foam and Nelly, and Baksh and Chittaranjan.

Harbans seemed more concerned about the loss of Baksh and the thousand Muslim votes than about the loss of honour of his prospective daughter-in-law. Dhaniram wasn't surprised.

'In the old days,' Dhaniram said, talking about Nelly, and sounding Harbans further, 'you coulda trust a Hindu girl. Now everything getting modern and mix up. Look, Harichand tell me just the other day that he went to San Fernando and went to a club place up there and he see Indian girls'—Dhaniram had begun to whisper—'he see Indian girls openly soli-citing.' He made the word rhyme with reciting. 'Openly soli-citing, man.'

'Openly soli-citing, eh,' Harbans said absently. 'Ooh, ooh. Send for some pencil and paper.'

'*Doolahin!*' Dhaniram called, loosening his black leather belt and sitting on the bench. 'Pencil and paper. And make it quick sharp.'

The *doolahin* brought out some brown paper and the old pencil with the string attached to the groove at the top. She said irritably, 'Why you don't keep the pencil tie round your waist?' And before Dhaniram could say anything she ran back to the kitchen.

'See?' Dhaniram said. 'Only two years she husband leave she to go to England to study, and you see how she getting on. In the old days you think a daughter-in-law coulda talk like that to a father-in-law? In fact'—Dhaniram was whispering again—'it wouldn't surprise me if *she* ain't got somebody sheself.'

'Ooh, ooh, Dhaniram, you musn't talk like that!' Harbans was sitting cross-legged on the floor, making calculations on the brown paper. 'We lose the Muslim vote. That is one thousand. We can't get the Negro vote. Two thousand and one thousand make three thousand. About a thousand Hindus going to vote for Preacher because of that traitor Lorkhoor. So, Preacher have four thousand votes. I have three thousand Hindus and the Spanish ain't voting.' He flung down the pencil. Dhaniram picked it up. Harbans said calmly, 'I lose the election, Pundit.'

Dhaniram laughed and loosened his belt a bit more. 'Lemmesee that paper,' he said, and lay down flat on his belly and worked it out. He looked perplexed. 'Yes, you lose. It *look* like if you lose.' He passed his hand over his face. 'Can't make it out, man. It did look like a sure thing to me. Sure sure thing.'

Harbans cracked his fingers, turned his palm downwards and studied the grey hairs and wrinkles on the back. 'I is a old man,' he said. 'And I lose a election. That is all. Nothing to cry about.' He looked up and smiled with his false teeth at Dhaniram.

Dhaniram smiled back.

Harbans broke down. 'How much money Preacher spend for him to beat me in a election?'

Dhaniram said, 'This democracy is a damn funny thing.'

At that moment Lorkhoor came up in his loudspeaker van. 'Preacher is gaining new support. Ladies and gentlemen, this is the voice of Lorkhoor. The enemy's ranks are thinning and Preacher will win . . .'

From her room Dhaniram's wife asked in Hindi, 'What is he saying?'

Dhaniram translated for her.

The *doolahin*, adjusting her veil, rushed out on bare feet.

'Back inside, *doolahin*,' Dhaniram said. 'Is not the sort of thing a married woman should listen to.'

She didn't obey right away.

'Here,' Dhaniram said. 'Take back this paper. *And* the pencil.'

She practically snatched them.

'See?' Dhaniram said. 'See what I was telling you? It only want for she to hear a man voice and she excited long time.'

Lorkhoor drove off noisily, shouting, 'Yaah! We will bury Harbans!'

Harbans all the while kept looking down at his hands.

Dhaniram sat on the bench again, lit a cigarette and began shaking his legs. The gravity of the situation thrilled him; he couldn't dim the twinkle in his eyes; he smiled continually.

A visitor came.

Harbans said, 'Go away, if is me you want to see. I ain't got no more money to give.'

The visitor was Mahadeo, still in his uniform, holding a sweated khaki topee in his hands. His big eyes shone mournfully at the floor; his cheeks looked swollen; his thick moustache gave an occasional twitch over his small full mouth.

'Sit down,' Dhaniram said, as though he was inviting Mahadeo to a wake.

Mahadeo said, 'I have a message from the goldsmith.'

Harbans shook away his tears. 'You is faithful, Mahadeo.'

Mahadeo's sad eyes looked sadder; his full mouth became fuller;

his eyebrows contracted. 'Is about Rampiari husband,' he said hesitantly. 'He sick. Sick like anything.'

'Rampiari husband is a Hindu, as you damn well know,' Dhaniram said.

'Aah, Mahadeo,' Harbans said, smiling through his tears. 'You is unfaithful, too?'

'Yes, Mr Harbans. No, Mr Harbans. But the goldsmith, Mr Chittaranjan, did promise Rampiari husband that you was going to see him. He sick bad bad. He cut his foot with a hoe.'

Harbans looked down at his hands. 'I ain't got no more money for nobody. All it have for me to do is to settle Ramlogan rum-account and leave Elvira for good. Why *I* fighting election for?'

Dhaniram said, 'Is God work.'

'How the hell is God work? Is God work for Preacher to beat me in a election? How much money Preacher spend? You call that God work?'

Mahadeo said, 'Preacher gone to see Rampiari husband.'

Harbans jumped up. 'Preacher ain't got no *right* to meddle with the Hindu sick.' He paced so thunderously about the veranda that Dhaniram's wife, inside, complained. 'All right,' he said. 'What about that list of Negro sick you was going to make?'

Mahadeo hesitated.

Dhaniram, who had suggested the care of sick Negroes, stopped shaking his legs.

Mahadeo explained about Mr Cuffy.

Harbans was silent for a while. Then he exploded: 'Traitors! Spies! Haw-Haw! I ask you, Mahadeo, to keep a eye on Negro sick and I come today and find that you is *feeding* them.' He wagged a long thin finger. 'But don't worry your head. I not going to cry. I going to fight all of all-you. I not going to let any of all-you make me lose my election, after all the hard work I put in for Elvira.'

Dhaniram's legs began to shake again; he pulled at his cigarette; his eyes twinkled.

Then Harbans's fight seemed to die. 'All right,' he said resignedly.

'All right, suppose I go to see Rampiari husband'—he gave a short grim laugh—'and I pay the entrance fee, what guarantee I have that Rampiari husband going to vote for me?'

Dhaniram stood up and crushed his cigarette under his shoe. 'Ah, the main thing is to *pay* the entrance fee.'

Harbans went absent-minded.

'The people of Elvira,' Dhaniram said, tightening his belt, 'have their little funny ways, but I could say one thing for them: you don't have to bribe them twice.'

'But what about Baksh?'

'Baksh,' Dhaniram said, 'is a damn disgrace to Elvira.'

They went to see Chittaranjan.

*

They found Chittaranjan unruffled, bland, in his home clothes, rocking in his veranda. Obviously he was in the highest spirits.

'Who say the Spanish ain't voting?' Chittaranjan said. And he told them about the five dead puppies in Cordoba. 'Bright and early those two white woman Witnesses come up on their fancy bike. The Spanish ain't talk to them, ain't look at them. The five dead puppies alone remain in the road and the Spanish go inside their house and lock up the door. The white woman had to go away. Who say the Spanish ain't voting?'

Harbans hid his joy. He didn't want to tempt fate again.

Dhaniram calculated. 'We draw up even with Preacher now. Four thousand apiece.'

Chittaranjan rocked. 'Wait. Watch and see if Preacher don't lose his deposit.'

Harbans said, 'Goldsmith, I shoulda tell you this a long time now.' And he disclosed the sign he had had weeks before: the Witnesses, the black bitch, the engine stalling.

Chittaranjan gave his corrosive titter. 'You *shoulda* tell me, Mr Harbans. You woulda save both of we a lot of worry. One sign is bad. But when you get *two* signs in one day, is different. They does cancel out one another. Just as how the dog cancel out the Witnesses.'

Dhaniram wanted Chittaranjan to talk about the row with Baksh. He said, 'I did always say we could give Preacher the Muslim vote. We could do without Baksh and Baksh son.'

'Dhaniram,' Chittaranjan said, 'you know me. I does say my mind, and who want to vex, let them vex. But you talking like a fool. Those dead puppies in Cordoba, who you think put them there?'

'Foam?' Harbans said. 'Ooh. You mean Foam is still faithful?'

'But I thought you did have a row with the father, man,' Dhaniram said.

'With the father, yes. But not with the son.' Chittaranjan glanced at Harbans. 'Is the father who put him up to *try*.'

Dhaniram frowned and began to shake his legs, slowly. 'Don't like it. Baksh want something more. He got something at the back of his mind.'

Chittaranjan clacked his sabots. 'Course he got! Baksh ain't no fool. Baksh have everything calculate already.'

Dhaniram tried once more. He cocked his head to one side and said, 'I feel I hearing little Nelly walking inside. She ain't gone to school today?'

Chittaranjan didn't look at Dhaniram but at Harbans who, his head bent, had gone absent-minded. Chittaranjan said, 'No school for she today. After all, she practically engage already.'

Harbans didn't look up.

'I say,' Chittaranjan said, slowly, incisively, 'how you want me to still send Nelly to school, when she practically *engage?*'

Harbans woke up. 'Wouldn't be right,' he said hurriedly, 'especially when the girl practically engage already.'

Chittaranjan looked triumphantly at Dhaniram.

*

The Witnesses stayed away from Cordoba and Elvira.

10. The New Candidate

THE CAMPAIGNS BEGAN to swing.

Preacher made his house-to-house visits. Mr Cuffy preached political sermons on Friday evenings. Lorkhoor blazed through the district.

Chittaranjan revisited Cordoba and won back the votes the Witnesses had seduced. Foam, loyal to Harbans, toured with his loudspeaker van, and neither Baksh nor Mrs Baksh objected. Harichand got orders for posters. Whenever Pundit Dhaniram officiated at a Hindu ceremony he urged his listeners to vote for Harbans.

Mahadeo kept a sharp, panicky eye on Old Sebastian. The man seemed to wilt more and more every day, and Mahadeo was giving him five shillings, sometimes two dollars a week to buy medicines.

Harbans resigned himself to visiting the Hindu sick. Whenever he came to Elvira and saw Mahadeo, he asked first, 'Well, how much Hindu sick today? And what-and-what is the various entrance fee?' Mahadeo would take out his little red notebook and say, 'Mungal not so good today. Two dollars go settle him. Lutchman complaining about a pain in his belly. He got a big family and the whole house have six votes. I think you better give him ten dollars. Five dollars for the least. Ramoutar playing the fool too. But he so ignorant, he can't even make a X and he bound to spoil his vote. Still, give him a dollar. It go make people feel that you interested.'

Harbans's rum-account with Ramlogan rose steeply. But Ramlogan maintained to all the drinkers that he was impartial. 'Once this election bacchanal over,' he said, 'I have to live with everybody, no matter who they vote for.' Chittaranjan never went inside the shop.

He and Foam devised rum-vouchers that could be exchanged only at Ramlogan's. Harichand printed the vouchers.

And, secure in the cocoa-house, Tiger began to flourish.

*

But Baksh was doing nothing at all about the election. The thousand Muslim voters of Elvira looked to him in vain for a lead. He wasn't campaigning for Preacher and he wasn't campaigning against Harbans. He remained in his shop and sewed dozens of khaki shirts, working with a new, sullen concentration. He refused to talk about the election, refused almost to talk at all. This sudden reticence won him a lot of attention and respect in Ramlogan's rumshop. But if he didn't talk much, his actions were larger. He brought down his thick glass heavily on the counter; he smacked his lips and twisted his face as though the puncheon rum tasted like castor oil; he spat copiously and belched often, bending forward, blowing out his cheeks and rubbing his belly, like one who suffers. When people asked him about the election he only gave an odd, ironic little smile. Altogether he behaved like a deep man with a deep secret.

This finally annoyed Mrs Baksh. 'You have everybody laughing at you. When this election nonsense did first begin, you ain't ask nobody, you ain't look right, you ain't look left, you jump in. Now, when everybody washing their foot and jumping in, you remaining quiet, sitting on your fat tail like a hatching fowl.'

'Well, all right I ain't doing nothing. What you want me to do? You think I would let two shot of cheap grog fool me? Look, is not for my sake I worrying, you know. If I trying to make anything outa this election, is for you and the children, you hear, not for me.'

Mrs Baksh would say with scorn, 'Even little Foam bringing home seventy-five dollars when the month end.'

Baksh's silent inactivity worried Harbans and his committee as much as Preacher's silent campaigning.

Messages from Baksh were always reaching the committee.

Some were boastful. 'Baksh say he just got to walk around Elvira *one* time, saying all that he know, and everybody going to forget Harbans.'

Some were cryptic. 'Baksh say *he* ain't got to do nothing to make Harbans lose. Harbans doing that hisself.'

Some were threatening. 'Baksh say Harbans could do what he want before the elections, but Harbans going to lose the election on election day itself.'

But Baksh himself did nothing.

Chittaranjan alone refused to be alarmed. He said, 'Baksh ain't no fool. Baksh know what he want. And the sad thing is that he going to get what he want. But *we* mustn't make the fust move. We would be low-rating weself if we do that.'

*

Foam wasn't happy about two things.

He would have liked to confess to Chittaranjan that it was he who had run over the clean-necked chicken; but he just didn't have the courage. Then there was Nelly. He felt especially guilty about her. Chittaranjan had taken her out of school and stopped her going anywhere; she remained in the house all day.

Perhaps Foam would have confessed about the chicken if Chittaranjan had been at all cool towards him; but Chittaranjan showed himself surprisingly, increasingly amiable. He encouraged Foam to visit the Big House and gave him many sweet drinks. Only, Mrs Chittaranjan did the honours now; not Nelly. Foam responded by making it clear that he wasn't interested in Nelly. He said, often and irrelevantly, that he couldn't understand why people got married, that he wasn't interested in marriage at all, hardly interested in girls even. Chittaranjan seemed to approve. 'Well, what happen between your father and me ain't have nothing to do with you.'

Then, when Chittaranjan thought he had proved to everyone in Elvira that Nelly's honour was safe; that Foam was a good boy whom he trusted absolutely; that Baksh was the envious troublemaker; then he sent Nelly off to Port of Spain, to stay with his brother, the barrister.

He was a lonely man after that. Outside, canvassing in his visiting outfit, he was the powerful goldsmith, the great controller of votes. But at home, in his torn khaki trousers, patched shirt and sabots, Foam knew him as a sad humiliated man. He never rushed to the veranda wall to shout at Ramlogan. He heard his chickens being shooed and struck and made to squeal in Ramlogan's yard, and he did nothing.

When Foam was in the Big House one day, a breadfruit and three over-ripe zabocas fell on the roof. Foam waited. Chittaranjan kept on rocking and pretended he hadn't heard.

Foam decided to confess

He said, 'Goldsmith, that clean-neck fowl . . .'

'Oh, that.' Chittaranjan waved a hand, anxious to dismiss the subject. 'That cook and eat long time now. Didn't have no disease you know.'

'Shoulda say this before, but was me who kill it. Knock it down with the loudspeaking van.'

Chittaranjan paused, just perceptibly, in his rocking; a look of surprise, relief passed over his face; then he rocked again. When he spoke he didn't look at Foam. 'All right, you kill it right enough. But who did want to see it dead?'

Foam didn't answer.

Chittaranjan waved a tired hand towards Ramlogan's yard. 'He. He wanted to see it dead. If the chicken dead now and eat, that not on your conscience.'

Foam didn't follow the reasoning; but it pleased him to see Chittaranjan look a little less oppressed. A little less grieved.

Foam said, 'It did grieve Ramlogan like anything to see it dead. He tell Pa so the day after. Is what he tell Pa and is what Pa tell me. Ramlogan say he did know the chicken from the time it hatch, and he did watch it grow up. He say it was like a child to him, and when it dead it was a pussonal loss.'

Chittaranjan looked even less grieved.

*

The big quarrel, coming after three years of intermittently explosive hostility, had in fact purged Chittaranjan of much of his animosity towards Ramlogan. He had never been sure that it was Ramlogan who had killed the chicken; but coming upon it so soon after discovering Tiger in the cupboard, he had felt that he had to do something right away. Now he realized the enormity of his accusation. Ramlogan had, justly, got the better of him in that quarrel; and would always get the better of him in any future quarrel: Nelly's dishonour was a more devastating argument than his ownership of the fence or his appearance in the Supreme Court.

He had had his fill of enmity. He wanted to change his relationship with the man. He called Mrs Chittaranjan and said, 'That breadfruit that fall, and those three zaboca, pick them up and put them in the basket I bring back from San Fernando and take them over to Ramlogan.'

Mrs Chittaranjan didn't show surprise. She was beyond it.

She packed the fruit in the basket and took it across. Ramlogan's shop was open. It was early morning and there were no customers.

Ramlogan was reading the *Sentinel,* his large hairy head down, his large hairy hands pressing on the chipped and greasy counter. When he saw Mrs Chittaranjan he went on reading with an air of absorption, reading and saying, 'Hm!' and scratching his head, aromatic with Canadian Healing Oil. In truth, he was deeply moved and trying to hide it. He too was ripe for reconciliation. He had always wanted to wound Chittaranjan; but now that he had, he regretted it. He knew he had gone too far when he attacked the honour of the man's daughter; he felt ashamed.

'Ah, *maharajin*,' he said at last, looking up and smoothing out the *Sentinel* on the counter.

Mrs Chittaranjan placed the basket of fruit on the counter and pulled her veil decorously over her forehead.

'Breadfruit,' Ramlogan said, as though he had never seen the fruit before. 'Breadfruit, man. And zaboca, eh? Zaboca. One, two, three zaboca.' He pressed a zaboca with a thick forefinger. 'Ripe too.'

Mrs Chittaranjan said, 'He send it.'

'It have nothing I like better than a good zaboca and bread. Nothing better.'

'Yes, it nice,' Mrs Chittaranjan said.

'Nice like anything.'

'He send it. He tell me to take up the breadfruit and the three zaboca and bring it for you in this basket.'

Ramlogan passed a hand over the basket. 'Nice basket.'

'He bring it from San Fernando.'

Ramlogan turned the basket around on the greasy counter. 'Very nice basket,' he said. 'It make by the blind?'

'He say I have to bring back the basket.'

Ramlogan emptied the basket, hugging the fruit to his breast. Mrs Chittaranjan saw the basket empty, saw the fruit in a cluster against Ramlogan's dirty shirt. Then she saw the cluster jog and heave and heave and jog.

Ramlogan was crying.

Mrs Chittaranjan began to cry in sympathy.

'We is bad people, *maharajin*,' Ramlogan sobbed.

Mrs Chittaranjan pressed a corner of her veil over her eyes. 'It have some good in everybody.'

Ramlogan clutched the fruit to his breast and shook his head so violently that tears fell on the breadfruit. 'No, no, *maharajin*, we is more bad than good.' He shook down some more tears and lifted his head to the sooty galvanized-iron roof. 'God, I is asking You. Tell me why we is bad.'

Mrs Chittaranjan stopped crying and took the basket off the counter. 'He waiting for me.'

Ramlogan brought his head down. 'He waiting?'

She nodded.

Ramlogan ran with the fruit to the back room and then followed Mrs Chittaranjan out of the shop.

Chittaranjan was leaning on the wall of his veranda.

Ramlogan shouted, 'Hello, brothers!'

Chittaranjan waved and widened his smile. 'You all right, brothers?'

'Yes, brothers. She bring the breadfruit and the zaboca for me. Ripe zaboca too, brothers.'

'They did look ripe to me too.'

Ramlogan was near the wire fence. He hesitated.

'Is all right, brothers,' Chittaranjan said. 'Is much your fence as mine.'

'Nice fence, brothers.'

Chittaranjan's two workmen were so astonished they stopped working and looked on, sitting flat on the concrete terrace under the awning, the bracelets which they were fashioning held between their toes.

Ramlogan spoke sharply to them: 'What the hell happen to all-you? The goldsmith paying all-you just to meddle in other people business?'

They hurriedly began tapping away at their bracelets.

From the veranda Chittaranjan said, 'Let them wait until I come down.' He clattered down the front steps. 'Is this modern age. Everybody want something for nothing. I work for every penny I have, and now you have these people complaining that they is poor and behaving as though other people depriving them.'

Ramlogan, grasping the fence firmly, agreed. 'The march of time, brothers. As the saying goes. Everybody equal. People who ain't got brain to work and those who use their brain to work. Everybody equal.'

Ramlogan invited Chittaranjan over to the shop and seated him on an empty rum crate in front of the counter. He gave him a glass of grapefruit juice because he knew Chittaranjan didn't drink hard liquor.

They talked of the degeneracy of the modern age; they agreed that democracy was a stupid thing; then they came to the elections and to Baksh.

Chittaranjan, sipping his grapefruit juice without great relish—he still had a low opinion of Ramlogan's cleanliness—said: 'This democracy just make for people like Baksh. Fact, I say it just make for Negro and Muslim. They is two people who never like to make anything for theyself, and the moment *you* make something, they start begging. And if you ain't give them, they vex.'

Ramlogan, thinking of Haq, assented with conviction.

'And if you give them,' Chittaranjan went on, 'they is ungrateful.'

'As the saying goes, however much you wash a pig, you can't make it a cow. *As* the saying goes.'

'Look at Baksh. Everybody else in Elvira just asking for one little piece of help before they vote for any particular body. Baksh is the only man who want three.'

Ramlogan scratched his head. 'Three bribe, brothers?'

'Three. Baksh done calculate everything ready.'

'The old people was old-fashion, but they was right about a lot of things. My father, when he was deading, tell me never to trust a Muslim.'

'Muslim, Negro. You can't trust none of them.'

They told tales of the ingratitude and treachery of these races. When Chittaranjan left, he and Ramlogan were good friends.

After that, every morning when Ramlogan got up he went out into his yard and called, 'How you is, brothers?' And Chittaranjan came to his veranda and said, 'All right, brothers. And how *you* is?'

Soon they started calling each other 'bruds'.

*

Then Ramlogan had an unfortunate idea. He wanted among other things to make some gesture that would seal his friendship with Chittaranjan. One day he announced that he was going to give a case of whisky to the committee of the winning candidate. He didn't make it more specific than that because he wished to preserve his impartiality, but he had no doubt that Harbans would win. Chittaranjan understood and was grateful. And the rest of Elvira was astonished by this act of the laxest generosity from someone who was not even a candidate. Which was one of Ramlogan's subsidiary intentions.

He talked a lot about his offer. This was to have disastrous consequences.

*

It was not until the week before nomination day that Baksh showed his hand. Two indirect messages came from him.

First, Foam announced: 'Pa say he thinking of going up for the elections hisself.'

'Damn traitor!' Harbans said, and added calmly, 'But he ain't got a chance. He only control the thousand Muslim votes.'

'Is that he say hisself,' Foam said. 'He say is the only thing that keeping him back.'

And then Ramlogan hurried across to Chittaranjan one lunchtime and said in a whisper, although there was no need to whisper: 'Bruds, Baksh was in the shop today. He ask me whether I would vote for him if he went up for the elections.'

Chittaranjan said, 'He ask you to tell me?'

Ramlogan said in a softer whisper, 'He particularly ask me *not* to tell you, bruds.'

'But he ask you about three four times not to tell me?'

Ramlogan looked surprised at Chittaranjan's sagacity. 'He did *keep* on asking me not to tell you. Is the reason *why* I come over to tell you.'

Chittaranjan said simply, 'Well, Baksh just got to get bribe number two now, that is all.'

And when Harbans came to Elvira Chittaranjan told him, 'Mr Harbans, you could take it from Chittaranjan that you win the elections.'

Harbans preferred not to show any excitement.

Chittaranjan said, 'Baksh send a message.'

'Another message again?'

'He want to go up.'

'Ooh.'

'You have to go and see him and make it appear that you begging him to go up for the elections hisself. Once the Muslims don't vote for Preacher, we all right.'

Harbans smiled and wagged a finger at Chittaranjan. 'Ooh, but you is a smart man, Goldsmith. Ooh, ooh. Split the opposition vote, eh?'

Chittaranjan nodded. 'But when you go to see him, don't just dip your hand in your pocket. Don't do nothing until you see everything in black and white.'

Harbans went to see Baksh.

He was sitting at his sewing-machine near the door, to get the light, and working with honest concentration.

Harbans cooed. 'Aah, Baksh. How you is? I hear that you thinking of going up for this election stupidness yourself.'

Baksh bit off a piece of loose thread from the shirt he was making. Thread between his teeth, he gave a dry laugh. 'Ho! Me? Me go up for election, a poor poor man like me? Whoever give you that message give it to you wrong. I ain't got no money to go up for no election. Election ain't make for poor people like me.'

Harbans cooed again. 'Still, the fact that you was even thinking of going up show, Baksh, that you is a ambitious man. I like people with ambition.'

'Is very nice of you to say those few kind words, Mr Harbans. But the fact is, and as the saying goes, I just ain't got the money. Two hundred and fifty dollars deposit alone. Posters. Canvassers. Agents. Is a lot of money, Mr Harbans.'

'Ooh, not more than five hundred dollars.' Harbans paused. 'For a fust try.'

'Don't forget the two hundred and fifty dollars deposit.'

'No, man. Two hundred and fifty and five hundred. All right?'

The machine hummed again. Baksh sewed thoughtfully, shaking his head. 'Elections is a lot more expensive than that, Mr Harbans. You know that yourself.' He took up the shirt and bit off another piece of thread. 'I would say three thousand dollars, plus the deposit money.'

Harbans laughed nervously and almost put his hand on Baksh's bowed shoulder. 'Ooh, ooh, Baksh. You making joke, man. Three thousand for your fust little try? A thousand.'

'Two thousand five hundred, plus the deposit money.'

'Two five. Ooh, Baksh. Come, man. One five.'

Baksh was sewing again. 'In the old days, as you know, Mr Harbans, before the war, you coulda take up six cents and go in a shop and buy a bread and some butter and a tin of sardine, and even a pack of cigarettes into the bargain. Today all you could buy with six cents is a Coca-Cola. I is a man with a big family. I can't fight elections with one thousand five hundred dollars.'

'You don't *want* more than two thousand dollars, Baksh,' Harbans said, the coo gone from his voice. 'And if you ain't careful you damn well have to find the deposit money out of that same two thousand.' He cooed again: 'Two thousand, eh, Baksh?'

'*Plus* the deposit money.'

'Plus the deposit money.'

'It not going to be much of a fight for two thousand dollars, Mr Harbans. I warning you. I is a man with a big big family.'

'Is a fust try,' Harbans said. 'You could always try again. This democracy not going to get up and run away.'

Baksh sewed and bit thread, sewed and bit thread. 'It would be nice if I could start off my campaign right away.'

Harbans remembered Chittaranjan's warning. 'Ooh, but you is

impatient, man. Right away? Give it a little time, man, Baksh. We never know what could happen between now and nomination day, eh?'

Baksh was surprisingly complaisant. 'Fair is fair. Nothing until after nomination day. Two thousand, plus the deposit money.'

'Plus the deposit money.'

Mrs Baksh came into the shop, combing out her long hair with a large gap-toothed comb.

Harbans went absent-minded.

Mrs Baksh held her hair in front of her bodice and combed. Particles of water sped about the room. She cleared the comb of loose hair, rolled the hair into a ball, spat on it a few times and flung it among the dusty scraps in a corner.

The sewing-machine hummed.

Mrs Baksh said, 'I was wondering who was doing all the talking.'

Harbans looked up. 'Ah. Ooh. How you is, Mrs Baksh?'

'Half and half. How the campaign?'

'Ooh, so-so. We trying to get your husband to go up hisself.'

Mrs Baksh stopped combing and tossed her hair over her shoulders.

Baksh sewed, not stopping to bite thread.

'Baksh, what the hell I hearing?'

'Hearing, man? Mr Harbans here come and beg me to go up for elections, that is all.'

'Mr Harbans beg you? Baksh, you know you talking arseness?'

'It go be a good experience for him.' Harbans smiled at Mrs Baksh. He got no response. 'Ooh. Two thousand dollars.'

'Plus the deposit money,' Baksh said to Mrs Baksh.

'It look as if your brains drop to your bottom, Baksh. This election riding you like a fever.'

'Is for your sake I doing it, man. For your sake and the children sake. And I doing it to help out Mr Harbans here.'

This was too much for Mrs Baksh.

'Oh God, Baksh! You go land me in court before this election over. Oh God! Sweetness! Sourness!'

*

And that was not all. When Harbans went back to his committee he found Harichand the printer with them.

'If Baksh going up, you go want new posters,' Harichand said. 'In all your present posters your symbol is the star and your slogan is "Hitch your wagon to the star". But they does give out the symbols in alphabetical order. Your name was fust and your symbol was the star. Now Baksh name going to be fust and *his* symbol going to be the star. Yours going to be the heart. Preacher going to be the shoes.'

Chittaranjan said, 'We want a new slogan.'

But Harbans had gone absent-minded.

'Do your part and vote the heart,' Foam said.

'Fust-class,' Harichand said.

Harbans was talking to the back of his hands. 'New symbol eh? New slogan. New posters. What sin I do to get myself in this big big mess in my old old age?'

Chittaranjan saw the danger sign of approaching tears. 'Is nothing, Mr Harbans. Nothing at all if it make you win the election. And Foam here give you a much nicer slogan. Do your part and vote the heart. Is much nicer.'

'He should take up poetry,' Harichand said.

Harbans looked up from his hands to Harichand. 'I know why you so damn glad, Harichand. I ain't got to go to a university to know why you glad.'

'Glad? Me? Me glad? I ain't glad, Mr Harbans.'

'You sorry?'

'Mr Harbans, it have no reason why you should start getting suckastic and insultive in my pussonal. Is only help I want to help you out.'

[153]

When Harbans was leaving Elvira he was stopped by Mahadeo, and lacked spirit even to make his little joke: 'How much Hindu sick today? And what-and-what is the various entrance fee?' Mahadeo offered his list sadly and received the entrance fees a little more sadly.

When Harbans had left Elvira and was in County Caroni, he stopped the lorry and shook his small fist at the dark countryside behind him.

'Elvira!' he shouted. 'You is a bitch! A bitch! A bitch!'

11. A Departure

EVERYONE IN ELVIRA now knew about Tiger and almost everyone accepted him as a mascot against future evil and *obeah*. Tiger thrived. His coat became thicker; not that he was a hairy, fluffy puppy, for after all he was only a common mongrel; but his coat became thick enough. His strength increased. He could sit and get up and walk and run and jump without pain and with increasing zest. But no amount of feeding and care could make him put on flesh to hide his ribs. No amount of feeding could make him lose his rangy figure. He looked the sort of puppy who would grow up into the perfect street dog, noisy but discreet, game for anything, from chasing a chicken to nosing about a dustbin at night. Still, he was Tiger and he was healthy and he was friendly. Herbert was pleased. So was Foam. Mrs Baksh was relieved. The growing health of the dog she interpreted as the weakening of any *obeah* and magic against her family.

Tiger still lived in the cocoa-house. In the early days of his recovery he had been anxious to leave it for the wider world; but stern talkings-to, some slaps and finally a length of rope had taught him that the cocoa-house was home. In time he appreciated his position. He had all the freedom of the freelance with none of the anxieties. But he never tired of reproaching Herbert and Foam. When they were leaving him for the night he would look at them and whine, softly, almost apologetically; and when they came to him in the morning he would wag his tail at first, then lie down and whine, loudly this time, looking away from them.

And now Tiger had to have his first bath. It couldn't be hidden from anyone, not even Herbert, that Tiger was full of fleas. You had only to pass a finger down Tiger's back to see whole platoons of fleas dispersing and taking cover.

Bathing Tiger was no easy business. First Foam and Herbert had to steal a block of Mrs Baksh's strong blue soap. Then they changed into old trousers and shirts because they were going to bath Tiger at the stand-pipe in the main road.

They went to the cocoa-house.

Outside the cocoa-house they saw Lorkhoor's van parked on the wide verge. The grass went up to the hubs of the wheels.

'Hope he not interfering with Tiger,' Herbert said.

On a signal from Foam Herbert fell silent and both boys made their way through the intricate bush to the cocoa-house. They heard Tiger bark. A little snap of a sound, high-pitched but ambitious. They heard someone muttering and then they saw Lorkhoor and the girl. Apparently they had been there some time because Tiger had grown used to their presence and had barked, not at them, but at Foam and Herbert.

The girl said, 'Oh God!' pulled her veil over her face and ran out of sight, through the bush, behind the cocoa-house and then, as Foam imagined, to the road.

Lorkhoor remained behind to brazen it out.

In his excitement he dropped his educated tone and vocabulary and slipped into the dialect. 'Eh, Foreman! You take up *maquereauing* now?'

'You ain't got no shame, Lorkhoor. Using words like that in front of a little boy.'

Herbert pretended he hadn't heard anything.

Lorkhoor turned vicious. 'You tell anything, and see if I don't cripple you.'

'I is not a tell-tale. And at the same time I is not a hide-and-seek man.'

'Go ahead. Open your mouth once, and I'll have the police on your tail, you hear.'

'Police?'

'Yes, police. You drive a van. You have a driving licence? If I lay one report against you, I would cripple you for life, you hear.'

Foam laughed. 'Eh, but this is a funny world, man. Whenever people wrong, they start playing strong.'

Lorkhoor didn't stay to reply.

'Eh!' Herbert shouted after him. 'But he too bold.'

Tiger, wagging his tail at Foam's feet, barked continually at Lorkhoor. Every now and then he made abortive rushes at him, but he never seriously courted danger.

Foam pursued Lorkhoor with his words. 'You disappoint me, Lorkhoor. For all the educated you say you educated, you ain't got no mind at all. You disappoint me, man.'

They heard Lorkhoor drive off.

Foam said, 'You see the girl who was with him, Herbert?'

'Didn't exactly see she. But . . .'

'All right. You ain't see nothing, remember. We don't want to start another bacchanal in Elvira now. Catch this dog.'

But Tiger wasn't going to be caught without making a game of it. He seemed to sense too that something disagreeable was in store for him. He ran off and barked. Herbert chased. Tiger ran off a little further and barked again.

'Stop, Herbert. Let him come to we.'

Foam put his hands in his pockets. Herbert whistled. Tiger advanced cautiously. When he was a little distance away—a safe distance—he gave his snapping little bark, stood still, cocked his head to one side and waited. Herbert and Foam were not interested. Tiger pressed down his forepaws and began to bark again.

'Don't do nothing, Herbert.'

Hearing Foam, Tiger stopped barking and listened. He ran off a little, stopped and looked back, perplexed by their indifference. He ran up to Herbert, barking around his ankles. Herbert bent down and caught him. Tiger squirmed and used an affectionate tongue as a means of attack. Herbert leaned backwards, closing his eyes and frowning. Tiger almost wriggled out of his hands and ran up his sloping chest.

'Take him quick, Foam.'

Foam took Tiger. Tiger recognized the stronger grasp and resigned himself.

They took him to the stand-pipe in the main road. To get a running flow from it you had to press down all the time on the brass knob at the top. Herbert was to do the pressing down. Foam the bathing and soaping of Tiger.

'It will drown the fleas,' Herbert said.

Foam wasn't so sure. 'These fleas is like hell to kill.'

'I don't think Tiger going to like this, you know, Foam.'

Tiger hated it. As soon as he felt the water he started to cry and whine. He shivered and squirmed. From time to time he forgot himself and tried to bite, but never did. The water soaked through his coat until Foam and Herbert could see his pink pimply skin. He looked tiny and weak still. Then the blue soap was rubbed over him.

'Careful, Foam. Mustn't let the soap get in his eye.'

The fleas hopped about in the lather, a little less nimble than usual.

Before they could dry him, Tiger slipped out of Foam's hands and ran dripping wet down the Elvira main road. Water had given him a strong attachment to dry land, the dustier the better. He rolled in the warm sand and dirt of the main road and shook himself vigorously on passers-by. Dirt stuck to his damp coat and he looked more of a wreck than he had before his bath.

Foam and Herbert chased him.

The patch of dirt before Mr Cuffy's house appealed to Tiger. He flung himself on it and rolled over and over. Mr Cuffy stood up to watch. Tiger rose from the dirt, ran up to Mr Cuffy, gave himself a good shake, spattering Mr Cuffy with water and pellets of dirt, and tried to rub against Mr Cuffy's trousers.

Mr Cuffy raised his boot and kicked Tiger away. And for a kick on a thin dog it made a lot of noise. A hollow noise, a *dup!* the noise you would expect from a slack drum. Tiger ran off whining. He didn't run far. He ran into the main road, turned around when he judged it safe to do so; then, taking a precautionary step backwards, let out a sharp snap of a bark. He turned away again, shook himself and ambled easily off.

Herbert, running up, saw everything.

'God go pay you for that, Mr Cawfee,' Herbert said. 'He go make you dead like a cockroach, throwing up your foot straight and stiff in the air. God go pay you.'

'Dirty little puppy dog,' said Mr Cuffy.

Foam came up. 'Yes, God go pay you back, Cawfee. All you Christians always hot with God name in your mouth as though all-you spend a week-end with Him. But He go pay you back.'

'Puppy dog,' Mr Cuffy said.

'He go make you dead like a cockroach,' Herbert said. 'Just watch and see.'

*

Nomination day came. The three candidates filled forms and paid deposits. There were only two surprises. Preacher supplied both. The first was his name, Nathaniel Anaclitus Thomas. Some people knew about the Nathaniel, but no one suspected Anaclitus. Even more surprising was Preacher's occupation, which was given on the nomination blank as simply, 'Proprietor'.

Harbans described himself as a 'Transport Contractor', Baksh as a 'Merchant Tailor'.

The night before, Pundit Dhaniram had suggested a plan to prevent the nomination of the other candidates.

'Get in fust,' he told Harbans. 'And pay them your two hundred and fifty dollars in coppers. Only in coppers. And make them check it.'

'You go want a salt bag to carry all that,' Foam said.

For an absurd moment Harbans had taken the idea seriously. 'But suppose they tell me wait, while they attend to Preacher and Baksh?'

Dhaniram shook his legs and sucked at his cigarette. 'Can't tell you wait. You go fust, they got to attend to you fust. Facts is facts and fair is fair.'

Chittaranjan squashed the discussion by saying drily, 'You can't give nobody more than twelve coppers. More than that is not legal tender.'

Harbans paid in notes.

He paid Baksh his two thousand dollars election expenses only after the nominations had been filed.

'Like I did tell you, boss, can't give you much of a fight with this alone,' Baksh said ungraciously. 'I is a man with a big family.'

That evening Baksh went to Ramlogan's rumshop to celebrate his new triumph. They treated him like a hero. He talked.

*

At the end of that week, the last in July, the Elvira Government School closed for the holidays and Teacher Francis was glad to get away to Port of Spain. Elvira had become insupportable to him. Lorkhoor's behaviour was one thing; and then, as he had feared, most of the Elvira parents had followed Chittaranjan's example and stopped sending their children to him for private lessons.

The children were now free to give more of their time to the election. In their tattered vests and shirts and jerseys they ran wild over Elvira, tormenting all three candidates with their encouragements; impartially they scrawled new slogans and defaced old ones; they escorted Preacher on his house-to-house visits until Mr Cuffy frightened them off.

And the campaigns grew hot.

Lorkhoor roared into the attack, slandering Baksh, slandering Harbans. He spent the whole of one steamy afternoon telling Elvira what Elvira knew: that Harbans had induced Baksh to stand as a candidate.

'A man who gives bribes,' Lorkhoor said, 'is also capable of taking bribes.'

'This Lorkhoor is a real jackass,' Chittaranjan commented. 'If he think that by saying that he going to make Harbans lose. People *like* to know that they could get a man to do little things for them every now and then.'

Lorkhoor turned to Baksh. 'A man who takes bribes,' Lorkhoor said, 'is also capable of giving them.'

'*Give?*' Chittaranjan said. '*Baksh* give anything? He ain't know Baksh.'

*

Photographs of Baksh and Harbans sprang up everywhere, on houses, telegraph-poles, trees and culverts; they were promptly invested with moustaches, whiskers, spectacles and pipes.

'Making you famous girl,' Baksh told Mrs Baksh. 'Pictures all over the place. Mazurus Baksh. Hitch your wagon to the star. Mazurus Baksh, husband of Mrs Baksh. Mazurus Baksh, the poor man friend. Mazarus Baksh, everybody friend.'

'Mazurus Baksh,' Mrs Baksh said, 'the big big ass.'

But he could tell that she was pleased.

*

Harban's new slogan caught on. When Harbans came to Elvira children shouted at him, 'Do your part, man!' And Harbans, his shyness gone, as Foam had prophesied, replied, 'Vote the heart!'

Foam was always coming up with fresh slogans. 'The Heart for a start.' 'Harbans, the man with the Big Heart.' 'You can't live without the Heart. You can't live without Harbans.' He got hold of a gramophone record and played it so often, it became Harban's campaign song:

> And oh, my darling,
> Should we ever say goodbye,
> I know we both should die,
> My heart and I.

Every day Chittaranjan put on his visiting outfit and campaigned; Dhaniram campaigned, in a less spectacular way; and Mahadeo entered the names of sick Hindus in his red notebook.

*

For some time Preacher stuck to his old method, the energetic walk-ing tour. But one day he appeared on the Elvira main road with a large stone in his hand. He stopped Mahadeo.

'Who you voting for?'

'Preacher? You know I campaigning for Harbans . . .'

'Good. Take this stone and kill me one time.'

Mahadeo managed to escape. But Preacher stopped him again two days later. Preacher had a Bible in his right hand and a stone—the same stone—in his left hand.

'Answer me straight: who you voting for?'

'*Every*body know I voting for you, Preacher.'

Preacher dropped the stone and gave Mahadeo the Bible. 'Swear!'

Mahadeo hesitated.

Preacher stooped and picked up the stone. He handed it to Mahadeo. 'Kill me.'

'I can't swear on the Bible, Preacher. I is not a Christian.'

And Mahadeo escaped again.

*

Lorkhoor, copying Foam, gave Preacher a campaign song which fea-tured Preacher's symbol, the shoe:

> I got a shoe, you got a shoe,
> All God's chillun got a shoe.
> When I go to heaven,
> Going to put on my shoe
> And walk all over God's heaven.

Baksh, whose symbol was the star, went up to Harbans one day and said, 'I want a song too. Everybody having song.'

'Ooh, Baksh. You want song too? Why, man?'

'Everybody laughing at me. Is as though I ain't fighting this election at all.'

In the end Harbans allowed Foam to play a song for Baksh:

> How would you like to swing on a star?
> Carry moonbeams home in a jar?
> You could be better off than you are.
> You could be swinging on a star.

Rum flowed in Ramlogan's rumshop. Everyone who drank it knew it was Harbans's rum.

Dhaniram, exultant, consoled Harbans. 'The main thing is to *pay* the entrance fee. Now is your chance.'

And Ramlogan encouraged the drinkers, saying, inconsequentially and unwisely, 'Case of whisky for winning committee. Whole case of whisky.'

*

And in the meantime Harbans's committee did solid work, Foam and Chittaranjan in particular. They canvassed, they publicized; they chose agents for polling day and checked their loyalty; they chose taxi-drivers and checked their loyalty. They visited warden, returning officer, poll clerks, policemen: a pertinacious but delicate generosity rendered these officials impartial.

With all this doing Harbans, with his moods, his exultations, depressions and rages, was an embarrassment to his committee. They wished him out of the way and tried, without being rude, to tell him so.

'You could stay in Port of Spain and win your election in Elvira,' Pundit Dhaniram told him. 'Easy easy. Just leave everything to your party machine,' he added, savouring the words. 'Party machine.'

At his meetings on the terrace of Chittaranjan's shop Harbans gave out bagfuls of sweets to children; and talked little. It was Foam and Chittaranjan and Dhaniram and Mahadeo who did most of the talking.

First Foam introduced Mahadeo; then Mahadeo introduced Dhaniram; and Dhaniram introduced Chittaranjan. By the time Chittaranjan introduced Harbans the meeting was practically over and Harbans could only receive deputations.

'Boss, the boys from Pueblo Road can't play no football this season. Goalpost fall down. Football bust.'

Harbans would write out a cheque.

'Boss, we having a little sports meeting and it would look nice if you could give a few of the prizes. No, boss, not give them out. Give.'

Another cheque.

It was Harbans, Harbans all the way. There could be no doubt of that.

Dhaniram repeatedly calculated: 'Three thousand Hindu votes and one thousand Spanish make four thousand. Preacher getting three thousand for the most. Baksh getting the thousand Muslim votes.'

Harbans didn't like this sort of talk. He said it gave people wrong ideas, encouraged them not to vote; and when he made a personal plea to some voter for the fourth or fifth time and the voter said, 'But Mr Harbans, you *know* I promise you,' Harbans would say, 'This democracy is a strange thing. It does make the great poor and the poor great. It make me a beggar—yes, don't stop me, I *is* a beggar— and I *begging* for your vote.'

*

Rumours began to fly. Mr Cuffy had deserted Preacher. Preacher was selling out to Baksh, but was going to do so only on the day before the election. Baksh was selling out to Preacher. Mahadeo was selling out to Preacher. Chittaranjan was selling out to Baksh. Everybody, it seemed, was selling out to somebody. Elvira thrilled to rumour and counter-rumour. Voters ran after candidates and their agents and warned that so-and-so had to be watched. It was agreed on all sides that Dhaniram had to be watched; he was interested only in his tractor and was just waiting to see which side was going to win before throwing in his full weight with it. The most persistent rumour was that Lorkhoor wanted to leave Preacher. That rumour Chittaranjan took seriously.

He said, 'I did always have a feeling that Lorkhoor wanted something big outa this election, but I couldn't rightly make out what it was.'

*

Chittaranjan was rocking in his veranda late one evening, thinking about going to bed, when he heard someone whisper from the terrace. He got up and looked down.

It was Dhaniram. He held a hurricane lantern that lit up his pundit's regalia. 'Message, Goldsmith,' Dhaniram whispered, barely controlling his excitement.

Chittaranjan whispered back. 'From Baksh?'

'Lorkhoor, Goldsmith. He say he have a matter of importance— said words he use—matter of importance to discuss with you.'

'Wait.'

Dhaniram stood on the terrace, swinging the lantern, humming:

> So he called the multitude,
> Turned the water into wine,
> Jesus calls you. Come and dine!

Presently Chittaranjan came down. In his visiting outfit.

They went to Dhaniram's house.

Lorkhoor was waiting for them. He sat on the balustrade of the veranda, smoking and swinging his legs, not looking in the least like a perplexed traitor. He said, 'Ah, Goldsmith. Sorry to get you up.'

'Yes, man,' Dhaniram said. 'It give me a big big surprise. I was just coming back from Etwariah place—Rampiari mother, you know: she was having a little *kattha:* I was the pundit—and I see Lorkhoor van outside.'

Lorkhoor said, 'Goldsmith, I'm tired of talking.'

Dhaniram was beside himself with delight. He lit a cigarette and smoked noisily.

'I could give you eight hundred votes,' Lorkhoor said. 'If I keep my mouth shut. Worth anything?'

Chittaranjan took off his hat and considered it in the light of the hurricane lantern. 'I don't know if it worth anything at all.'

Lorkhoor laughed. 'Silence is golden, Goldsmith.'

Dhaniram said tremulously, 'Eight hundred more for we and eight hundred less for Preacher. Is a sure sure win, Goldsmith.' He wanted the deal to go through; it would be dramatically proper.

Chittaranjan said, 'You did always think of selling out in the end, not so?'

'That's right.' Lorkhoor didn't sound abashed. 'I have no daughter to marry off.'

Dhaniram gave a nervous giggle.

'And I have no tractor.'

Dhaniram pulled at his cigarette.

Lorkhoor took out some typewritten electoral lists from his hip pocket. 'Eight hundred votes. Checked and signed and sealed. You can check up on them yourself, if you wish. A dollar a vote?'

Dhaniram shouted, '*Doolahin*, bring the Petromax.'

Inside, Dhaniram's wife woke up, complained and fell silent again.

Chittaranjan examined his hat. 'You think you could live in Elvira after the elections?'

Lorkhoor changed his position on the balustrade. 'I was thinking of leaving Elvira altogether.'

'Oh?' Dhaniram shook his legs. 'Where you was thinking of going?'

The *doolahin* brought the Petromax and blew out the hurricane lantern. She behaved with much modesty and Dhaniram was pleased.

No pert remarks, no stamping on the shaky floor. She pulled her veil over her forehead and hung up the Petromax.

Lorkhoor watched her walk off with the hurricane lantern. Watching her, he said, 'I was thinking of going to Port of Spain. Get a job on a paper. The *Guardian* or the *Sentinel* or the *Gazette*.'

Chittaranjan stood with his back to the Petromax and studied the lists Lorkhoor gave him. 'How we know these eight hundred Hindus going to do what you say?'

'You will see for yourself. But if I tell them that Preacher has betrayed me, and if I tell them to vote for a Hindu like Harbans, who do you think they'll vote for? Baksh?'

'How we know you not going to change your mind?'

Lorkhoor shrugged. 'I will leave on the Saturday before the elections.'

'Five hundred dollars,' Chittaranjan said.

'Splendid,' said Lorkhoor. 'That suits me fine.'

12. More Departures

THAT HAPPENED ONE WEEK before polling day. Harbans and Chittaranjan were confident but didn't show it. Dhaniram was shamelessly exultant. Mahadeo was beyond caring. He still had to endure Mr Cuffy's watchful eye, and still had to keep his own vigil over Old Sebastian. And there was his eternal anxiety that some other Negro might fall ill. Hindus were falling ill by the score every day now; Muslims had begun to join them, and even a few Spaniards. But no Negro became infirm. Mahadeo didn't have time to be thankful.

*

And then Baksh began to play the fool again.

'Bribe number three coming up,' Chittaranjan said.

Baksh told Ramlogan and Ramlogan told Chittaranjan. Baksh told Foam and Foam told Chittaranjan. Baksh told Harichand and Harichand told Chittaranjan.

'Say he ain't got a chance,' Harichand said. 'Not a chance in hell. Say, by asking Muslim people to vote for him, he wasting good good votes. Say it ain't fair to the Muslim to ask them to waste their good good votes. Say that it would look to a lot of people like a Hindu trick to waste good good Muslim votes. Say he thinking that, weighing up everything and balancing it, Preacher is still the better man. Say he thinking of selling out to Preacher. Say is the only thing to give back the Muslim their pride. Say . . .'

'Say he could kiss my arse,' Harbans said. 'Say he could go to hell afterwards.'

'Say,' Harichand went on unperturbed, 'that he willing to talk things over fust.'

'Give them the Muslim vote,' Dhaniram said. 'With the Spanish voting and with Lorkhoor telling the other Hindus not to vote for Preacher, we could give them the Muslim vote.'

Harbans paced about Chittaranjan's veranda with his jerky clockwork steps. 'It go against my heart to give that man another penny. Against my heart, man.'

Chittaranjan said, 'Harichand, tell Baksh we not going to see him until Saturday night.'

'But election is on Monday,' Harichand said.

'We know that,' Chittaranjan said. 'We don't want Baksh to tired out hisself changing his mind *four* times. Three times in one election is enough for one man.'

'Is your election, pappa.' Harichand shook his head, laughed and left.

Harbans fell into one of his unsettling depressive moods. He continued to walk up and down Chittaranjan's tiled veranda, muttering to himself, cracking his fingers.

'It don't matter who the Muslim vote for now,' Dhaniram said. 'Work it out for yourself, Mr Harbans. We getting *all* the Hindu votes and the Spanish vote. Five thousand. If the worst come to the worst and Baksh sell out to Preacher, Preacher could still only get three thousand. Two thousand Negro and a thousand Muslim.'

Harbans refused to be comforted.

And Chittaranjan rocking, rocking in his morris chair, wasn't as cool as he looked. It wasn't Baksh's message. He had expected that. And, as Dhaniram had said, Baksh wasn't important now anyway; though it would have been worthwhile, just to make absolutely sure, to see that the Muslims didn't vote for Preacher. But the message had come at a bad time. Chittaranjan had called Harbans to the committee meeting that Wednesday evening to tell him all about the big motor-car parade on Sunday, the eve of polling day.

Harbans knew nothing about the parade. Chittaranjan, Foam and Dhaniram had planned it among themselves. They were afraid that if Harbans got to know about it too early he might object: the parade was going to be a grand, expensive thing. But the committee wanted it—a final flourish to an impressive campaign.

Big motor-car parades were not new to Trinidad. Up to 1946, however, they had been used only for weddings and funerals. At weddings the decorated cars raced through the main roads with streamers flying and horns blaring. In their sombre way funeral processions were equally impressive; they always had right of way and often dislocated traffic; an important man could paralyse it. In 1946 the political possibilities of the motor-car parade were exploited for the first time by the P.P.U., the Party for Progress and Unity. On the day before the first general election the P.P.U. hired five hundred cars and toured the island. It was the P.P.U.'s finest moment. The party had been founded two months before the parade; it died two days after it. It won one seat out of twelve; ten of the candidates lost their deposits; the president and the funds disappeared. But Trinidad had been impressed by the parade and after that no election, whether for city council, county council or local road board, was complete without a parade.

But parades were expensive.

Chittaranjan, seeing Harbans work his way back and forth across the veranda, wished once again he could manage the campaign without having to manage the candidate as well.

He thought he would be casual. He said, 'You doing anything on Sunday, Mr Harbans?'

Harbans didn't reply.

Chittaranjan said, 'I hope you not doing anything, because we having a little parade for you.'

Harbans stopped walking.

'Small parade really.'

Harbans locked his fingers, looked at them and then at his shoes, cracked his fingers, and continued to walk.

'Motorcade,' Dhaniram said.

'About fifty cars.' Chittaranjan began to write. 'Fifteen dollars a car. And you could give them a few gallons of gas. You got to have food to give the people. And you have to have music.'

Harbans, still jerking about the veranda, only cracked his fingers.

'You can't disappoint the people, Mr Harbans,' Chittaranjan said. 'It go cost you about fifteen hundred dollars, but at the same time it going to make the people who want to vote for you feel good, seeing their candidate at the head of a big big parade.'

'Must have a motorcade,' Dhaniram said. 'Must must. Keep up with the times.' He laughed. '*Pay* the entrance fee.'

Harbans sat down.

When Foam came in they worked out details.

*

The only member of the committee who didn't turn up for that meeting was Mahadeo. Of late he had begun to stay away from committee meetings. It embarrassed him to be continually offering up lists of sick Hindus; much of Harbans's anger had been directed against him and he had had to defend himself more than once: '*I* didn't start up this democracy business, Mr Harbans.'

Old Sebastian was getting more difficult too. Concurrently with a series of unexpected ailments Sebastian had developed a sprightliness that should have heartened Mahadeo. It sickened him with worry. He could no longer rely on Sebastian to stay at home and make fish-pots. He often found him now in Ramlogan's rumshop, drinking free rum with the rest. Mahadeo didn't know where Sebastian got his rum vouchers. (He got them from Harichand, who had printed the vouchers and kept a few.) It didn't take much to get Sebastian drunk. He had lived for too long on an old age pension that had cramped his drinking style.

Mahadeo said, 'This democracy ain't a good thing for a man like Sebastian, you hear.'

And Mr Cuffy said, 'Mahadeo, I ain't know what sort of magic you working on Sebastian, but he acting damn funny. A candle does burn bright bright before it go out, remember. And Sebastian burning it at both ends.'

Sebastian's behaviour also distressed his drinking companion, Haq. Haq had with relief sacrificed his religious scruples so far as to drink in public. It wasn't the drink, he said; he wanted to be in a crowd, otherwise Foam would beat him up. He and Sebastian sat silently side by side on the bench against one wall of Ramlogan's rumshop and drank. They looked curiously alike; only, Sebastian smiled all the time, while Haq looked grumpy and uncompromising behind his spectacles; and Haq's bristle of white beard and whiskers was more impressive than the stray kinky brownish-grey hairs on Sebastian's chin that looked as though they had been despairingly planted by someone who hadn't enough seed to go round.

Mahadeo did his best. He bribed Sebastian to stay home; but Sebastian insisted that one bribe was good enough for only one day; and the days he stayed away from the rumshop he was very ill and alarmed Mahadeo more. He gave Sebastian money to go to the D.M.O. for a check-up. Sebastian said he went but Mahadeo didn't believe him. He bribed the D.M.O. to go to Sebastian. The D.M.O. reported, 'He'll last for a bit,' and left Mahadeo just as worried. 'A candle does burn bright bright before it go out,' he thought, and remembered Mr Cuffy and the whitewash brush on his face.

Mahadeo was a devout Hindu. He did his *puja* every morning and evening. In all his prayers now, and through all the ritual, the *arti* and bell-ringing and conch-blowing—which seemed in the most discouraging way to have nothing to do with what went on in Elvira— Mahadeo had one thought: Sebastian's health.

*

On the evening of the Saturday before the election Mahadeo noted that Sebastian was not at home. His vigil would be over in two days; he couldn't risk anything happening now. He went straight to Ramlogan's rumshop. It was full of the Saturday night crowd, merrier than usual because they still had rum vouchers; in two days they would have to start paying for their rum again. The floor was wet— the floors of rumshops are always wet. Ramlogan was busy, happy. Mahadeo forced his way through to the bench where Haq and Sebastian normally sat. He caught bits of election gossip.

'The British Government don't want Harbans to win this election.'

'They going to spoil all the poor people votes once they get them inside the Warden Office. Lights going out all over the place.'

'No, I not going to bet you, but I still have a funny feeling that Baksh going to win.'

'When Harbans done with this election, he done with Elvira, I telling all-you.'

'Chittaranjan in for one big shock when this election over, you hear.'

Mahadeo saw Haq, overshadowed by the standing drinkers and looking lost, fierce, but content.

'Where Sebastian?'

Rampiari's husband, his right foot emphatically bandaged, put his big hand on Mahadeo's shoulder. 'Sebastian! I never see a old man get so young so quick.'

Somebody else said, 'Take my word. Sebastian going to dead in harness.'

'Haq, you see Sebastian?'

'Nasty old man. Don't want to see him.'

Rampiari's husband said, 'Yes. In harness.'

'This ain't no joke, you know. Where Sebastian?'

'At home. By you. Go back and see after your wife, Mahadeo boy.'

'Two three years from now some Negro child running down Elvira main road calling Mahadeo Pa.'

'All-you ain't see Sebastian? Ramlogan!'

'Mahadeo, who the arse you think you is to shout at me like that? A man only got two hands.'

'Where Sebastian?'

'He take up a little drink and he gone long time.'

'For oysters.'

Mahadeo ran out of the shop, dazed by worry and the smell of rum. He ran back to Sebastian's hut. It was dead, lightless. No Sebastian. He made his way in the dark through the high grass to the latrine at the back of the yard. The heavy grey door—it came from one of the dismantled American Army buildings at Docksite in Port of Spain and heaven knows how Sebastian had got hold of it—the door was open. In the dark the latrine smell seemed to have grown in strength many times over. Mahadeo lit a match. No Sebastian. The hole was too small for Sebastian to have fallen in. He ran back to the road.

'Mahadeo, choose.'

It was Preacher, smelling of sweat and looking somewhat bedraggled.

'You see Sebastian?'

'The stone or the Bible?'

'The stone, man. The Bible. Anything. You see Sebastian?'

'Take the stone and kill me one time.'

'Let me go, man, Preacher. I got one dead on my hands already.' Then Mahadeo paused. 'Sebastian choose tonight?'

'Like Cawfee.'

'Aha! I did always believe that Cawfee was putting him up to everything. Let me *go,* man, Preacher, otherwise I going to hit you for true with the stone, you know.'

Mahadeo was released. On his way to Mr Cuffy's he passed a crowd on Chittaranjan's terrace, taxi-drivers waiting for instructions about the motorcade tomorrow. They were drinking and getting noisy. Mahadeo looked up and saw the light from Chittaranjan's drawing-room. He knew he should have been there, discussing the final election plans with Harbans and the rest of the committee. Guiltily he hurried away.

There was no light in Mr Cuffy's house. Normally at this time

Mr Cuffy sat in his small veranda reading the Bible by the light of an oil-lamp, ready to say 'Good night' to disciples who greeted him from the road.

Mahadeo passed and repassed the house.

'Mr Mahadeo.'

It was Lutchman. Mahadeo couldn't make him out right away because Lutchman wore a hat with the brim most decidedly turned down, as protection against the dew. Lutchman lived in the house with six votes. He was one of the earliest Hindus to report sick to Mahadeo. He had been succoured.

Mahadeo remembered. 'How the pain in your belly?'

'A lil bit better, Mr Mahadeo. One of the boys gone and fall sick now.'

'He fall sick a lil too late. Election is the day after tomorrow.'

Lutchman laughed, but didn't give up. 'You waiting for somebody, Mr Mahadeo?'

'You see Sebastian?'

Lutchman buttoned up his shirt and screwed down his hat more firmly. He held the brim over his ears. 'He sick too?'

'You meet anybody these days who *ain't* sick?'

'Is a sort of flu,' Lutchman said.

There was a coughing and a spluttering behind them.

Mahadeo started, ready to move off.

Lutchman said, 'Look him there.'

A cigarette glowed in Mr Cuffy's dark veranda.

Mahadeo whispered, 'Sebastian, is you?'

There was some more coughing.

'He smoking,' Mahadeo said angrily. 'Picking up all sort of vice in his old age.'

Lutchman said, 'He can't be all that sick if he smoking. Is a funny thing, you know, Mr Mahadeo, but I could always tell when *I* going to fall sick. I does find it hard to smoke. The moment that happen I does say, "Lutchman, boy, it look like you going to fall sick soon." True, you know, Mr Mahadeo.'

'Sebastian!'

'These days I can't even take a tiny little pull at a cigarette, man.'

Sebastian came into the road and Mahadeo knocked the cigarette from his hand.

Then Sebastian spoke.

'Dead,' Sebastian said. 'Dead as a cockroach.' He said it with a sort of neutral relish.

Mahadeo was confused by fear and joy.

'Dead?' Lutchman uncorked his hat.

Sebastian spoke again. 'Put back your hat on. You going to catch cold.'

'As a cockroach?' Mahadeo said.

'As a cockroach.'

The three men went into the lightless house. Mahadeo lit a match and they found the oil-lamp on a corner shelf. They lit that. The floorboards were worm-eaten and unreliable, patched here and there with the boards from a Red Cow condensed milk box. The pea-green walls were hung with framed religious pictures and requests to God, in Gothic letters, to look after the house.

Mr Cuffy sat in a morris chair as though he were posing for a photographer who specialized in relaxed attitudes. His head was slightly thrown back, his eyes were open but unstaring, his knees far apart, his right hand in his lap, his left on the arm of the chair.

'As a cockroach,' Sebastian said. He lifted the left hand and let it drop.

Lutchman, his hat in his hand, wandered about the tiny drawing-room like a tourist in a church. 'Old Cawfee Bible, man. Eh! Mr Mahadeo, look. Cawfee in technicolor, man.' He pointed to a framed photograph of a young Negro boy looking a little lost among a multitude of potted palms and fluted columns. It was a tinted black and white photograph. The palms were all tinted green; the columns were each a different colour; the boy's suit was brown, the tie red; and the face, untinted, black.

Mahadeo wasn't looking. It overwhelmed him just to be in Mr Cuffy's house. He felt triumph, shame, relief and awe. Then the shame and the awe went, leaving him exhausted but cool.

'Lutchman.'

'Mr Mahadeo.'

'Stay here with Sebastian. Don't let him go nowhere. Preacher mustn't get to know about Cawfee right now.'

He hurried over to Chittaranjan's, pushed his way through the drunken taxi-drivers on the terrace and went up the red steps. He saw Baksh at the top. Baksh was saying, with unconvincing dignity, 'Is not *you* I come to see, Goldsmith, but Mr Harbans.'

Mahadeo followed Baksh and Chittaranjan into the drawing-room. Harbans was there with his committee. Foam was sitting at the polished cedar table, looking at a very wide sheet which contained all the committee's dispositions for polling day: the names of agents and their polling stations, agents inside the stations and agents out-side; taxis, their owners, their drivers, their stations.

Mahadeo said, 'Goldsmith, I have to see you right away.'

Chittaranjan, honouring the occasion by wearing his visiting outfit (minus the hat) at home, looked at Mahadeo with surprise and some contempt.

'Pussonal,' Mahadeo insisted.

Chittaranjan felt the force of Mahadeo's eyes. He led him to the back veranda.

Baksh said, 'Mr Harbans, answer me this frank: if I go up, ain't I just making the Muslims and them waste their good good vote?'

Dhaniram said, 'Ach! You could keep the Muslim vote.'

'I know,' Baksh said. 'You ain't want the Muslim vote *now*. But you think it would look nice? When next election come round, and you *ain't* want the Muslim to waste their vote, what you going to do then?'

Harbans said, '*Next* election? This is the fust and last election I fighting in Elvira.'

Foam studied his chart. He wasn't going to take any part in the discussion.

Baksh knew he was pushing things too far. But he knew he was safe because Foam was there. Otherwise he stood a good chance of being beaten up. Not by Harbans or Dhaniram or Chittaranjan, but by helpers. He could hear the din from Ramlogan's shop next door: the curses and the quarrels, swift to flare up, swift to die down. He could hear the taxi-drivers downstairs, drunk and getting drunker; they were making a row about petrol for the motorcade tomorrow.

Baksh said, 'If the Muslims vote for Preacher, it going to make a little trouble for you, Mr Harbans. You is a old man and I ain't want to trouble you. But is the only proper thing to do.'

'And the only proper thing for *you* to do is to make haste and haul your tail away.' It was Chittaranjan, returning to the drawing-room. 'Dhaniram, at long last we could use your plan. Cawfee dead.'

'Aha! What I did tell you?' Dhaniram was so excited he lit a cigarette. 'One Negro was bound to dead before elections. You in luck, Mr Harbans. Lorkhoor going away tonight. And tonight self you get a chance to start paying the Negroes *their* entrance fee.'

Harbans was too stupefied by his good fortune to react.

'Wake,' Dhaniram said. 'Coffee. *We* coffee. Ha! Coffee for Cawfee. Coffee, rum, biscuits.'

Chittaranjan remained poised. 'Foam, take the van and run down to Chaguanas and get Tanwing to come up here with a nice coffin and a icebox and everything else. And telephone Radio Trinidad so they could have the news out at ten o'clock. You could make up the wordings yourself. Dhaniram, go home and get your daughter-in-law to make a lot of coffee and bring it back here.'

'How I go *bring* back a lot of coffee here?'

'Is a point. Foam, when you come back, go and pick up the coffee from Dhaniram place. Nelly mother going to make some more.'

Baksh saw it was no use threatening to sell out to Preacher now. He said, 'Funny how people does sit down and dead, eh? Since I was a boy so high in short pants I seeing Cawfee sitting down in his house, repairing shoe. All sorta shoe. Black shoe, brown shoe, two-tone shoe, high-heel, wedge-heel.' Baksh became elegiac: 'I remember one day, when I was a boy, taking a shoe to Cawfee. Heel was dropping off. One of those rubber heels. I take it to Cawfee and he tack back the heel for me. I offer him six cents but he ain't take it.'

No one listened. Foam was folding up his election chart in a business-like way. Dhaniram was buckling his belt, ready to go and see about the coffee. Harbans was still bemused. Mahadeo, relieved, exhausted, didn't care.

'He ain't take it,' Baksh repeated.

Chittaranjan said, 'Mahadeo, you better go and keep a sharp eye on the house. I going to talk to those taxi-drivers. We go want them for the funeral. I think it would be better to have the funeral before the motorcade.'

Mahadeo went back to Mr Cuffy's house.

Sebastian was sitting in a morris chair, leaning forward and grimacing.

Lutchman said, 'Sebastian ain't too well, Mr Mahadeo. Just now, just before you come, he take in with one belly pain. He sick.'

'Serve him damn right. And let me tell you one thing, Sebastian. If *you* dead, nobody not going to bury you, you hear.'

Sebastian only grimaced.

Lutchman said, 'Food and everything spread out in the kitchen, you know, Mr Mahadeo. Nothing ain't touch. Mr Cawfee,' Lutchman said, feeling for the words, 'get call away rather sudden.'

Sebastian straightened his face and got up. He stood in front of the tinted photograph. He said, 'I did know Cawfee when he take out that photo. Always going to Sunday School.' Abruptly his voice was touched with pathos. 'They use to give out cakes and sweet drinks. Then he get take up with this shoemaking.'

They sat and waited until they heard a van stop outside. Foam, Chittaranjan, the D.M.O. and Tanwing came in. The D.M.O. was a young Indian with a handsome dissipated face. He hadn't forgotten his association with England and continued to wear a Harris tweed jacket, despite the heat.

Foam asked, 'You going to cut him up, Doctor?'

The D.M.O. pursed his lips and didn't reply. He did two things. He took off Mr Cuffy's stout black boots, said, 'Good boots,' turned up Mr Cuffy's right eyelid, then closed both eyes.

'Heart,' he said, and filled the form.

'Was that self I did think,' Lutchman said.

Tanwing, the undertaker, was pleased by the D.M.O's dispatch, though nothing showed on his face. Tanwing was an effervescent little Chinese who had revolutionized burial in Central Trinidad. He had a big bright shop in Chaguanas with a bright show window. In the window he had coffins of many sizes and many woods, plain and polished, with silver handles or without any handles at all, with glass windows on the lid through which you could look at the face of the deceased, or without these windows. Every coffin had its price tag, sometimes with a hint like: 'The same in cyp, $73.00.' There were also tombstones, with tags like this: 'The same with kerbs, $127.00.' The slogan of Tanwing's was Economy with Refinement; because of the former he had abandoned horse-drawn hearses for motor ones. Refined economy paid. Tanwing was able to sponsor a weekly fifteen-minute programme on Radio Trinidad. The other programme of this sort was a hushed, reverent thing called 'The Sunshine Hour'. Tanwing gave his audience fifteen lively minutes of songs from many lands on gramophone records, and called his programme 'Faraway Places'.

Tanwing fell to work at once. He wasted no time sympathizing with anybody. But he was anxious to do his best; Mr Cuffy was being laid out in one of his more expensive coffins.

By now it could no longer be hidden from Elvira that something had happened to Mr Cuffy.

Shortly after the D.M.O. had signed the death certificate, Foam and Chittaranjan had taken over quantities of rum, coffee and biscuits to the house; and the news was broken. People began to gather, solemn at first, but when the rum started to flow all was well. Harbans mingled with the mourners as though they were his guests; and everyone knew, and was grateful, that Harbans had taken all the expenses of the wake upon himself. Some of Mr Cuffy's women disciples turned up in white dresses and hats, and sat in the drawing-room, singing hymns. The men preferred to remain in the yard. They sat on benches and chairs under Mr Cuffy's big almond tree and talked and drank by the light of flambeaux.

Baksh came, rebuffed but unhumbled. He said nothing about the election and was full of stories about the goodness of Mr Cuffy. The mourners weren't interested. Baksh was still officially a candidate and still the controller of the thousand Muslim votes; but politically he was a failure and everybody knew it. He knew it himself. He drank cup after cup of Harbans's weak black coffee and maintained a strenuous sort of gaiety that fooled no one.

He felt out of everything and ran from group to group in the yard, trying to say something of interest. 'But I telling all-you, man,' he said over and over. 'I see old Cawfee good good just last night. I pass by his house and I give him a right and he give me back a right.'

Baksh was romancing and no one paid attention. Besides, too many people had seen Mr Cuffy the day before.

Baksh drank. Soon the rum worked on him. It made him forget electioneering strategy and increased his loquaciousness. It also gave him an inspiration. 'All-you know why Cawfee dead so sudden?' he asked. 'Come on, guess why he dead so sudden.'

Lutchman said, 'When your time come, your time come, that is all.'

Harichand the printer was also there. He said, 'The way Cawfee dead remind me of the way Talmaso dead. Any of all-you here remember old Talmaso? Talmaso had the laziest horse in the whole wide world . . .'

'So none of all-you ain't going to guess why Cawfee dead?' Baksh said angrily. Then he relented. 'All right, I go tell you. Was because of that dog.'

Harichand pricked up his ears. 'That said dog?'

Baksh emptied his glass and rocked on his heels. 'Said said dog.' When Baksh drank his full face lost its hardness; his moustache lost its bristliness and drooped; his eyebrows drooped; his eyelids hung wearily over reddened eyes; his cheeks sagged. And the man spoke with a lot of conviction. 'Said dog. Cawfee run the dog down and give the poor little thing five six kicks. Herbert did warn him that if he kick the dog he was going to dead. But you know how Cawfee was own way and harden, never listening to anybody. Well, he kick the dog and he dead.'

Rampiari's husband, heavy with drink, said, 'Still, the man dead and I ain't want to hear nobody bad-talking him.'

'True,' Harichand said. 'But the way Cawfee just sit down and dead remind me of how Talmaso dead. Talmaso was a grass-cutter. Eh, but I wonder when the hell Talmaso did get that horse he had. Laziest horse in the world. Lazy lazy. Tock. Tock. Tock.' Harichand clacked his tongue to imitate the horse's hoofbeats. 'Tock. Tock. So it uses to walk. As if it was in a funeral. Lifting up his foot as though they was make of lead: one today, one tomorrow. Tock. Tock. Tock. And then Talmaso uses to take his whip and lash out *Pai! Pai! Pai!* And horse uses to go: tocktock-tock-tock-tock-tock-tock. Tock. Tock. Tock. *Pai!* Tock-tocktock-tock-tock. Tock. Tock. But you couldn't laugh at Talmaso horse. Talmaso run you all over the place. Every morning horse uses to neigh. As if it did want to wake up Talmaso. Horse neigh. Talmaso get up. One morning horse neigh. Talmaso *ain't* get up. Only Talmaso wife get up. Talmaso wife uses to give Talmaso hell, you know. Horse neigh again. Still, Talmaso sleeping. Sound sound. Like a top. Wife start one cussing-off. In Hindi. She shake up Talmaso. Horse neigh. Still, Talmaso sleeping. Like a baby. Wife push Talmaso. Talmaso roll off the bed. Stiff. Wife start one bawling. Horse neighing. Wife bawling. Talmaso dead. Horse never move again.'

'What happen to it?'

'Horse? Like Talmaso. Sit down and dead.'

Rampiari's husband exclaimed, 'Look! Preacher coming. All three candidates here now.'

Preacher didn't bustle in. He came into the yard with a solemn shuffle, kissing his right hand and waving languid benedictions to the crowd. They looked upon him with affection as a defeated candidate. His long white robe was sweat-stained and dusty; but there was nothing in his expression to show regret, either at the election or at Mr Cuffy's death: his tolerant eyes still had their bloodshot faraway look.

In the interest which greeted Preacher's arrival there was more than the interest which greets the newly defeated. Preacher was without staff, stone or Bible. And he was not alone. He had his left arm around Pundit Dhaniram, who was in tears and apparently inconsolable.

Mahadeo said, 'I know this wake was Dhaniram idea. But he taking this crying too damn far, you hear.'

Foam followed. 'No coffee from Dhaniram,' he announced.

'Dhaniram wife dead too?' Harichand asked, and got a laugh.

Chittaranjan staggered in with a large five-valve radio. It was his own and he didn't trust anyone else with it.

The women sang hymns in the drawing-room. In the yard some men were singing a calypso:

> O'Reilly dead!
> O'Reilly dead and he left money,
> Left money, left money.
> O'Reilly dead and he left money
> To buy rum for we.

Chittaranjan and Foam fiddled with wires from the loudspeaker van, attaching them to the radio. The radio squawked and crackled.

'Shh!'

The hymn-singers fell silent. The calypsonians fell silent. Only Dhaniram sobbed.

The radio was on. A woman sang slowly, hoarsely:

> I've found my man,
> I've found my man.

Then an awed chorus of men and women sang:

> She's in love:
> She's lovely:
> She uses Ponds.

There was a murmur of disappointment among the mourners, which was silenced by the radio announcer. *'This is Radio Trinidad and the Rediffusion Golden Network.'* He gave the time. Some trumpets blared.

'Shh!'

A fresh blare.

'Listen.'

> Time for a Carib!
> Time for a Carib
> La-ger!

The mourners became restless. Chittaranjan, responsible for the radio, felt responsible for what came out of it. He looked appeasingly at everybody.

Solemn organ music oozed out of the radio.

'Aah.'

The announcer was as solemn as the music. *'We have been asked to announce the death . . .'*

Rampiari's husband had to be restrained from giving a shout.

But the first announcement was of no interest to Elvira.

The organ music drew Tanwing out of the bedroom where he had been busy on Mr Cuffy. The hymn-singers made room for him and looked at him with respect. He held his hands together and looked down at his shoes.

The organ music swelled again.

'Now.'

'We have also been asked to announce the death of Joseph Cuffy . . .'

There was a long, satisfied sigh. Rampiari's husband had to be restrained again.

'. . . which occurred this evening at The Elvira in County Napa-roni. The funeral of the late Joseph Cuffy takes place tomorrow morning, through the courtesy of Mr Surujpat Harbans, from the house of mourning, near Chittaranjan's Jewellery Establishment, Elvira main road, and thence to the Elvira Cemetery. Friends and relations are kindly asked to accept this intimation.'

Then there was some more music.

As soon as the music was over Tanwing unclasped his hands and disappeared into the bedroom and set to work on Mr Cuffy again. A woman sang:

> Brush your teeth with Colgate,
> Colgate Dental Cream.

'Take the damn thing off,' Rampiari's husband shouted.

> It cleans your breath
> (One, two),
> While it guards your teeth.

The radio was turned off. The hymn-singers sang hymns.

Pundit Dhaniram's grief was beginning to be noticed. A lot of people felt he was showing off: 'After all, Cawfee was Preacher best friend, and Preacher ain't crying.' Preacher was still consoling Dhaniram, patting the distraught pundit; while the announcement was coming over the radio Preacher had held on to him with extra firmness and affection. Now he took him to the bedroom.

It was close in the bedroom. The window was shut, the jalousies blocked up. The pictures had been turned to the wall and a towel thrown over the mirror. Tanwing and his assistants worked by the light of an acetylene lamp which was part of the equipment they had brought; candles burned impractically at the head of the bulky bed. The assistants, noiseless, were preparing the icebox for Mr Cuffy. Mr Cuffy's corpse was without dignity. The man's grumpiness, his fierce brows—all had gone for good. He just looked very dead and very old. The body had already been washed and dressed, with a curious clumsiness, in the shiny blue serge suit Elvira had seen on so many Friday evenings.

Preacher released Pundit Dhaniram and looked at Mr Cuffy as though he were looking at a picture. He put his hand to his chin, held his head back and moved it slowly up and down.

Dhaniram still sobbed.

This didn't perturb Tanwing. He looked once at Dhaniram and looked no more. He was still fussing about the body, putting on the finishing touches. He was trying to place camphor balls in the nostrils and the job was proving a little awkward. Mr Cuffy had enormous nostrils. Tanwing had to wrap the camphor balls in cotton wool before they would stay in. Tanwing had the disquieting habit of constantly passing a finger under his own nostrils as though he had a runny nose, or as though he could smell something nobody else could.

When Dhaniram and Preacher left the room they were met by Chittaranjan. Dhaniram almost fell on Chittaranjan's shoulder, because he had to stoop to embrace him.

'You overdoing this thing, you know, Dhaniram,' Chittaranjan said. 'You ain't fooling nobody.'

'She gone, Goldsmith,' Dhaniram sobbed. 'She gone.'

'Who gone, Dhaniram?'

'The *doolahin* gone, Goldsmith. She run away with Lorkhoor.'

'Come, sit down and drink some coffee.'

'She take up she clothes and she jewellery and she gone. She gone, Goldsmith. Now it ain't have nobody to look after me or the old lady.'

Outside, the men were singing a calypso about the election:

> And I tell my gal,
> Keep the thing in place.
> And when they come for the vote,
> Just wash down their face.

The drinking and singing continued all that night and into the morning. Then they buried Mr Cuffy. Preacher did the preaching.

13. Democracy Takes Root in Elvira

IN MR CUFFY'S YARD the flambeaux had burned themselves out and were beaded with dew. The smell of stale rum hung in the still morning air. Under the almond trees benches lay in disorder. Many were overturned; all were wet with dew and coffee or rum. Around the benches, amid the old, trampled almond leaves, there were empty bottles and glasses, and enamel cups half full of coffee; there were many more in the dust under the low floor of Mr Cuffy's house. The house was empty. The windows and doors were wide open.

It was time for the motorcade.

Outside Chittaranjan's the taxis were parked in jaunty confusion, banners on their radiators and backs, their doors covered with posters still tacky with paste. The taxi-drivers too had a jaunty air. They were all wearing cardboard eyeshades, printed on one side, in red, DO YOUR PART, and on the reverse, VOTE THE HEART.

Some taxis grew restless in the heat and prowled about looking for more advantageous parking places. Disputes followed. The air rang with inventive obscenities.

Then a voice approached, booming with all the authority of the loudspeaker: 'Order, my good people! My good people, keep good order! I am begging you and beseeching you.'

It was Baksh.

Without formal negotiation or notification he was campaigning for Harbans. In the loudspeaker van he ran up and down the line of taxis, directing, rebuking, encouraging: 'The eyes of the world is on you, my good people. Get into line, get into line. Keep the road clear. Don't disgrace yourself in the eyes of the world, my good people.'

His admonitions had their effect. Soon the motorcade was ready to start.

Harbans, Chittaranjan, Dhaniram and Mahadeo sat in the first car. Dhaniram was too depressed, Mahadeo too exhausted, to respond with enthusiasm to the people who ran to the roadside and shouted, 'Do your part, man! Vote the heart!'

Mrs Baksh and the young Bakshes had a car to themselves. Mrs Baksh was not only reconciled to the election, she was actually enjoying it, though she pretended to be indifferent. She had decked out the young Bakshes. Carol and Zilla had ribbons in their hair, carried small white handbags which contained nothing, and small paper fans from Hong Kong. The boys wore sock and ties. Herbert and Rafiq waved to the children of poorer people until Zilla said, 'Herbert and Rafiq, stop low-rating yourself.'

Baksh was with Foam in the loudspeaker van. He did his best to make up to Harbans for all the damage and distress he had caused him. He said, 'This is the voice of . . . Baksh. Mazurus Baksh here. This is the voice of . . . Baksh, asking each and every one of you, the good people of Elvira, to vote for your popular candidate, Mr Surujpat Harbans. Remember, good people of Elvira, I, Mazurus Baksh, not fighting the election again. I giving my support to Mr Surujpat Harbans. For the sake of unity, my good people. This is the voice of . . . Baksh.'

Then Foam played the Richard Tauber record of the campaign song:

And oh, my darling,
Should we ever say goodbye,
I know we both should die,
My heart and I.

And Baksh added, 'Don't let nobody fool you, my good people. Vote the heart. Make your X with a black lead pencil, my good people. A black lead pencil. Not a red pencil or a pen. Do your part. This is the voice of . . . Baksh.'

The motorcade was well organized. One van alone carried food—*roti, dalpuri* and curried goat. Another carried hard liquor and soft drinks. There were small mishaps. Two or three cars broke down and had to be pushed out of the way. Once the motorcade enthusiastically went beyond Elvira, snarled with the motorcades of other candidates in the next constituency, and when the dust settled Chittaranjan saw that the first half of the motorcade, which contained the candidate, the committee and the loudspeaker van, had got detached from the second half, which carried the food and the liquor.

A long grey van pulled up. It belonged to the Trinidad Film Board, who were shooting scenes for a Colonial Office documentary film about political progress in the colonies, the script of which was to be written, poetically, in London, by a minor British poet. Apart from the driver and an impressive tangle of equipment behind the front seat, the van carried a Negro cameraman dressed for the job: green eyeshade, unlit cigar, wide, brilliant tie, broad-collared shirt open at the neck, sleeves neatly rolled up to mid-forearms. The cameraman chewed his cigar, sizing up Harbans's diminished motorcade.

Chittaranjan went to him. 'You drawing photo?'

The cameraman chewed.

'If is photo you drawing, well, draw out a photo of *we* candidate.'

Harbans smiled wanly at the cameraman.

The cameraman chewed, nodded to his driver and the van moved off.

'Everybody want bribe these days,' Chittaranjan said.

He sent Foam off in the loudspeaker van to look for the rest of the motorcade. Foam came upon them parked not far off in a side road near Piarco Airport. The food van had been plundered; the liquor van was being noisily besieged. Harichand was there, Lutchman, Sebastian, Haq, and Rampiari's husband, moving about easily on a bandaged foot.

Foam broke the party up. All went smoothly after that.

*

Baksh made one last attempt to cause trouble.

It happened after the motorcade, early in the evening, when Harbans was sitting in Chittaranjan's drawing-room, signing voucher after petrol voucher. He was giving each car six gallons for polling day. Baksh said it wasn't enough.

Harbans said, 'Ooh. When that finish, Baksh, come back to me and I go give you another voucher.'

Baksh snorted. 'Ha! Is *so* you want to fight elections? You mean, when my gas finish, I must put down whatever I doing? Put it down and come running about looking for you? Look for you, for you to give me another voucher? Another voucher for me to go and get more gas? Get gas to go back and take up whatever it was I was doing before I put it down to come running about looking for you . . .' He completed the argument again.

The taxi-drivers were drunk and not paying too much attention, and nothing would have come of Baksh's protests but for a small accident.

Chittaranjan had, at his own expense, got his workmen to make heart-shaped buttons for Harbans's agents and taxi-drivers to wear on polling day. Shortly after the motorcade Foam came downstairs to distribute the buttons. They were in a shoebox. A taxi-driver at the bottom of the steps tried to grab a handful. The man was drunk and his action was high-spirited, nothing more. But Foam turned nasty; he was thoroughly tired out by all the festivities, first Mr Cuffy's wake, then the motorcade.

He said, 'Take your thiefing hand away!' That was bad enough, but as Foam spoke his temper rose, and he added, 'I going to make you wait till last for your button.'

When he finally offered, the man declined. 'I don't want none.'

'Come on. Ain't you was grabbing just now? Take the button.'

'Not going to take no damn button. All you people running about behaving like some damn civil servant, pushing away people hand as if people hand dirty.' He raised his voice: 'My hand ain't dirty, you hear. You hearing me good? I is a taxi-driver, but I does bathe every day, you hear. My hand ain't dirty, you hear.'

A crowd began to gather.

Foam said, 'Take your button, man.'

The other taxi-drivers were already sporting theirs.

Foam tried to pin the button on the driver's shirt.

The driver pushed him away and Foam almost fell.

The taxi-driver addressed his audience: 'They want to use people car, but they don't want to give people no button. I ask for one little button and the man push away my hand and practically threaten to beat me up. Giving button to everybody. Everybody. And when he come to me, passing me. I is a dog? My name is Rex? I does go bow-wow-wow? Well, I is *not* a dog, and my name *ain't* Rex, and I ain't taking no damn button.'

Foam's tactics were wrong. He tried to be reasonable. He said, 'I threaten to beat you up? Or you mean that you try to grab the whole shoebox of button?'

The driver laughed. He turned his back on Foam and walked away, the taxi-drivers making a path for him; then he turned and walked back to Foam and the ring of taxi-drivers closed again. 'Is so all you people does get on. So much money all-you spend for this election and now, on the second to-last night, all-you start offending people and start getting insultive and pussonal.'

Foam continued to be reasonable. 'I was insultive?'

But nobody was listening.

Another taxi-driver was saying, 'And today, when they was sharing out food, I ain't even get a little smell. When I go and ask, they tell me it finish. When I go and ask for a little shot of grog, they drive me away. Harbans spending a lot of money, but is the people that helping him out who going to be responsible if he lose the election. I mean, man, no food, no grog. Things like that don't sound nice when you say it outside.'

And then came this talk about petrol.

'Six gallons ain't enough,' Baksh said.

Somebody else said, 'You know how much they giving taxi-drivers in Port of Spain? Thirty dollars a day. And then in addition too besides, they fulling up your tank for you, you hear. And it have good good roads in Port of Spain that not going to lick up your car.'

That at once made matters worse.

Chittaranjan, Mahadeo and Harbans were upstairs, besieged by more taxi-drivers. Harbans was filling in petrol vouchers as Chittaranjan called out the amount, the number of the taxi, the name of the driver. They were not using the cedar dining-table; it was too good for that; Chittaranjan had brought out the large kitchen table, spread it over with newspapers and jammed it, like a counter, in the doorway between the drawing-room and the veranda. The drivers pressed around the table, waiting for Harbans to fill in and sign their vouchers. Mahadeo was trying to keep some order among the drivers, fruitlessly. They shouted, they cursed, laughed, complained; their shoes grated and screeched on the tiled floor. Harbans filled in and signed, filled in and signed, in a daze, not looking up.

Through all the press Chittaranjan sensed that something was wrong downstairs, and he sent Mahadeo to see what was happening. Mahadeo came back with the news that unless the men were given at least ten gallons of petrol they were going to go on strike the next day.

The taxi-drivers around the table took up the cry.

'Ten gallons, man. I got a big American car. No English match-box. I does only do fifteen miles to the gallon. Six gallons is like nothing to my car, man.'

'In Port of Spain they fulling up your tank for you.'

'Let Harbans watch out. He think he only saving two gallons of gas. If he ain't careful he saving hisself the trouble of going up to Port of Spain every Friday afternoon to sit down in that Legislative Council.'

Not even Chittaranjan's authority could quell the unrest.

'Mahadeo,' Chittaranjan called. 'Go down and tell them that they going to get their ten gallons. Those that get six tell them to come up for another voucher.'

Harbans didn't stop to think.

Chittaranjan just whispered to him, 'Ten gallons. Driver name Rapooch. He taxi number is HT 3217.'

And Harbans wrote, and wrote. If he stopped to think he felt he would break down and cry. His wrinkled hand perspired and shook; it had never done so much writing at one time.

Mahadeo went downstairs and spread the healing word.

*

Elvira was stirring before dawn. A fine low mist lay over the hills, promising a hot, thundery day. As the darkness waned the mist lifted, copying the contours of the land, and thinned, layer by layer. Every tree was distinct. Soon the sun would be out, the mist would go, the trees would become an opaque green tangle, and polling would begin.

Polling was to begin at seven; but the fun began before that. The Elvira Estate had given its workers the day off; so had the Public Works Department. Chittaranjan gave his two workmen the day off and put on a clean shirt. Baksh gave himself the day off. He rose early and went straight off to start celebrating with Rampiari's husband and the others. As soon as he was up Foam went over to Chittaranjan's. Harbans was there already. Harbans had wanted to spend the night in Elvira, but Chittaranjan had advised him not to, considering the irreverent mood of the taxi-drivers.

Mahadeo, according to Chittaranjan, was behaving even at that early hour in an entirely shameless way. He was drunk and, what was worse, drinking with the enemy.

Chittaranjan, his hat on, his shirt hanging nice and clean on him, said, 'I did feel like lifting up my hand and giving Mahadeo one good clout with my elbow. I meet him drinking with some good-for-nothing and I say, "Why for you drinking with these good-for-nothing, Mahadeo?" I did expect a straight answer. But the man drunk too

bad, man. He tell me he drinking with them because he want to find
out which way the wind blowing.'

*

At seven, or thereabouts, the polling stations opened. Presently there
were queues. Agents sat on the roots of trees still cool with dew, tick-
ing off names on duplicated electoral lists, giving cards to voters,
instructing the forgetful in the art of making an X. 'No, old man,
they ain't want two X.' 'Ah, *maharajin*, it ain't a scorpion they want
you to draw. Is a X. Look . . .' 'No, man. They ain't want you to vote
for *everybody*. You just put your little X by the heart. Do your part,
man.' 'You want to kill him or what? Not *inside* the heart, man.'

*

Foam's job was to see that the organization worked smoothly. He had
to see that the food van made regular rounds; officially, this was to
feed agents and other accredited representatives, but many other
people were to benefit. He had to make periodic tours of the polling
stations to see that no one played the fool.

At ten o'clock Foam reported: 'They staggering the voting at the
school.'

'Staggering?'

'Taking six seven minutes over one vote.'

Chittaranjan said, 'I did always feel that man was going to make
trouble. You better go and see him, Mr Harbans.'

Harbans knew what that meant.

He went to the school, Teacher Francis's domain, but now in the
holidays without Teacher Francis, who was in Port of Spain.

There was a long complaining queue.

Foam said, 'A lot of people leave because they didn't want to
stand up all this time.'

The clerk, a cheerful young Negro, greeted Harbans with un-
abashed warmth. 'Is a big big day for you today, Mr Harbans.'

'Ooh, I hear you having a little trouble here.'

'People ain't even know their own name, Mr Harbans.'

'But ain't they got a number?'

The clerk didn't stop smiling. 'I ain't want to know their number. Want to know their name.'

'Ooh. And when they tell you their name, you spend a long long time finding out whether they on the list, and then sometimes you does ask them to spell out their name? Let we look at the election regulations together.'

The clerk brightened.

From his hip pocket Harbans pulled out an orange pamphlet folded in two. He opened it so that only he and the clerk could see what was inside. It was a ten-dollar note.

The clerk said, 'Hm. I see what you mean. My mistake. Just leave these regulations here, Mr Harbans.'

Foam was still anxious. 'You can't be too careful in this place. In Trinidad you can't say anybody win election until they draw their first pay. We have to follow the ballot-boxes back to the Warden Office, otherwise you don't know what sort of chicanery they not going to try.'

For that task he and Chittaranjan had chosen men of tried criminality.

One man asked, 'You want me take my cutlass, Goldsmith?'

'I don't want you to land yourself in the Supreme Court again,' Chittaranjan said. 'Just take a good stick.'

*

Dhaniram stayed at home all morning. With no *doolahin* about, he had to empty his wife's spitting-cup; he had to cook for her; he had to lift her from her bed, make the bed, and put her back on it. He had no time to think about the election, yet when he went to Chittaranjan's he announced, 'Things going good good for you up Cordoba way, Mr Harbans. I spend the whole morning there.'

Chittaranjan barely widened his smile. 'Is a funny thing that you didn't see Foam. Foam going around everywhere all morning.'

Dhaniram changed the subject. 'I too break up by the *doolahin* and Lorkhoor.' He did indeed look ravaged; his skin was yellower, his eyes smaller, redder, without a twinkle.

But he was going to get no sympathy from Harbans. Foam's reports from the polling stations had convinced Harbans that he had practically won the election.

He kept making little jokes with Chittaranjan and Dhaniram.

'I wonder what colour the cheque going to be.'

Chittaranjan couldn't enter into the spirit of the game. 'I don't think they does pay members of the Legislative Council by cheque. I think you does get a sorta voucher. You got to cash it at the Treasury.'

'But what colour you think *that* is?'

'All government voucher white,' Chittaranjan said.

'Ooh, ooh. Least I did expect it woulda be pink or green or something nice like that. Eh, Goldsmith? Ooh, ooh. Just white, eh?' He laughed and slapped Chittaranjan on the back.

Chittaranjan preserved his gravity.

'The thing to make sure you win now,' he said, 'is rain.'

'Ooh, ooh.' Harbans poked Dhaniram in the ribs. Dhaniram laughed painfully. 'Listen to the goldsmith, Pundit. Rain! Ooh, ooh.'

'Rain,' Chittaranjan explained, 'going to keep back all those people who going to vote for Preacher. Preacher ain't got cars to take them to the polling station. We got all the cars.'

'Ooh, Goldsmith, how you could wish that for the poor man? I ain't have nothing against Preacher, man. Eh, Dhaniram?'

'I ain't got nothing against him neither,' Dhaniram said.

Chittaranjan said, 'Talking about taxi remind that the ringleader last night ain't even turn out this morning.' He consulted his chart. 'Oumadh. HV 5736.'

'Ooh. HV 5736, eh?' Harbans laughingly noted the number in a small notebook. 'We go fix him up, Goldsmith. Going to put the police on his tail. Parking. Speeding. Overloading. From now on he going to spend more time in court than driving taxi. Eh, Goldsmith? Eh, Dhaniram?'

*

Baksh spent the morning drinking with Mahadeo, and Rampiari's husband and Harichand. Mahadeo didn't even vote. He had clean forgotten.

*

At noon Ramlogan closed his shop and came across.

'Ooh, Ramlogan, man,' Harbans greeted him. 'Look out, man!' Ramlogan roared with laughter.

'Look out, man, Ramlogan. Ooh, you getting fat as a balloon. Ooh, he go bust. Ooh.' Harbans poked Ramlogan in the belly.

Ramlogan laughed even louder. 'You done win already, Mr Harbans.'

Harbans showed his neat false teeth and dug Dhaniram in the ribs. 'How he could say so, eh, Pundit? How he could say so? Ooh, Ramlogan!'

'But you done win, man.'

'Ooh, Ramlogan, you mustn't talk like that, man. You putting goat-mouth on me.'

And many more people kept coming to congratulate Harbans that afternoon. Even people who had announced that they were going to vote for Preacher and had in fact voted for Preacher, even they came and hung around Chittaranjan's shop. One man said, to nobody in particular, 'I is a kyarpenter. Preacher can't afford to give me no kyarpentering work. Preacher and people who voting for Preacher don't build house.'

The attitude of the policemen changed. In the morning they had been cautious and reserved: most of them had come from outside districts and didn't know much about the prospects of the candidates. In the afternoon they began to treat Harbans and his agents with respect. They waved and smiled and tried to keep their batons out of sight.

And then Chittaranjan had his wish. It rained. The roads became muddy and slippery; agents had to leave their positions under trees and move under houses; taxis, their windows up and misted over, steamed inside.

By three o'clock nearly everyone who was going to vote had voted. It was a fantastically high poll, more than eighty-three per cent. The fact was noted with approval in official reports.

*

Foam's last duty was to keep an eye on the ballot-box at the polling station in the school. At five o'clock he went with a taxi-driver and waited. Through the open door he could see the poll clerk, the staggerer of the morning's vote, sitting at Teacher Francis's own table, flanked by Harbans's agent and a Negro girl, one of Preacher's few agents. The ballot-box looked old and brown and unimportant. Foam could see the clerk taking out the ballot-papers and counting them.

Harbans's agent came to the door and waved to Foam.

Foam shouted, 'You is a ass. Go back and see what they doing.'

The agent was a slim young man, almost a boy, with a waist that looked dangerously narrow. He said, 'Everything under control, man,' but he went back to the table.

The watch lasted until dark.

The policeman who had been hanging about outside the school went up the concrete steps. The clerk said something to him. The policeman came down the steps, went across the road and called, 'Bellman!' He spoke with a strong Barbadian accent.

A middle-aged Negro in washed-out khaki trousers and a thick flannel vest came out into his veranda.

'Bellman, you got a lamp? They want it borrow over here.'

Bellman brought out an oil lamp. Unprotected, the flame swayed and rose high, smoking thickly.

Bellman said, 'I sending in my account to the Warden.'

The policeman laughed and took the lamp to the school. The checking was still going on. Apparently there had been some mistake in the checking because the ballot-box had been emptied again and the ballot-papers lay in a jagged white pile on the table.

The taxi-driver said, 'If that agent don't look out, they work some big big sort of trick here, you know.'

The policeman looked at Foam and the taxi-driver and swung his long baton, a casual warning.

Another of Harbans's taxis came up. The driver leaned out and asked, 'You got the score here yet?'

Harbans's agent, hearing the noise, came out with a sheet of paper. 'Preliminary,' he said, smiling, handing it over.

'Haul your tail back quick,' Foam said. 'See what they doing.'

The agent smiled and ran back up the steps.

Foam's taxi-driver said, 'What you want for elections is strong agents. Strong strong agents.'

They looked at the paper.

Foam read: 'Harbans 325, Thomas 57, Baksh 2.'

The other taxi-driver whistled. 'We giving them licks on all fronts. But some people don't listen at all, man. Baksh get two votes after the man ask them not to vote for him.' Then he delivered his own news: 'At Cordoba, Harbans 375, Thomas 19, Baksh 0. At Cordoba again, the second polling station, is Harbans 345, Thomas 21, Baksh 0.'

Foam's taxi-driver said, 'Yaah!' and took a drink of rum from the bottle on the dashboard shelf.

The other taxi-driver drove away.

The box was being sealed and signed.

Foam couldn't help feeling sorry for Preacher's agent. She was one of those who had sung the hymns at Mr Cuffy's wake. She sat unflinchingly at the table, being brave and unconcerned; while Harbans's agent, to the disgust of Foam and the taxi-driver, was jumping about here and there, doing goodness knows what.

Bellman pushed his head through his window curtain and said, 'Look, all-you finish with my lamp? That costing the Warden six cents, you know. I sure all-you done burn six cents' pitch-oil already.'

They were finished. The box was sealed, signed and brought out to the steps. The policeman took the lamp back to Bellman; then he rejoined the girl, Harbans's agent and the ballot-box. The clerk was padlocking the school door.

Foam shouted, 'What the hell all-you waiting for?'

Harbans's agent smiled.

They waited for about twenty minutes.

The clerk went home. The girl, Preacher's agent, went home. Harbans's agent said, 'This is a lot of arseness. Foreman, you could look after the ballot-box now yourself. I hungry like hell.'

Foam said, 'Good. Go. But I marking you for this. You hungry? You ain't eat? The food van ain't bring you nothing?'

'What food van? I ain't even see the food van. Everybody did tell me about this famous food van, but I ain't see nothing.' And he went home.

Foam said to his taxi-driver, 'Let that teach you a lesson. Never pay people in advance.'

The policeman kept on coughing in the darkness.

'Put on your lights,' Foam said.

When the lights went on, the policeman stopped coughing.

The taxi-driver went for a little walk. Then Foam went for a little walk. The policeman was still waiting.

When it was nearly half past seven and it seemed that no one had even honourable designs on the ballot-box, Foam lost his patience.

He went to the policeman. 'What you waiting for?'

The policeman said, 'I ain't know. They did just tell me to wait.'

'You want a lift to the Warden Office?'

'You going there?'

They took the policeman and the ballot-box to the Warden's Office.

In the asphalt yard next to the Warden's Office, Foam heard the loudspeaker—his father's voice; and he heard the enthusiastic shouts of the crowd. Apparently some results had already been rechecked and given out as official.

They delivered the policeman and the ballot-box; then they drove through the crowd to a free place in the yard.

Baksh was announcing: 'Kindly corporate with the police. Keep death off the roads. Beware of the Highway Code. This is the voice of Baksh telling you to beware of the Highway Code and keep death off the roads. Come in a lil bit more, ladies and gentlemen. Come in a lil bit. Another result just come in. But come in a lil bit more fust. This is the voice of Baksh begging you and beseeching you to corporate with the Highway Code and keep death off the roads. Another result. From Cordoba, station number one. Another result. From Cordoba One. Final result. Baksh nought. Baksh nought.'

The crowd appreciated the joke.

'Harbans 364, Harbans 364.'

Clamour.

'Come in a lil bit, ladies and gentlemen. Be aware of the Highway Code. Beware of the Highway Code. Thomas 45 .'

Shouts of 'Yaah!' Spontaneous drumming on car bonnets.

Baksh took advantage of the pause to have another drink. The gurgling noises were magnified by the loudspeaker. Someone was heard saying, 'Give *me* a chance at the loudspeaker. Beware of the Highway Code, ladies and gentlemen. Beware . . .' Baksh's voice broke in, conversationally, 'Is for the government I working tonight, you know. Not for any-and everybody. But for the government.' Then officially: 'Thomas 45. Thomas 45.'

What Baksh said was true. He was working for the government, as an official announcer; he had paid well to get the job.

The loudspeaker was silent for some time.

Then there was a shout, and sustained frenzied cheering. Harbans had appeared. In his moment of triumph he managed to look sad and absent-minded. The crowd didn't mind. They rushed to him and lifted him on their shoulders and they took him to the loudspeaker van and made him stand on one of the wings and then they grabbed the microphone from Baksh and thrust it into Harbans's hands and shouted, 'Speech!'

Baksh tried to get the microphone back.

'This is government business, man. All-you want me to get in trouble or what?'

Harbans didn't object. 'Is true, eh, Baksh?' and he passed the microphone back.

'Ladies and gentlemen, corporate with the police. Beware of the Highway Code. Be aware of the Highway Code, ladies and gentlemen.'

The crowd shouted obscene abuse at Baksh. Some of it was picked up by the loudspeaker.

'Ladies and gentlemen, unless you corporate with the government and unless and until you corporate with the police and start bewaring of the Highway Code, I cannot give out the last and final result which I have at this very present moment in my own own hand. Ladies and gentlemen, come in a lil bit fust, ladies and gentlemen. Keep the road clear. Keep death off the roads. Think before you drink. Drive slowly. 'Rrive safely. Come in a lil bit fust. Last result. Last result. Corporate with the police. Last result. Final grand total. Ladies and gentlemen, come in a lil bit.'

Harbans remained on the wing of the van, almost forgotten.

'Baksh 56. Baksh 56.'

Boos. Ironical cheers. Laughter.

'Repeat. Final result. Baksh 56. Harbans five thousand . . .'

Tumult.

'Beware of the Highway Code. Harbans five thousand, three hundred and thirty-six. Five three three six.'

The crowd swarmed around the van, grabbed at Harbans's ankles, knees. Some offered up hands. Harbans grabbed them with astonishing vigour and shook them fervently.

Baksh tried to carry on calmly, like a man on government business. 'Thomas seven hundred . . .'

They wanted to hear no more.

Baksh shouted at them without effect. He shouted and shouted and then waited for them to calm down.

'Ladies and gentlemen, you is *not* corporating. Thomas seven hundred and sixteen. Seven one six. And so, ladies and gentlemen, I give you your new Onble Member of the Legislative Council, Mr Surujpat Harbans. But before I give him to you, let me make a final appeal to corporate with the police. Beware of the Highway Code.'

Harbans, on the wing, was in tears when he took the microphone. His voice, coming over the loudspeaker, was a magnified coo. 'I want to thank everybody. I want to thank you and you and you . . .'

Somebody whispered, 'The police.'

'. . . and I want to thank the police and the Warden and the clerks and I want to thank everybody who vote for me and even people who ain't vote for me. I want to thank . . .' Tears prevented him from going on.

Baksh recovered the microphone. 'Corporate, ladies and gentlemen. That was your new Onble Member of the Legislative Council, Mr Surujpat Harbans.'

Foam wandered among the crowd looking for members of the committee. Mahadeo was drunk and useless. Dhaniram he couldn't see. At the edge of the yard, in the darkness, he saw Chittaranjan, leaning against the radiator of a car.

'Well, Goldsmith, we do it. We win.'

Chittaranjan pressed down his hat and folded his arms. 'What else you did expect?'

*

At that moment Preacher was going round briskly from house to house, thanking the people.

*

And so democracy took root in Elvira.

Epilogue: The Case of Whisky

HARBANS SPENT THE REST of that night settling his bills. The taxi-drivers had to be paid off, Ramlogan's rum-account settled, petrol vouchers honoured, agents given bonuses. And when all that was done, Harbans left Elvira, intending never to return.

But he did return, once.

It was because of that case of whisky Ramlogan had promised the committee of the winning candidate. Ramlogan wanted the presentation to be made in style, by the new Member of the Legislative Council. Chittaranjan thought it was fitting. He hadn't always approved of the publicity Ramlogan gave the case of whisky; but now he was glad of the excuse to get Harbans back in Elvira. Harbans hadn't dropped a word about marrying his son to Nelly. Chittaranjan knew the rumours that had been going around Elvira during the campaign, knew that people were laughing at him behind his back. But that had only encouraged him to work harder for Harbans. He had made those heart-shaped buttons at his own expense. He had worn his visiting outfit nearly every day; he had used up one shirt; his shoes needed half-soling. Harbans had taken it all for granted.

The presentation was fixed for the Friday after polling day; it was to take place outside Chittaranjan's shop. Benches and chairs were brought over from the school. Dhaniram lent his Petromax. Chittaranjan lent a small table and a clean tablecloth. On the tablecloth they placed the case of whisky stencilled WHITE HORSE WHISKY PRODUCE OF SCOTLAND 12 BOTTLES. On the case of whisky they placed a small Union Jack—Ramlogan's idea: he wanted to make the whole thing legal and respectable.

Haq and Sebastian came early and sat side by side on the bench against Chittaranjan's shop. Harichand came, Rampiari's husband, Lutchman. Tiger came and sniffed at the table legs. Haq shooed him off, but Tiger stayed to chase imaginary scents all over Chittaranjan's terrace.

Foam dressed for the occasion as though he were going to Port of Spain.

Mrs Baksh asked, 'And what you going to do with the three bottle of whisky? Drink it?'

'Nah,' Foam said. 'Keeping it. Until Christmas. Then going to sell it in Chaguanas. You could get anything up to eight dollars for a bottle of White Horse at Christmas.'

'You say that. But I don't think it would please your father heart to see three bottle of whisky remaining quiet in the house all the time until Christmas.'

'Well, you better tell him not to touch them. Otherwise it going to have big big trouble between me and he.'

Mrs Baksh sighed. Only three months ago, if Foam had talked like that, she could have slapped him. But the election had somehow changed Foam; he was no longer a boy.

Ramlogan prepared with the utmost elaborateness. He rubbed himself down with coconut oil; then he had a bath in lukewarm water impregnated with leaves of the *neem* tree; then he rubbed himself down with Canadian Healing Oil and put on his striped blue three-piece suit. A handkerchief hung rather than peeped from his breast pocket. His enormous brown shoes were highly polished; he had even bought a pair of laces for them. He wore no socks and no tie.

Chittaranjan put on his visiting outfit, Mahadeo his khaki uniform.

Dhaniram wasn't going to be there. He was so distressed by the loss of the *doolahin* that he had lost interest even in his tractor. He didn't see how he could replace the girl. He was a fussy Brahmin; he couldn't just get an ordinary servant to look after his food. Ideally, he would have liked another daughter-in-law.

Outside Chittaranjan's shop the crowd thickened. People were coming from as far as Cordoba and Pueblo Road. It was like Mr Cuffy's wake all over again.

Foam told the other members of the committee, sitting in Chittaranjan's drawing-room, 'I feel it going to have some trouble tonight.'

Chittaranjan felt that himself, and despite his friendship with Ramlogan, snapped out, 'Well, if people must show off . . .'

Ramlogan took it well. He laughed, took out his handkerchief and fanned his face. 'Gosh, but these three-piece suit hot, man. What trouble it could have? Whisky is for the committee, not for everybody in Elvira. Election over, and they know that.'

It was Friday evening; the people downstairs were in the week-end mood. Talk and laughter and argument floated up to the drawing-room.

'They could say what they want to say. But I know that Baksh coulda win that election easy easy.'

'What I want to know is, who put Harbans in the Council? Committee or the people?'

'No, man. Is not *one* case of whisky. Is twelve case.'

'Hear what I say. Preacher lose the election the night Cawfee dead. I was backing the man strong, man. Had two dollars on him.'

'That one case under the Union Jack is just a sort of *sign* for all the twelve case.'

'If Cawfee didn't throw up his four foot and dead, you think Harbans coulda win?'

'Yes, twelve case of whisky on one small table wouldn't look nice.'

Then Harbans came.

'Pappa! Eh, but what happen to the old Dodge lorry?'

Harbans had come in a brand-new blue-and-black Jaguar.

'Lorry! What happen to Harbans?'

He wasn't the candidate they knew. Gone was the informality of dress, the loose trousers, the tie around the waist, the open shirt. He was in a double-breasted grey suit. The coat was a little too wide and a little too long; but that was the tailor's fault. Harbans didn't wave. He looked preoccupied, kept his eye on the ground, and when he hawked and spat in the gutter, pulled out an ironed handkerchief and wiped his lips—not wiped even, patted them—in the fussiest way.

The people of Elvira were hurt.

He didn't coo at anybody, didn't look at anybody. He made his way silently through the silent crowd and went straight up the steps into Chittaranjan's drawing-room. The crowd watched him go up and then they heard him talking and they heard Ramlogan talking and laughing.

They didn't like it at all.

Presently the committee appeared on the veranda. Foam looked down and waved. Mahadeo looked down and waved. Harbans didn't look down; Chittaranjan didn't look down; and Ramlogan, for a man who had just been heard laughing loudly, looked ridiculously solemn.

The walk down the polished red stairs became a grave procession. Foam and Mahadeo, at the back, had to clip their steps.

'Tock. Tock. Tock,' Harichand said. *'Pai! Pai! Pai!* Tocktock-tocktocktock.'

The crowd laughed. Tiger barked.

Chittaranjan frowned for silence, and got it.

Harbans looked down at his shoes all the time, looking as miserable as if he had lost the election. Ramlogan would have liked to match Harbans's dignity, but he wanted to look at the crowd, and whenever he looked at the crowd he found it hard not to smile.

The chairs and benches had been disarrayed. The crowd had spread out into the road and formed a solid semicircle around the case of whisky draped with the Union Jack.

Harbans sat directly in front of the whisky. Ramlogan was on his right, Chittaranjan on his left. Foam was next to Ramlogan, Mahadeo next to Chittaranjan. Not far from Foam, on his right, Haq and Sebastian sat.

As soon as the committee had settled down a man ran out from the crowd and whispered to Harbans.

It was Baksh.

He whispered, urgently, 'Jordan can't come tonight. He sick.'

The word aroused bitter memories.

'Jordan?' Harbans whispered.

'Sick?' Mahadeo said.

Baksh ran back, on tiptoe, to the crowd.

Sebastian looked on smiling. Haq sucked his teeth and spat.

Chittaranjan stood up. 'Ladies and gentlemen'—there were no ladies present—'tonight Mr Harbans come back to Elvira, and we glad to welcome him again. Mr Harbans is a good friend. And Mr Harbans could see, by just looking at the amount of people it have here tonight, how much all-you think of him in Elvira.'

Harbans was whispering to Ramlogan, 'Jordan sick? Who is Jordan? He fall sick too late.'

Ramlogan roared, for the audience.

Chittaranjan shot him a look and went on, 'I want to see the man who could come up to me and tell me to my face that is only because Mr Harbans win a election that everybody come to see him. I know, speaking in my own pussonal, that even if Mr Harbans *didn't* win *no* election, Mr Harbans woulda *want* to come back to Elvira, and all-you woulda *want* to come and see him.'

There was some polite clapping.

'And so, ladies and gentlemen, without further ado, let me introduce Mr Foreman Baksh.'

Foam said, 'Ladies and gentlemen, it nice to see so much of all-you here. Tonight Mr Ramlogan'—he nodded towards Ramlogan, but Ramlogan was too busy talking to Harbans to notice—'Mr Ramlogan going to present a case of whisky to the committee. The committee, ladies and gentlemen, of which I am proud and happy to be a member. Ladies and gentlemen, times changing. People do the voting, is true. But is the committee that do the organizing. In this modern world, you can't get nowhere if you don't organize. And now let me introduce Mr Mahadeo.'

Foam's references to the whisky and the committee caused so much buzzing that Mahadeo couldn't begin.

Baksh used the interval to run forward again.

'Don't forget,' he whispered to Harbans. 'Jordan ain't here. He sick.'

Chittaranjan stood up and said sternly, 'Ladies and gentlemen, Mr Mahadeo want to say a few words.'

Mahadeo said, 'Well, all-you must remember . . .'

Chittaranjan pulled at Mahadeo's trousers.

Mahadeo broke off, confused, 'I sorry, Goldsmith.' He coughed. 'Ladies and gentlemen.' He swallowed. 'Ladies and gentlemen, Mr Harbans ain't have nothing to do with the whisky. I ain't really know how the rumour get around, but this case of whisky'—he patted the Union Jack—'is for the committee, of which I am proud and happy to be a member. The whisky ain't for nobody else. Is not Mr Harbans whisky. Is Mr Ramlogan whisky.'

The buzzing rose again.

Mahadeo looked at Ramlogan. 'Ain't is your whisky, Mr Ramlogan?'

Ramlogan stood up and straightened his striped blue jacket. 'Ladies and gentlemen, what Mr Mahadeo say is the gospel truth, as the saying goes. Is my whisky. Is my idea.' He sat down and immediately began to talk to Harbans again.

The murmurings of the crowd couldn't be ignored. Mahadeo remained standing, not saying anything.

Rampiari's husband, bandageless, came out from the crowd. 'Wasn't what *we* hear. We didn't hear nothing about no whisky for no committee. And I think I must say right here and now that Elvira people ain't liking this bacchanal at all. Look at these poor people! They come from all over the place. You think a man go put on his clothes, take up his good good self and walk from Cordoba to Elvira in the night-time with all this dew falling, just to see committee get a case of whisky?'

Harichand said, 'Everybody think they could kick poor people around. Let them take back their whisky. The people of Elvira ain't got their tongue hanging out like dog for nobody whisky, you hear. The people of Elvira still got their pride. Take back the damn whisky, man!'

The people of Elvira cheered Harichand.

Ramlogan stopped talking to Harbans. Harbans's hands were tapping on his knees.

Mahadeo, still standing, saying nothing, saw the crowd break up into agitated groups. He sat down.

Ramlogan didn't smile when he looked at the crowd.

Suddenly he sprang up and said, 'I have a damn good mind to mash up the whole blasted case of whisky.' He grabbed the case and the Union Jack slipped off. 'Go ahead. Provoke me. See if I don't throw it down.'

The silence was abrupt.

Ramlogan scowled, the case of whisky in his hands.

Rampiari's husband walked up to him and said amiably, 'Throw it down.'

The crowd chanted, '*Throw it down! Throw it down!*' Tiger barked.

Chittaranjan said, 'Sit down, bruds.'

Ramlogan replaced the case of whisky and picked up the Union Jack.

Baksh ran to Harbans. He didn't whisper this time. 'Don't say I didn't tell you. Jordan sick. Remember that.'

Harbans was puzzled.

'Why Jordan sick?' he asked Ramlogan.

Ramlogan didn't laugh.

The crowd became one again. Harichand and Rampiari's husband came to the front.

Harichand said, 'Mr Harbans, I think I should tell you that the people of Elvira not going to take this insult lying down. They work hard for you, they waste their good good time and they go and mark X on ballot-paper for your sake.'

Rampiari's husband tightened his broad leather belt. 'They putting money in your pocket, Mr Harbans. Five years' regular pay. And the committee get pay for what they do. But look at these poor people. You drag them out from Cordoba and Ravine Road and Pueblo Road. I can't hold back the people, Mr Harbans.'

Harbans yielded. He rose, held his hands together, cracked his fingers, shifted his gaze from his feet to his hands and said, cooing like the old Harbans, 'The good people of Elvira work hard for me and I going to give Ramlogan a order to give ten case of whisky to the committee to give you.' It would cost him about four hundred dollars, but it seemed the only way out. He couldn't make a run for his Jaguar. 'Ten case of whisky. Good whisky.' He gave a little coo and showed his false teeth. 'Not White Horse, though. You can't get that every day.'

Almost miraculously, the crowd was appeased. They laughed at Harbans's little joke and chattered happily among themselves.

But Chittaranjan was in the devil of a temper. He was annoyed with the crowd; annoyed with Harbans for giving in so easily to them; annoyed because he knew for sure now that Harbans never had any intention of marrying his son to Nelly; annoyed with Ramlogan for offering the whisky and making so much noise about it.

He jumped up and shouted, 'No!' It was his firm fighting voice. It stilled the crowd. 'You people ain't got no shame at all. Instead of Mr Harbans giving you anything more, you should be giving *him* something, for a change.'

The crowd was taken by surprise.

'Most of you is Hindus. Mr Harbans is a Hindu. He win a election. *You* should be giving him something. You should be saying prayers for him.'

There was a murmur. Not of annoyance, but incomprehension.

'Say a *kattha* for him. Get Pundit Dhaniram to read from the Hindu scriptures.'

The effect was wonderful. Even Rampiari's husband was shamed.

He took off his hat and came a step or two nearer the case of whisky. 'But Goldsmith, a *kattha* going to cost a lot of money.'

'Course it going to cost money!'

Rampiari's husband withdrew.

Harbans got up, cooing. 'Ooh, Goldsmith. If they want to honour me with a *kattha*, we must let them honour me with a *kattha*. Ooh. Tell you what, eh, good people of Elvira. Make a little collection among yourself fust.'

The crowd was too astonished to protest.

Only Haq staggered up and said, 'Why for we should make a collection for a Hindu *kattha?* We is Muslims.'

But no one heard him. Harbans was still speaking: 'Make your collection fust.' He flashed the false teeth again. 'And for every dollar you collect, I go put a dollar, and with the money *all* of we put up, we go have the *kattha*.' Harbans had heard Haq though; so he turned to Foam, as a Muslim, for support 'Eh, Foreman? You don't think is the best idea?'

Foam rose. 'Is the best thing. And I agree with the goldsmith that the people of Elvira should give something to their own Onble Member.'

That really caused the trouble.

Rampiari's husband didn't mind when Chittaranjan had said it. Everyone respected Chittaranjan as an honourable man, and everyone knew that he hadn't got a penny from Harbans. But when Foam said it, that was different.

'Is all right for *you* to talk, Foreman Baksh,' Rampiari's husband said. 'Your pocket full. You get your two hundred dollars a month campaign-managing for Harbans.'

'And your father get a whole loudspeaking van,' Harichand chipped in. 'And everybody in Elvira damn well know that out of the fifty-six votes your father get, your father vote was one.'

Baksh danced to the front of the crowd.

'What loudspeaking van?' he asked.

Chittaranjan was on his feet again. 'And we, the members of the committee, going to give back the case of whisky to Mr Ramlogan.'

This made Mahadeo lose his temper.

'Why? Why for we must give back the case of whisky?'

'And how the hell you know I ain't vote for Harbans, Harichand?'

'The clerk tell me,' Harichand said.

For a moment Baksh was nonplussed. Than he shouted, 'Harbans, if you going to give money for a Hindu *kattha*, you damn well got to give the Muslims a *kitab*.'

Mahadeo said, 'Goldsmith, why for we must give back the whisky?'

'Hush your mouth, you damn fool,' Chittaranjan whispered. 'We not giving it back really.'

Haq had limped right up to the whisky and was saying, 'Muslim vote for Harbans too. What happen? They stop counting Muslim vote these days?'

'All right,' Harbans cooed. 'All you Muslim make your collection for your *kitab*. And for every dollar you put, I go put one. Eh?'

Then somebody else leapt up and asked what about the Christians.

Rampiari's husband shouted, 'Haq, what the hell you doing there? You vote for Harbans?'

'Who I vote for is my business. Nobody ain't make you a policeman yet.'

Then it was chaos. Rampiari's husband switched his attack to Baksh. Baksh was attacking Harbans. Foam was being attacked by innumerable anonymous people. Mahadeo was being attacked by people whose illness he had spurned. Haq was poking questions directly under Harbans's nose. Harbans was saying, 'Ooh, ooh,' and trying to pacify everybody. Only two objects remained immovable and constant: Chittaranjan and the case of whisky.

Somehow, after minutes of tortuous altercation, something was decided. The committee were to give back the case of whisky. The people of Elvira were to get religious consolation. The Muslims were to get their *kitab,* the Hindus their *kattha,* the Christians their service.

But nobody was really pleased.

Ramlogan insisted that Harbans should give him back the case of whisky ceremonially.

Harbans said, "Ladies and gentlemen, was nice of all-you to ask me down here today to give away this whisky. But I can't tell you how happy and proud it make me to see that the committee ain't want it. Committee do their duty, and duty is their reward.'

There was some derisory cheering.

'So, Mr Ramlogan, I give you back your whisky. And I glad to see that at this moment the people of Elvira putting God in their heart.'

Foam said, 'Three cheers for the Onble Surujpat Harbans. Hip-hip.'

He got no response.

Only, Baksh ran up.

'Jordan sick, Mr Harbans.'

'I hope he get better.'

'For the last time, Mr Harbans. Jordan sick.'

The crowd pressed forward silently around the committee.

Harbans buttoned his over-large coat and prepared to leave. He put his hand on the arm of Rampiari's husband, to show that he wasn't cowed. 'Give me a little break. Let me get through.'

Rampiari's husband folded his arms.

'Give me a break, man. Last time I come to Elvira, I telling you. All you people driving me away.'

Rampiari's husband said, 'We know you is a Onble and thing now, but you deaf? You ain't hear what the man saying? Jordan sick.' Rampiari's husband turned his back to Harbans and addressed the crowd. 'All-you see Jordan tonight?'

The reply came in chorus: *'No, we ain't see Jordan.'*

'What happen to Jordan?' Rampiari's husband asked.

'Jordan sick,' the crowd replied.

Harbans looked at Chittaranjan.

Chittaranjan said, 'You better go.'

Jordan lived in one of the many traces off the main road. It was a moonless night and the occasional oil lamps in the houses far back from the trace only made the darkness more terrible. At the heels of Harbans and his committee there was nearly half the crowd that had gathered outside Chittaranjan's shop. Tiger ran yapping in and out of the procession. One horrible young labourer with glasses, gold teeth and a flowerpot hat pushed his face close to Harbans and said, 'Don't worry with the old generation. Is the young generation like me you got to worry about.'

Jordan was waiting for them, reclined on a couch in his front room, a plump sleepy-faced young Negro with a pile of stiff kinky hair. He wore pyjamas that looked suspiciously new. Chittaranjan was surprised. Nobody in Elvira wore pyjamas.

'Jordan,' Harbans called. 'You sick?'

'Yes, man,' Jordan said. 'Stroke. Hit me all down here.' He ran his hand along his left side.

'The man break up bad,' Rampiari's husband said. 'He can't do no more work for a long time to come.'

'It come sudden sudden,' Jordan said. 'I was drinking a cup of water and it come. Bam! just like that.'

An old woman, a young woman and a boy came into the room.

'Mother, wife, brother,' Baksh explained.

'Jordan supporting all of them,' Harichand said.

Chittaranjan regarded Jordan and Jordan's family with contempt. He said, 'Give him ten dollars and let we go.'

'Ten!' Jordan exclaimed acidly. 'Fifty.'

'Fifty at least,' Baksh said.

'At least,' said Rampiari's husband.

'Is not something just for Jordan,' Baksh said. 'You could say is a sort of thank-you present for everybody in Elvira.'

'Exactly,' Harichand said. 'Can't just come to a place and collect people good good vote and walk away. Don't look nice. Don't sound nice.'

Harbans said, 'This election making me a pauper. They should pass some sort of law to prevent candidates spending too much money.' But he pulled out his wallet.

Jordan said, 'God go bless you, boss.'

Harbans took two twenty-dollar notes and one ten-dollar note, crackled them separately and handed them to Jordan.

Without warning Tiger sprang on the couch, trampled over Jordan's new pyjamas, put his front paws on the window-sill and barked.

Almost immediately there was a loud explosion from the main road. Seconds later there were more explosions.

The crowd in the trace shouted, 'Fire!'

Jordan's stroke was forgotten. Everybody scrambled outside, committee, mother, wife, brother. Jordan himself forgot about his stroke and knelt on his couch to look out of the window. In the direction of the main road the sky was bright; the glare teased out houses and trees from the darkness.

Somebody cried, 'Mr Harbans! Goldsmith!'

But Harbans was already in the trace and running, awkwardly, like a woman in a tight skirt.

He found the crowd standing in a wide silent circle around the burning Jaguar. It was a safe spectacle now; the petrol tanks had blown up. The firelight reddened unsmiling, almost contemplative, faces.

Harbans stopped too, to watch the car burn. The fire had done its work swiftly and well, thank to the Jaguar's reserve petrol tank, which Harbans liked to keep full. That was little smoke now; the flames burned pure. Behind the heat waves faces were distorted.

The people from the trace ran up in joyful agitation, flowed around the car, settled, and became silent. Harbans was wedged among them.

Foam acted with firmness.

He beat his way through to Harbans.

'Mr Harbans, come.'

Harbans followed without thinking. They got into the loud-speaker van. It wasn't until Foam drove off that the people of Elvira turned to look. They didn't cheer or boo or do anything. Only Tiger, missing Foam, ran barking after the van.

'Is okay now, Mr Harbans,' Foam said. 'If you did stay you woulda want to start asking questions. If you did start asking questions you woulda only cause more trouble.'

'Elvira, Elvira.' Harbans shook his head and spoke to the back of his hands, covered almost up to the knuckles by the sleeves of his big grey coat. 'Elvira, you is a bitch.'

And he came to Elvira no more.

The Jaguar was less than a week old. The insurance company bought him a new one.

*

It made Lorkhoor's reputation. He was living with the *doolahin* in a dingy furnished room in Henry Street in Port of Spain. He had already applied, without success, for jobs on the *Trinidad Guardian* and the *Port of Spain Gazette* when, on Saturday, the news of the burning Jaguar broke. Lorkhoor took a taxi down to Harichand's printery in Couva and got the facts from Harichand. That, and his own inside knowledge, gave him material for a splendid follow-up story which he submitted to the *Trinidad Sentinel*. It appeared in the Sunday issue. Lorkhoor wrote the headline himself: 'A Case of Whisky, the New Jaguar and the Suffrage of Elvira'. He had fallen under the influence of William Saroyan.

On Monday Lorkhoor was on the staff of the *Sentinel*. He began to contribute a regular Sunday piece for the *Sentinel*'s magazine section, *Lorkhoor's Log*.

*

Foam had his wish. He got Lorkhoor's old job, announcing for the cinemas in Caroni. In addition, he had earned two hundred and twenty-five dollars as Harbans's campaign manager; and he had been able to snub Teacher Francis.

Teacher Francis deteriorated rapidly. In the Christmas holidays he married into one of the best coloured families in Port of Spain, the Smiths. He renounced all intellectual aspirations, won the approval of the Education Department and an appointment as Schools Inspector.

And Ramlogan. He had won his largest rum-account. He could buy that refrigerator now. Now, too, he could pick his own flowers and eat his own breadfruit and zaboca.

And Dhaniram. He had some luck. His brother-in-law died in September, and his sister came to live with him.

And Tiger. He had won a reprieve. He was to live long and querulously.

And Chittaranjan. But he had lost. He sent many messages to Harbans but got no reply. At last he went to see Harbans in Port of Spain; but Harbans kept him waiting so long in the veranda and greeted him so coldly, he couldn't bring himself to ask about the marriage. It was Harbans who brought the point up. Harbans said, 'Chittaranjan, the Hindus in Trinidad going downhill fast. I say, let those who want to go, go quick. If only one hundred good Hindu families remain, well, all right. But we can't let our children marry people who does run about late at night with Muslim boys.' Chittaranjan accepted the justice of the argument. And that was that.

But if Chittaranjan had lost, Nelly had won. In September of that year she went to London and joined the Regent Street Polytechnic. She went to all the dances and enjoyed them. She sent home presents that Christmas, an umbrella for her father, and a set of four china birds for her mother. The birds flew on the wall next to the picture of Mahatma Gandhi and King George V. The umbrella became part of Chittaranjan's visiting outfit.

*

So, Harbans won the election and the insurance company lost a Jaguar. Chittaranjan lost a son-in-law and Dhaniram lost a daughter-in-law. Elvira lost Lorkhoor and Lorkhoor won a reputation. Elvira lost Mr Cuffy. And Preacher lost his deposit.

Mr Stone and the

Knights Companion

I

It was Thursday, Miss Millington's afternoon off, and Mr Stone had to let himself in. Before he could switch on the hall light, the depthless green eyes held him, and in an instant the creature, eyes alone, leapt down the steps. Mr Stone cowered against the dusty wall and shielded his head with his briefcase. The cat brushed against his legs and was out through the still open door. Mr Stone stood where he was, the latchkey in one ungloved hand, and waited for the beating of his heart, the radiation of fine pain through his body, to subside.

The cat belonged to the family next door, people who had moved into the street just five years before and were still viewed by Mr Stone with suspicion. It had come to the house as a kitten, a pet for the children; and as soon as, ceasing to chase paper and ping-pong balls and balls of string, it began to dig up Mr Stone's garden, its owners having no garden worth digging up, Mr Stone had transferred his hostility from the family to their cat. When he returned from the office he examined his flowerbeds—strips of earth between irregular areas of crazy paving—for signs of the animal's obscene scuttlings and dredgings and buryings. 'Miss Millington! Miss Millington!' he would call. 'The cat pepper!' And heavy old Miss Millington, aproned down to her ankles, would shuffle out with a large tin of pepper dust (originally small tins had been thought sufficient: the picture of the terrified cat on the label looked so convincing) and would ritually sprinkle all the flowerbeds, the affected one more than the others, as though to obscure rather than prevent the animal's activities. In time the flowerbeds had become discoloured; it was as if

[223]

cement had been mixed with the earth and dusted on to the leaves and stems of plants.

Now the cat had penetrated into the house itself.

The beating of Mr Stone's heart moderated and the shooting pain receded, leaving a trail of exposed nerves, a lightness of body below the heavy Simpson's overcoat, and an urge to decisive action. Not closing the front door, turning on no lights, not taking off his overcoat or hat, depositing only his gloves and briefcase on the hall table, he went to the kitchen, where in darkness he opened the larder door and took out the cheese, still in its Sainsbury wrapping, from its accustomed place—Miss Millington shopped on Thursday mornings. He found a knife and carefully, as though preparing cocktail savouries, chopped the cheese into small cubes. These he took outside, to the front gate; and glancing about him in the sodden murk—some windows alight, no observer about—he laid a trail of cheese from gate to door, up the dark carpeted hall, now bitterly cold, and up the steps to the bathroom. Here, sitting on the cover of the lavatory bowl, still in his hat and overcoat, he waited, poker in hand. The poker was not for attack but self-defense. Often, walking down that cat-infested street, he had been surprised by a cat sitting sedately on a fence post at the level of his head, and he had always made as if to shield his face. It was a disgraceful action, but one he could never control. He feared the creatures; and there were all those stories of cornered cats, of cats growing wild and attacking men.

The damp air filled the hall and invaded the bathroom. The darkness and the silence emphasized the cold. He had visions of dipping the cat's paws in boiling oil, of swinging the creature by its tail and flinging it down to the pavement below, of scalding it in boiling water. He got up from the lavatory seat and turned on the geyser. Instant hot water! The water ran cold, then after the *whoomph!* as the jets caught, lukewarm, then at last warm. The geyser needed cleaning; he must remind Miss Millington. He filled the basin and sat down again on the lavatory bowl. The water-pipes ceased to hum; silence returned.

Some minutes later, five, perhaps ten, he remembered. It was rats that ate cheese. Cats ate other things. He put on lights everywhere, closed the front door, and turned on fires.

The cheese he forgot. It was a pleasurably agitated Miss Millington who reported the next morning on the disappearance of her cheese from the larder, and its conversion into cubes laid in a wavering line from gate to bathroom. He offered no explanation.

*

This incident, which might be said to have led to his undoing, did not arise out of Mr Stone's passion for gardens. Gardening as he practised it was no more than a means, well suited to his age, which was sixty-two, of exhausting the spare time and energy with which his undemanding duties in one of the departments of the Excal company, his status as a bachelor and his still excellent physique amply provided him. The habit had come late to him. He relished the activity rather than the results. It mattered little to him that his blooms were discoloured by pepper dust. His delight lay more in preparing the ground for planting than in the planting, which sometimes never occurred. Once his passion had been all for digging. When this came to an end—after he had punctured a water main—he decided to hoard his refuse, to spare none for the local council. Strict instructions were given to Miss Millington; and the refuse of his household, dutifully presented by her for his daily inspection, he spread afternoon after afternoon, with a miser's delight in its accumulation, over the front garden. The following year he planted grass; but so ferociously did he mow the tender shoots—with a mower bought for the purpose—that before the end of the spring what he had thought of as his lawn had been torn to bare and ragged earth. It was after this that he had covered most of the garden with crazy paving, which proved to be a great absorber of moisture, so that even in a moderate summer his plants wilted as in a drought.

Still he persevered, finding in his activity a contented solitude and opportunity for long periods of unbroken reflection. And the

incident of that evening could be said to have arisen out of his solitude, the return to a house he knew to be empty. It was in the empty
house, on these occasions of Miss Millington's absence, that he found
himself prey to fancies which he knew to be grotesque but which he
ceaselessly indulged. He thought of moving pavements: he saw himself, overcoated and with his briefcase, standing on his private moving strip and gliding along, while walkers on either side looked in
amazement. He thought of canopied streets for winter, the pavements perhaps heated by that Roman system he had seen at Bath.
One fantasy was persistent. He was able to fly. He ignored traffic
lights; he flew from pavement to pavement over people and cars and
buses (the people flown over looking up in wonder while he floated
serenely past, indifferent to their stupefaction). Seated in his armchair, he flew up and down the corridors of his office. His imagination had people behave exaggeratedly. The dour Evans trembled and
stammered; Keenan's decadent spectacles fell off his face; wickedly
giving Miss Menzies a wig, he had that jump off her head. Everywhere there was turmoil, while he calmly went about his business,
which completed, he as calmly flew away again.

Miss Millington, returning on Friday mornings, sometimes
found the fruit of her master's solitude: a rough toy house, it might
be, painstakingly made from a loaf of bread which, bought on
Thursday morning, was on Thursday evening still new and capable
of easy modelling; the silver paper from a packet of cigarettes being
flattened by every large book in the house, the pile rising so high that
it was clear that the delicately balanced structure had in the end
become her master's concern; objects left for her inspection, admiration and eventual dismantling, but which by an unspoken agreement
of long standing neither he nor she mentioned.

That she should mention the cheese was unusual. But so was the
incident, which was, moreover, not to be buried like the others. For
how often, by a person still to him unknown, was the incident of
that Thursday evening to be repeated in his presence, as a funny,
endearing story, to which he would always listen with a smile of self-

satisfaction, though on the evening itself, in the cold darkness of the empty house, he had acted throughout with the utmost seriousness and, even on the discovery that cats did not eat cheese, had found nothing absurd in the situation.

*

Exactly one week later, on the twenty-first of December, Mr Stone went, as he did every year at this time, to the Tomlinsons' dinner party. He had been to teacher training college with Tony Tomlinson, and though their paths had since diverged, their friendship was thus annually renewed. Tomlinson had remained in education and was a figure of some importance in his local council. From initialing the printed or duplicated signatures of others he had risen to having other people initial his, which was now always followed by the letters T.D. On their first appearance these letters had led Mr Stone to suggest at one of these annual dinner parties that Tomlinson had become either a teacher of divinity or a doctor of theology; but the joke was not repeated the following year, for Tomlinson took his Territorial Decoration seriously.

According to Tomlinson, Mr Stone had 'gone into industry'. And it was also Tomlinson who designated Mr Stone as 'head librarian'. 'Richard Stone,' he would say. 'An old college friend. Head librarian with Excal.' The 'with' was tactful; it concealed the unimportant department of the company Mr Stone worked for. The title appealed to Mr Stone and he began using it in his official correspondence, fearfully at first, and then, encountering no opposition from the company or the department (which was in fact delighted, for the words lent a dignity to their operations), with conviction. And so, though Tomlinson's dinners had increased in severity and grandeur with the years, Mr Stone continued to be invited. To Tomlinson his presence was a pole and a comfort, a point of rest; more, it was a proof of Tomlinson's loyalty; it acknowledged, at the same time, that their present exalted positions made respectable a past which might otherwise have encouraged speculation.

The guest of honour changed from year to year, and Tomlinson in his telephone invitation always reminded Mr Stone that if he came he might make a few useful contacts. It seemed to Mr Stone that both he and Tomlinson were past the time for useful contacts. But Tomlinson, in spite of his age and an advancement which must have exceeded all his hopes, was still restless with ambition, and it amused Mr Stone to see him 'in action'. It was easy at these dinners to distinguish the 'contact'. Tomlinson stuck close to him, in his presence looked pained, sometimes distracted, as though awaiting punishment or as though, having cornered his contact, he didn't know quite what to do with him; and he spoke little, contenting himself with asking questions that required no answer or with repeating the last three or four words of the contact's sentences.

But when Mr Stone went to the dinner this year, he found that Tomlinson's word about the contact had been only a matter of habit; that there was no one to whom Tomlinson stuck close and whose words he echoed; and that the centre of attention, the leader of talk, was Mrs Springer.

Mrs Springer was over fifty, striking in her garnets, a dark red dress of watered silk, cut low, the skirt draped, and a well-preserved gold-embroidered Kashmir shawl. Her manner went contrary to her dress; it was not a masculinity she attempted, so much as an arch and studied unfemininity. Her deep voice recalled that of a celebrated actress, as did her delivery. Whenever she wished to make a telling point she jerked herself upright from the waist; and at the end of one of her little speeches she subsided as abruptly, her knees slightly apart, her bony hand falling into the sink of the skirt thus created. So that the old-fashioned jewellery and the dress, which, though of irreproachable cut, appeared to accommodate rather than fit her body, seemed quite distinct from the personality of the wearer.

She had already established herself as a wit when Mr Stone arrived. There were smiles as soon as she began to speak, and Grace Tomlinson appeared to be acting as cheer-leader. What Tomlinson did for the 'contact' in previous years, Grace was now doing for Mrs Springer who, Mr Stone learned, was her friend.

They were talking about flowers. Someone had expressed admiration for Grace's floral decorations (which, with her corsage and her dinner-party arrangements, were the result of a brief course at the Constance Spry school in St John's Wood).

'The only flower I care about,' Mrs Springer said, cutting across the muttered approvals, 'is the cauliflower.'

Grace laughed, everyone laughed encouragingly, and Mrs Springer, subsiding into her seat and seeming to rock, within her dress, on her bottom, widened her knees and briskly rearranged her skirt into the valley, a crooked smile playing about her face, emphasizing the squareness of her jaws.

So, destroying silences, hesitations, obliterating mumblings, she held them all.

The talk turned to shows lately seen. Up to this time, apart from an occasional loud *Mmm,* which could have meant anything, Tomlinson had been silent, his long thin face more pained, his eyes more worried than usual, as though without his contact he was lost. But now he sought to raise the discussion, which had already declined into an exchange of titles, to a more suitable intellectual level; this was acknowledged as his prerogative and duty. He had been, he said, to *Rififi,* had gone, as a matter of fact, on the recommendation of a person of importance.

'Extraordinary film,' he said slowly, losing nothing of his suffering appearance, looking at none of them, fixing his eyes on some point in space as though drawing thoughts and words out of that point. 'French, of course. Some things these French films do extremely well. Most extraordinary. Almost no dialogue. Gives it quite an impact, I must say. No dialogue.'

'I for one would be grateful,' Mrs Springer said, tearing into Tomlinson's reflections, which he at once abandoned, looking a little relieved. 'I hate these subtitles. I always feel I'm missing all the naughty bits. You see people waving their hands and jabbering away. Then you look at the subtitles and all you see is. "Yes".' She spoke some gibberish to convey the idea of a foreign language and garrulousness. 'Then you look and you see "No".'

The observation struck Mr Stone as deliciously funny and accurate. It corresponded so exactly to his own experience. He longed to say, 'Yes, yes, *I*'ve felt like that.' But then Grace was offering sherry again and, infected by the witty mood, said when she filled Mrs Springer's glass, 'Especially for you, Margaret. Untouched by hand.'

Mrs Springer jerked herself up again. 'When you hear that anything is untouched by hand,' she said, 'you can be pretty sure it has been touched by foot.' And she took her glass to her lips, as though about to drain it.

Mr Stone sat speechless with admiration. When his own glass was being refilled he was emboldened to try one of the office jokes.

'I see,' he said, 'that you are anxious to get me under the affluence of incohol.'

There was no response. Tomlinson looked distressed, Grace pretended not to hear, Mrs Springer didn't hear. Mr Stone put his glass to his lips and sipped long and slowly. The joke wasn't even his own; it was one of Keenan's, of Accounts. People in the office pretended to groan when Keenan said it—that ought to have warned him—but Mr Stone had always thought it extremely funny. He knew that puns were in bad taste, though he didn't know exactly why. He resolved to be silent, and his resolve was strengthened when, as they were getting ready to go to the dining-room, Grace informed him, with a touch of reproof, that Mrs Springer was in fact in profound mourning, having not long before buried her second husband. This then explained Grace's solicitude, and the licence Mrs Springer appeared to enjoy. It also invested Mrs Springer with a glamour over and above her own brilliance, a glamour of which she appeared not unaware.

So far Mrs Springer had taken little notice of Mr Stone, and at dinner they were far apart, each barely perceptible to the other, in the candle-lit gloom, through the candles and flowers and the innumerable novelties in carved wood, manger scenes, pine trees, tarnished relics of an Austrian holiday which the Tomlinsons had managed to turn into their traditional decorations. On two small tables in the outer circle of gloom there were those Christmas cards, selected from the cards of more than a decade, which Grace said she couldn't bear to throw away. They were either very large or very ornate, one or two edged with lace; and every year they were thus taken out and displayed. It was this display which now held the attention of the table, of Mrs Springer and Mr Stone. And indeed for him it was a pleasure and a reassurance to enter this festive room after twelve months, to find himself in the same atmosphere and to see the same decorations.

It wasn't until after dinner, when the men joined the ladies, that Mrs Springer spoke directly to Mr Stone.

'Here,' she said flirtatiously, patting the seat beside her. 'You sit next to me.'

He did as she asked. No subject of conversation immediately presented itself, and he noticed that she had the appearance, as he had seen three or four times that evening, of someone lost in thought or of someone thinking of something to say. And before the silence became embarrassing she had spoken.

'Do you,' she asked, turning upon him with that suddenness he had begun to associate with her, 'like cats?'

'Cats,' he said. 'Well, I suppose it depends. This thing happened the other day. Just last week, as a matter of fact——'

'I think all these animal lovers talk'——she paused, and a mischievous light came into her eyes, as it did whenever she was about to use an improper word (she had already used bitch and bloody)——'a lot of rubbish.' She spoke these last words with a curious emphasis, as though they were in themselves witty; she made them sound like *a lotta rubbish*.

'This one attacked me the other day,' Mr Stone said. 'Attacked——'

'I'm not surprised. They're creatures of the jungle.'

'Jumped down the steps at me as soon as I opened the door. Gave me quite a fright, really. And then——it's very funny, really . . .'

He paused, not sure whether to go on. But encouragement was in her eyes. And he told the story. He told it all. He caricatured himself, finding in this a delight long forgotten. He described, with gruesome elaboration, his visions of boiling the cat in oil or water; he mentioned the turning on of the geyser, the filling of the sink, the sitting on the lavatory seat with the poker in his hand. And he held her! She listened; she was silent.

'Cheese,' she said at the end. 'You foolish man! Cheese! I must tell Grace about this.'

She made the story her own. She told it slowly and told it well. He noted her additions and ornamentations with pleasure and gratitude; and while she spoke, sitting forward and upright, he leaned back on the sofa, his broad shoulders rounded, looking down at his lap, smiling, cracking walnuts, looking up from time to time when there were exclamations, his eyes bright and gentle below his high, projecting forehead.

Thereafter she possessed him. She brought him into all her conversations. 'Cheese, Mr Stone?' she would say. Or, 'Mr Stone prefers cheese, though.' And the word always raised a laugh.

It was for him a new sensation; he luxuriated in it. And when towards the end of the evening, after the musical interlude, they again found themselves sitting side by side, and Mrs Springer said, 'Have you noticed how these walnuts look like brains?' he felt confident enough to say, loudly, 'I imagine that's why they're called nuts.'

The words hushed the room. Someone handling the crackers hesitated; then in the silence came the involuntary cracking of the nut.

'*I* think that's very funny,' Mrs Springer said.

But even she was too late to give the lead.

He left the house feeling unhappy, disgraced, dissatisfied. He was overcome by a sense of waste and futility and despair.

*

Mr Stone liked to think in numbers. He liked to think, 'I have been with Excal for thirty years.' He liked to think, 'I have been living in this house for twenty-four years.' He liked to think of the steady rise of his salary, since he had gone into industry, to its present £1,000 a year; and he liked to think that by earning this sum he was in the top five per cent of the country's wage-earners (he had read this fact somewhere, possibly in the *Evening Standard*). He liked to think he had known Tomlinson for forty-four years. And though it was an occasion of grief—the sharpest he had known—he liked to think that it was forty-five years since his mother had died.

His life, since his recovery from that disturbance, he saw as a period of protracted calm which, by reference to what had gone before, he had never ceased to savour in his special way. Life was something to be moved through. Experiences were not to be enjoyed at the actual moment; pleasure in them came only when they had been, as it were, docketed and put away in the file of the past, when they had become part of his 'life', his 'experience', his career. It was only then that they acquired colour, just as colour came truly to Nature only in a coloured snapshot or a painting, which annihilated colourless, distorting space. He was in the habit in odd moments of solitude of writing out neatly tabulated accounts of his career such as might have been submitted to a prospective employer; and it always was a marvel to him that the years had gone on, had rolled by so smoothly, that in spite of setbacks and alarms his life had arranged itself with a neatness and order of which the boy of seventeen had never dreamed.

Cherishing the past in this way, he cherished his appearance. He was a big man, well-made; his clothes sat well on him. The performance of a habitual action he never rushed, whether it was the putting on of a coat or the unfolding of a paper after dinner. For these two reasons he looked older than he was: there was about him the not excessive but always noticeable tidiness of the very old who are yet able to look after themselves. And he cultivated his habits. He shaved the right side of his face first; he put on his right shoe first. He was strict about his food, observing the régime he had laid down for himself as punctiliously as if it had been ordered by a trusted doctor. He read the first page and no more of the *Telegraph* at breakfast; the rest he went through at the office. He bought two evening newspapers, the *News* and the *Standard*, from a particular vendor at Victoria; without glancing at them he folded them and put them in his briefcase; they were not to be read on the train (he mentally derided those who did so), but were to be read at leisure after dinner, the news to be savoured not as news, for he instantly forgot most of what he read, but as part of a *newspaper*, something which day by day produced itself for his benefit during this after-dinner period, an insulation against the world out of which it arose.

The present was flavourless; its passing was not therefore a cause for alarm. There was a tree in the school grounds at the back of his house by which he noted the passing of time, the waxing and waning of the seasons, a tree which daily when shaving he studied, until he had known its every branch. The contemplation of this living object reassured him of the solidity of things. He had grown to regard it as part of his own life, a marker of his past, for it moved through time with him. The new leaves of spring, the hard green of summer, the naked black branches of winter, none of these things spoke of the running out of his life. They were only a reminder of the even flowing of time, of his mounting experience, his lengthening past.

All around him were such reminders of solidity, continuity and flow. There were the Christmas decorations of the Tomlinsons, each year more tarnished. In the office Miss Menzies, his assistant (over whom he was 'head librarian': the department now had no librarian proper), had exactly eighteen 'business' outfits, a variety and number that had at first stupefied him, unused though he was to noticing women's clothes, but a number which in the end had formed part of the soothing pattern of his existence. Individual outfits faded and were replaced, but the number remained constant, one outfit for each day of the week until three weeks had passed and the cycle began again. In time he had grown to recognize the days of the week from these outfits. Their passing away, their conversion into rough clothes (impossible, though, to imagine Miss Menzies in rough clothes, and uncorseted), their disintegration, as he imagined, into dusters, were like the shedding of the leaves of his tree; her new garments were like the leaves of spring.

And at home, Miss Millington. Every Thursday afternoon the old soul went to the cinema to the cheap show for pensioners; and she continued to do so even after he had bought a television set. He suspected that she slept through the films, and it always gave him pleasure on Friday morning to have her say the fiery or romantic titles. 'What was the film you saw yesterday, Miss Millington?' '*To Hell and Back*, sir,' she would say, no expression on her square, pallid face, her hoarse, indistinct voice making him think of a gasping fish.

Now, this Friday morning, shaving in the cold bathroom, he saw through the window, just beginning to stream, the familiar winter view. Beyond the bare tree were the sodden, smoking grounds of the girls' school. This portion of it, removed from the buildings and the tennis courts, was much used in summer by the very young pupils, creatures who took a delight in the feel of their companions' bodies and always in their games contrived to come together in little heaps; but now in winter it was empty except on some mornings for a hard-calved games mistress and her red-legged band. Beyond the school grounds were the backs of the two houses of people he didn't know and had mentally christened The Male (a small stringy man with a large family) and The Monster (an enormously fat woman who hibernated in winter and in the spring tripped out daintily among her flowers in what looked like a gym slip, wielding a watering can like a choric figure). The Male was always hanging out of windows, painting, sawing, hammering, running up tall ladders, making improvements to his nest. Mr Stone watched him whenever he could, hoping he would one day fall. Such frenzied home-making he detested almost as much as the sight of the men of the street cleaning their cars on a Sunday morning. He took pleasure instead in the slow decay of his own house, the time-created shabbiness of its interiors, the hard polish of old grime on the lower areas of the hall wallpaper, feeling it right that objects like houses should age with their owners and carry marks of their habitation.

But this morning the familiarity of the scene did not soothe him. He felt only a faint unease, whose origin he couldn't place and which, persisting, gave him a twinge of alarm, for it seemed that all the ordered world was threatened.

Miss Millington was downstairs, heavy, slow, too old for work, too helpless to retire, her face unhealthily pale and puffy, the small eyes watering and sleepy. Her long white apron hung over her shiny black skirt which reached down to her swollen ankles.

'What was the film you saw yesterday, Miss Millington?'

'*A Night to Remember*, sir. It was a very good film, sir. About the *Titanic*.' One of the rare comments she had volunteered on films she hadn't slept through, the *Titanic* still for her a disaster over-riding those of two wars.

In the neat tabulations of his life he had taken Miss Millington into account: she had been with him for twenty-eight years. That she must one day die had occurred to him, but it was not a thought that stayed with him for long. This morning, probing his unease, he persuaded himself, as he had never done before, that the woman before him, slowed down by age and by flesh which was bulky but not robust, was soon to die. And at once everything about the morning ritual, even as it happened, seemed to belong to the past. It was not an event which was attaching itself to his hoard of experience, but something to which he was saying good-bye.

This was a fancy, foolish as he knew most of his fancies to be. But it refused to be dispelled.

He folded the *Telegraph*, running his thumb-nail down the folds, and inserted it into his leather briefcase, which was dark in patches and shining in others, ageing well, like its owner. (He had had it for twenty-two years, and resented as an affront and a piece of trickery the advertisement he saw in the train about men 'like you' needing a new *leather* briefcase.) Then, with the putting on of the heavy Simpson's overcoat and his bowler, he was ready.

It was a time of year when routine was everywhere broken, the streets impossible, when for a whole week life was dislocated, Christmas week, with little work done, for the lonely and the unhappy tedious days to be lived through until the holidays were over and routine returned. Miss Menzies was in an outfit he recognized; she was as plumply corseted, as powdered and perfumed, as high-heeled and brisk, as 'business'-like as ever; even on this morning she managed to look occupied, though there was little to do. A letter from Sir Harry, the head of Excal, to *The Times* had to be attended to. This letter was in Sir Harry's finest vein of irony; he criticized the sluggishness of the shops in not having any Easter goods, and complained of his difficulty in making his Easter purchases because of the crowds of Christmas shoppers. The letter was a tailpiece to the correspondence he had initiated in late September, under the heading, 'The Antipodean Advance of Christmas'. A request from one of the department's 'writers' unearthed yet another of those folders which Miss Menzies's male predecessor, appointed shortly after the end of the war, had so woefully mismanaged. The man was barely literate; his idea of filing a magazine article was to tear the pages out and staple them at the top, so that consecutive reading was as difficult as it was infuriating. (In an unusual burst of anger and energy, Mr Stone had managed to have the man degraded to Stores, in the basement; and from the basement, as well as from the dingy restaurant of the nearby LCC cookery school where some of the staff had lunch for a few ill-spent pence, the man had for many years afterwards issued warnings about the imminent collapse of the department's filing system.) After the folder had been put right, there was nothing more to do. The pub, where Mr Stone went for his lunchtime glass of Guinness, was unbearably hot and overcrowded. The glasses, hastily dipped in water, were not clean. He stood in the open doorway, drinking the drink he could not relish, struggling with the new sensation of threat which he could not subdue and which was nagging him at last into an awareness of his own acute unhappiness, standing at the edge of the boisterous, beery crowd.

Shuffling that evening with the damp, steaming queue into the Underground station, to get a train to Victoria, his attention was caught by a London Transport poster. It was a new one, and had possibly been released for this midwinter's day.

In these dark damp days it is hard for us, daily pacing city pavements, to believe that winter is on the wane, that the days steadily lengthen. Below the frozen earth, however, and in the stripped black trees, life goes on. A trip to London's countryside, where the winter-dun wrapping of buds conceals all the season's muted preparation, will reassure those who doubt the coming of Spring.

Those who doubt the coming of Spring: the words magnified and gave a focus to his uneasiness. They recalled a moment—then, memory and fear quickening, he saw that they recalled several moments, which had multiplied during the last year—of unease, unsettlement: a fleeting scene in a film, a remark in the office, an item in the newspaper, one of his stray thoughts: moments he had thought buried, for they formed no part of the pattern of his life, but which now, through all the mechanical actions and unseen sights of the familiar journey home, rose revivified, one after the other, to be examined, discarded, taken up again.

And on this day of upset and disorder something else occurred which sent him scuttling home to Miss Millington in what was almost fear.

He was walking down the High Road. It was dark, the pavements in a cold sweat of mud. He was passing the dimly-lit entrance of the public library when just for a moment he saw a woman standing with a boy on the steps. Just for a moment he saw, and looked away in horror. The boy had fangs instead of teeth. And in the attitude of the woman there was all the lonely solicitude of a mother for her deformed child. A boy, with limbs like other boys! He thought of rats that must nibble to keep their teeth from transfixing their brains. He was unwilling to believe what he had just seen. He dared not look back. He carried the picture with him: the foolish face, the yellow fangs: the impulses of growth turned sour and virulent.

Seconds later he passed the well-known shop, its windows lighted and streaming. He stopped, breathed deeply, a theatrical gesture, and closed his eyes.

An old man, neat with overcoat, briefcase and hat, standing before the window of the joke-shop, seeming to smile at the imitation glasses of Guinness, the plastic faeces, the masks, the rubber spiders, the joke teeth.

*

Abandoning the garden to the cat, Miss Millington to her relations (he believed she had a number of grandnieces for whom during the Thursday morning shopping she sometimes bought little gifts of sweets), and abandoning the few worn Christmas decorations which Miss Millington put up every year in the hall, the dining-room and a little way up the stairs, decorations which suggested the end rather than the beginning of a festival and which neither of them stayed to enjoy on the day, Mr Stone went to Banstead, to his widowed sister, a former schoolteacher, with whom he always spent Christmas.

He believed that his absence in Banstead over the Christmas holidays was a secret, and he did his best to keep it so. In spite of the notices on the board in front of the police station, in spite of the leaflets and advertisements, he never informed the police, for it was his conviction that they were in league with the thieves of the neighbourhood. Burglars were always on his mind when he went to visit his sister. She was harassed by them, and a good deal of her conversation was about burglaries, abortive or successful, and measures against burglaries. Her fear of burglars was one of the reasons she gave for her frequent moves. In twelve years she had moved from Balham to Brixton to Croydon to Sutton to Banstead, each move taking her farther out of the city, and though she was always up to the last minute full of plans for each house, her houses had an unfinished look, which Mr Stone could not help contrasting with the appearance of his own.

But it was always a pleasure to go to Olive's. Between Mr Stone and his sister there existed a relationship which had scarcely changed since childhood. The female attentions, over and above those provided by Miss Millington, of which he occasionally felt the need, were supplied by Olive during their brief visits to each other. And he was the man whose opinions she quoted, whose habits she studied and humoured and built stories around, whose occasional jokes she passed off as her own. The relationship had suffered during the war when suddenly, at the age of thirty-seven, Olive had married. Less than a year later Olive's husband died, and shortly afterwards Gwen was born. The relationship survived, though the birth of Gwen brought into it an element of falsity, for Mr Stone did not greatly care for children and did not care at all for Gwen. But for Olive he had grown to care more. The events of that year had marked her. Her hair went grey. Her fine teeth were destroyed; her lips, adapting themselves to their protective function, lost their shape and still after all these years suggested vulnerable gums and exposed nerves. Spittle gathered at the corners of her mouth when she spoke; her speech became slower and was sometimes slurred.

Mr Stone had, however, tried with Gwen. He knew, having heard and read it often enough, that children were like dogs: they 'knew' when adults or 'grown-ups', a word he had had to add to his vocabulary, didn't like them. He knew that the handling of children required a rare skill which was compounded of simplicity and complete honesty. And he knew that the whole tedious business was a test of the grown-up's character. He had tried. He had talked seriously to her and played games seriously with her. But he could not always gauge the level at which she was momentarily operating, and it was not infrequent for her to ask him to stop being stupid. These afternoons, 'with children', of whose relaxing charms he had heard so much, left him exhausted and occasionally with feelings that were murderous. But what fixed his distaste for the child was when, on a visit to a fairground just three years ago, she had rejected his offer to go on the big dipper because, as she said, 'I have no intention of screaming like a shop assistant on holiday.' The words came out pat, just like that; they were clearly not her own. She was thirteen then, and it had given him a deep pleasure to see her grow fat and ungainly, with those plump forearms and short, stupid fingers which always irritated him in women. Puppy fat, Olive said; but it showed no sign of melting and he did what he could to encourage it. Chocolate, for example, which Olive forbade, was effective. Gwen was inordinately fond of it and he secretly gave her half-pound bars whenever he could. Even this did not improve their relations, for she made it plain that she regarded these gifts as bribes and that her affection was too important a thing to be bartered.

Suitable gifts, though, had been another of the problems that came with the creature. The Enid Blyton stage had seemed to be going on safely for eternity; but without warning the creature's tastes changed, rendering futile and laughable the 'Five' book he had stood in a long queue in Selfridge's to get autographed by the writer, together with her personal expression of good wishes to Gwen. Once he had brought ridicule on himself by giving her a toy hand-bag which was suitable for a girl of eight but not for one of fifteen. Last year he had solved the problem by giving a two-pound cheque, money down the drain; this year he would do the same.

So, though he had never come to accept her as part of Olive, he accepted her as part of Olive's home. As Gwen had grown older Olive had seemed to reassert her separate identity, and he felt that the element of falsity in his relationship with her sister had diminished. Olive could still give him solace; she could still exercise his protective pity. To go to her was like going home; to get away from her was a recurring liberation.

But not even Olive could remove the unease with which he had come to her this year. She was welcoming and ministering and calm and slow as always. She wore the brown slacks he associated with her, a habit of dress dating from the war, which always inspired him with tenderness for her. She had the height and slim hips for slacks, but she wore them with such apparent disregard for her appearance that Mr Stone would have found them slightly comic if they didn't reveal her stiff-waisted walk, the upper half of her body bent forward a little, so that she always had a purposeful air, as though about to rearrange things.

The days took their usual course. On Christmas eve he helped with the decorations, enduring the snappish criticisms of Gwen. (Who were such a creature's friends? He had a vision of her, brows contracted until she was almost cross-eyed, walking down the street in her school uniform, hugging her satchel to her stomach, and chattering away between sucks on a sweet about an 'enemy' to a smaller, silent companion, who would soon become an 'enemy' as well.) Then he drank Guinness and watched television while Olive was busy in the kitchen. At meal after meal he watched Gwen, fat and sickly with unfulfilled urges, putting away sweets and potatoes with relish. Olive objected. But: 'It's Christmas,' Mr Stone said.

Of these familiar things, however, he could no longer feel himself part. They had the heightened reality, which is like unreality, that a fever gives to everyday happenings. And at last it was time to leave. He took one of Olive's puddings, as he did every year. The bowls he never returned. They remained, washed and white, in one of Miss Millington's cupboards, this year's bowl fitting into the pile of all the previous years', stacked away as neatly as his experience, his past.

*

He returned to see the garden freshly covered with pepper dust: Miss Millington in command of the house, the cat at it again. But what a few days before would have roused him to pleasurable anger now left him unmoved. The naked tree permitted a clear view of The Male's back window, curtained and lighted in its sickly green frame (a colour chosen by The Male last spring and applied with loving care to all the exterior woodwork of his establishment). The Monster's house was unlighted. On this evening, the mists gathering in the silent school grounds, the day dying with the feel of the death of the holiday, it seemed that the world was in abeyance.

Next morning there was a letter for him. It was from Mrs Springer. She expressed her delight at meeting him and wondered whether he would like to come to a small New Year's eve gathering. She promised biscuits and cheese, which word was followed by a mark of exclamation in parenthesis. And the letter ended, 'As you can imagine, I am trying to cheer myself up, I do hope you can make it.'

Several things about the letter irritated him. He was a purist in matters of punctuation, and Mrs Springer had used a comma where she should have used a full stop. Her attempts at wit fell flat in her sloping old-fashioned writing, which was prim and characterless. He thought the reference to the cheese, and the exclamation mark, foolish, and the reference to her mourning ostentatious and insincere. But he was flattered that she should write. And it was the novelty, the break in his routine, to which to his own surprise he found himself looking forward. So the invitation, which perhaps from a person better known would have caused no such reaction, became of importance. It was a peak in time to which he could anchor himself over the intervening days. A new person, a new relationship: who knew what might come of that?

Mrs Springer lived in Earl's Court. A disreputable, overcrowded area Mr Stone had always thought it, and he thought no better of it now. The entrance to the Underground station was filthy; in a street across the road a meeting of the British National Party was in progress, a man shouting himself hoarse from the back of a van. Behind neon lights and streaming glass windows the new-style coffee houses were packed; and the streets were full of young people in art-student dress and foreigners of every colour.

The address Mrs Springer gave turned out to be a private hotel in one of the crescents off the Earl's Court Road. A small typewritten 'Europeans Only' card below the bell proclaimed it a refuge of respectability and calm. It also turned out to be a refuge of age. A lift, as aged and tremulous as most of the people Mr Stone saw in the small lobby, took him up to Mrs Springer's room, where the bed was imperfectly disguised as a sofa, and the window, open because of the fug, framed a view of roofs and chimney pots against the murkily glowing sky. It was not what he expected, and the shabbiness was only partly redeemed by the presence of an elderly white-coated hotel servant whom Mrs Springer called Michael. Still, he passed a reasonable evening, was encouraged as before by Mrs Springer's brilliance, by the re-telling twice of the story of the cat and the cheese, to make a few witticisms of his own; though, as always now after brilliance, there came gloom.

He invited Mrs Springer to tea two Sundays afterwards, and made careful preparations to receive her. In these preparations Miss Millington, moving with what for her was sprightliness, showed an unwonted zeal. The fireplace was cleaned up, the cracked, uneven tiles polished to reveal their true discoloration, and a good fire got going. The cakes and scones were made ready, the table laid. Then, in the growing darkness, they waited.

When the bell rang they both went out to the draughty hall. The door was opened, Mrs Springer was revealed smiling crookedly, and Mr Stone, slightly confused, introduced Miss Millington.

'So this is the garden!' Mrs Springer said, lingering outside. With her shoe she touched a low leaf that was coated with pepper dust. At her touch the dust came off in flakes, and the leaf, somewhat wan, feebly reasserted its springiness.

'I suppose this is what is known as a shrub,' she said in her party way. 'What do you call it?'

'I don't really know,' Mr Stone said. 'It's been there for some years. It is a sort of evergreen, I imagine.'

'Miss Millington, what do the common people call this?'

In that moment Mr Stone lost Miss Millington.

'I don't know, mum,' Miss Millington said, 'what the proper name is. But the common people—'

But Mrs Springer had already moved on, having, even before entering the house, made herself mistress of it, as she had made herself mistress of both its occupants.

In the second week of March Mr Stone and Mrs Springer were married, when on the tree in the school grounds the buds had swollen and in sunshine were like points of white.

2

ANXIETY WAS REPLACED by a feeling of deflation, a certain fear and an extreme shyness, which became acute as the ritual bathroom hour approached on their first evening as man and wife, words which still mortified him. He waited, unwilling to mention the matter or to make the first move, and in the end it was she who went first. She was a long time and he, sucking on his burnt-out pipe, savoured the moments of privacy as something now to be denied him forever.

'Yours now, Richard.'

Her voice was no longer deep and actressy. It was attempting to tinkle, and emerged a blend of coo and halloo.

In the bathroom, which before had held his own smell, to him always a source of satisfaction, there was now a warm, scented dampness. Then he saw her teeth. It had never occurred to him that they might be false. He felt cheated and annoyed. Regret came to him, and a prick of the sharpest fear. Then he took out his own teeth and sadly climbed the steps to their bedroom.

He had never cared for the opinion of the street, refusing to bid anyone on it good-day for fear that such greeting might be imposed on him in perpetuity, leading to heaven knows what intimacy. But he did not want the street to suspect that his household had been modified, and it was his intention to have Margaret move in in instalments. He thought his plan had so far been successful. Two suitcases were almost enough for what Margaret had at the Earl's Court hotel, where their procession through the small dark lobby had attracted discreet stares from the old and frank, uncomprehending stares from the very old, making Mr Stone feel that he was engaged in an abduction, though Margaret's triumphant gravity suggested that the operation was one of rescue. They had arrived at their house in the early evening, as though for dinner; and Mr Stone had handled the suitcases with a certain careless authority to hint to whoever might be watching that the suitcases were his own.

They had scarcely settled down in bed, each silent in his own cot (Margaret in the one taken from the room where Olive occasionally slept), when she sat up, almost with her party brightness, and said, 'Richard, do you hear anything?'

Something he had heard. But now there was only silence. He settled down again, fearing speech from her.

Flap!

It was undeniable.

Thump! Creak! Measured noises, as of someone ascending the thinly-carpeted staircases firmly, cautiously.

'Richard, there is a man in the house!'

At her words the steps ceased.

'Go and look, Richard.'

He disliked the repetition of his name. But he dragged himself up to a sitting position. He thought she was relishing the role of the frightened woman, and he noted with distaste that she had pulled the blankets right up to her neck.

The responsibility was new. It wearied, irritated him. And though he was alarmed himself, he at that moment hoped that someone was in the house, standing right behind the door, and that he would come in and batter them both to death and release.

Flap, thump, flap.

He flung off the bedclothes and ran to the landing and put on the light, hoping by his speed and violence to still the noise, to drive it away.

'Hello!' he called. 'Who is it? Is there anyone there?'

There was no reply.

Carefully he approached the banister and looked down the well of the stairs upon a gloom made sinister by the elongated leaning shadows of the rails. Far below him he saw the telephone, its dial dully gleaming.

He hurried back to the room. He closed the door, turned on the light. She was standing directly below the lampshade in her frilly nightdress, her mouth collapsed, her bed disarrayed, the inadequate sheet already peeling off the three large cushions (red, white and blue, and arranged by Miss Millington in that order) that served as mattress.

'I didn't see anyone,' he said with mild irritation, and sat down on his bed.

For some time they remained as they were, saying nothing. He looked about the room, avoiding her eye. He had always thought of his bedroom as comfortable. Now that it held a second person, he took it in detail by detail, and as he did so his irritation grew. The tasselled lampshade had been painted green by Miss Millington at his orders, not to cover grime but simply for the sake of the green; the lighted bulb now revealed the erratic distribution of all her labouring, overcharged brushstrokes. The curtains were made of three not quite matching pieces of brown velvet, chosen by Miss Millington to hide dirt. The carpet was worn, its design and colours no longer of importance; the cracked, ill-fitting linoleum surrounds (hard as metal) had lost their pattern and were a messy dark brown. The wallpaper was dingy, the ceiling cracked. Next to the dark, almost black wardrobe a ruined armchair, which had not been sat on for years, served as a receptacle for miscellaneous objects.

Flap! Creak! Thump!

'Richard! Dial 999, Richard!'

He realized the necessity, but was greatly afraid.

'Come down with me to the telephone,' he said.

He would willingly have had her precede him down the steps, but his new responsibility did not permit this. Arming himself with a bent poker, dusty to the touch, he tiptoed down the stairs ahead of her, expecting a blow from every dark corner of his once familiar house. Arriving at the hall, he telephoned, poker in hand, regretting his action as soon as he heard the cool, unhurried inquiries.

They went upstairs to wait, turning on all lights on the way and recovering their teeth from the bathroom. Except for their own movements there was now silence.

When the bell rang Mr Stone went down to the door with the poker in his hand. The officer, armed only with an electric torch, gave the poker an amused look, and Mr Stone began to apologize for it.

The officer cut him short. 'I've sent my man round to the back,' he said, and proceeded, expertly and reassuringly, to dive into all the corners that had held such threat.

They found no one.

The constable who had been sent round to the back came in through the front door; and they all sat in the still warm sitting-room.

'With some of these semi-detached houses noises next door often sound as though they're coming from this side,' the officer said.

The constable smiled, playing with his torch.

'There was a man in the house,' Margaret said argumentatively.

'Is there any door or entrance in the back he could get in by?' the officer asked.

'I don't know,' she said. 'I only came to the house tonight.'

There was a silence. Mr Stone looked away.

'Would you like a cup of tea?' he asked. From the films he had seen he believed that police officers always drank tea in such circumstances.

'Yes,' Margaret said, 'do have a cup of tea.'

The tea was declined, their apologies politely brushed aside.

But the house blazed with lights, and the police car attracted attention. So that on the following day, far from attempting to hide his marriage, Mr Stone was compelled to proclaim it and to endure the furtive glances, the raised curtains of the street.

Even Miss Millington, used to curious happenings in the house during her absence, could not hide her excitement at the police visit.

*

One thing relieved him. They had come to one another as wits. And when, towards the end of their pre-marriage acquaintance (the word 'courtship' did not appeal to him), his efforts grew febrile, he had sought to establish himself as someone with a rich sense of humour and an eye for the ridiculous in 'life'. He feared, then, that marriage might mean a lifelong and exhausting violation of his personality. But to his surprise he found that Margaret required no high spirits from him, no jocularity, no wit; and again to his surprise he discovered that her party manner, which he had thought part of her personality, was something she discarded almost at once, reserving it for those of her friends who knew her reputation. And often during their after-dinner silence (he reading the paper, Margaret writing letters or knitting, thin-rimmed spectacles low down her nose, ageing her considerably) he would think with embarrassment for both their sakes of the brightness of her first remark to him, its needle-sharp enunciation ('Do you . . . like *cats?*'), and of the unexpected brilliance of his last remark at that meeting ('I imagine that's why they're called nuts'). For never again was she so impressively abrupt or 'brittle' (a word whose meaning he thought he fully understood only after meeting Margaret), and never again was he so brilliant.

Of Margaret's history he never inquired, and she volunteered little. The thought sometimes arose, though he suppressed it, for Margaret by her behaviour had signalled that what they had said during their 'courtship' was to be discounted, that she was not as grand as she had made out. Neither was he; and this was more painful. For his own secrets, which had never been secrets until the night of their meeting, had to be revealed. His head librarianship, for example, and his £1,000 a year. Margaret asked no questions. But secrets were burdensome; he lacked the patience or the energy to conceal or deceive. Neither his position nor salary was negligible, but he felt that Margaret had expected more and that secretly she mocked at him, as he secretly mocked at her, though his own mockery he considered harmless.

Secretly she might mock, but of this nothing escaped her in speech or expression. And it was astonishing to what degree he was able to recreate his former routine. He was out all day at the office as before; and Margaret at home became an extension, a more pervading extension, of Miss Millington, who had accepted the new situation and her new mistress with greater calm than her master. Certain things he lost. His solitude was one; never again would he return to an empty house. And there was the relationship with Olive. Though she was all goodwill and though he might try to pretend that their relationship remained what it was, he knew that a further falsity, more corroding than that introduced by the birth of Gwen, had invaded it. And then there was the smell, the feel of his house.

The mustiness, the result of ineffectual fussings with broom and brush by Miss Millington, in which he had taken so much pleasure, was replaced not by the smell of polish and soap but by a new and alien mustiness. The sitting-room for some weeks he could scarcely call his own, for it was dominated by a tigerskin, which came out of store in excellent condition and which Margaret explained by producing a framed sepia photograph of a dead tiger on whose chest lay the highly polished boot of an English cavalry officer, moustached, sitting bolt upright in a heavy wooden armchair (brought from goodness knows where), fighting back a smile, one hand caressing a rifle laid neatly across his thighs, with three sorrowful, top-heavily turbanned Indians, beaters or bearers or whatever they were, behind him. Many little bits of furniture came with the tigerskin as well. Very fussy frilly bits he thought them, and they looked out of place among the bulky nineteen-thirty furniture which was his own. But Miss Millington, falling on them with a delight as of one rediscovering glories thought dead and gone, regularly and indefatigably heightened their gloss, using a liquid polish which, drying in difficult crevices, left broken patterns of pure, dusty white. To accommodate the new furniture there had to be rearrangements. Miss Millington and Margaret consulted and rearranged, Miss Millington with painful joy, eyes closed, lips compressed, wisps of grey wet hair escaping from her hair net, doing the pushing and hauling about. So afternoon after afternoon Mr Stone returned home to a disturbing surprise, and the expectant glances of the two women waiting approval.

Before his marriage he had been to Miss Millington an employer. Now he became The Master. And to the two women he was something more. He was a 'man', a creature of particular tastes, aptitudes and authority. It was as a man that he left the house every morning—or rather, was sent off, spick and span and spruce and correct in every way, as though the world was now his audience—and it was as a man that he returned. This aspect of his new responsibility deepened his feeling of inadequacy; he even felt a little fraudulent. Miss Millington, in particular, appeared confidently to await a change in his attitude and behaviour towards her, and he felt that he was continually letting her down. He had been a 'man' in a limited way and only for a few days at a time with his sister Olive; it was an intermittent solace which he welcomed but which he was at the end always glad to escape. Now there was no escape.

From his role as their brave bull, going forth day after day to 'business' (Miss Menzies's word, which was Margaret's as well), he hoped to find rest in the office. But rest there was none, for increasingly his manner, to his disquiet, reflected his role. The neatness on which he prided himself became a dapperness. And even if one forgot the irreverent allusions of the young to his married state, in the beginning a source of much pain to him, there was a noticeable change in the attitude of the office people. The young girls no longer petted him or flirted with him, and he could not imagine himself making as if to hit them on the bottom with his cylindrical ruler, the weapon with which he repelled their playful advances. And as he progressively lost his air of freedom and acquired the appearance of one paroled from a woman's possession, the young men, even those who were married, no longer tolerated him as before, no longer pretended that he might be one of them. He attracted instead the fatiguing attentions of Wilkinson, the office Buddhist, whose further eccentricity was sometimes to walk about the office corridors in stockinged feet.

He had fallen into the habit of staying in the office later than was usual or necessary, as though to recapture a little of the privacy and solitude he had lost. Turning off the library lights one evening, and going into the darkened corridor, he bumped into a man as tall as himself. The man's clothes felt rough; he was a guardsman. And a girl's voice (he recognized one of the typists) said a little breathlessly, 'We can't find the light switch, Mr Stone.' He showed where it was. He did more: he turned the lights on. And it was only when he was on the train, his briefcase containing the evening papers resting lightly on his lap, that he realized the truth of the situation. 'Damned fool,' he thought, his anger directed as much towards himself as towards them. He took a dislike to that typist and was glad when not long afterwards she left the office.

The office not offering refuge, he was driven to seek it at home, so that his goings forth and returnings were both in the nature of flights, until at length he found that he had settled down into the new life, had grown to expect that as soon as he opened the garden gate the front door should be opened by a sprucer Miss Millington, that Margaret, who had given the signal for the opening, should be in the front window and should from that point advance, at first as though to receive him, and then to embrace him, brushing off some of the fresh powder from her cheeks on to his. She dressed every afternoon for his return as carefully as she dressed him for his departure in the mornings.

The street still watched, especially for this evening encounter. And, as an aid to composure, it became his custom to start whistling as soon as he came within sight of the house. 'That was very nice, Richard,' Margaret said one day as she kissed him. 'This doggie is for sale.' He had been whistling, 'How Much is That Doggie in the Window?' So he whistled it every evening. And that was how he became 'Doggie' and, more rarely, she became 'Doggie'.

Yet, communing with his tree, he could not help contrasting its serenity with his disturbance. It would shed its leaves in time; but this would lead to a renewal which would bring greater strength. Responsibility had come too late to him. He had broken the pattern of his life, and this break could at best be only healed. It would not lead to renewal. So the tree no longer comforted. It reproached.

This summer the Male was busier than ever, building an out-house. More fervently than before, Mr Stone wished for some accident that would put an end to the man's never-ending improvements to his nest, which improvements were watched with unabating admiration by the man's numerous brood.

He was a man, then. Bravely every morning he ventured forth into the rigorous world of business. And now he learned that Margaret was a woman. She attached the greatest importance to her functions as a woman and a wife. These were to feed, dress, humour, encourage, occasionally to seduce and never to let down. She rested in the mornings to recover from her exertions in seeing him off; she rested in the afternoons before getting ready for his return; she was concerned about getting her sleep at night so that she did not look a fright in the morning. Many creams and skin-foods supplemented her rest. And he was not grateful. He refused to notice. He began to think her idle, lazy, vain. When he thought of the responsibility she had imposed on him, when he thought of her pulling the blankets up to her neck on their first night, he could not help feeling that in the division of their functions she had got the better bargain.

The emphasis on the separateness of their functions as man and woman was a standing irritation. He would have liked her to relieve him of the garden, but she was unwilling to do so. Not only because she didn't care for gardening—the pre-marriage statement turned out to have a grain of truth—but also because she thought it suitable that a man should have a hobby and that gardening should be the hobby of Mr Stone, who had no other aptitude. Twice a day (thrice on Sundays) he faced her across the dining table; and these moments, which in no consideration of marriage he had envisaged, were moments of the greatest strain. She, the feeder, ate with voracious appetite, continually apologizing for being slow. He could see the powder on the hairs of her taut cheeks. Her lipstick became oily; then, as it grew fainter, spread over areas not originally painted. Reflecting at the dining table on her idleness and frivolity, the hours she spent preparing herself for him, he feared he might say something offensive. But their first quarrel occurred for another, ridiculous reason.

*

At Margaret's suggestion, and against his wishes, they gave a dinner party, which to a large extent recreated one of the Tomlinsons' dinner parties. It was, inevitably, somewhat shabbier, even Margaret's improving zeal having failed to make any great impression on the house which had been so carefully neglected for so long. The Tomlinsons themselves came, radiating patronage and benevolence, their manner suggesting that they regarded themselves as creators of the new establishment. There were various friends of Margaret's, some picked up from the Tomlinsons', one or two from the Earl's Court hotel. (How little he knew of her!) Among the friends was a tall, heavy woman of forty or fifty with a face scrubbed of all attraction and expression; she didn't speak, little attention was paid to her, and yet, sitting primly where she was put, she appeared content.

Mr Stone had been urged to get some of his business colleagues. But he could think of no one. Evans, Keenan, Wilkinson, none of them was really suitable. Evans might have done, but he would have accepted, if he had accepted, as one doing a favour. With his colleagues Mr Stone had only an office relationship, of the utmost cordiality, but over the years of his bachelorhood the relationship had hardened in this way, so that any visiting now would have appeared an intrusion; such visiting in any case seemed more in evidence among the young. Nor did Mr Stone relish meeting his colleagues outside the office. After the initial boisterous greeting, which suggested that there was so much in common, so much to say, after the cracking of the current office joke, conversation faded, having little to feed on, until one of them said with brisk joviality, 'Well, see you at the office.' It was only at the office that such relationships could flourish; they were like hothouse plants, needing the protection of their artificial setting.

From Mr Stone's side, then, the only persons who came were Olive and Gwen. He was outnumbered. He couldn't count Miss Millington as one of his allies. She, donning hair net and scarf, and panting and sighing and breaking into cold sweat, had zestfully worked all day long under Margaret's directions. And then, to her own gasping delight, she had been dressed for the dinner by Margaret in a new apron and new cap which, tilting sharply back from her low brow, had given a touch of rakishness to her aged baby-face. Nor could Mr Stone count Gwen on his side. Pallid and pimply and sour, the fat creature sought to convey her impatient contempt for everyone. She deeply disturbed Mr Stone, already vulnerable in his new role as husband and host.

With the wine—'I think a good Beaujolais would do,' Margaret had said, trespassing on the role of her husband after he had shown no wish to take it on—there were toasts. Not many, for only one bottle of Beaujolais had been bought and this was poured out like a liqueur, one small glass per guest, as was the custom at the Tomlinsons'. Then, as was also customary at the Tomlinsons', the men and women separated. With all the delight of a fulfilled woman in the segregation of the sexes, Margaret shooed the women away from the dining-room, leaving Mr Stone, Tomlinson and one other man (the party was unbalanced, many of the women being widows) in silence, Mr Stone not knowing what to say, Tomlinson looking anguished, clearing his throat, the other man (an accountant, a chief accountant) beginning to speak but only a squeak issuing from a throat clogged after a long silence.

'Very good dinner you gave us,' Tomlinson said at last, in encouraging commendation.

'Yes,' the chief accountant said hurriedly. 'Very good.'

They listened to the shuffle and contented babble of the women.

Margaret's voice was deep, Grace drawled. There was nothing to drink in the dining-room (there was none at the Tomlinsons'). Once, several Christmas-week dinners ago, Tomlinson had attempted to tell a dirty story. Everyone had dutifully prepared to listen, smile and perhaps even make laughter that would be heard outside the room. But Tomlinson had told his story so precisely, with such calculated pauses and smiles, yet with such evident distaste on his thin, tormented face, that the story had fallen flat, no one knowing when it had ended, no one laughing, everyone embarrassed and slightly shocked, for without wit the story had appeared only as a piece of wilful obscenity. Tomlinson had thereafter abandoned his role of male-amuser. So now they stood, waiting.

'I think we can go outside now,' Mr Stone said. He was unwilling to use the phrase about joining the ladies; he did not feel he could manage it with Tomlinson's ease and conviction.

'Not yet,' Tomlinson said, as though his authority had been appealed to.

And indeed at that moment came the sound of the lavatory flush.

The chief accountant cleared his throat.

When at last they did go outside, Margaret greeted them with, 'Well, what have you men been guffawing about?'

They seated themselves around the tigerskin like participants in some form of combat. Mr Stone submitted with outward good humour and inward fury to the badinage about his marriage, though he could not help contracting his brows in annoyance when Grace Tomlinson said, 'I see you've already trained him well, Margaret.'

The entertainment was like that at the Tomlinsons'. There was singing. And, as at the Tomlinsons', the women were expected to sing well and to be applauded seriously. Occasionally, very occasionally, there might be an acknowledged comedienne. But the men were supposed to clown, savage creatures who, presenting forbidding fronts to the world of business, relaxed thus in the privacy of their hearths for their mates and friends alone, revealing benignant or childish aspects of their character which the outside world never suspected. So he did ridiculous things to the lapels of his jacket, pulled his hair down his forehead, rolled up one trouser leg, and with the two other sad men did his comic song.

It was after this that Margaret asked Gwen to recite 'something nice'. To Mr Stone's surprise Gwen rose at once, the back of her flared skirt crumpled from the clumsy weight so recently on it, and took up her position on the tigerskin. She did a scene from *The Importance of Being Earnest*, affecting a deep voice not for the male role but, in imitation of the celebrated actress, for the female. Mr Stone looked on in wonder; up till that moment he had not thought Gwen capable of doing anything. Her sour expression had been replaced by one of blankness, as though she had removed herself from the room. With complete absorption she acted out the scene, turning her head abruptly this way and that to indicate the changing of roles. She never faltered or lost her composure, even when, attempting an excessive throatiness for *In a Handbag*, she emitted *hand* as a squeak. There was a good deal of approval, which Mr Stone shared.

It then occurred to him that it was perhaps indelicate of Gwen to imitate the actress whom Margaret imitated, in a circle which had for so long accepted Margaret's imitation. He glanced at Margaret and saw that she was suffering slightly. The line that ran from nose to mouth had deepened; her lips had tautened over her false teeth. He was filled with sympathy for her. But when the performance came to an end it was Margaret who led the applause, crying 'Bravo! Bravo!'

With a well-trained bow Gwen acknowledged the applause, not seeming, however, to see anyone in the room. And then to the general surprise she launched into a fresh recitation, the court scene from *The Merchant of Venice*. This was less successful. Whereas before she had spoken prose as though it were rhetoric, now she spoke rhetoric as though it were everyday speech. Mr Stone could hardly recognize Portia's speech. Then, turning her head to indicate the new speaker, Gwen attempted Shylock, and attempted Shylock in a Jewish accent.

Something told Mr Stone this was wrong and, looking about the room, he saw proof on every face. Grace Tomlinson, whose lips were invariably slightly parted, now had her mouth clamped shut. Tomlinson looked stern. Margaret's eyes held definite anger. Everyone shot brief covert glances at the chief accountant, whose eyes were fixed on Gwen.

The recitation went on, only Olive in her pride unaware of the currents of disapproval and embarrassment.

The recitation was over. Without waiting for applause, Gwen bowed and returned to her seat, smoothing her dress below her and then looking down at her lap like one annoyed, like one whose modesty had been violated, while shufflings and rustlings broke through the room.

'Miss Banks,' Margaret said coldly, 'did you bring your music?'

The person addressed was the tall woman with the scrubbed face. Little attention had been paid to her, but she had remained all evening in her own pool of contentment. At the dining table she had shown herself a silent and steady eater. Now, without replying, she took out her music from her very large bag, rose, seated herself at the piano and began to play.

*

In the stillness that followed—Miss Banks's music received exaggerated attention—Mr Stone had much time for thought. He thought about Miss Banks and he thought about his house. What changes had come to it! The neighbours could now hear piano music. Yet from the outside his house had not changed at all. What strange things must happen behind the blank front doors of so many houses! And just as sometimes when travelling on a train he had mentally stripped himself of train, seats and passengers and seen himself moving four or five feet above ground in a sitting posture at forty miles an hour, so now he was assailed by a vision of the city stripped of stone and concrete and timber and metal, stripped of all buildings, with people suspended next to and above and below one another, going through all the motions of human existence. And he had a realization, too upsetting to be more than momentarily examined, that all that was solid and immutable and enduring about the world, all to which man linked himself (The Monster watering her spring flowers, The Male expanding his nest), flattered only to deceive. For all that was not flesh was irrelevant to man, and all that was important was man's own flesh, his weakness and corruptibility.

*

The dinner party had its ridiculous sequel two weeks later. Every four weeks or so Olive sent Mr Stone a fruit cake of her own making. The custom had survived Olive's marriage, had survived Gwen. Mr Stone was glad that it had survived his own marriage as well and that Margaret, however much she might dislike this reminder of an additional claim on her husband's manhood, had lent herself happily to the ritual of cutting Olive's cake.

But this evening when, the cake cut, the coffee ready, they sat before the electric fire, Margaret did a strange thing. She speared a large piece of the cake with her knife and held it close to the guard of the fire.

'You will electrocute yourself!' Mr Stone cried.

The rich cake had already caught. Margaret jerked it off on to the reflector. It burned steadily and well, like good fuel. Even when completely charred it continued to burn, the metal around it turning brown from the oozing fat.

'In India,' Margaret said, gazing at the cake, 'they always offer little bits like this to the fire before they cook or eat anything.'

Mr Stone was outraged. Starting to put down his plate gently, as he always did, but changing his mind right at the last moment and setting it down hard, he got up and made for the door, kicking at the tiger's head, against which he had nearly tripped.

'Doggie!'

He held the door open. 'I—I don't believe you've ever been to India.'

'Doggie!'

He locked himself in the former junk room, which Margaret had furnished with some of her furniture and presented to him as a 'study', a place for male solitude. And there, despite Margaret's knocks and calls and coos, he remained, thinking in the dark of the past, of Olive, himself, childhood. He beheld a boy of seventeen walking back alone from school on a winter's day, past the shops of the High Street. The boy was going home, unaware of what awaited him there. Whether the picture was true or composite he no longer knew; whether there was a reason for remembering this stretch of the way home he couldn't say. But it was what he saw when he wished to think of his childhood in a tender way. This boy didn't know that his life would unroll without disturbance, the years flow evenly; and for him Mr Stone felt an ache of pity.

At length the passion passed. It was quite late and he was stiff and cold. He nevertheless prolonged his stay in the study until past ten. Then, for no reason, he went down to the sitting-room. Margaret did not speak; she was reading a library book. He said nothing to her. He went up to the bathroom. It had become the rule that he should go first. It was also a rule that he should smoke his pipe there; it warmed the room up, Margaret said, and she loved the smell of his tobacco. It was his custom therefore to puff vigorously on his pipe four or five times before leaving the bathroom. Tonight, because of their quarrel, he went without his pipe.

From the bedroom he listened to her own preparations. When she came in he was under the sheets, motionless. She did not put the light on. She set the alarm and got into bed.

He was falling off to sleep when he heard her.

'Doggie.'

He didn't reply.

Minutes later she spoke again.

'Doggie.'

He mumbled.

'Doggie, you've made me very unhappy.'

Whereat he almost lost his temper. Fatigue alone kept him silent.

She started to sob.

'Doggie, I want to eat a piece of your cake.'

'Why don't you go and eat the damned thing?'

She sobbed a little more.

'Won't you come and eat a little piece with me, Doggie?'

'No.'

'A little piece, Doggie.'

'For heaven's sake!' he said, throwing the bedclothes off.

She was sitting up.

They went to the bathroom and got their teeth. They went down to the sitting-room, almost stuffy after the cold bedroom, and ate large pieces of Olive's cake in silence.

Then they went up to the bathroom and took out their teeth, and went to bed, still silent.

He was now wide awake.

'Doggie,' she said.

'Doggie.'

It was some time before they could fall asleep, and they suffered frightfully from indigestion.

Olive continued to send her cakes. But Mr Stone knew that the relationship between his sister and himself belonged to the past.

*

So step by step he became married; and step by step marriage grew on him. For Margaret revealed a plasticity of character which abridged and rendered painless the process of getting to know her, getting used to her. He was at the core of their relationship; she moulded herself about him so completely and comfortably that it was with surprise, when he observed her with her friends, that he remembered she did have a character of her own, and views and attitudes. And just as at first it seemed that Margaret had become an extension of Miss Millington, so he now saw them both as extensions of himself. It was, too, with a growing pleasure, which he did not in the beginning care to acknowledge even to himself, that he thought of the suspension that came to the house as soon as he left it in the morning, and of its reanimation in the afternoon in preparation to receive him.

His habits were converted into rituals; they grew sacred even to him. He succumbed to gardening, of the type that Margaret desired, his attentions to beds and bulbs being regarded as sacramental by both Margaret and Miss Millington, willing acolytes (Miss Millington, whose only concern with the garden before had been to dust it, in her uncontrolled, deluging and expensive way, with pepper dust, and perhaps, when flowers appeared, to make some reference to their loveliness). So it was established that he was 'fond of gardening'. But he drew the line when Margaret, saying, 'Something for you, Doggie,' tried to get him to become a regular listener to *Country Questions* and *In Your Garden*. He soothed her disappointment by repeating, what he had heard in the office, that the people who spoke on the radio with rustic accents about country matters lived in Mayfair; window-boxes were the only land *they* knew. This became one of his 'sayings'; his statements had never before been regarded as 'sayings'.

It was established, too, that the black cat next door was an enemy. The two women entered into a sweet conspiracy to conceal the creature's activities from the Master. An intermittent afternoon watch was kept and ravages hastily repaired so that the Master might not be upset when he returned. The women succeeded better than they knew. The war taken out of his hands, Mr Stone's hostility towards the cat diminished, leaving him with a sense of something lost.

But beneath the apparent calm which marriage had once more brought to him, there grew a new appreciation of time. It was flying by. It was eating up his life. Every week—and how quickly these Sundays followed one another on the radio: *Coast and Country* after the news, or *The Countryside in October, The Countryside in November,* monthly programmes that seemed like weekly programmes: Sundays which made him feel that the last one was yesterday—every racing week drew him nearer to retirement, inactivity, corruption.

Every ordered week reminded him of failure, of the uncreative years once so comfortingly stacked away in his mind. Every officeless Sunday sharpened his anxiety, making him long for Monday and the transient balm of the weekdays, false though he knew their fullness to be, in spite of the office diary he had begun to keep, tabulating appointments, things to be done, to flatter himself that he was busily and importantly occupied.

The tree, changing, developing with the year, made its point every day. And when, sitting at the Sunday tea, trying to reassure himself by his precise, neat, slow gestures, he sometimes said, 'You are part of me, Margaret. I don't know what I would do without you,' he spoke with an urgency and gratitude she did not fully understand.

3

LATE IN MARCH, the buds white in sunlight on the black branches and daily acquiring a greenish tinge, Mr Stone and Margaret left London for a fortnight. It was his holiday—he who would soon be in need of no holiday—and it was also their honeymoon. They went to Cornwall. Mr Stone preferred to spend his holidays in England. He had thought after the war that he would go abroad. In 1948 he went to Ireland; but the most enjoyable part of that holiday was the journey from Southampton to Cobh in a luxurious, rationing-free American liner. A fortnight in Paris two years later had been, after the first moment of pleasure at being in the celebrated city, a tedious torment. He had dutifully gone sightseeing and had been considerably fatigued; he often wondered afterwards why he followed the guidebook so slavishly and went to places as dreary as the Panthéon and the Invalides. He had sat in the cafés, but hated the coffee, and to sit idling in an unfamiliar place was not pleasant, and the cups of coffee were so small. He had tried aperitifs but had decided they were a waste of time and money. He was very lonely; his pocket was playfully picked by an Algerian, who warned him to be more careful in future; everything was hideously expensive; the incessant cries from men and women of *le service, monsieur, le service!* had given him a new view of the French, whom he had thought a frivolous, funloving people made a little sad by the war. And for the last two days he was afflicted by a type of dysentery which made it impossible for him to take anything more solid than mineral water.

So Cornwall it was. Margaret suppressed her disappointment in reflections about the need to economize, which, already delicately acknowledged, had begun to obtrude more and more into their conversation, now that Mr Stone was only eighteen months or so from retirement. She told Grace Tomlinson, and Grace agreed, that it was high time they got to know their own country.

They put up at the Queen's Hotel in Penzance. The season had not properly begun. The weather was unusually bad, the hotel people said, as though assuring them they had not done a foolish thing; and they received much attention.

They took buses and went for walks, Mr Stone feeling conspicuous in his black city overcoat (Simpsons's, and twenty years old: Simpson's clothes, as he and Tomlinson had long ago agreed, were worth the extra money, and it had once been a source of satisfaction to Mr Stone that he was often, so far as dress went, a complete Simpson's man). In another part of England he might have felt less conspicuous in his black overcoat. But in that landscape it was like an emblem of softness and inaptitude. Human habitation had scarcely modified the land; it was not as if a race had withdrawn but as if, growing less fit, it had been expunged from the stone-bound land, which remained to speak of discord between man and earth.

Once on a bare cliff they came upon a dead fox, as whole as the living animal, no marks of death or violence on it, lying on its side as if in sleep, its fur blown about by the wind.

On Sunday they went to Chysauster. It was a difficult walk, and for part of the way led down a murderous rocky lane. The wind was sharp and naggingly irregular, the sunshine thin and fitful. By the time they arrived they were both bad-tempered, in no mood for abandoned Celtic dwellings. They sat against a low stone wall in the lee of the wind, Mr Stone reckless of his overcoat, and worked through the tea they had brought, the carrying of which had added to their discomfort. From time to time, but never long enough to warm them, the sun came out.

Afterwards, like giants entering the houses of men, they examined the cluster of solid stone hovels. How thick the walls, how clumsy, how little space they enclosed, as though built for people sheltering from more than the elements! Mr Stone thought of the Monster with her watering can, the nest-building of the Male: this was not their setting. Then he remembered his own Simpson's coat. He saw himself, a cartoon figure, with knotted club and leopard skin: he could not hold the picture for long. The hovels were indefinably depressing. He wanted to get away.

They had planned to get a bus to St Ives and from there to get another back to Penzance. In the hotel room, with maps and bus time-tables, such an adventurous return had seemed simple enough. But the walk to Chysauster had taken longer than they expected; and now they could not determine where they were. Margaret, proclaiming her stupidity in these matters, left the fixing of their position to him, and with wind and cheating sun his temper was wearing thin again.

Then they saw the fire. Across the dry bare field at the back of the hut-cluster it advanced silently towards them with much clean white smoke.

And they saw they were not alone. To their left, considering the fire and not them, was a very tall, big-boned man in a dark-blue beret and a tattered, unbuttoned army tunic. He looked like a farm labourer. His elongated heavy face was dark red; his eyes were small, the lips puffed and raw.

Mr Stone felt urgently now that they should be off.

'How do we get to the road for St Ives?' he asked, and found himself shouting, as though his words would otherwise be overcome by the smoke of the silent fire.

The man in the army tunic didn't speak. He glanced at them, then started walking briskly away with long-legged strides. Over the wall that separated the huts from the field he went, and along a white path in the field itself, walking into the smoke.

And hurriedly, not willing to lose sight of him, they followed, scrambling over the wall.

The man was disappearing into the smoke.

Mr Stone knew panic.

The man stopped, turned towards them, and was lost in smoke. And they followed.

They heard the low, contented crackle of the fire. Smoke enveloped them. They were robbed of earth and reality. He was robbed of judgement, of the will to act.

Then Margaret's cry, 'Doggie!' recalled him to questioning and fear, and they ran back to the wall, out of the smoke, into the clear open air, to rocks and earth and sky.

Behind the wall they stood, watching the fire. It came right up to the wall and before their eyes burnt itself out. The smoke was dissipated in the air. And it was as if there had been no fire, and all that had happened a hallucination.

Reality was completed by the arrival of a Morris Minor. Mr Stone inquired about the road to St Ives. The new visitors offered a lift to Penzance.

It was only when they were in the car that they saw, not far from the stone huts, the man in the army tunic. He was gazing at the only slightly charred field. He did not look at them.

'Well, of course,' the desk-clerk said confidently, when Margaret gave him an account of the afternoon's happenings, 'the thing about Cornwall'—his Birmingham accent prolonging the *g* like a piano pedal—'is that it is steeped in legend. Positively steeped.'

Mr Stone never doubted that the incident could be rationally and simply explained. But that hallucinatory moment, when earth and life and senses had been suspended, remained with him. It was like an experience of nothingness, an experience of death.

*

They decided to give the Cornwall of legend the miss—the desk-clerk told with relish of a man he knew whose house had been burned down after a visit to Chysauster—and they were helped by the weather, which continued cold, drizzly and uncertain. The day before they left, however, the skies cleared and in the afternoon they went for a walk. Their way led along cliffs which, rimmed with deep white footpaths, fell to the sea in partial ruin, on a principle of destruction that was easy to comprehend but was on such a scale that the mind could not truly grasp it. It was still cold, and they encountered no more than half a dozen people on the way, among them a man who, to Mr Stone's satisfaction, was wearing a black city overcoat. Just when they were getting tired and craving for sweet things, they saw a neat sign promising tea fifty yards on.

The establishment was as neat as the sign. A clean white card on each crisp checked tablecloth, a blue cloth alternating with a red, announced the owner as Miss Chichester. Miss Chichester was what her name, her establishment and her card promised. She was middle-aged, stout, with a large bosom. Her brisk manner proclaimed the dignity of labour as a discovery she expected to be universally shared; her accent was genteel without exaggeration; in her dress and discreet make-up there was the hint, that though perhaps widowed and in straitened circumstances, she was not letting herself go.

Only one of the tables was occupied, by a party of three, a man and two women. The women were as stout as Miss Chichester, but an overflow of flesh here and there, a coarseness in legs, complexion and hair, in coats, hats and shiny new bags suggested only a cosy grossness, as well as the fixed stares through spectacles in ill-chosen frames, and the smooth swollen hands firmly grasping bags on thighs whose fatness was accentuated by the opened coats, lower buttons alone undone. The man was a wizened creature with narrow, sloping shoulders loose within a stiff new tweed jacket, his thin hair, the flex of his hearing-aid and the steel rims of his spectacles contributing to a general impression of perilous attenuation, as did the hand-rolled cigarette which, thin and wrinkled like the neck of the smoker, lay dead and forgotten between thin lips. He showed no interest in the arrival of Margaret and Mr Stone, and continued to stare at the checked tablecloth; sitting between the two women (one his wife, the other—what?) who looked like his keepers.

Their silence imposed silence on Margaret and Mr Stone as well, and even when Miss Chichester brought out tea for the party the silence continued. The man fell wordlessly on plates and pots and tasteful jugs as though he had been sparing his energies for this moment. He attacked the dainty sandwiches, the fresh scones, the homemade jam; and with every mouthful he appeared to grow more energetic, restless and enterprising. His thin, hairy hand shot out in all directions, making to grab teapots, cake-plates, jam-bowls, gestures so decisive and of such authority that his keepers, who were at first inclined to deflect his pouncing actions, surrendered entirely, and contented themselves with salvaging what food they could. Abruptly the eater finished. He worked his lips over his teeth, made a few sucking noises, and perceptibly the expression of blind eagerness gave way to the earlier sour dejection. He stared straight ahead, at nothing; while his keepers, rescuing their tea interlude from premature extinction, intermittently nibbled at bread and butter as if without appetite. Throughout there had been no speech at the table.

The habit of examining people older than himself was one into which Mr Stone had been falling during the past year. It was something he fought against; observation told him that only women, very young children and very old men inspected and assessed others of their group with such intensity. But now in spite of himself he stared with horror and fascination, and found that, as the eater's actions had grown more frenzied, his own had grown exaggeratedly slow.

Their own tea arrived and they prepared to begin. Attempting to break the silence Mr Stone found that he whispered, and the whisper was like gunshot. Silence continued, except for the kitchen clatter and the thumps of Miss Chichester's shoes.

And then silence vanished. The door was pushed vigorously open and there entered a very tall fair man and a very small fair girl. The man was in mountaineering clothes, like one equipped for a Himalayan or at least Alpine expedition. He carried rucksack and ropes; his thick rough trousers were tucked into thick woollen socks, and these disappeared into massive lustreless boots with extraordinarily thick soles. He created, by his masculine entry and the laying down of detachable burdens, as much noise as for two or three. The girl was soft and mute. Her slacks, imperfectly and tremulously filled, suggested only fragility; so did her light-blue silk scarf. The pale colours of her clothes, the milky fawn of her raincoat, and the style of her pale tan shoes marked her as a European.

Sitting at the table, his rough-trousered knees reaching to the tablecloth, dwarfing the table and the flower vase, the mountaineer extended a greeting, accompanied by a bow, to the room. His English was only slightly accented.

The eater and his keepers nodded. Mr Stone's eyebrows dropped, like one surprised and affronted. Margaret was only momentarily distracted from scones and jam.

But the man filled the room. His speech created a conversational momentum on its own; the silence of others did not matter. He said that he was Dutch; that in his country there were no mountains; that Cornwall was indescribably picturesque. All this in English which, because he was Dutch, was perfect; and the linguistic performance was made more impressive by his occasional sentences in Dutch to his mute scarfed companion.

He required no replies, but the eater and his keepers were steadily drawn into his talk. From nods and exclamations of 'Yes' and 'Oh!' they went on to speak approvingly of his English. These remarks the Dutchman translated to his companion, who, raising embarrassed eyes, appeared to receive the compliments as her own.

'S-so—' the eater began, and rolled his wrinkled cigarette between his lips. 'S-so you're on holiday?' His voice was thin and curiously querulous.

'A fortnight's holiday,' the Dutchman said.

The eater chewed at his cigarette. 'I—I retired last Friday.'

The Dutchman spoke to his companion in Dutch.

'Forty years with the same firm,' the eater said joylessly.

His keepers glanced at Margaret and Mr Stone, inviting them to take cognition of the information just given.

'Forty years,' Margaret said, swallowing cake. 'That's very nice.'

'Very nice indeed,' said the Dutchman.

And now the keepers had broad smiles for everyone.

'Show them, Fred,' one said.

'On Friday,' Fred said, his face as sourly dejected as before, his voice as querulous, 'I had a party. They gave it for me.' He was having difficulty with his words and his throat. He paused, swallowed and added, 'In my honour.' His hand went to his vest pocket. 'They gave me this.'

A keeper passed the watch to the Dutchman.

'Forty years,' Fred said.

'Very nice,' said the Dutchman, and spoke in Dutch.

His companion looked up, reddening, and smiled at Fred.

The keeper, recovering the watch, passed it to Margaret.

'Now isn't . . . that . . . *nice?*' Margaret said, looking from the watch to Fred and speaking as to a child who must be encouraged. 'Isn't this nice, Richard?'

'Very nice.'

'They gave it to me on Friday,' Fred said. 'Retired on Friday—'

'Brought him down here on Saturday,' the head keeper said triumphantly.

Now Fred was really unwinding. 'Read the inscription,' he said, handing the watch back to Mr Stone. 'It's on the back. It was a sort of surprise, you know. Of course there was a lot of whispering—'

'Very nice,' Mr Stone said, holding out the watch.

'Show it to her,' Fred commanded, indicating Margaret. 'But what's so funny about a last day, I said. Last day's same as any other. Last day's just another—'

'Very nice,' Margaret said.

'May I?' the Dutchman said, reaching out.

'I wasn't looking for medals. That's all that a lot of these young fellows are doing these days. Looking for medals. Young fellow comes up to me and asks for the keys. I say, "You take them, mate. *I* ain't looking for no medals."'

*

Noticing his moodiness on the way back, Margaret said, 'Don't worry. Doggie, I'll buy you a watch.'

It was the sort of joke they had begun to make, a residue of their wit. But she saw from his unchanging expression, the slight shift of his shoulder from hers, and his silence that he was annoyed. So she too fell silent and stared out of the window.

His annoyance went deeper than she imagined. It wasn't only the grotesque scene in the teashop, the sight of the men, both mountaineer and mouse, reduced to caricature. In the teashop he had been seized by a revulsion for all the women. For Miss Chichester, corseted and fat and flourishing, however distressed, however widowed. For the eater's keepers, gross in their cosiness. And the blushing little mute in soft colours he had hated most of all. The decorative little creeper would become the parasite; the keeper would become the kept, permitted to have his sayings, to perform his tricks.

For a fortnight, for twenty-four hours a day, except when he or she went to the bathroom, he and Margaret had been together. It was a new and disturbing experience. In the teashop this disturbance had reached its climax, and Margaret's playful sentence—'I'll buy you a watch'—spoken in the tone of one encouraging a child, which was permissible in the circumstances (after the observation of something humorous in 'life'), had released all his resentment.

Yet mingled with this was the feeling that his thoughts about women and his marriage as they drove through the darkening countryside, where darkness still conveyed threat, were a betrayal of her who sat beside him, not at all fat, not at all parasitic, full only of loving, humiliating, killing concern.

Their silence, their quarrel, continued at the hotel, the desk-clerk noting their mood with satisfaction.

Towards the end of the evening, however, her presence, which at the teashop he had wished away, had developed, because of this very silence, into a comfort. When in bed he wilfully stimulated the return of that moment of hallucination in the white void, the loss of reality, his alarm was real, and he said, 'Doggie.'

'Doggie.'

Her own hardness had vanished. He could tell she had been crying.

4

IT WAS ON THAT NIGHT that the idea of the Knights Companion—the name came later and was the creation of young Whymper, the PRO—came to Mr Stone. The idea came suddenly when he was in bed, came whole, and to his surprise in the morning it was still good. All the way to London he turned it over in his mind, adding nothing, experiencing only the anxious joy of someone who fears that his creation may yet in some way elude him.

As soon as he got home he announced that he was going to 'work' in the study. Such an announcement had been long hoped for, and the two women hastened to supply his wants, Margaret's delight touched with relief that the silence she had noted all day was not moodiness. She adjusted the reading lamp, sharpened pencils; without being asked she took in a hot drink. Unwilling herself to withdraw, until she noticed Mr Stone's impatience, she gave instructions to Miss Millington that the Master was working and was not to be disturbed. Miss Millington compressed her lips and attempted to walk on tiptoe. Her long black skirts made it difficult to tell whether she was succeeding; but so she persevered, whispering in hoarse explosions that carried farther than her normal gasping speech.

While, in the study, aware only of the baize-covered desk (Margaret's) as a pool of light in the darkness, Mr Stone wrote, soft pencil running smoothly over crisp white paper.

Until late that night he worked. When he returned from the office on the following day he went directly to the study; and again it was announced that he was working. And so for more than a week it went on. He wrote, he corrected, he re-wrote; and fatigue never came to him. His handwriting changed. Losing its neatness, becoming cramped and crabbed, some of its loops wilfully inelegant, it yet acquired a more pleasing, more authoritative appearance, even a symmetry. The lines were straight; the margins made themselves. The steady patterning of each page was a joy, the scratch of soft pencil on receiving paper, the crossings out, the corrections in balloons in the margin.

And then the writing was finished. And though Mr Stone might go up in the evenings to the study, there was now nothing there to occupy him as before. The fair copy made, he put it in his briefcase one morning (giving that object a purpose at last), and took it out of the house to the office, where he persuaded one of the girls from the pool to type it. Two or three days later, receiving the typescript on rich Excal paper, he was struck anew by the perfection and inevitability of what he had written. And now he was overcome by shyness. He was unwilling to submit the typescript to the head of his department. He did not think he was a good advertisement for his work, and preferred it to be sent to someone who did not know him. This was why, ignoring correct procedure, he some days later addressed what he had written to Sir Harry, the head of Excal, enclosed a covering letter, and let the envelope fall into the Internal Post tray.

He felt exhausted, sad and empty. He might garden, watch television or read the newspapers: his evenings remained a blank.

He expected nothing to happen, but was not surprised when Keenan, from Accounts, a man who knew everything before it happened and took pleasure in making a secret of facts that were well known, came into the library one day and, negotiating the last steps to his desk on a ridiculous tiptoe, said in a whisper, 'I believe they'll be wanting you at Head Office, Stoney.'

Keenan didn't say more, but it was clear he believed that Mr Stone was guilty of a misdemeanour. His moustache curled up above his small well-shaped teeth; his eyes twinkled behind his spectacles with one arm missing (a dereliction he cultivated); within his baggy trousers his long, thin legs appeared to be twitching at the knees.

And quickly the word went round the office. Mr Stone was wanted at Head Office! As though Mr Stone had committed an offence of such enormity that the department was incapable of handling it and had passed it on to Head Office, resulting in the present summons, such as only the head of the department received.

Mr Stone was aware of the talk. He caught the looks. And he pretended to an indifference which he knew would be interpreted as an unexpected bravery. The situation was oddly familiar. Then he remembered the eater in the Cornwall teashop. 'Of course there was a lot of whispering. But what's so funny about a last day, I said.' This was unsettling. But the familiarity went deeper. All the events of the morning seemed to have been lived through before.

And it was only towards the end of the morning, when he was walking past Evans's open door, that he realized what it was. Evans was ex-RAF, a fact he never mentioned but which others invariably did. He wore dark-blue double-breasted suits, moved briskly on his short legs, leather heels giving each step a military sharpness, and he had the severe manner of an importantly busy man. He was suspect even when he descended among the 'boys', for he was a type of head-boy, a self-appointed office watchdog who permitted himself jokes about superiors and office organization which on analysis could always be seen to be harmless but which occasionally encouraged some of the boys to be indiscreet. Walking, then, past the always open door of Evans, Mr Stone found himself carrying the needless papers which, to give himself the appearance of being busy, he carried whenever he left the library. And it occurred to him that on that day of all days the papers were not really necessary, that the look Evans, sitting frowning at his desk, gave him was not the everyday look, but the look of awe which he had been receiving from everyone that morning. And at last he was able to place the familiarity of the morning's happenings. What he felt now was the sensation he enjoyed in his fantasies when he flew calmly about in his armchair and the people in the office stared in astonishment.

So he exaggerated his calm, and it was only when he was on the train, the briefcase on his lap, that he relaxed. The delicate lines about his deep-set eyes became lines of humour; the lips curved. He smiled, a tired, elderly office worker oblivious of the crowd, his eyes fixed unseeing on the insurance poster.

After dinner that evening, when he was filling his pipe and Margaret was knitting, in light of painful dullness (she was sensitive to harsh light), he said, 'I believe they'll be wanting me at Head Office.'

The words meant little to her. And she simply said, 'That's very nice, Doggie.'

He fell silent. She did not notice it, so it did not develop into one of their silences. However, he resolved to tell her nothing more.

*

Old Harry—as he was known to those who did not know him, but Sir Harry to those whom he admitted to converse which they hoped to suggest was intimate—was a terrifying figure. In the eyes of their wives, men like Mr Stone and Tomlinson and Tomlinson's friends had their forbidding public image as well. But whereas they dropped the public mask in private, Old Harry, such was his importance, dropped his public mask in public. He wrote letters to *The Times*. He wrote on the number of pins in new shirts, the number of matches in matchboxes; he wrote on concrete lamp-standards. He never entered the first cuckoo competition, but he made important contributions to 'The Habits of the No. 11 Bus' and initiated the correspondence on the London Transport bus ticket. ('The smudged curling scrap of paper with which I am presented neither looks nor feels like an omnibus ticket, which is after all a certificate of travel, however humdrum. It is scarcely suitable for tucking into the hatband, like any respectable ticket. Rather, its flimsiness and general disreputable appearance encourage one heedlessly to crumple it into a ball or, in more creative moments, neatly to fold it into a miniature accordion, both ball and accordion vanishing at the moment when the omnibus inspector makes a request for their appearance.') Transport was in fact his special subject, and he had built up a reputation, nowhere more formidable than at Excal, for his knowledge of the country's railway system. (What he said to Miss Menzies at the garden party was famous. 'So you live in Streatham? But that's where the main line trains branch off for Portsmouth.') Every letter Old Harry wrote to *The Times* was cut out by Miss Menzies together with the correspondence contents column, which made the title of the writer plain, pasted on to a sheet of thin white paper and circulated round the department, returning from its round impressively initialled in a variety of handwritings, inks and pencils. The effect of these frivolous letters over the years was to turn Old Harry into a figure of awe. With every letter he receded; his occasional references to himself as 'a member of the travelling public' were shattering; and the impression of grandeur and inaccessibility was completed by his reported left-wing leanings.

So Mr Stone's departure for his interview with Old Harry at Head Office, for a reason neither Evans nor anyone else in the department knew, was in the nature of a solemn send-off. He was in his best Simpson's suit; Margaret, with an appreciation of Sir Harry rather than the occasion, had chosen his tie. For a moment Mr Stone felt it was like going to a wedding, and the feeling was encouraged by the tearful appearance in the library of one of the typists, a broad-framed young slattern whose main topic of conversation was the refusal of the LCC to put her down on their housing list (in fact she and her husband ran a car). She had had a difficult morning; she had been 'reprimanded' by Evans; and now she said almost angrily to Mr Stone, 'It's people like you who make it hard for the rest of us.'

He paid no attention and, walking down the middle of the corridor, not at the side, as he had done in the past to escape detection, and carrying no papers in his hand, went out of the office, in the middle of the workday morning.

*

He had hardly sat down in his chair in the library that afternoon when Keenan came tiptoeing in.

'Well, what did Old Harry have to say?' Keenan's knees were twitching; his hands, in his pockets, appeared to be fondling his private parts; and the concern in his whispered question was belied by the delight in his eyes, his lips, his moustache.

'Sir Harry and I,' Mr Stone said, 'discussed a project I had put up for the creation of a new department.'

And again Mr Stone had the delicious sensation of flying in his chair. Keenan's reaction was a caricature of astonishment and incredulity. For seconds he held himself in his conspiratorial stoop, held his smile. Then he straightened, his hands and knees went still, his smile grew empty and disappeared, and it was as if the distance between the two men had become unbridgeable. Keenan's joviality vanished. The lines of good humour in his face became fussy lines of worry and suppressed hysteria. In his thin, shapeless trousers, his broken spectacles, he appeared, beside Mr Stone in his Simpson's suit, quite abject and mean. The almost immediate return of his restless jollity did not efface that moment.

Another relationship had been adjusted, changed. But Mr Stone flew. For the rest of that afternoon, for the rest of that week, he walked about the corridors of the office as one who sat in his chair and flew.

At the end of the month Mr Stone was moved to Welfare, to a new office in a new building, where the furniture was brand-new from Heal's and where there was no Miss Menzies to signal the passing of the days by her costume. His salary was raised to £1,500 a year. His transfer but not his salary was mentioned in the house magazine; there was also a photograph. And it was the house magazine that he casually showed Margaret on the day of its publication (some half a dozen copies in his briefcase), saying, 'Something about me here.'

Around him the world was awakening to green and sun. The tree in the school grounds at the back became flecked, then brushed, with green. And this was no mere measuring of time. He was at one with the tree, for with it he developed from day to day, and every day there were new and inspiring things to do. At Welfare there were the long sessions with Whymper, the young PRO who had been assigned to the new department. The idea, Whymper said, was good, very good. He was 'excited' by it, but it had to be 'licked into shape'. These last words he spoke with almost physical relish, passing a thick tongue over his top lip, tapping a cigarette in his own manner on his silver cigarette case. Whymper saw himself as a processor of raw material. He spoke as one whose chief delight lay in sifting, cleaning, removing impurities. He said he made nothing. 'But,' he added, 'I make something out of nothing.'

For someone who took pride in his ability to refine, his appearance was strangely coarse, and Mr Stone's first impressions were not good. The squarish jaws were slack and a little too fleshy, the lips bruised-looking with rims like welts (having tapped his cigarette in that way of which he was so proud, he rolled it between these lips, and sometimes the cigarette came out wet at the end); the eyes were soft and brown and unreliable, as of someone made uncertain by suffering. He was of medium height and average physique. For such men ready-to-wear suits are made by the hundred thousand, but nothing Whymper wore appeared to fit. His clothes had the slackness of his jaw; they suggested that the flesh below was soft, never exposed, unhardened. His jacket, always awry, made him look round-shouldered and sometimes even humped. And his fancy waistcoats—for Whymper was interested in clothes—were only startling and ridiculous.

Mr Stone did not like being told that his idea had to be licked into shape. And his displeasure grew when at their first meeting in Welfare Whymper abruptly said, 'I hope you don't mind my saying so, Stone, but I find the way you tap a cigarette profoundly irritating.'

Cigarette in hand, Mr Stone paused.

'Go on,' Whymper said. 'Let's see you tap it.'

Mr Stone held the cigarette between forefinger and thumb and struck.

This, Whymper said, was wrong. The correct way was to let the cigarette drop from a height of half an inch, so that it bounced back into the grip of forefinger and thumb.

For two or three minutes they tapped cigarettes, Whymper the instructor, Mr Stone the pupil.

Distaste for Whymper was, however, quickly replaced by pleasure in the man's quick mind, his capacity for hard work and above all his enthusiasm, which Mr Stone took as a compliment to himself, though it very soon became clear that Whymper's 'excitement' differed from his own.

'How about this?' Whymper said. 'Our pensioners visit the pensioners of clients. Take them a little gift from the company and so on. It wouldn't break Excal. And look. Word will get around. "Our relationships are more than business relationships. They are relationships between friends".' He spoke the words as if they were already a slogan. 'That sort of thing will do a lot more good than all those Christmas cards. Nobody likes a PRO. You don't have to tell me. But who will suspect these old boys? And think. Men working for Excal even after they retire. A whole army of Excal old boys on the march, in every corner of the country.'

Mr Stone allowed himself to play with the idea. He gave the pensioners of his fantasy long white beards, thick, knotted sticks and Chelsea Hospital uniforms. He saw them tramping about country lanes, advancing shakily through gardens in full bloom, and knocking on the doors of thatched cottages.

'Thousands of unpaid PROs,' Whymper was saying. 'Welcome wherever they go. One in every village.'

'Unrealistic.'

Always there was this difference in their approaches, Whymper talking of benefits to Excal, Mr Stone having to conceal that his plan had not been devised to spread the fame of Excal, but simply for the protection of the old.

And in Whymper's attitude lay this especial irritant, that he seemed not to acknowledge the concern and fear out of which the plan had arisen, or the passion which had supported Mr Stone during its elaboration, going up night after night to his study. Whymper did not acknowledge this; Mr Stone was unwilling to state it. And as they endlessly discussed modifications and alternatives Mr Stone found that he was beginning, however slightly, to adopt Whymper's position that the venture was one of public relations.

'I am excited by this thing,' Whymper said every day during their discussions. 'I feel that something big can be made of it.'

He was full of ideas. It amused him to exercise his inventiveness, and he described even the wildest idea at length, with much tangential detail. When these ideas ran down or were otherwise disposed of, he returned to the duplicated memorandum that lay before him and asked Mr Stone to outline his scheme afresh.

'We write to our pensioners,' Mr Stone said. 'We invite those who want to do so to become Visitors or Companions. In this way we sort out the active from the inactive. We send our Visitors or Companions or whatever we call them details of the people they have to visit. The inactive. Age, department, date of retirement, length of service and so on.'

'That's where we'll need staff,' Whymper said.

'Our Visitors report cases of special need. We investigate those. But for the normal visit nothing more is required than the Visitor's travelling expenses and a refund for the small gift—flowers or chocolate—that he takes. In this way we organize our pensioners into a self-sufficient, self-help unit. All we provide is the administration.'

Always they came back like this to Mr Stone's original points, so that it seemed that by 'licking into shape' Whymper meant only wandering away from a point before returning to it.

This perversity of Whymper's encouraged Mr Stone to speak

with increasing enthusiasm. Fear of being too explicit about his motives led him to vagueness. But he steadily revealed more of what he truly felt, and to his surprise Whymper neither derided nor looked puzzled.

'This is interesting,' Whymper would say intently; his eyes narrowing. 'You are holding me. This is what I want.'

Mr Stone expanded. He had solved some of the problems of old age. He rescued men from inactivity; he protected them from cruelty. He preserved for men the comradeship of the office, which released them from the confinement of family relationships. He kept alive loyalty to the company. And he did all this at almost no cost: his scheme would cost Excal no more than £20,000 a year.

'A society,' Whymper said, 'for the protection of the impotent male.'

Whymper's talk was full of sexual references like this. Mr Stone had learned to ignore them, but at this remark he could not hide his embarrassment and disgust.

Whymper was delighted. 'This is what I want,' he said. 'You've got me interested. Go on.'

More and more, in the process of licking into shape, Whymper placed Mr Stone in the position of the defender, the explainer, until at length, passion exhausted, Mr Stone was driven to make easy statements which were like insincerities. But these impressed Whymper no less.

Once, towards the end of the week, Mr Stone heard himself saying, 'It is a way, you see, of helping the poor old people.'

It was ridiculous and cheap, and far from what he felt. But Whymper only said in an earnest, matter-of-fact way, 'The treatment of the old in this country is scandalous.'

And it was at this level that their discussions remained, as though they had both decided not to open their minds fully and had tacitly agreed not to point this out to one another.

They came to discuss the name of the project.

'We want something really inspiring,' Whymper said. 'Something that will actually get the old boys out on the road and up to the various front doors.'

Mr Stone had not thought of a name at all. And now, sitting at the desk with Whymper, Whymper tapping his cigarette and rolling it between his lips, he felt he did not want to think of a name. He feared a further cheapening of his idea.

'Luncheon Vouchers are big business,' Whymper said. 'And you know why? The name. Luncheon voucher. In those words you have lunch, crunch, munch, mouth, rich. You even have belch. Why, the words are like a rich meal. That's what we want. Something that would explain. Something that would inspire. Something memorable.'

'Veterans,' Mr Stone said.

Whymper shook his head tolerantly. 'Just what we don't want. The name we want will suggest youth. Youth and comradeship and the protection of the male.'

Mr Stone thought he saw how Whymper processed his raw material.

'Something like Knights,' Whymper said.

'Scarcely for the protection of the male.'

Whymper paid no attention. ' Knights of the something. Knights of the open road. Knights-errant. That's just what they're going to be, aren't they? Knights-errant.'

Mr Stone thought the suggestion ridiculous. He felt like sweeping the Heal's table clear of memoranda and paper, saying something offensive to Whymper, and returning to the peace of his library desk.

There was silence, while Mr Stone inwardly raged and Whymper thought. Then, as sometimes happened when he thought, Whymper grew lightheaded.

'Door-knockers,' he said. 'The Company's Door-Knockers. The Most Worshipful Company of Door-Knockers.'

Mr Stone lit a cigarette, tapping it in his own way and rather hard. But the suggestion went home. He stripped his pensioners of their red uniforms and gave them elaborate ones in dark brown with yellow stripes; they wore knee breeches and black stockings and knocked on doors with poles carved with some meaningful ancient design.

'The Knight Visitors,' Whymper said.

'That's another sort of night.'

'I am not a child, Stone.'

'You're behaving like one.'

Whymper's uncertain eyes went appealing. 'The Good Companions.'

'Knight Companions,' Mr Stone said wearily.

'Scarcely at their age.' Whymper gave a little titter.

Mr Stone looked at the window.

'Knights Companion,' Whymper said.

Mr Stone was silent.

'Right in every way,' Whymper said. 'Youth in the Knight. The Company in Companion. And then the association with those titles. KCVO and something else. Knight Companion of the something. Suggesting age and dignity. So we have youth and age, dignity and good companionship. *And* the Company. Knights Companion. God! The thing is full of possibilities. Your Knights Companion can form a Knights' Circle. A Round Table. They can have a dinner every year. They can have competitions. You know, Stone, I believe we've licked this thing into shape.'

*

And now Margaret took on a new role, and took it on as easily as she had always taken on new roles. She ceased to be merely the wife who waited for her husband at home; she became the wife who encouraged and inspired her husband in his work. Whereas before the nature of Mr Stone's employment was scarcely mentioned, a little of the fraudulence of the designation of 'head librarian' remaining to remind them both of their spurious attitudes at their first meeting, now they talked about his work incessantly, and the subject of his retirement receded. Her dress subtly changed: when she welcomed Mr Stone in the evenings she might also without disgrace have received visitors. (And what affection he had begun to feel for her clothes, for the garnets and the red dress of watered silk, once the arresting attributes of a new person, now the familiar, carefully looked-after parts of a limited wardrobe.) She still moulded herself around him, but she expanded, regaining something of her earlier manner. She saw, before Mr Stone did, that her responsibilities had widened, and she spoke of these responsibilities as of a bother which yet had to be squarely faced. She spoke of 'entertaining' as of an imminent and awful possibility; and she became graver and more insistent as the references to Mr Stone and the Knights Companion became more frequent, longer and self-congratulatory in the house magazine. Duty called her, called them both; and duty must not be shirked.

So then, like any young couple (as Margaret herself said, laughing to counter ridicule and destroy embarrassment), they discussed the changes that had to be made in the house. They needed new carpets, new pictures, new wallpaper, and Margaret was full of suggestions. Mr Stone listened with only half a mind, saying little, savouring Margaret's feminine talk in that room with the tigerskin as part of his new situation. His gestures became more leisured; he exaggerated them, acting them out for his own pleasure. The reading of the evening paper was no longer the exercise of 'a habit which solaced and without which the evening was incomplete. It was with a delicious sense of patronage that he read about the rest of the wonderful world. He was more easily amused and more easily touched. He often read items out to Margaret; and it was a relief, so tight were they with emotion, to laugh or be moved. Every sensation was heightened. They even fabricated little quarrels, which they never, however, allowed to develop into one of their silences.

About the improvements to the house Mr Stone said little. Playfully adopting her attitude, he said that these things were for the woman; just as she, in spite of all Mr Stone's expositions, pretended to know little about the Knights Companion and at times even claimed to be slightly bored or irritated by all the talk about them.

So gradually the house began to change again. Gradually, because it was discovered that if the repairs were to be thorough whole areas of the house would have to be rebuilt. Part of the roof had subsided, the attic floor was dangerous, the window frames had buckled. Uncompensated war damage, Mr Stone said—he told her how the planes came over this part of South London every Saturday night—and it roused Margaret to perfect fury against the government. They decided, therefore, to do up only those sections which might be exposed to the view of distinguished guests: the hall, the sitting-room, the dining-room, the bathroom, and those parts of the stairs which were visible from the highest stage of ascent that might reasonably be considered legitimate. The kitchen, on the ground floor, and their own bedroom, on the first, they decided to leave untouched.

Miss Millington was thought to be competent to undertake the redecorating. First of all she painted. Her fussy, ineffectual and inaccurate brush marks were to be seen everywhere. She proclaimed herself thereafter ready for the papering, hinting at the same time at the availability of Eddie and Charley, who, she said, were just finishing the fish shop. And that very afternoon a neat white card— E. Beeching and C. Bryant, Builders and Decorators—came into the letter box. They called that evening. They were elderly but spry. Bryant, round-faced and with spectacles, smiled. Beeching, the cadaverous-faced spokesman, said they were freelances, anxious to build up a reputation. Their prices were high; but Beeching said the prices of the firm they had previously worked for were higher. They were engaged. And gradually, section by section, one patch of building and decorating separated from the other by a week or a fortnight, during which Beeching and Bryant went off to do other jobs and Miss Millington was encouraged to try her hand again, the public areas of the house, or the areas soon to be public, were done.

Margaret had envisaged dinner parties spreading out on to the lawn in summer. It was a small lawn, and in spite of views of the backs of houses might have been suitable, particularly with the openness of the adjacent school grounds. But the neighbours were not co-operative. The keeper of the black cat was no handyman; his fence was in an appalling condition, wobbling and sagging; and his garden was rank, with a few hollyhocks and overgrown rose trees rising out of much bush. The people on the other side went in for desert rather than jungle; they also took in lodgers, and their back garden was strung with clothes lines. Their own back fence, too, was not what it might have been, being steadily forced out of true by the roots of the tree Mr Stone considered every day when shaving.

So the changes that came to the house did not alter its character. To the alien mustiness brought in by Margaret's possessions, which had now grown familiar, there was added only a gloss. The redecorated portions of the house did not lose their smell of old dirt, rags and polish. And every evening when they climbed up the stairs to their bedroom, to the brown velvet curtains, the tasselled lampshade painted green, the nondescript carpet and linoleum, it was like re-entering the old house, the past.

Change also came to Miss Millington. Whereas before she was an old servant whose inefficiency and physical failings were getting more and more troublesome, now she became precious; she added lustre to the establishment. In how many houses these days were front doors opened by uniformed maids? And now to summon her, who had previously only been shouted or ullulated for, there appeared, on the table in the hall, next to the flowerpot in the brass vase, a brass bell on a brass tray; and to enable her to summon them, there appeared at the same time on the wall a large gong of beaten brass, which the failing old soul managed with great difficulty, compressing her lips, closing her eyes, and striking in a daze with a slow curving gesture until the sound she created penetrated her consciousness and reminded her to stop. So now she existed in the changed house, shuffling steadily in and out of her roles as drudge and ornament, a pensioner only on Thursdays, when she went to the pensioners' cinema show to sleep through the afternoon.

*

'All we provide is the administration,' Mr Stone had told Whymper, and now they were occupied with the administering of the pilot scheme. So Whymper called it. He had a flair for urgent, important names. It was his suggestion that the Knights Companion Department of Welfare should be called a 'Unit'. The Unit was conducting an 'operation', for which it needed 'intelligence'. This accumulation of military metaphor, combined with the frequency with which Whymper called him by his name and referred to the large-scale wall-map of the area chosen for the pilot scheme, occasionally led Mr Stone to indulge in the fantasy that they were both in general's uniform, in a high panelled room such as Mr Stone had seen in some films: they spoke softly, but at their word pensioners deployed all over the country.

He relished Whymper's words. He relished the urgency Whymper, by his manner, his bulging briefcase and his talk of paperwork as of something tedious but vitally important, gave to the operation. He relished the words 'administration' and 'staff'. And staff was recruited, the word and the concept declining into three typists whose ordinariness and near-illiteracy robbed them of the charm of typists in films and cartoons (which, in spite of his experience, was what he expected), four male clerks whose advanced age diminished and somehow mocked the urgency of the project and whose appearance of unremitting diligence went with a strangely limited output, and a junior accountant from Yorkshire, a young man of ridiculous sartorial and social pretensions.

Letters had to be written, replies sorted. Knights Companion appointed, short biographies of the inactive prepared, machinery set up for the handling of accounts. And in spite of the staff, diligently tapping, diligently turning over pages, bustling about corridors with sheaves of paper, a good deal of this work had to be done by Mr

Stone himself. At the same time a continuous stream of propaganda on behalf of the project had to be maintained. This was Whymper's job. And Mr Stone was grateful for Whymper. Whymper had flair. All the ideas which had seemed theatrical and cheap were those that caught on.

It was Whymper's idea that a Knight Companion should be issued with a scroll of appointment on hand-made paper with rough edges. For this words had to be composed, archaic but not whimsical, and authoritative; and Whymper composed them. A special visit had to be made to Sir Harry to get his approval for the use of the Excal seal on the scrolls, and to Mr Stone's surprise Sir Harry was not annoyed or amused by their play, but enthusiastic and commending. It was Whymper's idea that Knights Companion should carry in their lapels little silver figures of knights, armoured and visored, charging at full gallop, lances tilted—that and nothing else, no word or letter. It was his further idea, though this was not adopted, that all Excal pensioners should wear little metal roses, of varying colours to indicate their length of service with the Company, to facilitate recognition by other pensioners and by Knights Companion. And so always Whymper's mind sparked, racing ahead of the Unit's schedule and occasionally wasting much time thereby (for days, for example, he played with the design of the charging knight, though he was no artist), but always generating enthusiasm.

And by his work of administration, of creating out of an idea—words written on paper in his study—an organization of real people, Mr Stone never ceased to be thrilled. Now his worn, shiny briefcase carried documents that mattered. Now, too, he caught himself looking at briefcases in shop windows, ready to discard the once fraudulent container that had given him so much pleasure in the days when the weeks were to be got through and numbered and hoarded. His talk became exclusively of the Knights Companion. Margaret knew as well as anyone of the problems of staff, and Grace Tomlinson responded with tales of staff problems that Tomlinson had silently endured for years. Now, Grace seemed to say, she could speak: Mar-

garet and Richard could understand. And Margaret gave a ready ret-
rospective sympathy.

*

The pilot scheme ran into certain difficulties.

A former head of an Excal department, scenting old blood on his
appointment as a Knight Companion, took a leisurely tour through
Wales, visited eight widely scattered pensioners of his acquaintance,
and sent in a bill for £249 17s 5½d, neatly worked out, the bills of
expensive hotels enclosed together with restaurant bills, garage bills
and receipts for the gifts he had bought. For one pensioner he had
bought a radio. He regretted his inability to buy a television set for
another, who had gone deaf; and in his letter strongly urged the Unit
to do so.

Twenty Knights Companion were on the road. Letters were
hastily dispatched to nineteen. And the bill of the former department
head, rejected in horror by official after higher official, had to go up
to Sir Harry himself. It was decided to refund the sum demanded;
but with the cheque went a letter, composed after much labour by
Whymper and Mr Stone, outlining the limited scope of the project.
A Knight Companion, the letter said, was not expected unduly to
exert himself; he was to visit only those pensioners—and they were
within easy reach—whose names were supplied to him; and only
token gifts were to be made. Energy such as the former department
head had displayed was admirable, but for eight visits he was entitled
to no more than £4, and they could not hide from him that his request
for more than sixty times that sum had gravely embarrassed them
with their accountants and threatened the continuance of the scheme
itself.

Promptly the reply came, in a large envelope: the scroll of
appointment was inside. In a long confused letter, indignant and hurt
and apologetic, the former department head thanked the Unit and
Excal for the cheque. But, he said, he felt obliged to return the scroll
of appointment. In his day he encouraged his staff to believe, as he

himself was encouraged, that Excal did a thing well or not at all. As for the silver pin, he was keeping that for the time being; he awaited their instructions.

They urged him to keep the pin. And nothing more was heard from him until the end of the year.

Less disastrous, though perhaps more embarrassing, was the administrative error which sent an inadequately briefed Knight Companion, a former messenger, to visit a retired Excal director. The short biography provided was democratically defective and the messenger knew nothing of the eminence of the person he journeyed to succour. Pertinacious in the face of kindly surprise, his chivalry at last turned to doubt and then was dissipated in anxiety. The former director appeared; the messenger bowed low, presented a packet of Co-op tea, and withdrew.

Whymper had made much in his handouts of having a messenger and a department head as Knights Companion. But now they decided that there ought to be some parity between the visitor and the visited. It was also decided to abandon the fixed gift allowance for a sliding scale related to the status of the person visited. It was, too, at this time, disillusionment with the Knights Companion momentarily going deep, that the Yorkshire accountant suggested that bills for gifts should be sent direct to the Unit. This would mean more work, but the accountant produced some figures to show that if as a result of this precaution two or three shillings were saved per visit— and it might be more, for some shops could be persuaded to give Excal a discount—the Unit would gain or at worst break even.

'What we need,' he said, 'is more staff.'

The request for more staff, enthusiastically put up by Whymper and Mr Stone, was as enthusiastically greeted by Sir Harry. And more staff was recruited, so that the female flurry towards the lavatories between twelve-thirty and one and five and five-thirty became disturbing: tock-tock-tock on brisk heels, pause, flush, tock-tock-tock: like a lazy sea whipped to spasmodic but towering fury on a steep rocky shore.

Two further irregularities came to light, and to the first there
appeared to be no solution. A series of aggrieved complaining letters
in various shaky hands revealed that a Knight Companion was using
his right of entry to homes to propagate the creed of the Jehovah's
Witnesses. The gifts he took, and for which the Unit had been paying for some weeks, were copies of *Let God Be True* and an annual
subscription to a magazine called *Awake!* Eighteen letters were
hastily dispatched, warning the Knights Companion against such
practices, and to the Witness himself there went a letter informing
him that he was struck off the roll of Knights Companion. A calm
reply was received. The Witness wrote that what he had done was
legitimate, since the truth had to be spread by whatever means.
Authority always feared the truth and the action of the Unit did not
surprise him; but he would continue with his 'preaching and pub-
lishing work'. He carried out his threat, and for long the district
remained disturbed, as could be seen from the concentration of red
on the wall-map, where blue pins indicated satisfaction, red dissatis-
faction, and yellow cases to be investigated by the Unit itself.

It was decided that in future Knights Companion would be carefully sounded for the depth of their religious convictions. More work
was involved, because Personnel did not have the necessary information. And Whymper, saying it in much the same way as he used to
say, 'The treatment of the old in this country is scandalous', said,
'That's the terrible thing about living in a pagan country.' (This was
Mr Stone's first intimation that Whymper might be a Roman
Catholic.) 'A man works forty, fifty years for a firm, and no one cares
whether he is Muslim or Buddhist.'

The other irregularity was discovered by chance. A Knight
Companion claimed to have visited ten persons in his area, and was
sent £5. The very day the cheque was sent, however, Pensions
reported that one of the pensioners had moved to another address a
fortnight before the date mentioned by the Knight Companion.
Investigation revealed that the pensioner had not been visited at all.
A further stern letter was sent, a further set of insignia recalled, and

Whymper decreed that in every list of pensioners sent out thereafter to Knights Companion one dead pensioner should be included.

*

At the dinner parties they had begun to give—the guests senior officials from Welfare, Personnel and Pensions, Miss Millington despairingly praised by her mistress for her chips and her fish—these were the stories that Margaret and Mr Stone told. They had thought their life's store of stories completed; now they had the joy of acquiring new stories almost every week. The story of the cat and the cheese, through which Mr Stone and the Tomlinsons had sat so often, was forgotten, almost as completely as the cat: the animal had ceased to dig up the garden, which Mr Stone on free evenings and on weekends diligently cultivated, with the now superfluous but still reverential encouragement of Margaret and Miss Millington.

To some of these dinners Whymper came. He astonished them the first time by appearing in formal wear, his jacket sitting uncomfortably as always on his soft round shoulders. At the first meeting he was excessively courtly towards Margaret, and displayed none of the brusqueness or desire to shock which Mr Stone had feared. He was courtly, but he was severe. His eyes were narrowed; his mouth determinedly set, giving an unconvincing tightness to his jaw. He smoked innumerable cigarettes, tapping them in his way and rolling them slowly between his lips. He said little. He resisted all Margaret's brightness, and she was intimidated by him. She thought she had failed with Whymper, and so did Mr Stone. But he came again, and again, accepting each invitation with alacrity; and each time he appeared in formal clothes. Margaret persevered in her brightness, and gradually Whymper thawed, acquiring something of his office manner. He sprawled in his chair, his legs wide apart, his back humped; his eyes lost their severity and uncertainty; and he occasionally gave that titter which Mr Stone found coarse and irritating in the office but which he was now glad to hear in his home.

'Tell me, Mr Whymper,' Margaret said one evening, in her best imitation of the actress, 'what do you think of all this talk about virgin birth?'

'What they call virgin birth I call grudge birth,' Whymper said. 'Somebody had it in for the husband.'

Margaret saw it before Mr Stone. She forgot the actress, her mouth went square with delight, and she gave a great guffawing laugh, widening her knees and leaning towards Whymper.

Their friendship grew firm. He became a regular visitor to the house and often had dinner alone with them, so that at times Mr Stone wondered whether Whymper, in spite of his smart, busy appearance, had no other friends. In his usual way of not letting civility stand in the way of honesty, Whymper spoke his mind about Margaret's clothes and the food she offered. Mr Stone suffered, but Margaret was delighted. It was 'just like Whymper'. This recognition pleased him, and he made an effort to please. He became Bill to Margaret, and she Margaret to him, while Mr Stone remained simply Stone, spoken in a mock-formal, affectionate way at home, seriously at the office.

Sometimes Olive and Gwen were among the guests. Gwen was as sour-sweet as ever. But she had been slimming—it showed in the slight looseness of skin about her neck—and she had at last managed to impose some shape on her body. She wore her brassières tight, so that her large breasts were pushed upwards. They impended; they dominated. But they were shapely, and she was not without attraction when she was seated. When she stood up the impression was spoilt. For her hips were wide, and though not disproportionately so, the foolish child, in an effort to emphasize her breasts, wore tight-waisted dresses and sometimes broad belts which exaggerated the broadness of her hips.

Gwen was always a strain, and so now Mr Stone began to find Olive. He wanted her admiration, but he thought her only tepid. In spite of all the show of friendship, the exclamations at this new decoration and that, in spite of the ease with which she and Margaret spoke, it was as if Olive had withdrawn from the household, and could no longer fully participate in its joys or sadness. Even when Margaret was out of the room she spoke as if Margaret were still there. And Mr Stone was disappointed. He expected something sweeter and more conspiratorial.

*

The leaves on the tree in the school grounds faded and fell, revealing once more the houses of the Monster and the Male (ferreting this autumn into the earth for a purpose which Mr Stone in spite of long observation could not ascertain). The pilot scheme ran its course and could be pronounced a success. Impressive sums had been spent; but the achievements were impressive. The Unit had been licked into shape. Administration had been simplified, liaison with Pensions and other departments regularized; and expansion could be easy. The usefulness of the scheme had been proved beyond doubt. The Knights Companion not only uncovered cases of distress and need; they also uncovered many cases of neglect and cruelty. Whymper fell on these with zeal, wrote them up in *Oyez! Oyez!*, the Unit's cyclostyled newsletter, and reproduced photographs of the Knights Companion concerned, encouraging the others to a more rigorous investigation of their charges. The protective function of the Unit became increasingly important, beyond what Whymper or even Mr Stone had envisaged. And the name of the Knights Companion, in which Mr Stone had at first discerned only Whymper's irreverence and professional enthusiasm, though Whymper always spoke it with the utmost earnestness and had indeed once roundly abused the junior accountant for speaking it with a smile of complicity, the name of the Knights Companion became a reality. For the operation had become a crusade.

It was another example of Whymper's flair, and Mr Stone was admiring. And such was Whymper's zeal, so great his delight at proofs of the scheme's usefulness, that Mr Stone could not be sure that Whymper had not committed himself without reserve to the cause. It was hard to tell with Whymper. In this respect he was a little like Evans, ex-RAF. He permitted himself moments of mockery, particularly at the petty crookedness which came to light, but he was quick to snub anyone, even Mr Stone, who attempted to do likewise. So that there were occasions when Mr Stone felt that he, absorbed in administration, and Whymper, speaking with the accents of passion, had exchanged roles.

'The thing's a success,' Whymper said, looking at the map with its blue pins everywhere, its obstinate patch of red, and its now liberal sprinkling of yellow. 'But what is success? We have a lot of letters, we can quote a lot of figures, the Knights are as happy as sandboys. But it isn't enough. Stone. A rescue here and a rescue there is all very well. But in a few months even that will become routine. Everyone will become bored, even the Knights. We want something big. Something explosive. Something that will drive the whole thing along on its steam for a year or so.'

This was Whymper, dissatisfied with a thing as soon as it began to run smoothly, needing the stimulus of fresh ideas, and always slightly unsettling to Mr Stone, who was content but not surprised at the proofs of the usefulness of his project, and whose delight in the creation of the Unit was doubled by its smooth functioning and the daily contemplation of real men and women, with serious lives of their own, engaged in the working out of a project he had sketched in words, in the pool of light in his study.

Then they discovered the Prisoner of Muswell Hill.

Late one afternoon Mr Stone received a telephone call from a man who announced himself as Mr Duke. Mr Duke was distracted and much of what he said was unintelligible. But Mr Stone gathered that Mr Duke had been recently appointed a Knight Companion, that he had on that day sported the silver knight on his lapel for the first time and gone out to pay his visits. The first two pensioners he called on were dead, and had been dead for years.

'I bought a walnut cake for them,' he said repeatedly, as though distressed by its perishable quality.

One of the pensioners was indeed dead. But Pensions reported that the other was alive, or that at any rate pensions were still being sent to him. A yellow button went up like a quarantine flag over Muswell Hill, and an investigator was sent out the next morning. She returned just before lunch, quite shaken, and told this story.

The address had turned out to be in one of the respectable red-brick streets of Muswell Hill. The house was not noticeable if one walked past it quickly, for red brick is red brick and there are more rank gardens in Muswell Hill than the borough of Hornsey would care to admit. It was only on scrutiny that one noticed that the house was derelict, the window frames washed of all paint, that the curtains had a curious colourlessness, and that about the structure there was that air of decay which comes from an absence of habitation. The walk up to the front door had strengthened that impression. The bells were rusted; so was the knocker. She had knocked and knocked. At length there was movement, and as soon as the door was opened she was assailed by the smell of dirt and mustiness and cats and rags, which came partly from the house and partly from the cheap fur coat that the woman who opened was wearing. This woman was about fifty, of medium height, with pale-blue eyes behind pink-framed spectacles. Her eyes were searching but held no suspicion. Behind her in the dark hallway there was continuous movement, and she held the door as much to prevent the escape of what was behind her as to deny entry to the investigator. The movement continued, little rubbings, bristlings, soft thumps. The house was full of cats. Her father, the woman said, was dead. She had already told them he was dead. Why did they want to hear it again?

The investigator forced her way into the hall. Cats rubbed against her legs, and to the protests of the woman in the fur coat she responded with something like bullying. There were many letters in the hall: a mound of football coupons, letters from various government departments, and all the literature the Knights Companion Unit had sent out. Breathing with difficulty, the investigator had searched the house, and in a room bolted from the outside had found her pensioner. The smell was even more disagreeable than that downstairs. The man did not see her; the room was in darkness; he was lying on a bed of rags. 'He doesn't like cats,' the woman in the fur coat said. The man appeared to have lost the gift of speech; what he uttered were gruff little noises. The investigator pulled down curtains, an easy task; with greater difficulty she opened windows. And then at last the man spoke, a sentence of pure foolishness. But here the investigator broke down and sobbed.

What did the man say, from the mound of rags on the bed?

'Going to put you up for the MCC.'

The story shocked and frightened Mr Stone. It awakened all the unease which he had lost sight of since joining Welfare, which he had submerged in the creation of the Unit, in the thrill of authorship and the savouring of his good fortune.

It was not one of the stories he told Margaret. And it was no consolation that evening to be in his own brightened home, where everything spoke of newness and the possibility of rapid change, where the bedroom with the green lampshade could become a prison. Its mustiness was again unfamiliar and threatening.

He was glad when morning came and he could get away to the office.

From his gloom he was rescued by Whymper, on whom the story of the Prisoner of Muswell Hill—as the newspapers later called the affair—had had an altogether stimulating effect. He too was shocked and horrified, but his fury was translated into energy, into a desire, as he said, 'to shame the country which permits this sort of thing to happen'.

'This is too big and disgraceful for *Oyez! Oyez!*,' he said. 'I think we should call in the Press.'

Mr Stone wished to dissociate himself from Whymper's zeal. He saw the advantages of publicity, but at the same time he feared, as he had feared the previous evening to reveal anything to Margaret, to publicize a humiliation which was so close to them all, a humiliation which rendered the threatened more vulnerable.

But he didn't say this. He only said, what Whymper expected him to say, 'I think we should move cautiously. I think this is a matter for higher authority.'

And Whymper agreed, not as one who had had an unexpectedly easy success but as one who out of deference and a desire for harmony was accepting a brake on his enthusiasm.

Once again it was as though unspoken words lay between them.

Higher authority was approached; higher authority was approving; and the story was given to the Press. In this way the Knights Companion scheme came to the notice of the public. The story was released in time for the Sundays, and there was enough interest for follow-up stories to appear in the dailies, national and provincial. The local Muswell Hill paper, whose posters, while photographers and reporters were in the area, proclaimed nothing more exciting than 'Boy, 11, Bitten by Alsatian', had solider fare for its readers.

In the commendations that followed, both from within Excal and without, Mr Stone found himself rejoicing. The Unit had established itself; its future was assured; the crusade would go on. He fended off congratulations by saying they had had a lot of luck. Whymper said as much. And Mr Stone revealed to Tomlinson and Tomlinson's friends the high-level discussions that had taken place before they had 'released the story'—speaking the words as one who had earned the right to speak them—to the Press.

*

Some time later Mr Stone travelled north on business. He took the opportunity to visit the Yorkshire asylum, called a hospital, where the daughter of the Prisoner of Muswell Hill was lodged. The Prisoner himself had died shortly after his release. The daughter had been freed of her fur coat and cats. She missed neither. She was entirely harmless and was allowed to look after the room of one of the doctors. Every morning she presented him with a bouquet of flowers from the hospital gardens. Every day she bought two sweets from the canteen. One she kept for herself, the other for a person she was unwilling to name. For this person she looked all morning. She did not find him. Then sadly she gave the sweet to the staff nurse.

5

WITH THIS SUCCESS there came a change in Mr Stone's attitude to Whymper. Nothing was said, and their relationship continued as before, but Mr Stone found himself more and more reassessing Whymper. He found himself studying Whymper's face and mannerisms, attempting to see them as if for the first time, and he wondered how he had come to suppress his initial distaste, how he had managed to feel affection for Whymper, to enjoy his obscene laugh and obscene jokes (Whymper on the types of fart, Whymper on the types of female walk), his puns ('equal pay for equal shirk'), the aphorisms ('soup is the best substitute for food I know') which were probably not his own, the violence of his socialist-fascist political views. He felt he had been made a fool of by Whymper and had succumbed to the man's professional charm. In these moods he was unwilling to concede honesty to any of Whymper's actions. He saw only that his own folly and softness were complementary to Whymper's cleverness and ruthlessness.

Of all this he told Margaret nothing. She and Whymper had become great friends. For Whymper's benefit Margaret had extended her party manner: she dropped daring words and was 'unshockable'. She gauged Whymper well. They enjoyed one another's jokes, and each rejoiced that to the other he was a 'character'.

Nor could Mr Stone tell Margaret of his irritation, annoyance, and in some moments his anguish, to find, as he thought, that Whymper was 'riding to success on his back'. These were the words that came to his mind, and they created a picture of almost biblical pitifulness: a lusty, fat-cheeked young man on the back of someone very old, very thin, in rags, supporting his feebleness on a staff. Mr Stone could no longer hide from himself his displeasure at finding their names, Whymper and Stone, coupled so frequently. Always in such items in the house magazine it was Whymper who was quoted, so that over the months it had begun to appear that Whymper was the Unit. His own contribution, his passion and anguish had gone for nothing, had gone to magnify Whymper. Out of his life had come this one idea; for this single creation his life had been changed for good, perhaps destroyed. And it had gone to magnify Whymper, young Whymper, whose boast was that he made nothing.

Yet with this there remained the concern for Whymper that had grown out of their relationship, a concern that was almost parental and at times was like pity. Between what Whymper saw himself to be and what he was the gap was too great. His attempts at smartness were pathetic. His clothes were good; he wore them badly. He tapped his cigarette with such careful elegance; when the cigarette came out from between his bruised lips it was wet and disagreeable to see. Attempting authority, he frequently only invited rebuff; and though he seemed always half to expect rebuff, he had never learned to handle it. And like a reproach to Mr Stone was Whymper's growing and often proclaimed affection for Margaret and himself, an affection for which, in spite of everything, Mr Stone found that he was grateful and pleased, and perhaps a little surprised, for in the office their relationship continued to be formal.

About himself Whymper spoke continually, but about his family he had little to say. He was a Londoner. His father still lived in Barnet, but when Whymper spoke of him it was as of someone far away and unimportant. His mother he never mentioned. He was a man without a family, someone who belonged only to the city. As secret as his parents he kept his house. He seldom spoke of it except to indicate that it was fully owned by him. All his important activities appeared to take place outside it, and Margaret and Mr Stone began to feel that his house was not a place to which Whymper invited anyone. They were both surprised, then, when one evening after dinner he said, 'I just can't keep on eating this muck of Margaret's. You must come and have dinner with me, just to see what can be done with food.'

His house was Kilburn, on that side of the High Road which gave him a Hampstead telephone number. It was an undistinguished terrace house with no garden. Whymper lived on the ground floor; the basement and other floors he rented out. Margaret and Mr Stone sat in the front room while Whymper busied himself in the kitchen, which was at the end of the hallway, on the landing of the basement stairs. The front room was roughly and sparsely furnished. There was a type of buff-coloured matting on the floor. The two armchairs were perfunctorily modern, their simplicity already turned to shabbiness. A bullfighting poster, dusty at the top, was fixed with yellowing adhesive tape to one wall; the other walls were bare. The bookcase was a jumble of paperbacks, old newspapers and copies of *Esquire, Time* and the *Spectator*; separate from this was a neat shelf of green Penguins. To Margaret and Mr Stone, who had expected something grander, something more in keeping with Whymper's clothes, the room spoke of loneliness. While they sat waiting, they heard footsteps in the hall and on the stairs: Whymper's tenants.

He brought in the food plate by plate. His plates and dishes had been chosen with greater care than his furniture. The first thing he offered was a plateful of cold sliced beef below a thick layer of finely chipped lettuce, cabbage, carrots, capsicums and garlic, all raw. Then he brought out a tall, slender bottle.

'Olive oil,' he said.

Margaret let a few drops fall onto her plate.

'It isn't going to explode,' he said, taking the bottle away from her. 'Like this.' He poured with a slow, circular motion. 'Go on. Eat it up.' He did the same for Mr Stone, then went out to the kitchen.

Margaret and Mr Stone sat silently in the dim light, staring at the plates on their napkined knees.

'You remember during the war,' Whymper said, coming back, 'how those starving Poles didn't have nice white bread like ours and were living on *black* bread? It's just ten times as good as our cotton wool, that's all. Don't have a *slice*, Margaret. Break off a hunk. None of your fish-and-chips graces tonight, dear. Have some butter with it. You too, Stone.'

They broke off hunks.

He left them again.

'What are we going to do, Doggie?'

He returned with a label-less bottle of yellow fluid.

'Don't wait for me,' he said. He filled three tumblers. 'This used to be a great wine-drinking country. Today you people with your one bottle of Beaujolais think it's something you sip. What do you think of that, Stone? It's the resin that gives it the flavour.'

He sat opposite them. 'Mm!' he said, sniffing at his plate with mock disgust. 'Those dirty foreigners, eating all this garlic and grease. Where's the tomato ketchup?' He started champing through his chipped grass and olive oil, drinking retsina, biting at his hunk of black bread, and maintained a steady flow of cheerful talk, mainly about food, while they nibbled and sipped.

Afterwards they had biscuits with brie and camembert. And then he gave them turkish coffee out of a long-handled, shining copper jug.

They returned home extremely hungry, but feeling extraordinarily affectionate towards the ridiculous young man. A day or two later they were agreeing that the dinner was 'just like Whymper'.

And it was as though, having invited Mr Stone to his home, he had decided that there was no longer to be any reserve between them. Now they often had lunch together, Whymper initiating Mr Stone into the joys of traveling about London by taxi in the middle of the day at Excal's expense. And Mr Stone was subjected to Whymper's confessions.

It turned out in the first place that Whymper had a 'mistress'. He used the word with a tremendous casualness. She was a radio actress whose name Mr Stone knew only vaguely but which for Whymper's sake he pretended to know very well. Whymper spoke of her as a public figure, and was full of stories of her sexual rapacity. It appeared that food had a disturbing effect on her. Once, according to Whymper, when they were in a restaurant she had suddenly abandoned her main course, picked up her bag and said, 'Pay the bill and let's go home and—'

'She tears the clothes off you,' Whymper added.

Mr Stone regretted encouraging Whymper, for Whymper's talk became increasingly of sex. The details he gave of his actress mistress were intimate and embarrassing. And once, after a dinner at the Stones', he said of Gwen, 'I feel that if I squeeze that girl she will ooze all sorts of sexual juices.'

Overwhelmed by the word 'mistress' and by Whymper's talk, Mr Stone was beginning to doubt that the actress existed, when Whymper arranged a meeting one lunchtime in a pub. ('Daren't give her lunch,' Whymper said.) She was, disappointingly, over thirty, with a face that was overpowdered, lips that were carelessly painted, and teary eyes. She gave an impression of length: her face was thin and long, she had no bust to speak of, and her bottom, long rather than broad, hung very low. There was nothing of the actress, as Mr Stone had imagined the type, about her, either in looks or voice. He could not imagine her tearing the clothes off anyone, but he was glad that she was sufficiently excited by Whymper to wish to tear off his clothes; and he was glad that Whymper was sufficiently excited by her to permit this. Towards them both he felt paternal: he thought they were lucky to find one another.

'She's a very charming person,' he said afterwards.

And Whymper said: 'I can put my head between her legs and stay there for hours.'

He spoke with an earnestness that was like sadness. And thereafter the sight of Whymper rolling a cigarette between his lips always brought back this unexpected, frightening, joyless sentence.

After this meeting, Mr Stone heard nothing of the actress for some time. Instead Whymper let drop talk, disconnected and vague, as though the humiliations were still close, of his childhood and army experiences. 'We were listening to the Coronation on the wireless, with some of my mother's friends. And I was quite big, you know. My mother said, "Come and look, Bill. They're coming down the street." And I went and looked. I went. They all roared with laughter. I could have killed her.' 'They say the army makes a man. It nearly broke me. You know the old British soldier. "Terribly" stupid and "frightfully" brave. I was neither.'

Sometimes he kept up a running commentary of contempt on everything he saw. This could be amusing. Once, just as they turned into a street, he said, 'Look at that idiot.' And before them, as though conjured up by Whymper's words, was a man in bloated motorcyclist's garb, the low-hanging seat of which was stained with monkey-like markings. There were days when the sight of black men on the London streets drove him to fury; he spent the whole of one lunchtime walk loudly counting those he saw, until both he and Mr Stone burst out laughing. But these midday walks with Whymper also had their embarrassments. Well-dressed women with their daughters infuriated him as much as black men; and once, when they were behind such a couple on a traffic island at Oxford Circus, Mr Stone heard him mutter, 'Get out of the way, you old bitch.' He frequently muttered abuse like this in crowds. But this time he had spoken too loudly. The woman turned, gave him a slow look of deep contempt, at which he seemed to cringe; and the depression that came upon him persisted until they returned to the office.

He was going through a difficult time. He appeared to cling to Mr Stone. One day, when they were having lunch, Whymper said with sudden passion, 'I wish I were like you, Stone. I wish my life was over. I wish everything had already happened.'

'How do you know my life is over?'

'I can't bear the thought of having to go on. It must be so nice to look back, to be what one is. To have done it all, to know that one had done it all. To be calm, blissfully calm, day after day, having tea on a fresh clean tablecloth on a green lawn.'

His words pierced Mr Stone, rousing him out of his concern for Whymper, recalling a past that was so near and now so inaccessible. How right Whymper was, and how wrong! And these words of Whymper's, which he thought almost poetic, remained with him like the words of a song, with the power always to move.

Day by day, then, Whymper's confidences became disquieting.

'I am a changed man,' he said one lunchtime. 'As from today. How can I *signalize* this change, Stone?'

'I can't really think.'

'A hat, Stone. A man needs a hat. A hat makes a man. Look at you. Look at the people wearing hats. Where can I buy one?'

'I buy mine at Dunn's. There's a branch at the end of Oxford Street.'

'Good. We'll go to Dunn's.'

They hustled through the lunchtime crowd, Whymper chanting, 'A hat, a hat. Must get a hat.'

And when they got to the Dunn's window Whymper stopped dead and gaped, his determination abruptly gone, his new character abandoned.

'I didn't know,' he said softly, 'that hats were so expensive.'

For some time they stood, their back to the window, studying the crowded street, until Mr Stone said they had better be getting on.

Whymper had not been looking well, his eyes sunken, his face sallow; and one morning he came into the office looking ravaged and ill.

'I was in her garden all night,' he said to Mr Stone at lunch.

This was the first reference to his mistress since the meeting in the pub.

'I saw them have dinner'—remembering the effect of food on Whymper's mistress, Mr Stone prepared to smile, but Whymper was telling it as no joke—'and I watched until they drew the curtains. Then I stayed until he left. I couldn't leave. It was hell.'

'Who was this other—chap?'

Whymper gave the name of a minor and declining television personality, speaking it with the casualness he used for the word 'mistress'.

Mr Stone permitted himself to be impressed. But Whymper's pride had already vanished in his distress, and Mr Stone very much wanted to comfort him.

'I should think,' he said, 'that that settles that. She sounds a most unreliable person, and if I were you I shouldn't see her again.'

'Very well!' Whymper said angrily. 'I will see that you don't meet her again. Ever.'

And that was the end not only of Whymper's stories about his mistress, but also of his confidences and their lunchtime outings. With Mr Stone in the office Whymper was again the efficient hard man of action, and there was nothing in his manner to indicate that he had once damagingly revealed himself to Mr Stone.

*

The crisis or crises in Whymper's personal life in no way affected his work for the Knights Companion. His mind continued as restless and inventive as ever. He established a competition for Knights Companion. It was difficult to work out a basis for awarding points and in the end they decided that the prize should go to someone of his and Mr Stone's choice. *Oyeʒ! Oyeʒ!* continued to encourage the belief that a carefully marked competition was afoot, and late in November announced that the prize was to be presented by Sir Harry at a Christmas Round Table dinner.

This dinner greatly exercised and stimulated Whymper, and he had continually to be restrained by Mr Stone. His first idea was that the Knights Companion should appear in antique costume of some sort. When this was rejected he suggested that the toastmaster should wear chainmail, real or imitation, that the waiters should wear Elizabethan dress (Whymper's feeling for period was romantic and inexact), and that there should be musicians, also in Elizabethan dress, playing Elizabethan music.

'The music would be just right,' he said. 'You know it? Tinkle, tinkle, scrape and tinkle. The old boys being bowed to their seats. Tinkle, tinkle. We could hire the costumes from the Old Vic.'

Mr Stone said he didn't think any self-respecting restaurant or waiter would care for that.

'Hire costumes from the Old Vic?' Whymper said, growing light-headed. 'We'll hire the Old Vic.'

Calmer, he pleaded for the toastmaster in chainmail, then for a doorman in armour, and finally for a suit of armour in the doorway. He settled for archaically worded invitations in gothic lettering on parchment-like paper.

On the night nearly all of those who had promised to attend turned up, many bearing their scroll-like invitations. Among the earliest was the former department head of whom nothing had been heard since his acknowledgement of the cheque for £249 17s 5½d. He entered with the appearance of someone deeply offended. But his name aroused no recognition in Whymper or Mr Stone, who, though passingly puzzled by his frown and two-finger handshake, were more interested in his companion. It seemed that a fresh humiliation awaited the former department head, for contrary to the explicit men-only instructions of the invitation and the Round Table publicity, he had brought his wife, who was even now, having shaken hands with Whymper and Mr Stone, penetrating deeper into the chamber where elderly men, variously dressed in lounge suits and dinner jackets, were standing in subdued, embarrassed groups. Whymper acted quickly.

'Ladies in the bower,' he said, catching up with her and blocking her progress.

A few words to the head-waiter had their effect. The lady was led, surprised but unprotesting, to another room on the same floor, where for some little time she sat in solitude.

Whymper's action proved a blessing. For a number of Knights Companion ('What can you do with the bastards?' Whymper muttered) brought their ladies, and the bower gradually filled.

Sir Harry arrived. His presence gave depth and meaning to the silence. Such a small man, though, to be so important!

Names were looked for on charts, places found and the dinner began. Now and again camera bulbs flashed and the diners blinked. The Press was represented in force and their effect on the waiters was profound.

The meal over, the Queen toasted ('God bless her,' Whymper said with a straight face), it was time for Sir Harry to make his speech. He pulled out some typewritten sheets from his breast pocket and the room was hushed. It was known that he prepared his speeches carefully, writing down every word, and it was an article of faith in Excal that his English could not be bettered.

They were meeting, Sir Harry said, to celebrate their fellowship and to do honour to one of their number. That they had gathered together to do this had, however, a deeper significance. He thought it proved three things. It proved in the first place that Excal did not consider its obligations to an employee ended when the employee's own responsibilities were over. In the second place it proved that in Excal it was possible for anyone with drive and determination to rise, regardless of his age. Mr Stone was an example of this. (At this there was applause and Mr Stone didn't know where to look.) It also proved that teamwork was of the essence in an organization like Excal. That the Unit was a success could not be denied. That it had been successful was due to the effort and faith of three persons. If congratulations were in order, and he thought they were, then congratulations, like Gaul, ought to be divided into three parts. Congratulations to Mr Stone. Congratulations to Mr Whymper.

'And last—aha!' He looked up roguishly from his typewritten script. 'You thought I was going to say "and last but not least"! And last and *also* least, the person who intends to keep you no longer from the main business and true star of the evening.'

He sat down amid frenzied applause, a little wiping of rheumy eyes, and cries of 'Good old Harry!' from those whom the occasion roused to a feeling of fellowship greater than they had known during their service. As soon as he sat down he looked preoccupied and indifferent to the applause and busied himself with a grave conversation with the man beside him.

Whymper was the next speaker. He spoke of the competition and of the difficulty they had had in coming to a decision. One man would get the prize, but the prize was in a way for all of them, since they were meeting, as Sir Harry had so rightly stressed, to celebrate their fellowship.

And the climax came.

'Silence! Silence!' the toastmaster called.

There was silence.

'Let Jonathan Richard Dawson, Knight Companion, rise and advance!'

(The ritual and words had been devised by Whymper.)

From one end of the horse-shoe table an old man in a tweed suit arose, bespectacled, vaguely chewing and looking rather wretched. Followed by hundreds of watery eyes, and in absolute silence, he advanced right up to the centre to Sir Harry, who, standing once more, took a sword from an attendant and presented it. A score of camera bulbs flashed, and in the newspapers the next morning the scene appeared: the presentation of the sword *Excal*ibur to the Knight Companion of the year.

*

It was a week of Christmas lunches and dinners and staff parties, and on the next evening Mr Stone and Margaret had to go to the Tomlinsons'. To this Mr Stone looked forward with greater pleasure than he had to the Round Table dinner. For he was going as a private person among friends who had not that day had the advantage of seeing their names, and a photograph in which they were clearly visible, in the newspapers; and he was going as someone who was not at all puffed up by such publicity but was taking it calmly, someone who still among his friends could be natural and unspoilt.

Mr Stone could tell, from the welcome they received at the door and from Tony Tomlinson's lingering attentions, that he and Margaret were the stars of the party. The photograph was not mentioned, and it was with an indescribable pleasure that he led the conversation to perfectly normal and even commonplace subjects. His gestures became slower and more relaxed. He studied himself, and the word that came to him was 'urbane'. He was perceptibly fussy and longwinded in deciding between sweet and dry sherry, as one who felt that his decision was of importance and was being watched by many. Still, he felt, with the steady erosion of the main course and the imminent approach of the dessert, that the determination of Tomlinson and Tomlinson's guests to maintain a silence on the issue which he felt was consuming them was a little excessive. He even slightly withdrew from the commonplace talk in which he had earlier so actively participated. And it was with relief that he heard Grace say, 'It's so nice for Richard and Margaret, don't you think?'

There was an instant chorus of undemonstrative approval.

'You wouldn't believe it,' Grace went on. 'But they met under this very roof just two years ago.'

'. . . just two years ago,' Tomlinson echoed.

Margaret at once took over.

'For the last six months I've been hearing about nothing else,' she said. 'If I hear another word about those doddering old men of Richard's I believe I'll scream.'

'Well, of course, it's your own fault, Margaret,' Grace said. 'We've been telling Richard for years that every man needs a woman behind him.'

'How unsatisfactory!' Margaret said, rocking in her seat, as she did after delivering a witticism.

Mr Stone recognized the influence of Whymper and covertly examined the table for reactions. But there was only pleasure. Even the demure, unspeaking wife of the unspeaking chief accountant, though red to the tips of her ears, was smiling at her plate. At this dinner, it was clear, Margaret could set the tone and dictate her own terms.

And if he needed further proof of their position of command that evening, it came when the ladies had been led away, and the men, standing drinkless and cigarless, with funny hats on their heads, prepared to make conversation. Now all the delight he had bottled up throughout the evening overflowed. His funny hat pushed to the back of his head, his face a constant smile, absently taking the nuts which Tomlinson gravely pressed on him, he led the talk. And now it was his words that Tomlinson listened to, it was his words that Tomlinson echoed.

'It's like a religious movement,' he said, rising on his toes, making a lifting gesture with both arms and throwing a handful of nuts into his mouth.

'. . . yes, a religious movement,' Tomlinson said, with the pained expression with which he always uttered his echoes.

'Why not get our old boys to visit the old boys of clients, they said. But'—wagging a nut-filled hand and chewing—'"Why?" I said. "This is not to help Excal. This is to help all those poor old people without friends, without relations, without—without *any-thing*."' He threw more nuts into his mouth.

'. . . of course, helping the poor old people . . .'

'Of course,' said the chief accountant, speaking through a mouthful of half-chewed nut and swallowing hurriedly when his words issued blurred, 'an idea is one thing, but the packaging is another. And that's where I hand it to you. Packaging. Everybody's interested in packaging these days.'

'Packaging, of course,' Mr Stone said, momentarily faltering before delight again swept him on. 'We had to get the old boys out on the road and up to the various front doors.'

'. . . yes, packaging . . .'

But before Mr Stone could modify his views on packaging Tomlinson said they ought to be joining the ladies.

And to the ladies Margaret was saying, 'Well, that's what I tell Richard when he gets depressed.' (When was he depressed?) 'It's so much better to have success now than to have a flash in the pan at thirty.'

Dear Doggie! When did they ever discuss the point? When did she ever say such words to him?

It was an evening of pure delight. He would look back and see that it marked the climax of his life.

6

FOR AS SOON as the door closed behind them and they were alone in the empty lamplit street, he no longer wished to talk. He wished only to savour the unusual mood. Margaret, sensing the change in him, was silent. And as the minutes passed, steadily separating him from the brilliance, it was as though the brilliance was something already lost, a hallucination that could never be captured again; and his silence developed into a type of irritability, which might never have found expression had not Margaret, no longer able to keep herself in, begun to talk, party platitudes, party comments, while they were in the taxi. By that shrug of his shoulders with which he expressed his distaste for her, his wish to be alone and separate from her, he forced her to silence, and in silence they returned home. So, unexpectedly, the evening ended.

And the further the brilliance receded the more clearly he recognized its unusual quality. It was a brilliance which was incapable of being sustained, yet a brilliance of which every diminution was a loss to be mourned, a reminder of darkness that had been lived through and a threat of the darkness that was to come.

It was again that difficult time of year when with Christmas and the New Year the workaday world was in abeyance, the season of rest and goodwill which throws everyone more deeply into himself and makes the short days long. The holiday was not at all what they had planned. His mood did not lift. The brilliance he sought to repossess grew more shadowy; and with helpless rage, both rage and helplessness stimulated by the absence of the people against whom he raged, his mind returned again and again to certain things which during his brilliance he had ignored but which now could not be denied. There was Sir Harry's speech. There was Whymper. There was the chief accountant's knowing little remark about packaging, doubtless picked up from some magazine or newspaper. Other people had made his idea their property, and they were riding on his back. They had taken the one idea of an old man, ignoring the pain out of which it was born, and now he was no longer necessary to them. Even if he were to die, the Whympers and Sir Harrys would continue to present *Excal*iburs. He would be forgotten together with his pain: a little note in the house magazine, then nothing more.

So impotently during these festive days he raged, and could tell Margaret nothing of what he felt. He feared to make himself ridiculous, and he feared Margaret's impatience: he was sure that she would take the other side and make out quite a case for the Whympers and Sir Harrys. So at last the brilliance dimmed, and all that remained was this anxiety, anger and sense of loss. Any reference to his success reminded him of his present emptiness. 'It has nothing to do with me at all,' he said, the modesty, thought proper, concealing a bitterness that was already turning to sorrow.

And then late one evening, less than a week after the Tomlinsons' party, the telephone rang, shattering the silence. Margaret took off her spectacles and went out to answer it. Her words, few and widely separated, came to him muffled.

When the door opened and Margaret reappeared, he knew.

'That was Grace. Tony's dead.'

He put his pipe down slowly, hearing the slight tap as it touched the table.

'He was watching television at half past eight. At nine o'clock he was dead.'

Tony! So whole, so complete, so Tony-like, so live in the often recollected incidents of that evening!

Margaret came to the back of his chair and put her arms around his neck, her cheek on his head. It was a theatrical gesture. He appreciated it. But it did not console him.

He went to his study. It was very cold. He turned on the electric
fire, sat down and watched its ever-brightening glow, saw the dust on
the electric bars make its tiny flares and smelled its burning.

Downstairs Margaret was telephoning.

'He was watching television at half past eight. At nine o'clock he
was dead.'

*

The new year did not bring Mr Stone the reassurance he had been
half expecting. There was nothing new to excite or absorb him, and
much of the work he was called upon to do was simple routine. So,
barring the discussions with Whymper about the Round Table dinner, it had been for many weeks past; but now, with his new eyes, he
thought he saw his own position more clearly. He was in the office
what he had been in the library, a gentle, endearing man nearing
retirement, of no particular consequence. Now he saw how often
in a crisis the instinct of the 'staff' was to turn to Whymper, for
Whymper's quick thinking, his ability to see his way out of a jam,
was legendary—'ladies in the bower' had already become an office
story—and though not liked, he was respected. He saw that he was
entrusted with what might be considered safe: the supervision of
lists, the overlooking of accounts. He had declined into 'staff' himself. To this assumption there was nothing with which he could reply.
He did not have Whymper's restless mind; he had no new idea to
offer; he was unable to handle the public relations—and this aspect
of the Unit's work had grown more important since the publicity—
with Whymper's skill. He became snappish in the office; he became
rude. And there occurred a row with Whymper over a typist of
Polish origin.

Enraged by her inadequate grammar, sloppy dress and what he
thought was her insolence, he had quarrelled with her in public and
gone so far as to refer to her as 'that D.P. girl'. He was in his office
scourging himself for his behaviour when Whymper entered in a
tremendous temper, his eyes narrow, his lips quivering, Whymper of

all people, the man who during those lunchtime walks had spoken with so much feeling about 'foreigners cluttering up the place'. His performance was melodramatic and self-appraising from start to finish, from 'What's this I hear, Stone?' to 'Don't you dare talk to any of the staff like that again, do you hear?' Mr Stone saw through it all but was none the less cowed. It occurred to him that the girl might be Whymper's new mistress, and several replies to Whymper's threat came into his head. But he had the lucidity to remain silent.

He thought, however, to revenge himself on them the following day. The girl had typed 'artillery' for 'itinerary' in a letter to a distinguished Knight Companion. He did not point out the error to her. Instead, he put an asterisk after the word and wrote a footnote: 'I leave this in because I feel that this example of our typists' literacy will amuse you. The word should, of course, be "itinery".' It was a heavy joke, made at the end of the day; perhaps the judgement of early morning might have shown him as much. Two days later the reply came: 'It seems that typists' literacy is catching. By "itinery" I imagine you mean "itinerary".' Now he knew very well how the word ought to be spelt; and in this swift rebuke he saw some sort of judgement, which made him desist from his war against the girl and made him less anxious to impose himself in the office.

His relationship with Whymper underwent a further change. Whymper's attitude was now one of strict formality, and in view of their respective power in the office this formality was like indifference. The quarrel over the typist was scarcely the reason. It seemed, rather, that in the days since the Round Table dinner Whymper had progressively lost interest in the Knights Companion, and having lost interest in them, had lost interest in Mr Stone as well. And this to Mr Stone was additionally galling, that though Whymper's interest in the Unit had declined, his power and fame as its representative steadily increased.

From the office, then, once the source of so much excitement, the source of his new vigour, he turned once more to his home. Here everything spoke of the status which he could not fully feel in the office: the re-decorated rooms, the organization of his household, Miss Millington's banging of the dinner gong (a process that ever lengthened), Margaret's dinner parties.

At these parties, to which Whymper continued to come, though less often than before, there was now a new fixture: Grace. Margaret was performing with zest for her what she had once performed for Margaret. And Grace was as radiant a widow as Margaret had been. From the first wan, teary-eyed appearance, with a brave sad smile, the gaunt creature had in spite of fogs and wintry drizzles visibly blossomed from week to week. The gradual attenuation which, as though to approximate to the appearance of her husband, she had been undergoing was abruptly arrested. The lined, thin face filled out; the neck lost some of its scragginess; the eyes brightened; the voice, always deep, grew deeper and more positive. Even in her movements there was freedom, as though some restraint had been removed. Whereas before she had been content to sit vaguely round-shouldered and apparently enervated in a chair, drawling out comments, often her husband's, with an occasional baring of very white false teeth, now there was a liveliness, a pertness, an independence. Her hairstyle changed. And, at first noticed by Margaret alone, who did not think it fair to Grace to mention it or to betray her to Mr Stone, new clothes and new ornaments began appearing on the aged creature. This taste, once released, became an obsession. Margaret continued only to observe until, no longer able to bear the silence, Grace spoke. And it was at a display of recent acquisitions that Mr Stone surprised them one Sunday afternoon in a childish huddle, those two women who, meeting at the door, had been so world-weary, one brave, the other grave.

Then for ten whole days there was no visit from Grace. When she reappeared she looked fit but saddened. She had been, she said, to Paris; and she suggested that her action was partly the result of her distracted state. She was walking down Bond Street in the middle of the day and had seen the Air France building. Yielding to impulse, she had gone in and inquired whether there was a seat on any of the

Paris planes that day, behaving as though the matter was one of urgency; had booked and paid; had raced home in a taxi to get passport, had raced in the taxi to the bank to get traveller's cheques, and then, with minutes to spare, had made the West Kensington air terminal for the airport bus. Throughout she had had no control of herself and had acted as one crazed. The trip, not surprisingly, had given her little pleasure. But for Margaret she had a gift: a bottle of 'Robe d'un Soir' perfume by Carven (one of a set of three bottles bought on the BEA plane back). She had bought a number of other things as well: she had in her haste forgotten to pack all the clothes she needed. Some of the things she was wearing; a number of the smaller items she had brought with her; and Margaret, with an approval that diminished as the display lengthened, made approving comments.

This was the first of Grace's disappearances. When in the middle of March she returned tanned, with cheeks almost full, from Majorca, she said to Mr Stone, 'You have to do *some*thing, haven't you?'

At last even Margaret's loyalty, in spite of Grace's gifts, was strained. Mr Stone's stupefaction turned to downright disapproval. But nothing could be said, for with each succeeding escapade Grace showed herself more anxious for their support.

Tony was never mentioned. At first this had been due to delicacy. Later it seemed that, as a result of Grace's strenuous efforts to forget, he had indeed been forgotten.

And sometimes it occurred to Mr Stone that he was surrounded by women—Margaret, Grace, Olive, Gwen, Miss Millington—and that these women all lived in a world of dead or absent men.

*

Winter still ruled, but there was the promise of spring in the morning sunshine which each day grew less thin. Slanting through the black branches of the tree it fell, the palest gilding, on the decaying grey-black roof of the outhouse next door. And there one morning Mr Stone saw his old enemy, the black cat. It was asleep. Even as Mr

Stone watched, the cat woke, stretched itself in a slow, luxurious, assured action, and rose. It was as if the world was awakening from winter. Then, leisurely, still drowsy from its sleep in the sunshine, the cat made its way along the length of board which the man next door had attached from outhouse to fence (perhaps to keep the fence from complete collapse, or the outhouse, or to support each to the other). Along the top of the broken fence the cat walked to the back, and leapt lightly down into the grounds of the girls' school. Idly, frequently pausing to look, it paced about the damp grass until, bored, it returned to its own ruinous garden and licked itself. It looked up and Mr Stone was confronted with the eyes that had stared at him two years before from the top of his dark steps. He tapped on the window. The cat turned, walked to its back fence and settled itself in a gap, sticking its head out into the school grounds, revealing only the caricature of a cat's back to Mr Stone.

For Mr Stone this appearance of the cat marked the end of winter, and morning after morning he watched the cat stretch and rise and make its aimless perambulation about its garden and the school grounds. His hostility to the animal had long ago died, living only in the almost forgotten story of Margaret's. And now he was taken not only by the animal's idle elegance, but also by its loneliness. He came to feel that the cat watched for him every morning just as he watched for it. One morning when he tapped on the window the cat did not turn and walk away. So he tapped on the window every morning, and the cat unfailingly responded, looking up with blank patient eyes. He played games with it, tapping on the window, crouching behind the wall, then standing up again. 'You're behaving like an old fool,' he sometimes thought. And indeed one day when he had been knocking and making noises through the glass at the cat, he heard Margaret say, 'What's the matter, Doggie? You'll be late if you don't hurry up.'

One of her recent complaints was that he was taking longer and longer to do simple things, and the slowness of his gestures was degenerating into absent-mindedness.

His communion with the cat, stretching every morning in the warming sunshine, made him more attentive to the marks of the approaching spring. It extended his observations from the tree in the school grounds to every tree and shrub he saw on the way to work. He took an interest in the weather columns of the newspapers, studying the temperatures, the times of the rising and setting of the sun, noting how, though the days seemed equally short, the afternoons frequently dissolving in rain and fog, the newspapers each day announced a lengthening of daylight. He noticed the approaching spring in the behaviour of people on the streets and in the train, in the advertisements in the newspapers and even in the letters to the editor. One letter in particular he remembered, from the chatty letter column of a popular newspaper he sometimes read in the office. It was by a girl who had taken care to indicate her age, which was sixteen, in brackets after her name. She protested sternly at the behaviour of men in springtime. Men, she wrote, stared so 'hungrily'. 'Sometimes,' she ended fiercely, 'I feel I would really like to give them an eyeful.' It was such a joyous letter. It spoke with such innocent assurance of the coming of spring.

*

He observed. But participation was denied him. It was like his 'success', from which at its height he had felt cut off, and which reminded him only of his emptiness and the darkness to come. A new confirmation of his futility presently arrived. For reasons which in his own mind were confused—his restlessness, his fear of imprisonment at home, his hope that given more time he might do something that would be his very own, something that would truly release him—he had been making vague inquiries about the possible deferment of his retirement, which was to take place that July. He had been met, as it seemed he had always been met, with a gentle humouring, a statement that he had done enough, and a joke that there would be no trouble about his appointment as a Knight Companion and that he stood a good chance of getting *Excal*ibur next year.

He did not relish the joke. It deepened his distaste for the work he did day by day; deepened his distaste for Whymper, now curiously withdrawn and adding an abruptness to his formality, all of which Mr Stone thought he saw through but which nevertheless annoyed him; it deepened his sense of loss, and made him hug more closely the anxiety and anger which was all that remained of that evening of brilliance.

Beyond spring lay summer and retirement and those days of which Whymper had spoken: 'To be calm, blissfuly calm, day after day, having tea on a fresh clean tablecloth on a green lawn.'

For these days Margaret was already preparing. She spoke of the need for activity: idleness was to be kept at bay. She was already planning visits and tours, and Grace, whose helpfulness suggested that she might not be unwilling to accompany them, was full of advice. It was clear, however, that one preliminary was unavoidable. Miss Millington would have to go. The old woman had aged and thickened considerably during the last few months, possibly because of the labours that had been imposed on her and which she had willingly undertaken. Though she had not lost any of her enthusiasm and did her best to conceal the failing of her flesh, not even the smartest uniform could now hide the fact that she had ceased to be an ornament and had declined far beyond the stage of the old retainer occasionally called in to help. Her shuffle had become a painful crawl, and it could not be denied that she smelled. She was often found dozing in the kitchen where she had once made her inimitable chips. One day she dropped the dinner gong on her foot. The gong was dented, and for this she was dreadfully sorry. Her own pain she concealed, but her foot swelled, and remained swollen; the flesh, progressively failing, could only yield. Once she slopped some soup over the jacket of a high official from Welfare, and in a feeble reflex of concern had poured the remainder into his lap.

And once she nearly killed Margaret. The brass bell had been rung to summon her. And presently, shuffling out of the Master's study, Miss Millington appeared at the top of the stair well with the bread knife in her hand. What was she doing up there with the bread knife? But so it was now with the aged soul: she had some minutes before been making sandwiches in the kitchen downstairs for the Master's tea. She appeared, then, holding the bread knife. And even as Margaret looked up the bread knife slipped out of Miss Millington's grasp and, steadied by the weight of its bone handle, plummeted dagger-like down, not more than two inches from Margaret's head, and stuck upright and quivering, as though thrown by an expert knife-thrower, into the telephone table. Margaret had stood transfixed, had refused to touch the knife, which had sunk in quite deep. And by the time Miss Millington had descended the stairs, step by step, at every step uttering garbled apologies in her gasping voice, the door bell had rung, Mr Stone had been admitted by a shaken Margaret, and there, next to the telephone, like the emblem of a secret society, the bread knife stood before him.

So Miss Millington had to go. But before she went there were discussions, which enabled Margaret to taste power and even sweeter compassion. Whereas before the two women had entered into conspiracies to keep disagreeable things from the Master, now Margaret attempted to engage Mr Stone in conspiratorial discussions about Miss Millington. But he was not interested; he appeared reluctant to come to a decision. So Margaret turned to Grace. And often, in whispers, when Miss Millington was out of the room, the old servant's failings were talked over, and it was agreed that firmness was as much in order as compassion. When Miss Millington entered the room there was silence. For a moment the women stared at the creature's pallid, puffy baby-face, her netted hair below her scarf, her long skirts. Then Margaret would speak to her in a voice that was just too loud, as one might do when requiring an animal to perform its tricks. And the decrepit creature, like an animal scenting the slaughterhouse, would make hurried, gasping and unintelligible talk, still anxious to prove her activity and usefulness, appealing, it seemed, not to Margaret but to Grace, whose full tanned face remained as seeming-smiling and full of teeth as always.

There came a day when Margaret was out of the house—she had gone to a sale with Grace, such shopping occasions having become more important to them both—and Mr Stone was alone at home with Miss Millington. He announced that he was going up to the study. He did nothing there which he could not have done more easily in the office, but he preferred now to bring some of his work home, as though hoping to find again in the study the passion and vigour which had once driven him night after night, working in the warm pool of light at the desk that had come to the house with Margaret.

It was while he was there that he heard a voice booming up indistinctly through the house. He called: 'Miss Millington!' But the booming did not abate. He opened the door and went out to the landing.

It was Miss Millington. He saw her below him in the hall, sitting in the chair next to the telephone table, talking into the telephone in a voice which held conspiracy and which she must have felt to be a whisper, but which was a breathless shouting that echoed and re-echoed in the hall and up the stairs. She was wearing her white apron. Her head scarf was on the table, and he could see the net on her grey hair.

'She thinks I tried to kill her,' she was saying. 'With the bread knife. She doesn't say so. But I know that's what's on her mind. It will be stealing next. Though there's precious little of hers to steal. I believe she's gone mad. The Master? He's gone very strange. To tell the truth, I don't know what's happening to the place. I don't see how I can stay on here, not with all that's going on.'

To whom was she speaking? Who, in all the huge city, was the person to whom Miss Millington could turn for comfort, to whom she was speaking with such security, such an assurance of sympathetic reception? Of her life outside the house—her relationship with Eddie and Charley, 'just finishing the fish shop', the children for whom she bought sweets, the nephew in Camden Town she sometimes went to see—he knew very little. And now this saddened him. But more than this was the warmth that started in him for the creature who could scarcely disguise her hurt by her show of dignity, which both he and Margaret had assumed to be dead.

And all he could say was, 'Miss Millington! Miss Millington!'

But she was deafened by her own booming.

It wasn't until he was half way down the stairs, shouting her name ever more loudly as he approached her own thundering, that she looked up, tears drying on her cheeks, less like the marks of emotion than of physical decay, no guilt on her face, no realization of having been caught out.

'Yes, sir,' she said into the telephone. And in the same soft tone, which was like silence, she said, 'I have to ring off now.' Then, as though there was still need for secrecy, she pressed her lips together and put the telephone lightly into its cradle, pressing her lips harder when the telephone bell gave its tinkle.

He said, 'I wonder what's keeping Mrs Stone?'

What could he say?

And Miss Millington, by a reflex action dusting the telephone table with her head scarf, quite ineffectually, said, 'Well, you know how it is with these sales, sir. And Mrs Tomlinson is with her.'

*

Margaret sometimes talked to Grace about moving to the country after Mr Stone retired. She had no intention of doing so—she never spoke of it to Mr Stone—but she felt that such talk was suitable. It also enabled her to indicate to Grace her helpless awareness that the street was no longer what it was. For some time, in fact, and even before Margaret came to it, the street had been changing. Once the habitation mainly of the old and the settled, it was now being invaded by the married young. More prams were pushed about the street. Houses were being turned into flats. Bright 'To Let' and 'For Sale' notices in red, white and black appeared with growing frequency amid the green of hedges, and were almost fixtures in the gardens of some houses which continually changed hands: petty speculators had moved in. Eddie and Charley—E. Beeching and

C. Bryant, Builders and Decorators—cheerful red faces between grey caps and white overalls, popped up regularly in the street, now painting this wall, now mending that roof, now visible through uncurtained windows in some stripped front room. A Jamaican family of ferocious respectability (they received no negro callers, accepted no negro lodgers for the room they let, and they kept a budgerigar) moved into one of the houses, which Eddie and Charley promptly repainted, inside and out: its gleaming black-pointed red brick was like a reproach to the rest of the street.

In this ferment the people next door decided to move. So Margaret reported. The house, she said, was too big for the Midgeleys. She had found out their name, and was quoting Mrs Midgeley, with whom, in spite of the black cat, the rank garden and the ruined fence, she appeared to be on cordial terms. They were moving to a new town, where, Margaret said, sticking up for the street, they would be 'more comfortable'.

To Mr Stone the Midgeleys were still newcomers—he slightly resented learning their name—and he did not realize the importance of Margaret's news until the following morning, when he saw the cat sitting in the gap in the fence, its back expressive of boredom, waiting for those early arrivals among the young girls who, with the warmer weather, now drifted up to this end of the school grounds.

At breakfast he said, 'Well, I imagine we'll soon be seeing the last of that cat.'

'They're having it destroyed,' Margaret said. 'Mrs Midgeley was telling me.'

He went on spooning out his egg.

'The children liked him when he was a kitten. But they don't care for him now. Mrs Midgeley was telling me. My dear'—she seemed to be echoing Mrs Midgeley's tone, which was oddly touched with pride—'they say he is an absolute terror among the lady-cats of the street.'

His morning play with the cat acquired a new quality. Every morning the animal awakened in sunshine, all its grace intact, all its instincts correct, and all awaiting extinction. He wished to see these instincts exercised, to reassure himself that they had not begun to wither, to wonder at their continuing perfection. He tapped; the cat was instantly alert. He studied its body, followed its sure-footed walk, gazed into its bright eyes. He felt anger and pity. The anger was vague and diffused, only occasionally and by an effort of will focusing on the Midgeleys and their dreadful children. The pity was like love, a desire to rescue and protect and cause to continue. But at the same time there was a great lassitude, an unwillingness to act. And his impulse of love never survived the bathroom.

He observed the cats of the street more closely, seeking the lady-cats among which the black cat had done such damage. Perhaps they were those creatures that sat so sedately on the window-ledges of front rooms, on the tops of fence-posts, on steps, the very creatures that in back gardens became so frivolous and unrestrained, for these animals, as he now saw, had one set of manners for the street and another for back gardens. He sought, too, for possible offspring. One he thought he did see, prowling about in the school grounds, a creature like its sire, black, but furrier and more restless.

Taking over Mrs Midgeley's pride, he saw, at the centre of all the cat activity of the street, his own black cat, which every morning waited for him in attitudes of repose and longing. And gradually, what he had at first thought with such anger and pity—'You will soon be dead'—became mere words, whose import he had to struggle fully to feel, for they released only a pure sweet emotion of sadness in which the object of his thoughts was forgotten, a short-lived emotion that he sought to stimulate by additional words, which he at first rejected but later came to accept with sad satisfaction: 'You will soon be dead. Like me.' For now the leaves of the spring had hardened and the year would soon be racing to its summer height, and he was left out of this cycle, with which just a year ago he had felt himself so happily in tune.

Thus absorbed, he paid little attention to the preparations of the Midgeleys for departure. There was, indeed, little to see. Shortly after Margaret's announcement the Midgeley's front room had been dismantled and had since shown itself curtainless and bare, with a few desolate-looking sticks of furniture and one stained and tattered mattress. This front room gave the house an abandoned air, as did the front garden, where the non-gardening Midgeleys had a single, untended rose tree that continued dutifully to bear its annual white blooms, pure and startling in their isolated beauty. In this garden there was now always to be seen a collection of cats in the late afternoon. It was as if they had already sensed the neglect of the house and its coming emptiness. They were always on their best front-of-house behaviour, but their number, their silent fellowship in the midst of dereliction, and their seeming vigilance unsettled Mr Stone; and they ignored all his muted attempts to frighten them away.

The uncharacteristic behaviour of one of these cats struck him one afternoon as he came down the street, swinging his new brief-case. The cat, white with brown patches, was restlessly pacing about the garden. Its belly was heavy, and from time to time it did a veritable dance of anguish, throwing itself up in the air. The frenzy of the animal alarmed Mr Stone. He made a threatening gesture, in such a way that an onlooker might have thought he was only changing his briefcase from one hand to another with an unnecessarily large action. The cat's frenzy was stilled; then, surprisingly, it leapt up the fence and fled.

He did not think of this incident again until the following morning, when there was no cat on the outhouse roof, when nothing answered his call, and he knew that the black cat, so whole until the morning before, had been destroyed.

No sweet emotion came to him. He was struck with horror. He was filled with self-disgust and, what he had never expected, fear. Fear made the hair on his arms stand on end. Every familiar gesture of the bathroom ritual became meaningless, a mockery of himself. There was reproach and fear in every reminder of his ability to feel, in the touch of the razor on his chin, the chafing of the towel. He feared to touch or be touched.

'Hurry up, Doggie. You'll miss the news headlines.'

He had been holding the towel in his hands and staring at the mirror.

At breakfast Margaret spoke of her plan. Now that the Midgeleys had gone she intended to break down the collapsing fence before the new people arrived. It wouldn't take much to break it down, and the new people would then be compelled to repair it.

*

They were in the garden some four weeks later, on a Sunday afternoon. Mr Stone was doing his gardening. Margaret was supervising and encouraging the exercise of this passion, which—men being what they are—had caused a cessation of all other activity in the house. Miss Millington was holding a box of petunia seedlings which Margaret had bought the previous morning, less for Mr Stone's benefit than for that of the very old and despairing man who offered them at the door. Squatting, and advancing with a crab-like motion along the bed, Mr Stone was followed step by step by Miss Millington, who held out the seedling box like a nurse offering instruments to a surgeon. She, poor soul, would not see the flowers that might come: she had not yet been told, but she was leaving in a fortnight. Their conversation while they gardened was mainly about the recent depredations of the young black cat, the offspring of that which had been destroyed. He had, it appeared, inherited the habits of his sire. Miss Millington expressed herself fiercely on the subject, and Margaret looked at her with distant approval and encouragement, in which surprise, amusement and regret were all mingled.

It was a restricted, unnatural conversation, with Miss Millington doing most of the talking. It was made so partly by the presence of Miss Millington herself, and partly by their awareness of the new people next door, whose strangeness had not yet worn off and was still a strain. For Mr Stone the arrival of the new people had at once converted the house next door into enemy territory. From the security of his bathroom window he stared with disapproval at everything that went on. And it was, it seemed, with a similar disapproval of his neighbours that the new owner went frowningly about his tasks. He was short, fat and bald. He smoked a pipe and strutted about his property in his waistcoat with his sleeves rolled up. Mr Stone found him as offensive as his dog, a short, corgi-type mongrel that was as round as a sausage and appeared to sleep all day, his white, excessively washed body dazzling in the sunlight. The animal's reaction to noise was negligently to raise its head, then let it drop down again: the cats remained in possession of the front garden. And as much as Margaret had regretted the unmasculine inactivity of Mr Midgeley, so she now regretted the improving zeal of the new owner. Within days of his arrival Eddie and Charley, traitors, had been called in, and had busied themselves with apparent pleasure about the property. They put up a fence so new, so straight, so well-built, that their own now looked shabby and weathered. The back fence in particular, twisted by the spreading roots of the tree in the school grounds, was almost disgraceful.

So in the back garden, which felt so strange, Mr Stone bedded out his petunias, Miss Millington talked about the black cat, and Margaret occasionally made a whispered comment about the folly of the neighbour in not creosoting his fence. Then in the gathering darkness, still squatting beside the bed, Mr Stone began to speak, negligently. He spoke of the lengthening days. He spoke of the tree in whose shade on hot summer afternoons they would soon be sitting. He spoke of flowers.

The aqueous light deepened to darkness. Lights went on about them, in the neighbour's, and across the school grounds in the Monster's and the Male's.

'Doesn't it make you think, though?' he said. 'Just the other day the tree was so bare. And that dahlia bush. Like dead grass all winter. I mean, don't you think it's just the same with us? That we too will have our spring?'

He stopped. And there was silence. About them outlines blurred, windows brightened. The words he had just spoken lingered in his head. They embarrassed him. The silence of the women embarrassed him. Miss Millington was still holding out the empty box. He stood up, dusted his hands, said he was going to have a wash, and walked through the back door into the dark house.

'Miss Millington,' he heard Margaret say, 'did you hear what the Master's just been saying? What do you think?'

He slackened his step.

He heard Miss Millington begin, 'Well, mum——' and after that the diplomatic old soul only pretended to speak and made a series of gasps which could have stood for anything.

He walked on, was going up the steps. A light came on, feet were wiped on the wire mat, and then there was Margaret saying in her party voice:

'Well, I think it's a lotta rubbish.'

*

One Sunday twelve years before, when Olive was living in Balham, Mr Stone went to have tea with her and Gwen, who was then just six. He had learned the importance of tea in their lives from an incident that had occurred not long before. They had gone for a walk on Clapham Common. About four Olive said they should be getting back; but he insisted on going on, to prolong the pleasure he felt at taking them both out. 'You can go on if you wish,' Olive said. 'But Gwen will be wanting her tea.' There was a sharpness in the words, a distinct ruffling of feathers, and Mr Stone felt himself heavily rebuked for his thoughtlessness. The incident did not increase his affection for the fat child who was 'wanting her tea'. And tea with Gwen and Olive became an entertainment he dreaded, particularly as in those days Olive was 'living for her child', and facing life with a degree of bravery Mr Stone thought excessive.

At the tea table in Balham, then, he was constrained. There was nothing to constrain Gwen, and Olive herself was fully and happily occupied with Gwen, supplying food as well as the occasional sharp word. (What delight Olive had taken in the food ritual imposed by a government so conscious of Gwen: the milk and orange juice and cod-liver oil beneficently doled out, sacramentally received and administered!) At length, the feeding drawing to a close, his constraint became noticeable and Olive asked him to tell Gwen about the holiday in Ireland from which he had just come back.

He had so far failed miserably in his attempts to amuse Gwen, and he knew that the performance which Olive required would be carefully assessed, for Olive was at the stage where, with the instincts of the school-teacher and the widowed mother forbiddingly allied, she graded people according to their ability to 'get on' with children and with Gwen in particular.

So after the tea things had been cleared away, and Olive had seated herself in her brown-leather armchair (typical of her furniture) and taken out her knitting—how, in her bravery, Olive had tried to age herself! Did he ever see her with knitting needles nowadays?—Mr Stone took Gwen on his lap, and the ordeal began.

Trying to see it all with the eye of a child, he told as simply as he could of the train journey and the boarding of the great liner. He had a good time giving her an idea of the size of the liner, and he thought he was doing well. Then he came to the first glimpse of Cobh. It had been a misty, drizzling morning, and on a hill of the palest rain-blurred green there had appeared a tall, white building, rising like a castle in a storybook. It was an enchantment which he thought a child might share, and as he spoke he re-lived that moment at dawn on the rainswept deck of the liner, the sea grey and restless, men in oilskins in small, tossing boats, the lines of sea and land and sky all blurred by rain and mist.

'Too self-conscious and namby-pamby,' Olive said at the end.

And there was something in what she said. What he felt now, standing in the dark bathroom, watching the lights of the houses brightening in that period of pause between the activity of day and the activity of evening, was something like what he felt then. Nothing that came out of the heart, nothing that was pure ought to be exposed.

'Well, I think it's a lotta rubbish.'

And of course Margaret was right.

Nothing that was pure ought to be exposed. And now he saw that in that project of the Knights Companion which had contributed so much to his restlessness, the only pure moments, the only true moments were those he had spent in the study, writing out of a feeling whose depth he realized only as he wrote. What he had written was a faint and artificial rendering of that emotion, and the scheme as the Unit had practised it was but a shadow of that shadow. All passion had disappeared. It had taken incidents like the Prisoner of Muswell Hill to remind him, concerned only with administration and success, of the emotion that had gone before. All that he had done, and even the anguish he was feeling now, was a betrayal of that good emotion. All action, all creation was, a betrayal of feeling and truth. And in the process of this betrayal his world had come tumbling about him. There remained to him nothing to which he could anchor himself.

*

In the routine of the office, as in the rhythm of the seasons, he could no longer participate. It all went without reference to himself. Soon it would go on without his presence. His earlier petulance—'Why do you ask *me?* Why don't you ask Mr Whymper?' At which the ridiculous young man from Yorkshire with the ridiculous clothes had actually sniggered, and reported that 'Pop', the foolish and common nickname which that foolish and common boy had succeeded in popularizing, wasn't in a good mood that morning—his earlier petulance had given way to weariness and indifference and then at last to a distaste for the office which was like fear.

There were days when the office was made unbearable for him by the knowledge that Whymper was present. He felt that Whymper's indifference had turned to contempt, of the sort which follows affection; he thought it conveyed reassessment, rejection and offended disgust. There were times when he felt that he had brought this contempt on himself, that his own revulsion and hostility had been divined by Whymper, who was demonstrating his disregard for the judgement by an exaggerated heartiness with the other members of the staff. He had certainly unbent considerably towards them in these last weeks, and the Whymperish gambit of joviality followed by coldness was less in evidence. 'Tell them a joke,' Whymper used to say in the early days. 'They will laugh. The fresh ones will try to tell you a joke in return. You don't laugh.'

The young accountant had frequently fallen victim to this tactic. Now, fortified by Whymper's friendship—he was Whymper's new lunch companion—he attempted to use it on more junior staff. He also tried to embarrass typists by staring at their foreheads, an 'executive's' gambit which Mr Stone had heard of but had never seen practised. The detestable young man now tapped his cigarettes—it was his affectation to smoke nothing but Lambert and Butler's Straight Cut, with the striped paper—in the Whymper manner. And—these young men appeared to be having an effect on one another—Whymper came back to the office one afternoon wearing an outrageous bowtie: the junior accountant sometimes wore bowties. Mr Stone could imagine the abrupt decision, the marching off to the shop with the young accountant, the determined yet slack-jawed expression as Whymper bought perhaps half a dozen. Thereafter Whymper always wore bowties; and, since he was Whymper, they were invariably askew. Mr Stone thought they looked a perfectly ridiculous pair of young men, particularly on Saturday mornings, when the young accountant came to work in a 'county' outfit, with a hat far above his station. The hat Mr Stone especially loathed. It was green, with a green feather, as though the boy might at any moment be setting off across the moors.

On calmer days Mr Stone felt that Whymper might only be reacting against his former indiscretions, though he was convinced that these indiscretions and perhaps others were being repeated to the junior accountant. He also saw in Whymper's strange behaviour proof of the now persistent rumour that Whymper was soon going to leave the Unit and might indeed be resigning from Excal.

Altogether, it was a relief when Whymper left for his holiday, though the presence of his familiar never ceased to be irritating.

*

Margaret appeared to be unusually excited when she let Mr Stone in that evening—such duties no longer being performed by Miss Millington, who had been dismissed with a standing invitation, so far not taken up, to come back and watch television whenever she liked—and it was with an unusually businesslike air that she hustled Mr Stone into the sitting-room. There he found Olive. She was dressed as for a morning's shopping, in clothes formal yet festive. But she looked grave and exhausted, and Margaret wore a careful expression in which concern was mingled with the plain desire not to be thought interfering. With her subdued impresario-like manner Margaret seated Mr Stone, then settled down herself. It was clear that Olive had brought news of importance and that this news—there were cups of tea about—had already been given. But it was not immediately forthcoming, for first there were the inquiries about the office from Margaret and Olive, and there were offers of tea and the things that went with tea. Then, the scene prepared, Margaret glanced at Olive as though encouraging her to begin, and then glanced at Mr Stone, almost, it seemed—Mr Stone couldn't help being reminded of the infants' radio programme—to see whether he was 'comfortable'. She herself sat forward in her chair, restlessly rocking about and rearranging her skirt over her knees as though she had made several witticisms.

At last it came out, and the calmest person appeared to be Olive.

Gwen wanted to go away on holiday with Whymper.

Margaret, watching them both anxiously like a referee, asked, 'Did you know about this, Richard?'

He didn't reply. But his mind, ranging far and fast, instantly settled on various incidents which, though ignored at the time, now turned out to have registered. The deceptions of the young never took in the young; they took in only the old. So much about Whymper's recent behaviour was now explained. The burden of such secrecy had been too great, even for Whymper. And Mr Stone had no doubt that this secrecy had been maintained at the instance of Gwen: he could see the sour foolish face as, mistaking her own fulfilment for power, she childishly exacted promises and made threats in Whymper's shabby front room with the bullfighting poster, Whymper's tenants moving about the hall outside.

But Whymper!

'Well, of course you'll refuse. Gwen's just being very foolish.'

He noted their hesitation.

Then Olive said that Gwen had left home that morning and gone to Whymper's house.

'This is ridiculous. Utterly ridiculous.' He got up and walked about the tigerskin. 'And if you knew what I know about him you wouldn't both be sitting there looking so pleased with yourselves.' They were, in fact, both looking up at him with some apprehension. 'Whymper! Bill! The man is—the man is immoral. I know him better than any of you. Immoral,' he repeated, adding with satisfaction, 'and common. Immoral and common.'

His violence startled them. The saliva in the corners of Olive's mouth was perceptible.

'We are as shocked and upset as you are, Richard,' Margaret said unconvincingly. 'But I don't imagine Olive came here to hear you talk like this.'

'All this talk about a pagan country,' Mr Stone said.

There was a pause.

'Wanting her tea,' he said reflectively. 'Well, she's got it now. Running off with this man just like any shop assistant on holiday. And now you come to see me. Why don't you go to *Bill?* But I imagine you want me to go and bring her home and read her a little Enid Blyton and tell her a little story about what I did at the office today.'

He saw himself entering Whymper's house, saw Whymper's frightened, contemptuous face; saw Gwen sulky, satisfied, triumphant; saw Whymper being 'firm' and offensive. It was too much. 'But that's something you and Margaret can see about. *You* can tell her about the big red bus and the choo-choo train.'

'Richard!' Margaret cried. The solemn scene she had visualized was all but destroyed.

Too late, then, it came out that Gwen was pregnant.

'I'm not surprised! I'm not surprised!' He was, deeply. 'But the welfare state hasn't run short of milk and orange juice and cod-liver oil.'

And incapable of further irony, he grew so violent in his language that it was all Margaret could do to prevent an open breach between brother and sister.

It was only later, when Olive had left, with nothing settled or even talked over, that he calmed down.

'I don't understand you, Richard,' Margaret said that evening when they were getting ready for bed. 'If you hate them both so much, why should you be so upset?'

'You are quite right,' he said, looking out of the bedroom window past the old thick brown velvet curtains. 'You are quite right. They deserve one another. And I loathe them both.' He even managed a laugh. 'Poor Olive.'

*

Before the end of the week Whymper's resignation was officially announced.

'Bill's had an offer from Gow's,' the junior accountant said importantly. 'Sacred Gow's, the gondemporary people.'

His master's voice, Mr Stone thought.

And on Thursday afternoon the boy came into Mr Stone's office with a copy of the *World's Press News*.

'Have you seen this about Bill?'

Next to a photograph of a presentation of antique furniture to a retiring executive, Mr Stone read:

BILL WHYMPER JOINS GOW'S

Bill Whymper is leaving Excal at the end of this month to take up the newly created executive position of publicity director with Gow's. 'The appointment emphasizes the importance attached to progressive marketing and publicity policies in Gow's expanding operations, and Mr Whymper will advise in the overall formulation and review of plans,' a spokesman said.

Mr Whymper moves to this top post with the asset of years of success in Excal's P.R. division. He will be remembered as the man behind the energetic and resourceful promotion of Excal's signally successful 'Knights Companion' scheme last year.

When at last he put the paper down, the office was silent. He went out into the corridor. Traffic noises came up from the street unchallenged. The typists' room was empty, lights turned off, the machines all draped with black covers. The clock said twenty past four.

LONDON WAS WALKING that day. He had forgotten the one-day transport strike which, only partial in the morning, had steadily mounted in drama, the evening papers issuing breathless front-page bulletins on the dislocation and suspension of services. He found the Embankment choked with unmoving cars and buses. People who had stood in hopeless queues and fought to get seats in buses remained where they were and stewed in the heat: the strikers had chosen a fine day. And still, scarcely noticeable in the slow two-way movement on the crowded pavements, the queues remained. At first he stood in a queue. Then he pursued a rogue bus down a side street into the Strand, boarded it without difficulty and discovered it was going no farther. So he decided to walk. And he walked with the city. Along the Embankment, across the bridge, losing all sense of time and distance in the steady tread of thousands of feet, here in the openness of the glinting river crisper and more resonant, he walked with swinging strides, enjoying the exertion, not looking forward to the end, wishing to exhaust himself, to numb the pain within him, hardly aware of the people about him, faceless, their clothes in the mass so uniform, the military-minded and the officerly alone distinguishing themselves by their stride and the little competitive knots about them. Across the river, many disappeared into Waterloo Station, and corner by corner thereafter the noise of feet diminished and the pavement cleared. The signs of commonplace public houses, open doors revealing empty cream-and-brown interiors, were like invitations to rest and relief. And now the walk required will, for it led through long streets of dark brick and stucco peeling like the barks of the pollarded plane trees, past rows of small bright shops made more mean by signboards and display cards and samples bleaching in the windows. Nightly, from the warm, bright heart where they worked and to which they went back for their pleasures, the people of the city returned to such areas, such streets, such houses.

And as he walked through the long, dull streets, as with each step he felt his hips and thighs and calves and toes working, his mood changed, and he had a vision of the city such as he had had once before, at the first dinner party he and Margaret had given. (Gwen was there, and Olive, and Grace and Tony Tomlinson, and Miss Millington had cooked and served her inimitable chips.) He stripped the city of all that was enduring and saw that all that was not flesh was of no importance to man. All that mattered was man's own frailty and corruptibility. The order of the universe, to which he had sought to ally himself, was not his order. So much he had seen before. But now he saw, too, that it was not by creation that man demonstrated his power and defied this hostile order, but by destruction. By damming the river, by destroying the mountain, by so scarring the face of the earth that Nature's attempt to reassert herself became a mockery.

He had now reached Brixton, with its large, glass-fronted shops, its modernistic police station and antique food stalls, its crowds of black and white. Here the walkers were not noticeable. There were long but manageable queues at the bus stops. Several buses arrived; many people got off. He jumped a queue, found himself within the warding-off arm of a conductor on a 109 bus, and rode home. He was grateful for the ride. He was beginning to be fatigued and his breath was failing.

As he walked up the street to his home with long, hard strides, he felt himself grow taller. He walked as the destroyer, as the man who carried the possibility of the earth's destruction within him. Taller and taller he grew, firmer and firmer he walked, past the petty gardens of petty houses where people sought to accommodate themselves to life, past the blank, perceptive faces of cats, past the 'To Let' and 'For Sale' signs, and all the transient handiwork of Eddie and Charley.

At his door he rang. Harder, and longer. The house was empty. Margaret was with Olive and Grace. Happy band of sisters! He fetched out his own key, opened, let himself into the dark hall.

The eyes were green.

Fear blended into guilt, guilt into love.

'Pussy.'

But before the word was fully uttered the young black cat was down the steps, and before any further gesture could be made was out through the open door.

*

He was no destroyer. Once before the world had collapsed about him. But he had survived. And he had no doubt that in time calm would come to him again. Now he was only very tired. In the empty house he was alone. He took the briefcase up to the study, to wait there and perhaps to do a little work until Margaret arrived.

Srinagar, August 1962

A Flag on the Island

To Diana Athill

Contents

My Aunt Gold Teeth

I NEVER KNEW her real name and it is quite likely that she did have one, though I never heard her called anything but Gold Teeth. She did, indeed, have gold teeth. She had sixteen of them. She had married early and she had married well, and shortly after her marriage she exchanged her perfectly sound teeth for gold ones, to announce to the world that her husband was a man of substance.

Even without her gold teeth my aunt would have been noticeable. She was short, scarcely five foot, and she was very fat. If you saw her in silhouette you would have found it difficult to know whether she was facing you or whether she was looking sideways.

She ate little and prayed much. Her family being Hindu, and her husband being a pundit, she, too, was an orthodox Hindu. Of Hinduism she knew little apart from the ceremonies and the taboos, and this was enough for her. Gold Teeth saw God as a Power, and religious ritual as a means of harnessing that Power for great practical good, her good.

I may have given the impression that Gold Teeth prayed because she wanted to be less fat. The fact was that Gold Teeth had no children and she was almost forty. It was her childlessness, not her fat, that oppressed her, and she prayed for the curse to be removed. She was willing to try any means—any ritual, any prayer—in order to trap and channel the supernatural Power.

And so it was that she began to indulge in surreptitious Christian practices.

She was living at the time in a country village called Cunupia, in County Caroni. Here the Canadian Mission had long waged war against the Indian heathen, and saved many. But Gold Teeth stood firm. The Minister of Cunupia expended his Presbyterian piety on her; so did the headmaster of the Mission school. But all in vain. At no time was Gold Teeth persuaded even to think about being converted. The idea horrified her. Her father had been in his day one of the best-known Hindu pundits, and even now her husband's fame as a pundit, as a man who could read and write Sanskrit, had spread far beyond Cunupia. She was in no doubt whatsoever that Hindus were the best people in the world, and that Hinduism was a superior religion. She was willing to select, modify and incorporate alien eccentricities into her worship; but to abjure her own faith—never!

Presbyterianism was not the only danger the good Hindu had to face in Cunupia. Besides, of course, the ever-present threat of open Muslim aggression, the Catholics were to be reckoned with. Their pamphlets were everywhere and it was hard to avoid them. In them Gold Teeth read of novenas and rosaries, of squads of saints and angels. These were things she understood and could even sympathize with, and they encouraged her to seek further. She read of the mysteries and the miracles, of penances and indulgences. Her scepticism sagged, and yielded to a quickening, if reluctant, enthusiasm.

One morning she took the train for the County town of Chaguanas, three miles, two stations and twenty minutes away. The Church of St Philip and St James in Chaguanas stands imposingly at the end of the Caroni Savannah Road, and although Gold Teeth knew Chaguanas well, all she knew of the church was that it had a clock, at which she had glanced on her way to the railway station nearby. She had hitherto been far more interested in the drab ochre-washed edifice opposite, which was the police station.

She carried herself into the churchyard, awed by her own temerity, feeling like an explorer in a land of cannibals. To her relief, the church was empty. It was not as terrifying as she had expected. In the gilt and images and the resplendent cloths she found much that reminded her of her Hindu temple. Her eyes caught a discreet sign: CANDLES TWO CENTS EACH. She undid the knot in the end of her veil, where she kept her money, took out three cents, popped them into the box, picked up a candle and muttered a prayer in Hindustani. A brief moment of elation gave way to a sense of guilt, and she was suddenly anxious to get away from the church as fast as her weight would let her.

She took a bus home, and hid the candle in her chest of drawers. She had half feared that her husband's Brahminical flair for clairvoyance would have uncovered the reason for her trip to Chaguanas. When after four days, which she spent in an ecstasy of prayer, her husband had mentioned nothing, Gold Teeth thought it safe to burn the candle. She burned it secretly at night, before her Hindu images, and sent up, as she thought, prayers of double efficacy.

Every day her religious schizophrenia grew, and presently she began wearing a crucifix. Neither her husband nor her neighbours knew she did so. The chain was lost in the billows of fat around her neck, and the crucifix was itself buried in the valley of her gargantuan breasts. Later she acquired two holy pictures, one of the Virgin Mary, the other of the crucifixion, and took care to conceal them from her husband. The prayers she offered to these Christian things filled her with new hope and buoyancy. She became an addict of Christianity.

Then her husband, Ramprasad, fell ill.

Ramprasad's sudden, unaccountable illness alarmed Gold Teeth. It was, she knew, no ordinary illness, and she knew, too, that her religious transgression was the cause. The District Medical Officer at Chaguanas said it was diabetes, but Gold Teeth knew better. To be on the safe side, though, she used the insulin he prescribed and, to be even safer, she consulted Ganesh Pundit, the masseur with mystic leanings, celebrated as a faith-healer.

Ganesh came all the way from Fuente Grove to Cunupia. He came in great humility, anxious to serve Gold Teeth's husband, for Gold Teeth's husband was a Brahmin among Brahmins, a *Panday*, a man who knew all five Vedas; while he, Ganesh, was a mere *Chaubay* and knew only four.

With spotless white *koortah,* his dhoti cannily tied, and a tasselled green scarf as a concession to elegance, Ganesh exuded the confidence of the professional mystic. He looked at the sick man, observed his pallor, sniffed the air. 'This man,' he said, 'is bewitched. Seven spirits are upon him.'

He was telling Gold Teeth nothing she didn't know. She had known from the first that there were spirits in the affair, but she was glad that Ganesh had ascertained their number.

'But you mustn't worry,' Ganesh added. 'We will "tie" the house—in spiritual bonds—and no spirit will be able to come in.'

Then, without being asked, Gold Teeth brought out a blanket, folded it, placed it on the floor and invited Ganesh to sit on it. Next she brought him a brass jar of fresh water, a mango leaf and a plate full of burning charcoal.

'Bring me some ghee,' Ganesh said, and after Gold Teeth had done so, he set to work. Muttering continuously in Hindustani he sprinkled the water from the brass jar around him with the mango leaf. Then he melted the ghee in the fire and the charcoal hissed so sharply that Gold Teeth could not make out his words. Presently he rose and said, 'You must put some of the ash of this fire on your husband's forehead, but if he doesn't want you to do that, mix it with his food. You must keep the water in this jar and place it every night before your front door.'

Gold Teeth pulled her veil over her forehead.

Ganesh coughed. 'That,' he said, rearranging his scarf, 'is all. There is nothing more I can do. God will do the rest.'

He refused payment for his services. It was enough honour, he said, for a man as humble as he was to serve Pundit Ramprasad, and she, Gold Teeth, had been singled out by fate to be the spouse of such a worthy man. Gold Teeth received the impression that Ganesh spoke from a first-hand knowledge of fate and its designs, and her heart, buried deep down under inches of mortal, flabby flesh, sank a little.

'Baba,' she said hesitantly, 'revered Father, I have something to say to you.' But she couldn't say anything more and Ganesh, seeing this, filled his eyes with charity and love.

'What is it, my child?'

'I have done a great wrong, Baba.'

'What sort of wrong?' he asked, and his tone indicated that Gold Teeth could do no wrong.

'I have prayed to Christian things.'

And to Gold Teeth's surprise, Ganesh chuckled benevolently. 'And do you think God minds, daughter? There is only one God and different people pray to Him in different ways. It doesn't matter how you pray, but God is pleased if you pray at all.'

'So it is not because of me that my husband has fallen ill?'

'No, to be sure, daughter.'

In his professional capacity Ganesh was consulted by people of many faiths, and with the licence of the mystic he had exploited the commodiousness of Hinduism, and made room for all beliefs. In this way he had many clients, as he called them, many satisfied clients.

Henceforward Gold Teeth not only pasted Ramprasad's pale forehead with the sacred ash Ganesh had prescribed, but mixed substantial amounts with his food. Ramprasad's appetite, enormous even in sickness, diminished; and he shortly entered into a visible and alarming decline that mystified his wife.

She fed him more ash than before, and when it was exhausted and Ramprasad perilously macerated, she fell back on the Hindu wife's last resort. She took her husband home to her mother. That venerable lady, my grandmother, lived with us in Port-of-Spain.

Ramprasad was tall and skeletal, and his face was grey. The virile voice that had expounded a thousand theological points and recited a hundred *puranas* was now a wavering whisper. We cooped him up in a room called, oddly, 'the pantry'. It had never been used as a pantry and one can only assume that the architect had so designated it some forty years before. It was a tiny room. If you wished to enter the pantry you were compelled, as soon as you opened the door, to climb on to the bed: it fitted the room to a miracle. The lower half of the walls were concrete, the upper close lattice-work; there were no windows.

My grandmother had her doubts about the suitability of the room for a sick man. She was worried about the lattice-work. It let in air and light, and Ramprasad was not going to die from these things if she could help it. With cardboard, oil-cloth and canvas she made the lattice-work air-proof and light-proof.

And, sure enough, within a week Ramprasad's appetite returned, insatiable and insistent as before. My grandmother claimed all the credit for this, though Gold Teeth knew that the ash she had fed him had not been without effect. Then she realized with horror that she had ignored a very important thing. The house in Cunupia had been tied and no spirits could enter, but the house in the city had been given no such protection and any spirit could come and go as it chose. The problem was pressing.

Ganesh was out of the question. By giving his services free he had made it impossible for Gold Teeth to call him in again. But thinking in this way of Ganesh, she remembered his words: 'It doesn't matter how you pray, but God is pleased if you pray at all.'

Why not, then, bring Christianity into play again?

She didn't want to take any chances this time. She decided to tell Ramprasad.

He was propped up in bed, and eating. When Gold Teeth opened the door he stopped eating and blinked at the unwonted light. Gold Teeth, stepping into the doorway and filling it, shadowed the room once more and he went on eating. She placed the palms of her hand on the bed. It creaked.

'Man,' she said.

Ramprasad continued to eat.

'Man,' she said in English, 'I thinking about going to the church to pray. You never know, and it better to be on the safe side. After all, the house ain't tied—'

'I don't want you to pray in no church,' he whispered, in English too.

Gold Teeth did the only thing she could do. She began to cry. Three days in succession she asked his permission to go to church, and his opposition weakened in the face of her tears. He was now, besides, too weak to oppose anything. Although his appetite had returned, he was still very ill and very weak, and every day his condition became worse.

On the fourth day he said to Gold Teeth, 'Well, pray to Jesus and go to church, if it will put your mind at rest.'

And Gold Teeth straight away set about putting her mind at rest. Every morning she took the trolley-bus to the Holy Rosary Church, to offer worship in her private way. Then she was emboldened to bring a crucifix and pictures of the Virgin and the Messiah into the house. We were all somewhat worried by this, but Gold Teeth's religious nature was well known to us; her husband was a learned pundit and when all was said and done this was an emergency, a matter of life and death. So we could do nothing but look on. Incense and camphor and ghee burned now before the likeness of Krishna and Shiva as well as Mary and Jesus. Gold Teeth revealed an appetite for prayer that equalled her husband's for food, and we marvelled at both, if only because neither prayer nor food seemed to be of any use to Ramprasad.

One evening, shortly after bell and gong and conch-shell had announced that Gold Teeth's official devotions were almost over, a sudden chorus of lamentation burst over the house, and I was summoned to the room reserved for prayer. 'Come quickly, something dreadful has happened to your aunt.'

The prayer-room, still heavy with fumes of incense, presented an extraordinary sight. Before the Hindu shrine, flat on her face, Gold Teeth lay prostrate, rigid as a sack of flour. I had only seen Gold Teeth standing or sitting, and the aspect of Gold Teeth prostrate, so novel and so grotesque, was disturbing.

My grandmother, an alarmist by nature, bent down and put her ear to the upper half of the body on the floor. 'I don't seem to hear her heart,' she said.

We were all somewhat terrified. We tried to lift Gold Teeth but she seemed as heavy as lead. Then, slowly, the body quivered. The flesh beneath the clothes rippled, then billowed, and the children in the room sharpened their shrieks. Instinctively we all stood back from the body and waited to see what was going to happen. Gold Teeth's hand began to pound the floor and at the same time she began to gurgle.

My grandmother had grasped the situation. 'She's got the spirit,' she said.

At the word 'spirit,' the children shrieked louder, and my grandmother slapped them into silence.

The gurgling resolved itself into words pronounced with a lingering ghastly quaver. 'Hail Mary, Hail Ram,' Gold Teeth said, 'the snakes are after me. Everywhere snakes. Seven snakes. Rama! Rama! Full of grace. Seven spirits leaving Cunupia by the four o'clock train for Port-of-Spain.'

My grandmother and my mother listened eagerly, their faces lit up with pride. I was rather ashamed at the exhibition, and annoyed with Gold Teeth for putting me into a fright. I moved towards the door.

'Who is that going away? Who is the young *caffar*, the unbeliever?' the voice asked abruptly.

'Come back quickly, boy,' my grandmother whispered. 'Come back and ask her pardon.'

I did as I was told.

'It is all right, son,' Gold Teeth replied, 'you don't know. You are young.'

Then the spirit appeared to leave her. She wrenched herself up to a sitting position and wondered why we were all there. For the rest of that evening she behaved as if nothing had happened, and she pretended she didn't notice that everyone was looking at her and treating her with unusual respect.

'I have always said it, and I will say it again,' my grandmother said, 'that these Christians are very religious people. That is why I encouraged Gold Teeth to pray to Christian things.'

*

Ramprasad died early next morning and we had the announcement on the radio after the local news at one o'clock. Ramprasad's death was the only one announced and so, although it came between commercials, it made some impression. We buried him that afternoon in Mucurapo Cemetery.

As soon as we got back my grandmother said, 'I have always said it, and I will say it again: I don't like these Christian things. Ramprasad would have got better if only you, Gold Teeth, had listened to me and not gone running after these Christian things.'

Gold Teeth sobbed her assent; and her body squabbered and shook as she confessed the whole story of her trafficking with Christianity. We listened in astonishment and shame. We didn't know that a good Hindu, and a member of our family, could sink so low. Gold Teeth beat her breast and pulled ineffectually at her long hair and begged to be forgiven. 'It is all my fault,' she cried. 'My own fault, Ma. I fell in a moment of weakness. Then I just couldn't stop.'

My grandmother's shame turned to pity. 'It's all right, Gold Teeth. Perhaps it was this you needed to bring you back to your senses.'

That evening Gold Teeth ritually destroyed every reminder of Christianity in the house.

'You have only yourself to blame,' my grandmother said, 'if you have no children now to look after you.'

1954

The Raffle

THEY DON'T PAY primary schoolteachers a lot in Trinidad, but they allow them to beat their pupils as much as they want.

Mr Hinds, my teacher, was a big beater. On the shelf below *The Last of England* he kept four or five tamarind rods. They are good for beating. They are limber, they sting and they last. There was a tamarind tree in the schoolyard. In his locker Mr Hinds also kept a leather strap soaking in the bucket of water every class had in case of fire.

It wouldn't have been so bad if Mr Hinds hadn't been so young and athletic. At the one school sports I went to, I saw him slip off his shining shoes, roll up his trousers neatly to mid-shin and win the Teachers' Hundred Yards, a cigarette between his lips, his tie flapping smartly over his shoulder. It was a wine-coloured tie: Mr Hinds was careful about his dress. That was something else that somehow added to the terror. He wore a brown suit, a cream shirt and the wine-coloured tie.

It was also rumoured that he drank heavily at weekends.

But Mr Hinds had a weak spot. He was poor. We knew he gave those 'private lessons' because he needed the extra money. He gave us private lessons in the ten-minute morning recess. Every boy paid fifty cents for that. If a boy didn't pay, he was kept in all the same and flogged until he paid.

We also knew that Mr Hinds had an allotment in Morvant where he kept some poultry and a few animals.

The other boys sympathized with us—needlessly. Mr Hinds beat us, but I believe we were all a little proud of him.

I say he beat us, but I don't really mean that. For some reason which I could never understand then and can't now, Mr Hinds never beat me. He never made me clean the blackboard. He never made me shine his shoes with the duster. He even called me by my first name, Vidiadhar.

This didn't do me any good with the other boys. At cricket I wasn't allowed to bowl or keep wicket and I always went in at number eleven. My consolation was that I was spending only two terms at the school before going on to Queen's Royal College. I didn't want to go to QRC so much as I wanted to get away from Endeavour (that was the name of the school). Mr Hinds's favour made me feel insecure.

At private lessons one morning Mr Hinds announced that he was going to raffle a goat—a shilling a chance.

He spoke with a straight face and nobody laughed. He made me write out the names of all the boys in the class on two foolscap sheets. Boys who wanted to risk a shilling had to put a tick after their names. Before private lessons ended there was a tick after every name.

I became very unpopular. Some boys didn't believe there was a goat. They all said that if there was a goat, they knew who was going to get it. I hoped they were right. I had long wanted an animal of my own, and the idea of getting milk from my own goat attracted me. I had heard that Mannie Ramjohn, Trinidad's champion miler, trained on goat's milk and nuts.

Next morning I wrote out the names of the boys on slips of paper. Mr Hinds borrowed my cap, put the slips in, took one out, said, 'Vidiadhar, is your goat,' and immediately threw all the slips into the wastepaper basket.

At lunch I told my mother, 'I win a goat today.'

'What sort of goat?'

'I don't know. I ain't see it.'

She laughed. She didn't believe in the goat, either. But when she finished laughing she said: 'It would be nice, though.'

I was getting not to believe in the goat, too. I was afraid to ask Mr Hinds, but a day or two later he said, 'Vidiadhar, you coming or you ain't coming to get your goat?'

He lived in a tumbledown wooden house in Woodbrook and when I got there I saw him in khaki shorts, vest and blue canvas shoes. He was cleaning his bicycle with a yellow flannel. I was overwhelmed. I had never associated him with such dress and such a menial labour. But his manner was more ironic and dismissing than in the classroom.

He led me to the back of the yard. There *was* a goat. A white one with big horns, tied to a plum tree. The ground around the tree was filthy. The goat looked sullen and sleepy-eyed, as if a little stunned by the smell it had made. Mr Hinds invited me to stroke the goat. I stroked it. He closed his eyes and went on chewing. When I stopped stroking him, he opened his eyes.

Every afternoon at about five an old man drove a donkey-cart through Miguel Street where we lived. The cart was piled with fresh grass tied into neat little bundles, so neat you felt grass wasn't a thing that grew but was made in a factory somewhere. That donkey-cart became important to my mother and me. We were buying five, sometimes six bundles a day, and every bundle cost six cents. The goat didn't change. He still looked sullen and bored. From time to time Mr Hinds asked me with a smile how the goat was getting on, and I said it was getting on fine. But when I asked my mother when we were going to get milk from the goat she told me to stop aggravating her. Then one day she put up a sign:

RAM FOR SERVICE
Apply Within For Terms

and got very angry when I asked her to explain it.

The sign made no difference. We bought the neat bundles of grass, the goat ate, and I saw no milk.

And when I got home one lunch-time I saw no goat.

'Somebody borrow it,' my mother said. She looked happy.

'When it coming back?'

She shrugged her shoulders.

It came back that afternoon. When I turned the corner into Miguel Street I saw it on the pavement outside our house. A man I didn't know was holding it by a rope and making a big row, gesticulating like anything with his free hand. I knew that sort of man. He wasn't going to let hold of the rope until he had said his piece. A lot of people were looking on through curtains.

'But why all-you want to rob poor people so?' he said, shouting. He turned to his audience behind the curtains. 'Look, all-you, just look at this goat!'

The goat, limitlessly impassive, chewed slowly, its eyes half-closed.

'But how all you people so advantageous? My brother stupid and he ain't know this goat but I know this goat. Everybody in Trinidad who know about goat know this goat, from Icacos to Mayaro to Toco to Chaguaramas,' he said, naming the four corners of Trinidad. 'Is the most uselessest goat in the whole world. And you charge my brother for this goat? Look, you better give me back my brother money, you hear.'

My mother looked hurt and upset. She went inside and came out with some dollar notes. The man took them and handed over the goat.

That evening my mother said, 'Go and tell your Mr Hinds that I don't want this goat here.'

Mr Hinds didn't look surprised. 'Don't want it, eh?' He thought, and passed a well-trimmed thumb-nail over his moustache. 'Look, tell you. Going to buy him back. Five dollars.'

I said, 'He eat more than that in grass alone.'

That didn't surprise him either. 'Say six, then.'

I sold. That, I thought, was the end of that.

One Monday afternoon about a month before the end of my last term I announced to my mother, 'That goat raffling again.'

She became alarmed.

At tea on Friday I said casually, 'I win the goat.'

She was expecting it. Before the sun set a man had brought the goat away from Mr Hinds, given my mother some money and taken the goat away.

I hoped Mr Hinds would never ask about the goat. He did, though. Not the next week, but the week after that, just before school broke up.

I didn't know what to say.

But a boy called Knolly, a fast bowler and a favourite victim of Mr Hinds, answered for me. 'What goat?' he whispered loudly. 'That goat kill and eat long time.'

Mr Hinds was suddenly furious. 'Is true, Vidiadhar?'

I didn't nod or say anything. The bell rang and saved me.

At lunch I told my mother, 'I don't want to go back to that school.'

She said, 'You must be brave.'

I didn't like the argument, but went.

We had Geography the first period.

'Naipaul,' Mr Hinds said right away, forgetting my first name, 'define a peninsula.'

'Peninsula,' I said, 'a piece of land entirely surrounded by water.'

'Good. Come up here.' He went to the locker and took out the soaked leather strap. Then he fell on me. 'You sell my goat?' Cut. 'You kill my goat?' Cut. 'How you so damn ungrateful?' Cut, cut, cut. 'Is the last time you win anything I raffle.'

It was the last day I went to that school.

1957

A Christmas Story

THOUGH IT IS CHRISTMAS Eve my mind is not on Christmas. I look forward instead to the day after Boxing Day, for on that day the inspectors from the Audit Department in Port-of-Spain will be coming down to the village where the new school has been built. I await their coming with calm. There is still time, of course, to do all that is necessary. But I shall not do it, though my family, from whom the spirit of Christmas has, alas, also fled, have been begging me to lay aside my scruples, my new-found faith, and to rescue us all from disgrace and ruin. It is in my power to do so, but there comes a time in every man's life when he has to take a stand. This time, I must confess, has come very late for me.

It seems that everything has come late to me. I continued a Hindu, though of that religion I saw and knew little save meaningless and shameful rites, until I was nearly eighteen. Why I so continued I cannot explain. Perhaps it was the inertia with which that religion deadens its devotees. It did not, after all, require much intelligence to see that Hinduism, with its animistic rites, its idolatry, its emphasis on mango leaf, banana leaf and—the truth is the truth—cowdung, was a religion little fitted for the modern world. I had only to contrast the position of the Hindus with that of the Christians. I had only to consider the differing standards of dress, houses, food. Such differences have today more or less disappeared, and the younger generation will scarcely understand what I mean. I might even be reproached with laying too great a stress on the superficial. What can I say? Will I be believed if I say that to me the superficial has always symbolized the profound? But it is enough, I feel, to state that at eighteen my eyes were opened. I did not have to be 'converted' by the Presbyterians of the Canadian Mission. I had only to look at the work they were doing among the backward Hindus and Moslems of my district. I had only to look at their schools, to look at the houses of the converted.

My Presbyterianism, then, though late in coming, affected me deeply. I was interested in teaching—there was no other thing a man of my limited means and limited education could do—and my Presbyterianism was a distinct advantage. It gave me a grace in the eyes of my superiors. It also enabled me to be a good teacher, for between what I taught and what I felt there was no discordance. How different the position of those who, still unconverted, attempted to teach in Presbyterian schools!

And now that the time for frankness has come I must also remark on the pleasure my new religion gave me. It was a pleasure to hear myself called Randolph, a name of rich historical associations, a name, I feel, thoroughly attuned to the times in which we live and to the society in which I found myself, and to forget that once—I still remember it with shame—I answered, with simple instinct, to the name of—Choonilal. That, however, is so much in the past. I have buried it. Yet I remember it now, not only because the time for frankness has come, but because only two weeks ago my son Winston, going through some family papers—clearly the boy had no right to be going through my private papers, but he shares his mother's curiosity—came upon the name. He teased, indeed reproached me, with it, and in a fit of anger, for which I am now grievously sorry and for which I must make time, while time there still is, to apologize to him, in a fit of anger I gave him a sound thrashing, such as I often gave in my school-teaching days, to those pupils whose persistent shortcomings were matched by the stupidity and backwardness of their parents. Backwardness has always roused me to anger.

*

As much as by the name Randolph, pleasure was given me by the stately and *clean*—there is no other word for it—rituals sanctioned by my new religion. How agreeable, for instance, to rise early on a Sunday morning, to bathe and breakfast and then, in the most spotless of garments, to walk along the still quiet and cool roads to our place of worship, and there to see the most respectable and respected, all dressed with a similar purity, addressing themselves to the devotions in which I myself could participate, after for long being an outsider, someone to whom the words *Christ* and *Father* meant no more than *winter* or *autumn* or *daffodil*. Such of the unconverted village folk who were energetic enough to be awake and alert at that hour gaped at us as we walked in white procession to our church. And though their admiration was sweet, I must confess that at the same time it filled me with shame to reflect that not long before I too formed part of the gaping crowd. To walk past their gaze was peculiarly painful to me, for I, more perhaps than anyone in that slow and stately procession, *knew*—and by my silence had for nearly eighteen years condoned—the practices those people indulged in in the name of religion. My attitude towards them was therefore somewhat stern, and it gave me some little consolation to know that though we were in some ways alike, we were distinguished from them not only by our names, which after all no man carries pinned to his lapel, but also by our dress. On these Sundays of which I speak the men wore trousers and jackets of white drill, quite unlike the leg-revealing dhoti which it still pleased those others to wear, a garment which I have always felt makes the wearer ridiculous. I even sported a white solar topee. The girls and ladies wore the short frocks which the others held in abhorrence; they wore hats; in every respect, I am pleased to say, they resembled their sisters who had come all the way from Canada and other countries to work among our people. I might be accused of laying too much stress on superficial things. But I ought to say in my own defence that it is my deeply held conviction that progress is not a matter of outward show, but an attitude of mind; and it was this that my religion gave me.

It might seem from what I have so far said that the embracing of Presbyterianism conferred only benefits and pleasure. I wish to make no great fuss of the trials I had to endure, but it is sufficient to state that, while at school and in other associations my fervent adherence to my new faith was viewed with favour, I had elsewhere to put up with the constant ridicule of those of my relations who continued, in spite of my example, in the ways of darkness. They spoke my name, Randolph, with accents of the purest mockery. I bore this with fortitude. It was what I expected, and I was greatly strengthened by my faith, as a miser is by the thought of his gold. In time, when they saw that their ridiculing of my name had not the slightest effect on me—on the contrary, whereas before I had in my signature suppressed my first name behind the blank initial C, now I spelt out Randolph in full—in time they desisted.

But that was not the end of my trials. I had up to that time eaten with my fingers, a manner of eating which is now so repulsive to me, so ugly, so unhygienic, that I wonder how I managed to do it until my eighteenth year. Yet I must now confess that at that time food never tasted as sweet as when eaten with the fingers, and that my first attempts to eat with the proper implements of knife and fork and spoon were almost in the nature of shameful experiments, furtively carried out; and even when I was by myself I could not get rid of the feeling of self-consciousness. It was easier to get used to the name of Randolph than to knife and fork.

Eating, then, in my determined manner one Sunday lunchtime, I heard that I had a visitor. It was a man; he didn't knock, but came straight into my room, and I knew at once that he was a relation. These people have never learned to knock or to close doors behind them.

I must confess I felt somewhat foolish to be caught with those implements in my hand.

'Hello, Randolph,' the boy Hori said, pronouncing the name in a most offensive manner.

'Good afternoon, *Hori*.'

He remained impervious to my irony. This boy, Hori, was the greatest of my tormentors. He was also the grossest. He strained charity. He was a great lump of a man and he gloried in his brutishness. He fancied himself a debater as well, and many were the discussions and arguments we had had, this lout—he strained charity, as I have said—insisting that to squat on the ground and eat off banana leaves was hygienic and proper, that knives and forks were dirty because used again and again by various persons, whereas the fingers were personal and could always be made thoroughly clean by washing. But he never had *his* fingers clean, that I knew.

'Eating, Randolph?'

'I am having my lunch, *Hori*.'

'Beef, Randolph. You are progressing, Randolph.'

'I am glad you note it, *Hori*.'

I cannot understand why these people should persist in this admiration for the cow, which has always seemed to me a filthy animal, far filthier than the pig, which they abhor. Yet it must be stated that this eating of beef was the most strenuous of my tests. If I persevered it was only because I was strengthened by my faith. But to be found at this juncture—I was in my Sunday suit of white drill, my prayer book was on the table, my white solar topee on the wall, and I was eating beef with knife and fork—to be found thus by Hori was a trifle embarrassing. I must have looked the picture of the over-zealous convert.

My instinct was to ask him to leave. But it occurred to me that that would have been too easy, too cowardly a way out. Instead, I plied my knife and fork with as much skill as I could command at that time. He sat, not on a chair, but on the table, just next to my plate, the lout, and gazed at me while I ate. Ignoring his smile, I ate, as one might eat of sacrificial food. He crossed his fat legs, leaned back on his palms and examined me. I paid no attention. Then he took one of the forks that were about and began picking his teeth with it. I was angry and revolted. Tears sprang to my eyes, I rose, pushed away my plate, pushed back my chair, and asked him to leave. The violence of my reaction surprised him, and he did as I asked. As soon as he had gone I took the fork he had handled and bent it and stamped on it and then threw it out of the window.

*

Progress, as I have said, is an attitude of mind. And if I relate this trifling incident with such feeling, it is because it demonstrates how difficult that attitude of mind is to acquire, for there are hundreds who are ready to despise and ridicule those who they think are getting above themselves. And let people say what they will, the contempt even of the foolish is hard to bear. Let no one think, therefore, that my new religion did not bring its share of trials and tribulations. But I was sufficiently strengthened by my faith to bear them all with fortitude.

My life thereafter was a lonely one. I had cut myself off from my family, and from those large family gatherings which had hitherto given me so much pleasure and comfort, for always, I must own, at the back of my mind there had been the thought that in the event of real trouble there would be people to whom I could turn. Now I was deprived of this solace. I stuck to my vocation with a dedication which surprised even myself. To be a teacher it is necessary to be taught; and after much difficulty I managed to have myself sent to the Training College in Port-of-Spain. The competition for these places was fierce, and for many years I was passed over, because there were many others who were more fitting. Some indeed had been born of Presbyterian parents. But my zeal, which ever mounted as the failures multiplied, eventually was rewarded. I was twenty-eight when I was sent to the Training College, considerably older than most of the trainees.

It was no pleasure to me to note that during those ten years the boy Hori had been prospering. He had gone into the trucking business and he had done remarkably well. He had bought a second truck, then a third, and it seemed that to his success there could be no limit, while my own was always restricted to the predictable contents of the brown-paper pay-packet at the end of the month. The clothes in which I had taken such pride at first became less resplendent, until I felt it as a disgrace to go to church in them. But it became clear to me that this was yet another of the trials I was called upon to undergo, and I endured it, until I almost took pleasure in the darns on my sleeves and elbows.

At this time I was invited to the wedding of Hori's son, Kedar. They marry young, these people! It was an occasion which surmounted religious differences, and it was a distinct pleasure to me to be again with the family, for their attitude had changed. They had become reconciled to my Presbyterianism and indeed treated me with respect for my profession, a respect which, I fear, was sometimes missing in the attitude of my superiors and even my pupils. The marriage rites distressed me. The makeshift though beautiful tent, the coconut-palm arches hung with clusters of fruit, the use of things like mango leaves and grass and saffron, the sacrificial fire, all these things filled me with shame rather than delight. But the rites were only a small part of the celebrations. There was much good food, strictly vegetarian but somehow extremely tempting; and after a period of distaste for Indian food, I had come back to it again. The food, I say, was rich. The music and the dancers were thrilling. The tent and the illuminations had a charm which not even our school hall had on concert nights, though the marriage ceremony did not of course have the grace and dignity of those conducted, as proper marriages should be, in a church.

Kedar received a fabulous dowry, and his bride, of whose face I had just a glimpse when her silk veil was parted, was indeed beautiful. But such beauty has always appeared to me skin deep. Beauty in women is a disturbing thing. But beyond the beauty it is always necessary to look for the greater qualities of manners and—a thing I always remind Winston of—no one is too young or too old to learn—manners and *ways*. She was beautiful. It was sad to think of her joined to Kedar for life, but she was perhaps fitted for nothing else. No need to speak of the resplendent regalia of Kedar himself:

his turban, the crown with tassels and pendant glass, his richly embroidered silk jacket, and all those other adornments which for that night concealed so well the truck-driver that he was.

*

I left the wedding profoundly saddened. I could not help reflecting on my own position and contrasting it with Hori's or even Kedar's. I was now over forty, and marriage, which in the normal way would have come to me at the age of twenty or thereabouts, was still far from me. This was my own fault. Arranged marriages like Kedar's had no part in my scheme of things. I wished to marry, as the person says in *The Vicar of Wakefield*, someone who had qualities that would wear well. My choice was severely restricted. I wished to marry a Presbyterian lady who was intelligent, well brought up and educated, and wished to marry me. This last condition, alas, I could find few willing to fulfil. And indeed I had little to offer. Among Hindus it would have been otherwise. There might have been men of substance who would have been willing to marry their daughters to a teacher, to acquire respectability and the glamour of a learned profession. Such a position has its strains, of course, for it means that the daughter remains, as it were, subject to her family; but the position is not without its charms,

You might imagine—and you would be correct—that at this time my faith was undergoing its severest strain. How often I was on the point of reneging I shudder to tell. I felt myself about to yield; I stiffened in my devotions and prayers. I reflected on the worthlessness of worldly things, but this was a reflection I found few to share. I might add here, in parenthesis and without vanity, that I had had several offers from the fathers of unconverted daughters, whose only condition was the one, about my religion, which I could not accept; for my previous caste had made me acceptable to many.

In this situation of doubt, of nightly wrestling with God, an expression whose meaning I came only then fully to understand, my fortune changed. I was appointed a headmaster. Now I can speak!

How many people know of the tribulations, the pettiness, the intrigue which schoolteachers have to undergo to obtain such promotion? Such jockeying, such jealousy, such ill-will comes into play. What can I say of the advances one has to make, the rebuffs one has to suffer in silence, the waiting, the undoing of the unworthy who seek to push themselves forward for positions which they are ill-qualified to fill but which, by glibness and all the outward shows of respectability and efficiency and piety, they manage to persuade our superiors that they alone can fill? I too had my adversaries. My chief rival—but let him rest in peace! I am, I trust, a Christian, and will do no man the injustice of imagining him to persist in error even after we have left this vale of tears.

In my fortune, so opportune, I saw the hand of God. I speak in all earnestness. For without this I would surely have lapsed into the ways of darkness, for who among us can so steel himself as to resist temptation for all time? In my gratitude I applied myself with renewed dedication to my task. And it was this that doubtless evoked the gratification of my superiors which was to lead to my later elevation. For at a time when most men, worn out by the struggle, are content to relax, I showed myself more eager than before. I instituted prayers four times a day. I insisted on attendance at Sunday School. I taught Sunday School myself, and with the weight of my influence persuaded the other teachers to do likewise, so that Sunday became another day for us, a day of rest which we consumed with work for the Lord.

And I did not neglect the educational side. The blackboards all now sparkled with diagrams in chalks of various colours, projects which we had in hand. Oh, the school was such a pretty sight then! I instituted a rigid system of discipline, and forbade indiscriminate flogging by pupil teachers. All flogging I did myself on Friday afternoons, sitting in impartial judgement, as it were, on the school, on pupils as well as teachers. It is surely a better system, and I am glad to say that it has now been adopted throughout the island. The most apt pupils I kept after school, and for some trifling extra fee gave them private lessons. And the school became so involved with work as an ideal that had to be joyously pursued and not as something that had to be endured, that the usefulness of these private lessons was widely appreciated, and soon larger numbers than I could cope with were staying after school for what they affectionately termed their 'private'.

*

And I married. It was now in my power to marry virtually anyone I pleased and there were among the Sunday School staff not a few who made their attachment to me plain. I am not such a bad-looking fellow! But I wished to marry someone who had qualities that would wear well. I was nearly fifty. I did not wish to marry someone who was much younger than myself. And it was my good fortune at this juncture to receive an offer—I hesitate to use this word, which sounds so much like the Hindu custom and reminds one of the real estate business, but here I must be frank—from no less a person than a schools inspector, who had an unmarried daughter of thirty-five, a woman neglected by the men of the island because of her attainments—yes, you read right—which were considerable, but not of the sort that proclaims itself to the world. In our attitude to women much remains to be changed! I have often, during these past days, reflected on marriage. Such a turning, a point in time whence so many consequences flow. I wonder what Winston, poor boy, will do when his time comes.

My establishment could not rival Hori's or Kedar's for splendour, but within it there was peace and culture such as I had long dreamed of. It was a plain wooden house, but well built, built to last, unlike so many of these modern monstrosities which I see arising these days: and it was well ordered. We had simple bentwood chairs with cane bottoms. No marble-topped tables with ball-fringed lace! No glass cabinets! I hung my treasured framed teaching diploma on the wall, with my religious pictures and some scenes of the English countryside. It was also my good fortune at this time to get an old auto-graphed photograph of one of our first missionaries. In the decoration of our humble home my wife appeared to release all the energy and experience of her thirty-five years which had so far been denied expression.

To her, as to myself, everything came late. It was our fear, confirmed by the views of many friends who behind their expressions of goodwill concealed as we presently saw much uncharitableness, that we would be unable to have children, considering our advanced years. But they, and we, underestimated the power of prayer, for within a year of our marriage Winston was born.

*

The birth of Winston came to us as a grace and a blessing. Yet it also filled me with anxiety, for I could not refrain from assessing the difference between our ages. It occurred to me, for instance, that he would be thirty when I was eighty. It was a disturbing thought, for the companionship of children is something which, perhaps because of my profession, I hold especially dear. My anxiety had another reason. It was that Winston, in his most formative years, would be without not only my guidance—for what guidance can a man of seventy give to a lusty youngster of twenty?—but also without my financial support.

The problem of money, strange as it might appear, considering my unexpected elevation and all its accruing benefits, was occupying the minds of both my wife and myself. For my retirement was drawing near, and my pension would scarcely be more than what I subsisted on as a simple pupil teacher. It seemed then that like those pilgrims, whose enthusiasm I admire but cannot share, I was advancing towards my goal by taking two steps forward and one step back, though in my case a likelier simile might be that I was taking one step forward and one step back. So success always turns to ashes in the mouth of those who seek it as ardently as I had! And if I had the vision and the depth of faith which I now have, I might have seen even then how completely false are the things of this world, how much they flatter only to deceive.

We were both, as I say, made restless. And now the contemplation of baby Winston was a source of much pain to both of us, for the poor innocent creature could scarcely know what anguish awaited him when we would both be withdrawn from this vale of tears. His helplessness, his dependence tortured me. I was past the age when the taking out of an insurance policy was a practicable proposition; and during my days as a simple teacher I never had the resources to do so. It seemed, then, that I was being destroyed by my own good fortune, by the fruits of all my endeavour. Yet I did not heed this sign.

I continued while I could giving private lessons. I instituted a morning session as well, in addition to the afternoon one. But I did so with a heavy heart, tormented by the thought that in a few years this privilege and its small reward would be denied me, for private lessons, it must be understood, are considered the prerogative of a headmaster: in this way he stamps his character on the school. My results in the exhibition examinations for boys under twelve continued to be heartening; they far surpassed those of many other country schools. My religious zeal continued unabated; and it was this zeal which, burning in those years when most men in my position would have relaxed—they, fortunate souls, having their children fully grown—it was this surprising zeal, I say, which also contributed, I feel, to my later elevation which, as you will see from the plain narration of these events, I did not seek.

My retirement drew nearer. I became fiercer at school. I wished all the boys under me could grow up at once. I was merciless towards the backward. My wife, poor creature, could not control her anxiety with as much success as myself. She had no occupation, no distracting vocation, in which her anxiety might have been consumed. She had only Winston, and this dear infant continually roused her to fears about his future. For his sake she would, I believe, have sacri-

ficed her own life! It was not easy for her. And it required but the
exercise of the mildest Christian charity to see that the reproaches
she flung with increased acerbity and frequency at my head were but
expressions of her anxiety. Sometimes, I must confess, I failed! And
then my own unworthiness would torment me, as it torments me
now.

We confided our problems to my wife's father, the schools
inspector. Though we felt it unfair to let another partake of our troubles, it is none the less a recognized means of lightening any load
which the individual finds too heavy to bear. But he, poor man,
though as worried on his daughter's behalf as she was on Winston's,
could offer only sympathy and little practical help. He reported that
the authorities were unwilling to give me an extension of my tenure
as headmaster. My despondency found expression in a display of
temper, which he charitably forgave; for though he left the house,
promising not to do another thing for us, he presently returned, and
counselled patience.

So patient we were. I retired. I could hardly bear to remain at
home, so used had I been to the daily round, the daily trials. I went
out visiting, for no other reason than that I was afraid to be alone at
home. My zeal, I believe, was remarked upon, though I took care to
avoid the school, the scene of my late labours. I sought to take in for
private lessons two or three pupils whose progress had deeply interested me. But my methods were no longer the methods that found
favour! The parents of these children reported that the new headmaster had expressed himself strongly, and to my great disfavour, on
the subject, to such a degree, in fact, that the progress of their children at school was being hampered. So I desisted; or rather, since the
time has come for frankness, they left me.

*

The schools inspector, a regular visitor now at our humble, sad
home, continued to counsel patience. I have so far refrained in this
narrative from permitting my wife to speak directly; for I wish to do

nothing that might increase the load she will surely have to bear, for my wife, though of considerable attainments, has not had the advantages of a formal education on which so much stress is nowadays laid. So I will refrain from chronicling the remark with which she greeted this advice of her father's. Suffice it to say that she spoke a children's rhyme without any great care for its metre or rhyme, the last of which indeed she destroyed by accidentally, in her haste, pulling down a vase from the centre-table on to the floor, where the water ran like one of the puddles which our baby Winston so lately made. After this incident relations between my wife and her father underwent a perceptible strain; and I took care to be out of the house as often as possible, and indeed it was pleasant to forget one's domestic troubles and walk abroad and be greeted as 'Headmaster' by the simple village folk.

*

Then, as it appears has happened so regularly throughout my life, the clouds rolled away and the sky brightened. I was appointed a School Manager. The announcement was made in the most heartwarming way possible, by the schools inspector himself, anticipating the official notification by a week or so. And the occasion became a family reunion. It was truly good to see the harassed schools inspector relaxing at last, and to see father and daughter reasonably happy with one another. My delight in this was almost as great as the delight in my new dignity.

For a school managership is a good thing to come to a man in the evening of his days. It permits an exercise of the most benign power imaginable. It permits a man at a speech day function to ask for a holiday for the pupils; and nothing is as warming as the lusty and sincere cheering that follows such a request. It gives power even over headmasters, for one can make surprise visits and it is in one's power to make reports to the authorities. It is a position of considerable responsibility as well, for a school manager manages a school as much as a managing director manages a company. It is in his power to decide whether the drains, say, need to be remade entirely or need simply be plastered over to look as new; whether one coat of paint or two are needed; whether a ceiling can be partially renovated and painted over or taken out altogether and replaced. He orders the number of desks and blackboards which he considers necessary, and the chalks and the stationery. It is, in short, a dignity ideally suited to one who has led an active life and is dismayed by the prospect of retirement. It brings honour as well as reward. It has the other advantage that school managers are like civil servants; they are seldom dismissed; and their honours tend to increase rather than diminish.

I entered on my new tasks with zeal, and once again all was well at our home. My wife's father visited us regularly, as though, poor man, anxious to share the good fortune for which he was to a large measure responsible. I looked after the school, the staff, the pupils. I visited all the parents of the pupils under my charge and spoke to them of the benefits of education, the dangers of absenteeism, and so on. I know I will be forgiven if I add that from time to time, whenever the ground appeared ripe, I sowed the seed of Presbyterianism or at any rate doubt among those who continued in the ways of darkness. Such zeal was unknown among school managers. I cannot account for it myself. It might be that my early austerity and ambition had given me something of the crusading zeal. But it was inevitable that such zeal should have been too much for some people to stomach.

*

For all his honour, for all the sweet cheers that greet his request for a holiday for the pupils, the school manager's position is one that sometimes attracts adverse and malicious comment. It is the fate of anyone who finds himself in a position of power and financial responsibility. The rumours persisted; and though they did not diminish the esteem in which I was so clearly held by the community—at the elections, for example, I was approached by all five candidates and asked to lend my voice to their cause, a situation of peculiar difficulty, which I resolved by promising all five to remain neutral, for which they were effusively grateful—it is no good thing for a man to walk among people who every day listen eagerly— for flesh is frail, and nothing attracts our simple villagers as much as scurrilous gossip—to slanders against himself. It was beneath my dignity, or rather, the dignity of my position, to reply to such attacks; and in this situation I turned, as I was turning with growing frequency, to my wife's father for advice. He suggested that I should relinquish one of my managerships, to indicate my disapproval of the gossip and the little esteem in which I held worldly honour. For I had so far succeeded in my new functions that I was now the manager of three schools, which was the maximum number permitted.

I followed his advice. I relinquished the managership of a school which was in a condition so derelict that not even repeated renovations could efface the original gimcrackery of its construction. This school had been the cause of most of the rumours, and my relinquishing of it attracted widespread comment and was even mentioned in the newspapers. It remained dear to me, but I was willing for it to go into other hands. This action of mine had the effect of stilling rumours and gossip. And the action proved to have its own reward, for some months later my wife's father, ever the bearer of good tidings, intimated that there was a possibility of a new school being put up in the area. I was thoroughly suited for its management; and he, the honest broker between the authorities and myself, said that my name was being mentioned in this connection. I was at that time manager of only two schools; I was entitled to a third. He warmly urged me to accept. I hesitated, and my hesitations were later proved to be justified. But the thought of a new school fashioned entirely according to my ideas and principles was too heady. I succumbed to temptation. If now I could only go back and withdraw that acceptance! The good man hurried back with the news; and within a fortnight I received the official notification.

*

I must confess that during the next few months I lost sight of my doubts in my zeal and enthusiasm for the new project. My two other schools suffered somewhat. For if there is a thing to delight the heart of the school manager, it is the management of a school not yet built. But, alas! We are at every step reminded of the vanity of worldly things. How often does it happen that a person, placed in the position he craves, a position which he is in every way suited to fill, suddenly loses his grip! Given the opportunity for which he longs, he is unable to make use of it. The effort goes all into the striving.

So now it happened with me. Nearly everything I touched failed to go as it should. I, so careful and correct in assessments and estimates, was now found repeatedly in error. None of my calculations were right. There were repeated shortages and stoppages. The school progressed far more slowly than I would have liked. And it was no consolation to me to find that in this moment I was alone, in this long moment of agony! Neither to my wife nor to her father could I turn for comfort. They savoured the joy of my managership of a new school without reference to me. I had my great opportunity; they had no doubt I would make use of it; and I could not bear disillusioning them or breaking into their happiness with my worries.

My errors attracted other errors. My errors multiplied, I tell you! To cover up one error I had to commit twenty acts of concealment, and these twenty had to be concealed. I felt myself caught in a curious inefficiency that seemed entirely beyond my control, something malignant, powered by forces hostile to myself. Until at length it seemed that failure was staring me in the face, and that my entire career would be forgotten in this crowning failure. The building went up, it is true. It had a respectable appearance. It looked a building. But it was far from what I had visualized. I had miscalculated badly, and it was too late to remedy the errors. Its faults, its weaknesses would be at once apparent even to the scantily trained eye. And now night after night I was tormented by this failure of mine.

With the exercise of only a little judgement it could so easily have been made right. Yet now the time for that was past! Day after day I was drawn to the building, and every day I hoped that by some miracle it would have been effaced during the night. But there it always stood, a bitter reproach.

Matters were not made easier for me by the reproaches of my wife and her father. They both rounded on me and said with justice that my failure would involve them all. And the days went by! I could not—I have never liked bickering, the answering of insult with insult—I could not reproach them with having burdened me with such an enterprise at the end of my days. I did it for their glory, for I had acquired sufficient to last me until the end of my days. I did it for my wife and her father, and for my son Winston. But who will believe me? Who will believe that a man works for the glory of others, except he work for the glory of God? They reproached me. They stood aside from me. In this moment of need they deserted me.

*

They were bitter days. I went for long walks through our villages in the cool of the evening. The children ran out to greet me. Mothers looked up from their cooking, fathers from their perches on the roadside culverts, and greeted me, 'Headmaster!' And soon my failure would be apparent even to the humblest among them. I had to act quickly. Failures should be destroyed. The burning down of a school is an unforgiveable thing, but there are surely occasions when it can be condoned, when it is the only way out. Surely this was such an occasion! It is a drastic step. But it is one that has been taken more than once in this island. So I argued with myself. And always the answer was there; my failure had to be destroyed, not only for my own sake, but for the sake of all those, villagers included, whose fates were involved with mine.

Once I had made up my mind, I acted with decision. It was that time of year, mid-November, when people are beginning to think of Christmas to the exclusion of nearly everything else. This served my purpose well. I required—with what shame I now confess it—certain assistants, for it was necessary for me to be seen elsewhere on the day of the accident. Much money, much of what we had set aside for the future of our son Winston, had to go on this. And already it had been necessary to seal the lips of certain officials who had rejoiced in my failure and were willing to proclaim it to the world. But at last it was ready. On Boxing Day we would go to Port-of-Spain, to the races. When we returned the following day, the school would be no more. I say 'we', though my wife had not been apprised of my intentions.

With what fear, self-reproach, and self-disgust I waited for the days to pass! When I heard the Christmas carols, ever associated for me with the indefinable sweetness of Christmas Eve—which I now once more feel, thanks to my decision, though underneath there is a sense of doom and destruction, deserved, but with their own inevitable reward—when I heard carols and Christmas commercials on the radio, my heart sank; for it seemed that I had cut myself off from all about me, that once more I had become a stranger to the faith which I profess. So these days passed in sorrow, in nightly frenzies of prayer and self-castigation. Regret assailed me. Regret for what might have been, regret for what was to come. I was sinking, I felt, into a pit of defilement whence I could never emerge.

Of all this my wife knew nothing. But then she asked one day, 'What have you decided to do?' and, without waiting for my reply, at once drew up such a detailed plan, which corresponded so closely to what I had myself devised, that my heart quailed. For if, in this moment of my need, when the deepest resource was needed, I could devise a plan which might have been devised by anyone else, then discovery was certain. And to my shame, Winston, who only two or three days before had been teasing me with my previous unbaptized name, Winston took part in this discussion, with no appearance of shame on his face, only thrill and—sad am I to say it—a pride in me greater than I had ever seen the boy display.

How can one tell of the workings of the human heart? How can one speak of the urge to evil—an urge of which Christians more than anyone else are so aware—and of the countervailing urge to good? You must remember that this is the season of goodwill. And goodwill it was. For goodwill was what I was feeling towards all. At every carol my heart melted. Whenever a child rushed towards me and cried, 'Headmaster!' I was tormented by grief. For the sight of the unwashed creatures, deprived, so many of them, of schooling, which matters so much in those early years, and the absence of which ever afterwards makes itself felt, condemning a human being to an animal-like existence, the sight of these creatures, grateful towards me who had on so many evenings gone among them propagating the creed with what energy I could, unmanned me. They were proud of their new school. They were even prouder of their association with the man who had built it.

Everywhere I felt rejected. I went to church as often as I could, but even there I found rejection. And as the time drew nearer the enormity of what I proposed grew clearer to me. It was useless to tell myself that what I was proposing had been often done. The carols, the religious services, the talk of birth and life, they all unmanned me.

I walked among the children as one who had it in his power to provide or withhold blessing, and I thought of that other Walker, who said of those among whom I walked that they were blessed, and that theirs was the kingdom of heaven. And as I walked it seemed that at last I had seized the true essence of the religion I had adopted, and whose worldly success I had with such energy promoted. So that it seemed that these trials I was undergoing had been reserved to the end of my days, so that only then I could have a taste of the ecstasy about which I had so far only read. With this ecstasy I walked. It was Christmas Eve. It was Christmas Eve. My head felt drawn out of my body. I had difficulty in assessing the size and distance of objects. I felt myself tall. I felt myself part of the earth and yet removed.

And: 'No!' I said to my wife at teatime. 'No, I will not disgrace myself by this action of cowardice. Rather, I will proclaim my failure to the world and ask for my due punishment.'

She behaved as I expected. She had been busy putting up all sorts of Christmas decorations, expensive ones from the United States, which are all the rage now, so unlike the simple decorations I used to see in the homes of our early missionaries before the war. But how changed is the house to which we moved! How far has simplicity vanished and been replaced by show! And I gloried in it!

She begged me to change my mind. She summoned Winston to her help. They both wept and implored me to go through with our plan. But I was firm. I do believe that if the schools inspector were alive, he would also have been summoned to plead with me. But he, fortunate man, passed away some three weeks ago, entrusting his daughter and grandson to my care; and this alone is my fear, that by gaining glory for myself I might be injuring them. But I was firm. And then there started another of those scenes with which I had become only too familiar, and the house which that morning was filled with the enthusiasm of Winston was changed into one of mourning. Winston sobbed, tears running down his plump cheeks and down his well-shaped nose to his firm top lip, pleading with me to burn the school down, and generally behaving as though I had deprived him of a bonfire. And then a number of things were destroyed by his mother, and she left the house with Winston, vowing never to see me again, never to be involved in the disgrace which was sure to come.

And so here I sit, waiting not for Christmas, but in this house where the autographed photograph of one of our earliest missionaries gazes down at me through his rich beard and luxuriant eyebrows, and where the walls carry so many reminders of my past life of endeavour and hardship and struggle and triumph and also, alas, final failure, I wait for the day after Boxing Day, after the races to which we were to have gone, for the visit of the inspectors of the Audit Department. The house is lonely and dark. The radios play the

Christmas songs. I am very lonely. But I am strong. And here I lay down my pen. My hand tires; the beautiful letters we were taught to fashion at the mission school have begun to weaken and to straggle untidily over the ruled paper; and someone is knocking.

*

December 27. How can one speak of the ways of the world, how can one speak of the tribulations that come one's way? Even expiation is denied me. For even as I wrote the last sentence of the above account, there came a knocking at my door, and I went to open unto him who knocked. And lo, there was a boy, bearing tidings. And behold, towards the west the sky had reddened. The boy informed me that the school was ablaze. What could I do? My world fell about my ears. Even final expiation, final triumph, it seemed, was denied me. Certain things are not for me. In this moment of anguish and despair my first thought was for my wife. Where had she gone? I went out to seek her. When I returned, after a fruitless errand, I discovered that she and Winston had come back to seek me. Smiling through our tears, we embraced. So it was Christmas after all for us. And, with lightened heart, made heavy only by my wrestling with the Lord, we went to the races on Boxing Day, yesterday. We did not gamble. It is against our principles. The inspectors from the Audit Department sent word today that they would not, after all, come.

1962

The Mourners

I WALKED UP the back stairs into the veranda white in the afternoon sun. I could never bring myself to enter that house by the front stairs. We were poor relations; we had been taught to respect the house and the family.

On the right of the veranda was the kitchen, tiled and spruce and with every modern gadget. An ugly Indian girl with a pockmarked face and slack breasts was washing some dishes. She wore a dirty red print frock.

When she saw me she said, 'Hello, Romesh.' She had opened brightly but ended on a subdued tone that was more suitable.

'Hello,' I said softly. 'Is she there?' I jerked my thumb towards the drawing-room that lay straight ahead.

'Yes. Boy, she cries all day. And the baby was so cute too.' The servant girl was adapting herself to the language of the house.

'Can I go in now?'

'Yes,' she whispered. Drying her hands on her frock, she led the way. Her kitchen was clean and pure, but all the impurities seemed to have stuck on her. She tiptoed to the jalousied door, opened it an inch or two, peered in deferentially and said in a louder voice, 'Romesh here, Miss Sheila.'

There was a sigh inside. The girl opened the door and shut it behind me. The curtains had been drawn all around. The room was full of a hot darkness smelling of ammonia and oil. Through the ventilation slits some light came into the room, enough to make Sheila distinct. She was in a loose lemon housecoat; she half sat, half reclined on a pink sofa.

I walked across the polished floor as slowly and silently as I could. I shifted my eyes from Sheila to the table next to the sofa. I didn't know how to begin.

It was Sheila who broke the silence. She looked me up and down in the half-light and said, 'My, Romesh, you are growing up.' She smiled with tears in her eyes. 'How are you? And your mother?'

Sheila didn't like my mother. 'They're all well—all at home are well,' I said. 'And how are you?'

She managed a little laugh. 'Still *living*. Pull up a chair. No, no—not yet. Let me look at you. My, you are getting to be a handsome young man.'

I pulled up a chair and sat down. I sat with my legs wide apart at first. But this struck me as being irreverent and too casual. So I put my knees together and let my hands rest loosely on them. I sat upright. Then I looked at Sheila. She smiled.

Then she began to cry. She reached for the damp handkerchief on the table. I got up and asked whether she would like the smelling salts or the bay rum. Jerking with sobs, she shook her head and told me, in words truncated by tears, to sit down.

I sat still, not knowing what to do.

With the handkerchief she wiped her eyes, pulled out a larger handkerchief from her housecoat and blew her nose. Then she smiled. 'You must forgive me for breaking down like this,' she said.

I was going to say, 'That's all right,' but the words felt too free. So I opened my mouth and made an unintelligible noise.

'You never knew my son, Romesh?'

'I only saw him once,' I lied; and instantly regretted the lie. Suppose she asked me where I had seen him or when I had seen him. In fact, I never knew that Sheila's baby was a boy until he died and the news spread.

But she wasn't going to examine me. 'I have some pictures of him.' She called in a gentle, strained voice: 'Soomintra.'

The servant girl opened the door. 'You want something, Miss Sheila?'

'Yes, Soomin,' Sheila said (and I noticed that she had shortened the girl's name, a thing that was ordinarily not done). 'Yes, I want the snapshots of Ravi.' At the name she almost burst into tears, but flung her head back at the last moment and smiled.

When Soomintra left the room I looked at the walls. In the dim light I could make out an engraving of the Princes in the Tower, a print of a stream lazing bluely beautiful through banks cushioned with flowers. I was looking at the walls to escape looking at Sheila. But her eyes followed mine and rested on the Princes in the Tower.

'You know the story?' she asked.

'Yes.'

'Look at them. They're going to be killed, you know. It's only in the past two days I've really got to understand that picture, you know. The boys. So sad. And look at the dog. Not understanding a thing. Just wanting to get out.'

'It is a sad picture.'

She brushed a tear from her eye and smiled once more. 'But tell me, Romesh, how are you getting on with your studies?'

'As usual.'

'Are you going away?'

'If I do well in the exams.'

'But you're bound to do well. After all, your father is no fool.'

It seemed overbearingly selfish to continue listening. I said, 'You needn't talk, if you don't want to.'

Soomintra brought the snapshot album. It was an expensive album, covered in leather. Ravi had been constantly photographed from the time he had been allowed into the open air to the month before his death. There were pictures of him in bathing costume, digging sand on the east coast, the north coast and the south coast; pictures of Ravi dressed up for Carnival, dressed up for tea parties; Ravi on tricycles, Ravi in motor cars, real ones and toy ones; Ravi in the company of scores of people I didn't know. I turned the pages with due lassitude. From time to time Sheila leaned forward and commented. 'There's Ravi at the home of that American doctor. A wunnerful guy. He looks sweet, doesn't he? And look at this one: that boy always had a smile for the camera. He always knew what we were doing. He was a very smart little kid.'

At last we exhausted the snapshots. Sheila had grown silent towards the end. I felt she had been through the album many times in the past two days.

I tapped my hands on my knees. I looked at the clock on the wall and the Princes in the Tower. Sheila came to the rescue. 'I am sure you are hungry.'

I shook my head faintly.

'Soomin will fix something for you.'

Soomintra did prepare something for me, and I ate in the kitchen—their food was always good. I prepared to face the farewell tears and smiles. But just then the Doctor came. He was Sheila's husband and everyone knew him as 'The Doctor'. He was tall with a pale handsome face that now looked drawn and tired.

'Hello, Romesh.'

'Hello, Doctor.'

'How is she?'

'Not very happy.'

'She'll be all right in a couple of days. The shock, you know. And she's a very delicate girl.'

'I hope she gets over it soon.'

He smiled and patted me on the shoulder. He pulled the blinds to shut out the sun from the veranda, and made me sit down.

'You knew my son?'

'Only slightly.'

'He was a fine child. We wanted—or rather, I wanted—to enter him in the Cow and Gate Baby Contest. But Sheila didn't care for the idea.'

I could find nothing to say.

'When he was four he used to sing, you know. All sorts of songs. In English and Hindi. You know that song—*I'll Be Seeing You?*'

I nodded.

'He used to sing that through and through. He had picked up all the words. Where from I don't know, but he'd picked them up. And even now I don't know half the words myself. He was like that. Quick. And do you know the last words he said to me were "I'll be seeing you in all the old familiar places"? When Sheila heard that he was dead she looked at me and began to cry. "I'll be seeing you," she said.'

I didn't look at him.

'It makes you think, doesn't it? Makes you think about life. Here today. Gone tomorrow. It makes you think about life and death, doesn't it? But here I go, philosophizing again. Why don't you start giving lessons to children?' he asked me abruptly. 'You could make tons of money that way. I know a boy who's making fifty dollars a month by giving lessons one afternoon a week.'

'I am busy with my exams.'

He paid no attention. 'Tell me, have you seen the pictures we took of Ravi last Carnival?'

I hadn't the heart to say yes.

'Soomin,' he called, 'bring the photograph album.'

1950

The Nightwatchman's Occurrence Book

November 21. 10.30 p.m. C. A. Cavander takes over duty at C—Hotel all corrected. *Cesar Alwyn Cavander*

7 a.m. C. A. Cavander hand over duty to Mr Vignales at C—Hotel no report. *Cesar Alwyn Cavander*

November 22. 10.30 p.m. C. A. Cavander take over duty at C—Hotel no report. *Cesar Alwyn Cavander*

7 a.m. C. A. Cavander hand over duty to Mr Vignales at C—Hotel all corrected. *Cesar Alwyn Cavander*

This is the third occasion on which I have found C. A. Cavander, Nightwatchman, asleep on duty. Last night, at 12.45 a.m., I found him sound asleep in a rocking chair in the hotel lounge. Nightwatchman Cavander has therefore been dismissed.

Nightwatchman Hillyard: This book is to be known in future as 'The Nightwatchman's Occurrence Book'. In it I shall expect to find a detailed account of everything that happens in the hotel tonight. Be warned by the example of ex-Nightwatchman Cavander. *W. A. G. Inskip, Manager*

Mr Manager, remarks noted. You have no worry where I am concern sir. *Charles Ethelbert Hillyard, Nightwatchman*

November 23. 11 p.m. Nightwatchman Hillyard take over duty at C— Hotel with one torch light 2 fridge keys and room keys 1, 3, 6, 10 and 13. Also 25 cartoons Carib Beer and 7 cartoons Heineken and 2 cartoons American cigarettes. Beer cartoons intact Bar intact all corrected no report. *Charles Ethelbert Hillyard*

7 a.m. Nightwatchman Hillyard hand over duty to Mr Vignales at C—Hotel with one torch light 2 fridge keys and room keys, 1, 3, 6, 10 and 13. 32 cartoons beer. Bar intact all corrected no report. *Charles Ethelbert Hillyard*

Nightwatchman Hillyard: Mr Wills complained bitterly to me this morning that last night he was denied entry to the bar by you. I wonder if you know exactly what the purpose of this hotel is. In future all hotel guests are to be allowed entry to the bar at whatever time they choose. It is your duty simply to note what they take. This is one reason why the hotel provides a certain number of beer cartons (please note the spelling of this word). *W. A. G. Inskip*

Mr Manager, remarks noted. I sorry I didnt get the chance to take some education sir. *Chas. Ethelbert Hillyard*

November 24. 11 p.m. N.W. Hillyard take over duty with one Torch, 1 Bar Key, 2 Fridge Keys, 32 cartons Beer, all intact. 12 Midnight Bar close and Barman left leaving Mr Wills and others in Bar, and they left at 1 a.m. Mr Wills took 16 Carib Beer, Mr Wilson 8, Mr Percy 8. At 2 a.m. Mr Wills come back in the bar and take 4 Carib and some bread, he cut his hand trying to cut the bread, so please dont worry about the stains on the carpet sir. At 6 a.m. Mr Wills come back for some soda water. It didn't have any so he take a ginger beer instead. Sir you see it is my intention to do this job good sir, I cant see how Nightwatchman Cavander could fall asleep on this job sir. *Chas. Ethelbert Hillyard*

You always seem sure of the time, and guests appear to be in the habit of entering the bar on the hour. You will kindly note the exact time. The clock from the kitchen is left on the window near the switches. You can use this clock but you MUST replace it every morning before you go off duty. *W. A. G. Inskip*

Noted. *Chas. Ethelbert Hillyard*

November 25. Midnight Bar close and 12.23 a.m. Barman left leaving

Mr Wills and others in Bar. Mr Owen take 5 bottles Carib, Mr Wilson 6 Bottles Heineken, Mr Wills 18 Carib and they left at 2.52 a.m. Nothing unusual. Mr Wills was helpless, I don't see how anybody could drink so much, eighteen one man alone, this work enough to turn anybody Seventh Day Adventist, and another man come in the bar, I dont know his name, I hear they call him Paul, he assist me because the others couldn't do much, and we take Mr Wills up to his room and take off his boots and slack his other clothes and then we left. Don't know sir if they did take more while I was away, nothing was mark on the Pepsi Cola board, but they was drinking still, it look as if they come back and take some more, but with Mr Wills I want some extra assistance sir.

Mr Manager, the clock break I find it break when I come back from Mr Wills room sir. It stop 3.19 sir. *Chas. E. Hillyard*

More than 2 lbs of veal were removed from the Fridge last night, and a cake that was left in the press was cut. It is your duty, Nightwatch-man Hillyard, to keep an eye on these things. I ought to warn you that I have also asked the Police to check on all employees leaving the hotel, to prevent such occurrences in the future. *W. A. G. Inskip*

Mr Manager, I don't know why people so anxious to blame servants sir. About the cake, the press lock at night and I dont have the key sir, everything safe where I am concern sir. *Chas. Hillyard*

November 26. Midnight Bar close and Barman left. Mr Wills didn't come, I hear he at the American base tonight, all quiet, nothing unusual.

Mr Manager, I request one thing. Please inform the Barman to let me know sir when there is a female guest in the hotel sir. *C. E. Hill-yard*

This morning I received a report from a guest that there were screams in the hotel during the night. You wrote All Quiet. Kindly explain in writing. *W. A. G. Inskip*

Write Explanation here:

EXPLANATION. Not long after midnight the telephone ring and a woman ask for Mr Jimminez. I try to tell her where he was but she say she cant hear properly. Fifteen minutes later she came in a car, she was looking vex and sleepy, and I went up to call him. The door was not lock, I went in and touch his foot and call him very soft, and he jump up and begin to shout. When he come to himself he said he had Night Mere, and then he come down and went away with the woman, was not necessary to mention.

Mr Manager, I request you again, please inform the Barman to let me know sir when there is a female guest in the hotel. *C. Hillyard*

November 27. 1 a.m. Bar close, Mr Wills and a American 19 Carib and 2.30 a.m. a Police come and ask for Mr Wills, he say the American report that he was robbed of $200.00¢, he was last drinking at C—— with Mr Wills and others. Mr Wills and the Police ask to open the Bar to search it, I told them I cannot open the Bar for you like that, the Police must come with the Manager. Then the American say it was only joke he was joking, and they try to get the Police to laugh, but the Police looking the way I feeling. Then laughing Mr Wills left in a garage car as he couldn't drive himself and the American was waiting outside and they both fall down as they was getting in the car, and Mr Wills saying any time you want a overdraft you just come to my bank kiddo. The Police left walking by himself. *C. Hillyard*

Nightwatchman Hillyard : 'Was not necessary to mention'!! You are not to decide what is necessary to mention in this nightwatchman's occurrence book. Since when have you become sole owner of the hotel as to determine what is necessary to mention? If the guest did not mention it I would never have known that there were screams in the hotel during the night. Also will you kindly tell me who Mr Jimminez is? And what rooms he occupied or occupies? And by what right? You have been told by me personally that the names of all hotel guests are on the slate next to the light switches. If you find Mr Jimminez's name on this slate, or could give me some information about him, I will be most warmly obliged to you. The lady you ask about is Mrs Roscoe, Room 12, as you very well know. It is your duty to see that guests are not pestered by unauthorized callers. You should give no information about guests to such people, and I would be glad if in future you could direct such callers straight to me. *W. A. G. Inskip*

Sir was what I ask you two times, I dont know what sort of work I take up, I always believe that nightwatchman work is a quiet work and I dont like meddling in white people business, but the gentleman occupy Room 12 also, was there that I went up to call him, I didn't think it necessary to mention because was none of my business sir. *C.E.H.*

November 28. 12 Midnight Bar close and Barman left at 12.20 a.m. leaving Mr Wills and others, and they all left at 1.25 a.m. Mr Wills 8 Carib, Mr Wilson 12, Mr Percy 8, and the man they call Paul 12. Mrs Roscoe join the gentlemen at 12.33 a.m., four gins, everybody calling her Minnie from Trinidad, and then they start singing that song, and some others. Nothing unusual. Afterwards there were mild singing and guitar music in Room 12. A man come in and ask to use the phone at 2.17 a.m. and while he was using it about 7 men come in and wanted to beat him up, so he put down the phone and they all ran away. At 3 a.m. I notice the padlock not on the press, I look inside, no cake, but the padlock was not put on in the first place sir. Mr Wills come down again at 6 a.m. to look for his sweet, he look in the Fridge and did not see any. He took a piece of pineapple. A plate was covered in the Fridge, but it didn't have anything in it. Mr Wills put it out, the cat jump on it and it fall down and break. The garage bulb not burning. *C.EH.*

You will please sign your name at the bottom of your report. You are in the habit of writing Nothing Unusual. Please take note and think before making such a statement. I want to know what is meant by nothing unusual. I gather, not from you, needless to say, that the police have fallen into the habit of visiting the hotel at night. I would be most grateful to you if you could find the time to note the times of these visits. *W. A. G. Inskip*

Sir, nothing unusual means everything usual. I dont know, nothing I writing you liking. I don't know what sort of work this nightwatchman work getting to be, since when people have to start getting Cambridge certificate to get nightwatchman job, I ain't educated and because of this everybody think they could insult me. *Charles Ethelbert Hillyard*

November 29. Midnight Bar close and 12.15 Barman left leaving Mr Wills and Mrs Roscoe and others in the Bar. Mr Wills and Mrs Roscoe left at 12.30 a.m. leaving Mr Wilson and the man they call Paul, and they all left at 1.00 a.m. Twenty minutes to 2 Mr Wills and party return and left again at 5 to 3. At 3.45 Mr Wills return and take bread and milk and olives and cherries, he ask for nutmeg too, I said we had none, he drink 2 Carib, and left ten minutes later. He also collect Mrs Roscoe bag. All the drinks, except the 2 Carib, was taken by the man they call Paul. I don't know sir I don't like this sort of work, you better hire a night barman. At 5.30 Mrs Roscoe and the man they call Paul come back to the bar, they was having a quarrel, Mr Paul saying you make me sick, Mrs Roscoe saying I feel sick, and then she vomit all over the floor, shouting I didn't want that damned milk. I was cleaning up when Mr Wills come down to ask for soda water, we got to lay in more soda for Mr Wills but I need extra assistance with Mr Wills Paul and party sir.

The police come at 2, 3.48 and 4.52. They sit down in the bar a long time. Firearms discharge 2 times in the back yard. Detective making inquiries. I don't know sir, I thinking it would be better for me to go back to some other sort of job. At 3 I hear somebody shout Thief, and I see a man running out of the back, and Mr London, Room 9, say he miss 80 cents and a pack of cigarettes which was on his dressing case. I don't know when the people in this place does sleep. *Chas. Ethelbert Hillyard*

Nightwatchman Hillyard: A lot more than 80 cents was stolen. Several rooms were in fact entered during the night, including my own. You are employed to prevent such things occurring. Your interest in the morals of our guests seems to be distracting your attention from your duties. Save your preaching for your roadside prayer meetings. Mr Pick, Room 7, reports that in spite of the most pressing and repeated requests, you did not awaken him at 5. He has missed his plane to British Guiana as a result. No newspapers were delivered to the rooms this morning. I am again notifying you that papers must be handed personally to Doorman Vignales. And the messenger's bicycle, which I must remind you is the property of the hotel, has been damaged. What do you *do* at nights? *W. A. G. Inskip*

Please don't ask me sir.

Relating to the damaged bicycle: I left the bicycle the same place where I meet it, nothing took place so as to damage it. I always take care of all property sir. I dont know how you could think I have time to go out for bicycle rides. About the papers, sir, the police and them read it and leave them in such a state that I didn't think it would be nice to give them to guests. I wake up Mr Pick, room 7, at 4.50 a.m. 5 a.m. 5.15 a.m. and 5.30. He told me to keep off, he would not get up, and one time he pelt a box of matches at me, matches scatter all over the place I always do everything to the best of my ability sir but God is my Witness I never find a nightwatchman work like this, so much writing I dont have time to do anything else, I dont have four hands and six eyes and I want this extra assistance with Mr Wills and party sir. I am a poor man and you could abuse me, but you must not abuse my religion sir because the good Lord sees All and will have His revenge sir, I don't know what sort of work and trouble I land myself in, all I want is a little quiet night work and all I getting is abuse. *Chas. E. Hillyard*

November 30. 12.25 a.m. Bar close and Barman left 1.00 a.m. leaving Mr Wills and party in Bar. Mr Wills take 12 Carib Mr Wilson 6, Mr Percy 14. Mrs Roscoe five gins. At 1.30 a.m. Mrs Roscoe left and there were a little singing and mild guitar playing in Room 12. Nothing unusual. The police come at 1.35 and sit down in the bar for a time, not drinking, not talking, not doing anything except watching. At 1.45 the man they call Paul come in with Mr McPherson of the SS Naparoni, they was both falling down and laughing whenever anything break and the man they call Paul say Fireworks about to begin tell Minnie Malcolm coming the ship just dock. Mr Wills and party scatter leaving one or two bottles half empty and then the man they call Paul tell me to go up to Room 12 and tell Minnie Roscoe that Malcolm coming. I don't know how people could behave so the thing enough to make anybody turn priest. I notice the padlock on the bar door break off it hanging on only by a little piece of wood. And when I went up to Room 12 and tell Mrs Roscoe that Malcolm coming the ship just dock the woman get sober straight away like she dont want to hear no more guitar music and she asking me where to hide where to go. I dont know, I feel the day of reckoning is at hand, but she not listening to what I saying, she busy straightening up the room one minute packing the next, and then she run out into the corridor and before I could stop she run straight down the back stairs to the annexe. And then 5 past 2, still in the corridor, I see a big man running up to me and he sober as a judge and he mad as a drunkard and he asking me where she is where she is. I ask whether he is a authorized caller, he say you don't give me any of that crap now, where she is, where she is. So remembering about the last time and Mr Jimminez I direct him to the manager office in the annexe. He hear a little scuffling inside Mr Inskip room and I make out Mr Inskip sleepy voice and Mrs Roscoe voice and the red man run inside and all I hearing for the next five minutes is bam bam bodow bodow bow and this woman screaming. I dont know what sort of work this nightwatchman getting I want something quiet like the police. In time things quiet down and the red man drag Mrs Roscoe out of the annexe and they take a taxi, and the Police sitting down quiet in the bar. Then Mr Percy and the others come back one by one to the bar and they talking quiet and they not drinking and they left 3 a.m. 3.15

Mr Wills return and take one whisky and 2 Carib. He asked for pineapple or some sweet fruit but it had nothing.

6 a.m. Mr Wills came in the bar looking for soda but it aint have none. We have to get some soda for Mr Wills sir.

6.30 a.m. the papers come and I deliver them to Doorman Vignales at 7 a.m. *Chas. Hillyard*

Mr Hillyard: In view of the unfortunate illness of Mr Inskip, I am temporarily in charge of the hotel. I trust you will continue to make your nightly reports, but I would be glad if you could keep your entries as brief as possible. *Robt. Magnus, Acting Manager*

December 1 10.30 p.m. C. E. Hillyard take over duty at C—Hotel all corrected 12 Midnight Bar close 2 a.m. Mr Wills 2 Carib, 1 bread 6 a.m. Mr Wills 1 soda 7 a.m. Nightwatchman Hillyard hand over duty to Mr Vignales with one torch light 2 Fridge keys and Room Keys 1, 3, 6 and 12. Bar intact all corrected no report. *C.E.H.*

1962

The Enemy

I HAD ALWAYS considered this woman, my mother, as the enemy. She was sure to misunderstand anything I did, and the time came when I thought she not only misunderstood me, but quite definitely disapproved of me. I was an only child, but for her I was one too many.

She hated my father, and even after he died she continued to hate him.

She would say, 'Go ahead and do what you doing. You is your father child, you hear, not mine.'

The real split between my mother and me happened not in Miguel Street, but in the country.

My mother had decided to leave my father, and she wanted to take me to her mother.

I refused to go.

My father was ill, and in bed. Besides, he had promised that if I stayed with him I was to have a whole box of crayons.

I chose the crayons and my father.

We were living at the time in Cunupia, where my father was a driver on the sugar estates. He wasn't a slave-driver, but a driver of free people, but my father used to behave as though the people were slaves. He rode about the estates on a big clumsy brown horse, cracking his whip at the labourers and people said—I really don't believe this—that he used to kick the labourers.

I don't believe it because my father had lived all his life in Cunupia and he knew that you really couldn't push the Cunupia people around. They are not tough people, but they think nothing of killing, and they are prepared to wait years for the chance to kill someone they don't like. In fact, Cunupia and Tableland are the two parts of Trinidad where murders occur often enough to ensure quick promotion for the policemen stationed there.

At first we lived in the barracks, but then my father wanted to move to a little wooden house not far away.

My mother said, 'You playing hero. Go and live in your house by yourself, you hear.'

She was afraid, of course, but my father insisted. So we moved to the house, and then trouble really started.

A man came to the house one day about midday and said to my mother, 'Where your husband?'

My mother said, 'I don't know.'

The man was cleaning his teeth with a twig from a hibiscus plant. He spat and said, 'It don't matter. I have time. I could wait.'

My mother said, 'You ain't doing nothing like that. I know what you thinking, but I have my sister coming here right now.'

The man laughed and said, 'I not doing anything. I just want to know when he coming home.'

I began to cry in terror.

The man laughed.

My mother said, 'Shut up this minute or I give you something really to cry about.'

I went to another room and walked about saying, 'Rama! Rama! Sita Rama!' This was what my father had told me to say when I was in danger of any sort.

I looked out of the window. It was bright daylight, and hot, and there was nobody else in all the wide world of bush and trees.

And then I saw my aunt walking up the road.

She came and she said, 'Anything wrong with you here? I was at home just sitting quite quiet, and I suddenly feel that something was going wrong. I feel I had to come to see.'

The man said, 'Yes, I know the feeling.'

My mother, who was being very brave all the time, began to cry.

But all this was only to frighten us, and we were certainly frightened. My father always afterwards took his gun with him, and my mother kept a sharpened cutlass by her hand.

Then, at night, there used to be voices, sometimes from the road, sometimes from the bushes behind the house. The voices came from people who had lost their way and wanted lights, people who had come to tell my father that his sister had died suddenly in Debe, people who had come just to tell my father that there was a big fire at the sugar-mill. Sometimes there would be two or three of these voices, speaking from different directions, and we would sit awake in the dark house, just waiting, waiting for the voices to fall silent. And when they did fall silent it was even more terrible.

My father used to say, 'They still outside. They want you to go out and look.'

And at four or five o'clock when the morning light was coming up we would hear the tramp of feet in the bush, feet going away.

As soon as darkness fell we would lock ourselves up in the house, and wait. For days there would sometimes be nothing at all, and then we would hear them again.

My father brought home a dog one day. We called it Tarzan. He was more of a playful dog than a watch-dog, a big hairy brown dog, and I would ride on its back.

When evening came I said, 'Tarzan coming in with us?'

He wasn't. He remained whining outside the door, scratching it with his paws.

Tarzan didn't last long.

One morning we found him hacked to pieces and flung on the top step.

We hadn't heard any noise the night before.

My mother began to quarrel with my father, but my father was behaving as though he didn't really care what happened to him or to any of us.

My mother used to say, 'You playing brave. But bravery ain't going to give any of us life, you hear. Let us leave this place.'

My father began hanging up words of hope on the walls of the house, things from the Gita and the Bible, and sometimes things he had just made up.

He also lost his temper more often with my mother, and the time came when as soon as she entered a room he would scream and pelt things at her.

So she went back to her mother and I remained with my father.

During those days my father spent a lot of his time in bed, and so I had to lie down with him. For the first time I really talked to my father. He taught me three things.

The first was this.

'Boy,' my father asked. 'Who is your father?'

I said, 'You is my father.'

'Wrong.'

'How that wrong?'

My father said, 'You want to know who your father really is? God is your father.'

'And what you is, then?'

'Me, what I is? I is—let me see, well, I is just a second sort of father, not your real father.'

This teaching was later to get me into trouble, particularly with my mother.

The second thing my father taught me was the law of gravity.

We were sitting on the edge of the bed, and he dropped the box of matches.

He asked, 'Now, boy, tell me why the matches drop.'

I said, 'But they bound to drop. What you want them to do? Go sideways?'

My father said, 'I will tell why they drop. They drop because of the laws of gravity.'

And he showed me a trick. He half filled a bucket with water and spun the bucket fast over his shoulder.

He said, 'Look, the water wouldn't fall.'

But it did. He got a soaking and the floor was wet.

He said, 'It don't matter. I just put too much water, that's all. Look again.'

The second time it worked.

The third thing my father taught me was the blending of colours. This was just a few days before he died. He was very ill, and he used to spend a lot of time shivering and mumbling; and even when he fell asleep I used to hear him groaning.

I remained with him on the bed most of the time.

He said to me one day, 'You got the coloured pencils?'

I took them from under the pillow.

He said, 'You want to see some magic?'

I said, 'What, you know magic really?'

He took the yellow pencil and filled in a yellow square.

He asked, 'Boy, what colour this is?'

I said, 'Yellow.'

He said, 'Just pass me the blue pencil now, and shut your eyes tight tight.'

When I opened my eyes he said, 'Boy, what colour this square is now?'

I said, 'You sure you ain't cheating?'

He laughed and showed me how blue and yellow make green.

I said. 'You mean if I take a leaf and wash it and wash it and wash it really good, it go be yellow or blue when I finish with it?'

He said, 'No. You see, is God who blend those colours. God, your father.'

I spent a lot of my time trying to make up tricks. The only one I could do was to put two match-heads together, light them, and make them stick. But my father knew that. But at last I found a trick that I was sure my father didn't know. He never got to know about it because he died on the night I was to show it him.

It had been a day of great heat, and in the afternoon the sky had grown low and heavy and black. It felt almost chilly in the house, and my father was sitting wrapped up in the rocking chair. The rain began to fall drop by heavy drop, beating like a hundred fists on the roof. It grew dark and I lit the oil lamp, sticking a pin in the wick, to keep away bad spirits from the house.

My father suddenly stopped rocking and whispered, 'Boy, they here tonight. Listen. Listen.'

We were both silent and I listened carefully, but my ears could catch nothing but the wind and the rain.

A window banged itself open. The wind whooshed in with heavy raindrops.

'God!' my father screamed.

I went to the window. It was a pitch black night, and the world was a wild and lonely place, with only the wind and the rain on the leaves. I had to fight to pull the window in, and before I could close it, I saw the sky light up with a crack of lightning.

I shut the window and waited for the thunder.

It sounded like a steamroller on the roof.

My father said, 'Boy, don't frighten. Say what I tell you to say.'

I went and sat at the foot of the rocking chair and I began to say, 'Rama! Rama! Sita Rama!'

My father joined in. He was shivering with cold and fright.

Suddenly he shouted, 'Boy, they here. They here. I hear them talking under the house. They could do what they like in all this noise and nobody could hear them.'

I said, 'Don't fraid, I have this cutlass here, and you have your gun.'

But my father wasn't listening.

He said, 'But it dark, man. It so dark. It so dark.'

I got up and went to the table for the oil lamp to bring it nearer. But just then there was an explosion of thunder so low it might have been just above the roof. It rolled and rumbled for a long long time. Then another window blew open and the oil lamp was blown out. The wind and the rain tore into the dark room.

My father screamed out once more, 'Oh God, it dark.'

I was lost in the black world. I screamed until the thunder died away and the rain had become a drizzle. I forgot all about the trick I had prepared for my father: the soap I had rubbed into the palms of my hands until it had dried and disappeared.

*

Everybody agreed on one thing. My mother and I had to leave the country. Port-of-Spain was the safest place. There was too a lot of laughter against my father, and it appeared that for the rest of my life I would have to bear the cross of a father who died from fright. But in a month or so I had forgotten my father, and I had begun to look upon myself as the boy who had no father. It seemed natural.

In fact, when we moved to Port-of-Spain and I saw what the normal relationship between father and son was—it was nothing more than the relationship between the beater and the beaten—when I saw this I was grateful.

My mother made a great thing at first about keeping me in my place and knocking out all the nonsense my father had taught me. I don't know why she didn't try harder, but the fact is that she soon lost interest in me, and she let me run about the street, only rushing down to beat me from time to time.

Occasionally, though, she would take the old firm line.

One day she kept me home. She said, 'No school for you today. I just sick of tying your shoe-laces for you. Today you go have to learn that!'

I didn't think she was being fair. After all, in the country none of us wore shoes and I wasn't used to them.

That day she beat me and beat me and made me tie knot after knot and in the end I still couldn't tie my shoe-laces. For years afterwards it was a great shame to me that I couldn't do a simple thing like that, just as how I couldn't peel an orange. But about the shoes I made up a little trick. I never made my mother buy shoes the correct size. I pretended that those shoes hurt, and I made her get me shoes a size or two bigger. Once the attendant had tied the laces up for me, I never undid them, and merely slipped my feet in and out of the shoes. To keep them on my feet, I stuck paper in the toes.

To hear my mother talk, you would think I was a freak. Nearly every little boy she knew was better and more intelligent. There was one boy she knew who helped his mother paint her house. There was another boy who could mend his own shoes. There was still another boy who at the age of thirteen was earning a good twenty dollars a month, while I was just idling and living off her blood.

Still, there were surprising glimpses of kindness.

There was the time, for instance, when I was cleaning some tumblers for her one Saturday morning. I dropped a tumbler and it broke. Before I could do anything about it my mother saw what had happened.

She said, 'How you break it?'

I said, 'It just slip off. It smooth smooth.'

She said, 'Is a lot of nonsense drinking from glass. They break up so easy.'

And that was all. I got worried about my mother's health.

She was never worried about mine.

She thought that there was no illness in the world a stiff dose of hot Epsom Salts couldn't cure. That was a penance I had to endure once a month. It completely ruined my weekend. And if there was something she couldn't understand, she sent me to the Health Officer in Tragarete Road. That was an awful place. You waited and waited and waited before you went in to see the doctor.

Before you had time to say, 'Doctor, I have a pain—' he would be writing out a prescription for you. And again you had to wait for the medicine. All the Health Office medicines were the same. Water and pink sediment half an inch thick.

Hat used to say of the Health Office, 'The Government taking up faith healing.'

My mother considered the Health Office a good place for me to go to. I would go there at eight in the morning and return any time after two in the afternoon. It kept me out of mischief, and it cost only twenty-four cents a year.

But you mustn't get the impression that I was a saint all the time.

I wasn't. I used to have odd fits where I just couldn't take an order from anybody, particularly my mother. I used to feel that I would dishonour myself for life if I took anybody's orders. And life is a funny thing, really. I sometimes got these fits just when my mother was anxious to be nice to me.

The day after Hat rescued me from drowning at Docksite I wrote an essay for my schoolmaster on the subject, 'A Day at the Seaside'. I don't think any schoolmaster ever got an essay like that. I talked about how I was nearly drowned and how calmly I was facing death, with my mind absolutely calm, thinking, 'Well, boy, this is the end.' The teacher was so pleased he gave me ten marks out of twelve.

He said, 'I think you are a genius.'

When I went home I told my mother, 'That essay I write today, I get ten out of twelve for it.'

My mother said, 'How you so bold-face to lie brave brave so in front of my face? You want me give you a slap to turn your face?'

In the end I convinced her.

She melted at once. She sat down in the hammock and said, 'Come and sit down by me, son.'

Just then the crazy fit came on me.

I got very angry for no reason at all and I said, 'No, I not going to sit by you.'

She laughed and coaxed.

And the angrier she made me.

Slowly the friendliness died away. It had become a struggle between two wills. I was prepared to drown rather than dishonour myself by obeying.

'I ask you to come and sit down here.'

'I not sitting down.'

'Take off your belt.'

I took it off and gave it to her. She belted me soundly, and my nose bled, but still I didn't sit in the hammock.

At times like these I used to cry, without meaning it, 'If my father was alive you wouldn't be behaving like this.'

*

So she remained the enemy. She was someone from whom I was going to escape as soon as I grew big enough. That was, in fact, the main lure of adulthood.

Progress was sweeping through Port-of-Spain in those days. The Americans were pouring money into Trinidad and there was a lot of talk from the British about colonial development and welfare.

One of the visible signs of this progress was the disappearance of the latrines. I hated the latrines, and I used to wonder about the sort of men who came with their lorries at night and carted away the filth; and there was always the horrible fear of falling into a pit.

One of the first men to have decent lavatories built was Hat, and we made a great thing of knocking down his old latrine. All the boys and men went to give a hand. I was too small to give a hand, but I went to watch. The walls were knocked down one by one and in the end there was only one remaining.

Hat said, 'Boys, let we try to knock this one down in one big piece.'

And they did.

The wall swayed and began to fall.

I must have gone mad in that split second, for I did a Superman act and tried to prevent the wall falling.

I just remember people shouting, 'O God! Look out!'

*

I was travelling in a bus, one of the green buses of Sam's Super Service, from Port-of-Spain to Petit Valley. The bus was full of old women in bright bandanas carrying big baskets of eddoes, yams, bananas, with here and there some chickens. Suddenly the old women all began chattering, and the chickens began squawking. My head felt as though it would split, but when I tried to shout at the old women I found I couldn't open my mouth. I tried again, but all I heard, more distinctly now, was the constant chattering.

Water was pouring down my face.

I was flat out under a tap and there were faces above me looking down.

Somebody shouted, 'He recover. Is all right.'

Hat said, 'How you feeling?'

I said, trying to laugh, 'I feeling all right.'

Mrs Bhakcu said, 'You have any pains?'

I shook my head.

But, suddenly, my whole body began to ache. I tried to move my hand and it hurt.

I said, 'I think I break my hand.'

But I could stand, and they made me walk into the house.

My mother came and I could see her eyes glassy and wet with tears.

Somebody, I cannot remember who, said, 'Boy, you had your mother really worried.'

I looked at her tears, and I felt I was going to cry too. I had discovered that she could be worried and anxious for me.

I wished I were a Hindu god at that moment, with two hundred arms, so that all two hundred could be broken, just to enjoy that moment, and to see again my mother's tears.

1955

Greenie and Yellow

AND BLUEY IS the hero of this story.

At first Bluey belonged to the Welsh couple in the basement. We heard him throughout the house but we hardly saw him. I used to see him only when I went down to the dustbins just outside the basement window. He was smoky blue; lively, almost querulous, with unclipped wings, he made his cage seem too small.

When the Welsh couple had to go back to Wales—I think Mrs Lewis was going to have a baby—they decided to give Bluey to Mrs Cooksey, the landlady. We were surprised when she accepted. She didn't like the Lewises. In fact, she didn't like any of her tenants. She criticized them all to me and I suppose she criticized me to them. You couldn't blame her: the house was just too full of tenants. Apart from a sittingroom on the ground floor, a kitchen on the landing at the top of the basement steps, and a bedroom somewhere in the basement, the whole of the Cookseys' house had been let. The Cookseys had no children and were saving up for old age. It had come but they didn't know.

Mrs Cooksey was delighted with Bluey. She used to lie in wait behind her half-opened door and spring out at us as we passed through the hall; but now it wasn't to ask who had taken more than his share of the milk or who had left the bath dirty; it was to call us into her room to look at Bluey and listen to him, and to admire the improvements she had made to his cage.

The cage, when I had seen it in the basement window, was an elegant little thing with blue bars to match Bluey's feathers, two toy trapezes, a seed-trough, a water-trough and a spring door. Now every Friday there were additions: Mrs Cooksey shopped on Friday. The first addition was a toy ferris wheel in multicoloured plastic. The second was a seed-bell; it tinkled when Bluey pecked at it. The third was a small round mirror. Just when it seemed that these additions were going to leave little room for Bluey, Mrs Cooksey added something else. She said it was a friend for Bluey. The friend was a red-beaked chicken emerging from a neatly serrated shell, all in plastic and weighted at the bottom to stay upright.

Bluey loved his toys. He kept the chicken and shell swaying, the trapezes going, the ferris wheel spinning, the seed-bell ringing. He clucked and chattered and whistled and every now and then gave a zestful little shriek.

But he couldn't talk. For that Mrs Cooksey blamed Mrs Lewis. 'They're just like children, d'you see? You've got to train them. But she didn't have the time. Very delicate she was. Just a romp and a giggle all day long.'

Mrs Cooksey bought a booklet, *Your Budgie,* and kept it under the heavy glass ashtray on the table. She said it was full of good hints; and when she had read them, she began to train Bluey. She talked and talked to him, to get him used to her voice. Then she gave him a name: Joey. Bluey never recognized it. When I went down to pay for the milk one Saturday Mrs Cooksey told me that she was also finger-training him, getting him to come out of his cage and remain on her finger. Two or three days later she called me in to get Bluey down from the top of the curtains where he was squawking and shrieking and flapping his wings with energy. He wouldn't come down to calls of 'Joey!' or to Mrs Cooksey's cluckings or at her outstretched finger. I had a lot of trouble before I got him back into his cage.

The finger-training was dropped and the name Joey was dropped. Mrs Cooksey just called him Bluey.

Spring came. The plane tree two back-gardens away, the only tree between the backs of the houses and the back of what we were told was the largest cinema in England, became touched with green.

The sun shone on some days and for an hour or two lit up our back-garden, or rather the Cookseys' garden: tenants weren't allowed. Mrs Cooksey put Bluey and his cage outside and sat beside him, knitting a bedjacket. Sparrows flew about the cage; but they came to dig up Mr Cooksey's cindery, empty flowerbeds, not to attack Bluey. And Bluey was aware of no danger. He hopped from trapeze to trapeze, spun his ferris wheel, rubbed his beak against his little mirror and cooed at his reflection. His seed-bell tinkled, the red-beaked chicken bobbed up and down. Bluey was never to be so happy again.

*

Coming into the hall late one Friday afternoon I saw that Mrs Cooksey's door was ajar. I let her take me by surprise. Behind her pink-rimmed glasses her watery blue eyes were full of mischief. I followed her into the room.

Bluey was not alone. He had a companion. A live one. It was a green budgerigar.

'He just flew into the garden this morning,' Mrs Cooksey said. 'Really. Oh, he must have been a smart fellow to get away from all those naughty little sparrows. Smart, aren't you, Greenie?'

Greenie was plumper than Bluey and I thought he had an arrogant breast. He wasted no time showing us what he could do. He fanned out one wing with a series of small snapping sounds, folded it back in, and fanned out the other. He could lean over sideways on one leg too, and when he pecked at a bar it didn't look so strong. He was noisier than Bluey and, for all his size, more nimble. He looked the sort of budgerigar who could elude sparrows. But his experience of freedom and his triumph over danger had made him something of a bully. Even while we stood over the cage he baited Bluey. By shrieks and flutterings he attracted Bluey to the ferris wheel. Bluey went, gave the wheel a spin with his beak and stood by to give another. Before he could do so, Greenie flew at him, flapping his wings so powerfully that the sand on the floor of the cage flew up. Bluey retreated, complaining. Greenie outsquawked his complaints.

The ferris wheel meant nothing to Greenie; in his wanderings he hadn't picked up the art of making a wheel spin. After some moments he flew away from the wheel and rested on a trapeze. He invited Bluey to the wheel again. Bluey went, and the whole shameful squabble began all over.

Mrs Cooksey was giving little oohs and ahs. 'You have a real friend now, haven't you, Bluey?'

Bluey wasn't listening. He was hurrying away from the wheel to the red-beaked chicken. He pecked at it frenziedly.

'Just like children,' Mrs Cooksey said. 'They'll quarrel and fight, but they are good friends.'

Life became hard for Bluey. Greenie never stopped showing off; and Bluey, continually baited and squawked at, retaliated less and less. At the end of the week he seemed to have lost the will even to protest. It was Greenie now who kept the little trapeze going, Greenie who punched the seed-bell and made it ring, Greenie who filled the room with noise. Mrs Cooksey didn't try to teach Greenie to talk and I don't imagine the thought of finger-training him ever entered her head. 'Greenie's a big boy,' she said.

It gave me some pleasure to see how the big boy fretted at the ferris wheel. He shook it and made it rattle; but he couldn't make it spin.

'Why don't you show him, Bluey?' Mrs Cooksey said.

But Bluey had lost interest in all Mrs Cooksey's embellishments, even in the plastic chicken. He remained on the floor of the cage and hardly moved. Finally he stood quite still, his feathers permanently ruffled, shivering from time to time. His eyes were half-shut and the white lined lids looked tender and vulnerable. His feet began to swell until they became white and scaly.

'He's just hopeless,' Mrs Cooksey said, with surprising vehemence. 'Don't blame Greenie. I did my best to train Bluey. He didn't care. And who's paying for it now?'

She was contrite a few days later. 'It isn't his fault, poor little Bluey. He's got ingrowing toe-nails. And his feet are so dirty too. He hasn't had a bath for a long time.'

I stayed to watch. Mrs Cooksey emptied the glass ashtray of pins and paper-clips and elastic bands and filled it with warm water. She turned on the electric fire and warmed a towel in front of it. She put a hand into the cage, had it pecked and squawked at by Greenie, pulled Bluey out and dropped him into the water in the ashtray. Instantly Bluey dwindled to half his size. His feathers stuck to him like a second skin. He was rubbed with carbolic soap, rinsed in the ashtray and dried in the warm towel. At the end he looked damp and dishevelled. 'There you are, Bluey. Dry. And now let's have a look at your nails.' She put Bluey on the palm of her left hand and held a pair of nail scissors to his swollen feet. A month before, given such freedom, Bluey would have flown to the top of the curtains. Now he lay still. Suddenly he shrieked and gave a little wriggle.

'Poor little Bluey,' Mrs Cooksey said. 'We've cut his little foot.'

Bluey didn't recover. His feet became scalier, more swollen and gnarled. A paper-thin growth, shaped like a fingernail, appeared on his lower beak and grew upwards, making it hard for him to eat, impossible for him to peck. The top of his beak broke out into a sponge-like sore.

And now even Greenie no longer baited him.

*

In summer Mr Cooksey did something he had been talking about for a long time. He painted the hall and the stairs. The paint he used was a dull ordinary blue which quickly revealed extraordinary qualities. It didn't dry. The inside of the door became smudged and dirty and all up the banisters there were streaks of sticky blue from the fingers of tenants. Mr Cooksey painted the door again, adding a notice: WET PAINT PLEASE, with the PLEASE underlined three times. He also chalked warnings on the steps outside. But after a fortnight the paint hadn't dried and it looked as though the door would have to be painted again. Mr Cooksey left notices on the glass-topped table in the hall, each note curter than the last. He had a good command of curt language. This wasn't surprising, because Mr Cooksey was a commissionaire or caretaker or something like that at the head office of an important public corporation. Anyway, it was a big position: he told me he had thirty-four cleaners under him.

I never got used to the wet paint and one day, as I came into the hall, wondering in my exasperation whether I shouldn't wipe the paint off on to the wallpaper, the Cookseys' door opened and I saw Mr Cooksey.

''Ave a drink,' he said. 'Cocktail.'

I feared Mr Cooksey's cocktails: they were too obviously one of the perquisites of his calling. But I went in, wiping my fingers on my evening paper. The room smelled of paint and linseed oil.

Mrs Cooksey sat in her armchair and beamed at me. Her hands were resting a little too demurely on her lap. She clearly had something to show.

The cage on the sewing machine was covered with a blue cloth, part of one of Mrs Cooksey's old dresses. It was late evening, still light outside, but dark inside: the Cookseys didn't like to use more electricity than was strictly necessary. Mr Cooksey passed around his cocktails. Mrs Cooksey refused with a shake of the head. I accepted but delayed sipping, Mr Cooksey sipped.

Muted rustlings and tumblings and cheeps came from behind the blue cloth. Mr and Mrs Cooksey sat silent and listened. I listened.

'Got a new one,' Mr Cooksey said, sipping his cocktail and smacking his lips with a little *pop-pop* sound.

'He came into the garden too?' I asked.

'It's a *she!*' Mrs Cooksey cried.

'*Pop-pop.* Ten bob,' said Mr Cooksey. 'Man wanted twelve and six.'

'And we've got a nesting-box for her too.'

'But we didn't pay for that, Bess.'

Mrs Cooksey went and stood by the cage. She rested her hands on the blue cloth, delaying the unveiling. 'She's the daintiest little thing.'

'Yellow,' said Mr Cooksey.

'Just the sort of mate for Greenie.' And, with a flourish, Mrs Cooksey lifted the blue cloth from the cage.

It wasn't the cage I had known. It was a bigger, cruder thing, made from wire netting, with rudimentary embellishments—just two bars supported on the wire netting. And I saw Greenie alone. He had composed himself to sleep. Yellow I didn't see.

Mrs Cooksey giggled, enjoying my disappointment. 'She's there all right. But *in her nesting-box!*' I saw a small wooden box hanging at the back of the cage. Mrs Cooksey tapped it. 'Come out, Yellow. Let Uncle have a look at you. Come out, come out. We know where you are.' Through the round hole of the box a little yellow head popped out, restlessly turning this way and that. Mrs Cooksey tapped the box again, and Yellow slipped out of the box into the cage.

Yellow was smaller than Greenie or Bluey. She wandered about the cage fussily, inquisitively. She certainly had no intention of going to sleep just yet, and she wasn't going to let Greenie sleep either. She hopped up to where he stood on his bar, his head hunched into his breast, and pecked at him. Greenie shook himself but didn't open his eyes. Yellow gave him a push. Perhaps it was chivalry—though I had never credited Greenie with that—or perhaps he was just too sleepy. But Greenie didn't fight back. He yielded and yielded until he could move no further. Then he went down to the other bar. Yellow followed. When she had dislodged him a second time she lost interest in him and went back into her nesting-box.

'D'you see?' Mrs Cooksey said. 'She's interested. The man at the shop says that when they're interested you can expect eggs in ten days.'

'Twelve, Bess.'

'He told *me* ten.'

I tried to get them off the subject. I said, 'They've got a new cage.'

'Mr Cooksey made it.'

Mr Cooksey pop-popped.

He had painted it too. With the blue paint.

Yellow pushed her head through the hole of her box.

'Oh, she *is* interested.' Mrs Cooksey replaced the blue cloth on the cage. 'We mustn't be naughty. Leave them alone.'

'One of my cleaners,' Mr Cooksey said, pausing and throwing the possessive adjective into relief, 'one of my cleaners keeps chickens and turkeys. Makes a packet at Christmas. Nabsolute packet.'

Mrs Cooksey said, 'I wouldn't like to sell any of my little Greenies and Yellows.'

Abruptly I remembered. 'Where's Bluey?'

I don't think Mrs Cooksey liked being reminded. She showed me where Bluey's cage was, on the floor, over-shadowed by an armchair and the bookcase that had few books and many china animals. Alone among the luxurious furnishings of his cage, Bluey stood still, on one foot, his feathers ruffled, his head sunk low.

'I can't throw him out, can I?' Mrs Cooksey shrugged her shoulders. 'I've done my best for him.'

*

The love life didn't agree with Greenie.

'She's taming him,' Mrs Cooksey said.

He had certainly quietened down.

'P'raps he's missing Bluey,' Mr Cooksey said.

'Hark at him,' said Mrs Cooksey.

Yellow was still eager, restless, inquisitive, going in and out of her box. Mrs Cooksey showed me how cleverly the box had been made: you could slide out the back to see if there were eggs. She counted the days.

'Seven days now.'

'Nine, Bess.'

'Seven.'

Then : 'Greenie's playing the fool,' Mr Cooksey said.

'Look who's talking,' Mrs Cooksey said.

Two days later she met me in the hall and said, 'Something's happened to Greenie.'

I went to look. Greenie had the same unhealthy stillness as Bluey now: his feathers were ruffled, his eyes half-closed, his head sunk into his breast. Yellow fussed about him, not belligerently or playfully, but in puzzlement.

'She *loves* him, d'you see? I've tried to feed him. Milk from an eye-dropper. But he isn't taking a thing. Tell me where it hurts, Greenie. Tell Mummy where.'

It was Friday. When Mrs Cooksey rang up the RSPCA they told her to bring Greenie in on Monday. All during the week-end Greenie deteriorated. Mrs Cooksey did her best. Although it was warm she kept the electric fire going all the time, a luxury the Cookseys denied themselves even in winter. A towel was always warming in front of the fire. Greenie was wrapped in another towel.

On Monday Mrs Cooksey wrapped Greenie in a clean towel and took him to the doctor. He prescribed a fluid of some sort and warned Mrs Cooksey against giving Greenie milk.

'He said something about poison,' Mrs Cooksey said. 'As though I would want to do anything to my Greenie. But you should have seen the doctor. Doctor! He was just a boy. He told me to bring Greenie again on Friday. That's four days.'

When I came in next evening, my fingers stained with blue paint from the door, Mrs Cooksey met me in the hall. I followed her into the room.

'Greenie's dead,' she said. She was very calm.

The door opened authoritatively and Mr Cooksey came in, mackintoshed and bowler-hatted.

'Greenie's dead,' Mrs Cooksey said.

'*Pop-pop.*' Mr Cooksey took off his hat and mackintosh and rested them carefully on the chair next to the sideboard.

In the silence that followed I didn't look at the Cookseys or the cage on the sewing machine. It was dark in the corner where Bluey's cage was and it was some moments before I could see things clearly.

Bluey's cage was empty. I looked up at the sewing machine. He was in the cage with Yellow; he drooped on the floor, eyes closed, one swollen foot raised. Yellow paid him no attention. She fussed about from bar to bar, with a faint continuous rustle. Then she slipped through the hole into the nesting-box and was silent.

'She's still *interested*,' Mr Cooksey said. He looked at Bluey. 'You never know.'

'It's no good,' Mrs Cooksey said. 'She loved Greenie.' Her old woman's face had broken up and she was crying.

Mr Cooksey opened doors on the sideboard, noisily looking for cocktails.

Mrs Cooksey blew her nose. 'Oh, they're like children. You get so fond of them.'

It was hard to think of something to say. I said, 'We were all fond of Greenie, Mrs Cooksey. I was fond of him and I am sure Mr Cooksey was too.'

'*Pop-pop.*'

'Him? He doesn't care. He's *tough*. D'you know, he had a look at Greenie this morning. Told me he looked better. But he's always like that. Look at him. Nothing worries him.'

'Not true, Bess. Was a trific shock. Trific.'

*

Yellow never came out of her nesting-box. She died two days later and Mrs Cooksey buried her in the garden, next to Greenie. I saw the cage and the nesting-box, smashed, on the heap of old wood Mr Cooksey kept in the garden shed.

In the Cookseys' sitting-room Bluey and his cage took their place again on the sewing machine. Slowly, week by week, Bluey improved. The time came when he could stand on both feet, when he could shuffle an inch or two on the floor of his cage. But his feet were never completely well again, and the growths on his beak didn't disappear. The trapezes never swung and the ferris wheel was still.

*

It must have been three months later. I went down one Saturday morning to pay Mrs Cooksey for the milk. I had to get some change and she had to hunt about for her glasses, then for the vase in which she kept small change. She poured out buttons from one vase, pins from another, fasteners from a third.

'Poor old lady,' she kept on muttering—that was how she had taken to speaking of herself. She fumbled about with more vases, then stopped, twisted her face into a smile and held out her open palm towards me. On it I saw two latch keys and a small white skull, finished, fragile.

'Greenie or Yellow,' she said. 'I couldn't really tell you which. The sparrows dug it up.'

We both looked at Bluey in his cage.

1957

The Perfect Tenants

WE HEARD ABOUT the Dakins before they arrived. 'They're the perfect tenants,' Mrs Cooksey, the landlady, said. 'Their landlady brought them to me personally. She says she's sorry to lose them, but she's leaving London and taking over a hotel in Benson.'

The Dakins moved in so quietly it was some days before I realized they were in the house. On Saturday and Sunday I heard sounds of washing and scrubbing and carpet-sweeping from the flat above. On Monday there was silence again.

Once or twice that week I saw them on the steps. Mrs Dakin was about forty, tall and thin, with a sweet smile. 'She used to be a policewoman,' Mrs Cooksey said. 'Sergeant, I think.' Mr Dakin was as old as his wife and looked as athletic. But his rough, handsome face was humourless. His greetings were brief and firm and didn't encourage conversation.

Their behaviour was exemplary. They never had visitors. They never had telephone calls. Their cooking never smelled. They never allowed their milk bottles to accumulate and at the same time they never left an empty milk bottle on the doorstep in daylight. And they were silent. They had no radio. The only sounds were of scrubbing brush, broom and carpet-sweeper. Sometimes at night, when the street fell silent, I heard them in their bedroom: a low whine punctuated infrequently with brief bass rumbles.

'There's respectable people in every class,' Mrs Cooksey said. 'The trouble these days is that you never know where you are. Look at the Seymours. Creeping up late at night to the bathroom and splashing about together. You can't even trust the BBC people. Remember that Arab.'

The Dakins quickly became the favourite tenants. Mr Cooksey invited Mr Dakin down to 'cocktails'. Mrs Dakin had Mrs Cooksey up to tea and Mrs Cooksey told us that she was satisfied with the appearance of the flat. 'They're very fussy,' Mrs Cooksey said. She knew no higher praise, and we all felt reproached.

*

It was from Mrs Cooksey that I learned with disappointment that the Dakins had their troubles. 'He fell off a ladder and broke his arm, but they won't pay any compensation. The arm's bent and he can't even go to the seaside. What's more, he can't do his job properly. He's an electrician, and you know how they're always climbing. But there you are, d'you see. *They* don't care. What's three hundred pounds to *them?* But will they give it? Do you know the foreman actually burned the ladder?'

I hadn't noticed any disfigurement about Mr Dakin. He had struck me as a man of forbidding vigour, but now I looked on him with greater interest and respect for putting up so silently with his misfortune. We often passed on the stairs but never did more than exchange greetings, and so it might have gone on had it not been for the Cookseys' New Year's Eve party.

At that time I was out of favour with the Cookseys. I had left a hoard of about fifteen milk bottles on the doorstep and the milkman had refused to take them all at once. For a whole day six partly washed milk bottles had remained on the doorstep, lowering Mrs Cooksey's house. Some unpleasantness between Mrs Cooksey and the milkman had followed and quickly been passed on to me.

When I came in that evening the door of the Cookseys' sitting-room was open and through it came laughter, stamping and television music. Mr Cooksey, coming from the kitchen with a tray, looked at me in embarrassment. He brought his lips rapidly over his false teeth and made a popping sound.

'*Pop-pop*. Come in,' he said. 'Drink. Cocktail.'

I went in. Mrs Cooksey was sober but gay. The laughter and the stamping came from the Dakins alone. They were dancing. Mrs Dakin shrieked whenever Mr Dakin spun her around, and for a man whose left arm was permanently damaged he was doing it quite well. When she saw me Mrs Dakin shrieked, and Mrs Cooksey giggled, as though it was her duty to cheer the Dakins up. The couple from the flat below mine were there too, she on the seat of an armchair, he on the arm. They were dressed in their usual sub-county manner and looked constrained and unhappy. I thought of this couple as the Knitmaster and the Knitmistress. They had innumerable minor possessions: contemporary coffee tables and lampstands, a Cona coffee machine, a record-player, a portable television-and-VHF set, a 1946 Anglia which at the appropriate season carried a sticker: FREE LIFT TO GLYNDEBOURNE AT YOUR OWN RISK, and a Knitmaster machine which was never idle for long.

The music stopped, Mrs Dakin pretended to swoon into her husband's injured arms, and Mrs Cooksey clapped.

''Elp yourself, 'elp yourself,' Mr Cooksey shouted.

'Another drink, darling?' the Knitmaster whispered to his wife.

'Yes, yes,' Mrs Dakin cried.

The Knitmistress smiled malevolently at Mrs Dakin.

'Whisky?' said Mr Cooksey. 'Beer? Sherry? Guinness?'

'Give her the cocktail,' Mrs Cooksey said.

Mr Cooksey's cocktails were well known to his older tenants. He had a responsible position in an important public corporation—he said he had thirty-four cleaners under him—and the origin and blend of his cocktails were suspect.

The Knitmistress took the cocktail and sipped without enthusiasm.

'And you?' Mr Cooksey asked.

'Guinness,' I said.

'Guinness!' Mr Dakin exclaimed, looking at me for the first time with interest and kindliness. 'Where did you learn to drink Guinness?'

We drew closer and talked about Guinness.

'Of course it's best in Ireland,' he said. 'Thick and creamy. What's it like where you come from?'

'I can't drink it there. It's too warm.'

Mr Dakin shook his head. 'It isn't the climate. It's the Guinness. It can't travel. It gets sick.'

Soon it was time to sing Auld Lang Syne.

The next day the Dakins reverted to their exemplary behaviour, but now when we met we stopped to have a word about the weather.

*

One evening, about four weeks later, I heard something like a commotion in the flat above. Footsteps pounded down the stairs, there was a banging on my door, and Mrs Dakin rushed in and cried, 'It's my 'usband! 'E's rollin' in agony.'

Before I could say anything she ran out and raced down to the Knitmasters.

'My husband's rollin' in agony.'

The whirring of the Knitmaster machine stopped and I heard the Knitmistress making sympathetic sounds.

The Knitmaster said, 'Telephone for the doctor.'

I went and stood on the landing as a sympathetic gesture. Mrs Dakin roused the Cookseys, there were more exclamations, then I heard the telephone being dialled. I went back to my room. After some thought I left my door wide open: another gesture of sympathy.

Mrs Dakin, Mrs Cooksey and Mr Cooksey hurried up the stairs. The Knitmaster machine was whirring again.

Presently there was a knock on my door and Mr Cooksey came in. '*Pop-pop*. It's as hot as a bloomin' oven up there.' He puffed out his cheeks. 'No wonder he's ill.'

I asked after Mr Dakin.

'A touch of indigestion, if you ask me.' Then, like a man used to more momentous events, he added, 'One of my cleaners took ill sudden last week. Brain tumour.'

The doctor came and the Dakins' flat was full of footsteps and conversation. Mr Cooksey ran up and down the steps, panting and pop-popping. Mrs Dakin was sobbing and Mrs Cooksey was comforting her. An ambulance bell rang in the street and soon Mr Dakin, Mrs Dakin and the doctor left.

'Appendix,' Mr Cooksey told me.

The Knitmaster opened his door

'Appendix,' Mr Cooksey shouted down. 'It was like an oven up there.'

'He was cold,' Mrs Cooksey said.

'Pah!'

Mrs Cooksey looked anxious.

'Nothing to it, Bess,' Mr Cooksey said. ''Itler had the appendix took out of all his soldiers.'

The Knitmaster said, 'I had mine out two years ago. Small scar.' He measured off the top of his forefinger. 'About that long. It's a nervous thing really. You get it when you are depressed or worried. My wife had to have hers out just before we went to France.'

The Knitmistress came out and smiled her terrible smile, baring short square teeth and tall gums, and screwing up her small eyes. She said, 'Hallo,' and pulled on woollen gloves, which perhaps she had just knitted on her machine. She wore a tweed skirt, a red sweater, a brown velveteen jacket and a red-and-white beret.

'Appendix,' Mr Cooksey said.

The Knitmistress only smiled again, and followed her husband downstairs to the 1946 Anglia.

'A terrible thing,' I said to Mrs Cooksey tentatively.

'*Pop-pop.*' Mr Cooksey looked at his wife.

'Terrible thing,' Mrs Cooksey said.

Our quarrel over the milk bottles was over.

Mr Cooksey became animated. 'Nothing to it, Bess. Just a lot of fuss for nothing at all. Gosh, they kept that room like an oven.'

Mrs Dakin came back at about eleven. Her eyes were red but she was composed. She spoke about the kindness of the nurses. And then, to round off an unusual evening, I heard—at midnight on a weekday—the sound of the carpet-sweeper upstairs. The Knit-mistress complained in her usual way. She opened her door and talked loudly to her husband about the nuisance.

*

Next morning Mrs Dakin went again to the hospital. She returned just before midday and as soon as she got into the hall she began to sob so loudly that I heard her on the second floor.

I found her in Mrs Cooksey's arms when I went down. Mrs Cooksey was pale and her eyes were moist.

'What's happened?' I whispered.

Mrs Cooksey shook her head.

Mrs Dakin leaned against Mrs Cooksey, who was much smaller.

'And my brother is getting married tomorrow!' Mrs Dakin burst out.

'Come now, Eva,' Mrs Cooksey said firmly. 'Tell me what happened at the hospital.'

'They're feeding him through a glass tube. They've put him on the danger list. And—his bed is near the door!'

'That doesn't mean anything, Eva.'

'It does! It does!'

'Nonsense, Eva.'

'They've got him screened round.'

'You must be brave, Eva.'

We led Mrs Dakin to Mrs Cooksey's sittingroom, made her sit down and watched her cry.

'It burst inside 'im.' Mrs Dakin made a wild gesture across her body. 'They had to cut him clean open, and—*scrape* it out.' Having uttered this terrible word, she abandoned herself to her despair.

'Come now, Eva,' Mrs Cooksey said. 'He wouldn't like you to behave like this.'

*

We all took turns to look after Mrs Dakin between her trips to the hospital. The news didn't get better. Mrs Dakin had tea with the Cookseys. She had tea with the Knitmistress. She had tea with me. We talked gaily about everything except the sick man, and Mrs Dakin was very brave. She even related some of her adventures in the police force. She also complained.

'The first thing Mr Cooksey said when he came up that evening was that the room was like an oven. But I couldn't help that. My husband was cold. Fancy coming up and saying a thing like that!'

I gave Mrs Dakin many of the magazines which had been piling up on the enormous Victorian dresser in my kitchen. The Knitmistress, I noticed, was doing the same thing.

Mr Cooksey allowed himself to grow a little grave. He discussed the operation in a sad but clinical way. 'When it bursts inside 'em, you see, it poisons the whole system. That's why they had to cut 'im open. Clean it out. They hardly ever live afterwards.'

Mrs Cooksey said, 'He was such a nice man. I am so glad now we enjoyed ourselves on New Year's Eve. It's her I'm really sorry for. He was her second, you know.'

'Aah,' Mr Cooksey said. 'There are women like that.'

I told the Knitmistress, 'And he was such a nice man.'

'Wasn't he?'

I heard Mrs Dakin sobbing in everybody's rooms. I heard her sobbing on the staircase.

Mrs Cooksey said, 'It's all so terrible. Her brother got married yesterday, but she couldn't go to the wedding. She had to send a telegram. They are coming up to see Mr Dakin. What a thing to happen on anybody's honeymoon!'

*

Mrs Dakin's brother and his bride came up from Wales on a motorbike. Mrs Dakin was at the hospital when they came and Mrs Cooksey gave them tea.

I didn't see Mrs Dakin that evening, but late that night I saw the honeymoon couple running upstairs with bottles wrapped in tissue paper. He was a huge man—a footballer, Mrs Cooksey said—and when he ran up the steps you heard it all over the house. His bride was small, countrified and gay. They stayed awake for some time.

Next morning, when I went down to get the paper, I saw the footballer's motorbike on the doorstep. It had leaked a lot of oil.

Again that day Mrs Dakin didn't come to our rooms. And that evening there was another party in the flat above. We heard the footballer's heavy footsteps, his shouts, his wife's giggles, Mrs Dakin's whine.

Mrs Dakin had ceased to need our solace. It was left to us to ask how Mr Dakin was getting on, whether he had liked the magazines we had sent, whether he wanted any more. Then, as though reminded of some sadness bravely forgotten, Mrs Dakin would say yes, Mr Dakin thanked us.

Mrs Cooksey didn't like the new reticence. Nor did the rest of us. For some time, though, the Knitmaster persevered and he had his reward when two days later Mrs Dakin said, 'I told 'im what you said about the nervousness, and he wondered how you ever knew.' And she repeated the story about the fall from the defective ladder, the bent arm, the foreman burning the ladder.

We were astonished. It was our first indication that the Dakins were taking an interest in the world outside the hospital.

'Well, really!' Mrs Cooksey said.

The Knitmistress began to complain about the noise in the evenings.

'Pah!' Mr Cooksey said. 'It *couldn't* 'ave burst inside him. Feeding through a glass tube!'

We heard the honeymoon couple bounding down the stairs. The front door slammed, then we heard the thunderous stutter of the motorbike.

'He could be had up,' Mr Cooksey said. 'No silencer.'

'Well!' Mrs Cooksey said. 'I am glad *somebody's* having a nice time. So cheap too. Where do you think they're off to?'

'Not the hospital,' Mr Cooksey said. 'Football, more likely.'

This reminded him. The curtains were drawn, the tiny television set turned on. We watched horse-racing, then part of the football match. Mrs Cooksey gave me tea. Mr Cooksey offered me a cigarette. I was back in favour.

*

The next day, eight days after Mr Dakin had gone to the hospital, I met Mrs Dakin outside the tobacconist's. She was shopping and her bulging bag reflected the gaiety on her face.

'He's coming back tomorrow,' she said.

I hadn't expected such a rapid recovery.

'Everybody at the hospital was surprised,' Mrs Dakin said. 'But it's because he's so strong, you see.' She opened her shopping bag. 'I've got some sherry and whisky and'—she laughed—'some Guinness of course. And I'm buying a duck, to have with apple sauce. He loves apple sauce. He says the apple sauce helps the duck to go down.'

I smiled at the little family joke. Then Mrs Dakin asked me, 'Guess who went to the hospital yesterday.'

'Your brother and his wife.'

She shook her head. 'The foreman!'

'The one who burned the ladder?'

'Oh, and he was ever so nice. He brought grapes and magazines and told my husband he wasn't to worry about anything. They're frightened now all right. As soon as my husband went to hospital my solicitor wrote them a letter. And my solicitor says we stand a good chance of getting more than three hundred pounds now.'

I saw the Knitmaster on the landing that evening and told him about Mr Dakin's recovery.

'Complications couldn't have been serious,' he said. 'But it's a nervous thing. A nervous thing.'

The Knitmistress opened the kitchen door.

'He's coming back tomorrow,' the Knitmaster said.

The Knitmistress gave me one of her terrible smiles.

'Five hundred pounds for falling off a ladder,' Mr Cooksey said. 'Ha! It's as easy as falling off a log, ain't it, Bess?'

Mrs Cooksey sighed. 'That's what the Labour has done to this country. They didn't do a thing for the middle class.'

'Bent arm! Can't go to the seaside! Pamperin', that's what it is. You wouldn't've found 'Itler pampering that lot.'

A motorbike lacerated the silence.

'Our happy honeymooners,' Mr Cooksey said.

'They'll soon be leaving,' Mrs Cooksey said, and went out to meet them in the hall.

'Whose key are you using?'

'Eva's,' the footballer said, running up the stairs.

'We'll see about that,' Mrs Cooksey called.

*

Mrs Dakin said: 'I went down to Mrs Cooksey and I said, "Mrs Cooksey, what do you mean by insulting my guests? It's bad enough for them having their honeymoon spoilt without being insulted." And she said she'd let the flat to me and my 'usband and not to my brother and his wife and they'd have to go. And I told her that they were leaving tomorrow anyway because my husband's coming back tomorrow. And I told her I hoped she was satisfied that she'd spoiled their honeymoon, which comes only once in a lifetime. And she said some people managed to have two, which I took as a reference to myself because, as you know, my first husband died during the war. And then I told her that if that was the way she was going to behave then I could have nothing more to say to her. And she said she hoped I would have the oil from my brother's bike cleaned up. And I said that if it wasn't for my husband being so ill I would've given notice then and there. And she said it was *because* my husband was ill that she didn't give me notice, which any other landlady would've done.'

*

Three things happened the next day. The footballer and his wife left. Mrs Dakin told me that the firm had given her husband four hundred pounds. And Mr Dakin returned from hospital, no more noticed by the rest of the house than if he had returned from a day's work. No sounds came from the Dakins' flat that evening except for the whine and rumble of conversation.

Two days later I heard Mrs Dakin racing down to my flat. She knocked and entered at the same time. 'The telly's coming today,' she said.

Mr Dakin was going to put up the aerial himself. I wondered whether he was as yet strong enough to go climbing about the roof.

'They wanted ten pounds to do it. But my husband's an electrician and he can do it himself. You must come up tonight. We're going to celebrate.'

I went up. A chromium-plated aeroplane and a white doily had been placed on the television set. It looked startlingly new.

Mrs Dakin emptied a bottle of Tio Pepe into three tumblers.

'To good 'ealth,' she said, and we drank to that.

Mr Dakin looked thin and fatigued. But his fatigue was tinged with a certain quiet contentment. We watched a play about a 400-year-old man who took certain drugs and looked no more than twenty. From time to time Mrs Dakin gave little cries of pleasure, at the play, the television set, and the quality of the sherry.

Mr Dakin languidly took up the empty bottle and studied the label. '*Spanish* sherry,' he said.

Mr Cooksey waylaid me the following day. 'Big telly they've got.'

'Eighteen inch.'

'Those big ones hurt the eyes, don't you find?'

'They do.'

'Come in and have a drink. BBC and Commercial?'

I nodded.

'Never did hold with those commercials. Ruining the country. We're not going to have ours adapted.'

'We're waiting for the colour,' Mrs Cooksey said.

Mrs Cooksey loved a battle. She lived for her house alone. She had no relations or friends, and little happened to her or her husband. Once, shortly after Hess had landed in Scotland, Mr Cooksey had been mistaken by a hostile crowd at Victoria Station for Mussolini, but for the most part Mrs Cooksey's conversation was about her victories over tenants. In her battles with them she stuck to the rules. *The Law of Landlord and Tenant* was one of the few books among the many china animals in the large bookcase in her sittingroom. And Mrs Cooksey had her own idea of victory. She never gave anyone notice. That was almost an admission of defeat. Mrs Cooksey asked me, 'You didn't throw a loaf of stale bread into the garden, did you?'

I said I hadn't.

'I didn't think you had. That's what the other people in this street do, you know. It's a fight to keep this house the way it is, I can tell you. There's the mice, d'you see. You haven't any mice up here, have you?'

'As a matter of fact I had one yesterday.'

'I knew it. The moment you let up these things start happening. All the other houses in this street have mice. That's what the sanitary inspector told me. He said this was the cleanest house in the whole street. But the moment you start throwing food about you're bound to get mice.'

That evening I heard Mrs Dakin complaining loudly. She was doing it the way the Knitmistress did: talking loudly to her husband through an open door.

'Coming up here and asking if I had thrown a loaf of bread into 'er 'orrible little garden. And talking about people having too much to eat these days. Well, if it's one thing I like, it is a warm room. I don't wrap myself up in a blanket and *'uddle* in front of cinders and then come and say that somebody else's room is like an oven.'

Mrs Dakin left her kitchen door open and did the washing up with many bangs, jangles, and clatters. The television sound was turned up and in my room I could hear every commercial, every

song, every scrap of dialogue. The carpetsweeper was brought into
action; I heard it banging against walls and furniture.

The next day Mrs Cooksey continued her mice hunt. She went
into all the flats and took up the linoleum and put wads of newspaper
in the gaps between the floorboards. She also emptied Mrs Dakin's
dustbin. 'To keep away the mice,' she told us.

I heard the Dakins' television again that night.

The next morning there was a large notice in the hall. I recog-
nized Mr Cooksey's handwriting and style: WILL THE PERSON OR PER-
SONS RESPONSIBLE SEE ABOUT THE IMMEDIATE REMOVAL OF THE OIL
STAINS ON THE FRONT STEPS. In the bathroom there was a notice tied
to the pipe that led to the geyser: WILL THE PERSON OR PERSONS WHO
HAVE BEEN TAMPERING WITH THIS TAP PLEASE STOP IT. And in the
lavatory: WE NEVER THOUGHT WE WOULD HAVE TO MAKE THIS
REQUEST BUT WILL THE PERSON OR PERSONS RESPONSIBLE PLEASE
LEAVE THESE OFFICES AS THEY WOULD LIKE TO FIND THEM.

The Dakins retaliated at once. Four unwashed milk bottles were
placed on the stains on the steps. An empty whisky bottle was placed,
label outwards, next to the dustbin.

I felt the Dakins had won that round.

'Liquor and football pools,' Mr Cooksey said. 'That's all that
class spends its money on. Pamperin'! You mustn't upset yourself,
Bess. We're giving them enough rope to hang themselves.'

The television boomed through the house that evening. The
washing-up was done noisily, the carpet-sweeper banged against
walls and furniture, and Mrs Dakin sang loudly. Presently I heard
scuffling sounds and shrieks. The Dakins were dancing. This went
on for a short time. Then I heard a bath being run.

There was a soft knock on my door and Mrs Cooksey came in. 'I
just wanted to find out who was having the bath,' she said.

For some moments after she left the bath continued to run. Then
there was a sharper sound of running water, hissing and metallic.
And soon the bath was silent.

There was no cistern to feed the geyser ('Unhygienic things, cisterns,' Mr Cooksey said) and the flow of water to it depended on the taps in the house. By turning on a tap in your kitchen you could lessen the flow and the heat of the water from the geyser. The hissing sound indicated that a tap had been turned full on downstairs, rendering the geyser futile.

From the silent bathroom I heard occasional splashes. The hissing sound continued. Then Mr Dakin sneezed.

The bathroom door opened and was closed with a bang. Mr Dakin sneezed again and Mrs Dakin said, 'If you catch pneumonia, I know who your solicitor will have to be writing to next.'

And all they could do was to smash the gas mantle in the bathroom.

It seemed that they had accepted defeat, for they did nothing further the next day. I was with the Cookseys when the Dakins came in from work that afternoon. In a few minutes they had left the house again. The light in the Cookseys' sittingroom had not been turned on and we stared at them through the lace curtains. They walked arm in arm.

'Going to look for a new place, I suppose.' Mrs Cooksey said.

There was a knock and the Knitmistress came in, her smile brilliant and terrible even in the gloom. She said, 'Hullo.' Then she addressed Mrs Cooksey: 'Our lights have gone.'

'Power failure,' Mr Cooksey said. But the street lights were on. The light in the Cookseys' room was turned on but nothing happened.

Mrs Cooksey's face fell.

'Fuse,' Mr Cooksey said briskly. He regarded himself as an electrical expert. With the help of a candle he selected fuse wire, went down to the fuse box, urged us to turn off all lights and fires and stoves, and set to work. The wire fused again. And again.

'He's been *up* to something,' Mr Cooksey said.

But we couldn't find out what that was. The Dakins had secured their rooms with new Yale locks.

The Knitmistress complained.

'It's no use, Bess,' Mr Cooksey said. 'You'll just have to give them notice. Never *did* hold with that class of people anyway.'

*

And defeat was made even more bitter because it turned out that victory had been very close. After Mrs Cooksey asked them to leave, the Dakins announced that they had used part of the compensation money to pay down on a house and were just about to give notice themselves. They packed and left without saying goodbye.

Three weeks later the Dakins' flat was taken over by a middle-aged lady with a fat shining dachshund called Nicky. Her letters were posted on from a ladies' club whose terrifying interiors I had often glimpsed from the top of a number sixteen bus.

1957

The Heart

WHEN THEY DECIDED that the only way to teach Hari to swim would be to throw him into the sea, Hari dropped out of the sea scouts. Every Monday afternoon for a term he had put on the uniform, practised rowing on the school grounds, and learned to run up signals and make knots. The term before he had dropped out of the boy scouts, to avoid going to camp. At the school sports the term before that he had entered for all the races for the under-elevens, but when the time came he was too shy to strip (the emblem of his house had been fancifully embroidered on his vest by his mother), and he didn't run.

Hari was an only child. He was ten and had a weak heart. The doctors had advised against over-exertion and excitement, and Hari was unexercised and fat. He would have liked to play cricket, fancying himself as a fast bowler, but he was never picked for any of the form teams. He couldn't run quickly, he couldn't bowl, he couldn't bat, and he threw like a girl. He would also have liked to whistle, but he could only make hissing noises through his small plump lips. He had an almost Chinese passion for neatness. He wrote with a blotter below his hand and blotted each line as he wrote; he crossed out with the help of a ruler. His books were clean and unmarked, except on the fly-leaf, where his name had been written by his father. He would have passed unnoticed at school if he hadn't been so well provided with money. This made him unpopular and attracted bullies. His expensive fountain pens were always stolen; and he had learned to stay away from the tuck shop.

Most of the boys from Hari's district who went to the school used Jameson Street. Hari wished to avoid this street. The only way he could do this was to go down Rupert Street. And at the bottom of that street, just where he turned right, there was the house with the Alsatians.

The house stood on the right-hand corner and walking on the other side would have made his cowardice plain, to dogs and passers-by. The Alsatians bounded down from the veranda, barking, leapt against the wire fence and made it shake. Their paws touched the top of the fence and it always seemed to Hari that with a little effort they could jump right over. Sometimes a thin old lady with glasses and grey hair and an irritable expression limped out to the veranda and called in a squeaky voice to the Alsatians. At once they stopped barking, forgot Hari, ran up to the veranda and wagged their heavy tails, as though apologizing for the noise and at the same time asking to be congratulated. The old lady tapped them on the head and they continued to wag their tails; if she slapped them hard they moved away with their heads bowed, their tails between their legs, and lay down on the veranda, gazing out, blinking, their muzzles beneath their forelegs.

Hari envied the old lady her power over the dogs. He was glad when she came out; but he also felt ashamed of his own fear and weakness.

The city was full of unlicensed mongrels who barked in relay all through the day and night. Of these dogs Hari was not afraid. They were thin and starved and cowardly. To drive them away one had only to bend down as though reaching for a stone; it was a gesture the street dogs all understood. But it didn't work with the Alsatians; it merely aggravated their fury.

Four times a day—he went home for lunch—Hari had to pass the Alsatians, hear their bark and breath, see their long white teeth, black lips and red tongues, see their eager, powerful bodies, taller than he when they leapt against the fence. He took his revenge on the street dogs. He picked up imaginary stones; and the street dogs always bolted.

When Hari asked for a bicycle he didn't mention the boys in Jameson Street or the Alsatians in Rupert Street. He spoke about the sun and his fatigue. His parents had misgivings about the bicycle, but Hari learned to ride without accident. And then, with the power of his bicycle, he was no longer afraid of the dogs in Rupert Street. The Alsatians seldom barked at passing cyclists. So Hari stopped in front of the house at the corner, and when the Alsatians ran down from the veranda he pretended to throw things at them until they were thoroughly enraged and their breath grew loud. Then he cycled slowly away, the Alsatians following along the fence to the end of the lot, growling with anger and frustration. Once, when the old lady came out, Hari pretended he had stopped only to tie his laces.

Hari's school was in a quiet, open part of the city. The streets were wide and there were no pavements, only broad, well-kept grass verges. The verges were not level; every few yards there were shallow trenches which drained off the water from the road. Hari liked cycling on the verges, gently rising and falling.

Late one Friday afternoon Hari was cycling back from school after a meeting of the Stamp Club (he had joined that after leaving the sea scouts and with the large collections and expensive albums given him by his father he enjoyed a continuing esteem). It was growing dark as Hari cycled along the verge, falling and rising, looking down at the grass.

In a trench he saw the body of an Alsatian.

The bicycle rolled down into the trench and over the thick tail of the dog. The dog rose and, without looking at Hari, shook himself. Then Hari saw another Alsatian. And another. Steering to avoid them he ran into more. They lay in the trenches and all over the verge. They were of varying colours; one was brown-black. Hari had not pedalled since he had seen the first dog and was now going so slowly he felt he was losing his balance. From behind came a low, brief bark, like a sneeze. At this, energy returned to him. He rode on to the asphalt and it was only then, as though they too had just recovered from their surprise, that the Alsatians all rose and came after him. He pedalled, staring ahead, not looking at what was behind him or beside him. Three Alsatians, the brown-black one among them, were running abreast of his bicycle. Calmly, as he pedalled, Hari waited for their attack. But they only ran beside him, not barking. The bicycle hummed; the dogs' paws on the asphalt sounded like pigeons' feet on a tin roof. And then Hari felt that the savagery of the Alsatians was casual, without anger or malice: an evening gathering, an evening's pleasure. He fixed his eyes on the main road at the end, with the street lamps just going on, the lighted trolley-buses, the motorcars, the people.

Then he was there. The Alsatians had dropped behind. He didn't look for them. It was only when he was in the main road, with the trolley-poles sparking blue in the night already fallen, that he realized how frightened he had been, how close to painful death from the teeth of those happy dogs. His heart beat fast, from the exertion. Then he felt a sharp pain he had never known before. He gave a choked, deep groan and fell off the bicycle.

*

He spent a month in a nursing home and didn't go to school for the rest of that term. But he was well enough again when the new term began. It was decided that he should give up the bicycle; and his father changed his hours of work so that he could drive Hari to and from the school.

His birthday fell early that term, and when he was driven home from school in the afternoon his mother handed him a basket and said, 'Happy birthday!'

It was a puppy.

'He won't bite you,' his mother said. 'Touch him and see.'

'Let me see you touch him,' Hari said.

'You must touch him,' his mother said. 'He is yours. You must get him used to you. They are one-man dogs.'

He thought of the old lady with the squeaky voice and he held out his hand to the puppy. The puppy licked it and pressed a damp nose against it. Hari was tickled. He burst out laughing, felt the puppy's hair and the puppy rubbed against his hand; he passed his hand over the puppy's muzzle, then he lifted the puppy and the puppy licked his face and Hari was tickled into fresh laughter.

The puppy had small sharp teeth and liked to pretend that he was biting. Hari liked the feel of his teeth; there was friendliness in them, and soon there would be power. His power. 'They are one-man dogs,' his mother said.

He got his father to drive to school down Rupert Street. Sometimes he saw the Alsatians. Then he thought of his own dog, and felt protected and revenged. They drove up and down the street with grass verges along which he had been chased by the Alsatians. But he never again saw any Alsatian there.

The puppy was always waiting when they got back home. His father drove right up to the gate and blew his horn. His mother came out to open the gate, and the puppy came out too, wagging his tail, leaping up against the car even as it moved.

'Hold him! Hold him!' Hari cried.

More than anything now he feared losing his dog.

He liked hearing his mother tell visitors about his love for the puppy. And he was given many books about dogs. He learned with sadness that they lived for only twelve years; so that when he was twenty-three, a man, he would have no dog. In the circumstances training seemed pointless, but the books all recommended training, and Hari tried it. The puppy responded with a languor Hari thought enchanting. At school he was moved almost to tears when they read the poem beginning 'A barking sound the shepherd hears'. He went to see the film *Lassie Come Home* and wept. From the film he realized that he had forgotten an important part of the puppy's training. And, to prevent his puppy eating food given by strangers, he dipped pieces of meat in peppersauce and left them about the yard.

The next day the puppy disappeared. Hari was distressed and felt guilty, but he got some consolation from the film; and when, less than a week later, the puppy returned, dirty, scratched and thinner, Hari embraced him and whispered the words of the film: 'You're my Lassie—my Lassie come home.'

He abandoned all training and was concerned only to see the puppy become healthy again. In the American comic books he read, dogs lived in dog-houses and ate from bowls marked DOG. Hari didn't approve of the dog-houses because they looked small and lonely; but he insisted that his mother should buy a bowl marked DOG.

When he came home for lunch one day she showed him a bowl on which DOG had been painted. Hari's father said he was too hot to eat and went upstairs; his mother followed. Before Hari ate he washed the bowl and filled it with dog-food. He called for the puppy and displayed the bowl. The puppy jumped up, trying to get at the bowl.

Hari put the bowl down and the puppy, instantly ignoring Hari, ran to it. Disappointed, Hari squatted beside the puppy and waited for some sign of recognition. None came. The puppy ate noisily, seeming to catch his food for every chew. Hari passed his hand over the puppy's head.

The puppy, catching a mouthful of food, growled and shook his head.

Hari tried again.

With a sharper growl the puppy dropped the food he had in his mouth and snapped at Hari's hand. Hari felt teeth sinking into his flesh; he could sense the anger driving the teeth, the thought that finally held them back. When he looked at his hand he saw torn skin and swelling blobs of blood. The puppy was bent over the bowl again, catching and chewing, his eyes hard.

Hari seized the bowl marked DOG and threw it with his girl's throw out of the kitchen door. The puppy's growl abruptly ended.

When the bowl disappeared he looked up at Hari, puzzled, friendly, his tail swinging slowly. Hari kicked hard at the puppy's muzzle and felt the tip of his shoe striking the bone. The puppy backed away to the door and looked at Hari with bewilderment.

'Come,' Hari said, his voice thick with saliva.

Swinging his tail briskly, the puppy came, passing his neat pink tongue over his black lips, still oily from the food. Hari held out his bitten hand. The puppy licked it clean of blood. Then Hari drove his shoe up against the puppy's belly. He kicked again, but the puppy had run whining out of the kitchen door, and Hari lost his balance and fell. Tears came to his eyes. His hands burned at those points where the puppy's teeth had sunk, and he could still feel the puppy's saliva on his hand, binding the skin.

He got up and went out of the kitchen. The puppy stood by the gate, watching him. Hari bent down, as though to pick up a stone. The puppy made no move. Hari picked up a pebble and flung it at the puppy. It was a clumsy throw and the pebble rose high. The puppy ran to catch it, missed, stopped and stared, his tail swinging, his ears erect, his mouth open. Hari threw another pebble. This one kept low and struck the puppy hard. The puppy whined and ran into the front garden. Hari followed. The puppy ran around the side of the house and hid among the anthurium lilies. Hari aimed one stone after another, and suddenly he had a sense of direction. Again and again he hit the puppy, who whined and ran until he was cornered below the narrow trellis with the Bleeding Heart vine. There he stood still, his eyes restless, his tail between his legs. From time to time he licked his lips. This action infuriated Hari. Blindly he threw stone after stone and the puppy ran from tangle to tangle of Bleeding Heart. Once he tried to rush past Hari, but the way was too narrow and Hari too quick. Hari caught him a drumming kick and he ran back to the corner, watching, faintly whining.

In a choked voice Hari said, 'Come.'

The puppy raised its ears.

Hari smiled and tried to whistle.

Hesitantly, his legs bent, his back curved, the puppy came. Hari stroked his head until the puppy stood erect. Then he held the muzzle with both his hands and squeezed it hard. The puppy yelped and pulled away.

'Hari!' He heard his mother's voice. 'Your father is nearly ready.'

He had had no lunch.

'I have no appetite,' Hari said. They were words his father often used.

She asked about the broken bowl and the food scattered about the yard.

'We were playing,' Hari said.

She saw his hand. 'Those animals don't know their own strength,' she said.

*

It was his resolve to get the puppy to allow himself to be stroked while eating. Every refusal had to be punished, by beating and stoning, imprisonment in the cupboard below the stairs or imprisonment behind the closed windows of the car, when that was available. Sometimes Hari took the puppy's plate, led the puppy to the lavatory, emptied the plate into the toilet bowl and pulled the flush. Sometimes he threw the food into the yard; then he punished the puppy for eating off the ground. Soon he extended his judgement to all the puppy's actions, punishing those he thought unfriendly, disobedient or ungrateful. If the puppy didn't come to the gate when the car horn sounded, he was to be punished; if he didn't come when called, he was to be punished. Hari kept a careful check of the punishments he had to inflict because he could punish only when his parents were away or occupied, and he was therefore always behindhand. He feared that the puppy might run away again; so he tied him at nights. And when his parents were about, Hari was enraged, as enraged as he had been by that licking of the oily lips, to see the puppy behaving as though unaware of the punishments to come: lying at his father's feet, yawning, curling himself into comfortable positions, or wagging his tail to greet Hari's mother. Sometimes, then, Hari stooped to pick up an imaginary stone, and the puppy ran out of the room. But there were also days when punishments were forgotten, for Hari knew that he controlled the puppy's power and made it an extension of his own, not only by his punishments but also by the complementary hold of affection.

Then came the triumph. The puppy, now almost a dog, attacked Hari one day and had to be pulled back by Hari's parents. 'You can never trust those dogs,' Hari's mother said, and the dog was permanently chained. For days, whenever he could get the chance, Hari beat the dog. One evening, when his parents were out, he beat the dog until it ceased to whine. Then, knowing he was alone, and wishing to test his strength and fear, he unchained the dog. The dog didn't attack, didn't growl. It ran to hide among the anthurium lilies. And after that it allowed itself to be stroked while it ate.

Hari's birthday came again. He was given a Brownie 6-20 camera and wasted film on absurd subjects until his father suggested that a photograph should be taken of Hari and the dog. The dog didn't stand still; eventually they put its collar on and Hari held on to that and smiled for the camera.

Hari's father was busy that Friday and couldn't drive Hari home. Hari stayed at school for the meeting of the Stamp Club and took a taxi home. His father's car was in the drive. He called for the dog. It didn't come. Another punishment. His parents were in the small dining-room next to the kitchen; they sat down to tea. On the dining table Hari saw the yellow folder with the negatives and the prints. They had not come out well. The dog looked strained and awkward, not facing the camera; and Hari thought he himself looked very fat. He felt his parents' eyes on him as he went through the photographs. He turned over one photograph. On the back of it he saw, in his father's handwriting: *In memory of Rex*. Below that was the date.

'It was an accident,' his mother said, putting her arms around him. 'He ran out just as your father was driving in. It was an accident.'

Tears filled Hari's eyes. Sobbing, he stamped up the stairs.

'Mind, son,' his mother called, and Hari heard her say to his father, 'Go after him. His heart. His heart.'

1960

The Baker's Story

Look at me. Black as the Ace of Spades, and ugly to match. Nobody looking at me would believe they looking at one of the richest men in this city of Port-of-Spain. Sometimes I find it hard to believe it myself, you know, especially when I go out on some of the holidays that I start taking the wife and children to these days, and I catch sight of the obzocky black face in one of those fancy mirrors that expensive hotels have all over the place, as if to spite people like me.

Now everybody—particularly black people—forever asking me how this thing start, and I does always tell them I make my dough from dough. Ha! You like that one? But how it start? Well, you hearing me talk, and I don't have to tell you I didn't have no education. In Grenada, where I come from—and that is one thing these Trinidad black people don't forgive a man for being: a black Grenadian—in Grenada I was one of ten children, I believe—everything kind of mix up out there—and I don't even know who was the feller who hit my mother. I believe he hit a lot of women in all the other parishes of that island, too, because whenever I go back to Grenada for one of those holidays I tell you about, people always telling me that I remind them of this one and that one, and they always mistaking me for a shop assistant whenever I in a shop. (If this thing go on, one day I going to sell somebody something, just for spite.) And even in Trinidad, whenever I run into another Grenadian, the same thing does happen.

Well, I don't know what happen in Grenada, but mammy bring me alone over to Trinidad when she was still young. I don't know

[448]

what she do with the others, but perhaps they wasn't even she own. Anyway, she get a work with some white people in St Ann's. They give she a uniform; they give she three meals a day; and they give she a few dollars a month besides. Somehow she get another man, a real Trinidad 'rangoutang, and somehow, I don't know how, she get somebody else to look after me while she was living with this man, for the money and the food she was getting was scarcely enough to support this low-minded Trinidad rango she take up with.

It used to have a Chinee shop not far from this new aunty I was living with, and one day, when the old girl couldn't find the cash no how to buy a bread—is a hell of a thing, come to think of it now, that it have people in this island who can't lay their hands on enough of the ready to buy a bread—well, when she couldn't buy this bread she send me over to this Chinee shop to ask for trust. The Chinee woman—eh, but how these Chinee people does make children!— was big like anything, and I believe I catch she at a good moment, because she say nothing doing, no trust, but if I want a little work that was different, because she want somebody to take some bread she bake for some Indian people. But how she could trust me with the bread? This was a question. And then I pull out my crucifix from under my dirty merino that was more holes than cloth and I tell she to keep it until I come back with the money for the bake bread. I don't know what sort of religion these Chinee people have, but that woman look impressed like anything. But she was smart, though. She keep the crucifix and she send me off with the bread, which was wrap up in a big old *châle-au-pain*, just two or three floursack sew together. I collect the money, bring it back, and she give me back the crucifix with a few cents and a bread.

And that was how this thing really begin. I always tell black people that was God give me my start in life, and don't mind these Trinidadians who does always tell you that Grenadians always praying. Is a true thing, though, because whenever I in any little business difficulty even these days I get down bam! straight on my two knees and I start praying like hell, boy.

Well, so this thing went on, until it was a regular afternoon work for me to deliver people bread. The bakery uses to bake ordinary bread—hops and pan and machine—which they uses to sell to the poorer classes. And how those Chinee people uses to work! This woman, with she big-big belly, clothes all dirty, sweating in front of the oven, making all this bread and making all this money, and I don't know what they doing with it, because all the time they living poor-poor in the back room, with only a bed, some hammocks for the young ones, and a few boxes. I couldn't talk to the husband at all. He didn't know a word of English and all the writing he uses to write uses to be in Chinee. He was a thin nashy feller, with those funny flapping khaki short pants and white merino that Chinee people always wear. He uses to work like a bitch, too. We Grenadians understand hard work, so that is why I suppose I uses to get on so well with these Chinee people, and that is why these lazy black Trinidadians so jealous of we. But was a funny thing. They uses to live so dirty. But the children, man, uses to leave that ramshackle old back room as clean as new bread, and they always had this neatness, always with their little pencil-case and their little rubbers and rulers and blotters, and they never losing anything. They leaving in the morning in one nice little line and in the afternoon they coming back in this same little line, still cool and clean, as though nothing at all touch them all day. Is something they could teach black people children.

But as I was saying this bakery uses to bake ordinary bread for the poorer classes. For the richer classes they uses to bake, too. But what they would do would be to collect the dough from those people house, bake it, and send it back as bread, hot and sweet. I uses to fetch and deliver for this class of customer. They never let me serve in the shop; it was as though they couldn't trust me selling across the counter and collecting money in that rush. Always it had this rush. You know black people: even if it only have one man in the shop he always getting on as if it have one hell of a crowd.

Well, one day when I deliver some bread in this *châle-au-pain* to

a family, there was a woman, a neighbour, who start saying how nice
it is to get bread which you knead with your own hands and not mix
up with all sort of people sweat. And this give me the idea. A oven
is a oven. It have to go on, whether it baking one bread or two. So I
tell this woman, was a Potogee woman, that I would take she dough
and bring it back bake for she, and that it would cost she next to nothing. I say this in a sort of way that she wouldn't know whether I
was going to give the money to the Chinee people, or whether it was
going to cost she next to nothing because it would be I who was
going to take the money. But she give me a look which tell me right
away that she wanted me to take the money. So matter fix. So. Back
in the *châle-au-pain* the next few days I take some dough, hanging it
in the carrier of the bakery bicycle. I take it inside, as though I just
didn't bother to wrap up the *châle-au-pain*, and the next thing is that
this dough mix up with the other dough, and see me kneading and
baking, as though all is one. The thing is, when you go in for a thing
like that, to go in brave-brave. It have some people who make so
much fuss when they doing one little thing that they bound to get
catch. So, and I was surprise like hell, mind you. I get this stuff push
in the oven, and is this said Chinee man, always with this sad and sorrowful Chinee face, who pulling it out of the oven with the long-
handle shovel, looking at it, and pushing it back in.

And when I take the bread back, with some other bread, I collect
the money cool-cool. The thing with a thing like this is that once you
start is damn hard to stop. You start calculating this way and that
way. And I have a calculating mind. I forever sitting down and working out how much say .50 a day every day for seven days, and every
week for a year, coming to. And so this thing get to be a big thing
with me. I wouldn't recommend this to any and everybody who want
to go into business. But is what I mean when I tell people that I make
my dough by dough.

The Chinee woman wasn't too well now. And the old man was
getting on a little funny in a Chinee way. You know how those Chinee fellers does gamble. You drive past Marine Square in the early

hours of the Sabbath and is two to one if you don't see some of those Chinee fellers sitting down outside the Treasury, as though they want to be near money, and gambling like hell. Well, the old man was gambling and the old girl was sick, and I was pretty well the only person looking after the bakery. I work damn hard for them, I could tell you. I even pick up two or three words of Chinee, and some of those rude black people start calling me Black Chinee, because at this time I was beginning to dress in short khaki pants and merino like a Chinee and I was drinking that tea Chinee people drinking all day long and I was walking and not saying much like a Chinee. And, now, don't believe what these black people say about Chinee and prejudice, eh. They have nothing at all against black people, provided they is hard-working and grateful.

But life is a funny thing. Now when it look that I all set, that everything going fine and dandy, a whole set of things happen that start me bawling. First, the Chinee lady catch a pleurisy and dead. Was a hell of a thing, but what else you expect when she was always bending down in front of that fire and then getting wet and going out in the dew and everything, and then always making these children too besides. I was sorry like hell, and a little frighten. Because I wasn't too sure how I was going to manage alone with the old man. All the time I work with him he never speak one word straight to me, but he always talking to me through his wife.

And now, look at my crosses. As soon as the woman dead, the Chinee man like he get mad. He didn't cry or anything like that, but he start gambling like a bitch, and the upshot was that one day, perhaps about a month after the old lady dead, the man tell his children to pack up and start leaving, because he gamble and lose the shop to another Chinee feller. I didn't know where I was standing, and nobody telling me nothing. They only packing. I don't know, I suppose they begin to feel that I was just part of the shop, and the old man not even saying that he sorry he lose me. And, you know, as soon as I drop to my knees and start praying, I see it was really God who right from the start put that idea of the dough in my head, because without that I would have been nowhere at all. Because the new feller who take over the shop say he don't want me. He was going to close the bakery and set up a regular grocery, and he didn't want me serving there because the grocery customers wouldn't like black people serving them. So look at me. Twenty-three years old and no work. No nothing. Only I have this Chinee-ness and I know how to bake bread and I have this extra bit of cash I save up over the years.

I slip out of the old khaki short pants and merino and I cruise around the town a little, looking for work. But nobody want bakers. I had about $700.00, and I see that this cruising around would do but it wouldn't pay, because the money was going fast. Now look at this. You know, it never cross my mind in those days that I could open a shop of my own. Is how it is with black people. They get so use to working for other people that they get to believe that because they black they can't do nothing else but work for other people. And I must tell you that when I start praying and God tell me to go out and open a shop for myself I feel that perhaps God did mistake or that I hadn't hear Him good. Because God only saying to me, 'Youngman, take your money and open a bakery. You could bake good bread.' He didn't say to open a parlour, which a few black fellers do, selling rock cakes and mauby and other soft drinks. No, He say open a bakery. Look at my crosses.

I had a lot of trouble borrowing the extra few hundred dollars, but I eventually get a Indian feller to lend me. And this is what I always tell young fellers. That getting credit ain't no trouble at all if you know exactly what you want to do. I didn't go round telling people to lend me money because I want to build house or buy lorry. I just did want to bake bread. Well, to cut a long story short, I buy a break-down old place near Arouca, and I spend most of what I had trying to fix the place up. Nothing extravagant, you understand, because Arouca is Arouca and you don't want to frighten off the country-bookies with anything too sharp. Too besides, I didn't have the cash. I just put in a few second-hand glass cases and things like that. I write up my name on a board, and look, I in business.

Now the funny thing happen. In Laventille the people couldn't have enough of the bread I was baking—and in the last few months was me was doing the baking. But now trouble. I baking better bread than the people of Arouca ever see, and I can't get one single feller to come in like man through my rickety old front door and buy a penny hops bread. You hear all this talk about quality being its own advertisement? Don't believe it, boy. Is quality plus something else. And I didn't have this something else. I begin to wonder what the hell it could be. I say is because I new in Arouca that this thing happening. But no. I new, I get stale, and the people not flocking in their hundreds to the old shop. Day after day I baking two or three quarts good and all this just remaining and going dry and stale, and the only bread I selling is to the man from the government farm, buying stale cakes and bread for the cows or pigs or whatever they have up there. And was good bread. So I get down on the old knees and I pray as though I want to wear them out. And still I getting the same answer: 'Youngman'—was always the way I uses to get call in these prayers—'Youngman, you just bake bread.'

Pappa! This was a thing. Interest on the loan piling up every month. Some months I borrow from aunty and anybody else who kind enough to listen just to pay off the interest. And things get so low that I uses to have to go out and pretend to people that I was working for another man bakery and that I was going to bake their dough cheap-cheap. And in Arouca cheap mean cheap. And the little cash I picking up in this disgraceful way was just about enough to keep the wolf from the door, I tell you.

Jeezan. Look at confusion. The old place in Arouca so damn out of the way—was why I did buy it, too, thinking that they didn't have no bakery there and that they would be glad of the good Grenadian-baked—the place so out of the way nobody would want to buy it. It ain't even insure or anything, so it can't get in a little fire accident or anything—not that I went in for that sort of thing. And every time I go down on my knees, the answer coming straight back at me: 'Youngman, you just bake bread.'

Well, for the sake of the Lord I baking one or two quarts regular every day, though I begin to feel that the Lord want to break me, and I begin to feel too that this was His punishment for what I uses to do to the Chinee people in their bakery. I was beginning to feel bad and real ignorant. I uses to stay away from the bakery after baking those quarts for the Lord—nothing to lock up, nothing to thief—and, when any of the Laventille boys drop in on the way to Manzanilla and Balandra and those other beaches on the Sabbath, I uses to tell them, making a joke out of it, that I was 'loafing'. They uses to laugh like hell, too. It have nothing in the whole world so funny as to see a man you know flat out on his arse and catching good hell.

The Indian feller was getting anxious about his cash, and you couldn't blame him, either, because some months now he not even seeing his interest. And this begin to get me down, too. I remember how all the man did ask me when I went to him for money was: 'You sure you want to bake bread? You feel you have a hand for baking bread?' And yes-yes, I tell him, and just like that he shell out the cash. And now he was getting anxious. So one day, after baking those loaves for the Lord, I take a Arima Bus Service bus to Port-of-Spain to see this feller. I was feeling brave enough on the way. But as soon as I see the old sea and get a whiff of South Quay and the bus touch the Railway Station terminus my belly start going pweh-pweh. I decide to roam about the city for a little.

Was a hot morning, *petit-carême* weather, and in those days a coconut uses still to cost .04. Well, it had this coconut cart in the old square and I stop by it. It was a damn funny thing to see. The seller was a black feller. And you wouldn't know how funny this was, unless you know that every coconut seller in the island is Indian. They have this way of handling a cutlass that black people don't have. Coconut in left hand; with right hand bam, bam, bam with cutlass, and coconut cut open, ready to drink. I ain't never see a coconut seller chop his hand. And here was this black feller doing this bam-bam business on a coconut with a cutlass. It was as funny as seeing a black man wearing dhoti and turban. The sweetest part of the whole business was that this black feller was, forgetting looks, just like an Indian. He was talking Hindustani to a lot of Indian fellers, who was giving him jokes like hell, but he wasn't minding. It does happen like that sometimes with black fellers who live a lot with Indians in the country. They putting away curry, talking Indian, and behaving just like Indians. Well, I take a coconut from this black man and then went on to see the feller about the money.

He was more sad than vex when I tell him, and if I was in his shoes I woulda be sad, too. Is a hell of a thing when you see your money gone and you ain't getting the sweet little kisses from the interest every month. Anyway, he say he would give me three more months' grace, but that if I didn't start shelling out at the agreed rate he would have to foreclose. 'You put me in a hell of a position,' he say. 'Look at me. You think I want a shop in Arouca?'

I was feeling a little better when I leave the feller, and who I should see when I leave but Percy. Percy was an old rango who uses to go to the Laventille elementary school with me. I never know a boy get so much cut-arse as Percy. But he grow up real hard and ignorant with it, and now he wearing fancy clothes like a saga boy, and talking about various business offers. I believe he was selling insurance—is a thing that nearly every idler doing in Trinidad, and, mark my words, the day coming when you going to see those fellers trying to sell insurance to one another. Anyway, Percy getting on real flash, and he say he want to stand me a lunch for old times' sake. He makes a few of the usual ignorant Trinidadian jokes about Grenadians, and we went up to the Angostura Bar. I did never go there before, and wasn't the sort of place you would expect a rango like Percy to be welcome. But we went up there and Percy start throwing his weight around with the waiters, and, mind you, they wasn't even a quarter as black as Percy. Is a wonder they didn't abuse him, especially with all those fair people around. After the drinks Percy say, 'Where you want to have this lunch?'

Me, I don't know a thing about the city restaurants, and when Percy talk about food all I was expecting was rice and peas or a roti off a Indian stall or a mauby and rock cake in some parlour. And is a damn hard thing to have people, even people as ignorant as Percy, showing off on you, especially when you carrying two nails in your pocket to make the jingling noise. So I tell Percy we could go to a parlour or a bar. But he say, 'No, no. When I treat my friends, I don't like black people meddling with my food.'

And was only then that the thing hit me. I suppose that what Trinidadians say about the stupidness of Grenadians have a little truth, though you have to live in a place for a long time before you get to know it really well. Then the thing hit me, man.

When black people in Trinidad go to a restaurant they don't like to see black people meddling with their food. And then I see that though Trinidad have every race and every colour, every race have to do special things. But look, man. If you want to buy a snowball, who you buying it from? You wouldn't buy it from a Indian or a Chinee or a Potogee. You would buy it from a black man. And I myself, when I was getting my place in Arouca fix up, I didn't employ Indian carpenters or masons. If a Indian in Trinidad decide to go into the carpentering business the man would starve. Who ever see a Indian carpenter? I suppose the only place in the world where they have Indian carpenters and Indian masons is India. Is a damn funny thing. One of these days I must make a trip to that country, to just see this thing. And as we walking I see the names of bakers; Coelho, Pantin, Stauble. Potogee or Swiss, or something, and then all those other Chinee places. And, look at the laundries. If a black man open a laundry, you would take your clothes to it? *I* wouldn't take my clothes there. Well, I walking to this restaurant, but I jumping for joy. And then all sorts of things fit into place. You remember that the Chinee people didn't let me serve bread across the counter?

I uses to think it was because they didn't trust me with the rush. But it wasn't that. It was that, if they did let me serve, they would have had no rush at all. You ever see anybody buying their bread off a black man?

I ask Percy why he didn't like black people meddling with his food in public places. The question throw him a little. He stop and think and say. 'It don't *look* nice.'

*

Well, you could guess the rest of the story. Before I went back to Arouca that day I made contact with a yellow boy call Macnab. This boy was half black and half Chinee, and, though he had a little brown colour and the hair a little curly, he could pass for one of those Cantonese. They a little darker than the other Chinee people, I believe. Macnab I find beating a steel pan in somebody yard—they was practising for Carnival—and I suppose the only reason that Macnab was willing to come all the way to Arouca was because he was short of the cash to buy his costume for the Carnival band.

But he went up with me. I put him in front of the shop, give him a merino and a pair of khaki short pants, and tell him to talk as Chinee as he could, if he wanted to get that Carnival bonus. I stay in the back room, and I start baking bread. I even give Macnab a old Chinee paper, not to read, because Macnab could scarcely read English, but just to leave lying around, to make it look good. And I get hold of one of those big Chinee calendars with Chinee women and flowers and waterfalls and hang it up on the wall. And when this was all ready, I went down on my knees and thank God. And still the old message coming, but friendly and happy now: 'Youngman, you just bake bread.'

And, you know, that solve another problem. I was worrying to hell about the name I should give the place. New Shanghai, Canton, Hongkong, Nanking, Yang-tse-Kiang. But when the old message came over I know right away what the name should be. I scrub off the old name—no need to tell you what that was—and I get a proper sign painter to copy a few letters from the Chinee newspaper. Below that, in big letters, I make him write:

YUNG MAN
BAKER

I never show my face in the front of the shop again. And I tell you, without boasting, that I bake damn good bread. And the people of Arouca ain't that foolish. They know a good thing. And soon I was making so much money that I was able to open a branch in Arima and then another in Port-of-Spain self. Was hard in the beginning to get real Chinee people to work for a black man. But money have it own way of talking, and when today you pass any of the Yung Man establishments all you seeing behind the counter is Chinee. Some of them ain't even know they working for a black man. My wife handling that side of the business, and the wife is Chinee. She come from down Cedros way. So look at me now, in Port-of-Spain, giving Stauble and Pantin and Coelho a run for their money. As I say, I only going in the shops from the back. But every Monday morning I walking brave brave to Marine Square and going in the bank, from the front.

1962

A Flag on the Island

A Fantasy for a Small Screen

I

IT WAS AN ISLAND around which I had been circling for some years. My duties often took me that way and I could have called there any time. But in my imagination the island had ceased to be accessible; and I wanted it to remain so. A lassitude always fell upon me whenever—working from the name made concrete and ordinary on say an airport board—I sought to recreate a visit. So easy then to get into a car, to qualify a name with trees, houses, people, their quaint advertisements and puzzling journeys. So easy to destroy more than a name. All landscapes are in the end only in the imagination; to be faced with the reality is to start again.

And now the island was upon me. It was not on our itinerary. But out there, among the tourist isles to the north, there was the big annual event of the hurricanes; and it was news of one of these hurricanes, called Irene, that was making us put in. The island, we were told in the ship's bulletin, was reasonably safe. There had been a hurricane here, and a mild one, only once, in the 1920s; and scientists at that time had said, in the way scientists have, that the island was safe for another hundred years. You wouldn't have thought so, though, from the excitement in the announcements from the local radio station, which our transistors had begun to pick up as we came slowly into the harbour through the narrow channel, still and clear and dangerous, between tall green-thatched rocky islets.

Channel and islets which I had never hoped or wished to see again. Still there. And I had been so calm throughout the journey northwards. Abstemiousness, even self-mortification, had settled on me almost as soon as I had gone aboard; and had given me a deep content. I had been eating little and drinking not at all. I fancied that I was shrinking from day to day, and this daily assessment had been pleasing. When I sat I tried to make myself as small as possible; and it had been a pleasure to me then to put on my spectacles and to attempt to read, to be the ascetic who yet knew the greater pleasure of his own shrinking flesh. To be the ascetic, to be mild and gentle and soft-spoken, withdrawn and ineffectual; to have created for one-self that little clearing in the jungle of the mind; and constantly to reassure oneself that the clearing still existed.

Now as we moved into the harbour I could feel the jungle press in again. I was jumpy, irritated, unsatisfied, suddenly incomplete. Still, I made an effort. I decided not to go ashore with the others. We were to stay on the island until the hurricane had blown itself out. The shipping company had arranged trips and excursions.

'What's the name of this place? They always give you the name of the place in airports. Harbours try to keep you guessing. I wonder why?'

'Philosopher!'

Husband and wife, playing as a team.

Already we were news. On the transistors there came a new announcement, breathless like the others: 'Here is an appeal from the Ministry of Public Order and Education. Five hundred tourists will be on our island for the next few days. The Ministry urges that these tourists be treated with our customary courtesy and kindness.'

'The natives are excited,' a tourist said to me.

'Yes,' I said, 'I think there is a good chance they will eat us. We look pretty appetizing.'

Red dust hung in a cloud above the bauxite loading station, dis-figuring the city and the hills. The tourists gazed, lining the rails in bermuda shorts, bright cotton shirts and straw hats. They looked vulnerable.

'Here is an appeal from the Ministry of Public Order and Educa-tion. . . .'

I imagined the appeal going to the barbershops, rumshops, cafés and back-yards of the ramshackle town I had known.

The radio played a commercial for a type of shirt; an organ moaned and some deaths were announced; there was a commercial for a washing powder; then the time was tremendously announced and there were details of weather and temperature.

A woman said, 'They get worked up about the time and the weather here too.'

Her husband, his bitterness scarcely disguised by the gaiety of his tourist costume, said, 'Why the hell shouldn't they?'

They were not playing as a team.

I went down to my cabin. On the way I ran into the happier team, already dressed as for a carnival.

'You're not going ashore?' asked the male.

'No. I think I will just stay here and read.'

And in my self-imposed isolation, I did try to read. I put on my spectacles and tried to savour my shrinking, mortified flesh. But it was no use; the jungle pressed; confusion and threat were already being converted into that internal excitement which is in itself fulfilment, and exhaustion.

Here on this Moore-McCormack liner everything was Moore-McCormack. In my white cabin the name called to me from every corner, from every article, from towels, from toilet paper, from writing paper, from table cloth, from pillow-cases, from bed sheets, from blankets, from cups and menus. So that the name appeared to have gone deep, to have penetrated, like the radiation we have been told to fear, the skin of all those exposed to it, to have shaped itself in living red corpuscles within bodies.

Moore-McCormack, Moore-McCormack. Man had become God. Impossible in this cabin to escape; yet I knew that once we were out of the ship the name would lose its power. So that my decision was almost made for me. I would go ashore; I would spend the night ashore. My mood was on me; I let it settle; I let it take possession of me. Then I saw that I too, putting away briefcase, papers, letters, passport, was capable of my own feeble assertions. I too had tried to give myself labels, and none of my labels could convince me that I belonged to myself.

This is part of my mood; it heightens my anxiety; I feel the whole world is being washed away and that I am being washed away with it. I feel my time is short. The child, testing his courage, steps into the swiftly moving stream, and though the water does not go above his ankles, in an instant the safe solid earth vanishes, and he is aware only of the terror of sky and trees and the force at his feet. Split seconds of lucidity add to his terror. So, we can use the same toothpaste for years and end by not seeing the colour of the tube; but set us among strange labels, set us in disturbance, in an unfamiliar landscape; and every unregarded article we possess becomes isolated and speaks of our peculiar dependence.

'You are going to spend the night ashore?'

The question came from a small intelligent-looking man with a round, kind face. He had been as withdrawn from the life of the ship as myself, and I had always seen him in the company of a big grey-suited man whose face I had never been able to commit to memory. I had heard rumours that he was very rich, but I had paid no attention; as I had paid no attention to the other rumour that we had a Russian spy on board as a prisoner.

'Yes, I am going to be brave.'

'Oh, I am glad,' he said, 'we are going to have lots of fun to-gether.'

'Thanks for asking me.'

'When I say fun, I don't mean what you mean.'

'I don't know what you mean either.'

He did not stop smiling. 'I imagine that you are going ashore for pleasure.'

'Well, I suppose that you could call it that.'

'I am glad we put in here.' His expression became that of a man burdened by duty. 'You see I have a little business to do here.' He spoke gravely, but his excitement was clear. 'Do you know the island?'

'I used to know it very well.'

'Well, I am so glad we have met. You are just the sort of person I want to meet. You could be of great help to me.'

'I can simplify matters for you by giving you a list of places you must on no account go to.'

He looked pained. 'I am really here on business.'

'You can do good business here. I used to.'

Pleasure? I was already exhausted. My stomach felt tight; and all the unexpended energy of days, of weeks, seemed to have turned sour. Already the craving for shellfish and seafood was on me. I could almost feel its sick stale taste in my mouth, and I knew that for all that had happened in the past, I would eat no complete meal for some time ahead, and that while my mood lasted the pleasures I looked for would quickly turn to a distressing-satisfying endurance test, would end by being pain.

I had been the coldest of tourists, unexcited by the unexpected holiday. Now, as we landed, I was among the most eager.

'Hey, that was a pretty quick read.'

'I read the last page—the butler did it.'

In the smart reception building, well-groomed girls, full of self-conscious charm, chosen for race and colour, with one or two totally, diplomatically black, pressed island souvenirs on us: toy steel-drums, market-women dolls in cotton, musicians in wire, totem-like faces carved from coconuts. Beyond the wire-netting fence, the taxi drivers of the city seethed. It seemed a frail barrier.

'It's like the zoo,' the woman said.

'Yes,' said her embittered husband. 'They might even throw you some nuts.'

I looked for a telephone. I asked for a directory. It was a small directory.

'A toy directory,' the happy tourist said.

'It's full of the numbers of dolls,' I said.

I dialled, I waited. A voice I knew said, 'Hullo.' I closed my eyes to listen. The voice said, 'Hullo, hullo.' I put the receiver down.

'Naughty.'

It was my friend from the ship. His companion stood at the other end of the room, his back to us; he was looking at books on a revolving bookstand.

'What do you think Sinclair is interested in? Shall we go and see?'

We moved over. Sinclair shuffled off.

Most of the books displayed were by a man called H. J. B. White. The back of each book had a picture of the author. A tormented writer's-photograph face. But I imagined it winking at me. I winked back.

'Do you know him?' my friend asked.

'I don't know whether any of us really knew Mr Blackwhite,' I said. 'He was a man who moved with the times.'

'Local writer?'

'Very local.'

He counted the titles with an awed finger. 'He looks tremendous. Oh, I hope I can see him. Oh, this looks very good.'

The book he picked up was called *I Hate You*, with the sub-title *One Man's Search for Identity*. He opened the book greedily and began moving his lips, '"I am a man without identity. Hate has consumed my identity. My personality has been distorted by hate. My hymns have not been hymns of praise, but of hate. How terrible to be Caliban, you say. But I say, how tremendous. Tremendousness is therefore my unlikely subject".'

He stopped reading, held the book out to the assistant and said, 'Miss, Miss, I would like to buy this.' Then, indicating one title after the other: 'And this, and this, and this, and this.'

He was not the only one. Many of the tourists had been deftly guided to the bookstall.

'Native author.'

'Don't use that word.'

'Lots of local colour, you think?'

'Mind your language.'

'But look, he's attacking us.'

'No, he's only attacking tourists.'

The group moved on, leaving a depleted shelf.

I bought all H. J. B. White's books.

The girl who sold them to me said, 'Tourists usually go for *I Hate You*, but I prefer the novels myself. They're heartwarming stories.'

'Good clean sex?'

'Oh no, inter-racial.'

'Sorry, I need another language.'

I put on my spectacles and read on the dedication page of one book: 'Thanks are due to the Haaker Foundation whose generous support facilitated the composition of this work.' Another book offered thanks to the Stockwell Foundation. My companion—he was becoming my companion—held all his own books under his arm and read with me from mine.

'You see,' he said, 'they're all after him. I don't imagine he'll want to look at me.'

We were given miniature rum bottles with the compliments of various firms. Little leaflets and folders full of photographs and maps with arrows and X's told us of the beauties of the island, now fully charted. The girl was especially friendly when she explained about the sights.

'You have mud volcanoes here,' I said, 'and that's pretty good. But the leaflet doesn't say. Which is the best whorehouse in town nowadays?'

Tourists stared. The girl called: 'Mr Phillips.' And my companion held my arm, smiled as to a child and said soothingly: 'Hey, I believe I am going to have to look after you. I know how it is when things get on top of you.'

'You know, I believe you do.'

'My name's Leonard.'

'I am Frank,' I said.

'Short for Frankenstein. Forget it, that's my little joke. And you see my friend over there, but you can't see his face? His name's Sinclair.'

Sinclair stood, with his back to us, studying some tormented paintings of black beaches below stormy skies.

'But Sinclair won't talk to you, especially now that he's seen me talking to you.'

In the turmoil of the reception building we were three fixed points.

'Why won't Sinclair talk to me?'

'He's jealous.'

'Hooray for you.'

I broke away to get a taxi.

'Hey, you can't leave me. I'm worried about you, remember?'

Below a wooden arch that said WELCOME TO THE COLOURFUL ISLAND the taxi drivers, sober in charcoal-grey trousers, white shirts, some even with ties, behaved like people maddened by the broadcast pleas for courtesy. They rushed the tourists, easy targets in their extravagantly Caribbean cottons stamped with palm-fringed beaches, thatched huts and grass skirts. The tropics appeared to be on their backs alone; when they got into their taxis the tropics went with them.

We came out into an avenue of glass buildings, airconditioned bars, filling stations and snappily worded advertisements. The slogan PRIDE, TOIL, CULTURE, was everywhere. There was a flag over the customs building. It was new to me: rays from a yellow sun lighting up a wavy blue sea.

'What did you do with the Union Jack?'

The taxi driver said, 'They take it away, and they send this. To tell the truth I prefer the old Union Jack. Now don't misunderstand me, I talking about the flag as a flag. They send us this thing and they try to sweeten us up with some old talk about *or, a pile gules, argenta bordure, barry-wavy*. They try to sweeten us up with that, but I prefer the old Union Jack. It look like a real flag. This look like something they make up. You know, like foreign money?'

Once the island had seemed to me flagless. There was the Union Jack of course, but it was a remote affirmation. The island was a floating suspended place to which you brought your own flag if you wanted to. Every evening on the base we used to pull down the Stars and Stripes at sunset; the bugle would sound and through the city of narrow streets, big trees and old wooden houses, every American serviceman would stand to attention. It was a ridiculous affirmation—the local children mocked us—but only one in a city of ridiculous affirmations. For a long time Mr Blackwhite had a coloured portrait of Haile Selassie in his front room; and in his corner grocery Ma-Ho had a photograph of Chiang Kai-shek between his Chinese calendars. On the flagless island we, saluting the flag, were going back to America; Ma-Ho was going back to Canton as soon as the war was over; and the picture of Haile Selassie was there to remind Mr. Blackwhite, and to remind us, that he too had a place to go back to. 'This place doesn't exist,' he used to say, and he was wiser than any of us.

Now, driving through the city whose features had been so altered, so that alteration seemed to have spread to the land itself, the nature of the soil, I felt again that the reality of landscape and perhaps of all relationships lay only in the imagination. The place existed now: that was the message of the flag.

The road began to climb. On a culvert two calypsonians, dressed for the part, sat disconsolately waiting for custom. A little later we saw two who had been successful. They were serenading the happy wife. The taxi driver, hands in pockets, toothpick in mouth, stood idle. The embittered husband stood equally idle, but he was like a man fighting an inward rage.

The hotel was new. There were murals in the lobby which sought to exalt the landscape and the people which the hotel's very existence seemed to deny. The noticeboard in the lobby gave the name of our ship and added: 'Sailing Indefinite'. A poster advertised

The Coconut Grove. Another announced a Barbecue Night at the Hilton, Gary Priestland, popular TV personality, Master of Ceremonies. A photograph showed him with his models. But I saw only Priest, white-robed Priest, handler of the language, handler of his six little hymn-singing girls. He didn't wink at me. He scowled; he threatened. I covered his face with my hand.

In my moods I tell myself that the world is not being washed away; that there is time; that the blurring of fantasy with reality which gives me the feeling of helplessness exists only in my mind. But then I know that the mind is alien and unfriendly, and I am never able to regulate things. Hilton, Hilton. Even here, even in the book on the bedside table. And The Coconut Grove again in a leaflet on the table, next to the bowl of fruit in green cellophane tied with a red ribbon.

I telephoned for a drink; then I telephoned again to hear the voice and to say nothing. Even before lunch I had drunk too much.

'Frank, your eye is still longer than your tongue.'

It was an island saying; I thought I could hear the words on the telephone.

Lunch, lunch. Let it be ordered in every sense. Melon or avocado to start, something else to follow—but what? But what? And as soon as I entered the diningroom the craving for oysters and shellfish became overpowering. The liveried page strolled through the diningroom beating a toy steel pan and calling out a name. I fancied it was mine: 'Frankie, Frankie.' But of course I knew better.

I saw Sinclair's back as he walked to a table. He sat at the far end like a man controlling the panorama.

'Are you feeling better?'

'Leonard?'

'Frank.'

'Do you like seafood, Leonard?'

'In moderation.'

'I am going to have some oysters.'

'A good starter. Let's have some, I'll have half a dozen.'

The waiter carried the emblem of yellow sun and wavy sea on his lapel; my eyes travelled down those waves.

'Half a dozen for him. Fifty for me.'

'Fifty,' Leonard said.

'Well, let's make it a hundred.'

Leonard smiled. 'Boy, I'm glad I met you. You believe me, don't you, Frank?'

'I believe you.'

'You know, people don't believe I have come here to work. They think I am making it up.'

The waiter brought Leonard his six oysters and brought me my hundred. The oysters were of the tiny island variety; six scarcely filled one indentation of Leonard's oyster plate.

'Are these six oysters?' Leonard asked the waiter.

'They are six oysters.'

'Okay, okay,' Leonard said soothingly, 'I just wanted to find out. Of course,' he said to me, 'it doesn't sound like work. You see—'

And here the liveried page walked back through the diningroom beating a bright tune on his toy pan and calling out a name.

'—you see, I have got to give away a million dollars.'

My oysters had come in a tumbler. I scooped up about a dozen and swallowed them.

'Exactly,' Leonard said. 'It doesn't sound like work. But it is. One wants to be sure that one is using the money sensibly. It's easy enough to make a million dollars, I always say. Much harder to spend it.'

'That's what I have always felt. Excuse me.'

I went up to my room. The oysters had been too many for me. The sick tightness was in my stomach. Even at this early stage it was necessary for me to drive myself on.

I was careful, as I always am on these occasions, to prepare sensibly. I lined the waist-band of my trousers with the new funny island money; I distributed notes all over my pockets; I even lay some flat in my shoes.

A letter from home among my papers. Nothing important; no news; just a little bit about the drains, the wonderful workmen who had helped. Brave girl. Brave.

I remembered again. I lifted the telephone, asked for a line, dialled. The same voice answered and again my courage left me and I listened to the squawks until the phone went dead.

I had stripped myself of all my labels, of all my assertions. Soon I would be free. Hilton, Hilton: man as God. Goodbye to that now. My excitement was high.

I went to the desk, transferred a fixed sum to the hotel vault. The final fraudulence that we cannot avoid: we might look for escape, but we are always careful to provide for escape from that escape.

While the clerk was busy I took the pen from the desk, blacked out the whites of Gary Priestland's eyes and sent an arrow through his neck. The clerk was well trained. It was only after I had turned that he removed the disfigured poster and replaced it by a new one.

The liveried doorman whistled up a taxi. I gave him a local dollar; too much, but I enjoyed his attempt to look unsurprised. He opened the taxi door, closed it, saluted. It was the final moment of responsibility. I did not give the taxi driver the name of any bar; I gave him the name of a department store in the centre of the city. And when I got off I actually went into the store, as though the taxi driver was watching me and it was important that I should not step out of the character which he must have built up for me.

The store was airconditioned. The world was cool and muffled. My irritation was sharpened.

'Can I help you, sir?'

'No thank you, I am just passing through.'

I spoke with unnecessary aggressiveness; one or two customers stared and I instinctively waited for Leonard's interjection.

'Leonard,' I whispered, turning.

But he wasn't there.

The shop girl took a step backwards and I hurried out through the other door into the shock of damp heat, white light, and gutter smells. Hooray for airconditioning. My mood had taken possession of me. I was drunk on more, and on less, than alcohol.

The money began to leak out of my fingers. This is part of the excitement; money became paper over which other people fought. Two dollars entrance here; one dollar for a beer there; cigarettes at twice the price: I paid in paper. Bright rooms, killing bright, and noisy as the sea. The colours yellow, green, red, on drinks, labels, calendars on the walls. On the television intermittently through a series of such bars, Gary Priestland, chairing a discussion on love and marriage. And from a totally black face, a woman's, black enough to be featureless, issued: 'Well, I married for love.' 'No, she married for hate.' Laughter was like the sea. Someone played with the knob on the set; and the thought, perhaps expressed, came to me. 'It is an unkind medium.'

In bright rooms, bright seas, I floated. And I explored dark caves, so dark you groped and sat still and in the end you found that you were alone.

'Where is everybody?'

'They are coming just now.'

In an almost empty room—dim lights, dark walls, dark chairs—the man sitting at the edge of the table invited us to come close up to him. We all six in the room moved up to him, as to a floor show. He crossed his legs and swung them. 'Is he going to strip?'

Confusion again. The door; the tiled entrance; the discreet board:

BRITISH COUNCIL
The Elizabethan Lyric
A Course of Six Lectures

I always feel it would be so much better if I could wait to pick and choose. Time after time I promise myself to do so. But when the girl came and said—so sad it seemed to me—'I am going to screw you,' I knew that this was how it would begin; that I wouldn't have the will to resist.

PRIDE, flashed the neon light across the square.

She ordered a stout.

'You are an honest girl.'

'Stout does build me up.'

TOIL

The stout came.

'Ah,' she said, 'my old bulldog.'

And from the neck label the bulldog growled at me. With the stout there also came two men dressed like calypsonians in the travel brochures, dressed like calypsonians on the climbing road to the hotel.

'Allow me to welcome the gentleman to our colourful island.'

CULTURE

'Get away,' I shouted.

She looked a little nervous; she nodded uncertainly to someone behind me and said, 'Is all right, Percy.' Then to me: 'Why you driving them away?'

'They embarrass me.'

'How you mean, they embarrass you?'

'They're not real. Look, I could put my hand through them.'

The man with the guitar lifted his arm; my hand went through.

The song went on: 'In two-twos, this gentleman got the alcoholic blues.'

'God!'

When I uncovered my face I saw a ringed hand before it. It was an expectant hand. I paid; I drank.

A fat white woman began to do a simple little dance on the raised floor. I couldn't look.

'What wrong with you?'

And when the woman made as if to discard the final garment, I stood up and shouted. 'No!'

'But how a big man like you could shame me so?'

The man who had been sitting with a stick at the top of the steps came to our table. He waved around the room, past paintings of steel-bands and women dancing on golden sand, and pointed to a sign:

> Patrons are requested to abstain from
> lewd and offensive gestures
> By order, Ministry of Order and Public Education

'Is all right, Percy,' the girl said.

Percy could only point. Speech was out of the question because of the steel orchestra. I sat down.

Percy went away and the girl said gently: 'Sit down and tell me why you finding everything embarrassing. What else you tourists come here for?' She beckoned to the waitress. 'I want a fry chicken.'

'No,' I said. 'No damn fry chicken for you.'

At that moment the band stopped, and my words filled the room. The Japanese sailors—we had seen their trawlers in the harbour—looked up. The American airmen looked up. Percy looked up.

And in the silence the girl shouted to the room, 'He finding everything embarrassing, and he damn mean with it.' She stood up and pointed at me. 'He travelling all over the world. And all I want is a fry chicken.'

'Frank,' I heard a voice whisper.

'Leonard,' I whispered back.

'O boy, I am glad I've found you. I've had such a time looking for you. I have been in so many different bars, so many. I've got all these nice names, all these interesting people I've got to assist and give money to. Sometimes I had trouble getting the names. You know how people misunderstand. I was worried about you. Sinclair was worried about you too.'

Sinclair was sitting at a table in the distance with his back to us, drinking.

Caught between Leonard and a demand for fried chicken, I bought the fried chicken.

'You know,' Leonard said confidentially, 'it seems that the place to go to is The Coconut Grove. It sounds terrific, just what I am looking for. You know it?'

'I know it.'

'Well look, why don't we all three of us just go there now.'

'Not me at The Coconut Grove,' the girl said.

Leonard said to me, 'I meant you and me and Sinclair.'

'What the hell you mean?' She stood up and held the bottle of stout at an angle over Leonard's head, as though ready to pour. She called, 'Percy!'

Leonard closed his eyes, passive and expectant.

'I'll be with you in a minute, Leonard,' I said, and I ran down the steps with the girl who was still holding the bottle of stout.

'How you get so impatient so sudden?'

'I don't know, but this is your big chance.'

The open car door at the foot of the steps was like an invitation. We got in, the door slammed behind us.

'I've got to get away from those people upstairs. They're mad, they're quite mad. You don't know what I rescued you from.'

She looked at me.

So it began: the walking out past tables; the casual stares; the refusal to walk the hundred yards to the hotel; the two-dollar taxi; the unswept concrete steps; the dimly lit rooms; the cheap wooden furniture; the gaudy calendars on the wall, mocking desire, mocking flesh; the blue shimmer of television screens; Gary Priestland, now with the news of the hurricane; the startling gentility of glass cabinets; the much-used bed.

And in lucid intermissions, the telephone: the squawks, the slams.

So it began. The bars, the hotels, pointless conversations with girls. 'What's your name? Where do you come from? What do you want?' The drinks; the bloated feeling in the stomach; the sick taste of island oysters and red pepper sauce; the airless rooms; the wastepaper baskets, wetly and whitely littered; and white wash-basins which, supine on stale beds, one associated with hospitals, medicines, operations, feverishness, delirium.

'No!'

'But I ain't even touched you yet.'

Above me a foolish face, the poor body offering its charms that were no charms. Poor body, poor flesh; poor man.

And again confusion. I must have spoken the words. A woman wailed, claiming insult and calling for brave men, and the bare wooden staircase resounded. Then among trellis and roses, dozens of luminous white roses, a dog barked, and growled. The offended black body turned white with insult. The same screams, the same call for vengeance. Down an aisle, between hundreds and hundreds of fully clothed men with spectacles and pads and pencils, the body chased me. To another entrance; another tiled floor; another discreet board:

ALLIANCE FRANÇAISE
Art Course
Paris Model
(Admission free)

And the glimpses of Leonard: like scenes imagined, the man with the million dollars to give away, the Pied Piper whom as in a dream I saw walking down the street followed by processions of steel-bandsmen, singers, and women calling for his money. At the head he walked, benign, stunned, smiling.

The day had faded, the night moved in jerks, in great swallows of hours. Lighted docks had wise and patient faces.

The bar smelled of rum and latrines. The beer and some notes and some silver were pushed at me through the gap in the wire-netting. My right hand was gripped and the black face, smiling, menacing, humorous, frightening, which I seemed to study pore by pore, hair by hair, was saying, 'Leave the change for me, nuh.'

Confusion. Glimpses of faces expressing interest rather than hostility. A tumbling and rumbling; a wet floor; my own shouts of 'No', and the repeated answering sentence: 'Next time you walk with money.'

And in the silent street off the deserted square, midnight approaching, the Cinderella hour, I was sitting on the pavement, totally lucid, with my feet in the gutter, sucking an orange. Sitting below the old straw-hatted lady, lit by the yellow smoking flame of a bottle flambeau. On the television in the shop window, Gary Priestland and the Ma-Ho Four, frantic and mute behind plate-glass.

'Better?' she said.

'Better.'

'These people nowadays, they never have, they only want.'

'What do they want?'

'What you have. Look.'

The voice was mock American: 'Man, I can get anything for you?'

'What do you have?'

'I have white,' the taxi driver said. 'I have Chinese, I have Portuguese, I have Indian, I have Spanish. Don't ask me for black. I don't do black.'

'That's right, boy,' the old lady said. 'Keep them out of mischief.'

'I couldn't do black or white now.'

'Was what I was thinking,' the orange lady said.

'Then you want The Coconut Grove,' the taxi driver said. 'Very cultural. All the older shots go there.'

'You make it sound very gay.'

'I know what you mean. This culture would do, but it wouldn't pay. Is just a lot of provocation if you ask me. A lot of wicked scanty clothing and all you doing with your two hands at the end is clapping. The spirit of the older shots being willing, but the flesh being weak.'

'That sounds like me. After mature consideration I think we will go to The Coconut Grove.'

'And too besides, I was going to say, they wouldn't take you in like this, old man. Look at you.'

'I don't know, I believe I have lost you somewhere. Do you want me to go to this place?'

'I don't want nothing. I was just remarking that they wouldn't take you in.'

'Let's try.'

'In these cultural joints they have big bouncers, you know.'

We drove through silent streets in which occasionally neon lights flashed PRIDE, TOIL, CULTURE. On the car radio came the news of midnight. Terrific news, from the way it was presented. Then came news of wind velocity and temperature, and of the hurricane, still out there.

'You see what I mean,' the taxi driver said when we stopped.

'It has changed,' I said. 'It used to be an ordinary house, you know. You know those wooden houses with gables and fretwork along the eaves?'

'Oh, the old-fashioned ones. We are pulling them down all the time now. You mustn't think a lot of them still remain.'

Henry's was new and square, with much glass. Behind the glass, potted greenery; and behind that, blinds. Rough stone walls, recessed mortar, a heavy glass door, heavy, too, with recommendations from clubs and travel associations, like the suitcase of an old-fashioned traveller. And behind the door, the bouncer.

'Big, eh?' the taxi driver said.

'He's a big man.'

'You want to try your luck?'

'Perhaps a little later. Just now I just want you to drive slowly down the street.'

The bouncer watched us move off. I looked back at him; he continued to look at me. And how could I have forgotten? Opposite The Coconut Grove, what? I looked. I saw.

Ministry of Order and Public Education
University College
Creative Writing Department
Principal: H. J. B. White
Grams: Olympus

'You don't mind going so slowly?' I asked the driver.

'No, I do a lot of funeral work when I'm not hustling.'

No overturned dustbins on the street now; no pariah dogs timidly pillaging. The street we moved down was like a street in an architect's drawing. Above the neat new buildings trees tossed. The wind was high; the racing clouds were black and silver. We came to an intersection.

'Supermarket,' the driver said, pointing.

'Supermarket.'

A little further on my anxiety dissolved. Where I had expected and feared to find a house, there was an empty lot. I got out of the car and went to look.

'What are you looking for?' the taxi driver asked.

'My house.'

'You sure you left it here? That was a damn careless thing to do.'

'They've pulled down my house.' I walked among the weeds, looking.

'The house not here,' the taxi-driver said. 'What you looking for?'

'An explanation. Here, go leave me alone.' I paid him off.

He didn't go. He remained where he was and watched me. I began to walk briskly back towards The Coconut Grove, the wind blowing my hair, making my shirt flap, and it seemed that it was just in this way, though not at night and under a wild sky, but in broad daylight, below a high light sky, that I had first come to this street. The terror of sky and trees, the force at my feet.

2

I used to feel in those days that it was we who brought the tropics to the island. When I knew the town, it didn't end in sandy beaches and coconut trees, but in a tainted swamp, in mangrove and mud. Then the land was reclaimed from the sea, and the people who got oysters from the mangrove disappeared. On the reclaimed land we built the tropics. We put up our army huts, raised our flag, planted our coconut trees and our hedges. Among the great wooden buildings with wire-netting windows we scattered pretty little thatched huts.

We brought the tropics to the island. Yet to the islanders it must have seemed that we had brought America to them. Everyone worked for us. You asked a man what he did; he didn't say that he drove a truck or was a carpenter; he simply said he worked for the Americans. Every morning trucks drove through the city, picking up workers; and every afternoon the trucks left the base to take them back.

The islanders came to our bit of the tropics. We explored theirs. Nothing was organized in those days. There were no leaflets telling you where to shop or where to go. You had to find out yourself. You found out quickly about the bars; it wasn't pleasant to be beaten up or robbed.

I heard about Henry's place from a man on the base. He said Henry kept a few goats in his backyard and sometimes slaughtered them on a Sunday. He said Henry was a character. It didn't seem a particularly enticing thing. But I got into a taxi outside the base one Thursday afternoon and decided to look. Taxi drivers know every-thing; so they say.

'Do you know a man called Henry?' I asked the taxi driver. 'He keeps a few goats.'

'The island small, boss, but not that small.'

'You must know him. He keeps these goats.'

'No, boss, you be frank with me, I be frank with you. If goats you after . . .'

I allowed him to take me where he wished. We drove through the old ramshackle city, wooden houses on separate lots, all decay, it seemed, in the middle of the brightest vegetation. It scarcely seemed a city where you would, by choice, seek pleasure; it made you think only of empty afternoons. All these streets look so quiet and alike. All the houses looked so tame and dull and alike: very little people attending to their very little affairs.

The taxi driver took me to various rooms, curtained, hot, stuffed with furniture, and squalid enough to kill all thoughts of pleasure. In one room there was even a baby. 'Not mine, not mine,' the girl said. I was a little strained, and the driver was strained, by the time we came to the street where he said I would find Henry's place.

The brave young man looking for fun. The spark had gone; and to tell the truth, I was a little embarrassed. I wished to arrive at Henry's alone. I paid the taxi driver off.

I imagine I was hoping to find something which at least looked like a commercial establishment. I looked for boards and signs. I saw nothing. I walked past shuttered houses to a shuttered grocery, the only clue even there being a small black noticeboard saying, in amateurish letters, that Ma-Ho was licensed to deal in spirituous liquors. I walked down the other side of the street. And here was something I had missed. Outside a house much hung with ferns a board said:

Premier Commercial College
Shorthand and Bookkeeping
H. J. Blackwhite, Principal

Here and there a curtain flapped. My walks up and down the short street had begun to attract attention. Too late to give up, though. I walked back past the Premier Commercial College. This time a boy was hanging out of a window. He was wearing a tie and he was giggling.

I asked him, 'Hey, does your sister screw?'

The boy opened his mouth and wailed and pulled back his head. There were giggles from behind the ferns. A tall man pushed open a door with coloured glass panes and came out to the veranda. He looked sombre. He wore black trousers, a white shirt, and a black tie. He had a rod in his hand!

He said in an English accent, 'Will you take your filth elsewhere. This is a school. We devote ourselves to things of the mind.' He pointed sternly to the board.

'Sorry, Mr—'

He pointed to the board again. 'Blackwhite. Mr H. J. Blackwhite. My patience is at an end. I shall sit down and type out a letter of protest to the newspapers.'

'I feel like writing some sort of protest myself. Do you know a place called Henry's?'

'This is not Henry's.'

'Sorry, sorry. But before you go away, tell me, what do you people do?'

'What do you mean, do?'

'What do you people do when you are doing nothing? Why do you keep on?'

There were more giggles behind the ferns. Mr Blackwhite turned and ran through the coloured glass doors into the drawingroom. I heard him beating on a desk with a rod and shouting: 'Silence, silence.' In the silence which he instantly obtained he beat a boy. Then he reappeared on the veranda, his sleeves rolled up, his face shining with sweat. He seemed willing enough to keep on exchanging words with me, but just then some army jeeps turned the corner and we heard men and women shouting. Overdoing the gaiety, I thought. Blackwhite's look of exaltation was replaced by one of distaste and alarm.

'Your colleagues and companions,' he said.

He disappeared, with a sort of controlled speed, behind the glass panes. His class began to sing, 'Flow gently, sweet Afton.'

The jeeps stopped at the unfenced lot opposite Mr Blackwhite's. This lot contained two verandaless wooden houses. Small houses on low concrete pillars; possibly there were more houses at the back. I stood on the pavement, the jeep-loads tumbled out. I half hoped that the gay tide would sweep me in. But men and girls just passed on either side of me, and when the tide had washed into the houses and the yard I remained where I was, stranded on the pavement.

Henry's, it was clear, was like a club. Everybody seemed to know everybody else and was making a big thing of it. I stood around. No one took any notice of me. I tried to give the impression that I was waiting for someone. I felt very foolish. Pleasure was soon the last thing in my mind. Dignity became much more important.

Henry's was especially difficult because it appeared to have no commercial organization. There was no bar, there were no waiters. The gay crowd simply sat around on the flights of concrete steps that led from the rocky ground to the doors. No tables outside, and no chairs. I could see things like this inside some of the rooms, but I wasn't sure whether I had the right to go into any of them. It was clearly a place to which you couldn't come alone.

It was Henry in the end who spoke to me. He said that I was making him nervous and that I was making the girls nervous. The girls were like racehorses, he said, very nervous and sensitive. Then, as though explaining everything, he said, 'The place is what you see it is.'

'It's very nice,' I said.

'You don't have to flatter me; if you want to stay here, fine; if you don't want to stay here, that's fine too.'

Henry wasn't yet a character. He was still only working up to it. I don't like characters. They worry me, and perhaps it was because Henry wasn't yet a character—a public performer, jolly but exclud-ing—that I fell in so easily with him. Later, when he became a character, I was one of the characters with him; it was we that did the excluding.

I clung to him that first afternoon for the sake of dignity, as I say. Also, I felt a little resentful of the others, so very gay and integrated, and did not wish to be alone.

'We went out,' Henry said. 'A little excursion, you know. That bay over the hills, the only one you people leave us. I don't know, you people say you come here to fight a war, and the first thing you do you take away our beaches. You take all the white sand beaches; you leave us only black sand.'

'You know these bureaucrats. They like things tidy.'

'I know,' he said. 'They like it tidy here too. I can't tell you the number of people who would like to run me out of town.'

'Like that man across the road?'

'Oh, you meet old Blackwhite?'

'He is going to type out a letter about me to the newspapers. And about you, too, I imagine. And your colleagues and companions.'

'They don't print all Blackwhite's letters. Good relations and all that, you know. He believe he stand a better chance with the type-writer. Tell me what you do to provoke him. I never see a man look as quiet as you.'

'I asked one of his boys whether he had a sister who screwed.'

Amusement went strangely on Henry's sour face. He looked the ascetic sort. His hair was combed straight back and his narrow-waisted trousers were belted with a tie. This was the one raffish, star-tling thing about his dress.

Henry went on: 'The trouble with the natives—'

I started at the word.

'Yes, natives. The troubles with the natives is that they don't like me. I don't belong here, you know. I am like you. I come from another place. A pretty island, if I tell you. I build up all this from scratch.' He waved at his yard. 'These people here lazy and they damn jealous with it too. They always trying to get me deported. Illegal immigrant and so on. But they can't touch me. I have all the shots in the palm of my hand. You hear people talk about Gordon? Black man; but the best lawyer we have. Gordon was always coming here until that divorce business. Big thing. You probably hear about that on the base.'

'Sure, we heard about it.'

'And whenever I have any little trouble about this illegal immigrant business, I just go straight, like man, to Gordon office. The clerks—you know, those fellows with ties—try to be rude, and I just telling them, "You tell Alfred"—his name is Alfred Gordon—"you tell Alfred that Henry here." And everybody falling back in amazement when Mr Gordon come out heself and shaking me by the hand and muching me up in front of everybody. "All you wait," he say, "I got to see my old friend Henry." And teeth.'

'Teeth?'

'Teeth. Whenever I want to have any teeth pull out, I just run up to old Ling-Wing—Chinee, but the best dentist we have in the place—and he pulling out the teeth straight way. You got to have a philosophy of life. Look, I go tell you,' he said, 'my father was a good-for-nothing. Always gambling, a game called wappee and all-fours. And whenever my mother complain and start bawling out, "Hezekiah, what you going to leave for your children?" my father he only saying, "I ain't got land. I ain't got money. But I going to leave my children a wonderful set of friends."'

'That's a fine philosophy,' I said.

'We all have to corporate in some way. Some people corporate in one way, some corporate another way. I think that you and me going to get on good. Mavis, pour this man a drink. He is a wonderful talker.'

Henry, sipping at rum-and-cokes all the time, was maudlin. I was a little high myself.

One of the Americans who had been on the excursion to the bay came up to us. He tottered a little. He said he had to leave.

'I know,' Henry said. 'The war etcetera.'

'How much do I owe you, Henry?'

'You know what you owe me. I don't keep no check.'

'Let me see. I think I had a chicken pilau. Three or four rum-and-cokes.'

'Good,' Henry said. 'You just pay for that.'

The man paid. Henry took his money without any comment. When the man left he said, 'Drink is never any excuse. I don't believe people ever not knowing what they do. He not coming back in here. He had two chicken pilaus, six rum-and-coke, five bottles soda water and two whiskies. That's what I call vice.'

'It is vice, and I am ashamed of him.'

'I will tell you, you know.' Henry said. 'When the old queen pass on—'

'The old queen?'

'My mother. I was in a sort of daze. Then I had this little dream. The old man, he appear to me.'

'Your father Hezekiah?'

'No. God. He say, "Henry, surround yourself with love, but avoid vice." On this island I was telling you about, pretty if I tell you, they had this woman, pretty but malevolent. She make two-three children for me, and bam, you know what, she want to rush me into marriage.'

The sun was going down. From the base, the bit of the tropics we had created, the bugle sounded Retreat. Henry snapped his fingers, urging us all to stand. We stood up and saluted to the end.

'I like these little customs,' he said. 'Is a nice little custom you boys bring with you.'

'About this woman on the pretty island with two or three children?'

Henry said, 'I avoided vice. I ran like hell. I get the rumour spread that I dead. I suppose I am dead in a way. Can't go back to my pretty little island. Oh, prettier than this. Pretty, pretty. But she waiting for me.'

We heard hymns from the street.

'Money,' Henry said, 'all you girls got your money ready?'

They all got out little coins and we went out to the pavement. A tall bearded man, white-robed and sandalled, was leading a little group of hymn-singers, six small black girls in white gowns. They were sweet hymns; we listened in silence.

Then the bearded man said, 'Brothers and sisters, it is customary on such occasions to say that there is still time to repent.' He was like a man in love with his own fluency. His accent was very English. 'It is, however, my belief that this, at this time, is one of the optimistic assertions of fraudulent evangelists more concerned with the counting of money than what I might call the count-down of our imminent destruction.' Suddenly his manner changed. He paused, closed his eyes, swayed a little, lifted up his arms and shouted, in an entirely different voice: 'The word of the Bible is coming to pass.'

Some of Henry's girls chanted back: 'What word?' And others. 'What part?'

The white-robed man said, 'The part where it say young people going to behave bad, and evil and violence going to stalk the land. That part.'

His little chorus began to sing; and he went round collecting from us, saying, 'It is nothing personal, you understand, nothing personal. I know you boys have to be here defending us and so on, but the truth is the truth.'

He collected his money, slipped it into a pocket of his robe, patted the pocket; then he seemed to go on patting. He patted each of his singers, either out of a great love, or to make sure that they had not hidden any of the coins they had received. Then: 'Right-wheel!' he called above their singing; and, patting them on the shoulder as they passed him, followed them to the grocery at the corner. His hymn meeting continued there, under the rusty corrugated-iron eaves.

It was now dark. A picnic atmosphere came to Henry's yard. Meals were being prepared in various rooms; gramophones were playing. From distant yards came the sound of steel-bands. Night provided shelter, and in the yard it was very cosy, very like a family gathering. Only, I was not yet of the family.

A girl with a sling bag came in. She greeted Henry, and he greeted her with a largeness of gesture which yet concealed a little reserve, a little awe. He called her Selma. I noted her. I became the third in the party; I became nervous.

I am always nervous in the presence of beauty; and in such a setting, faced with a person I couldn't assess, I was a little frightened. I didn't know the rules of Henry's place and it was clear that the place had its own rules. I was inexperienced. Inexperienced, I say. Yet what good has experience brought me since? I still, in such a situation and in such a place, move between the extremes of courtesy and loudness.

Selma was unattached and cool. I thought she had the coolness that comes either from ownership or from being owned. It was this as much as dress and manner and balance which marked her out from the others in the yard. She might have been Henry's girl, the replacement for that other, abandoned on the pretty little island; or she might have belonged to someone who had not yet appeared.

The very private greetings over, Henry introduced us.

'He's quite a talker,' he said.

'He's a good listener,' I said.

She asked Henry, 'Did he hear Priest talk?'

I answered, 'I did. That was some sermon.'

'I always like hearing a man use language well,' she said.

'He certainly does,' I said.

'You can see,' she said, 'that he's an educated man.'

'You could see that.'

There was a pause. 'He sells insurance,' she said, 'when he's not preaching.'

'It sounds a wonderful combination. He frightens us about death, and then sells us insurance.'

She wasn't amused. 'I would like to be insured.'

'You are far too young.'

'But that is just the time. The terms are better. I don't know, I would just like it. I feel it's nice. I have an aunt in the country. She is always making old style because she's insured. Whenever she buys a little more she always lets you know.'

'Well, why don't you buy some insurance yourself?'

She said, 'I am very poor.'

And she said the words in such a way that it seemed to put a full-stop to our conversation. I hate the poor and the humble. I think poverty is something we should all conceal. Selma spoke of it as something she was neither proud nor ashamed of; it was a condition which was soon to be changed. Little things like this occur in all relationships, little warning abrasions in the smoothness of early intercourse which we choose to ignore. We always deceive ourselves; we cannot say we have not been warned.

'What would you do if you had a lot of money?'

'I would buy lots of things,' she said after some thought. 'Lots of nice modern things.'

'What sort of things?'

'A three-piece suite. One of those deep ones. You sink into them. I'd buy a nice counterpane, satiny and thick and crisscrossed with deep lines. I saw Norma Shearer using one in *Escape*.'

'A strange thing. That's all I remember of that picture. What do you think she was doing in that bed then? But that was an eiderdown she had, you know. You don't need an eiderdown in this part of the world. It's too warm.'

'Well, whatever you call it, I'd like that. And shoes, I'd buy lots of shoes. Do you have nightmares?'

'Always.'

'You know mine?'

'Tell me.'

'I am in town, you know. Walking down Regent Street. People staring at me, and I feel: this is new. I don't feel embarrassed. I feel like a beauty queen. Then I see myself in a shop window. I am barefoot. I always wake up then. My feet are hanging over the bed.'

I was still nervous. The conversation always seemed to turn away from the point to which I felt I ought to bring it, though to tell the truth I had lost the wish to do so. Still, we owe a duty to ourselves.

I said, 'Do you come from the city?'

'I come from the country.'

Question, answer, fullstop. I tried again. Henry was near us, a bottle in his hand.

I said, 'What makes a girl like you come to a place like this?' And, really, I was ashamed of the words almost before I said them.

'That's what I call a vicious question,' Henry said.

At the same time Selma slapped me.

'You think that's a nice question?' Henry said. 'I think that's a vicious question. I think that's obscene.' He pointed through the open doorway to a little sign in one of the inner rooms: Be obscene but not heard. 'It's not something we talk about.'

'I am sorry.'

'It's not for me that I am worried,' he said. 'It's for Selma. I don't know, but that girl always bringing out the vice in people. She bring out the vice in Blackwhite across the road. Don't say anything, but I see it in his eye: he want to reform her. And you know what reform is? Reform mean: keep off, for me alone. She bring out the vice in Priest. He don't want to reform. He just want. Look, Frankie, one set of people come here and then too another set come here. Selma is a educated girl, you know. Cambridge Junior Certificate. Latin and French and geometry and all that sort of thing. She does work in one of the big stores. Not one of those little Syrian shops, you know. She come here every now and then, you come here. That is life. Let us leave the vice outside, let us leave the vice outside. A lot of these girls work in stores. Any time I want a shirt, I just pass around these stores, and these girls give me shirts. We have to help one another.'

I said, 'You must have a lot of shirts.'

'Yes, I have a lot of shirts. Look, I will tell you. Selma and one or two of the other people you see here, we call *wabeen*.'

'Wabeen?'

'One of our freshwater fish. A lil loose. A *lil*. Not for any and everybody. You understand? Wabeen is not *spote*.'

'Spote?'

'Spote is—don't make me use obscene language, man, Frank. Spote is what you see.' He waved his hands about the yard.

The steel-bands sounded nearer, and then through a gate in the corrugated iron fence at the back of the lot the musicians came in. Their instruments were made out of old dustbins, and on these instruments they played a coarse music I had never heard before.

'They have to hide, you know,' Henry told me. 'It's illegal. The war and so on. Helping the war effort.'

There was a little open shed at the back. It had a blackboard. I had noticed that blackboard and wondered about it. In this shed two or three people now began to dance. They drew watchers to them; they converted watchers into participants. From rooms in the houses on Henry's lot, from rooms in other back-yards, and from the sewerage trace at the back, people drifted in steadily to watch. Each dancer was on his own. Each dancer lived with a private frenzy. Women among the watchers tore twigs from the hibiscus hedges and from time to time, as though offering benediction and reward, beat the dancer's dusty feet with green leaves.

Henry put his arm over my shoulder and led me to where Selma was standing. He kept one hand on my shoulder; he put the other on her shoulder. We stood silently together, watching. His hands healed us, bound us.

A whistle blew. There were cries of 'Police!' and in an instant the yard was transformed. Dustbins appeared upright here and there; liquor bottles disappeared inside some; the dancers and the audience sat in neat rows under the shed and one man stood at the blackboard, writing. Many of Henry's girls put on spectacles. One or two carried pieces of embroidery.

It seemed to me that the police were a long time in entering. When they did, the Inspector shook Henry by the hand and said, 'The old Adult Education class, eh?'

'As you see,' Henry said. 'Each one teach one.'

The Inspector closed his fingers when he took away his hand from Henry's. He became chatty. 'I don't know, boy,' he said. 'We just have to do this. Old Blackwhite really on your tail. And that Mrs Lambert, she too lodge a complaint.'

*

I wonder, though, whether I would have become involved with Selma and the others, if, during that first evening after I had undressed and was lying with Selma, I hadn't seen my clothes dancing out of the window. They danced; it was as though they had taken on a life of their own.

I called out to Selma.

She didn't seem surprised. She said, 'I think they are fishing tonight.'

'Fishing?' I ran to the window after my disappearing clothes.

'Yes, you know, fishing through the windows. Lifting a shirt here, a pair of trousers there. It is no good chasing them. Carnival coming, you know, and everybody wants a pretty costume.'

She was right. In the morning I woke up and remembered that I had no clothes except for my pants and vest. I threw open the back window and saw naked Americans hanging out of windows. We looked at one another. We exchanged no words. The evening was past; this was the morning.

Boys and girls were going to Mr Blackwhite's college. Some stopped to examine contraceptives thrown into the gutters. Selma herself was fully dressed when I saw her. She said she was going to work. So it seemed after all that Henry's story about some of his girls working in stores was right. Henry himself brought me a cup of coffee.

'You can have one of my shirts. I just pass around and ask them for one, you know.'

The morning life of Henry's yard was different from the evening life. There was a subdued workaday bustle everywhere. A tall thin man was doing limbering-up exercises. He wore a vest and a pair of shorts, and from time to time he rubbed himself with oil from a little phial.

'Canadian Healing Oil,' Henry said. 'I like to give him a little encouragement. Mano is a walker, you know. But a little too impatient; he does always end up by running and getting disqualified.'

'This is terrible,' I said. 'But what about my clothes?'

'You've got to learn tolerance. This is the one thing you have got to learn on the island.'

Mano was squatting and springing up. All about him coalpots were being fanned on back steps and women were preparing morning meals. A lot of green everywhere, more than I had remembered. Beyond the sewerage trace I could see the equally forested backyards of the houses of the other street, and it was in some of these yards that I saw khaki uniforms and white sailor uniforms hanging limp from lines.

Henry followed my eyes. 'Carnival coming, Frank. And you people got the whole world. Some people corporate in one way, some in another.'

I didn't want Henry's philosophy just then. I ran out as I was on to the pavement. By the standards of the street I wasn't too badly dressed in my vest and pants. Next door an old negro sat sunning himself in the doorway of a room which looked like a declining secondhand bookshop. He was dressed in a tight-fitting khaki suit. The open door carried on its inside a flowery sign—MR W. LAMBERT, BOOKBINDER—so that I understood how, with the front door closed, the house was the respectable shuttered residence I had seen the day before, and how now, with the front door open, it was a shop. Beside Mr Lambert—I thought it safe to assume that he was Mr Lambert—was a small glass of rum. As I passed him he lifted the glass against the light, squinted at it, nodded to me and said, 'Good morning, my Yankee friend, may God all blessings to you send.' Then he drank the rum at a gulp and the look of delight on his face was replaced by one of total torment, as though the rum and the morning greeting formed part of an obnoxious daily penance.

'Good morning.'

'If it is not being rude, tell me, my good sir, why you are nude.'

'I don't have any clothes.'

'Touché, I say. Naked we come, and naked go away.'

This was interesting and worth exploring but just then at the end of the road I saw the jeep. I didn't know what the punishment was for losing your uniform and appearing naked in public. I ran back past Mr Lambert. He looked a little startled, like a man seeing visions. I ran into the side of Henry's yard and went up to the front house by the back steps. At the same time Mano, the walker, began walking briskly out from the other side of the house into the road.

I heard someone say from the jeep, 'Doesn't it look to you that he went in white and came out black?'

A window opened in the next room and an American voice called out, 'Did you see a naked white man running down here this morning, a few minutes ago?'

A woman's voice said, 'Look, mister, the morning is my period of rest, and the last thing I want to see in the morning is a prick.'

A pause, and the SPs drove off.

For me there remained the problem of clothing. Henry offered to lend me some of his. They didn't exactly fit. 'But,' he said, 'you could pass around by Selma's store and get a shirt. Look, I'll give you the address.'

A bicycle bell rang from the road. It was the postman in his uniform.

'Henry, Henry,' he said. 'Look what I bringing today.'

He came inside and showed a parcel. It was for Mr Blackwhite and had been sent to him from a publisher in the United States.

'Another one come back, another one.'

'O my God!' Henry said. 'I'm going to have Blackwhite crying on my hands again. What was this one about?'

'Usual thing,' the postman said. 'Love. I had a good little read. In fact, it was funny in parts.' He pulled out the manuscript. 'You want to hear?'

Henry looked at me.

'I am a captive audience,' I said.

'Make yourself comfortable,' the postman said. He began to read: '"Lady Theresa Phillips was the most sought-after girl in all the county of Shropshire. Beautiful, an heiress to boot, intelligent, well-versed in the classics, skilful in repartee and with the embroidery needle, superbly endowed in short, she had but one failing, that of pride. She spurned all who wooed her. She had sent frustrated lovers to Italy, to the distant colonies, there to pine away in energetic solitude. Yet Nemesis was at hand. At a ball given by Lord Severn, the noblest lord in the land, Lady Theresa met Lord Alistair Grant. He was tall, square-shouldered and handsome, with melancholy eyes that spoke of deep suffering; he had in fact been left an orphan."'

'Christ! Is this what he always writes about?'

'All the time,' Henry said. 'Only lords and ladies. Typing like a madman all day. And Sundays especially you hear that machine going.'

The front door was open and through it now came the voice of Mr Blackwhite. 'Henry, I have seen everything this morning, and Mrs Lambert has just been to see me. I shall be typing out a letter to the newspapers. I just can't have naked men running about my street.' He caught sight of the postman and caught sight of the manuscript in the postman's hand. His face fell. He raced up the concrete steps into the room and snatched the manuscript away. 'Albert, I've told you before. You must stop this tampering with His Majesty's mail. It is the sort of thing they chop off your head for.'

'They send it back, old man,' Henry said. 'If you ask me, Blackwhite, I think it's just a case of prejudice. Open-and-shut case. I sit down quiet-quiet and listen to what Albert read out, and it was really nice. It was really nice.'

Blackwhite softened. 'You really think so, Henry?'

'Yes, man, it was really nice. I can't wait to hear what happen to Lady Theresa Phillips.'

'No. You are lying, you are lying.'

'What happened in the end, Mr Blackwhite?' I slapped at an ant on my leg.

'You just scratch yourself and keep quiet,' he said to me. 'I hate you. I don't believe you can even read. You think that black people don't write, eh?'

Albert the postman said, 'It was a real nice story, Blackwhite. And I prophesy, boy, that one day all those white people who now sending back your books going to be coming here and begging you to write for them.'

'Let them beg, let them beg. I won't write for them when they beg. Oh, my God. All that worrying, all that typing. Not going to write a single line more. Not a blasted line.' He grew wild again. 'I hate you, Henry, too. I am going to have this place closed, if it's the last thing I do.'

Henry threw up his hands.

'To hell with you,' Blackwhite said. 'To hell with Lady Theresa Phillips.' To me he said pointing, 'You don't like me.' And then to Henry: 'And you don't like me either. Henry, I don't know how a man could change like you. At one time it was always Niya Binghi and death to the whites. Now you could just wrap yourself in the Stars and Stripes and parade the streets.'

'Niya Binghi?' I asked.

'Was during the Abyssinian War,' Henry said, 'and the old queen did just die. Death to the whites. Twenty million on the march. You know our black people. The great revenge. Twenty million on the march. And always when you look back, is you alone. Nobody behind you. But the Stars and Stripes,' he added. 'You know, Black-white, I believe you have an idea there. Good idea for Carnival. Me as sort of Uncle Sam. Gentleman, it have such a thing as Stars and Stripes at the base?'

'Oh, he's one of those, is he?' Blackwhite said. 'One of our American merchantmen?'

'I believe I can get you a Stars and Stripes,' I said.

Blackwhite went silent. I could see he was intrigued. His aggressiveness when he spoke wasn't very convincing. 'I suppose that you people have the biggest typewriters in the world, as you have the biggest everything else?'

'It's too early in the morning for obscene language,' Henry said.

'I am not boasting,' I said. 'But I am always interested in writing and writers. Tell me, Mr Blackwhite, do you work regularly, or do you wait for inspiration?'

The question pleased him. He said, 'It is a mixture of both, a mixture of both.'

'Do you write it out all in longhand, or do you use a typewriter?'

'On the typewriter. But I am not being bribed, remember. I am not being bribed. But if the naked gentleman is interested in our native customs and local festivals, I am prepared to listen.' His manner changed. 'Tell me, man, you have a little pattern book of uniforms? I don't want to appear in any and every sort of costume at Carnival, you know.'

'Some of those costumes can be expensive,' I said.

'Money, money,' Blackwhite said. 'It had to come up. But of course I will pay.'

*

This was how it started; this was how I began to be a purveyor of naval supplies. First to Mr Henry and to Mr Blackwhite and then to the street. I brought uniforms; money changed hands. I brought steel drums; money changed hands. I brought cartons of cigarettes and chewing gum; money changed hands. I brought a couple of Underwood standard typewriters. Money didn't change hands.

Blackwhite said, 'Frankie, I think art ought to be its own reward.'

It wasn't though. A new line went up on Blackwhite's board:

ALSO TYPING LESSONS

'Also typing lessons, Blackwhite?'

'Also typing lessons. Black people don't type?'

This had become his joke. We were in his room. His walls were hung with coloured drawings of the English countryside in spring. There were many of these, but they were not as numerous as the photographs of himself, in black and white, in sepia, in coarse colour. He had an especially large photograph of himself between smaller ones of Churchill and Roosevelt.

'The trouble, you know, Blackwhite,' I said, 'is that you are not black at all.'

'What do you mean?'

'You are terribly white.'

'God, I am not going to be insulted by a beachcomber.'

'Beachcomber. That's very good. But you are not only white. You are English. All those lords and ladies, Blackwhite. All that Jane Austen.'

'What's wrong with that? Why should I deny myself any aspect of the world?'

'Rubbish. I was wondering, though, whether you couldn't start writing about the island. Writing about Selma and Mano and Henry and the others.'

'But you think they will want to read about these people? These people don't exist, you know. This is just an interlude for you, Frankie. This is your little Greenwich Village. I know, I can read. Bam bam, bram, bram. Fun. Afterwards you leave us and go back. This place, I tell you, is nowhere. It doesn't exist. People are just born here. They all want to go away, and for you it is only a holiday. I don't want to be any part of your Greenwich Village. You beachcomb, you buy sympathy. The big rich man always behind the love, the I-am-just-like-you. I have been listening to you talking to people in Henry's yard about the States; about the big cinemas with wide screens and refrigerators as big as houses and everybody becoming film stars and presidents. And you are damn frightened of the whole thing. Always ready for the injection of rum, always looking for the nice and simple natives to pick you up.'

It was so. We turn experience continually into stories to lend drama to dullness, to maintain our self-respect. But we never see ourselves; only occasionally do we get an undistorted reflection. He was right. I was buying sympathy, I was buying fellowship. And I knew, better than he had said, the fraudulence of my position in the street.

He pointed to Churchill on the wall. 'What do you think would have happened to him if he was born here?'

'Hold your head that way, Blackwhite. Yes, definitely Churchillian.'

'Funny. You think we would have been hearing about him today? He would have been working in a bank. He would have been in the civil service. He would have been importing sewing machines and exporting cocoa.'

I studied the photograph.

'You like this street. You like those boys in the back-yard beating the pans. You like Selma who has nowhere to go, poor little wabeen. Big thing, big love. But she is only a wabeen and you are going back, and neither of you is fooling the other. You like Mr Lambert sitting on the steps drinking his one glass of rum in the morning and tacking up a few ledgers. Because Mr Lambert can only drink one glass of rum in the morning and tack up a few ledgers. You like seeing Mano practising for the walking race that is never going to come off. You look at these things and you say, "How nice, how quaint, this is what life should be." You don't see that we here are all mad and we are getting madder all the time, turning life into a Carnival.'

And Carnival came.

It had been permitted that year under stringent police supervision. The men from the yards near Henry's made up their bands in the uniforms I had provided; and paraded through the streets. Henry was Uncle Sam; Selma was the Empress Theodora; the other girls were slave girls and concubines. There were marines and infantrymen and airforce pilots on the Pacific atolls; and in a jeep with which I had provided him stood Mr Blackwhite. He stood still, dressed in a fantastically braided uniform. He wore dark glasses, smoked a corn-cob pipe and his left hand was held aloft in a salute which was like a benediction. He did not dance, he did not sway to the music. He was MacArthur, promising to return.

On the Tuesday evening, when the streets were full of great fig-ures—Napoleon, Julius Caesar, Richard the Lionheart: men parad-ing with concentration—Blackwhite was also abroad, dressed like Shakespeare.

*

Selma and I settled down into a relationship which was only occa-sionally stormy. I had taken Mr Henry's advice that first morning and had gone around to the store where she worked. She did not acknowledge me. My rough clothes, which were really Henry's, attracted a good deal of critical attention and much critical comment on the behaviour of Americans. She acknowledged me later: she was pleased that I had gone to see her in a period as cool and disenchanted as the morning after.

Henry's, as I said, seemed to have its own especial rules. It was a club, a meeting-place, a haven, a place of assignation. It attracted all sorts. Selma belonged to the type of island girl who moved from relationship to relationship, from man to man. She feared marriage because marriage, for a girl of the people, was full of perils and quick degradation. She felt that once she surrendered completely to any one man, she lost her hold on him, and her beauty was useless, a wasted gift.

She said, 'Sometimes when I am walking I look at these *warra-hoons,* and I think that for some little girl somewhere this animal is lord and master. *He. He* doesn't like cornflakes. *He* doesn't like rum. *He* this, *he* that.'

Her job in the store and Henry's protection gave her independence. She did not wish to lose this; she never fell for glamour. She was full of tales of girls she had known who had broken the code of their group and actually married visitors; and then had led dreadful lives, denied both the freedom they had had and the respectability, the freedom from struggle, which marriage ought to have brought.

So we settled down, after making a little pact.

'Remember,' she said, 'you are free and I am free. I am free to do exactly what I want, and you are free too.'

The pressing had always been mine. It wasn't an easy pact. I knew that this freedom might at any time embrace either Blackwhite, shy reformer in the background, or the white-robed preacher whom we called Priest. They both continued to make their interest in her plain.

But in the beginning it was not from these men that we found opposition after we had settled down in one of the smaller jalousied houses in the street—and in those days it was possible to buy a house for fifteen hundred dollars. No, it was not from these men that there was opposition, but from Mrs Lambert, Henry's neighbour, the wife of the man in the khaki suit who sipped the glass of rum in the mornings and spoke in rhyme to express either delight or pain.

Now Mrs Lambert was a surprise. I had seen her in the street for some time without connecting her with Mr Lambert. Mr Lambert was black and Mrs Lambert was white. She was about fifty and she had the manners of the street. It was my own fault, in a way, that I had attracted her hostility. I had put money in the Lamberts' way and had given them, too late in life, a position to keep up or to lose.

Mr Lambert had been excited by the boom conditions that had begun to prevail in the street. The words were Ma-Ho's, he who ran the grocery at the corner. Ma-Ho had begun to alter and extend his establishment to include a café where many men from the base and many locals sat on high stools and ate hot dogs and drank Coca-Colas, and where the children from several streets around congregated, waiting to be treated.

'Offhand,' Ma-Ho said, for he was fond of talking, 'I would say, boom.' And the words 'offhand' and 'boom' were the only really distinct ones. He began every sentence with 'offhand'; what followed was very hard to understand. Yet he was always engaged in conversation with some captive customer.

The walls of his grocery carried pictures of Chiang Kai-shek and Madame Chiang. They also had pictorial calendars, several years out of date, with delicately tinted Chinese beauties languid or coy against a background of ordered rocks and cultivated weeds, picturesque birds and waterfalls which poured like oil: incongruous in the shop with its chipped grimy counter, its open sacks of flour, its khaki-coloured sacks of sugar, its open tins of red, liquid butter. These pictures were like a longing for another world; and indeed, Ma-Ho did not plan to stay on the island. When you asked him, making conversation, especially on those occasions when you were short of change and wanted a little trust from him, 'You still going back?' the answer was: 'Offhand, I say two-four years.'

His children remained distinctive, and separate from the life of the street: a small neat crocodile, each child armed with neat bags and neat pencil boxes, going coolly off to school in the morning and returning just as coolly in the afternoon, as though nothing had touched them during the whole day, or caused them to be sullied. In the morning the back door of his shop opened to let out these children; in the afternoon the back door opened to swallow them in again; and nothing more was heard from them, and nothing more was seen of them.

The boom touched Ma-Ho. It touched Mrs Lambert. Mr Lambert called very formally one evening in his khaki suit and put a proposal to me.

'I don't want to see you get into trouble,' he said. 'Mrs Lambert and I have been talking things over, and we feel you are running an unnecessary risk in bringing these—what should I say?—these supplies to the needy of our poor island.'

I said, 'It's worked quite all right so far. You should see all the stuff we throw away.'

'Now don't misunderstand,' he said. 'I am not blaming you for what you are doing. But Mrs Lambert is particularly concerned about the trucks. She feels that by having them come out with these supplies and then having them go back, there is a chance of them being checked twice.'

'I see what you mean. Thanks, Mr Lambert. You mean that Mrs Lambert thinks that perhaps a truck might just slip out of the base and stay out?'

'Mrs Lambert thought it might be safer. Mrs Lambert has a relation who knows all there is to be known about trucks and motor vehicles generally.'

I said nothing just then, thinking of the possibilities.

Mr Lambert's manner broke up. It became familiar. All the people in the street had two sets of manners, one extremely formal, one rallying and casual.

'Look,' Mr Lambert said. 'The truck go back to the base, they start one set of questioning. It stay out here, ten to one they forget all about it. You people own the whole world.'

So into Mr Lambert's yard a truck one day rolled; and when, a fortnight or so later, it rolled out again, it was scarcely recognizable.

'Lend-lease, lease-lend,' Mr Lambert said with pure delight. 'The trend, my friend.'

And it was this truck that the Lamberts hired out to the contractors on the base. The contractors provided a driver and were willing—in fact, anxious—for the truck to work two shifts a day.

'We are getting twenty dollars a day,' Mr Lambert said. 'My friend, what luck! What luck you've given with a simple truck!'

Part of this luck, needless to say, I shared.

Yet all this while Mrs Lambert remained in the background. She was a figure in a curtained window; she was someone walking briskly down the street. She was never someone you exchanged words with. She never became part of the life of the street.

'That is one person whose old age you spoil,' Henry said. 'You see? She behaving as though they *buy* that truck. I don't think this is going to end good.'

Twenty dollars a day, minus commission and gasoline. The money was piling up; and then one day we saw a whole group of workmen around the Lamberts' house, like ants around a dead cockroach. The street came out to watch. The house, small and wooden, was lifted off its pillars by the workmen. The front door with the sign 'Mr W. Lambert, Bookbinder' swung open and kept on flapping while the house was taken to the back of the lot, to rest not on pillars but flat on the ground. The workmen drank glasses of rum to celebrate. The street cheered. But then we saw Mr Lambert pushing his way through the crowd. He looked like a man expecting news of death. He saw the pillars; he saw his house on the ground; and he said: 'My house! My house brought low! But I did not want a bungalow. Here the old pillars stand, in the middle of naked land.' He left and went to Ma-Ho's. He became drunk; he addressed verse to everyone. The habit grew on him. It seemed to us that he remained drunk until he died.

Henry said, 'Once upon a time—and really now it sounded like a fairy tale—once upon a time Mrs Lambert was a very poor girl. Family from Corsica. Living up there in the cocoa valleys with the tall *immortelle* trees. Times was hard. You couldn't even give away cocoa. And Lambert had this job in the Civil Service. Messenger. Uniform, regular pay, the old pension at the end, and nobody sacking you. Marriage up there in the hills with the bush and red *immortelle* flowers. Oh, happy! Once-upon-a-time fairy tale. Wuthering Heights. Hansel and Gretel in the witch-broom cocoa woods. Then the world sort of catch up with them.'

The pillars were knocked down, and where the old wooden house stood there presently began to rise a house of patterned concrete blocks. The house, I could see, was going to be like hundreds of others in the city: three bedrooms down one side, a veranda, drawingroom and diningroom down the other side, and a back veranda.

No longer a doorstep at which Mr Lambert could sit, greeting us in the morning with his glass of rum. The old wooden house was sold, for the materials; frame by frame, jalousie by jalousie, the house was dismantled and reerected far away by the man who had bought it, somewhere in the country. And then there was no longer a Mr Lambert in the morning. He left the yard early. In his khaki suit he was like a workman hurrying off to a full day. We often saw him walking with Mano. Mano, the walker in Henry's yard, who after his morning's exercise put on his khaki messenger's uniform and walked to the government office where he worked. Their dress was alike, but they were an ill-assorted pair, Mano lean and athletic, Mr Lambert even at that early hour shambling drunk.

Mr Lambert had a sideline. At sports meetings, on race days, at cricket and football matches, he ran a stall. He sold a vile sweet liquid of his own manufacture. On these occasions he appeared, not with his cork hat, but with a handkerchief knotted around his head. He rang a bell and sang his sales rhymes, which were often pure gibberish. 'Neighbour! Neighbour! Where are you? Here I am! Rat-tat-too.' Sometimes he would point to the poisonous tub in which hunks of ice floated in red liquid, and sing: 'Walk in! Jump in! Run in! Hop in! Flop in! Leap in! Creep in!'

This was the Mr Lambert of happier days. Now, after the degradation of his house, it seemed that he had given up his stall. But he had grown friendly with Mano and this friendship led him to announce that he was going to the sports meeting in which Mano was to take part.

Henry said, 'Mrs Lambert doesn't like it. She feel that this old black man hopping around with a handkerchief on his head and ringing his bell is a sort of low-rating, especially now that she building this new house. And she say that if he go and ring that bell any more she finish with him. She not going to let him set foot in the new house.'

So we were concerned about both Mr Lambert and Mano. We often went in the afternoons to the great park to cycle around with Mano as he walked, to help him to fight the impatience that made him run in walking races and get disqualified.

Henry said, 'Frankie, I think you trying too hard with Mano. You should watch it. You see what happen to Mrs Lambert. You know, I don't think people want to do what they say they want to do. I think we always make a lot of trouble for people by helping them to get what they say they want to get. Some people look at black people and only see black. You look at poor people and you only see poor. You think the only thing they want is money. All-you wrong, you know.'

One day while we were coming back in procession from the park, Mano pumping away beside us past the crocodile of Ma-Ho's children, we were horrified to see Mr Lambert stretched out on the pavement like a dead man. He was not dead; that was a relief. He was simply drunk, very complicatedly drunk. Selma ran to Mrs Lambert and brought back a cool message: 'Mrs Lambert says we are not to worry our heads with that good-for-nothing idler.'

Henry said, 'We are not doing Lambert any good by being so friendly with him. Mrs Lambert, I would say, is hostile to us all, definitely hostile.'

Mr Lambert at this stage revived a little and said, 'They say I am black. But black I am not. I tell you, good sirs, I am a Scot.'

Henry said, 'Is not so funny, you know. His grandfather was a big landowner, a big man. We even hear a rumour some years before the war that according to some funny law of succession Mr Lambert was the legal head of some Scottish clan.'

The house went up. The day of the sports meeting came. Mano was extremely nervous. As the time drew nearer he even began to look frightened. This was puzzling, because I had always thought him quite withdrawn, indifferent to success, failure or encouragement.

Henry said, 'You know, Mano never read the papers. On the road yesterday some crazy thing make him take up the evening paper and he look at the horoscope and he read: "You will be exalted today."'

'But that's nice,' I said.

'It get him frightened. Was a damn funny word for the paper to use. It make Mano think of God and the old keys of the kingdom.'

Mano was very frightened when we started for the sports

ground. There was no sign in the street of Mr Lambert and we felt that he had in the end been scared off by Mrs Lambert and that to save face he had gone away for a little. But at the sports ground, after the meeting had begun and Mano was started on his walk—it was a long walk, and you must picture it going on and on, with lots of other sporting activities taking place at the same time, each activity unrelated to any other, creating a total effect of a futile multifarious frenzy—it was when Mano was well on his walk that we heard the bell begin to ring. To us it rang like doom.

'Mano will not run today, Mano will walk to heaven today.'

Exaltation was not in Mr Lambert's face alone or in his bell or in his words. It was also in his dress.

'On me some alien blood has spilt. I make a final statement, I wear a kilt.' And then came all his old rhymes.

And Mano didn't run. He walked and won. And Mr Lambert rang his bell and chanted: 'Mano will not run today. He will walk into the arms of his Lord today.'

We had worked for Mano's victory. Now that it had come it seemed unnatural. He himself was like a stunned man. He rejected congratulations. We offered him none. When we looked for Mr Lambert we couldn't find him. And with a sense of a double and deep unsettling of what was fixed and right, we walked home. We had a party. It turned into more than a party. We did not notice when Mano left us.

Later that night we found Mr Lambert drunk and sprawling on the pavement.

He said, 'I led her up from the gutter. I gave her bread. I gave her butter. And this is how she pays me back. White is white and black is black.'

We took him to his house. Henry went to see Mrs Lambert. It was no use. She refused to take him in. She refused to come out to him.

'To my own house I have no entrance. Come, friends, all on my grave dance.'

*

We had a double funeral the next day. Mano had done what so many others on the island had done. He had gone out swimming, far into the blue waters, beyond the possibility of return.

'You know,' Henry said, as we walked to the cemetery, 'the trouble with Mano was that he never had courage. He didn't want to be a walker. He really wanted to be a runner. But he didn't have the courage. So when he won the walking race, he went and drowned himself.'

Albert the postman was in our funeral procession. He said, 'News, Frankie. They send back another one of Blackwhite's books.'

Blackwhite heard. He said to me, 'Was your fault. You made me start writing about all *this*. Oh, I feel degraded. Who wants to read about this place?'

I said, 'Once you were all white, and that wasn't true. Now you are trying to be all black and that isn't true either. You are really a shade of grey, Blackwhite.'

'Hooray for me, to use one of your expressions. This place is nowhere. It is a place where everyone comes to die. But I am not like Mano. You are not going to kill me.'

'Blackwhite, you old virgin, I love you.'

'Virgin? How do you know?'

'We are birds of a feather.'

'Frankie, why do you drink? It's only a craving for sugar.'

And I said to him: 'Dickie-bird, why do you weep? Sugar, sugar. A lovely word, sugar. I love its sweetness on my breath. I love its sweetness seeping through my skin.'

And in the funeral procession, which dislocated traffic and drew doffed hats and grave faces from passers-by, I wept for Mano and Lambert and myself, wept for my love of sugar; and Blackwhite wept for the same things and for his virginity. We walked side by side.

*

Selma said Henry was right. 'I don't think you should go around interfering any more in other people's lives. People don't really want what you think they want.'

'Right,' I said. 'From now on we will just live quietly.'

Quietly. It was a word with so many meanings. The quietness of the morning after, for instance, the spectacles on my nose, quiet in an abstemious corner. I was a character now. I had licence. Sugar sweetened me. In Henry's yard, in Selma's house, and on the sands of the desolate bay over the hills, the healing bay where the people of the island sought privacy from joy and grief.

Priest's denunciations of us, of me, grew fiercer. And Blackwhite, seen through the flapping curtain of his front room, pounded away at his typewriter in sympathetic rage.

Then one blurred aching morning I found on the front step a small coffin, and in the coffin a mutilated sailor doll and a toy wreath of rice fern.

They came around to look.

'Primitive,' Blackwhite said. 'Disgusting. A disgrace to us.'

'This is Priest work,' Henry said.

'I have been telling you to insure me,' Selma said.

'What, is that his game?'

Henry said, 'Priest does take his work seriously. The only thing is, I wish I know what his work is. I don't know whether it is preaching, or whether it is selling insurance. I don't think he know either. For him the two seem to come together.'

To tell the truth, the coffins on Selma's doorstep worried me. They kept on appearing and I didn't know what to do. Selma became more and more nervous. At one moment she suggested I should take her away; at another moment she said that I myself should go away. She also suggested that I should try to appease Priest by buying some insurance.

'Appease Priest? The words don't sound right. Henry, you hear?'

Henry said, 'I will tell you about this insurance. I don't know how it happen on the island, but it becoming a social thing, you know. Like having a shower, like taking schooling, like getting married. If you not insured these days you can't hold up your head at all. Everybody feel you poor as a church rat. But look. The man coming himself.'

It was Priest, wearing a suit and looking very gay and not at all malevolent.

'Dropping in for a little celebration,' he said.

Selma was awed, and it was hard to say whether it was because of Priest's suit, the coffins, or his grand manner.

'What are you celebrating?' I said. 'A funeral?'

He wasn't put out. 'New job, Frankie, new job. More money, you know. Higher commission, bigger salary. Frankie, where you say you living in the States? Well, look out for me. I might be going up there any day. So the bosses say.'

I said, 'I'd love to have you.'

'You know,' he said, 'how in this insurance business I have this marvellous record. But these local people'—and here he threw up his beard, scratched under his chin, screwed up his eyes—'but these local people, you know how mean they is with the money. Then this new company come down, you know, and they get to know about me. I didn't go to see them. They send for me. And when I went to see them they treat me as a God, you know. And a damn lot of them was white to boot. You know, man, I was like—what I can say?—I was like a *playboy* in that crowd, a playboy And look how the luck still with me, look how the luck still in my hand. You know what I come in here to celebrate especially? You know how for years I begging Ma-Ho to take out insurance. And you know how he, Ma-Ho, don't want to take out no insurance. He just saying he want to go back to China, back to the old wan-ton soup and Chiang Kai-shek. Well, he insured as from today.'

Henry said, 'He pass his medical?'

I said, 'Offhand, that man looks damn sick to me, you know.'

'He pass his medical,' Priest said.

'He went to the doctor?' Henry asked. 'Or the doctor went to him?'

'What you worrying with these *details?* You know these Chinese people. Put them in their little shop and they stay there until kingdom come. Is a healthy life, you know.'

Henry said, 'Ma-Ho tell me one day that when he come to the island in 1920 and the ship stop in the bay and he look out and he see only mangrove, he started to cry.'

Selma said, 'I can't imagine Ma-Ho crying.'

Henry said, 'To me it look as though he never stop crying.'

'Offhand,' I said, 'no more coffins, eh?'

'Let me not hear of death,' Priest said in his preaching manner. He burst out laughing and slapped me on the back.

And, indeed, no more coffins and dead sailors and toy wreaths appeared on Selma's steps.

I knocked on Selma's door one day two weeks later. 'Any coffins today, Ma'am?'

'Not today, thank you.'

Selma had become houseproud. The little house glittered and smelt of all sorts of polishes. There were pictures in passe-partout frames on the walls and potted ferns in brass vases on the marble-topped three-legged tables for which she had a passion. That day she had something new to show me: a marble-topped dresser with a clay basin and ewer.

'Do you like it?'

'It's lovely. But do you really need it?'

'I always wanted one. My aunt always had one. I don't want to use it. I just want to look at it.'

'Fine.' And after a while I said, 'What are you going to do?'

'What do you mean?'

'Well, the war's not going to go on for ever. I can't stay here for ever.'

'Well, it's as Blackwhite says. You are going to go back, we are going to stay here. Don't weep for me, and'—she waved around at all the little possessions in her room—'and I won't weep for you. No. That's not right. Let's weep a little.'

'I feel,' I said, 'that you are falling for old Blackwhite. He's talked you round, Selma. Let me warn you. He's no good. He's a virgin. Such men are dangerous.'

'Not Blackwhite. To tell you the truth, he frightens me a little.'

'More than Priest?'

'I am not frightened of Priest at all,' she said. 'You know, I always feel Priest handles the language like a scholar and gentleman.'

I was at the window. 'I wonder what you will say now.'

Priest was running down the street in his suit and howling: 'All-you listen, all-you listen. Ma-Ho dead, Ma-Ho dead.'

And from houses came the answering chant. 'Who dead?'

'Ma-Ho dead.'

'The man was good. Good, good.'

'Who?'

'Ma-Ho.'

'I don't mean he was not bad. I mean,' Priest said, subsiding into personal grief, 'I mean he was well. He was strong. He was healthy. And now, and now, he dead.'

'Who dead?'

'Ma-Ho. I not crying because I blot my book in my new job. I not crying because this is the first time I sell insurance to someone who dead on my hands. I not crying because those white people did much me up when I get this new job.'

'But, Priest, it look so.'

'It look so, but it wrong. O my brothers, do not misunderstand. I cry for the man.'

'What man?'

'Ma-Ho.'

'He did want to go back.'

'Where?'

'China.'

'China?'

'China.'

'Poor Ma-Ho.'

'You know he have those Chinese pictures in the back-room behind the shop.'

'And plenty children.'

'And you know how nice the man was.'

'The man was nice.'

'You go to Ma-Ho and ask for a cent red butter. And he give you a big lump.'

'And a chunk of lard with it.'

'And he was always ready to give a little trust.'

'A little trust.'

'Now he dead.'

'Dead.'

'He not going to give any lard again.'

'No lard.'

'He not going to China again.'

'Dead.'

Through the roused street Priest went, howling from man to man, from woman to woman. And that evening under the eaves of Ma-Ho's shop, before the closed doors, he delivered a tremendous funeral oration. And his six little girls sang hymns. Afterwards he came in, sad and sobered, to Henry's and began to drink beer.

Henry said, 'To tell you the truth, Priest, I was shocked when I hear you sell Ma-Ho insurance. Is a wonder you didn't know the man had diabetes. But with all these coffins all over the place, I didn't think it was any of my business. So I just keep my mouth shut. I ain't say nothing. I always say everybody know their own business.'

'Diabetes?' Priest said, almost dipping his beard into his beer. 'But the doctor pass him in everything.' He made circular gestures with his right hand. 'The doctor give him a test and everything was correct. Everything get test. The man was good, good, good, I tell

[513]

you. He was small, but all of all-you used to see him lifting those heavy sugar bags and flour bags over the counter.'

Henry asked, 'You did test his pee?'

'It was good. It was damned good pee.' Priest wept a little. 'You know how those Chinese people neat. He went into the little back-room with all those children, and he bring out a little bottle—a little Canadian Healing Oil bottle.' Still weeping, he indicated with his thumb and finger the size of the bottle.

'Was not his pee,' Henry said. 'That was why he didn't want to *go* to the doctor. That was why he wanted the doctor to come to *him*.'

'O God!' Priest said. 'O God! The Chinese bitch. He make me lose my bonus. And you, Henry. You black like me and you didn't tell me nothing. You see,' he said to the room, 'why black people don't progress in this place. No corporation.'

'Some people corporate in one way,' Henry said. 'Some people corporate in another way.'

'Priest,' I said, 'I want you to insure Selma for me.'

'No,' Selma said nervously. 'I don't want Priest to insure me. I feel the man blight.'

'Do not mock the fallen,' Priest said. 'Do not mock the fallen. I will leave. I will move to another part of the city. I will fade away. But not for long.'

And he did move to another area of the city. He became a nervous man, frightened of selling insurance, instilling terror, moreover, into those to whom he tried to sell insurance: the story of Ma-Ho's sudden death got around pretty quickly.

Ma-Ho went, and with him there also went the Chinese emblems in his shop. No longer the neat crocodile left and entered the back door of the shop; and from being people who kept themselves to themselves, who gave the impression of being only temporary residents on the island, always packed for departure, Ma-Ho's family came out. The girls began to ride bicycles. The insurance money was good. The boys began to play cricket on the pavement. And Mrs Ma-

Ho, who had never spoken a word of English, revealed that she could speak the language.

'I begin to feel,' Blackwhite said, 'that I am wrong. I begin to feel that the island is just about beginning to have an existence in its own right.'

*

Our own flag was also about to go down. The war ended. And, after all these years, it seemed to end so suddenly. When the news came there was a Carnival. No need to hide now. Bands sprang out of everywhere. A song was created out of nothing: *Mary Ann*. And the local men, who had for so long seen the island taken over by others, sang, but without malice, 'Spote, spote, Yankee sufferer,' warning everyone of the local and lean times to come.

The atmosphere at Henry's subtly changed. Gradually through the boom war years there had been improvements. But now, too, the people who came changed. Officers came from the base with their wives, to look at the dancing. So did some of the island's middle class. Men with tape recorders sometimes appeared in the audience. And in the midst of this growing esteem, Henry became more and more miserable. He was a character at last, mentioned in the newspapers. The looser girls faded away; and more *wabeens* appeared, so expensive as to be indistinguishable from women doomed to marriage. Henry reported one day that one of his drummers, a man called Snake, had been seized by somebody's wife, put into a jacket and tie, and sent off to the United States to study music.

Henry, now himself increasingly clean and increasingly better shaven, was despondent. Success had come to him, and it made him frightened. And Blackwhite, who had for years said that people like Snake were letting down the island, adding to the happy-go-lucky-native idea, Blackwhite was infuriated. He used to say, 'Snake is doing a difficult thing, beating out music on dustbins. That is like cutting down a tree with a penknife and asking for applause.' Now, talking of the kidnapping of Snake, he spoke of the corruption of the island's culture.

'But you should be happy,' I said. 'Because this proves that the island exists.'

'No sooner exists,' he said, 'than we start to be destroyed. You know, I have been doing a lot of thinking. You know, Frankie, I begin to feel that what is wrong with my books is not me, but the language I use. You know, in English, black is a damn bad word. You talk of a black deed. How then can I write in this language?'

'I have told you already. You are getting too black for me.'

'What we want is our own language. I intend to write in our own language. You know this patois we have. Not English, not French, but something we have made up. This is our own. You were right. Damn those lords and ladies. Damn Jane Austen. This is ours, this is what we have to work with. And Henry, I am sure, whatever his reasons, is with me in this.'

'Yes,' Henry said. 'We must defend our culture.' And sadly regarding his new customers, he added: 'We must go back to the old days.'

On the board outside Blackwhite's house there appeared this additional line: PATOIS TAUGHT HERE.

Selma began going to the Imperial Institute to take sewing lessons. The first lessons were in hemstitching, I believe, and she was not very good. A pillowcase on which she was working progressed very slowly and grew dirtier and dirtier, so that I doubted whether in the end any washing could make it clean again. She was happy in her house, though, and was unwilling to talk about what was uppermost in my own mind: the fact that we at the base had to leave soon.

We did talk about it late one night when perhaps I was in no position to talk about anything. I had gone out alone, as I had often done. We all have our causes for irritation, and mine lay in this: that Selma refused to exercise any rights of possession over me. I was free to come and go as I wished. This had been a bad night. I could not get the key into the door; I collapsed on the steps. She let me in in the end. She was concerned and sympathetic, but not as concerned as she might have been. And yet that tiny moment of rescue stayed with me: that moment of helplessness and self-disgust and total despair at the door, which soon, to my scratchings, had miraculously opened.

We began by talking, not about my condition, but about her sewing lessons. She said, 'I will be able to earn a little money with my sewing after these lessons.'

I said, 'I can't see you earning a penny with your sewing.'

She said, 'Every evening in the country my aunt would sit down by the oil lamp and embroider. She looked very happy when she did this, very contented. And I promised myself that when I grew up I too would sit down every evening and embroider. But really I wonder, Frank, who is afraid for who.'

Again the undistorted reflection. I said, 'Selma, I don't think you have ever been nicer than you were tonight when you let me in.'

'I did nothing.'

'You were very nice.' Emotion is foolish and dangerous; the sweetness of it carried me away. 'If anyone ever hurts you, I'll kill him.'

She looked at me with amusement.

'I really will, I'll kill him.'

She began to laugh.

'Don't laugh.'

'I am not really laughing. But for this, for what you've just said, let us make a bargain. You will leave soon. But after you leave, whenever we meet again, and whatever has happened, let us make a bargain that we will spend the first night together.'

We left it at that.

So now there gathered at Henry's, more for the company than for the pleasure, and to celebrate what was changing, the four of us whose interests seemed to coincide: Henry, Blackwhite, Selma and myself. What changes, changes. We were not together for long. Strangers were appearing every day now on the street, and one day there appeared two who split us up, it seemed, forever.

We were at Henry's one day when a finely-suited middle-aged man came up hesitantly to our table and introduced himself as Mr de Ruyter of the Council for Colonial Cultures. He and Blackwhite got on well from the start. Blackwhite spoke of the need to develop the new island language. He said he had already done much work on it. He had begun to carry around with him a few duplicated sheets: a glossary of words he had made up.

'I make up new words all the time. What do you think of *squinge?* I think that's a good word.'

'A lovely word,' Mr de Ruyter said. 'What does it mean?'

'It means screwing up your eyes. Like this.'

'An excellent word,' Mr de Ruyter said.

'I visualize,' Blackwhite said, 'an institute which would dedicate itself to translating all the great books of the world into this language.'

'Tremendous job.'

'The *need* is tremendous.'

I said to Henry and Selma: 'You know, I feel that all three of us are losing Blackwhite.'

'I think you are wrong,' Mr de Ruyter said. 'This is just the sort of thing that we must encourage. We have got to move with the times.'

'One of my favourite expressions,' Blackwhite said.

Mr de Ruyter said, 'I have a proposal which I would like to put to you, though I do so with great diffidence. How would you like to go to Cambridge to do some more work on your language? Oxford of course has a greater reputation for philology but—' Mr de Ruyter laughed.

And Blackwhite laughed with him, already playing the Oxford and Cambridge game. Almost before the question had been completed I could see that he had succumbed. Still he went down fighting. 'Cambridge, Oxford? But my work is here, among my people.'

'Indeed, indeed.' Mr de Ruyter said. 'But you will see the Cam.'

'A hell of a long way to go to see a Cam,' Henry said.

'It's a river,' Mr de Ruyter said.

'Big river?' Henry said.

'In England we think big things are rather vulgar.'

'It sounds a damn small river,' Henry said.

Mr de Ruyter went on, 'You will see King's College Chapel. You will see the white cliffs of Dover.'

With every inducement Blackwhite's eyes lit up with increased wattage.

Mr de Ruyter threw some more switches. 'You will cross the Atlantic. You will sail down the Thames. You will see the Tower of London. You will see snow and ice. You will wear an overcoat. You will look good in an overcoat.'

At the same time Henry, rising slowly and furtively, began to excuse himself. He said, 'I never thought I would see this.'

At the end of the room we saw a fat and ferocious woman who was looking closely at the darkened room as though searching for someone. She was the woman whose picture Henry often showed and around whom he had been in the habit of weaving stories of romance and betrayal. Even now, in this moment of distress, he found time to say, 'She wasn't fat when I did know she.'

Success, the columns in the newspapers, had betrayed him. He got away that evening, but within a fortnight he had been recaptured, cleaned up and brought back. And now it was Mrs Henry, if she was a Mrs Henry, who ruled. She worked like a new broom in the establishment, introducing order, cleanliness, cash registers, bill-pads, advertisements in the newspapers, and a signboard: THE COCONUT GROVE—*Overseas Visitors Welcome*.

No place for us now. Change, change. It was fast and furious. Through mine-free, dangerless channels ships came from Europe and the United States to the island: some grey, some still with their wartime camouflage, but one or two already white: the first of the tourist boats.

And on the base, where before there had been stern notices about a 5 mph speed limit and about the dangers to unauthorized persons, there now appeared a sign: TO BE SOLD BY PUBLIC AUCTION.

The base was sold and a time was fixed for local possession. Until that time my authority still mattered. From house to house in the street I went. And in that no man's time—between the last Retreat and the arrival of the local buyer who had put up a new board:

To Be Erected Here Shortly
THE FLORIDA SHIRT FACTORY

—in that no man's time, at dawn, through the open unguarded gates of the base the people of the street came in and took away whatever they could carry. They took away typewriters, they took away stoves, they took away bathtubs, wash-basins, refrigerators, cabinets. They took away doors and windows and panels of wire-netting.

I saw the buildings bulldozed. I saw the quick tropical grass spreading into the cracks on the asphalted roads. I saw the flowers, the bougainvillaea, poinsettia, the hibiscus, grow straggly in the tropics we had created.

In a house stuffed with refrigerators and wash-basins and stoves and typewriters I took my leave.

'It is our way,' Selma said. 'Better this than that.' She pointed to Henry's, where Henry stood, miserable in his own doorway, Mrs Henry, you could feel, oppressive in the background. 'That is how love and the big thing always ends.'

Blackwhite was typing when I left.

3

In the doorway now stood the bouncer.

'I've been keeping my eye on you.'

'Me too. You are very pretty.'

He made a gesture.

'As pretty as a picture in a magazine. What are you advertising today? Bourbon?'

'You can't come in here.'

'No, I don't think bourbon. I think rice.'

'Even with a tie I don't think you could come in here.'

'Bourbon, rice: I'm not interested. I'm turning the page over to the funnies.'

'You can't come in here.'

'You've a nice place to break up.'

It was lush inside, like the film set of an old musical. There were waiters dressed in fancy clothes which I took to be a type of folk costume. There were tourists at candlelit tables; there was a stage with a thatched roof. And sitting at a long table in the company of some expensively-dressed elderly men was Mr Blackwhite.

'You can't come in here without a tie.'

I pulled hard at his.

A voice said, 'You better lend him yours before you hang yourself on it.'

The voice was Henry's. Poor Henry, in a suit and with a tie; his eyes red and impotent with drink; thinner than I had remembered, his face more sour.

'Henry, what have they done to you?'

'I think,' another voice said, 'I think that is a question he might more properly put to you.'

It was Blackwhite. H. J. B. White, of the tormented winking writer's-photograph face. Very ordinary now.

'I have bought *all* your books.'

'Hooray for you, as the saying was. Frank, it is awfully nice seeing you here again. But you frighten us a little.'

'You frighten me too.' I lifted my arms in mock terror. 'Oh, I am frightened of you.'

Henry said, 'Do that more often and they will get you up on the stage.' He nodded towards the back of the room.

Blackwhite gave a swift, anxious look at the room. Some tourists, among them the happy team and the embittered team of the morning, were looking at me with alarm and shame. Letting down the side.

Blackwhite said, 'I don't think you only frighten us, you know.'

I was struggling with the tie the doorman had given me. Greasy.

'Look,' I said to Henry, pointing to the doorman. 'This man hasn't got a tie. Throw him out.'

'You are in one of your moods,' Blackwhite said. 'I don't think you can see that we have moved with the times.'

'Oh, I am frightened of you.'

'Drunkard,' Blackwhite said.

'It's only sugar, remember?'

'I believe, Frank, speaking as a friend, that you want another island. Another bunch of happy-go-lucky natives.'

'So you went to Cambridge?'

'A tedious place.'

'Still, it shows.'

The band began to tune up. Blackwhite became restless, anxious to get back to his guests. 'Come, Frankie, why don't you go down to the kitchen with Henry and have a drink and talk over old times? You can see we have some very distinguished guests from various foundations tonight. Very important negotiations on hand, boy. And we mustn't give them a wrong idea of the place, must we? Don't waste your time. Take a tip. Start looking for another island.' He looked at me; he softened. 'Though I don't think there is any place for you now except home. Take him down, Henry. And Henry, look, when Pablo and those other idlers come, clean them up a little bit in the kitchen first before you send them up, eh?'

Men and women in fancy costumes which were like the waiters' costumes came out on to the stage and began doing a fancy folk dance. They symbolically picked cotton, symbolically cut cane, symbolically carried water. They squatted and swayed on the floor and moaned a dirge. From time to time a figure with a white mask over his face ran among them, cracking a whip; and they lifted their hands in pretty fear.

'You see how us niggers suffered,' Henry said, leading me to a door marked STAFF ONLY. 'Is all Blackwhite doing, you know. He say it was you who give him the idea. You make him stop writing all those books about lords and ladies in England. You ask him to write about black people. You know, Frankie, come to think of it, you did interfere a damn lot, you know. Is a wonder you didn't try to marry me off: Is a *wonder?* Is a pity. Remember what you did use to say about what you would do if you had a million dollars? What you would do for the island, for the street?'

'A million dollars.'

Footsteps behind me. I turned.

'Frankie.'

'Leonard.'

'Frankie, I am glad I found you. I was really worried about you. But goodness, isn't this a terrific place? Did you see that last dance?'

From where we were we could hear the cracking of whips, orchestrated wails, the stamp and scuttling of feet. Then it came: muted, measured applause.

'Leonard, you'd better get back,' I said. 'There are some people from various foundations upstairs who have seized Mr White. If you aren't careful you will lose him.'

'Oh, is that who they were? Thanks for telling me. I will run up straight away. I don't know how I will make myself known to him. People just don't believe me . . .'

'You will think of something. Henry, where is the telephone?'

'You still play this telephone game. One day the police are going to catch up with you.'

I dialled. The telephone rang. I waited. A booming male voice shouted, 'Frankie. Stay away.' So loud that even Henry could hear.

'Priest,' I said. 'Gary Priestland. How do you think he knew?'

Henry said, 'From the way you've been getting on, I don't imagine there is a single person in town who doesn't know. You know you broke up the British Council lecture on Shakespeare or something?'

'My God.' I remembered the room. Six people, a man in khaki trousers swinging jolly, friendly legs over a table.

'You thought it was a bar.'

'But, Henry, what's happened to the place? You mean they've actually begun to give you culture now? Shakespeare and all the rest of it?'

'They give we, we give them. A two-way process, as old Black-white always saying. And they always saying how much they have to learn from us. I don't know how the thing catch on so sudden. You see the place is like a little New York now. I imagine that's why they like it. Everybody feel at home. Ice-cubes in the fridge, and at the same time they getting the exotic old culture. The old Coconut Grove even have a board of governors. I think, you know, the next thing is they going to ask me to run for the City Council. They already make me a MBE, you know.'

'MBE?'

'Member of the Order of the British Empire. Something they give singers and people in culture. Frankie, you don't even care about the MBE. Forget the telephone. Forget Selma. Sometimes you want the world to end. You can't go back and do things again. They begin just like that, they get good. The only thing is you never know they good until they finish. I wish the hurricane would come and blow away all this. I feel the world need this sort of thing every now and then. A clean break, a fresh start. But the damn world don't end. And we don't dead at the right time.'

'What about Selma?'

'You really want to know?'

'Tell me.'

'I hear she buy a mixmaster the other day.'

'Now this is what I really call news.'

'I don't know what else to tell you. I went the other day to the

Hilton. Barbecue night. I see Selma there, picking and choosing with the rest. Everybody moving with the times, Frankie. Only you and me moving backwards.'

Mrs Henry came into the room. She didn't have to say that she didn't like me. Henry cringed.

She said, 'I don't know, Henry. Leave you in charge in front for five minutes, and the place start going to pieces. I just had to sack the doorman. He didn't have no tie or anything. And Mr White did ask you to take special care this evening.'

I fingered the doorman's tie. When Mrs Henry left Henry sprayed the door with an imaginary tommy gun. I was aware of the room. We were among flowers. Hundreds of plastic blooms.

'You looking,' Henry said. 'Is not my doing. I like a flowers, but I don't like a flowers so bad.'

The back door was pushed open again. Henry cringed, lowered his voice. But it wasn't Mrs Henry.

'I is Pablo,' an angry man said. 'What that fat woman mean, telling we to come round by the back?'

'That was no woman,' Henry said. 'That was my wife.'

Pablo was one of three angry men. Three men of the people: freshly washed hair, freshly oiled, freshly suited. They looked like triplets.

Pablo said, 'Mr White sent for us specially. He send for me. He send for he.' He pointed to one of his friends.

The friend said, 'I is Sandro.'

'He send for he.'

'I is Pedro.'

'Pablo, Sandro, Pedro,' Henry said, 'cool down.'

'Mr White won't like it,' Pablo said.

'Making guests and artisses come through the back,' said Sandro.

'When they get invite to a little supper,' said Pedro.

Henry sized them up. 'Guests and artisses. A lil supper. Well, all-you look all right, I suppose. Making, as they say, the best of a bad job. Go up. Mr White waiting for you.'

They left, mollified. Determination to deter further insult was in their walk. Henry, following them, seemed to sag.

I noticed an angry face behind the window. It was the sacked doorman. I could scarcely recognize him without his tie. He made threatening gestures; he seemed about to climb in. I straightened his tie around my collar and hurried after Henry into the main hall.

At the long table the little supper seemed about to begin. Blackwhite rose to meet Pablo, Sandro and Pedro. The three expensively-suited men with Blackwhite rose to be introduced. Leonard and Sinclair were hanging around uncertainly.

Blackwhite eyed Leonard. Leonard flinched. He saw me and ran over.

'I don't have the courage,' he whispered.

'I'll introduce you.'

I led him to the table.

'I'll introduce you,' I said again. 'Blackwhite is an old friend.'

I pulled up two chairs from another table. I put one chair on Blackwhite's right. For Leonard. One chair on Blackwhite's left. For me. Astonishment on the faces of the foundation men; anxiety on Blackwhite's; a mixture of assessment and sympathy on the faces of Pablo, Sandro and Pedro, uncomfortable among the crystal and linen, the flowers and the candles.

A waiter passed around menus. I tried to take one. He pulled it back. He looked at Blackwhite, questioning. Blackwhite looked at me. He looked down at Leonard. Leonard gave a little smile and a little wave and looked down at the table at a space between settings. He drew forks from his right and knives from his left.

'Yes,' Blackwhite said. 'I suppose. Feed them.'

They hurried up with knives and forks and spoons.

Pablo and Sandro and Pedro were lip-reading the menus.

Pablo said, 'Steak Chatto Brian for me.'

'But, sir,' the waiter said. 'That's for two.'

Pablo said, 'You didn't hear me? Chatto Brian.'

'Chatto Brian,' Sandro said.

'Chatto Brian,' Pedro said.

'Oysters,' I said. 'Fifty. No, a hundred.'

'As a starter?'

'And ender.'

'Prawns for me,' Leonard said. 'You know. Boiled. And with the shells. I like peeling them.'

'He is a great admirer of yours, Blackwhite,' I said. 'His name is Leonard. He is a patron of the arts.'

'Yes, indeed,' Leonard said. 'Mr White, this is a great pleasure. I think *Hate* is wonderful. It is—it is—a most *endearing* work.'

'It was not meant to be an endearing work,' Blackwhite said.

'Goodness, I hope I haven't said the wrong thing.'

'You can't, Leonard,' I said. 'Leonard has got some money to give away.'

Blackwhite adjusted the nature of his gaze. Pablo, Sandro and Pedro looked up. The men from the foundations stared.

'Do you know him, Chippy?'

'Can't say I do. I'll ask Bippy.'

'I don't know him, Tippy.'

'Leonard,' Chippy said. 'I've never heard of that name in Foundationland.'

'This is possible,' Blackwhite said. 'But Leonard has the right idea.'

'Mr White,' Bippy said, affronted.

'We have never let you down,' said Tippy.

'You won't want to run out on us now, will you, Mr White?' Chippy asked.

'What about you, Mr White?' asked the waiter.

Blackwhite considered the menu. 'I think I'll start with the Avocado Lucullus.'

'Avocado Lucullus.' The waiter made an approving note.

'What do you mean by the right idea, Mr White?'

'Then I think I'll try a sole. What's the bonne femme like tonight? The right idea?'

The waiter brought his thumb and index finger together to make a circle.

'Well, let's say the sole bonne femme. With a little spinach. Gentlemen, I'll tell you straight. The artist in the post-colonial era is in a position of peculiar difficulty.'

'How would you like the spinach, Mr White?'

'En branches. And the way you or anyone else can help him is with—money. There it is, gentlemen. The way you can help Pablo here—'

'The wine list, Mr White.'

'Go on. We are listening.'

'The way to help Pablo—ah, sommelier. But let's ask our hosts.'

'No, no. We leave that to you, Mr White.'

'Is with—money. Shall we break some rules? Pablo, would you and your boys mind a hock? Or would you absolutely insist on a burgundy to go with your Chateaubriand?'

'Anything you say, Mr White.'

'I think the hock. Tell me, do you have any of that nice Rudesheimer left?'

'Indeed, Mr White. Chilled.'

'All right, gentlemen? A trifle sweet. But still.'

'Sure. Waiter, bring a couple of bottles of what Mr White just said. How do we help Pablo?'

'Pablo? You give Pablo ten thousand dollars. And let him get on with the job.'

'What does he do?' asked Bippy.

'That's a *detail*,' Blackwhite said. 'So far as my present argument goes.'

'I entirely agree,' Chippy said.

'Waiter,' Blackwhite called. 'I believe you have forgotten our hosts.'

'Sorry, gentlemen. For you?'

'But if you are interested, Pablo and his boys are a painting group. They work together at the same time on one canvas.'

'Steak tartare. Like the Italians. Or the Dutch.'

'Steak tartare. One man painting the face.'

'Steak tartare. The other painting the scenery. Steak tartare. What am I saying? Just a salad.'

'Not quite,' Blackwhite said. 'This is more an experiment in recovering the tribal subconscious.'

'Shall we say, en vinaigrette?'

'What do you mean?'

'You know about Jung and the racial memory.'

'With vinegar.'

'That's just about how I feel.'

'They have produced some very interesting results. A sort of artistic stream-of-consciousness relay. But in paint. A sort of continuous mutual interference.'

'This sounds very interesting, Mr White,' Bippy said.

'We don't want to offend Pablo,' Tippy said.

'Or Sandro or Pedro,' Chippy added.

'But we have to be sure, Mr White.'

'Foundationland has its own rules, Mr White.'

'Mr White, we have to write reports.'

'Mr White, help us.'

'Mr White, we have made this journey to see *you*.'

'I don't know, gentlemen. We can't just *brush* off Pablo and his boys just like that. An appropriate word, don't you think? Let us see how they feel.'

Bippy, Tippy and Chippy looked at Pablo, Sandro and Pedro.

'Ask them,' Blackwhite said. 'Go on, ask them.'

'What do you feel about this, Mr Pablo?' Bippy asked.

'If any money going, give it to Blackwhite,' Pablo said.

'Give it to Mr White,' Sandro said.

'Is what I say too,' said Pedro.

'You see, Mr White,' Chippy said. 'You must shoulder your responsibilities. We appreciate your desire to nurse struggling talent. But—'

'Exactly,' said Tippy.

Blackwhite didn't look disappointed.

The food came. Pablo and his friends began sawing. Blackwhite scooped avocado, poured wine.

Blackwhite said, 'I didn't want it to appear that I was pushing myself forward. I wanted you to meet Pablo and his boys because I thought you might want to encourage something new. I feel that you chaps have got quite enough out of me as it is.'

There was a little dismissing laughter. I swallowed oysters. Leonard peeled prawns.

'And also,' Blackwhite went on, 'because I felt that you might not be altogether happy with the experimental work I have on hand.'

'Experimental?' Tippy said.

'Oh, this sounds good,' Leonard said.

'Gentlemen, no artist should repeat himself. My interracial romances, though I say it myself, have met with a fair amount of esteem, indeed acclaim.'

'Indeed,' said Bippy, Tippy and Chippy.

'Gentlemen, before you say anything, listen. I have decided to abandon the problem.'

'This is good,' Leonard said. 'This is very good.'

'How do we abandon the problem?' Blackwhite said.

Pablo reached forward and lifted up a wine bottle. It was empty. He held it against the light and shook it. Chippy took the bottle from him and set it on the table. 'There is nothing more there,' he said.

'I have thought about this for a long time. I think I should move with the times.'

'Good old Blackwhite,' I said.

'I want,' Blackwhite said, 'to write a novel about a black man.'

'Oh, good,' Leonard said.

'A novel about a black man falling in love.'

'Capital,' said Bippy, Tippy and Chippy.

'With a black woman.'

'Mr White!'

'Mr White!'

'Mr White!'

'I thought you would be taken aback,' Blackwhite said. 'But I would regard such a novel as the statement of a final emancipation.'

'It's a terrific idea,' Leonard said.

'Tremendous problems, of course,' Blackwhite said.

'Mr White!' Bippy said.

'We have to write too,' said Chippy.

'Our reports,' said Tippy.

'Calm down boys,' Bippy said. 'Mr White, you couldn't tell us how you are going to treat this story?'

'That's my difficulty,' Blackwhite said.

'*Your* difficulty,' Chippy said. 'What about ours?'

'Black boy meets black girl,' Tippy said.

'They fall in love,' said Bippy.

'And have some black children,' said Chippy.

'Mr White, that's not a story.'

'It's more like the old-fashioned coon show. The thing we've been fighting against.'

'You'll have the liberals down your throat.'

'You will get us the sack. Mr White, look at it from our point of view.'

'Calm down, boys. Let me talk to him. This is a strange case of regression, Mr White.'

'I'll say. You've regressed right back to Uncle Remus, right back to Brer Rabbit and Brer Fox.'

'Do us another *Hate* and we'll support you to the hilt.'

'Give us more of the struggler, Mr White.'

'Calm *down* boys. Much depends on the treatment, of course. The treatment is everything in a work of art.'

'Of course,' Blackwhite said, scooping up the bonne femme sauce from the dish in the waiter's reverential hand.

'I don't know. You might just work something. You might have the black man rescued from a bad white woman.'

'Or the black woman rescued from a bad white man.'

Or *something*.'

'We've got to be careful,' Blackwhite said. 'I have gone into this thing pretty thoroughly. I don't want to offend any ethnic group.'

'What do you mean, Mr White?'

'He is right,' Leonard said. 'Mr White, I think you are terrific.'

'Thank you, Leonard. And also, I was toying with the idea of having a bad black man as my hero. Just toying.'

'Mr White!'

'Mr White!'

'Mr White!'

'I am sorry. I have used a foolish word. One gets into such a way of talking. Reducing the irreducible to simple terms. I don't mean bad. I just mean ordinary.'

'Mr White!'

'Calm down, Tippy.'

'What do you mean, Mr White? Someone bad at ball games?'

'And tone deaf?'

'You just want a cripple,' Leonard said.

'The thought occurred to me too, Leonard,' Blackwhite said. 'They just want a cripple.'

'Who the hell said anything about a cripple?'

'Calm down, Bippy.'

'Kid,' Chippy said. 'Forgive me for talking to you like this. But you are committing suicide. You've built up a nice little reputation. Why go and throw it away now for the sake of a few crazy ideas?'

'Why don't you go home and write us another *Shadowed Livery?*'

'Do us another *Hate*.'

Leonard said, 'I intend to support you, Mr White.'

Blackwhite said, 'I am rather glad this has turned out as it has. I believe I understand you gentlemen and what you stand for. It mightn't be a bad idea, after all, for you to extend your patronage to Pablo and his boys.'

'Anything to follow, Mr White?' the waiter said. 'A zabaglione? Crème de marrons?'

'I require nothing but the bill,' Blackwhite said. 'Though those boys look as though they require feeding.' He nodded towards Pablo and his friends.

The waiter produced the bill. Blackwhite waved towards Bippy, Tippy and Chippy, each of whom extended a trained hand to receive it.

'Mr White, we didn't mean to offend you.'

'But you have,' Leonard said.

'I hate you,' Blackwhite said to Bippy. He pointed to Chippy. 'I hate you.' He pointed to Tippy. 'And I hate you.'

They began to smile.

'This is the old H. J. B. White.'

'We might have lost a friend.'

'But we feel we have saved an artist.'

'Feed Pablo and his boys from now on,' Blackwhite said.

'Yes,' Leonard said, rising. 'Feed Pablo. Mr White, I am with you. I think your black idea is terrific. I will support you. You will want for nothing.'

'Who is this guy?' Bippy asked.

'Thanks for the oysters,' I said. 'He's got a million to play with. He's going to make you look pretty silly.'

'Who knows?' Chippy said. 'The mad idea might come off.'

'New York won't like it if it does,' Bippy said.

'Calm down,' said Tippy.

They walked towards the bar.

'No more winter trips.'

'Or extended journeys.'

'No more congresses.'

'By day or night.'

'No more chewing over literate-chewer.'

'Or seminars on cinema.'

'But wait,' said Bippy. 'Perhaps Blackwhite was right. Perhaps Pablo and his boys do have something. The tribal subconscious.'

They were still eating.

'Mr Pablo?'

'Mr Sandro?'

'Mr Pedro?'

*

I left Blackwhite and Leonard together. I left Sinclair too. He had been in the diningroom throughout. I went down to the kitchen.

On the TV screen Gary Priestland was announcing: 'Here is some important news. Hurricane Irene has altered course fractionally. This means the island now lies in her path. Irene, as you know'—he spoke almost affectionately—'has flattened the islands of Cariba and Morocoy.' On the screen there appeared stills. Flattened houses; bodies; motor-cars in unlikely places; a coconut grove in which uprooted coconut trees lay almost parallel to one another as though laid there by design, to await erection. Gary Priestland gave details of death and injuries and financial loss. He was like a sports commentator, excited by a rising score. 'To keep you in touch the Island Television Service will not be closing down tonight. ITS will remain on the air, to keep you in constant touch with developments. I have a message from the Red Cross. But first—'

The Ma-Ho girls came on in their frilly short skirts and sang a brisk little whinnying song for a local rum.

While they were singing the telephone rang.

Henry had been gazing at the television set, held, it seemed, by more than news. He roused himself and answered the telephone.

'For you.'

'Frankie.'

The voice was not that of Gary Priestland, TV compere, master of ceremonies. It was the voice of Priest.

'Frankie, I am telling you. Stay away. Do not interfere. My

thoughts are of nothing but death tonight. Leave Selma alone. Do not provoke her.'

On the TV I saw him put the telephone down, saw the manner change instantly from that of Priest to that of Priestland. Like a deity, then, he supervised more stills of disaster on the islands of Cariba and Morocoy.

The kitchen had a low ceiling. The light was fluorescent. No wind, no noise save that from the air extractor. The world was outside. Protection was inside.

Henry, gazing at the pictures of death and disorder, was becoming animated.

'Hurricane, Frankie. Hurricane, boy. Do you think it will really come?'

'Do you want it to come?'

He looked dazed.

I left him and made for the lavatories. The oyster sickness. One door carried a metal engraving of a man, the other of a woman. Their coyness irritated me. One at a time, they raced unsteadily up to me. I cuffed the woman. Squeals. I hurried through the door with the man.

The mirror was steamed over. I cleared part of it with my hand. For the first time that day, that night, that morning, I saw my face. My face, my eyes. My shirt, the doorman's tie. I was overwhelmed. The tribal subconscious. Portrait of the artist. I signed it in one corner.

'Yes. When all is said and done, I think you are pretty tremendous. Very brave. Moving among men like a man. You take taxis. You buy shirts. You run houses. You travel. You hear other people's voices and are not afraid. You are pretty terrific. Where do you get the courage?'

A hand on my elbow.

'Leonard,' I whispered, turning.

But it was Henry, a little firmer than he had been so far that evening, a little more rallying, a little less dejected.

'Hurricane coming, man. The first time. And you want to meet it here?'

I went out. And saw Selma.

'You,' I said.

'The mystery man on the telephone,' she said. 'No mystery to me, though, after the first few times. I knew it was you. Henry sent a message to me. I left the Hilton as soon as I could.'

'Barbecue night. Gary Priestland, master of ceremonies. I know. Selma, I have to talk to you. Selma, you have pulled down our house. I went and looked. You pulled it down.'

'I've got a nicer one.'

'Poor Selma.'

'Rich Selma,' Henry said. 'Poor Henry.'

We were in the kitchen. The television was blue. The air extractor roared.

'I sold the house to a foundation. They are going to put up a national island theatre.' She nodded towards the television set. 'It was Gary's idea. It was a good deal.'

'You've all done good deals. Who is going to write the plays? Gary?'

'It's only for happenings. No scenery or anything. Audiences walking across the stage whenever they want. Taking part even. Like Henry's in the old days.'

'Hurricane coming,' Henry said.

'It was all Gary's idea.'

'Not the hurricane,' I said.

'Even that.' She gazed at the screen as if to say, look.

Priestland, Priest, was lifting back his head. From details of death and destruction on other islands, details delivered with the messenger's thrill, he was rising to a type of religious exaltation. And now there followed not the Ma-Ho girls with their commercials but six little black girls with hymns.

She looked away. 'Come, shall I take you home?'

'You want me to see your home?'

'It is up to you.'

'Hurricane coming,' Henry said. He began to sway. 'All this is over. We all become new men.'

'Repent!' Priest cried from the television screen.

'Repent?' Henry shouted back. 'All this is over.'

'Rejoice!' Priest said. 'All this is over.'

'Why run away now?' Henry said.

'Why run away?' Priest said. 'There is nothing to run to. Soon there will be nothing to run from. There is a way which seemeth right unto a man but at the end thereof are the ways of death. Repent! Rejoice! How shall we escape, if we neglect so great a salvation.'

'Emelda!' Henry called. 'Emelda!' To Selma and to me he said, 'Not yet. Don't go. A last drink. A last drink. Emelda!' He wandered about the kitchen and the adjoining room. 'All these plastic flowers! All these furnitures! All these decorations! Consume them, O Lord!'

Mrs Henry appeared in the doorway.

'Emelda, my dear,' Henry said.

'What get into you now?'

He unhooked a flying bird from the wall and aimed it at her head. She ducked. The bird broke against the door.

'That cost forty dollars,' she said.

He aimed another at her. 'Eighty now.'

'Henry, the wind get in your head!'

'Let us make it a hundred.' He lifted a vase.

Selma said, 'Let us go.'

I said, 'I think the time has come.'

'No. You're my friends. You must have a farewell drink. Emelda, will you serve my friends?'

'Yes, Henry.'

'Call me mister, Emelda. Let us maintain the old ways.'

'Yes, Mr Henry.'

'Vodka and coconut water, Emelda.' He put down the vase.

The black girls sang hymns.

'You let me in that night, Selma,' I said. 'I've remembered that.'

'I remember. That was why I came.'

Emelda, Mrs Henry brought back a bottle, a pitcher and some tumblers.

Henry said, 'Emelda, after all this time you spend teaching me manners, you mean you want to give my friends glasses with hairs in it?'

'Then took after them yourself, you drunken old trout.'

'Old trout, old tout,' Henry said. And then, with shouts of pure joy, the hymns pouring out in the background, he smashed bottle, pitcher and tumblers. He went round breaking things. Emelda followed him, saying, 'That cost twenty dollars. That cost thirty-two dollars. That cost fifteen dollars. In a sale.'

'Sit down, Emelda.'

She sat down.

'Show them your mouth.'

She opened her mouth.

'Nice and wide. Is a big mouth you have, you know, Emelda. The dentist could just climb in inside with his lunch parcel and scrape away all day.'

Emelda had no teeth.

'Frankie, look at what you leave me with. Sit down, Emelda. She and she sister setting competition. Sister take out all her teeth. So naturally Miss Emelda don't want to keep a single one of she own. Look. I got to watch this morning, noon and night. I mad to hit you, mouth. Mouth, I mad to hit you.'

'No, Henry. That mouth cost almost a thousand dollars, you know.'

'All that, and the world ending!'

'Rejoice!' Priest called from the television screen. He lifted the telephone on his desk and dialled.

The telephone in Henry's kitchen rang.

'Don't answer,' Selma said. 'Come, our bargain. Our first evening. Let me take you home.'

Hymns from the blue screen; screams from Emelda; the crash of glasses and crockery. The main room of The Coconut Grove, all its lights still on, was deserted. The thatched stage was empty.

'The perfection of drama. No scenery. No play. No audience. Let us watch.'

She led me outside. People here. Some from the Coconut Grove, some from neighbouring buildings. They stood still and silent.

'Like an aquarium,' Selma said.

Low, dark clouds raced. The light ever changed.

'Your car, Selma?'

'I always wanted a sports model.'

'The car is the man, is the woman. Where are you taking me to?'

'Home.'

'You haven't told me. Where is that?'

'Manhattan Park. A new area. It used to be a citrus plantation. The lots are big, half an acre.'

'Lovely lawns and gardens?'

'People are going in a lot for shrubs these days. It's something you must have noticed. You'll like the area. It's very nice.'

It was a nice area, and Selma's house was in the modernistic style of the island. Lawn, garden, a swimming pool shaped like a teardrop. The roof of the veranda was supported on sloping lengths of tubular metal. The ceiling was in varnished pitchpine. The furnishings were equally contemporary. Little bits of driftwood; electric lights pretending to be oil lamps; irregularly shaped tables whose tops were sections of tree trunks complete with bark. She certainly hated straight lines and circles and rectangles and ovals.

'Where do you get the courage, Selma?'

'This is just your mood. We all have the courage.'

Local paintings on the wall, contemporary like anything.

'I always think women have a lot of courage. Imagine putting on the latest outrageous thing and walking out in that. That takes courage.'

'But you have managed. What do you sell? I am sure that you sell things.'

'Encyclopaedias. Textbooks. Inoffensive culture. *Huckleberry Finn* without nigger Jim, for ten cents.'

'You see. That's something I could never do. The world isn't a frightening place, really. People are playing a lot of the time. Once you realize that, you begin to see that people are just like yourself. Not stronger or weaker.'

'Oh, they are stronger than me. Blackwhite, Priest, you, even Henry—you are all stronger than me.'

'You are looking at the driftwood? Lovely things can be found in Nature.'

'But we don't leave it there. Lovely house, Selma. Lovely, ghastly, sickening, terrible home.'

'My home is not terrible.'

'No, of course not to you.'

'You can't insult me. You are too damn frightened. You don't like homes. You prefer houses. To fit into other people's lives.'

'Yes. I prefer houses. My God. I am on a treadmill. I can't get off. I am surrounded by other people's very big names.'

'You are getting worse, Frank. Come. Be a good boy. Bargain, remember. Let me show you my bedroom.'

'Adultery has its own rules. Never on the matrimonial bed.'

'Not matrimonial yet. That is to come.'

'I have no exalted idea of my prowess.'

'You were always lousy as a lover. But still.'

'What language, Selma. So snappy, man. Let me put on the old TV. I don't want to miss anything.'

The man on the screen had changed his clothes. He was wearing a white gown. He had abandoned news; he was only preaching.

He said, 'All we like sheep have gone astray; we have turned everyone to his own way.'

As if in sympathy with his undress, I began unbuttoning my shirt.

In the bedroom it was possible to hear him squawking on. On the bed lay a quilted satin eiderdown.

'You are like Norma Shearer in *Escape*.'

'Shut up. Come. Be good.'

'I will be good if I come.'

Our love-making was not a success.

'It was bad.'

'Drink is good for a woman,' Selma said. 'Bad for a man. You prepared yourself too well today, Frank. You waste your courage in fear.'

'I waste my courage in fear. "Now *look* what you have done."'

'Explain.'

'It was what a woman said to me many years ago. I was fifteen. She called me in one afternoon when I was coming back from school and asked me to get on top of her. And that was what she said at the end. "Now *look* what you have done." As though *I* had done the asking. Talking to me as though she was talking to a baby. Terrible. Sex is a hideous thing. I've decided. I'm anti-sex.'

'That makes two of us.'

'All I can say is that we've been behaving strangely for a very long time.'

'You started it. Tell me, did you expect me to keep our bargain?'

'I don't know. It is like one of those stories you hear. That a woman always sleeps with the man who took her maidenhead. Is it true? I don't know. Is it true?'

'It is,' Selma said, rising from the bed, 'an old wives' tale.'

In the drawingroom the television still groaned on. The black girls sang hymns. I went to the bathroom. The mat said RESERVED FOR DRIPS. On the lavatory seat there was a notice, flowers painted among the words: GENTLEMEN LIFT THE SEAT IT IS SHORTER THAN YOU THINK LADIES REMAIN SEATED THROUGHOUT THE PERFORMANCE. An ashtray; a little book of lavatory and bedroom jokes. The two so often going together. Poor Selma. I pulled the lavatory chain twice.

The wind was high.

'Selma, be weak like me. Henry is right. Priest is right. It is all going to be laid flat. Let us rejoice. Let us go to the bay. Let us take

Henry with us. And afterwards, if there is an afterwards, Henry will take us to his pretty little island.'

'There are no more islands. It's not you talking. It's the wind.'

The oil lamp which was really an electric lamp was overturned. Darkness, except for the blue of the television screen. And the wind drowned Priest's voice.

Selma became hysterical.

'Let us get out of here. Let us go back to town. In the street with the others.'

'No, let us go to the bay.'

Henry sat among disarrayed plastic flowers, in a deserted Coconut Grove.

'The bay!'

'The bay.'

We drove up and over the hills, the three of us. We heard the wind. We ran down onto the beach, and heard the sea. At least that couldn't be changed. Once the beach was dangerous with coconut trees, dropping nuts. Now most had been cut down to make a parking lot. Standing foursquare on the beach was a great concrete pavilion, derelict: a bit of modernity that had failed: a tourist convenience that had served no purpose. The village had grown. It had spread down almost to the beach, a rural marine slum. Lights were on in many of the shacks.

'I never thought you could destroy the bay.'

'We might have a chance to start afresh.'

We walked in the wind. Pariah dogs came up to wait, to follow fearfully. The smell of rotting fish came fitfully with the wind. We decided to spend the night in the tourist pavilion.

Morning, dark and turbulent, revealed the full dereliction of the beach. Fishing boats reclined or were propped up on the sand that was still golden, but there were also yellow oil drums on the beach for the refuse of the fishermen, whose houses, of unplastered hollow-clay bricks and unpainted timber, jostled right up to the limit of dry sand. The sand was scuffed and marked and bloody like an arena; it was littered with the heads and entrails of fish. Mangy pariah dogs, all rib and bone, all bleached to a nondescript fawn colour, moved listlessly, their tails between their legs, from drum to yellow drum. Black vultures weighed down the branches of coconut trees; some hopped awkwardly on the sand; many more circled overhead.

Henry was peeing into the sea.

I called out to him, 'Let us go back. It is more than I can stand.'

'I always wanted to do this,' he said. 'In public.'

'You mustn't blame yourself,' Selma said. 'It is never very good in the morning.'

It hadn't been good.

We drove back to the city. We drove, always, under a low dark sky. It was early, yet the island was alive. The streets were full of people. Their first hurricane, their first drama, and they had come out into the streets so as to miss nothing. All normal activity had been suspended. It was like a continuation of the night before; the streets were even more like aquaria, thick with life, but silent. Only the absence of the blackness of night seemed to have marked the passage of time; only that and the screens, now blank, of television sets seen through the open doors of houses—some still with useless lights on—and in cafés doing no business.

Then it was night again. The useless lights had meaning. Against the black sky blacker points moved endlessly: all the birds of the island, flying south. It was like the final abandonment. We were in the midst of noise, in which it was at times possible to distinguish the individual groans of houses, trees, and the metallic flapping of loose corrugated-iron sheets. No fear on any face, though. Only wonder and expectation.

The television screens shimmered. Priest reappeared, tired, shining with fatigue, telling us what we already knew, that the end of our world was at hand.

'Behold,' he said, 'now is the day of salvation.'

The city responded. Faintly at first, like distant temple bells, the sound of steel orchestras came above the roar of the wind. The pariah dogs, and those dogs that lived in houses, began to bark in relay, back and forth and crossways. Feet began to shuffle. Priest railed like a seer, exhausted by the effort of concentration. He railed; the city was convulsed with music and dance.

The world was ending and the cries that greeted this end were cries of joy. We all began to dance. We saw dances such as we had seen in the old days in Henry's yard. No picking of cotton, no cutting of cane; no carrying of water, no orchestrated wails. We danced with earnestness. We did contortions of which we had never thought ourselves capable.

We saw Blackwhite dancing with Leonard. Blackwhite not white, not black, but Blackwhite as we all would have liked to see him, a man released from endeavour, released from the strain of seeing himself (portrait of the artist: the tribal subconscious), at peace with the world, accepting, like Leonard. We saw Bippy, Tippy and Chippy arm in arm with Pablo, Sandro and Pedro, as though the wooing that had begun at The Coconut Grove had gone on all night: a gesture now without meaning, a fixed attitude of ritual in which news of the hurricane had caught them all. Occasionally the men from Foundationland pleaded with Blackwhite. Still, without malice or triumph, he spurned them, and did stylized stamps of simple negation: a private man, at last. As on a flat stage, stretching to infinity before our eyes, infinity the point where the painted floorboards met, companionship and wooing and pursuit and evasion played back and forth before us. But Leonard, obstinately dancing, dancing with earnestness, like the man anxious to catch the right mood and do the right thing: Leonard remained, in spite of his exertions, what he had always been, bemused, kind, blank. Arm in arm he danced with Blackwhite whenever they met; and Sinclair, big, heavy Sinclair, swung between them. And the tourist teams of the day before: the happy now like people who had forgotten the meaning of the word, which implied an opposite, the embittered, oh, infinitely less so. And for me, no terror of sky and trees: the courage of futility, the futility of courage, the empty, total response.

Through the streets, flattened to stage-boards, we danced, waiting for the final benediction. The sky hung low, grew high, hung low. The wind sweetly filled our ears, slackened, filled our ears again. We danced and waited. We waited and danced.

Benediction never came. Our dancing grew listless. Fatigue consumed anguish. But hope was not entirely consumed, even when on the television sets we saw Priest being transformed into Priestland, the seer into the newscaster, the man whose thoughts had only been of death, into the man who diminished life. But how could we deny?

We gave up the hurricane. We sat in the streets. Light was grey, then silver. The stage was becoming a street again; house took on volume. I heard Bippy, Tippy and Chippy wailing. Pablo and the boys comforted them.

Sinclair straightened his jacket and tie. In the light of a day that had now truly broken he went to Leonard, detached him from Blackwhite, and said, 'Come, Leonard. Come, boy. We have had our fun. It is time to go home!'

'Goodbye, Mr White,' Leonard said. 'Very well, Sinclair. You have been very good. Let us go.'

Blackwhite saw and understood. 'Leonard!' he said, stupefied. 'Leonard, what about my black novel? You promised help. You drove away the men from Foundationland. You said I was to want for nothing.'

'Goodbye, Mr White. How are you feeling, Sinclair?'

'Leonard! You promised support! Bippy, Tippy, Chippy. Wait, wait. Pablo, call off your idlers! Pablo! Bippy! Mr Tippy! Mr Chippy!'

He, once the pursued, now became the pursuer. Pablo, Sandro and Pedro fled before him, as did Bippy, Tippy and Chippy. He pursued them; they evaded him and often the six came together. On the stage stretching to infinity the chase took place, pursuer and the six pursued dwindling to nothing before us. The sun was bright; there were shadows.

I went with Selma to The Coconut Grove. Henry was cleaning

up the kitchen. Emelda stood over him. He rearranged plastic flowers; he put broken vases together.

On the television set Gary Priestland was announcing that the hurricane had not come. But he had news for us, news of the destruction of some other island. He had news. He had facts and the figures of death. He had stills.

In the harbour the ships blew the all-clear.

The Ma-Ho girls came on and did a commercial for a local cigarette.

The programmes for the day were announced.

'Home,' Selma said.

'The old driftwood calls. Lovely things can be found in Nature.'

'Gary will be tired.'

'I'll say.'

And in the city where each exhausted person had once more to accommodate himself to his fate, to the life that had not been arrested, I went back to the hotel.

Hilton, Hilton.
Sailing 1 p.m., the board said in the lobby.
Moore-McCormack, Moore-McCormack.

August 1965

ALSO BY V. S. NAIPAUL

AMONG THE BELIEVERS

On the basis of his seven-month journey across the Asian continent, V. S. Naipaul explores the life, the culture, and the ongoing ferment inside four nations of Islam: Iran, Pakistan, Malaysia, and Indonesia. In this brilliant account, Naipaul depicts an Islamic world at odds with the contemporary world and fueled by an implacable determination to believe.

Current Affairs

AN AREA OF DARKNESS

A classic of modern travel writing, *An Area of Darkness* is V. S. Naipaul's profound reckoning with his ancestral homeland and an extraordinarily perceptive chronicle of his first encounter with India. Traveling from the bureaucratic morass of Bombay to the ethereal beauty of Kashmir and a sacred ice cave in the Himalayas, Naipaul encounters a dizzying cross section of humanity and develops strikingly original and passionate responses to the subcontinent.

Travel

A BEND IN THE RIVER

V. S. Naipaul takes us deeply into the life of one man—an Indian who, uprooted by the bloody tides of Third World history, has come to live in an isolated town at the bend of a great river in a newly independent African nation. Naipaul gives us the most convincing and disturbing vision yet of what happens in a place caught between the dangerously alluring modern world and its own tenacious past and traditions.

Fiction/Literature

BETWEEN FATHER AND SON

In 1950, V. S. Naipaul, aged seventeen, took a two-week journey by steamer and arrived in Oxford, England, a world utterly removed from the one he had longed to escape and to which he would never really return. This collection of letters between a sacrificing father and his determined son gives us an intimate view of Naipaul's formative years and bears witness to the flowering of a literary genius.

Biography

BEYOND BELIEF

Fourteen years after the publication of his landmark travel narrative *Among the Believers*, V. S. Naipaul returned to the four non-Arab Islamic countries he reported on so vividly at the time of Ayatollah Khomeini's triumph in Iran. *Beyond Belief* is the result of his five-month journey through Indonesia, Iran, Pakistan, and Malaysia. In extended conversations with a vast number of people, including a rare survivor of the martyr brigades of the Iran-Iraq war and an intellectual training as a Marxist guerrilla, Naipaul deliberately effaces himself to let the voices of his subjects come through.

Religion/Islam

THE ENIGMA OF ARRIVAL

The story of a writer's singular journey—from one place to another, from the British colony of Trinidad to the ancient countryside of England and from one state of mind to another—this is perhaps V. S. Naipaul's most autobiographical work. Yet it is also woven through with remarkable invention to make it a rich and complex novel.

Fiction/Literature

GUERRILLAS

On a troubled Caribbean island—where Asians, Africans, Americans, and former British colonials coexist in a state of suppressed hysteria—a white man arrives with his mistress, an Englishwoman inflamed by fantasies of native power and sexuality, unaware of the consequences of her actions. Together with a young mulatto leader of the "Revolution," they act out a gripping drama of death, sexual violence, and political and spiritual impotence that illuminates the ravages of history on individual lives.

Fiction/Literature

HALF A LIFE

Half a Life is the story of Willie Chandran, whose father turned his back on his brahmin heritage and married a woman of low caste—a disastrous union he would live to regret. As an adult, Willie's flight from the travails of his mixed birth takes him to London, where, in the shabby haunts of immigrants and literary bohemians of the 1950s, he tries to contrive a new identity. His struggle to defeat self-doubt and become a writer bring him to the brink of exhaustion from which he is rescued only by the love of a good woman.

Fiction/Literature

A HOUSE FOR MR. BISWAS

Shuttled from one residence to another after the drowning of his father, Mr. Mohun Biswas yearns for a place he can call home. But when he marries into the domineering Tulsi family on whom he indignantly becomes dependent, Mr. Biswas embarks on an arduous and endless effort to weaken their hold over him and purchase a house of his own.

Fiction/Literature

IN A FREE STATE

It begins as a simple car trip through Africa. Two English people—Bobby, a civil servant with a guilty appetite for African boys, and Linda, a supercilious "compound wife"—are driving back to their enclave after a stay in the capital. But in between lies the landscape of an unnamed country whose squalor and ethnic bloodletting suggest Idi Amin's Uganda. And the farther V. S. Naipaul's protagonists travel into it, the more they find themselves crossing the line that separates privileged outsiders from horrified victims.

Fiction/Literature